TURF WAR

A DCI Jack Tyler thriller

Mark Romain

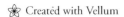 Created with Vellum

ACKNOWLEDGMENTS

Edited by Yvonne Goldsworthy

Cover design by Woot Han

I'd like to say a very special thank you to my brilliant team of Beta Readers, not only for volunteering to read the first draft of the manuscript, but also for all the great feedback they provided. They are: Clare R, Danny A, Cathie A, Darren H, Robert H, Tracie B, and Bejay R.

ALSO AVAILABLE FROM MARK ROMAIN IN THE DCI TYLER SERIES:

Turf War is set in May 1999... six months before the events described in Jack's Back.

CHAPTER ONE

Saturday 1st May 1999
THE RECRUITMENT

It was a warm Saturday night at the beginning of May, and the City Centre was buzzing with noise, lights, and a keen sense of expectation. There was music, laughter, the occasional blare of a horn or wail of a siren; a feeling that the night was young and full of potential – anything could happen, and probably would.

Already heaving, Cosmopolitan Manchester would only get busier as more people flocked in for a well-deserved night out, all intent on letting their hair down, blowing off some steam, and having a little fun.

The streets felt energised, and a party mood prevailed amongst the customers spilling out of jam-packed establishments onto adjoining pavements.

Although the Haçienda club in Whitworth Street West, on the south side of the Rochdale Canal, had closed in the summer of 1997 there were still plenty of other great clubs, bars and pubs in which to party away a Saturday night.

Unfortunately, the venue Conrad Livingstone was about to visit wasn't one of them.

The Gallagher brothers were belting out *Wonderwall* on the car radio and his idiot driver was singing along, tapping out an irritating drum beat on the top of the steering wheel with the palms of his hands.

For a while, Livingstone sat motionless in the front passenger seat of the sleek BMW M3 coupé, studying the club's entrance and contemplating how the evening would pan out.

His brooding was interrupted by a group of drunken girls who stumbled past the car, their off key singing easily drowning out Liam and Noel. Their party frocks were covered in glitter and tassels, and one of them wore a banner that proclaimed her as the bride to be. As Livingstone followed their erratic passage with his eyes, one of them suddenly lurched into the road and threw up. A couple of girls tottered over to help her while the rest of the group stood on the kerb, laughing and shouting profanities. His driver, Meeks, thought it was all very entertaining, but Livingstone wasn't in the mood to laugh. "Fucking skanks," he muttered under his breath.

Linking their arms through hers, the drunk's friends guided her back onto the relative safety of the pavement, and the group resumed its unsteady journey along the road.

Stepping out of the car, Livingstone told his driver to go back to the hotel and wait for him there; he didn't know how long he would be, but he would make his own way back after he'd concluded his business.

Livingstone crossed the busy road, nimbly dodging between cars that had no intention of slowing down for him, and walked towards the nightclub's garishly lit entrance.

The club might not be the most salubrious of establishments, but it was obviously very popular. A slow-moving line of between forty and fifty people hugged the wall to the left of the building, laughing and joking as they queued good naturedly to get in. Quite a few of them looked as though they were already half-cut.

The punters were being vetted at the entrance by three Eastern European looking bouncers who were checking to see that they met the age restriction and token dress code. All three men, Albanians or Romanians from the look of them, were big lumps, over six-foot tall, with shaven domes, facial scars and broken noses. One had a tattoo of a snake curling around a dagger running from the back of his ear all the way down the right side of his neck. Working in silent unison, they reminded Livingstone of a well-trained pack of attack dogs.

A nightclub would never have been Livingstone's first choice for such an important meeting but, for some unfathomable reason, the man whose particular skill set he'd driven all the way from London to hire had been adamant that they met there.

A flickering neon sign above the club's main entrance proclaimed its name was Crosby's, but two of the bulbs at the top of the O had shorted out, making the letter look like a U.

Two man-mountains in ill-fitting penguin suits were guarding the door to the VIP entrance on the opposite side of the building, and they watched Livingstone with undisguised suspicion as he approached them.

Attired as he was in an Armani suit of virgin wool, worn over a purple Givenchy silk shirt, there could be no doubting Livingstone's affluence, but as he reached the entrance the two doormen sidled up to each other, blocking his path. They regarded the well-dressed black man as though he were a vagrant begging for scraps. "This is a VIP only entrance," the one on the left said.

"Yeah, VIPs only," the one on the right echoed.

There was an air of lazy aggression about them. The man on his left flank made a point of sucking his teeth disrespectfully, while the man standing to his right repeatedly clenched and unclenched his fists as he stared menacingly at the visitor.

Livingstone was unmoved. He had been born in a rough London slum thirty-two years previously, and he had grown up immersed in the unforgiving violence of gang culture. These pussies didn't frighten him.

Both doormen were of African descent, with wide, chubby faces, and pronounced foreheads. They glared at him through spiteful, beady eyes that were bereft of intelligence or initiative.

"Do you know a man called Goliath, bruv?" Livingstone asked, unperturbed by their hostility.

"Who wants to know?" the one on the left demanded, jutting his head forward aggressively.

"Yeah, who wants to know?" the one on the right parroted.

Livingstone sighed impatiently and folded his arms. He hated dealing with lackeys. "Look, I'm here to meet with Goliath. I was told that if I mentioned his name at the VIP door someone would come out and collect me."

The two bouncers looked at each other, looked at Livingstone, shrugged. "Never heard of him," they said in tandem.

Anger flared. "Let me speak to your boss," Livingstone told them, allowing an edge to creep into his voice.

The doormen shared a glance. There was something about the coldness of the man's stare that made them uneasy. A clipboard magically appeared in the hand of the doorman standing on Livingstone's left. "Show me your name on this list," he demanded, belligerently thrusting it out towards Livingstone.

"My name's not on your stupid list," Livingstone said, waving the clipboard away impatiently.

That drew a scowl. "Then who should we say is calling?" the doorman demanded sullenly.

"Yeah, who should we say—"

"My name's not important," Livingstone snapped. "Just tell Goliath that the man who wants to hire him is outside, but won't be for much longer if he's not shown some FUCKING RESPECT!"

After a moment's hesitation, the bruiser with the clipboard clicked his tongue against the back of his teeth in agitation, then he lumbered over to a concealed panel in the wall beside the door. Flipping it open, he snatched out a red telephone on a long cord and dialled an extension inside the club.

When he returned several minutes later, Livingstone noticed that the bouncer's attitude had undergone a subtle change, and he now seemed marginally less confrontational, which seemed to confuse his intellectually challenged partner. "If you go and wait by the door, someone will be out to collect you shortly," he told Livingstone, indicating for his partner to move aside and let the smaller man pass.

A few moments later, the VIP door opened inward and, as the sound of music escaped, Livingstone found himself staring into the chest of a bald-headed black giant who was dressed in black trousers and a white shirt that was straining at the seams. The giant didn't bother Livingstone with pointless questions about who he was or why he was here. "Follow me," he simply said, and immediately headed back into the club without waiting for a response.

Livingstone followed the man through the VIP reception area, which was bigger and plusher than he'd expected it to be.

His guide, who appeared to be in a hurry, led him past a cloakroom staffed by a smiling attendant, a couple of fancy looking restrooms, and several plush sofas where well-dressed guests sat in small groups, nursing their drinks and chatting happily. The further into the club they went, the louder the trashy music became.

Up ahead, another gorilla in a dinner jacket was stationed by a set of doors that led into the club's murky interior, ensuring that only the entitled gained entry. They didn't get that far though, because the giant suddenly veered off to his left and keyed open a heavy wooden door marked "*Private – staff only*".

"The manager's office is the third door on your right, fam," he informed Livingstone, impatiently waving him on as he paused to close and re-lock the door that they had both just passed through. "Wait in there."

Livingstone did as he was bid.

The manager's office was a good size, well-lit and comfortably furnished. The walls were bare, but the magnolia paintwork looked clean, and the grey carpet was thick underfoot. Directly in front of him, a big mahogany desk dominated the room's centre. Apart from two telephones, it was devoid of clutter. Behind it, there stood a regal looking, gold framed King-Throne chair, complete with ornate carvings and a plush covering of red velvet. To the front of the desk, three cheap looking Wing-Backs with dark blue polyester upholstery had been arranged in a neat semi-circle.

Behind the desk was a solitary window. It was barred, making the room feel more like a plush prison cell than an office.

There was an informal seating area to Livingstone's right, which consisted of a three-seater leather sofa and two matching armchairs. These were arranged around a large glass-topped coffee table. Beyond this was a long, granite-topped bar with three padded swivel stools in front of it. A floor to ceiling drinks cabinet, crammed full of expensive looking bottles and an array of different shaped glasses, was secured to the wall immediately behind the bar.

The room's left-hand wall was home to several banks of CCTV monitors, each providing different internal and external views of the club. Beneath these, a steel table had been bolted to the wall, and this housed a large hard drive and the various toggle like controls for moving the cameras around and zooming them in or out. It was an impressive set up, allowing the manager to monitor everything that happened inside the club without ever having to leave his office.

Various feeds – some colour, some infrared – were currently show-ing. Livingstone could see live-time images of people gyrating under the strobe lighting of the packed dance floor; groups of animated guests standing around on the mezzanine level above them, cocktails in hand; the different themed bars within the club, all of which looked to be doing a roaring trade; the main foyer, where some of the people he'd seen outside were now paying to get in; the VIP reception and lounge he'd entered the club through; the staff only corridor he had just been shown along; both the VIP and regular customer entrances, still respectively manned by the Eastern Europeans and the Africans, and the car park at the rear, which contained several parked cars, all of which looked to be high end models.

The final camera showed what appeared to be a large empty base-ment, and Livingstone found himself wondering what possible reason the manager could have for wanting a live CCTV feed from down there? Perhaps it had been installed as a precaution in case the club was burgled out of hours, or to deter light-fingered staff from helping themselves to stock on delivery days?

Suddenly feeling in need of a stiff drink, Livingstone crossed to the bar to see what it had to offer. He was just pouring himself a large glass of eighteen-year-old Macallan whisky when the door opened and the black giant from earlier entered the room. Strutting over to the desk like he owned the place, he flopped down in the throne and hoisted his size fifteen feet onto the desk, setting them down with a loud thud.

"Ah, I see you found the drinks cabinet, Mr Livingstone. Good, good. Now, please have a seat and let's get down to business."

Livingstone chose the middle of the three chairs facing the desk. Sitting down slowly, he crossed his legs, tugged at a small crease that had appeared in his trousers, and took a sip of his drink, savouring the full-bodied taste. "My compliments to the owner, bruv," he commented, raising the glass appreciatively. "He has good taste in whisky."

The giant grinned broadly, revealing gold capped canines that made him look like a gangsta vampire. "I agree, but then again I would – I am the owner."

"Is that right?" Livingstone said, making a point of sounding unimpressed. "No offence, blud, but my time's precious, and my business is of a sensitive nature. The middleman I went through told me I would be able to speak directly to Goliath. When will I be able to do this?"

The giant grinned again. "Fam, I am Goliath. Surely my size gave you an inkling?"

Livingstone studied him dispassionately. For all he knew, the moniker had nothing to do with physical size. "Can you prove it?" Livingstone asked. "I apologise if the question seems rude, bruv," he added hastily, "but a person in my position has to be extremely careful."

Far from being offended, Goliath – if that was indeed who he really was – seemed to approve of the other man's caution.

"You're quite right to ask me," he said, nodding vigorously, "I would do exactly the same in your position. So, let me clear that up. You were pointed in my direction by a broker called Clive Middleton. He told you to come to the VIP entrance this evening and ask for Goliath. You were told my fees, which you said were exorbitant. He assured you that I was worth every penny, which I am by the way. You wanted to pay half up front, and the rest on completion. He said that I would expect the full amount to be paid up front, and that this was non-negotiable. Is that right?"

Livingstone gave a satisfied nod. That was pretty much how the conversation had gone down.

"I'm very much looking forward to being of service to you," Goliath said. "However, I am half-way through dealing with a little situation that has arisen, so would you mind if we talk while I work?"

Without waiting for a reply, he stood up.

Livingstone hesitated for a moment, but then followed suit. After all, what real choice did he have? As he watched, the giant went behind the bar and felt for a hidden switch on the side of the cabinet. Something clicked and, placing his enormous hands on one side, he gave it a firm pull. Rotating smoothly outward, the cabinet opened on concealed hinges like a conventional door. "Follow me," Goliath said, stepping inside the cavernous gap that had appeared.

Livingstone cautiously crossed the room to join his host, and discovered a dimly lit stairway that descended down to who knew where.

"I must apologise for those two idiots at the VIP entrance, fam," Goliath said, his words echoing all around them in the confined space. "I assure you the twins were told to expect you, and the way they behaved was unprofessional. I will speak to them about that, you can be assured."

Livingstone ignored the apology. "Where are we going, bruv?" he demanded, wondering if he was being dicked around. "I've come a long way to see you, and I'm very keen to discuss my business proposition, know what I'm saying? How long is this work you've got to do likely to take?"

"Don't worry, fam," Goliath soothed. "This won't take long at all, and then you can have my undivided attention."

When they reached the bottom of the stairs, Goliath pulled open a thickly padded door. He stepped into a deep recess and paused. "The room we are about to enter is completely soundproofed," he announced proudly. "You could be standing on one side of the door while I stood on the other, firing a machine gun, and you would not hear it." Motioning with his head for Livingstone to follow, Goliath pushed open an identically padded door and stepped into what appeared to be a brightly lit storage area.

As Livingstone followed him in, he immediately recognised the large open space as the basement area he had seen earlier on CCTV. Only it was no longer empty. The entire floor had been covered with thick plastic sheeting. Two men, both black, both in their late twenties, had been beaten and gagged, and they were bound to chairs that were bolted to the floor in the middle of the room. The men were clad only in their boxers, and their faces were bloodied and swollen.

The one nearest him was a runt of a man who seemed to be all skin and bone. He sported a big afro haircut like the ones that had been popular in the seventies, and from the smell of it, he had soiled himself. Thankfully, his incessant blubbering was being largely muffled by a filthy gag that had been forced deep into his mouth.

The head of the male furthest away, a short and rather plump individual with a receding hairline, was slumped forward onto his chest, which was covered in blood from where his nose and mouth had recently bled profusely. His chest rose and fell slowly, telling Livingstone that he wasn't dead, just unconscious.

This was madness. "What the fuck are you involving me in, bruv?" Livingstone demanded angrily.

"Don't worry, fam," Goliath assured him, "nothing that happens here will come back to bite you. Of that you have my word."

Livingstone had learned the hard way that you never took anyone's word for anything. For a moment, he seriously considered turning around and walking away, leaving the club while there was still time to distance himself from whatever was about to go down. But if he did that, his plan would be over, and he would have come all this way for nothing.

"Someone is going to die in this room tonight, fam," Goliath casually announced. "They will die brutally, and by my hand, but no one will ever be able to prove that I did it, or that the killing took place in this club."

Livingstone recalled that a live feed from this room was being recorded on the equipment up in the manager's office. His eyes urgently sought out the camera. When he found it, mounted high on the wall behind the two men, he breathed a sigh of relief.

Clever, he thought. Very clever.

A ten-by-eight-inch hi-resolution photograph had been expertly positioned in front of the camera's lens. Livingstone immediately realised that he had been looking at this photograph on the manager's monitor, and not at the actual basement itself. It had fooled Livingstone, and it would fool the police if they ever seized the club's CCTV.

"Let's begin," Goliath decreed, beaming his vampiric smile once more. "These men distribute product for an associate of mine," he explained. "Although they were well compensated for their services, one of them got greedy and started skimming the profits. My associate has asked me to establish who it is, and to deal with him appropriately. We were just getting started when Isaac called me to say you were outside."

Livingstone remained silent. He had witnessed violent deaths before and was completely unfazed by the prospect of seeing another. All that worried him was that he might be dragged into the ensuing police investigation if Goliath was sloppy about the clean-up.

Grabbing a handful of hair, Goliath yanked the first man's head back and stared down into his terror-stricken face. "I'm hoping it's you, Tyrone, and not Drake, here. I really am," he told his prisoner. "Just between you and me, I've never liked you, and I would very much enjoy killing you."

Shaking uncontrollably, the man called Tyrone's eyes widened, and a howl of anguish escaped his lips. His bladder gave way again, causing a dark stain to spread across his lap as a yellow liquid ran down the side of his leg to form a small pool by his feet

Goliath turned his nose up in disgust. "You do not endear yourself to me by doing that," he said.

Tyrone started wailing again. Goliath let him carry on like that for a few seconds, staring at him in mild amusement, and then he removed the material. "Choose your words wisely, fam, because this is the only chance that I'm going to give you to speak."

"Please," Tyrone sobbed, "I swear I haven't been ripping Marvin off. I would *never* do that, I promise."

Presumably, Marvin was the drug supplying associate Goliath was currently working for, Livingstone reasoned.

"I didn't even know the merchandise was being cut," Tyrone sobbed.

Goliath's eyes hardened. "I never said anything about it being cut," he said.

"Isn't that what's been happening?" Tyrone asked, confusion now competing with fear.

Goliath sighed. "No, it's not what was happening, you idiot. Cash is being stolen. The takings are way down on what they should be."

"It's not me," Tyrone blurted out.

Goliath regarded him with cynicism. "Yes, well, you would say that, wouldn't you, fam, but how do I know I can trust you?"

"You *can* trust me, bruv," Tyrone's quivering voice implored. "You can trust me with anything."

Goliath yawned, evidently bored, and turned to look at Livingstone. "I grow tired of this game. Ultimately, it doesn't matter to me which of these men is responsible, because I know that one of them definitely is. That makes the solution rather easy, don't you think?"

Livingstone shrugged. If this were his problem, he wouldn't have wasted time interrogating them. He would have ordered both men killed and be done with it. "How much longer is this going to take?" he demanded, looking at his Rolex impatiently.

The gesture was duly noted. "Not long at all," Goliath promised, walking over to a baseball bat that leaned against a wall behind the two dealers, just beyond the range of their peripheral vision. It was a wicked looking implement, with a large number of six-inch nails embedded at various angles in the head and along the first foot of the neck. Picking it up with one massive hand, he tested the weight and then, apparently satisfied, went and stood behind the two prisoners.

"For what it's worth," he said, running the fingers of his free hand through Tyrone's bushy hair to work out how far down his skull started, "I think I believe you when you say you are innocent."

On hearing this, Tyrone nearly fainted with relief. He scrunched his eyes shut and let out a long, pitiful moan of gratitude.

"Open your eyes, Tyrone," Goliath ordered. "I want you to watch what I do to people who steal from my associates."

As Tyrone tearfully complied, Goliath raised the baseball bat high above his gleaming dome and brought it down with tremendous force into the unconscious head of the fat man. The sound of the impact was sickeningly loud, reverberating around the basement like a thunderclap. The unconscious man's head jerked forward violently as the back of his skull was caved in. With a grunt of satisfaction, Goliath released his grip on the bat, which remained exactly where it was, having been nailed to his cranium.

"Jesus…" Livingstone breathed, startled by the sudden display of violence. He was immediately conscious of the giant's eyes turning on him to gauge his reaction, and he knew any show of emotion on his part would be perceived as a sign of weakness. That wasn't going to be a problem; Livingstone did what he always did in situations like this and put on his dead face, making it appear devoid of any feeling or humanity.

With the body still twitching, Goliath took a leisurely walk around to the front and knelt down to study Drake's face.

The left side of Tyrone's face was now covered with blood spatter, and he was shrieking hysterically as he tried to shake it off. "Oh God, oh God," he whimpered repeatedly." You killed Drake, man. You fucking killed Drake."

"Be quiet," Goliath snapped, raising a warning finger. "I won't be happy if you spoil this demonstration for our visitor."

Overcome by shock and revulsion, Tyrone was now crying uncontrollably. "I – I'm sorry," he stammered.

Goliath stood up and grasped the bat's handle in his right hand. Using it as a lever, he tilted Drake's head backwards, manipulating him like a gruesome puppeteer. The small-time drug dealer's eyes were half-open, but there was no longer any life in them.

Goliath tentatively tugged at the bat's handle to see how tightly the nails had become wedged into his victim's skull. All that achieved was to make Drake's head twist from side to side like he was having a violent disagreement with somebody.

The macabre sight made the giant smile.

"You stole Marvin's money, didn't you?" he accused the corpse. As soon as he'd finished speaking, he twisted the bat a couple of times to make Drake shake his head. Goliath looked at Tyrone and laughed. "Drake says no," he said.

"Please…" Tyrone begged, emitting the word as a long, anguished howl.

Livingstone watched on dispassionately. Instead of acting like a man, the stupid boy was making himself sound utterly pathetic to the psychotic giant.

Laughing at his captive's distress, Goliath took hold of the bat with both hands this time, and, placing his right foot against the back of Drake's chair, began violently twisting the handle: left, right, up, down. The muscles in his arms corded, and his breathing became faster. Finally, the bat came flying away, spraying blood, bone, and bits of dura mater everywhere.

"That's better," Goliath said, a little breathlessly. "Now that I've worked out how best to extract it, it'll be much easier next time."

Still sobbing, Tyrone glanced up at him, his face filling with dread. "You're not… you're not going to hit him again, are you?"

Goliath shook his head, solemnly. "No, Tyrone, I have finished with him."

All colour drained from Tyrone's tear streaked face. "So, w-what did y-you mean when you s-said 'next time'?"

"Well," Goliath said, walking behind him. "Do you remember I said that I didn't like you?"

"Y-yes," Tyrone sobbed, "but surely–"

Goliath swung the bat, sideways this time, like an American baseball star hitting a home run. The nails were driven into the terrified man's temple with incredible power. The bone was much thinner there, so the nails entered smoothly, hardly encountering any resistance at all. The sound of the impact was duller, too, more like a watermelon being dropped. Tyrone didn't even have time to cry out as the strike imploded his cheekbone and shattered his jaw, sending his disfigured head rocketing sideways at tremendous speed.

From across the room Livingstone watched on with calm detachment. Tyrone's fate had been sealed the moment Goliath had strapped him to the chair. What had just happened was sad, he supposed, but the ever-present risk of meeting a violent end was a consequence of the lifestyle they all embraced. Everyone who played the game knew the risks, but they all thought it would never happen to them. Tyrone had made his choices in life, and those choices had led to his death.

He should have made better choices.

Wrenching the bat free a moment later – Goliath had been right, it was much easier the second time around – he stood back and evaluated his handiwork.

"There. All done," he said contentedly.

Dropping the bat, Goliath ambled over to a metal dustbin at the far end of the room and began undressing. Everything went into the bin, even his shoes and underwear. When he was naked, he picked up a yellow packet of bleach wipes from a shelf and began vigorously rubbing his hands and arms with them. The used wipes also went into the bin. A new set of identical clothing was waiting for him on a plastic coated hanger next to the bin.

A few minutes later, he led Livingstone back up the secret staircase to the manager's office, poured them both a generous measure of Macallan whiskey, and invited his newest client to take a seat in one of the armchairs by the coffee table.

"So," he asked, once he had made himself comfortable on the sofa, "what would you have done in my place?"

"Exactly the same," Livingstone replied, keeping his tone neutral. "Except…"

Goliath smiled knowingly. "I know what you're thinking. Why kill them here?"

Livingstone nodded. It had been reckless to the point of stupidity, and he wasn't sure that he wanted someone like that working for him.

"Do you think I killed them here out of arrogance, a misguided belief that I am so good at my job that I can kill with impunity?"

"Is that why you did it?" Livingstone asked, turning the question around.

Goliath shook his head slowly but firmly. "No, fam, I killed them here because it is the safest place I could possibly have chosen." He sat back in his chair, a man totally at ease. "These men will eventually be reported missing," he explained. "Even scum like them have family who worry about them. Their bodies will never turn up, of course, but supposing the police did launch a missing person enquiry at some point, it would never go anywhere."

"You seem very confident."

"I am. There's nothing to link either of them to this club or to me. Our state-of-the-art CCTV system has been recording all night and, as it covers everywhere within the club, even the basement, any foul play would have been captured on film."

"The way you've fooled the basement camera is ingenious," Livingstone allowed. "But what happens when the Old Bill find footage of the dead men arriving at the club earlier in the day? That'll cause you problems, especially as there won't be any footage of them leaving."

Goliath smiled indulgently. "Don't worry, fam. I've got it all covered. Tyrone and Drake were picked up miles from here, well away from any CCTV cameras. The van used to grab them was on false plates, so if the Feds check DVLA records they'll be misdirected to a perfectly legitimate van that's registered to the local authority, and they won't find anything incriminating in that! As soon as the two fools were tasered and bundled into the van, my men took their mobile phones off them. The batteries and SIM cards were immediately removed, so the Feds won't be able to work out their movements from their phone records. My men rang ahead when they were nearing the club and, at that point, the cameras were turned off for precisely four minutes, which was all the time they needed to drive into the rear car park, unload the prisoners, and depart. The routine will be repeated in the morning in order to allow the bodies, which will be neatly wrapped up in the thick plastic sheeting you saw on the basement floor, to be removed. Everything will be taken straight to a nearby incinerator, where a man we pay an obscene amount of money to turn a blind eye to our activities every now and again will make sure that they are cremated."

It was incredibly clever, Livingstone had to admit. Although Goliath had killed two men on his property, the footage from the club's doctored CCTV would refute that fact.

Livingstone slowly nodded his approval. "Impressive, bruv," he said.

"Impressive enough to convince you to hire me, I hope?" the giant said.

"Before I answer that, tell me one thing. Why did you kill those men in front of me, a complete stranger? Surely the fewer witnesses the better?"

The giant chortled. "Mr Livingstone, I have checked you out thoroughly. You are no stranger to death – in fact, the word is that you have personally killed at least three men."

Livingstone had indeed killed three men, not that he was going to admit it. The first had tried to stab him because he was becoming too powerful; the second had sent the man who tried to stab him, and the third had shot at Livingstone during a botched drugs robbery. No bodies had ever been found; the men had just disappeared.

And then there was the loose-lipped junkie he'd disposed of a few years back. Well, strictly speaking, all he'd done was ensure the addict was given some contaminated smack, knowing that it would be injected without hesitation, causing a fatal reaction. There had been several similar deaths around the estate at that time and, as he'd predicted, the Feds had simply assumed the addict he'd killed was just another overdose.

"Nothing was ever proved," he said.

Goliath beamed. "Ha! Of course not. You and I are kindred spirits. I felt it the moment we met. I have a good nose for people," he said, tapping it, "and I instinctively knew that I could trust you with my secret, unlike Tyrone downstairs."

Goliath seemed to harbour an illusion that, because they were both murderers, they had something in common.

"Besides," Goliath said with a malevolent grin, "men like us know how dangerous talking to the wrong people can be for our health."

In other words, if Livingstone ratted Goliath out, he wouldn't live long enough to testify. That was fine. Goliath knew it worked both ways.

"So, you killed him because he might have talked, not because you didn't like him?" Livingstone said.

Goliath nodded. "Yes, that's why I killed Tyrone. He had a big mouth, and he would have sold me out to the Feds the first time that he got himself into trouble. So, you see, despite my reputation for being a little crazy, which I am very happy to encourage, I can assure you that there is always method to my madness."

"I believe you," Livingstone said, and he did.

"Good," Goliath said with a contented sigh. "So, shall we finally get down to business? Tell me, how can I be of service to you?"

"It's very simple," Livingstone said, knocking back his drink and holding the glass out for a refill, "I want you to come down to London and start a war for me."

CHAPTER TWO

Tuesday 25th May 1999
TROUBLE ARRIVES BY TRAIN

It was a gloriously sunny Tuesday in late May, and the forecasters were confidently predicting that the good weather would continue throughout the rest of the week, which probably meant that it would be raining by nightfall.

The Inter-City train from Manchester Piccadilly pulled into Euston main-line station dead on time at seventeen minutes past midday. As the alighting passengers wearily trudged along the lengthy platform towards the exit ramp, a slender black man stood on the gantry above them, watching with interest. The twenty-year old wore a faded pair of baggy jeans with the crotch sagging down almost as far as his knees, a grubby white sweatshirt with a faded cannabis leaf logo plastered across its chest, and a pair of blue Nike training shoes. His name was Tyson Meeks, but everyone called him 'Weasel.'

Weasel was feeling nice and mellow, thanks to the king sized spliff he'd smoked before entering the station. During last night's briefing, his handler had warned him to stay off the puff until today's task was out of the way, insisting that he needed to have his wits about him if he was going to be of any use to his paymasters at The Yard. Meeks had readily agreed, but as a prolific user, he could no more lay off the ganja than he could resist walking past a stray ten-pound note without picking it up.

He spotted his targets the moment the three men stepped out of their second-class carriage about halfway along the train. In truth, it would have been hard to miss the sinister looking trio of black men, partly due to their stature, but mostly because of the palpable aura of violence that surrounded them. The other passengers seemed to sense this too, for they all gave the surly looking group a wide berth.

Their leader was a towering brute of a man, with a glistening bald head the size of a bowling ball. Wrap-around sunglasses shielded his eyes, but Meeks imagined they would be actively scanning the concourse ahead, constantly seeking out any potential threats. He was talking into a mobile, the device seeming tiny in his huge paw.

The bald man moved with an exaggerated swagger, and his long, loping strides seemed to eat up distance effortlessly, so much so that his underlings were having to power-walk to keep up with him.

The two thugs struggling to keep pace were so strikingly similar in appearance that they had to be identical twins. Tweedle-fucking-dum and Tweedle-fucking-dee, Meeks thought, giggling to himself.

Without averting his eyes from the three men, Meeks pulled out his mobile and dialled a number from memory. It was answered on the second ring. "They've arrived," he said, and proceeded to describe them. He stayed on the phone until the man at the other end confirmed that his people had located the newcomers on camera.

All three of the men carried small holdalls, but as they were only staying overnight, he doubted that they would need too much in the way of clothing. Meeks wondered if they had brought any hardware with them, or if they were content to use the shooters that his boss had promised to supply when he'd hired them for the job.

Although his work was now officially done, Meeks continued to observe the three men when they reached the concourse, curious as to what they would do next.

After glancing around, presumably to get his bearings, the man called Goliath checked the time on the big electronic station clock and then, nodding for the others to follow him, set off towards the nearest men's room.

His overprotective handler had laboured the point that these men were extremely dangerous; he had warned Meeks that he was not, under any circumstances, to make direct contact with them. That advice was all very well and good, but it now occurred to Weasel Meeks that he might be able to earn himself a tidy little bonus if he could dig up some dirt on them. Seeing pound signs instead of potential danger, he gave them a few seconds to get ahead and then sauntered along behind at a leisurely pace.

He was so absorbed in monitoring the movements of the giant and his two cronies that he failed to notice the three strapping Eastern Europeans who stepped out of the rear carriage a few seconds after everyone else had alighted. Each wore non-branded jeans, sneakers and sweatshirts, and each carried a cheap satchel over his shoulder. Their leader had a silk scarf wrapped around his neck to conceal the eye-catching tattoo of a snake curled around a dagger. Like Goliath before him, he was talking into his mobile.

———

Tweedledum and Tweedledee were standing outside the washroom locked in an animated conversation about football when Meeks passed them, and he concluded that they either had much stronger bladders than their boss, or they had relieved themselves before leaving the train.

From the tiny snippet of conversation he overheard, it appeared that one twin supported United, the other City, demonstrating that they weren't identical in every aspect after all. An interesting discovery, perhaps, but not one that would earn him any extra wonga from the Feds. Engrossed in a debate about who was the better player, George Best or Dennis Law, they gave Meeks no more than a cursory glance as he strolled into the washroom.

Big, bad and bald was standing at the furthest urinal, relieving himself, when he entered. Apart from the two of them, the wash room appeared to be completely empty, but it always paid to be careful so, on the pretence of tying a shoelace, Meeks bent down and checked under the line of cubicles. Satisfied that they were all vacant, he shuffled over to a row of wash basins and began to scrub his hands, surreptitiously monitoring the giant in the mirror.

A few moments later, Goliath appeared beside him. He gave Meeks the once over out of the corner of his eye – an action borne more out of habit than suspicion – and then he commenced washing hands the size of snow shovels.

Almost immediately, the giant wrinkled his nose and turned to glower down at Meeks. "That's some strong shit you've been smoking, fam," he said in an African accent that contained subtle traces of Mancunian influence. The voice was nowhere near as deep as Meeks had expected it to be.

"I'm getting high just standing next to you," Goliath informed him with a grin.

Meeks smiled sheepishly, and gave his hands a quick shake to remove the excess water. "It was top quality stuff, bruv," he admitted, following Goliath across the room to a bank of wall mounted hot-air dryers. Mirroring the other man's actions, he inserted his – much smaller – hands and rubbed them together vigorously.

Another entrepreneurial thought struck Meeks. Perhaps he could top up the fee he was already receiving from the police informant's fund by selling some dope to the very man he was being paid to grass up. That would be pretty ballsy of him, he thought, quickly smothering the smirk that had begun to form on his face. "So, blud, do you prefer resin or herbal?" he asked. "I've got both, and you'll find my prices are very reasonable."

———

In the control car that was parked a short distance away from the station, Acting Detective Inspector Tony Dillon of SO7, the Organised Crime Group, spoke into the hand-held encrypted radio, his tone one of boredom. "Control to eyeball, can we have an update please?"

"*The two smaller Tangos–*" a Tango was a target "*–are waiting outside the men's room nearest the clock, and the third has gone inside.*" The voice belonged to DC Christine Taylor, who was currently sitting in the station's CCTV control centre monitoring the three black men remotely.

There was a loud crackle of static, and then Taylor was speaking again, and there was mischief in her voice. "*'Ere, guv, their leader's bloody massive. Compared to him, you look like a stick insect.*"

Dillon snorted. *Cheeky cow!*

Now in his late twenties, Dillon was a six-foot-two inches tall former powerlifter whose chest circumference was just shy of fifty inches when fully flexed. Grinning, he squeezed the press to talk – or PTT – button with his thumb. "He's probably on the gear," he retorted, naturally assuming that if Goliath really was significantly bigger than him, he could only have got that way by using steroids. "Won't do him any good in the long run, though, mark my words. He'll end up with an enlarged heart and a shrivelled dick. At least mine is all natural."

His driver gave him a strange look, apparently confused as to whether Dillon was referring to his heart or his dick.

"*I wouldn't know,*" Christine assured him in a prim and proper tone that suggested she didn't want to know either.

Dillon raised an eyebrow. That hadn't been her attitude when they were snuggled up in bed together last night!

"*Stand by,*" Christine said, suddenly serious. "*Tango One has just emerged from the toilets and all three of them are now heading towards the London Underground entrance.*"

"Received," Dillon said, lowering the radio and turning thoughtfully to his driver. "Well, it looks like the snout was bang on the money. Livingstone's drafted in outside muscle to carry out the contract, and we're going to have to move fast if we're going to be ready in time to stop them."

He pulled out his Job mobile and phoned DS Michael Moore, the man in charge of the surveillance unit waiting to follow the Mancunians from the station to the hotel they were going to be staying at while they were in London.

Moore had put one of his own people in the CCTV office with Christine and, as they were using their own communications network, Dillon knew that he would already be fully aware that the Mancs were on the move.

"Hello Mike, Dillon here. Listen, mate, it looks like that hit we were tipped off about last night is definitely going ahead, so I need to get back to base pronto, to get the proper authorities written up and signed off in time to deploy a firearms team this evening. Let me know as soon as they reach their hotel. I don't mean to harp on, but I need confirmation that they're definitely staying at the place the snout told us about as soon as possible, so I can get the OP up and running."

Thanks to a heads up from Weasel Meeks, the hotel had already been scoped out, and a suitable observation post – or OP – had been identified nearby.

Hanging up, Dillon let out a heartfelt sigh. It was going to be a very long day.

"Back to the factory?" his driver asked. He'd watched too many episodes of *The Sweeney*.

Dillon nodded, wearily. "As quick as you can please, Bill." The driver's name was actually Geoff but, as any fan of the cult 70s detective show knew, Regan's regular driver in *The Sweeney* had been called Bill.

"You'll miss all this when you get promoted next month and move across to AMIP," Geoff said, starting the car.

Although Dillon had been acting in the role of DI since passing the promotion exam earlier in the year, the rank would finally become permanent in a few weeks' time when he transferred to the Area Major Investigation Pool. His best friend, a DCI called Jack Tyler, was already over there and, with a little bit of luck, he would be able to wangle getting Dillon posted onto his team.

Bill – or rather Geoff – was right, though. He had enjoyed his time on the Organised Crime Group. However, as his dear old mum had often said, all good things must eventually come to an end. It was time to move on, and he was very much looking forward to the new challenge. "I suppose I will miss this firm," Dillon admitted, "but it'll be nice to be able to wear a suit again, and not have to dress like a tramp every day – something you pull off rather well, by the way."

Geoff grinned. "I do my best," he said.

"Trust me," Dillon said, grinning back, "you've got a natural talent for it."

As the car set off, Dillon dialled the number for Danny Flynn, his Detective Superintendent. Might as well give the grumpy old git a heads up that he was on his way in to seek authority to run a firearms operation. No doubt, Flynn would have a hissy fit when he found out just how much it was going to cost him. Dillon's shopping list included an SO19 team of Specialised Firearms Officers and an Alpha team – surveillance officers with an armed capacity – from C11.

If everything went according to plan, the SFOs would carry out the hard stop as soon as the suspects left the hotel. If it didn't, the surveillance team would have to follow the suspects away from the venue, with the SFOs holding back until an alternative spot for the armed intervention could be identified. Oh well, he thought, budgets were there to be spent, although he very much doubted that Mr tight-wad Flynn would see it that way.

———

After arriving from Manchester Piccadilly, Dritan Bajramovic, Valmir Demaci, and Lorik Kraja followed the instructions they had been given and caught a Victoria Line train from Euston to Finsbury Park, a region of North London where the Boroughs of Islington, Haringey and Hackney all converged. The journey, all three stops, took a total of eight-minutes, which they completed in silence.

Outside the station, traffic was nose to tail as it trundled along the Seven Sisters Road at a snail's pace, making a deafening noise and spewing out fumes. The pavements were equally congested, and everyone seemed to be in a rush, even those with nowhere to go.

When the lights changed, the three men quickly crossed to the other side of the road, carried along by the sea of people making the journey with them, and set off at a brisk pace towards Manor House.

They passed a few small retailers, none of whom seemed to be doing much business.

"I'm hungry," Valmir complained, drooling as he stared longingly through the window of a kebab shop. A nasty scar ran from the bridge of his nose all the way down the left side of his face to the corner of his upper lip, giving him a perpetual sneer.

"Me, too," Lorik agreed.

"Let's stop for some food," Valmir said aggressively, the way he said everything. He was a big man, and his bulky frame took a lot of calories to fuel.

"You're always hungry," Dritan chided, giving his associate a little nudge to get him moving again. "Stop complaining. There will be plenty of time to eat later. First, we book into our hotel."

Valmir was annoyed, but Dritan was the boss, and he wasn't a man to be messed with.

After a five-minute hike, they reached the bed and breakfast accommodation that had been booked for them in advance. It was a Victorian building with high metal railings surrounding the perimeter. The front had been freshly painted white, and there was a bright green canopy above the entrance. Three gold stars were prominently displayed on a plaque outside the door, but they were fooling no one; the establishment was basically a doss house.

The reception was dim and dingy, and the middle-aged woman behind the desk looked half asleep and totally disinterested. A pungent aroma filled the air; either someone had recently been spraying a powerful insecticide or it was the receptionist's perfume.

"What a dump," Valmir muttered under his breath. "Remind me to wipe my feet on the way out."

Their rooms had been reserved for them earlier in the day. Booking in under false names, they were given the keys for two adjoining rooms on the first floor towards the rear of the building. The crone behind the desk told them they were not allowed to bring women back to their rooms, and that there would be a room inspection before they left and they would be charged for any damage caused during their stay.

The lift was out of order, so they had to take the stairs.

"This place is a hovel," Lorik complained. "I've stayed in better gulags."

Dritan, as their leader, had a room all to himself. The other two had to share. The carpets were threadbare, the walls were damp, and the beds were lumpy, but it didn't matter to Dritan; they were only going to be there for a few hours and, in truth, they had all stayed in far worse accommodation than this.

Once they had settled in, Valmir was allowed to venture out, and he headed straight back to the kebab shop to get them all some food.

As soon as he was alone, Dritan called his boss on the burner phone he had been given to obtain further instructions.

———

As predicted, Detective Superintendent Flynn was not a happy bunny when Dillon appraised him of the developing situation upon his return from Euston, and for a while it was touch and go as to whether he would approve the job or not.

In his mid-fifties, with an unruly mop of silver hair and a bushy moustache that badly needed trimming, Danny Flynn had the craggy face and veined nose of a heavy drinker, and the nicotine stained fingers and chesty cough of an even heavier smoker. The first thing he'd wanted to know was why the Metropolitan Police Service couldn't just deliver an Osman warning to the intended victim.

Prior to 1998, there had been no legal obligation for police forces in the United Kingdom to provide a duty of care for victims of crime. However, that year the seemingly controversial case of Osman v United Kingdom had gone before the European Court of Human Rights seeking to rectify this. The ECHR had delivered their judgement on 28th October, ruling in favour of Osman, and creating a clear onus on the police to provide a duty of care from that moment onwards.

One of the first steps taken by UK law enforcement agencies in the wake of the ECHR ruling was to implement what became known as 'Osman warnings.' These were given in circumstances where credible intelligence indicated a realistic threat to life existed but there was insufficient evidence to make an arrest. In such circumstances, officers were required to provide a verbal or written notice – often both – to the potential victim, telling them that their life might be in danger.

Dillon patiently explained that they couldn't give out an Osman warning because they still weren't sure exactly who the intended target was, just that he was a relatively big player from an Albanian crime syndicate based in North London.

Flynn harrumphed at that. "Sounds pretty feeble to me. Just how credible is this so-called intelligence?" he demanded.

Dillon handed over a slim manila file marked 'Confidential'. "Here's the current intelligence picture on everyone connected to this job. Also, off the record, I've got a snout who's close to Livingstone. He drove Livingstone up to Manchester about three weeks ago, so that he could hire a guy called Samuel Adebanjo. His street name's Goliath, presumably because of his size, and the bloke's a total nutcase. Greater Manchester Police have a file on him a foot thick, and he's been the prime suspect in several particularly brutal gang related murders over the past few years, although they've never been able to pin anything on him."

Flynn seemed highly dubious. "And why exactly does this Livingstone chap need the services of a killer for hire anyway? He's a relatively big player himself. Couldn't he get one of his own people to do the dirty deed? Keep it in the family, so to speak."

Livingstone was a middle tier criminal who ran a thriving crime network in North London. He was known to be involved with prostitution, firearms and drug supply – mainly cannabis, amphetamine and cocaine – along with loan sharking and a bit of racketeering.

"You need to know the background story to understand that," Dillon said. "Earlier this year, the Regional Crime Squad closed down a North London criminal network who were up to their necks in drug trafficking, firearms importation, and white slavery. As you can imagine, when they were taken off the street, it created a bit of a void in the local drug and prostitution businesses."

"I bet it did," Flynn said.

"Livingstone's gang, an Albanian mob, and an element of the

Turkish mafia all moved quickly to try and fill the vacuum, hoping to claim the vacant turf as their own."

Flynn grunted. That was the trouble with nicking criminals; as soon as they were taken out of circulation, another parasite would step up to the plate and take over exactly where they had left off.

"From what my snout tells me," Dillon continued, "Livingstone and the Turks are willing to carve up the territory to avoid a turf war developing, but the Albanians are unhappy because they've been offered a much smaller stake than the other two gangs. Apparently, the last meeting became quite heated and the Albanian delegation stormed out. My snout says that Livingstone was deeply offended by this and has decided it can't go unpunished. However, he doesn't want to derail the talks, which taking direct action would obviously do, so his solution is to draft in an outside team to eliminate the offending Albanian in a way that can't be traced back to him."

"Alright then," Flynn countered. "Let's go and see Livingstone and this little crew from Manchester and give them a Reverse Osman." A Reverse Osman involved the police giving the verbal or written warning to the suspect, instead of the victim, making it clear that if anything happened to the intended victim, the recipient of the Reverse Osman warning would be held directly responsible.

Dillon shook his head wearily. He'd already explored that option. "Guv, as soon as I found out that these three villains were coming our way, I had a long chat with the GMP detective who's been after Adebanjo for years. When I mentioned that I was considering slapping a Reverse Osman on him the moment he stepped off the train, he just laughed. He reckons it would be tantamount to waving a red flag at a bull. In his opinion, which I trust, the man is completely unhinged, and us warning him off would just make him all the more determined to carry out the hit, if not today then tomorrow or the day after. Adebanjo's not silly, he knows we can't keep him under surveillance forever. All he's got to do is bide his time. Can you imagine the backlash if he kills this Albanian guy? They've got a reputation for extreme ruthlessness; they would hit back, and hard. Things would escalate quickly, and before we knew it, we'd be stuck in the middle of a three-way turf war, mopping up all the blood."

Flynn grimaced at the thought. He was starting to look a little brow beaten, Dillon thought with some satisfaction.

"Do we know what this Albanian gob-shite said to upset Livingstone?" Flynn asked, agitatedly flicking through the Intel file as he spoke.

Dillon shook his head. "The snout wasn't there when it happened."

There followed a lengthy silence, in which Dillon could almost hear the rusted cogs inside Flynn's head turning at a painfully slow speed. Eventually, his boss sighed unhappily and said, "Bollocks." Looking like he'd just received a terminal prognosis, he reached for the phone on his desk. "I suppose I'd better let the AC's office know that something big is likely to go down tonight," he grumbled, staring daggers at Dillon, whom he obviously blamed for the whole thing. Then, as an afterthought, he ominously added, "You'd better bloody well be right about all this."

———

The unfamiliar ringtone of the burner phone awoke Dritan with a start. For a moment, he didn't know where he was, and panic bloomed inside his chest. Sitting up quickly, his face covered in sweat, he instinctively reached out for an assault rifle that wasn't there. Nervously scanning the unfamiliar environment for signs of an incoming attack, he gradually realised that he was safely ensconced in a London hotel, and not back in some godforsaken war zone where he'd fallen into an exhausted sleep after taking shelter in a bombed-out building. Taking a deep breath to calm himself down, his shaking hand reached for the phone.

"Yes," he said, cautiously.

"*Get your team ready*," the voice of his employer instructed. "*A dark blue Ford Mondeo with a dented nearside rear wing will be waiting for you in the side street next to the hotel in half an hour's time. The doors will be open and the equipment you need is in the boot. Your target will be arriving at the location between eight-thirty and nine, tonight. You will get a call from our client's representative when his arrival is imminent, and you know what to do when he gets there?*"

"Of course," Dritan replied, frostily. The former mercenary was a professional, after all.

When the call finished, Dritan slipped the phone into the front pocket of his jeans and glanced down at this wristwatch. It was almost seven-thirty. Time to start getting ready.

————

Seven-forty-five p.m.

The lengthy main briefing for Operation Tulip – God knew who had come up with such a naff name? – was about to start. They were at East Ham police station, which was sufficiently far away from the suspect's hotel to ensure that they wouldn't become aware of any increased police activity, yet near enough to allow the units involved to reach their intended destination quickly once they deployed.

Detective Superintendent Felicity Knowles was a frizzy haired waif of a woman who looked about fourteen-years old, even though she was actually in her mid-thirties. Dressed in a crumpled grey business suit and flat shoes, her intelligent face was covered in freckles but devoid of make-up. A flyer who was destined for higher office, she had been appointed as Gold Commander for the deployment. This meant that she had overall strategic command and was responsible for achieving a safe resolution, which was a polite way of saying she would be held accountable for anything that went wrong.

Dillon, for his sins, had been appointed Silver, which meant he was responsible for developing and coordinating the tactical plan in order to achieve the Gold Commander's strategic intentions. In other words, his job was to make sure that Gold didn't end up with egg all over her freckled face. He would also have to 'double-hat' as the Senior Investigating Officer if tonight's operation resulted in a prosecution.

Pulling him aside just before they entered the briefing room, Knowles leaned in conspiratorially. "Don't forget, your first priority tonight is to make me look good!"

No pressure there, then, he thought, dutifully following her into the packed room.

When the briefing concluded thirty minutes later, most of the forty-three people involved in the operation stood up and slowly began to file out of the room, intent on using the loo or grabbing a quick cup of coffee before setting off.

What a roller-coaster ride of a day it had been so far, Dillon reflected as he waited behind to go through the final firearms instructions with the Tactical Adviser, a Chief Inspector from SO19, and the firearms officers.

The Tac Adviser had already had the venue discretely recced, and had drawn up a full deployment plan, including multiple contingencies to cater for the different ad hoc scenarios that might occur – the 'what ifs?' as they were referred to. When he'd finished going over these, it was Dillon's turn to address the assembled officers.

In his role as Silver, Dillon emphasised that the interception of the armed suspects before they left the confined area of the hotel car park remained the preferable option, but only if this could be achieved without placing any members of the public or police officers in unacceptable danger. If for any reason it wasn't possible, the surveillance team would slot in behind the stolen car that the suspects were going to be using and follow it until a suitable opportunity arose. The main problem with that scenario, he confided, was that they didn't know the address the three shooters were planning to hit, only that it was somewhere in North London, so they would have to act quickly if they wanted to prevent a shoot-out and all the carnage that came with it.

Before leaving them, Dillon reiterated the standard firearms warning, reading the blurb verbatim from his briefing notes: "If firearms are discharged, it will be the responsibility of the individual officer to justify why that level of force was necessary and proportionate."

The firearms officers listened impassively, having heard these words at every deployment they had ever been involved in, but Dillon still felt like a total git for saying them. It was as though, having pleaded with them to come along and clear his problem up, he was now warning them that unless they did it perfectly, they were likely to get in severe trouble and could even end up gripping the rail, a police euphemism for being prosecuted.

Feeling like a heel, Dillon wandered out into the back yard for some fresh air as soon as he had finished.

The small space was now heaving with police personnel. In addition to the firearms and surveillance teams, he also had a dog unit, a Traffic Patrol car, and a Police Support Unit containing a sergeant and six constables, which was on standby to deal with crowd or traffic displacement and cordon control.

Everyone was on overtime, but that was unavoidable, and none of them seemed to mind, except perhaps for the dog, a mean looking, long haired German Shepherd called 'Fluffy', who had already tried to bite several officers as they walked past him.

Ignoring everyone around him, Dillon leaned against a convenient wall, closed his eyes for a moment and reflected that it was a miracle the operation was still going ahead, because it had almost been completely derailed during the early afternoon when Meeks had called him in a real state of panic. Hardly pausing for breath, and stumbling over his words, Meeks had revealed that his boss, Conrad Livingstone, had just phoned him with a brand new set of instructions.

Livingstone now wanted Meeks to collect a package from a fellow gang member's house at nine p.m., and then run it over to the three goons at the hotel in a stolen car that had been boosted especially for the occasion. After delivering said car and package, Meeks was supposed to make himself scarce while keeping his phone on in case he was needed.

Later – after the job had been carried out – he was to meet the Africans back at the hotel and reclaim both the car and package. The former was to be taken somewhere remote and burnt out; the latter was to be returned from whence it came.

Meeks was, understandably, having a bit of a meltdown when he called. The low-level dealer knew that he was completely expendable as far as Livingstone was concerned, and he had a bad feeling that that was why he had been chosen. Dillon tried his best to reassure the informant, to keep him focused and onside, but secretly he agreed with him.

Livingstone hadn't said what the package was, but it stood to reason that it contained the weaponry that the out-of-town muscle was going to use to take down the Albanian.

Everything had immediately been put on hold. To continue, they would need authority to use Meeks as a participating informant, and there were all sorts of hoops to jump through before that proposal could be green lighted.

After typing out the relevant paperwork, Dillon had rushed straight up to The Yard to deliver a very stressful, 'in person' presentation to the Commander, taking with him the appropriate written support from DSU Flynn, who had almost suffered a coronary when Dillon asked him to put pen to paper and stick his own neck on the line by supporting his junior officer.

———

It was eight o'clock when Dritan led his small team out of the hotel. They had all changed into identical nondescript baggy tracksuits, and now all wore black leather gloves despite it being a warm night. Dritan had tied the scarf back around his neck to conceal his tattoo, and each man had a black balaclava tucked into their waistband, although they wouldn't need to don those until much later.

The dirty looking Mondeo was exactly where their employer had promised it would be, parked in Portland Rise facing away from Seven Sisters Road. It was easily recognisable by the dent in the rear wing. Lorik, who was their wheelman, tugged at the driver's door, and was relieved to see that it opened immediately. He leaned in and checked the ignition. As expected, the stolen car had been barrelled, and a screwdriver lay in the footwell ready to be used as a substitute key.

After looking around to make sure that no one was watching, Dritan went to the boot and rummaged around inside. There was a large red jerrycan full of petrol, which would be needed later, when the time came to dispose of the evidence. Other than that, it appeared to be empty, but when he lifted the lid to the compartment for the spare wheel, he saw a lumpy looking package wrapped in an old bath towel sitting in the hollow where the wheel should have been.

Unfolding the towel, he discovered a thick layer of bubble wrap beneath it. Tearing this open, he was pleased to see it contained three Škorpion machine pistols, each with two spare magazines, a loaded 9mm Baikal IZH-79 pistol, complete with a silencer, and two-hundred-and-seventy rounds of 7.65mm factory produced ammunition for the Škorpions, which equated to three full magazines for each gun. The weapons all looked to be in pristine condition, clean and well oiled. Folding the cloth back around the bundle, he scooped it up under one arm and closed the boot. Dritan barked out an order for Lorik to remain with the car, and then nodded for Valmir to accompany him back to the hotel.

As soon as they reached the privacy of his room, he laid the bundle on the bed and immediately began inspecting one of the Škorpions and the Baikal. He tossed the other two weapons over to his compatriot, who set to work examining them with the practiced ease of an ex-soldier.

When all the guns had been field-stripped, examined and reassembled, the two men checked the firing pins and the springs in the magazines. After loading them, they re-checked the firing mechanisms to make sure none of the weapons would jam on them when the trigger was pulled.

When he was satisfied that the guns were fit for purpose, Dritan gave the room a once over to make sure they hadn't inadvertently left anything behind that could be traced back to them at a later date. When that was done, he tucked the Baikal into the front of his waistband and pulled his top down to conceal it. Then, he went down to reception to settle their bill and organise the room inspections. While he did that, Valmir took the rest of the artillery back to the car.

————

By eight-thirty p.m., the nerves were starting to kick in as everyone formed up in the crammed rear yard, getting themselves ready to depart. The order had been given for all units to be 'on plot' by 20:45 hours at the latest. No one needed to be told twice; they all knew that lives depended on them being where they were supposed to be when they were supposed to be there.

For the umpteenth time, Dillon nervously checked his Job mobile to make sure that the battery was fully charged and that he had a strong signal. The plan was for Meeks to call him the moment he set off from his flat to collect the car and package. They had worked out that it would take him approximately fifteen-minutes to reach the other gang member's address and, even if he set off straight away, it would take around twenty-five minutes to drive across London to Adebanjo's hotel.

As Dillon watched the dog handler ushering a reluctant Fluffy into the rear of his van, the radio crackled, and the observation post transmitted the latest of their regular fifteen-minute updates. "*No change, no change,*" a reedy voice whispered, confirming that all three Mancunians were still inside the hotel.

Since their arrival earlier in the day, Adebanjo had left only once, making a short trip on foot. He had left the hotel at ten past seven that evening and had returned half an hour later, carrying a grocery bag with the name of a local store on it. The twins hadn't left since their arrival, and everyone was confident that the three men would remain there now until the weapons and the stolen car were delivered.

There were four SO19 vehicles, each crewed by three extremely fit looking SFOs who were dressed in scruffy plain clothes. Without exception, they stood by their rides, looking utterly relaxed as they gave their weapons a final once over.

Before the briefing, Dillon had asked the team leader what firepower they were packing. The Trojan skipper had explained that they all carried a standard issue Glock 17 Self Loading Pistol. In addition, the front passengers of each car were armed with a Heckler and Koch G36C carbine, which was a short-barrelled semi-automatic weapon chambered to fire a 5.65 rifle round, and the rear passengers had been issued with Hatton Guns. These were short-stock shotgun's that could be used to blow out tyres or blast off locks.

Checking his phone again, Dillon thought that the SFOs all looked ready for action, and he could imagine them going over their respective roles and responsibilities in their heads, conscious that they might be called upon to make life or death decisions in the blink of an eye during the coming hours; decisions that could not only have massive ramifications for the Metropolitan Police Service, but which could dramatically impact on themselves, their colleagues and their families.

Dillon didn't envy them their job and, as he recalled the 'on your heads be it if you fire your weapons' instructions that he had recently given them regarding the use of force, he felt another pang of guilt.

The SFO team leader was a seasoned police sergeant and former paratrooper called Tim Newman, whose call sign tonight was Bronze Trojan. Newman was in his mid-thirties, about five-foot-ten-inches tall, with cropped fair hair, hard grey eyes, and the wiry build of a marathon runner. Dillon watched him moving amongst his team, speaking quiet words of encouragement and satisfying himself that everything was as it should be. Exuding confidence from every pore, Newman's every movement was controlled, economical, and he struck Dillon as a strong leader who would remain focused under pressure and be as cool as ice if they came under fire.

The four vehicles, using the call signs Trojan Alpha, Trojan Bravo, Trojan Charlie and Trojan Delta, would travel in convoy, and would deploy for the hard stop using tried and tested methods they had all practiced a thousand times.

To Dillon's acute embarrassment, DSU Knowles had collared Newman straight after the tactical briefing, staring at him with her big blue eyes and wanting to know if he had any concerns over how his team would perform tonight if things went pear-shaped. Newman's eyes had narrowed to slits, and there had been steel in his voice as he'd informed her that he had no concerns whatsoever.

Dillon had pulled him to one side as soon as they were out of earshot and away from prying eyes, feeling the need to explain that Knowles hadn't meant any disrespect; it was just that this was her first real test since passing the Gold training, and she was understandably nervous. Despite her senior rank, she was still relatively young in service.

"It seems to me that the good old days, when guv'nors moved up the ranks at a slower rate and actually had the time to learn their trade, are rapidly becoming a thing of the past," Newman reminisced with some sadness. "I see it happening more and more: graduate entrants being pushed through the ranks too quickly, made to run before they can even walk, and given levels of responsibility they're nowhere near ready to handle."

Dillon could only shrug resignedly. He'd noticed it, too. "Get used to it, mate," he'd said. "Sadly, it's the future."

Just then, Dillon's phone rang, making him jump. The caller display said: *Weasel.*

"Shit," he said, pressing the green button and raising the phone to his ear. It looked like the show was about to begin.

CHAPTER THREE

HARD STOPS AND HIT MEN

"What do you mean, you can't open the bag?" Dillon asked, incredulously.

"*It's not my fault,*" Meeks complained, sounding like a petulant child. "*The bloody thing's padlocked, bruv.*"

After collecting the package, which had turned out to be a green vinyl duffle bag with a thirty litre capacity, Meeks had driven a short distance away from his fellow gang member's flat before pulling over into a bus stop to call Dillon.

"Well use your noggin and give it a good shake. See if it rattles like there's metal inside."

There was a pause, followed by a cheesed-off sigh. Meeks even had the audacity to tut.

Dillon rolled his eyes." Will you please just get on with it, you Muppet," he demanded impatiently.

A series of unpleasant grunting noises ensued, and Dillon visualised Meeks turning red-faced as he shook the bag about.

"*It's too well padded, bruv,*" Meeks bemoaned when he finally came back on the line, breathing heavily from his exertions. "*Nothing's rattling inside, though, innit.*"

Dillon shook his head in exasperation. Meeks definitely wasn't the brightest snout he'd ever had, although he was quite possibly the laziest. "Well give it a good squeeze, then," he cajoled, trying not to lose his temper. "Does it feel like there are any guns inside the bag to you?"

Meeks sucked through his teeth, cursed, and then put the phone down so that he could carry out Dillon's latest instruction. After a few seconds, the informant came back on the line, and his voice was full of frustration. "*Look, all I can tell you is that the bag is proper heavy, bruv. I think I can just about make out the shape of a couple of sawn-off shotguns, but I really can't be sure because everything's covered in fucking bubble wrap.*" To emphasise the point, he held his mobile phone against the bag and squeezed. The unmistakable sound of little air pockets in the bubble wrap popping under pressure travelled down the line to Dillon.

"Alright, that's enough," Dillon snapped after a couple of seconds. "I get the point."

"*So, what do you want me to do?*" Meeks demanded, sounding extremely stressed.

"Give me a minute to think," Dillon said, racking his brain. They had banked on him being able to take a sneak peek inside the bag to let them know what sort of firepower they'd be facing if things went wrong.

"*I don't have a fucking minute, bruv,*" Meeks shot back, and there was a real sense of panic in his voice. "*I'm telling you, blud, these people aint stupid. A phone call will have gone in the minute I breezed Jerome's place, and they'll know exactly how long it takes to get from his gaff to the hotel. If I'm late, they'll be suspicious.*"

"Okay, okay," Dillon said, accepting that Meeks was probably right. "You'd better get going, but before you do, quickly give me the details of the car you're driving."

"*I'm driving a red Golf GTI,*" Meeks informed him. "*Nice wheels, wouldn't mind one of these rides for myself. It's really nice looking, and the build quality —*"

"I don't need a bloody sales pitch," Dillon cut in, wondering whether his informant was high again or just plain stupid, "just the registration number."

Meeks didn't know it offhand, so he had to climb out of the car and walk around to the bonnet in order to read out the number plate. Dillon had to bite his tongue as he listened to the agitated snout grumbling to himself about the imposition.

"*Jerome told me it's a boosted car on false plates, bruv,*" Meeks said, getting back behind the steering wheel, "*so it won't show up as nicked on your computer. They've fitted a new ignition barrel to make it look legit, and I've even got an authentic set of VW keys.*"

Dillon was impressed. Some serious planning had gone into this job. "I'll get a check done anyway," he told Meeks. "Make sure you stop and call again when you're two minutes away from the hotel."

"*I can't keep stopping, bruv,*" Meeks protested, miserably.

"You'll do as you're bloody well told," Dillon snapped, and immediately regretted it. He took a deep breath and then continued speaking, forcing his voice to adopt a softer tone. "Just one more stop," he promised. "It'll literally take you thirty seconds. And remember, just hand over the package and the keys, and then walk away. Do not, under any circumstances, go into that hotel room. Do you understand?"

Meeks snorted. "*I'm not stupid, bruv. There aint no way I'm going in there.*"

———

It was a minute after nine p.m.

Dritan sat in the front passenger seat of the Mondeo, which Lorik had managed to park in Woodberry Grove, at the mouth of the junction with Green Lanes. Facing out into the main road, they had a perfect view of the little Turkish café, with its handful of customers, situated in the middle of a small parade of shops. The half-mile journey from Portland Rise to Woodberry Grove had taken them a paltry four minutes to complete, and they had been incredibly lucky to find this space, arriving just as another car pulled out.

Valmir was now dozing in the back, and his incessant snoring was really starting to irritate Dritan. So much so that he turned on the radio, which was tuned into a pre-set commercial station playing modern pop trash.

"The owner of this car has no taste," he complained, turning to face Lorik. "Can't you find something less painful for my ears to listen to?"

The driver shrugged. "I tried earlier, when you two went back to the hotel, but I think it's broken because I couldn't tune it into another station. Still, anything, even this rubbish, has to be better than listening to the noise he's making." He jerked his thumb backwards, towards the sleeping man as he spoke.

Dritan grunted. That was certainly true.

If their information was accurate, their target should be arriving within the next fifteen minutes. Dritan felt no nerves whatsoever. They were all professionals, and they had gone over the plan of action plenty of times, so all they had to do now was sit quietly and avoid drawing any attention until it was time to act.

———

Weasel Meeks was crapping himself with worry as he rapped on the door of the hotel room where the three Mancunians were staying. He had parked the Golf in the car park, leaving it in the exact location that Dillon had stipulated during the last call, four minutes ago. His legs almost turned to jelly at the thought of having to explain his presence at Euston this morning to the bald-headed giant, who was bound to be suspicious. He had deliberately withheld that information from his handlers during the debrief, knowing they would hit the roof. Should he claim that Livingstone had sent him there to make sure they arrived safely? That sounded good, but what if Goliath called Livingstone to verify this? He would be in dire trouble if that happened. Perhaps he should just say nothing, and hope they didn't recognise him. Perhaps…

The door was opened a fraction by one of the twins, Tweedledum or Tweedledee, he had no idea which. "What do you want?" the surly faced thug demanded.

A wave of relief washed over Meeks. With luck, he would be able to hand his cargo straight over to whichever Tweedle this was and make a swift retreat, thereby avoiding any contact with Goliath. Trying to stop his hands from shaking, Meeks held out the heavy bag in his left and the car keys in his right.

"It's cool, man. My boss told me to deliver these," Meeks said, nervously. "The car's a red VW Golf, and it's parked outside. You can't miss it."

The Tweedle grunted, and then snatched the two items from his outstretched hands. "Wait there," he ordered, and disappeared back inside, leaving the door slightly ajar.

Breeze outta here! A voice shouted in Weasel's head. *Breeze now, you dumb shit, before it's too late.* Deciding that this was a very good idea, he spun on his heels and started to walk away.

"Oi! You! Where d'ya think you're going?" an angry voice yelled, stopping Meeks in his tracks. He turned slowly, dejectedly, to see the twin – he assumed it was the same one he'd handed the stuff over to – waving him back. The man pointed towards the open door. "Get in there," he ordered. "The boss wants a word."

Swallowing hard, Meeks reluctantly did as he'd been told.

————

In the back of the control car, a Ford Galaxy people carrier with blacked out windows, Dillon sat in the dark with Christine Taylor, his loggist for the evening. Geoff, their driver, and the vehicle's only other occupant, had found a quiet little cul-de-sac to park up in, two streets away from the hotel. Geoff tended to eat when he was bored – or nervous, or stressed – and, so far, he had worked his way through two bars of Dairy Milk chocolate and a bag of cheese and onion crisps. He was just starting on a packet of Jaffa Cakes.

"Anyone want one?" he asked, passing the box back.

Dillon declined, but Christine took one and thanked him

"He should have been back out by now," Dillon whispered, his stomach churning with worry. Meeks was his informant, and although he didn't like the man, he didn't want anything bad to happen to him.

Christine, a slim brunette in her mid-twenties, popped the last of the Jaffa Cake into her mouth and picked up the encrypted radio. "Do you want me to check in with the OP?" she asked.

Dillon shook his head pensively. "No, we should probably give it a couple of minutes more."

Flynn had wanted Meeks to wear a wire so that they could monitor any conversations he had with the three shooters, but the informant had gone ballistic at the suggestion, and had flatly refused to cooperate. "Bruv, if they search me and find that, I'm brown bread," he had raged. "I'm taking a big enough risk as it is, without doing that." He was so upset by the request that he had threatened to walk away unless they changed their mind. In the end, they had been left with no choice but to back down. Dillon thought that Meeks had been one-hundred percent right to put his foot down, but if he had given in and worn a transmitter they wouldn't be sitting there now, fretting about what was going on inside the hotel.

The radio crackled into life, almost making Dillon jump out of his skin. "*Stand-by, stand-by,*" the voice of the officer inside the observation post sounded excited. "*OP to all units, Tangos One, Two, and Three emerging from the hotel. There's a fourth man with them. I can confirm this is Tango Four.*" That was the designation Meeks had been given when he'd arrived to drop off the Golf ten-minutes earlier. No one, apart from Dillon, Flynn and Taylor, his co-handler, knew that he was working for them. As far as everyone else was concerned, Meeks was just another gang member.

Dillon sat up straight as adrenaline surged through him, and he imagined that every other officer engaged in the deployment was doing likewise. They were approaching the moment of truth, when everything would either go brilliantly well or fall apart around them.

Dillon snatched the radio from the seat next to Christine, where she had deposited it in order to write the latest update in her log. "Silver to OP, can you see the guns at all, over?"

"*OP to Silver, Tango One is carrying the bag, and it looks pretty heavy, so presumably the weapons are still inside.*"

"Received," Dillon said. Then, taking a deep breath and praying he was making the right decision, he squeezed the PTT button again

"Bronze Trojan from Silver, we are now State Amber, repeat State Amber. Operational control now passes to you for tactical intervention."

Up until that moment, the operation had been at State Green, which meant the evidential threshold for armed intervention and arrest had not yet been reached. Dillon's announcement was a declaration that they now had sufficient grounds to act, and Trojan's deployment for a hard stop was warranted.

"*State Amber all received by Trojan Bronze,*" Newman replied calmly.

"Let's hope this doesn't turn into a bloody fiasco," Dillon said, placing the hand-held radio back on the seat between them.

"I'm sure it'll be fine," Christine assured him, although Dillon couldn't detect the slightest trace of conviction in her voice. Catching the questioning look he gave her, and making sure that Geoff couldn't see, she reached across and briefly squeezed his hand in the darkness.

"*All units from OP, all four men now walking across the lot towards the red Golf. Standby…*"

"What the hell is he playing at, accompanying them to the car?" Taylor asked, frantically scribbling the time of the transmission in her log.

"I wish I knew," Dillon said. Suddenly, he had a very bad feeling about this.

———

Less than five minutes after receiving a telephone call from an unknown man who spoke with a coarse London accent, informing them that the Turks would be arriving shortly, the target car pulled up outside the Turkish café in Green Lanes. Dritan knew the client had someone following the target, but he couldn't spot the tail car, which meant they were good at their job.

There were no spaces available against the kerb, so the driver of the silver E Class Mercedes just double parked it in the road and stuck on his hazards, not giving a toss about the obstruction he was now causing. Ignoring the honking horns from behind, three men, all Turkish, alighted, leaving the driver to wait with the vehicle.

"Here we go," Dritan said, turning around and nudging Valmir's knee roughly. "Wake up," he ordered. "The target has arrived."

Valmir was awake in an instant, showing no signs of sluggishness. "Do we take them now?" he asked, sitting forward to get a better look.

"No," Dritan said, thinking that the man's breath stank. "We hit them on the way out."

Lorik started the engine in anticipation, and then all three men busied themselves by carrying out a final check on their weapons.

With the selector switch set to fully automatic, the short-barrelled Škorpion machine pistols they carried had a discharge rate of 850 rounds per minute. Over longer distances, it wasn't terribly accurate, but for the close up work they were going to be doing tonight, it was perfect.

Looking through the café window into its well-lit interior, they watched the Turks saunter up to the counter as though they owned the place. Their leader was a smartly dressed man in a shiny grey cashmere suit, white shirt and black tie. In his early thirties, he had short, jet black, wavy hair and a thick, Omar Sharif style moustache. The two slovenly looking goons who stood either side of him, doing their best to look intimidating, were obviously just the hired muscle. Unshaven, they were clad in loose fitting jeans, casual shirts and leather bomber jackets – one black and the other brown.

Dritan estimated that they were both in their early to mid-forties. The beer bellies he could see hanging over their belts suggested they were both well out of shape, but he suspected they were still hard men, and the sidearms they were undoubtedly carrying would more than compensate for any lack of fitness.

There were two members of staff behind the serving counter. A young girl with her hair tied back in a ponytail was taking orders, while an older man with silver hair was working the grill. Their faces fell when they spotted the three men entering the shop. The man was obviously the proprietor, and he came over to the counter to speak to the suited Turk, whom he addressed with nervous respect. After a short conversation, the old man opened the till and reluctantly removed a wad of cash, which he duly handed over.

Nodding in satisfaction, the suited Turk bid the man goodnight, indicated for his men to follow him, and started walking towards the exit, pocketing the cash as he went. The girl followed behind to see them out.

Pulling his balaclava on, Dritan signalled for the others to do like-wise. "Pull out and stop right behind their car," he told Lorik. "And, remember, it is your responsibility to make sure the driver is disabled quickly. I do not want them getting away."

"I understand, and I will not let you down," Lorik promised, unfolding the metal stock of his weapon, which nestled comfortably on his lap.

————

"*All units from OP, Tango Four is getting into the driver's seat. Tango One is heading for the front passenger door. Tangos Two and Three are getting into the back. The bag containing the guns is being carried by Tango One. I repeat, Tango One has the weapons.*"

"What the fuck is he doing?" Dillon fumed. Meeks was supposed to drop the guns and car keys off and leave immediately, but for some strange reason he had disobeyed every instruction he'd been given. A horrible thought struck Dillon, and he scooped up the hand-held radio. "OP from Silver, does Tango Four seem to be accompanying the others willingly?"

"*Yes, yes,*" came the succinct reply.

"Received."

Almost immediately, Dillon's phone went. It was PS Newman. "*Anything I should be aware of?*" he asked tersely, having obviously thought the question was unusual.

"No," Dillon lied. "It just seemed odd to me that they were taking a stranger on a hit with them."

"*Well, perhaps they need a getaway driver with local knowledge,*" Newman suggested. "*It would make sense.*"

The radio crackled into life again. "*OP to all units. Lights on. I repeat vehicle lights on. The Golf is now manoeuvring slowly, reversing out of the parking space. Stand by for the off…"*

"*I've gotta go,*" Newman said, and hung up.

Meeks had been right about the car not showing up as stolen on the Police National Computer. According to the PNC check they had carried out after speaking to the snout, the car Jerome Norris had supplied him with was a relatively new red VW Golf GTI, which had no current keeper and no interest reports on it.

Why would they go to that much trouble? Dillon had wondered. He understood them swapping the plates, that made perfect sense, but changing the ignition barrel and providing a new set of keys as well – that just didn't add up. Then again, the work might not have been done specifically for this job. It was possible that they were just using a ringer that had previously been stolen to order and was scheduled for export. There was big money in that, Dillon knew.

"I wish there was some way to communicate with him," Dillon whispered to Christine, wondering if they ought to have arranged a visual panic signal for him to use in an emergency.

"I think the Trojan skipper's right," she said. "I think they've collared him to drive them to the target address because he has local knowledge."

"We can't show out when the interception goes in," Dillon said. "He'll have to be arrested like the others and go through the whole tiresome custody procedure."

"In that case, let's hope the SFOs don't rough him up too much when they take him to the floor during the hard stop," Christine said.

"Let's hope they don't bloody well shoot him," Dillon replied glumly.

"Oh," Christine said. She hadn't considered that.

––––––––

Inside the rear Trojan car, Trojan Delta, Newman was evaluating his options. If he let the Golf drive out of the relatively confined space of the hotel car park and onto the road it would make a hard stop far more difficult. The GTI was a very fast car, and it might outrun them if the conditions were favourable. That would be bad news; the last thing he wanted was a moving gunfight.

If he struck now, on the other hand, hitting the car while it was still contained within the car park, there was a good chance that they would be able to block it in with relative ease. Not only that, Tango One probably hadn't had time to distribute the firearms amongst his colleagues yet, and everyone inside the car was likely to be in a less heightened state of awareness than they would be in a few minutes time, when they were all tooled-up and en route to their intended target.

"OP from Bronze Trojan, confirm there are no civilians in the car park?" he transmitted.

"*Bronze Trojan from OP, I can confirm there are no civilians in the car park. Apart from the suspects, it's clear of people.*"

"Received," Newman said. Feeling the tension crank up a notch, he switched to the Trojan channel. "All units, we are now State Red, I repeat State Red. Move into the car park in convoy. Trojan Alpha, control goes to you. Acknowledge, please."

A gravelly voice responded immediately. "*Trojan Alpha acknowledges State Red. Moving into the car park now.*"

Their forward holding point was only a short distance away from the hotel perimeter, and as the convoy of four cars moved off, Newman rang Dillon again. "We're moving in now," he said as soon as the call was answered.

Thirty seconds later, Trojan Alpha pulled into the hotel's one-way system. Arriving cars entered via a gate to the far left of the property and drove along a short service road to a guest parking area. When it was time to leave, they continued along the service road until they reached the exit gate at the far right of the property. Both gates were barrier-controlled, and customers had to either use their electronic room keys to raise the barrier or buzz through to reception whenever they wanted to come in or go out. Earlier in the day, one of Dillon's officers had managed to procure a staff swipe card, which now allowed the Trojan vehicles to get in and out without having to buzz through to reception.

"*OP to all units, the Golf is now moving towards the exit gate,*" the latest update informed the Trojan officers, who were yet to acquire visual contact with the target.

"Trojan Delta from Trojan Alpha, stay on the road and carry on straight past us," the operator in the lead car immediately transmitted over the Trojan channel. *"We need you to block the exit gate ASAP."*

"Received," Newman replied, and pointed towards the exit gate approximately one-hundred-yards ahead. His driver nodded and accelerated past the other cars, the last of which was just turning into the entrance gate, coming to a halt across the exit a few moments later.

Things were moving quickly now, and Newman found himself listening to simultaneous broadcasts from the OP and from Trojan Alpha.

"All units from OP, the Golf is held at the exit gate. Repeat, the Golf is held at the exit gate."

And then, as Trojan Alpha gained visual control of the Golf, the words Newman and every other SFO was waiting for finally came over the radio: *"Trojan Alpha to all Trojan units, attack, attack, attack!"*

Erkan Dengiz was smiling contentedly as he waved goodbye to the pretty daughter of the café owner as she closed the door behind them. He paused on the pavement outside the café, and lit a cigarette. Drawing the smoke in deeply, he turned to his two compatriots. "She's pretty, no?"

They sniggered their agreement.

The next time they called to collect their dues here, he would ask her out, Dengiz decided. He thought it would be a great honour for the café owner to have a man like him show an interest in his daughter. If – no, when – she said yes, he might even allow them a temporary discount on what they were paying. He checked his watch, took a final drag, and threw the half smoked Camel Royal into the gutter. This had been a very good day. The round was almost over, and everything had gone smoothly, which wasn't always the case. He hated it when they begged and pleaded for more time, telling him their pathetic sob stories about how business had been slow this week, and how their takings were down.

He only had one more collection left to make, and then he would be free to enjoy the rest of his evening. He had a date arranged with a delicious little brunette he'd met at a club in Tottenham the previous weekend. They were meeting at ten o'clock, and he had promised to take her for a late dinner at his favourite restaurant, which was owned by a cousin. Dessert, he hoped, would come later, at her place.

His enforcers, Halil Kocadag and Kerim Bucak, stayed close to him as he crossed the pavement towards the car, behaving like a couple of dim witted but faithful dogs, which is effectively what they were. As he reached the passenger door his driver, Kemal Yucel, started the car.

At that moment, Erkan became aware of a car pulling up behind theirs. Glancing back, he saw it was a Mondeo, but he couldn't see who was inside because the cretinous fool of a driver had his main beams on, blinding him. "Amýn oðlu," he grumbled under his breath, calling the man a 'son of a pussy' in Turkish.

———

Inside the Mondeo, three doors opened as one, and the Eastern European hitmen, with their balaclavas now pulled down to conceal their faces, sprang out. As instructed, Lorik immediately ran to the front of the car and fired a sustained burst into the driver's window, which disintegrated inward. Yucel, wearing his seatbelt and unable to reach for the gun tucked into the front of his waistband, didn't stand a chance.

As the smoke cleared, Lorik peered inside, seeking visual confirmation that the Turkish driver was indeed dead. When he was satisfied that he was, Lorik ran straight back to the Mondeo so that he would be ready to pull away as soon as the others returned to the car.

Dritan and Valmir both alighted from the nearside of the car. Valmir immediately fanned out to the left to make sure that he had a clear line of fire, while Dritan advanced straight ahead, crouching down to ensure a steady aim and minimise the target area he would present in the unlikely event that any of the Turks managed to draw their weapons and return fire.

As per their plan, Dritan focused his sights on Erkan Dengiz. With the metal stock of the Škorpion comfortably tucked into his right shoulder, he opened fire as he advanced, emptying the whole magazine into his target from six-feet away.

The Škorpion produced very little recoil. Nonetheless, on automatic fire almost all weapons have a natural tendency to rise, so Dritan aimed low and allowed the gun to travel up on its own accord.

A fine pink mist appeared in front of the Turk as his body was riddled with holes, starting at his groin and travelling diagonally upwards towards his neck. The impact knocked him backwards, spinning him around and slamming him against the open door of the Mercedes. For a moment, he leaned against the door, and then he slowly sagged down to the floor, leaving a smeared trail of blood down the width of the windowpane.

One of the ejected rounds somehow managed to find its way inside the scarf that Dritan wore, burning his neck. Instinctively, he reached up with his left hand and tore the scarf off, freeing the trapped cartridge, which fell to the floor.

Valmir had two targets to nullify, so he was more economical with his trigger finger. Firing short controlled bursts, he pumped a stream of bullets into each man's central body mass, giving neither one the slightest chance to unholster their weapons and return fire. When they were both down, he walked forward slowly to administer the coup de grâce, putting each of them out of their misery with a single, precision head shot.

After confirming that all three Turks were dead, Dritan and Valmir ran back to the Mondeo, which pulled away with a loud wheelspin.

As soon as the assassin's car drove off, Bilal Yildiz, the elderly owner of the café, ran out onto the pavement and checked each of the enforcer's bodies for signs of life. His daughter, Tulay, had followed him out and was now standing by the door, her hands clasped to her mouth in shock.

"Call the police," Bilal shouted, waving for her to go back inside. When he reached Erkan's open eyed corpse, moments later, he had to resist the temptation to spit on the man. Instead, he quickly went through his pockets, retrieving the protection money he had so recently handed over. "May you rot in hell, you pig," he told the dead man.

———

Trojan Alpha screeched to a halt immediately behind the red Golf, stopping inches away from the rear bumper, a tactic designed to prevent the car from generating the momentum it needed to ram them out of the way should the driver decide to attempt this. Trojan Bravo and Trojan Charlie, following close behind, veered left and right, respectively, to flank the near and offsides of the target vehicle. The front seat passengers of all three cars, now wearing their blue baseball caps with 'POLICE' insignias prominently displayed on the front, were out of their cars and bringing their weapons to bear before the wheels had even stopped turning.

Directly in front of the Golf, on the other side of the exit gate, PS Newman sprang out of Trojan Delta and raised his carbine. His role was to bring Tango Four, the driver, under control. As his team moved forward to engage the car's other occupants, he aimed his G36C at Meeks and slid the selector from safety to 'fire'.

The SFOs were repeatedly shouting "ARMED POLICE!" at the top of their voices to ensure there was no confusion about who they were. As they took up station around the car, the shouts changed to cries of, "SHOW ME YOUR HANDS, SHOW ME YOUR HANDS!"

Meeks was so terrified that he somehow managed to rev the Golf's accelerator into the red. With no way of knowing that he had done this accidentally, and that he had no intention of trying to escape, the rear passenger of Trojan Delta stepped forward, knelt down, and fired a Hatton round into the front offside tyre, blowing it out and denting the wheel, making the car undriveable. Almost simultaneously, the rear passenger of Trojan Bravo fired a second Hatton round into the front nearside tyre.

Following the discharge of the Hatton guns, Newman stared at the shell-shocked driver, who had his hands in plain view and looked scared out of his wits. He quickly concluded that the man wasn't going to be a threat.

Hard stops were designed to shock dangerous suspects into rapid submission. To achieve this, they required a certain level of aggression to be demonstrated, both verbal and physical, and this show of force was enhanced by the brandishing of weapons, particularly the Hatton guns.

On this occasion, to the SFO team's relief, the tactic seemed to be working perfectly as the subdued suspects, now under control, were being fully compliant. Calling the occupants out of the car, the SFOs ordered them to lay face down on the floor, with their arms and legs spread out wide in the shape of a star. Then they instructed them to turn their heads so that they were looking in the opposite direction to the officers pointing guns at them.

When all four men were face down on the ground, the arrest team, a group of detectives from the Organised Crime Group who had travelled together in the back of an unmarked van at the rear of the convoy, were called forward to secure the suspects with plasticuffs and formally make the arrests.

Meeks found himself laying on a stretch of cold concrete on the opposite side of the car's bonnet to Goliath. As he lay there, listening to the arresting officer caution him, he glanced across at the giant and their eyes met. It was like staring into the face of the devil himself, and when Goliath suddenly smiled, it made Meeks blood run cold.

He knows! He knows I've sold him out.

CHAPTER FOUR

DEALING WITH THE FALLOUT

Once all four prisoners had been properly secured and the firearms officers had been stood down, a request was radioed through for cell space to be found, and suitable transport was summoned from the local borough to take them away.

Geoff drove the control car forward to the spot where the hard stop had occurred and, while he remained in the vehicle to finish off the last of his Jaffa Cakes, Dillon and Christine went in search of Newman for an update.

Newman was standing by the rear of the Golf, supervising his team's withdrawal and looking as chilled as ever. Because the Hatton guns had been discharged, he explained, there would have to be a Post Incident Procedure at Leman Street police station, and Dillon, as Silver, would be expected to attend.

One of Dillon's officers, DC Gurjit Singh, appeared carrying the bulky holdall Meeks had delivered to Goliath in one hand and a gigantic pair of bolt cutters in the other. Singh was a happy-go-lucky man in his late twenties. Short in stature, he was starting to get a little chubby around the middle, which he blamed on his wife's delicious cooking and her tendency to always serve extra-large portions. "Thought you'd want to be present when this was opened," he said in his thick Brummie accent.

Dillon nodded. "Go on then, Gurjit, do the honours. Let's see what hardware they've got in there."

Singh, who was already wearing blue nitrile gloves, placed the holdall on the ground, knelt down beside it, and applied the bolt cutters to the small padlock that prevented the zip from opening.

"Talk about using a sledgehammer to crack a walnut," Christine snorted as Gurjit effortlessly snipped off the padlock.

Gurjit smiled up at her with a mischievous twinkle in his eye. "As the actress said to the bishop, when it comes to the size of a man's tool, the bigger the better."

"Your wife must be constantly disappointed, then," Christine said, smiling back cattily.

Once the bag was unzipped, Gurjit started rummaging through the copious layers of bubble wrap that had been crammed inside it. "Bloody hell," he panted, "someone was having a laugh when they wrapped this up."

Eventually, he had removed enough padding to allow them to see the contents of the bag clearly. Unfortunately, these turned out to be nothing more sinister than three circular lengths of metal piping with a one-inch circumference, each gaffer taped to a length of wood about a foot long.

"There are no guns inside, boss," Gurjit said, looking up at him confused.

"I can bloody well see that," Dillon snapped, feeling gutted.

His head was spinning as he tried to analyse the situation.

Was it possible that Flynn had actually been right for once when he'd suggested that the informant was just stringing him along for a pay out? Dillon shook his head at the thought, dismissing it angrily. Everything Meeks had given them so far had been pure gold, and it made no sense for him to suddenly start lying.

Looking around for his informant, Dillon caught a glimpse of a burly uniformed constable ushering him into a marked station van that had just arrived. As Meeks took a seat in the caged area at the rear, having to lean forward at an awkward angle because his hands were cuffed behind his back, he struck Dillon as a broken man whose world had just fallen in on him, not someone who had concocted a fairy tale to earn himself some extra cash.

Dillon needed answers, and he desperately hoped that Meeks could provide them, but he couldn't confront the man here, in public, so he would just have to wait until he could get him into an interview room, alone.

"Search that bloody car from top to bottom," he told Gurjit, "and if you find anything, anything at all, I want to know immediately." As he turned to walk away, another thought occurred to him, and it wasn't a pleasant one. "While you're at it, get someone to check the Vehicle Identification Number on the Golf's engine and chassis. I urgently need to know if this car really is a ringer, or if that's a lie, too."

Leaving a confused looking Gurjit to crack on, Dillon stormed off back to the control car with Christine in tow.

"Tony, slow down," she protested, but he was so lost in thought that he didn't hear a word she said.

"I've sorted out cell space," Geoff said as he climbed into the rear of the people carrier. "The twins are being taken to Barking, while the other two are going to Forest Gate."

Dillon merely grunted. He was far too preoccupied to waste time talking. No firearms had been recovered. If it transpired that the car wasn't even stolen, they would have bugger-all evidence against the three men they'd just arrested. That would make tomorrow morning's interviews a complete waste of time; the streetwise Mancunians would just sit there with their arms folded, arrogantly smirking at the interviewing officers as they rattled off a string of 'no comment' replies.

What had gone wrong?

Assuming Meeks wasn't lying, he had to consider other possibilities. The first was that his snout had given them duff info, albeit in good faith. There was always a risk of this happening, and it was one of the reasons handlers tried so hard to verify the provenance of the information.

Then again, maybe Meeks had been right about Livingstone bringing in a team of hitters to take out a rival, but wrong about when it was going to happen. This might just have been a reconnaissance trip, with Adebanjo planning to come back and kill the target at some point in the near future.

Of course, there was one other possibility, but that was too ridiculous to even contemplate. And yet…

What if Livingstone wasn't planning a hit at all? What if he had worked out that there was a leak in the camp; a grass who was tipping the police off? What if he had deliberately provided Meeks with false information to see what he did with it, and this whole thing had been an elaborate charade concocted by Livingstone to unearth the spy in his midst?

"Geoff," Dillon said, looking up with a renewed sense of purpose. "Get straight on the radio and call off the team we've got standing by to enter Jerome Norris' place."

Upon learning that Livingstone wanted Meeks to ferry the stolen car and guns over to Goliath, he had immediately instructed one of his officers to obtain a search warrant for Jerome Norris' flat. A group of officers were, at this very moment, parked up at the base of Jerome's tower block, waiting for the green light to force entry and execute the warrant.

"Seriously?" Geoff asked, staring at Dillon in disbelief. "I don't understand, boss. We broke our backs getting that organised and assembling a team."

Dillon ran a large hand through his jet-black hair. "I know," he said through gritted teeth. "But it can't be helped. Call them off. Get them to head back to East Ham and await further instructions."

Christine climbed into the carrier, breathing heavily and looking flushed. "You took off like a bleeding rocket," she complained, breathlessly. "Where's the fire?"

Dillon ignored her. Pulling his mobile, he dialled the number for DC Coleen Perry, one of the two officers who had been inside the observation post keeping watch on the hotel. They had been instructed to head straight over to the hotel and search the rooms Goliath and his crew had occupied as soon as the arrests were made.

"Coleen, Dillon here," he said when she picked up. "Did you find anything of interest in their rooms?" He listened for a few moments, grimaced, and then grunted despondently. "Don't worry," he said, "so far we've drawn a big fat blank, too."

———

Detective Chief Inspector Jack Tyler arrived home at his little cottage on the outskirts of Blackmore in rural Essex just after nine-thirty p.m. that evening. A full day in the office, followed by a much longer than expected meeting with their Treasury Counsel, Dennis Prowler, QC in his chambers at Kings Bench Walk, had left him shattered and ready for bed. The meeting had started at 6 p.m., and although everyone in attendance had hoped they could whiz through the agenda, it had ended up dragging on for well over two-hours.

The cause of the emergency meeting had been a last-minute demand from defence counsel in an upcoming murder trial for the service of a huge amount of unused material. It was just a fishing expedition designed to unsettle them and create extra work, and the poor detective Tyler had appointed as disclosure officer was going to have his work cut out reviewing and serving that lot.

Kicking his shoes off, he draped his suit jacket over the banister at the bottom of the stairs, pulled his tie loose and made straight for the fridge. Helping himself to a cold beer, he stuck a frozen pizza in the oven, set the timer, and then flopped down on the sofa to watch the TV while he waited for it to cook.

He was just savouring the first swig of his beer when his Job mobile went off. Groaning inwardly, he retrieved the Nokia from the coffee table, where he'd dumped it only seconds earlier, and checked the display. DCI Andy Quinlan was calling him, which didn't bode well as Andy's team were performing the role of Homicide Assessment Team this week, and Jack's team were next in the frame to take on any new job that came in.

"Please tell me this isn't work related," Jack said after pressing the green button.

"*I really wish I could, Jack,*" Quinlan replied, doing his best to sound apologetic. "*A job's just come in on Stoke Newington's ground, right on the border with Haringey. Four Turks, all shot dead at close range. The shooters – we think there were three of them – used automatic weapons, and it's looking very much like a contract killing at this stage.*"

Recalling the conversation that he'd had with Tony Dillon the day before, about the team of hitmen who were supposed to be travelling down to London from up north, Jack swung his legs off the cushion and sat up straight. After fumbling around to find a coaster, he put his barely touched beer down on the coffee table. "Can you describe the gunmen, Andy? I don't suppose there was a large black man with a bald head amongst them?"

"*That's a bit of a random question,*" Quinlan said. "*From what I'm told they were all white. Why do you ask?*"

"I just wondered if it could have been connected to a murder suppression job a mate of mine from Organised Crime is working on, that's all."

"*Do you think there could be a link?*" Quinlan asked, sounding hopeful.

"Doesn't sound like it," Tyler said. "His suspects were all black."

"*Pity, but I suppose that would have been too good to be true,*" Quinlan said, clearly disappointed. "*Anyway, I need to press on, so are you ready to scribble down some details?*"

"Give me a minute," Jack said, his earlier tiredness now completely forgotten. Rushing out to the hall, he grabbed a notebook and biro from the oak sideboard. "Okay, fire away," he said, pen poised.

Quinlan proceeded to give Tyler a very quick overview of the current situation, pausing every few seconds to allow him to jot down notes.

"*As your team are in the frame to take it, I thought you might want to come out to the scene tonight to have a look for yourself,*" Quinlan suggested, "*before the official handover tomorrow morning.*"

"I think that's definitely a good idea," Jack agreed, heading into the kitchen. The tantalising aroma of the Four-Cheese Margherita pizza hit him as soon as he entered the room, and his stomach responded by growling hungrily. "It's probably going to take me the best part of an hour to get there," he said, bending down to turn the oven off. "Where's the RVP?"

"*Green Lanes, by the junction with Woodberry Grove. Make sure you come in from the Seven Sisters end as we've blocked the road off the other way.*"

Tyler slid his shoes back on and quickly popped to the loo. Then he grabbed his jacket, scooped his keys and warrant card up from the hall sideboard and headed for the door. He had been home for less than twenty-minutes.

With no wife, kids or animals to worry about, Tyler was free to come and go as he pleased. Five years ago, before the messy divorce, it would have been a very different story; his rushing back to work like this, less than half-an-hour after he'd arrived home, would have triggered another massive argument. Jenny, his ex, was a demanding woman who had expected total devotion from her husband; she hated Jack's job, which she came to think of as a mistress who rivalled her for his affections; she hated the people he associated with at work; but most of all, she hated the fact that he hadn't surrendered his independence when he'd taken his vows. The marriage had lasted just under a year, at which point she had left him for another man.

As he slid behind the wheel, his stomach was still gurgling for food. With any luck, there might be a few takeaways open near the crime scene. If not, he feared he was going to go very hungry tonight.

As was his wont when his team were in the frame, Tyler had brought a Job car home with him. The blue Ford Escort was pretty basic, but it did the job, and at least it was equipped with a Force Main-Set radio, so he could communicate with the Central Command Complex at New Scotland Yard if he needed to.

Before setting off, Jack dialled the number for DS Steve Bull, who was to be the Case Officer for this job. Steve had only been on the Command for a few weeks, having transferred in from – of all places – Stoke Newington. It was an uncanny coincidence how many times a new recruit's first murder case would occur on the ground that they had just left, and he hoped that Steve's familiarity with the area would work in their favour.

"*Hello,*" a soft-spoken voice said after the third ring.

"Stevie, Jack Tyler here. Listen, a job's just come in and I'm on my way in to Stoke Newington to visit the scene."

"*Anything good?*" Bull enquired, sounding excited.

"Could be," Jack said. "We've got four dead Turks, all shot with automatic weapons in what looks like a gangland hit."

"*Cool. Do you want me to come in?*" Steve asked, and Jack was pleased to hear the eagerness in his voice.

"No, there's no point in us both being knackered in the morning, but thanks for offering. What I would really appreciate is for you to send out the group pager and make sure the team is in the office for eight o'clock sharp tomorrow morning. Looks like we're in for a busy few days."

"*Leave it to me,*" Steve promised. "*I'll sort it out right now.*"

———

"*So, let me get this straight,*" Flynn asked, his voice dripping with scorn, "*the car isn't stolen, you've not recovered any firearms, and the suspect's room at the hotel is cleaner than a clean thing that's just been cleaned? Is that what you're telling me, Dillon?*"

"Yes, I'm afraid so, sir," Dillon replied, staring forlornly at the printout in his hand. The Vehicle Identification Number check he'd requested had confirmed that the car definitely wasn't stolen, as they had been led to believe. He was glad his boss was on the other end of a phone and not standing here in the room with him, staring down his bulbous, veined nose with utter contempt.

"*Well, don't say I didn't warn you that this informant of yours couldn't be trusted,*" Flynn gloated. "*He's been leading you around by your nose for weeks now, getting you to jump through hoops every time he snaps his fingers. You've made a complete cock up of handling this, and I must say that, although I'm disappointed, I'm not surprised in the slightest.*"

"Hang on a moment," Dillon protested, feeling a spark of anger ignite inside his chest. "My snout has a proven track record, and the first-rate information he's consistently provided us has enabled our team to make some major arrests over the past couple of months. Plus, thanks to him, we've made some substantial drug seizures and taken two illegal handguns out of circulation. That's hardly him leading me around by the nose, is it? That's intelligence led policing at its very best."

————

At the other end of the line, Flynn scoffed at that. Secretly, he thought of Dillon as a rambunctious child whose promotion ought to be put on hold until he learned to control the impulsive streak in his nature. Unfortunately, despite his off-the-record efforts to persuade the promotion board that Dillon should be overlooked on this occasion, the people making the decisions hadn't agreed with him. "If you have any grounds for concern regarding this officer's suitability," the chairman of the board had told him when they had met up for a quiet drink one evening, "you need to come forward officially, with documented proof."

Proof!

He didn't have any proof, just an instinctive dislike of the man, who was a maverick and a risk taker, and who didn't conform to his idea of a good leader. They had never gotten along. Flynn expected every person under his command to demonstrate blind obedience, following his orders without question, and agreeing with his every opinion, no matter how daft it might be. From day one, Dillon had made it clear he wasn't going to play that game, and it hadn't taken long for their working relationship to become strained.

"Acting Detective Inspector Dillon," he said, loading emphasis on the word 'acting,' "you need to face the facts, as unpleasant as they are. Your snout has hoodwinked you, and by acting blindly on what he told you, instead of taking the time to thoroughly research the information, you've made a complete fool out of yourself. The brutal truth is, you've been riding your luck for a while now, and tonight it finally ran out. Now, if that's all, we will talk further in the morning. Goodnight." With that, Flynn hung up on him.

Fuming about the waste of resources and the cost of the operation, he walked across his lounge to a small contemporary styled drinks cabinet next to the TV stand and removed a half-full bottle of Johnnie

Walker Blue Label. Pouring himself a liberal measure, he went through to the kitchen to get some ice.

He would look like a fool when he had to justify this to the AC in the morning, and it was all Dillon's fault.

"Are you coming to bed, dear?" his wife called from upstairs. "It's getting very late and you've got work in the morning."

Flynn pulled an unpleasant face and shook his fist at the ceiling. "I'll be up shortly," he called back, raising the tumbler and downing half the contents in one gulp. He really needed to cut back on the booze, he thought with a grimace.

And the fags.

Finishing off the drink, he rinsed the glass under the cold tap so his wife wouldn't know he'd been at the scotch again, and placed it on the draining board. As he trudged up the stairs, he decided that it wouldn't hurt to put in another call to his friend on the promotion board in the morning. Even putting aside his personal dislike of the man, which he had no intention of doing, Dillon really wasn't the sort of person the Job needed to promote in trying times like these.

––––––––

Staring at his mobile in disbelief, Dillon only just about resisted the urge to throw the damned thing against the wall. The muscles in his face rippled, and he ground his teeth together so tightly that his jaw began to ache.

Flynn's uncalled for dressing down had made his blood boil and, as he quietly seethed, he could feel his face becoming flushed with anger. The two-faced swine had been more than happy to wallow in all the glory when everything had been going well, but because there had been a minor hiccup, the spineless wanker was already trying to distance himself from any fallout that might result.

Okay, so Dillon's snout might not have come up trumps this time, he accepted that, but over the last couple of months the information provided by Meeks had led to a number of middle-tier criminals being charged with some extremely serious offences. And now, just because one job hadn't panned out, Flynn wanted to throw Dillon and his –

hitherto reliable – informant to the wolves. What really stung the most was the unjustified accusation that Dillon had rushed in, which he most definitely hadn't.

When Meeks had contacted him the day before, dropping the bombshell that Livingstone had hired a team of hitmen to travel down from Manchester the following morning, there had been no time to do more than carry out basic research, commission a full risk assessment, and speak to GMP about the potential suspects. Meeks had immediately been dragged in for a full intelligence interview, so that they could establish the provenance of the information.

What did Meeks know?

Who else knew about this?

Was there any corroborating evidence to support his claim?

They had asked him those questions and many more.

After checking it out as thoroughly as they could in the limited time they had, Dillon had concluded that the information was genuine, and they needed to act immediately if they were to stand any chance of thwarting the assassination attempt. But he hadn't rushed in, gung-ho, without consultation, as Flynn seemed to think. He had run the scenario by his own DCI, and then sought a second opinion from his best friend, Jack Tyler. Both had agreed that this information just couldn't be ignored. Luckily, the consultation process, along with his two senior colleague's recommendations, was fully documented.

With reluctance, Dillon left the tranquillity of the side office he'd used to call Flynn, emerging into the controlled chaos of Forest Gate's custody suite. The prisoner reception area was packed out with detainees and their escorting officers. A few were being well-behaved, but most were shouting, swearing and drunkenly protesting their innocence to anyone they thought might listen.

Behind a raised counter, three uniformed custody sergeants sat in a line, stoically ignoring everything and everyone except the person standing directly in front of them. Their fingers were furiously tapping away at the keyboards on their desks as they inputted data into the electronic custody sheets on their computer screens.

Goliath was standing on the other side of the room, facing the custody desk that was furthest away from Dillon. Towering over everyone around him, he looked calm, relaxed, and totally unworried.

Not a good sign.

Meeks, by contrast, was sitting on a cluttered bench at the rear of the room, waiting his turn to be booked in. He was nervous, jittery, full of fear. He visibly stiffened when he spotted Dillon; and he immediately looked away as though afraid the detective would acknowledge him in front of Goliath. He needn't have worried; Dillon walked straight past the anxious snout, pretending that he didn't exist.

Checking his watch, Dillon sighed despondently. He knew he needed to set off for Leman Street to attend the Post Incident Procedure for the firearms discharge, but he would have much preferred to stay where he was until a suitable opportunity arose for him to speak to Meeks. The trouble was, with Adebanjo at the same station, he would have to tread very carefully if he wanted to do this. Any out of the ordinary contact he had with the prisoner would stick out, and could endanger the snout.

Disheartened by the way things were turning out, he walked over to the exit. As he typed the four-digit code into the security keypad with a sausage shaped finger, he couldn't resist glancing back at the giant now giving his details to a grizzled custody sergeant. He hated to admit it, but Christine had been right when she'd pointed out how big he was. He looked at Goliath's biceps, mentally compared them to his own, and then shook his head smugly. "He's definitely on the gear," he said to himself.

CHAPTER FIVE

FOUR DEAD TURKS AND A CONSPIRACY THEORY

When he arrived at the crime scene, which was now full of police personnel, Tyler showed his warrant card to a female officer in a yellow reflective jacket who was diligently performing cordon duty. From her youthful appearance, he guessed that she was still under twenty. Jack had nothing against young recruits. In fact, he had joined the Job when he was only eighteen-and-a-half-years old, the minimum age for new entrants, and he had barely turned nineteen by the time he'd finished basic training at Hendon and been posted to his first station as a fresh-faced uniform probationer.

"DCI Tyler," he told her with a warm smile. "I'm the on-call Senior Investigating Officer from AMIP."

Clearly nervous in his presence, the young PC meticulously recorded his details in the scene log and then politely lifted the tape to allow him in.

In the distance, Tyler spotted a six-foot high wall of black canvas privacy screening that had been erected around the victim's car. As he set off towards it, DCI Andy Quinlan emerged from behind the screens, carrying a clipboard. Despite wearing full barrier clothing, his distinctive Joe 90 glasses made him immediately recognisable. Quinlan saw him and raised a hand in greeting.

When Tyler reached him, Quinlan pulled the hood of his overalls down and slipped off the Victoria face mask. His mop of curly black hair was plastered to his forehead with sweat. "Phew," he said, wiping his forehead with a sleeve. "Wearing this blooming outfit for any period of time is like being slow cooked in an oven."

There was a stark contrast between the two men. Tyler was tall and broad; Quinlan was short and skinny. Tyler, in his early thirties, was a fairly new DCI who was more interested in nicking villains than climbing the promotion ladder; Quinlan, a seasoned DCI with only a few years to go before he retired, was a man hungry for advancement. He wanted the next rank – and the one after that.

The first thing Quinlan did, after removing his horn-rimmed glasses and wiping the thick lenses on a tissue, was hand him a Computer Aided Dispatch printout of the incident, which had been clipped to his board. "There you, go," he said, passing it over. "Don't say I never give you anything."

As Jack read through the CAD incident log, he saw that there had been several calls about the shooting. The first had come from a female called Tulay Yildiz, and had been made from inside the Turkish café.

"How many witnesses do we have in total, Andy?" he asked.

"So far, we only have two. The café owner and his daughter, but at least they saw everything that happened. There were a few customers in the café as well, by all accounts, but they scarpered long before the local Old Bill showed up."

"Do we know their names?"

Quinlan shook his head. "Not yet, but we're working on it."

Tyler felt a pang of annoyance. Anyone who had seen the shooting was a key witness and needed to be interviewed as such. If they'd made themselves scarce before the police arrived, it was almost certainly because they didn't want to get involved. Now his team were going to have to invest valuable time, which would be better spent pursuing other lines of enquiry, trying to track them down. "What about

CCTV?" he asked, scanning the area for local authority cameras but not seeing any.

"None covering the scene itself, but there are a few cameras back at the junction with Seven Sisters Road, and a few of the other shops in the parade have private systems installed. Whether or not they actually work is another story but, as they're all closed, we'll have to wait until the morning to find out."

Jack grunted his frustration. It was more time wasted. "So, what do we know about the victims?" he asked next.

"Not a lot at the moment. The car's registered to someone called Erkan Dengiz from Wood Green. I've had intel checks carried out on the registered keeper's name and address, and it turns out that he's a really nasty piece of work. From what I can gather, he's a mid-level enforcer for one of the Turkish crime syndicates, with form for various assaults, demanding money with menaces and – last but not least – carrying weapons. I've had someone print out a custody imaging photo at Stoke Newington, and it's on its way here as we speak."

"Do we think this Dengiz character is the driver?" Jack asked.

Quinlan shook his head, emphatically. "If he's one of our victims, then it's most likely that he's the front seat passenger."

Jack was intrigued. "What makes you think that?" he asked.

"Basically, the driver and the two goons laying on the pavement are all dressed scruffily, like low level thugs. The guy slumped down beside the front seat passenger door, on the other hand, has a flashy suit, expensively cut hair and manicured hands. To me, he looks much more like a boss than the other three."

"So, what were they doing in the café?" Tyler asked cynically. "I don't suppose for one minute that they were just stopping off for a quick coffee on the way home from work?"

Quinlan snorted at that. "Yeah, right," he said, drawing the words out. "If you ask me, this is – or should I say was – a little team collecting protection money. It would certainly explain why three of the four were carrying shooters."

Jack cocked his head to one side, wondering if he'd heard right. "They were armed?"

Quinlan stared at him in confusion. "Didn't I mention that when I called you?"

Tyler shook his head. "No, Andy, you bloody well didn't."

"Sorry, mate," Quinlan said, having the decency to look embarrassed. "It must've slipped my mind. To be fair, it's been utter pandemonium here. Anyway, they've got sidearms, pistols as opposed to revolvers from what I could see, but they didn't have a chance to pull them out, which means the hitmen must have been on them before they could react."

Jack took a moment to absorb this information before passing comment. "That suggests to me," he eventually said, "that our shooters have experience at this sort of thing. I wonder if they're ex-military?" It was a worrying thought. Most gangland related shootings were carried out by brainless cretins who couldn't shoot straight and were lucky to have hit their target at all, not trained mercenaries. "Is there any intelligence to suggest a power struggle between rival gangs?"

"Well, it's funny you should say that," Quinlan said. "The local Duty Officer was telling me that tensions in the area are running a bit high right now because three separate gangs are all claiming rights to a disputed territory."

Jack raised an eyebrow at that. "Well, I'd say that the tension levels just went up several notches, wouldn't you?"

Quinlan nodded. "It does look that way," he agreed. "Let's hope it isn't the start of a tit-for-tat shooting spree."

Jack grimaced at the thought. "Do we know who these gangs are?" he asked.

"One's Turkish, another's Albanian, and the third is a black gang. The locals will know what they're called, and we'll have access to everything they've got by tomorrow morning."

"Who's the CSM?" Jack asked.

"It's Juliet Kennedy," Quinlan replied. "She was here a moment ago." He rotated a full 360 degrees in search of the Crime Scene Manager, but drew a blank. "Knowing her, she'll either be up to her elbows in gore, or sitting in her van, looking in a vanity mirror and applying an extra coat of war paint." Juliet was a firm favourite with all the SIOs, as much for her quirkiness as for her considerable knowledge and professionalism. Even when called to the most gruesome of scenes, knowing she'd be spending hours crawling around on her hands and knees in a rancid hole with nothing but a decomposing corpse for company, she habitually turned up dressed to the nines, with her hair and make-up looking immaculate. Of course, keeping it like that while working a crime scene required a lot of effort, so every now and again she would go AWOL for a few minutes in order to run a brush through her hair or touch up her makeup.

"It wouldn't surprise me," Jack admitted. "Have you appointed an exhibits officer, yet?"

Quinlan nodded. "Yes, DC Kevin Murray's been given that dubious honour. He'll make sure everything that happens tonight is properly documented, and he can go through everything with his oppo after the handover in the morning."

"Oi! Jack Tyler," an abrasive female voice called out, interrupting their conversation. "I hope you're not planning to go anywhere near my crime scene until you're properly attired?"

Tyler wheeled around to see the rake-thin figure of Juliet Kennedy striding towards him from the direction of her forensic van. Her Tyvek protective overalls, which looked way too big for her petite frame, rustled loudly with every step. In her mid-forties, with highlighted blonde hair, Juliet was an Ilford girl, born and bred. "There you go," she said, thrusting a bundle of protective overclothing into his hand. "Get that lot on, and hurry up. I haven't got all day."

"We were beginning to wonder where you were," Quinlan told her. "Thought you might've sneaked off for a quick cup of tea."

"I wish! I was just briefing the photographer," she told them. "He's going to get started as soon as you two are finished having a nose around."

As soon as Tyler was ready, Juliet led the two detectives past the screens and over to the driver's door of the Mercedes.

"Please be careful where you put those size twelve feet of yours, Jack," she warned. "The shell casings haven't been marked out yet, and I don't want any being disturbed before the ballistic expert arrives."

"I'll be careful," Tyler promised, bending down to peer inside.

Even though he'd known it would be grim, the sight still invoked a shudder. Forcing his face to remain impassive, and suppressing the revulsion he felt inside, he methodically ran his eyes over the driver. The man had slumped sideways towards the passenger seat, and the only thing keeping him from tipping over completely was the seat belt he wore.

The dead man's torso was peppered with ugly holes and stained a dark, wet red. His head and face, or rather what was left of them, had been transformed into a pulpy mess. There was an entry wound where his right eye had once been, leaving a bloody crater in its place. At least two more bullets had smashed straight through cranial bones on the way in and splattered skull fragments and sticky lumps of dura mater over the car's interior on the way out.

"Jesus," Tyler breathed, standing up to face Quinlan. "I doubt even his own family would recognise him now." He bent down and looked into the car again, and could just about make out a bulge at the front of the driver's trousers. "Is that a gun in his waistband?" he asked. "I can't tell from here?"

"Either it's a gun, Jack, or he's just very pleased to see you," Juliet said, winking at Tyler. Another thing most people liked about Juliet was her vulgar gallows humour. When dealing with violent death, it was sometimes the only thing that kept you sane.

Juliet stepped forward, unceremoniously pushed him aside, and poked her head through the window. "I don't want to move him until the record photography has been finished," she said, tentatively groping the area around the man's crotch with her gloved right hand. "Yep," she confirmed, after a few seconds of squeezing. "I can definitely make out the shape of a pistol. Unless, of course, he's just got a very deformed willy."

Quinlan shook his head as she emerged from the car. "That's what I like about you Essex girls," he said. "You can always be relied upon to conduct yourselves with decorum."

"Sod off," Juliet retorted, grinning wickedly. "You're just jealous because I've never fumbled your bollocks like that."

Quinlan, who was actually quite a shy man, blushed profusely. "Shall we look at the others?" he suggested quickly to cover his embarrassment.

They walked around the rear of the car and came to a halt beside the two men who had died so violently on the pavement. Both were lying flat on their backs, arms and legs akimbo.

Jack visualised what had happened. The well-placed groupings to their torsos had dropped them like stones. They were probably fatally wounded at that point, but the killer was clearly a professional, and he had finished the job by administering a single gunshot to each of their foreheads. He studied their open-eyed faces for a moment, wondering what – apart from the bullet that killed them – had passed through their heads immediately before they died.

Anger? Fear? Sadness?

No one would ever know.

"That's impressive shooting," he said, grudgingly. "Is that exactly how they were found?"

Juliet shook her head. "Not quite," she said. "This one," she nudged the shoulder of the body nearest the café entrance with her foot, "was lying in this spot, but he was curled up in a foetal position. That one," she nodded towards the second body, "was face down, about three feet to the left of where he is now. The first responders rolled them both onto their backs in order to check for signs of life and carry out emergency first aid."

Jack could see the long red stains on the pavement where the officers had hurriedly turned the fatally injured men over onto their backs so that they could examine them. He couldn't fault them for doing that. The preservation of life came before all else.

Telling the detectives to remain where they were, Juliet carefully walked through the gap between the two dead men, gingerly making her way over to the open front passenger door of the Mercedes. The last of the four victims was sitting on the pavement, back slumped against the inside of the open door, with one leg fully extended in front of him and the other folded underneath him at an odd angle. His head had sagged forwards onto his chest and his lifeless hands rested in his lap.

"That," Andrew Quinlan informed Tyler, "is the man we think is the car's registered keeper, Erkan Dengiz."

Juliet knelt down beside the body for a closer inspection. "He must have been shot a good twenty to thirty times," she told the two detectives. "Up close, the poor sod looks like a Swiss cheese. There's a diagonal line of entry wounds starting down by the right side of his groin and travelling up to the left side of his neck." As she spoke, she traced her forefinger through the air a few inches in front of the body to demonstrate.

"Was he shot at close range, too, do you think?" Tyler asked.

Juliet pointed to the sea of cases scattered around the pavement. "Based on where the cartridges landed, I would say so, yes. At a guess, I reckon the trigger man was only about six or seven feet away when he opened fire." She stood up, cursing as her knees creaked loudly, and made her way back to the others. "Right, if you've seen enough," Juliet said, "let's go back outside and find somewhere to talk in more comfort."

She led them over to her van, where Jack wasted no time in slipping out of the uncomfortable overalls. He gave them back to Juliet for disposal.

"So, Juliet," he said, "tell me where we are in terms of forensic support."

Kennedy scratched her head. "Well, all the record photography will be completed tonight. The forensic scientist specialising in firearms evidence has just arrived, and I'll brief him in a jiffy. He'll supervise the recovery of all the spent cartridges and take an initial look at the various trajectories and firing angles. Obviously, he'll do a more detailed examination of the car once it's taken to Charlton car pound."

"When's the car likely to be removed?" Tyler asked.

"I'll organise a full lift once the bodies are taken away. Hopefully, they can be removed overnight and we can get the car away in the morning."

"How long will we need to retain the scene?" Quinlan asked. "Only this is on a red route and I'll need to let Transport for London know so they can put diversions in place."

"At least until tomorrow afternoon, I'd say," she estimated.

Quinlan grimaced, knowing that a prolonged road closure would play havoc with rush hour traffic.

"I've got a POLSA team booked for the morning," Juliet continued, "but the search is going to take several hours at the very least." POLSA was an acronym for Police Search Adviser. This was usually an Inspector or a Sergeant, and their role was to supervise a team of specially trained search officers who were skilled at conducting fingertip and other intricate searches.

"It takes as long as it needs to take," Tyler said firmly. "I want this done properly."

"Unless either of you have strong views to the contrary, I don't see any point in calling out a pathologist or a BPA scientist; it'll take ages to organise and it won't tell us anything we don't already know."

Both Tyler and Quinlan nodded their agreement. They knew exactly what had happened to the deceased men and when it had happened. The services of a pathologist and a blood pattern analyst seemed surplus to requirements under the circumstances.

"Good," Juliet said, making a note in her blue daybook. "I'll get onto the Coroner's Officer in a minute and see if I can get the ball rolling on the SPMs."

A special post mortem was required following any suspicious death. Unlike standard post mortems, specials routinely took four or five hours to complete.

"It would be helpful if we could get the same pathologist to do them all," Tyler said, stating the obvious.

Juliet nodded. "I agree, but with four victims to get through, we might struggle to find someone who can fit them in for a day or two. Leave it with me, I'll see what I can do."

"Okay," Tyler said. "I'll leave you to get started. There'll be an office meeting at Arbour Square at eight tomorrow morning. I know this is going to be a very late finish for you, but…" he let the words trail off.

Juliet scrunched her face up. "Don't worry, I'll be there," she said. "I'll probably look like death warmed up, but I'll be there."

When Juliet had gone, Tyler turned to Andy Quinlan. "Any chance you can arrange for the café owner and his daughter to be key witness interviewed on tape tonight?" he asked.

Quinlan blew his cheeks out expressively. "I'll try," he said, not sounding overly optimistic, "but I'm running out of people."

When Dillon finally arrived back at Forest Gate after having attended the Post Incident Procedure at Leman Street, he found Christine Taylor sitting in the canteen, going through her log and updating her notes.

Apart from her, the large room was completely empty. He purchased two powdery cappuccinos from the hot drink dispenser, and then flopped down in a chair beside her.

"What's been happening?" he asked, sliding one across the table to her.

Christine looked shattered. "Not a lot," she said without looking up. "All the prisoners have had their fingerprints and DNA taken, and they've had their clothing seized. It was fun trying to find replacement clobber for Adebanjo. The track suit bottoms we gave him look like three-quarter length shorts on him." She grinned as she recalled the look on Adebanjo's face when he'd put them on. "Don't think he was very impressed. None of the Mancunians are asking for legal representation, by the way, which I find most concerning."

"It's very worrying," Dillon agreed, sounding depressed. "What about Meeks? Have you made sure his cell is as far away from Adebanjo's as possible?"

Christine stopped writing and glanced up at him, clearly peeved by the stupidity of the question. "No, I thought I'd let them share a cell," she said sarcastically.

Seeing the look on her face, Dillon took a sip of his coffee and sat there quietly, giving her a moment to calm down. That was the problem with getting romantically involved with junior officers, he reflected. It made them inclined to think they could ignore your rank and answer you back whenever you annoyed them. The clock on the canteen wall told him it was eleven-thirty. "Has the custody office quietened down yet?" he asked, hoping she wouldn't find that as contentious as his last question.

Christine, who had gone back to her log, shook her head. "Nope, it's busier than ever. They've just brought in a load of drunks following a punch up at the local curry house."

Dillon cursed under his breath. "I really need to speak to Meeks," he said. "I've got a horrible feeling that we've been played, and I need to get some answers from him quickly."

Christine picked up on his frustration. She stopped writing and looked at him questioningly. "Is there anything I can do to help?"

Dillon had been in a fractious mood since he'd spoken to Flynn and, although he hadn't said anything to her, she seemed to have picked up from his demeanour that the DSU had given him a hard time.

Dillon was quiet for a moment while he pondered what to do for the best. As he saw it, he had two choices. He could either speak to Meeks now, which might make Adebanjo suspicious, or wait until the morning, when it would probably look far more natural, although the down side to doing that was that his questions would remain unanswered for another twelve hours. In the end, he decided that it simply couldn't wait.

"Chrissy, go downstairs and book Meeks out for his first interview. I know it's busy, but sweet talk the skipper dealing with him into letting us crack on. I'll be down in ten minutes."

As soon as she'd gone, he pulled out his phone, intent on leaving Tyler a text message to call him in the morning. To his surprise, Tyler had sent him an almost identical request just five-minutes ago. He hadn't heard it as his phone was still in silent mode from where he'd attended the PIP. He rang his friend's number, and the call was picked up almost immediately.

"*Dill, thanks for calling back so quickly,*" Tyler said.

Dillon could hear street noises in the background, and it all sounded a bit hectic.

"*Listen, I'm at the scene of a quadruple shooting in Green Lanes, and the victims are all Turkish gang members. I thought you might be interested.*"

Dillon's eyes widened in surprise. "Damn right I am," he said, sitting up and reaching for a pen in case he needed to take notes. "Any idea who the shooters are yet?"

"*Not yet, mate. As you can imagine, when I first got the call, I thought it might be connected to the saga you're dealing with. Then, when I heard that the suspects were three white males in balaclavas, I dismissed the notion. Now, though, having attended the scene, seen the victims, and found out that there's trouble brewing between three gangs over a disputed territory, I'm beginning to wonder if there could actually be a connection after all. I don't suppose you'd be able to come over to HA in the morning for a briefing?*" HA was the phonetic code the police used for Arbour Square.

"Definitely," Dillon said.

"*Brilliant. The briefing starts at eight, but I'll be in the office from seven, so any time after that is good for me.*"

"I'll be there bang on seven," Dillon promised, "but do me a favour and try not to be your usual grumpy self." Tyler was always snappy when he had to get up early, whereas Dillon was routinely up at the crack of dawn, even on his days off. It was, he never tired of telling his friend, the best time of the day.

Tyler chortled. "*Can't promise that,*" he said, and hung up.

Talk about adding fuel to the fire, Dillon thought, pocketing his phone. The job Jack's team had just taken on had to be connected to whatever was going on between Livingstone and the other two gangs. The shooters were white – so, presumably, they were Albanians. If that was so, it was a no-brainer that the hit had occurred because the Albanians were pissed off about the way the other gangs were planning to carve up the disputed territory. Having hit out at the Turks, would they come after Livingstone next? It seemed likely. It struck Dillon that if Livingstone wasn't already planning an attack on the Albanians, he would be shortly.

When Dillon went down to the custody suite, which stank of alcohol and stale body odour, there was still a queue of raucous prisoners waiting to be booked in. One had the remains of a vindaloo spilt down his front and Dillon caught a whiff of it as he walked by the man. It didn't smell half-bad, and he wondered if it would be too late to order a takeaway after they finished the interview.

Just then, Christine popped her head out of one of the interview rooms and signalled for him to join her.

Inside the small, windowless room, which for some reason reeked of sweaty feet, Meeks was sitting at a coffee stained desk, squirming miserably. His hands were trembling, and the expression on his face was that of a man waiting to be led to the hangman's noose.

"What are you looking so bloody miserable about?" Dillon demanded, taking a seat opposite.

Burying his head in his hands, Meeks looked like he was about to start crying. "My life's over, bruv," he despaired. "Goliath knows. He knows I gave him up to you lot, so I'm as good as dead."

Dillon regarded him curiously. "Why do you say that?" he asked, resisting the urge to tell the man to pull himself together and grow a pair. "Has he said something to you?"

Meeks shook his head. "He didn't say anything," he said, his voice quivering. "He didn't need to."

"Then how do you know he's worked out that you're a grass?" Dillon asked, deliberately using a word that no informant likes to be called in order to test his reaction.

Meeks seemed genuinely offended by the question. "Trust me bruv," he moaned, "I just *know*. If you'd seen the way he looked at me when we woz both eating pavement, you'd know, too."

"Who paid for the hotel rooms for Goliath and his mates?" Dillon asked, switching topics. He planned to keep doing this throughout the interview to unsettle Meeks.

Meeks shrugged, confused by the randomness of the question. "How would I know that?"

"Did you pay for them?"

"No!" Meeks said, looking at Dillon as though he were mad. "Why would I pay for them?"

"Have you got a credit card, Tyson?" Dillon asked next.

"Nah, bruv. What would someone like me want plastic for? I only deal in paper, ya get me?"

Interesting, Dillon thought. He glanced at his watch, conscious that time was pressing on. "We don't have long," he said gruffly, "so let's go through what happened tonight. Firstly, why did you go into the hotel room, instead of just handing over the bag and keys and walking away like you were told to?"

"You think I wanted to go in there?" Meeks spluttered, sounding incredulous. "I *was* walking away, bruv, when I got called back and ordered inside. One of dem twins said Goliath wanted to speak to me, and he's not a man to be disobeyed. And then, when he saw me, he got all suspicious. Thought it was a bit of a coincidence that the brother who sold him weed at Euston should suddenly turn up in at his hotel room that same night. Know what I'm saying?"

"You did what?" Dillon exploded. He stood up and slammed the table with his clenched fist, making the informant flinch. "You sold him weed at Euston today? Are you fucking mad? I told you not to go anywhere near him!" His voice had risen with every sentence, and by the time he finished speaking he was leaning over the table, staring down at other man menacingly. "Why the fuck didn't you tell us that during the debrief?"

Meeks cowered back in his chair, staring up at Dillon in wide-eyed fear. "I didn't tell you because I was worried you'd lose your rag with me," he stammered. "You're not exactly the understanding type, know what I mean?"

Christine was standing by the door, making sure they weren't disturbed. "Boss," she said, gently and nodded towards his chair.

Taking the hint, Dillon sat down and took a deep breath to calm himself. "You're unbelievable, you know that?" he said, sounding deflated. Flynn would relish using this against him when he found out.

Meeks was unable to look his handler in the eye. "I'm sorry," he mumbled, the words barely audible.

"So, what did you tell him when he got suspicious?"

Meeks wriggled uncomfortably in his seat as he recalled the awkward conversation. "I told him Conrad had sent me to the station to make sure none of dem motherfuckers from the other gangs was waiting to follow dem mans off when they arrived."

Dillon pondered this. Considering it had come from a complete moron like Meeks, it was actually a half-decent excuse. "Did he buy that?" he asked.

Meeks shrug was full of nervous uncertainty. "He seemed to. I tell you, bruv, I was shitting myself in case he dialled Conrad's digits to check out my story, but he didn't."

Dillon nodded as he digested this. "So, having somehow managed to talk yourself out of an incredibly dangerous situation, why didn't you just leave?"

Meeks clucked his tongue against his teeth, and when he spoke, his tone was sheepish. "Goliath wouldn't let me, blud. Said he didn't know the area, so he needed me to drive dem mans to the place where the Albanian was going to be. He promised to let me go before they merked him."

"Merked?"

"Killed him, bruv."

"But you didn't know the address yourself," Dillon pointed out.

"I told him that, blud, but he wasn't having any of it. Told me he would bell Conrad and ask him for directions once we left the hotel."

That didn't make any sense at all.

From what GMP had told him about Adebanjo, Dillon knew the man was a meticulous planner. He would have worked everything out well in advance, including his routes to and from the target address. And he certainly wouldn't go out on a job without a secure means of contacting his employer, and yet none of the Mancs had mobile phones on them when they were arrested.

Dillon affected a bored look even though, inside, his mind was spinning. "Did he ask to use your phone?" he asked.

The question seemed to throw Meeks. "No. Why would he need to use my phone, bruv? He told me he's been speaking to Livingstone on and off all day, so he must have had a blower of his own. And, trust me, bruv, a *playa* like that aint gonna be relying on no public phone-box to chat with his bredrin."

Of course he wasn't, Dillon thought. Adebanjo obviously had a mobile phone on him when he arrived in London, but he had ditched it at some point before being arrested. Worryingly, that implied that he'd known the arrest was coming and had sanitised himself before-hand. Unfortunately, Dillon's team hadn't found any phones inside the hotel room or in the car, so where had the sly bugger dumped the burner?

And how could he possibly have known that the arrest was coming… unless he and Livingstone had set the whole thing up?

The more Dillon learned about this job, the more confused he became.

"Are you sure Livingstone told you that this Goliath bloke was definitely coming down to London to kill the Albanian today?"

"Hundred percent, bruv," Meeks said. "He was gonna merk the motherfucker tonight."

"Who told you that?"

"You know who told me that, bruv," Meeks said impatiently. "We musta gone through this shit a hundred times last night when I came to you with the information."

"Humour me," Dillon said. "Who told you?"

Meeks demonstrated his displeasure by sucking through his teeth. "Conrad Livingstone told me, innit."

"And you're sure he said the Albanians were the target, not Turks?"

"I think I can tell the difference," Meeks responded with heavy sarcasm.

"There were no guns in the bag," Dillon said, changing the direction of the conversation once again. "How do you explain that?"

Meeks spread his arms wide in a gesture of exaggerated perplexity. "I don't know, man. I was told to take the bag to Goliath and that's what I did."

Dillon leaned forward. "This is important and I need you to answer me truthfully. Did anyone ever actually say it contained firearms?"

Meeks found the question demeaning. "Are you saying I'm stupid, bruv?" he demanded accusingly.

Dillon folded his arms impatiently. "Just answer the damn question."

"Yes," Meeks confirmed, spitting the word out resentfully. "Jerome told me that the blammers the Mancs needed for the job were in the bag. Satisfied? Or do you want to ask me any other dumbass questions?"

"The car isn't stolen."

"It must be. I was told it was nicked and on false plates."

"By whom?"

"By Conrad on the phone, and by Jerome when I collected the car."

Dillon shook his head. "Not nicked. Not on false plates."

Meeks was flabbergasted. "For real?" he asked, looking utterly confused.

"For real," Dillon confirmed.

Meeks just sat there, open mouthed, looking from one to the other and not knowing what was going on or what to say.

Dillon knew exactly how he felt.

CHAPTER SIX

Wednesday 26th May 1999
TWO INVESTIGATIONS BECOME ONE

As he'd promised, Dillon arrived at Arbour Square police station dead on seven o'clock the following morning, unlike Jack Tyler, who didn't roll up until ten-past.

When he got there, Tyler looked tired and dishevelled, as Dillon had known he would.

The sky above them was a clear canopy of cerulean, and the promise of a glorious spring day was being duly celebrated by song-birds chirping in the trees around Arbour Square Gardens. All this pleasantness was wasted on Tyler, who was feeling hot, sticky, and very crotchety.

Tyler had remained at the crime scene until one a.m. When he'd arrived home, he'd slipped out of his clothes and climbed straight into bed, exhausted. Unfortunately, as much as he needed it, sleep wouldn't come and, in the end, he'd given up trying and had just lain there thinking about the new job and what needed to be done.

Removing his shades, he squinted against the brightness of the morning sun, yawned loudly and then stretched like an old man. When he clocked Dillon patiently waiting for him by the station doors, he just about managed to grunt out a monosyllabic greeting.

"Good morning to you, too, grump features," Dillon said in return.

"I need coffee," Tyler croaked.

Without another word, he led Dillon up to his office and put the kettle on. While it boiled, he stood by the mirror on his wall, running an electric shaver over his stubbled face.

"You might want to comb your hair, while you're at it," Dillon suggested, earning himself a sullen stare from Tyler, who begrudged the fact that his friend looked remarkably fresh despite having finished work a whole hour later than he had.

Clean shaven, hair gelled, smelling of expensive cologne, Dillon had swapped the scruffs he'd been wearing the previous day for an expensive single-breasted suit made from good quality material. His Windsor knot was tied to perfection and his handkerchief, folded into a triple square pocket point, protruded from his top pocket at just the right angle.

Jack, on the other hand, wore a cheap, crumpled suit he'd purchased from J. C. Penny's in Orlando during his visit last year. Because of his height, he had trouble buying off the peg suits in the UK, but it was never a problem in the States so, whenever he went there, he tended to come back with at least one new suit.

Tyler noticed that, unlike the single crisp folds running down the centre of Dillon's expensive trousers, the pair he wore had creases everywhere, so much so that they resembled a busy rail network in places. He made a mental note to hang them up from now on, instead of just flopping them over the back of a chair like he'd done last night.

Once the coffee was ready, they sat down together and Dillon talked him through what had happened the previous day. Tyler listened in silence, consuming two cups of coffee while his friend talked. By the end of the second, he was just about starting to feel human again. "So, let me get this straight," he said when Dillon had finished his narration. "Up until now your snout has been one-hundred-percent accurate and has always supplied quality information."

"Yep. We've had some really good results from him."

"But this time, for whatever reason, he gave you duff info and the job blew out."

"It's looking that way," Dillon agreed.

"And your boss–"

"Danny – the wanker – Flynn," Dillon interjected.

"–thinks he deliberately fed you a pack of lies to earn himself a pay-out?"

A contemptuous sneer appeared on Dillon's face. "Regardless of what Flynn thinks, I'm telling you Jack, I know my snout and he wouldn't do that."

"I believe you," Tyler said, smiling disarmingly. "Maybe he just got his facts wrong, Dill. Have you considered that?"

Dillon rolled his eyes impatiently. "Of course I bloody well have," he snapped. "I've spent the night thinking about little else. I hardly slept a wink, mate."

That's right, rub it in, Jack found himself thinking. *Why is it we both had sleepless nights but I'm the only one who looks like shit?*

Dillon continued. "Look, Jack, I know that the most obvious explanation to all this is that he just got his facts wrong, but I can't ignore the possibility that some insidious bastard deliberately gave him phony information."

"From the sound of it, I'm guessing that's exactly what you think happened?"

After a brief hesitation, Dillon nodded emphatically. "I do. If his information had been vaguer, I would have been more inclined to accept that he'd simply gotten the wrong end of the stick. No big deal; these things happen. However, I've rarely been given such specific information on a job that was about to go down. It just doesn't tally."

Tyler considered this. "You seem to have a lot of faith in this snout of yours, mate. Do you trust him that much?"

Dillon shook his head wearily. "I don't trust him at all, Jack. And I'm not making him out to be an angel. Far from it. I found out last night that the little shit approached Adebanjo at Euston and sold him weed, a fact that he deliberately withheld from us during the debrief."

Tyler's eyes narrowed. "So, he's a liar," he said.

Dillon waved this away dismissively. "All informants are to some extent, Jack. As a handler it goes with the territory."

"And you're comfortable with that? I know I wouldn't be."

Dillon shrugged. "I was fuming when I found out, but after I calmed down and put it into perspective, I realised that Meeks was just trying to avoid a bollocking for disobeying my instructions."

Jack didn't see it that way. "A lie's a lie, surely?"

Dillon allowed himself a wry smile. "Jack, I appreciate that by our standards his moral compass is deeply askew, but I really don't think he lied about the information he gave us, or where he got it from. I really don't."

Tyler still wasn't convinced, but he didn't see any point in saying so. "What's the score with the suspects?" he asked instead.

"They're being interviewed this morning, but we've got nothing so they'll get bail."

"Why not just NFA them?" Jack asked. "They can always be re-arrested if new evidence comes to light."

Dillon's face took on a pained expression. "If I release them with no further action, Flynn will find a way to stop me pursuing the investigation. And I can't let it die."

"You really think there's more to this than meets the eye?"

Dillon's nod was animated. "I do, Jack. I really do."

"Why? Be specific."

Dillon took in a deep breath, wondering where he should start. "For starters, lots of little things don't add up. Livingstone's a shrewd operator who plays his cards close to his chest. When Meeks drove him up to Manchester, he kept schtum about why they were going there."

"I would expect him to," Jack said. "Only a fool would reveal his plans to a low-level dealer like your informant, especially if those plans involved murder."

"Exactly, and yet the day before the shooters arrived, he pulled Meeks aside and opened up to him like he was confessing his sins to a priest.

Livingstone literally told Meeks everything, including the hitman's name and description, the time his train was arriving and the hotel he'd be staying at. Then, to make sure he'd been paying attention, Livingstone made him repeat it all back to him. Now, does any of that add up to you?"

"No," Jack admitted. "It stinks. There's no way that a career criminal like Livingstone would be that reckless."

"It gets better. Yesterday afternoon, Livingstone called Meeks and ordered him pick up a package–" he made air quotes to accompany the word "–and a boosted car from a fellow gang member, and deliver them both to Adebanjo at the hotel."

"Well, that bit of the story is feasible at least," Jack said.

"It is," Dillon agreed, "but get this: the hotel room was reserved the day before by someone phoning reception and paying with a credit card."

Jack shrugged. "Yeah, and…?"

"The caller gave his name as Tyson Meeks, and he paid with a credit card in that name. My boy is adamant that he doesn't even have a credit card."

Despite his reservation, Jack felt himself being drawn into Dillon's web of intrigue. "You need to get straight onto the company issuing the card to find out when it was applied for and to get a copy of the application."

"I've already tasked someone to do that the moment the banks open. It'll probably take a production order from a court to get a copy of the application, but I'm hoping they can be persuaded to give us a verbal steer over the phone."

"So, your theory is that Livingstone discovered Meeks was a snout and set this whole thing up to unearth him, is that right?"

"It's a lot more complicated than that," Dillon said. "I kept asking myself why, if Livingstone thought Meeks was a grass, he didn't just beat a confession out of him? The man's a dweeb, and he would have folded after the first punch. The only logical conclusion is that Livingstone left him alone because he realised that he could use Meeks to feed us false information."

"But why would he want to do that?" Jack asked.

"To send us on a wild goose chase, thereby ensuring that the real shooters would have a free run at their target."

Tyler's brow furrowed. "The real shooters being the team who gunned down the four Turks last night?"

"Yes."

Jack's head was starting to hurt. "But I thought you said he wanted the Albanians hit, not the Turks? Am I missing something here?"

"No, mate, you're not. I think Livingstone *wanted* Meeks to give us a load of misinformation so that we would be confused."

"Well, it's bloody well working," Jack said, tetchily.

"There's more. I stayed up most of the night reading through the file my mate from GMP sent me, and I've found something in it that's convinced me that Livingstone's ulterior motive is to instigate a war between the Albanians and the Turks."

Jack pinched his nose to alleviate the tension that was building behind his eyes. "Why would he want to do that?" he asked. It all sounded a bit far-fetched to him.

"Because it would be bloody good for his business, that's why. Think about it, mate. The Turks and Albanians are Livingstone's main competitors. If a war broke out between them, the Turks would obviously win, but their victory would come at a high price. The Albanians, on the other hand, would be annihilated. That's one competitor severely weakened and another completely eradicated. Livingstone's power base would increase exponentially, and he would have achieved the desired growth without firing a single shot. It's a bloody genius plan."

"And what about Adebanjo? What's his role in all this, or is he simply another pawn who's being manipulated by Livingstone in the same way that Meeks has been?"

Dillon blew out his cheeks in a mirthless laugh. "If Livingstone tried that on with Adebanjo, he'd be signing his own death warrant."

"So explain what Adebanjo's role is, because from where I'm sitting, it looks like he's not done anything wrong."

"I'm getting to that," Dillon assured him. "I've been liaising with a GMP detective called Jonny Murphy. He's spent five-years trying to build a solid case against Adebanjo but nothing ever sticks."

Tyler was always sceptical when he heard tales like that. "Yeah, but how much of an effort has he really put in, Dill?"

"A lot, and he hasn't made himself popular with his bosses, who think he's been neglecting his other cases to focus on Adebanjo. I'm not kidding, mate, putting that nutter behind bars has started to become an unhealthy obsession for Jonny."

Tyler raised a dubious eyebrow. "And you found something interesting in his files?"

"Yes. Last night I found a reference to a series of unsolved homicides that occurred in Rochdale, Oldham, and Tameside two-years ago; the circumstances are almost identical to what we've got going on here: three gangs fighting over a disputed territory. The first was a bunch of white neo-Nazi sympathisers, the second was Asian, and the last was a predominantly afro-Caribbean outfit. Anyway, acting on an anonymous tip off, the Old Bill executed a firearm's warrant at the home of the black gang leader, arresting him and three guests for conspiracy to murder the neo-Nazis. It didn't go anywhere, and after two days of intensive interviewing they were all released with no further action being taken. Meanwhile, a group of Asian gangsters were hit by three white shooters, who everyone presumed were neo-Nazis. The attack left four men dead. The Asians immediately retaliated, and within a week the two gangs were taking pot-shots at each other all over town. Eventually – another five homicides later – the madness stopped, but by the time it did, the Asians and the neo-Nazis were both considerably weaker, and the afro-Caribbean gang had taken over the vacant turf. Now, tell me, doesn't that sound familiar?"

Jack nodded reluctantly. It sounded worryingly similar.

Dillon reached down to the briefcase beside his chair. "I've got the file here if you want to read it," he said, pulling it out.

Tyler took the document and checked his watch. "I'll read it later," he said. It was seven-twenty already, and his staff were starting to arrive in dribs and drabs, getting ready for the eight o'clock briefing. Before that started, however, he needed to go down and speak to Detective Chief Superintendent George Holland, in order to put in a request for additional resources. He would need to allow a good fifteen minutes for that conversation.

"So you think Livingstone hired Adebanjo to do the same thing for him here as he did in Manchester, and set two rival gangs at each other's throats?"

Dillon nodded vigorously. "According to Murphy, Adebanjo has a big ego, and he sees himself as the Bobby Fischer of crime–"

"Who?" Tyler interrupted.

"Bobby Fischer was a chess grandmaster, one of the greatest tacticians of the game," Dillon explained impatiently. "In the GMP murders, the information provided to the Old Bill was given anonymously. I think that, when Livingstone told Adebanjo he had a leak inside his firm, Adebanjo came up with a clever way to exploit this to their advantage."

"But why would Adebanjo get himself arrested?" Tyler asked. "It was totally unnecessary. He could easily have used a minion as a decoy."

Having read the files Murphy had sent him, Dillon understood exactly why Adebanjo had done this. "The man's a megalomaniac," he explained, "and he wants to experience the spectacle of our confusion and disappointment up close and personal."

Tyler let out a low whistle. "Do you really think he would put himself through all that just so he could gloat?"

"I think he would, Jack. I think it would give him a fucking hard on."

Jack nodded, trying to process what his friend had just told him. If you were willing to do some lateral thinking, it made quite a lot of sense. If not, it sounded like a load of old bollocks.

"What do you think?" Dillon asked.

Tyler's breath was expelled in a sigh that was so strong it ruffled the papers lying on his desk. "My mind is reeling right now, and I honestly don't know what to think," he admitted, rubbing his temples and wondering where he could get some paracetamol from. "But I think the two investigations need to be merged so that we can pool resources."

Dillon shook his head sadly. "It's not going to happen, Jack. Flynn won't sanction it. He'd go spare if I told him what I just told you. And, to be fair to him, I only just about believe it myself."

"Then we need to speak to George Holland as soon as possible," Tyler said. "If this is going to work, we need him to be on side."

Almost eerily, George Holland chose that very moment to push open the door and stroll into the office. "Morning, Jack."

"Good morning, sir," Jack responded, standing up respectfully. "Can I get you a brew?"

Following his lead, Dillon did likewise.

"Yes, please, Jack. Coffee would be lovely," Holland replied with a curt smile. He gave Dillon an enquiring look, and then stared pointedly at Jack, obviously waiting to be introduced.

Tyler took the hint. "Boss, this is Tony Dillon. He's due to join us in a few weeks and, if you recall, I spoke to you a few days ago about the possibility of him coming on my team to replace Rex Tillerson."

Technically, Tillerson didn't retire for another four-weeks, but he had accrued so much unused leave that he had actually left the team a week ago.

Holland shook Dillon's bear like hand. "Good to meet you," he said. "I take it you've popped over to touch base with Jack and get a feel for how things work here?"

There was an awkward silence, during which Dillon and Tyler exchanged meaningful glances. Holland picked up on this at once.

"Actually, boss," Dillon said, "I think the job Jack's team have just taken might be linked to something I was already looking at."

"Really?" Holland said, immediately interested. "Would you care to elaborate." It wasn't a request.

"Perhaps you should have a seat first, boss," Tyler said, hurriedly. "I'll get us all a hot drink and then we can run you through it."

Holland's eyes narrowed suspiciously, and his craggy face took on a disapproving moue. "Why do I get the feeling you're only pampering me because you want something from me?" he asked.

Jack laughed nervously. "I'll get those drinks," he said.

———

When the incredibly annoying buzzer went off, Jenny Parker only just about resisted the urge to press the snooze button on her alarm clock and turn over for another fifteen minutes of glorious shut eye. Groaning, she threw the quilt cover back and rolled her legs over the edge of the mattress. Although she hadn't noticed him getting up, it was a weekday so Eddie would have risen well over an hour ago. Come rain or shine, his early morning Monday to Friday ritual consisted of a 5K run, after which he would stand under a steaming hot shower for ten-minutes until he resembled a prune.

As she sat there bleary eyed, enjoying the soothing sensation that repeatedly scrunching her manicured toes through the shag pile of their thick bedroom carpet gave her, she heard the patter of tiny feet running up the stairs. Seconds later, her precious black and tan miniature Dachshund burst into the room, tail wagging furiously.

"Morning Fritz," she said, bending down to stroke him affectionately.

As soon as she stood up to visit the en-suite, a sensation of nausea swept over her, just as it had done the previous day. "Oh dear," she said to the dog, "I really hope this doesn't mean what I think it does."

Before Fritz could answer, her mobile rang. She snatched it off of the bedside table and looked at the caller display. It was her father, Brendan Parker, QC. He was a highly respected Old Bailey judge, and some of his peers were already tipping him to become the next Commons Sergeant when the present incumbent retired. Most people addressed him as 'My Lord,' but to her he was just 'daddy'.

"Hi dad, what can I do for you?" she asked, wishing that the horrid queasiness would hurry up and pass.

"*Good morning Jennifer,*" he said, and she could almost hear the doting smile in his voice. "*I know how forgetful you are, so I thought it best to remind you that you and Edward are having dinner with your mother and I at our favourite restaurant this evening.*"

Jenny cringed. *Shit!* She had completely forgotten, and with the awful way that things were between her and Eddie at the moment, the last thing she wanted to do was go out with her folks. They would spot that something was wrong immediately.

"I haven't forgotten, daddy," she lied, "but I've woken up feeling really sick this morning, so I'll have to wait and see how I feel later, just in case I'm coming down with a bug."

"*Oh, you poor thing,*" he said, his rich voice immediately full of concern. "*Well, I'll be tucked up in court all day, so perhaps it's best if you speak to your mother when you decide. Hopefully, you'll be all better by lunchtime and we can carry on as planned, but if not, we will just have to reschedule for when you're well again.*"

"Thanks, dad. Listen, I've got to go as I'm running late. Hopefully, I'll see you later. Love you."

"*Love you too, pumpkin.*"

That settled it, she decided as she hung up. She would pop into the chemist in Station Parade on her way to the station. There was an easy way to find out whether she was just a little under the weather or suffering from an entirely different type of condition. She really hoped it would just turn out to be a mild stomach bug.

––––––––

It had taken considerably longer to brief Holland than Tyler had expected. Talking him through last night's quadruple shooting had been a fairly straightforward matter, but trying to sell Dillon's conspiracy theory was proving to be somewhat more problematic. Holland had spent the last thirty minutes scrutinising the file that Jonny Murphy had faxed over, refusing to discuss the feasibility of Livingstone and Adebanjo joining forces to replicate the Midlands scenario until he had finished.

At five to eight, Jack popped out into the main office, where his team were waiting for the briefing to begin. Quinlan and his HAT car crew were there too, as was a very sleepy, but immaculately turned out, Juliet Kennedy.

"Really sorry," he announced. "We're going to be fifteen minutes late starting. Feel free to grab a coffee, but don't wander off too far."

As he headed back towards his office, Quinlan made to join him. "Sorry, Andy," he said, "we're just dealing with a private issue that's arisen, so I'll have to ask you to wait here."

Quinlan seemed surprised. It wasn't often that a fellow DCI was excluded from a meeting, especially when it related to a job that they were waiting to formally hand over. "Oh, okay," he said, not knowing what else to say.

When Tyler returned to his office, Holland turned to Tony Dillon and explained that he needed a few moments alone with Tyler. Once Dillon left the room, he turned to Jack, his face deadly serious. "If I push for the two enquiries to merge, there will be fireworks. I know Danny Flynn of old, and there's no way he's going to agree to it. Danny always seeks the path of least resistance, and he'll just want to forget all about this and move on. So, before I go to bat for him, I need to know your friend is worth it. Tell me honestly, Jack, do you buy into this far-fetched theory of his?"

Jack's face became solemn. "I do, boss. I've known Dillon since he joined my relief as a fresh-faced probationer ten-years ago, and he's one of the most reliable, level-headed people you could ever want on your team. I know where you're coming from, and I don't mind telling you that I was a bit sceptical at first. But, having had a little time to digest his theory, I'm now behind it all the way."

Holland thought about this. "Well, in a few weeks' time he's going to be one of us, and you know I believe in supporting my staff. I suspect I'll have to refer this upwards for a decision, but I'd like to think I've got more sway at The Yard than Flynn, so I'm confident that we'll get our way in the end."

That was a big relief. "Do I need to postpone the meeting further?" Jack asked, hoping he wouldn't. There was so much to do, and he really wanted to make a start.

Holland shook his head. "No, I'll make a call to The Yard, to let the Commander know this is likely to be coming his way in due course for a decision, and then I'll come back up. If I'm not here by quarter past, start without me."

CHAPTER SEVEN

A BUSY DAY FOR EVERYONE

Holland hadn't returned by eight-fifteen, as Tyler had suspected would be the case, so he called the room to order. As was his preference when team meetings were being held, he sat with his back to the tea urn, his blue daybook folded open across his knees. He had invited Tony Dillon and Steve Bull to sit either side of him.

Andy Quinlan sat down next to Dillon. Twelve officers from Tyler's own team were present, along with a handful from Quinlan's. Juliet Kennedy was sat at the front, struggling to keep her eyes open.

Tyler began by introducing himself, then he turned to his friend. "And this big lug is DI Tony Dillon. He'll be joining us here at AMIP in a few weeks, and it's looking likely that he'll end up on this team as we're losing Rex Tillerson to retirement, so be nice to him."

"Good to meet you all," Dillon said, looking around the room. His eyes stopped when they reached an unhealthily thin male with a pale complexion who was sitting towards the rear of the group and doing his best not to get noticed by the new DI. The slim man had closely cropped brown hair and a goatee, which made his face look a little less sharp than it would otherwise. The smile on Dillon's face immediately faded, to be replaced with a frown as he recognised DC Kevin Murray; a face from the past.

"Okay," Tyler was saying. "Late last night four Turkish men were gunned down in cold blood as they left a small café at the Seven Sisters end of Green Lanes. All died at the scene in what we believe was a professional execution. We've established that the front seat passenger, Erkan Dengiz, was the registered keeper of the car. We're waiting on fingerprint comparisons to reveal the identities of the other three. Intelligence indicates that the shootings are linked to an escalation in tensions between three North London gangs involved in an ongoing dispute over territory."

"So, it's a turf war, is it?" DC George Copeland asked. The rotund Yorkshireman was going to be the exhibits officer for the job.

"It's complicated, George," Tyler explained, "but we think one of the gangs is trying to nudge the dispute that way, yes."

At that point, the door opened and Holland made his entry. "Don't mind me," he said, pulling up a chair next to Andy Quinlan.

"I'm going to start off by playing the scene video," Tyler said, fiddling with the remote control for the TV and video combo mounted on the wall behind his head until he got it to work.

"Okay," Tyler said when it had finished. "The good news is that all the victims were complete slags, so the streets of London are safer already. The bad news is that this enquiry is gang related, so it's going to be a real ball-ache." He looked around the room as he spoke, gauging his team's reaction. They were clearly disgruntled, and he really couldn't blame them for feeling that way. The reality was that, unless they got lucky with forensic evidence or CCTV, this job could easily end up as an unsolved – a sticker – and no detective liked being associated with cases like that.

Tyler's eyes settled on an athletic looking black male in his late twenties. "Colin, according to my list you're the dedicated CCTV officer for this job."

DC Colin Franklin nodded. "That's right, boss."

"We'll sit down together after the meeting and go through all the parameters in more detail, Colin, but the gist of it is this: I want all the CCTV for Hackney and Haringey boroughs downloaded for twenty-four-hours either side of the shooting. I know it's a big ask, and we probably won't end up having to view it all, but I want it in my possession."

"Yes, sir," Franklin said, already looking daunted.

"You'll have some assistance, I promise," Tyler said, seeing the look on his face. "Right, where's Dean?" he asked, keen to keep the momentum going.

In the middle of the room, DC Dean Fletcher reluctantly raised a hand. "Here, boss."

In his late forties, Fletcher was a solidly built man with a thatch of salt and pepper hair sitting atop a perpetually stern face. He was Jack's lead researcher on the team's Intelligence Cell.

"I've got a lot of work for you, too, I'm afraid," Tyler said, smiling ruefully. "I want a seven day ANPR check carried out on the victim's Mercedes. I want it to include the registration numbers of the ten vehicles travelling behind it on each occasion that it was clocked. If I'm right, whoever organised this had the Turks followed to the scene last night, and it's entirely possible that they also had them under surveillance during the days leading up to the hit."

When a vehicle passes an Automatic Number Plate Recognition camera, its details are automatically run through the database to see if there are any interest reports on it, such as it being reported stolen or involved in crime, but retrospective checks of the type Tyler had requested could also be carried out.

Fletcher was scribbling furiously in his daybook. "No problem," he said without looking up.

"There's a fair bit more, I'm afraid," Tyler said, sounding apologetic. "I want a detailed research docket completed on Erkan Dengiz. I'll also want dockets on the other three victims as soon as they've been identified. I want everything you can find on the gang they're affiliated to, and also on the two rival gangs involved in this territorial dispute. I suspect the Borough Intelligence Unit at Hackney will already have most of the info you need, and if you speak to them it might save you a lot of time."

"I suppose I'd better find you an analyst to evaluate all this data you're going to be gathering," Holland interjected.

"Thank you, that would be very helpful," Jack said. He turned his attention back to Fletcher. "The last thing I want you to do, Dean – at least for now – is to run a check on all burnt out cars that have shown up overnight. If I were the shooters, I'd torch that motor at the earliest opportunity. If you draw a blank, repeat the search every couple of hours."

"Leave it to me," Dean said, seemingly unfazed by the amount of work he'd been given.

"Right," Tyler said, moving on quickly. "Where's Reg?"

"Be gentle on me," Reg Parker piped up from somewhere near the back. A tubby man in his mid-thirties, with sandy coloured hair and a cherubic face, Parker was renowned for his technical prowess.

"You're not going to like this," Tyler said. "I want a cell dump from the mast covering the scene of the shooting." He raised a hand to stem the protest that was already spilling out of Parker's mouth. "I know the TIU will object, but tough. Four people are dead, and we need to move quickly if we're going to stop a turf war breaking out. Tell them I want a meeting to discuss tactics and options ASAP."

The Telephone Intelligence Unit at New Scotland Yard dealt with all phone related enquiries, liaising directly with the relevant industry service providers, and they would assign a single point of contact, referred to as a SPOC, to manage the case.

"I'll phone them straight after the meeting to give them a heads up," Parker said, but he didn't look like he was relishing the conversation.

Tyler turned to the sleepy headed Crime Scene Manager. "Juliet, am I right in saying all four victims had mobile phones on them?" he asked.

Kennedy yawned, nodded, and then yawned again. "They did," she confirmed. "Kevin seized them last night, I believe." She looked around, seeking confirmation from Murray.

"That's right, boss," Murray chipped in, still trying to keep his head down and studiously avoiding eye contact with Dillon, who shot daggers in his direction every time the man looked up.

"Reg, I want call data and cell site applications in on all four phones today, please."

Parker groaned. "Will do," he said.

Tyler turned to Quinlan. "Andy, how did you get on with the café owner and his daughter? Did you manage to get them key witness interviewed?"

Quinlan pushed his spectacles into the bridge of his nose. "Yes, both were done. A précis of what they said, along with their statements, have already been given to your Office Manager. They both saw the shooting. The girl was standing at the door when it happened, having escorted the victims out. She got a much better view than her father. From what she said, this was a slick operation carried out by three well-trained white men in balaclavas who appeared from nowhere, took all four Turks out with minimum effort, and then jumped into a dark coloured saloon that sped off."

"I don't suppose she got the car's index?" Tyler asked, knowing that even a partial index would be a good start.

Quinlan shook his head. "Afraid not."

"Does she at least know what type of saloon it was?" Tyler asked, hopefully.

Quinlan shook his head again, even more emphatically than before. "She's not good with cars, unfortunately. It was a five-door hatchback, blue or dark green. Although she did say it had a great big dent in the rear nearside wing."

Tyler turned to Franklin. "Colin, our CCTV viewers need to be aware of that," he said.

"They will be," Franklin promised.

"What did they say about why Dengiz and his cronies were there?" Tyler asked his opposite number.

Quinlan gave a resigned shrug. "They were both rather vague about that, I'm afraid. In fact, they were really uncomfortable speaking to us at all, and I got the distinct impression that they were afraid of repercussions from the Turkish mobsters they're paying protection money to."

Tyler nodded his understanding. Looking around the room, his eyes fell on DC Paul Evans, a slim Welshman who, despite his reputation for having a fiery temper, had a knack for talking to people and could, given enough time, charm any witness into confiding in him. "Paul, have a read of their statements and then pay them a visit. I want to know what those four Turks were really doing in that café, and I want to know if these witnesses are holding anything back about the shooters."

"I'll get right on it," Evans said.

"Right, Juliet, how are we doing with forensics?" Jack asked.

"We're doing alright," she told him. "The record photography is complete. The bodies were removed a little while ago. Wet sets will be taken from Erkan's driver and the two unidentified goons this morning, and they'll be rushed up to The Yard for fingerprint comparisons. Hopefully, we'll know who they are by mid-afternoon. The ballistic expert completed his scene examination overnight, and he'll be popping over to Charlton to take an in-depth look at the car tomorrow, after it's been examined by us. As soon as the lab have finished examining the bullets and shell casings, I'll get the striation and hammer marks from all three weapons run through NABIS to see if they've been used in any previous shootings."

Striation marks are caused by a bullet passing through a gun's barrel during discharge, and are unique to that weapon. Ejectors on semi or fully automatic weapons can also leave similar identifiable markings. Likewise, when the trigger is pulled, a gun's firing pin leaves a distinctive imprint on the cartridge case. The Forensic Science Service at Lambeth in South London would carefully examine the bullets retrieved from the four victim's bodies, along with the dozens of cases recovered at the scene, using special comparison microscopes. All the information gleaned would then be run though the National Ballistics Intelligence Service - or NABIS for short.

"Can we also get the shell casings checked for prints and DNA, please, Juliet?" Tyler asked.

"It's already in hand," she responded, unsuccessfully trying to stifle a yawn.

"Any luck arranging the specials?" Tyler enquired next.

The face Juliet pulled answered his question. "Afraid not," she said flatly. "I'm hoping they'll start tomorrow morning, but I still don't know for sure, and I have no idea who'll be carrying them out. I should have a definitive answer for you by lunchtime."

Tyler made a note in his daybook. He would chase that up if he hadn't heard anything by midday. "What about the POLSA search down at the crime scene?"

"It's being done as we speak."

"Okay," Tyler said. "We're confident the shooting's related to rising tensions between three North London based gangs competing to take over a vacant territory. One's Kurdish-Turkish, another is Albanian, and the final gang's an afro-Caribbean mob run by a bloke called Conrad Livingstone. Mr Dillon is currently with the Organised Crime Group. I can't go into specific detail but, acting on intelligence received, his team arrested three Mancunians at a hotel in Barking last night. Their names are-" he quickly glanced down at his notes, "- Samuel Adebanjo, Isaac Kalu and his brother, Andre. It was believed that Conrad Livingstone hired them to come down to London to kill an Albanian–"

"The shooters were white, boss," Steve Bull interrupted. "Does that mean the Albanians got word that trouble was coming and put in a pre-emptive strike?"

"Too early to say for sure," Tyler said, "but that's one possibility." During the pre-meeting conversation he'd had with Holland and Dillon, it had been decided that, unless an operational situation made disclosure unavoidable, it would be best to keep Dillon's theory between the three of them for the time being. It had also been agreed that there was to be no mention of Tyson Meeks' role as a source. "Anyway, Mr Dillon's team will continue to manage those enquiries and he'll share any information he gets with us."

"I can tell you," Holland said, cutting in, "that, following a lengthy conversation with DSU Flynn at SO7, Mr Dillon and four of his officers will be written off for the next few weeks to become part of a joint task force with us. They will be based here, but they will primarily explore the Manchester angle to start with."

As soon as the briefing concluded, Copeland and Franklin wandered off with their opposite numbers from the HAT crew to complete the formal hand over of all the exhibits and CCTV.

Leaving Bull to task the others, Tyler followed Holland and Dillon into his office and closed the door. "Were there any problems getting Dillon released?" he asked as they sat down.

Holland just smiled. "I don't think Danny was overly pleased, but we came to an accord." He left it at that.

"Dill, I've been thinking," Jack said. "Can you get onto your mate at GMP and get him to carry out a search at Adebanjo's club on our behalf? I want the club's CCTV for the last month seized."

"I'm sure he'll be happy to oblige."

"I also want him to visit the hotel Livingstone was staying at up there and get any CCTV they have – a day either side of Livingstone's visit should suffice. If we ever manage to prove he's behind all this, we'll need to be able to show clear association between Livingstone and Adebanjo. I also need an ANPR check carried out on the car your snout used to drive him up there, and a financial check run to see if Livingstone spent any money while he was away. Lastly, I want the CCTV from Euston seized for the hour either side of Adebanjo's train arriving."

"I can get that sorted," Dillon said, making frantic notes.

"There's more. I want Livingstone and Meeks' phone data, including cell-site, for the past month. You can speak to Reg, my tech guy, and see if he's willing to bolt that onto the other stuff he's doing. If not, though, you'll have to get one of your team to do it."

Dillon made more notes. Turning to Holland, he said," Sir, did Mr Flynn say who he was giving you from my team?"

"He did," Holland said, removing a folded sheet of paper from an inside jacket pocket. He had to squint to read the names he'd scribbled on it earlier. "Here we are… Christine Taylor, Coleen Perry, Gurjit Singh and Geoff Coles."

Dillon nodded his approval. "All good people," he told the others.

"Right," Holland said, standing up. "I'll handle all the media interest for you, but I want regular updates, Jack. Every morning and every evening, without fail – more frequently if anything significant happens. I have a horrible feeling that last night's shooting isn't going to be an isolated incident, and I don't want us being caught with our trousers down if something happens. In the meantime, I'm going to liaise with SO19 and ensure the area is flooded with ARVs."

Jack nodded his agreement. Armed Response Vehicles were going to be a far better deterrent than unarmed local patrols.

Holland turned to Dillon. "Nice to have you board," he said, and then added, "I don't want to put you under pressure before you've even arrived, but I've gone out on a limb for you this morning on the strength of Jack's word. Please make me glad that I did so."

Dillon swallowed hard. "I'll try," he promised.

———

Although Marcel Meeks was still only fifteen years old he already thought of himself as a man, and he resented being told what to do by people who weren't even his real family. Closing the door to his first-floor bedroom, he checked to make sure that the lock had engaged before setting off down the stairs of the local authority children's home in which he resided.

He had been placed in care when he was barely ten, following the death of his drug addict mum, who had overdosed on some bad smack that she'd been given. The only family he had left was an elder half-brother but, as far as he was concerned, Tyson was every bit as responsible for their mother's death as the dealer who provided the smack, and he wanted nothing more to do with him. They rarely saw each other, and when their paths did cross, they invariably fought.

As usual, he was the last one to come down to breakfast. Everyone else had already finished eating and they were now rushing around getting ready for school. Most of the other residents - or fellow inmates as he thought of them - were younger than him, although there were a couple of others who were of a similar age.

Marcel didn't care that he was late; he had no intentions of going to school today, or any other day for that matter. He would be sixteen soon, and he had long since decided that there was no gain to be had by studying for stupid exams. What was the point? He didn't want a dead-end job in a supermarket or fast food chain, earning minimum wage and being treated like dirt - not when he could earn much more money by *tiefing* and *shotting* drugs with his crew.

As he reached the communal dining room, he passed Leroy Apeloko on his way out. Leroy was cramming a piece of toast into his mouth, and he quickly wiped his right hand down the side of his trousers so that they could high-five.

"Wagwan," Marcel said, using the Jamaican patois for 'What's going on?'

Dotty Williams was hot on Leroy's tail. "Come on you two," she interjected, shooing the boys in different directions. "No time for idle chit-chat. You need to get ready for school." The roly-poly carer, whose head barely reached Marcel's shoulder, was a human whirlwind, and she stared at Meeks in exasperation as she passed him. "Marcel, I can't believe you're late down for breakfast *again*. *G*et a wiggle on!"

"Yes miss," he said with a smile of genuine warmth. Both boys liked Dotty; she didn't treat them like the orphans they were; she behaved as though they were family, and they responded by treating her with a degree of respect that was noticeably absent when they spoke to most of the other staff. "Laters bruv," he said, giving Leroy a farewell salute and heading into the dining room to scavenge whatever food was left.

Fifteen minutes later, he emerged from the front door of the children's home into a sunlit Queensbridge Road. As soon as a gap appeared in the traffic, he jogged across the busy road and cut through the estate until he came to a small green, adjacent to one of the parking lots. A few of the gang were already there, waiting for the others. Cries of "Wagwan," met him as he strutted over to them.

Before he'd left, Dotty had pulled him to one side, her kind face filled with concern as she pleaded with him to think of his future and go into school for a change, instead of bunking off to hang out with his gangsta boys. "You don't want to follow in the footsteps of your brother, do you?" she had warned, her finger wagging.

"No miss, definitely not," he'd replied. As far as he was concerned Tyson was a waste of space, a small time shotter who used more gear than he sold. He was a laughing stock on the streets; a gopher for the elders and an occasional driver for the Main Man, Conrad Livingstone. Marcel had no intentions of ending up like his loser of a brother. He had aspirations to make it big, to become a Face - maybe one day he'd end up a successful crime lord like Mr Livingstone.

"What we gonna do today?" someone asked.

"We're going tiefing, blud," came the reply. "Gonna get lots of Ps so I can buy some new jeans." Ps was street slang for money.

This drew laughter. "Whatcha wanna buy them for, bruv?" Meeks asked. "Let's just go down Mare Street and have some fun in the shops, innit." In their eyes, shoplifting wasn't so much a crime as a sport, something to do when they were bored, and a lot of the youngers got a real thrill from it.

"Can't," said Switch, a stocky seventeen-year-old with dead eyes and a bad attitude. He was second in command of their group. "Ziggy said we're gonna do the trains today."

"Cool," Meeks responded. There was good money to be made from doing that. Even if that hadn't been the case, Meeks would never have dared to challenge Switch. The boy was known for his violent disposition and was always looking for an excuse to dish out a beating to anyone who questioned him.

CHAPTER EIGHT

TOUGH DECISIONS

Although it was still early, the weather was already warm enough to make Jenny Parker regret having worn a jacket instead of a cardigan this morning. By the time she arrived at Chingford railway station, having had to power walk along Station Parade all the way from Boots, she was out of breath and perspiring – or glowing as her mother would have said.

The mad rush shouldn't have been necessary, but she had spent so long faffing around inside the chemist, trying to decide which tester to buy, that she had ended up making herself late. Now it was going to be touch and go as to whether she would actually catch her train.

As always seemed to happen to her when she fell behind with her schedule, the fates conspired against Jenny, doing their utmost to make her even later. Clearing the ticket inspector's booth with seconds to go before her train's scheduled departure, she found her onward path blocked by a group of doddering pensioners. They seemed to have all the time in the world and were totally oblivious to the fact that other people didn't.

Jenny raised her eyes to the heavens as if to ask, 'why me?' At that precise moment, as if God were mocking her, it came over the tannoy that the Liverpool Street bound train on platform two was about to depart.

Cursing under her breath, Jenny apologetically barged past the elderly group and broke into a trot. Face flushed from the effort, she just about managed to slip between the closing doors of the end carriage as they closed around her.

Halfway along, she found a seat between two burly men, and squeezed herself into the tight gap with an awkward smile. As the train lurched away from the platform, she leaned back, closed her eyes, and listened to the clackety-clack of the train's wheels passing over the tracks. Her mind was in such turmoil that she was only vaguely aware of her discomfort at being wedged in so tightly that it was difficult to breath.

She was almost a week late, and she was *never* late.

Although she was anxious to take the test, she had little doubt what the result would be. In addition to the nausea, she had started to feel a little fatigued over the last few days, which was most unusual for her as she was normally so full of energy. Of course, her symptoms could all be stress related, brought on by the trauma of her terrible ordeal. Her eyes misted as images of his face, so full of hatred, flashed into her mind. Taking a deep breath, she tried to calm herself; she couldn't lose it here, not in front of all these people.

Thankfully, when the train pulled into Highams Park the enormous man sitting to her left struggled to his feet and waddled off towards the doors, allowing her to spread out a little. He was quickly replaced by a diminutive elderly lady who hardly took up any space at all.

Jenny hadn't told anyone about that dreadful night five weeks earlier, in which her drunken fiancé had violated and humiliated the woman he supposedly loved. Waking up the following morning and claiming to have the hangover from hell, the bastard had acted as though nothing had happened. Neither of them had broached the subject since, and she wasn't even sure that he remembered it. Well lucky him if he didn't - it was a night Jenny would never be able to forget. She wasn't sure that she would ever be able to forgive either - or that she wanted to.

Since the incident, Jenny had noticed that she'd been having trouble concentrating and remembering things. There had been times when she'd felt detached from the world, the people in her life, and the activities she had always enjoyed so much. Her alcohol intake had also increased significantly, and she was starting to use it as a support mechanism to get her through the bad days.

When the train finally came to a halt at Liverpool Street, nine stops later, she exited her carriage in a daze.

It was even hotter by the time she left the station and, after removing her jacket and slipping her sunglasses on, she walked the short distance to the modern office block she worked in on autopilot. It was much cooler inside the glass fronted building thanks to the air conditioning. Jenny rode the swish elevator up twelve flights to the floor occupied by her company's senior management team. As soon as she reached her office, she hung her jacket up, grabbed the pharmacy bag, and disappeared into the toilet. Sitting down on the cold seat, she removed the wrapping and carefully read the instructions.

"Please God, let it be negative," she prayed aloud.

———

"Will your snout make a statement?" Jack asked.

Dillon raised his eyebrows at that. "Not a hope in hell, I would say. Why?"

"Listen Dill, if Livingstone's cottoned on to him, he's going to need protection, and the only way we can give it to him is if he's a prosecution witness."

"A witness to what? Without any evidence we can't charge anyone," Dillon pointed out acerbically.

"Doesn't matter. We think Livingstone and Adebanjo have conspired to commit murder, so we take a statement from our one and only witness, and then bail them pending further enquiries. That way,

I can get him into the witness protection scheme and we can ship him off somewhere safe until we manage to dig up some evidence. If we don't get anywhere, at least we won't have to worry about your informant ending up face down in a river somewhere."

"I don't think he'll buy into it, Jack."

"Then persuade him. Tell him we all have to make tough decisions in life, and sometimes every option available to us is shit; at least what we're offering him isn't as shitty as the only alternative he's got."

Dillon sighed. "You're right. I'll get Christine to speak to him this morning," he promised, but he didn't look hopeful.

The door to Jack's office opened and Dean Fletcher poked his head in. "Thought you'd want to know, a burnt-out Mondeo was found in Tottenham this morning, dumped on waste ground behind the A406. I've spoken to the locals on scene, and they reckon it's got a big dent in the rear wing."

Tyler and Dillon exchanged glances. "It's got to be the car our shooters used," the latter said. "Too much of a coincidence for it to be anything else."

"I'll ask Steve Bull to round up an exhibits officer and send them down to the scene if you like?" Fletcher offered.

Jack nodded gratefully. "Yes please, Dean."

When they were alone again, Tyler turned to Dillon. "Why don't you pop over to Forest Gate and speak to your snout yourself? While you're away, I'll phone the witness protection people and get the ball rolling."

————

Conrad Livingstone normally laid in until at least mid-morning, but not today. Unable to sleep, he had risen just before dawn and had spent the intervening hours sitting on his sofa playing mindless games on his PlayStation console – not that he'd been able to enjoy the experience. Thanks to that worthless bumbaclot, Meeks, he was half-expecting an unwelcome knock on the door from the Feds at any moment.

Every noise he heard made him jittery, and he promised himself that when this was all over, he was going to make Meeks wish he had never been born, and then he was going to kill him.

He had purposefully avoided having any contact with any of his crew since the previous evening, and now he was itching for an update. Picking up his phone, he called his right-hand man, Gunz, for a progress report.

"Wagwan?" a slurred voice asked. The prolonged exhalation that followed told Livingstone that his lieutenant was toking weed.

"Give me an update," he ordered.

The man called Gunz giggled; he was obviously high. *"Relax, blud, everything's sweet. I spoke to the whitey's after they dooked those Turkish motherfuckers, and they said it all went down like clockwork. They've torched the car, and taken a mini-cab to the second hotel. They're gonna wait there until their psycho boss gets released, and then they'll move on the second target just like we planned."*

"Bliss," Livingstone said, pleased that everything had gone according to plan.

Gunz went on to explain that, as instructed, he had followed the Turks on their debt collection round yesterday evening, and he had phoned the shooters when they were minutes away from the spot that had been chosen for the execution.

Livingstone knew that both Gunz and the Eastern European gunmen had been using burners, so there was no chance that the Feds would be able to link the phones back to anyone, least of all him. "That's good, bruv," he said. "You've done well."

"You can always rely on me, my bredrin, you know that," Gunz promised.

"I gotta breeze," Livingstone told him. "I'll call you when I need you."

The news that there hadn't been any complications seemed to lift a weight from Livingstone's shoulders. He stood up, stretched, and then lazily walked across the living room to one of the big sash windows. As soon as he pulled the heavy curtains back, light flooded into the room, making him wince. Shielding his eyes, he looked down onto Kingsland High Street, where a long line of early morning traffic was crawling its way south towards Crossway and the City.

Livingstone owned a spacious three-bedroom flat above a row of shops that were almost directly opposite the entrance to Ridley Road market. With all the money he had had made over the past five-years he could easily have afforded something grander in a more salubrious area, but these were his ends; he had been born here, and he would probably die here too.

Livingstone would never forget his humble beginnings, growing up on the Holly Street Estate, just the other side of Dalston Junction. His family had lived at the Queensbridge Road end, in one of the five low storey tower blocks what were known as the 'snake-blocks'. The place had been a ghetto, full of burnt out cars and crack houses. It had been a lawless and edgy place to live, and every day had been full of menace and despair.

Growing up in poverty, surrounded by violence, Livingstone had quickly realised that in those ends you were either the prey or the predator, and he had no intention of being the former. He had started running with the HSB – the Holly Street Boys – when he was just twelve. As a younger, he cut his teeth by *shotting* drugs for the elders, selling cannabis, crack or amphetamines to anyone who wanted to buy them. Then he'd progressed onto committing bag snatches, street robberies and group steamings. He'd loved the thrill of it; the exhilarating feeling of power he'd experienced as he'd stared down into the terrified eyes of his victims, *tiefing* whatever he wanted from them, and knowing there was nothing they could do to stop him.

As an elder, he started running lucrative county lines for the HSB; these drug networks had generated lots of money; enough that he could afford to splash out on fancy clothes, extravagant bling, and foreign cars.

By the time he reached his mid-twenties, Livingstone had become an established Face – a *Playa* – known and feared by youngers and elders alike, and treated with respect by his peers. Wherever he went in the Hood, he was instantly recognised by the young bucks who aspired to be just like him. His dangerous lifestyle and ready access to drugs and money had made him immensely popular with the girls, and he had taken full advantage of this.

His wake up call had come late one evening, some five years previously, during a time when the postcode feuds were at their craziest. He had been driving his shiny new BMW along Middleton Road, on his way back to the estate, when he spotted a group of people clustered around a dark shape on the pavement. Slowing to a crawl, he was horrified to see his best friend, Dwayne Nelson, laying on the floor in a pool of his own blood. Rushing from his car, Livingstone had cradled the dying man in his arms, knowing that there was nothing he could do to prevent him from bleeding out.

While waiting for the ambulance to arrive, Dwayne had breathlessly informed him that he'd been followed off and shived by a group of London Fields Boys just for cutting through their turf. "I... I didn't mean no disrespect, bruv," he'd stammered, choking on the words as blood spilled from his mouth. "I was just... on my way... to visit Cindy and Candice." Cindy was his baby mother, and she lived at the back of Broadway Market. Candice was their daughter, and she was going to be one year old the following day.

Up until then, Livingstone had considered himself impervious to danger, but the experience of Dwayne dying in his arms had provided a stark reminder of just how dangerous the streets of Hackney were for people like him. For years, his father had been warning him that the only 'gangsta boys' to reach forty were the ones 'dem Trident Boydem' had taken off the streets. They might be alive, he'd pointed out in his thick Jamaican accent, but they were serving an L-plate – a life sentence – which, frankly, wasn't much better than being planted six-feet under in a wooden box.

Dwayne's killer had been arrested within days, which made it impossible for Livingstone to extract the revenge he had so dearly craved, but as a consolation prize, he had personally seen to it that several of the killer's LFB friends were hunted down and beaten to within an inch of their lives. In the end, the London Fields elders had sued for a truce and, in order to prevent an all-out war from occurring, Livingstone had reluctantly agreed, drawing a line under the hostilities and moving on.

It wasn't until a couple of months later that he'd discovered Dwayne had been betrayed by a junkie from Holly Street, someone they both knew and trusted. Instead of receiving thirty pieces of silver, as Judas had for betraying Christ, Dwayne had been given up in exchange for a large bag of smack. The worthless junkie had put in a sneaky phone call to the London Fields Boys as Dwayne set off, alerting them that he would shortly be passing through their turf to visit his baby mother, which was a dangerous thing for anyone connected to HSB to do in those worrying times. The LFB had simply lain in wait for him, ready to pounce the moment he strayed into their territory.

Livingstone had made sure that the addict died a painful death, poisoned by an overdose of the very product his friend's life had been so callously traded for.

Things just hadn't been the same for him after Dwayne's passing and, following much soul searching, Livingstone had finally decided it was time for him to move on; to swap street level operations for a managerial role, where survival rates tended to be far higher. His parents were delighted when he told them he had abandoned his gangsta lifestyle in order to become a legitimate businessman.

"Perhaps you'll live to be forty after all," his father had said, smiling proudly.

"You can bank on it pops," he'd replied, hugging the old man.

Nowadays, Livingstone conducted his business from a comfortable office in his flat, leaving the sale of drugs and firearms to his cronies. He had branched out into prostitution, loan sharking, protection money, and illegal gambling. Racketeering, they called it. He even had a couple of legitimate shops on the go, where he laundered all his dirty money. It was a trick he had learned from the Turks.

Returning to the leather sofa, he made his second call of the day. It was time to test the waters and see how the Turks had taken the killing of four of their men. Not too well, he imagined, allowing himself a Machiavellian smile.

Livingstone took in a deep breath, counted to ten, and then released it slowly. Clearing his throat, he keyed in the personal number for Abdullah Goren, the forty-eight-year old leader of the Kurdish-Turkish crime gang he was in negotiation with over the disputed territory. Goren, he knew, had come to the UK as an asylum seeker in the late eighties, and, once settled, had lost no time in setting up a lucrative crime syndicate in North London. Livingstone knew he had to box clever, because Goren was loosely affiliated to the feared Abdullah Baybasin and his gang of bombacilars, which meant he could call on some serious clout if he needed backup.

The phone was answered after the fourth ring. "*Hello?*" a heavily accented voice said in an unfriendly tone. It did not belong to Goren.

"Is Mr Goren there?" Livingstone enquired.

"*Who wants to know?*" the gruff voice demanded.

"Tell him it's Conrad Livingstone."

A grunt. "*Wait,*" the man on the other end of the line said. He put his hand over the speaker, and there followed a series of muffled sounds while he spoke to someone in the room with him. "*A moment, please,*" the voice said when it came back on the line, and it sounded a little less hostile than before.

Seconds later, a new voice came through. Older, crueller, more authoritative. "*Mr Livingstone, this is Abdullah Goren. What is it that you want? I'm afraid this is not a convenient time for me.*" Goren had the rasping voice of a heavy smoker.

"I understand," Livingstone said. "I just saw it on the news, what happened to your nephew and his boys last night, and I wanted to call and offer my condolences."

"*Very thoughtful of you,*" Goren said. It was clear that the Turk wasn't in the mood for idle chat. "*Now, if you will excuse me.*"

"Have you got any idea who did it?" Livingstone asked quickly, before the older man could terminate the conversation. He hoped he didn't sound too eager.

There was a pause while the wily Turk gave careful thought to his response. "*We are working on that,*" Goren said after a moment of reflection. "*And, I assure you, once the truth is established, the matter will be resolved quickly.*"

"Do you think it was the Albanians?" Livingstone asked, pressing Goren for information.

"*What makes you think that?*" Goren demanded, suddenly sounding interested.

"Well," Livingstone said with a shrug. "Unless you've got a beef with anyone else, they seem like the logical culprits to me. I mean, they weren't exactly happy about the way we wanted to carve up the turf, were they? They didn't think twenty percent was enough, ungrateful bastards."

It was true, the Albanian crime boss had stormed out of the last meeting, enraged that his gang had been offered such paltry distribution rights. Demanding an equal division of the spoils, his parting shot was to issue an ultimatum: if Goren and Livingstone didn't give them a fair deal, the Albanians would be forced to take matters into their own hands.

Abdullah and his – now dead – nephew, Erkan, had harped on and on about it afterwards, claiming that the Albanian's disrespectful behaviour was an affront to their honour. It was their over-the-top reaction that had made Livingstone realise just how easily he could exploit this situation to his own advantage. With tensions already running high, it would only require a little push to launch the Albanians and the Turks into an all-out war. All he'd had to do was recruit the right man – Goliath – to organise everything.

"Ah, now I understand," Goren said. *"You are worried that the Albanians have grown tired of negotiation and are taking a more direct approach to staking their claim."*

Livingstone was very happy for Goren to think this. "Maybe," he said, guardedly.

"And I suppose it has also occurred to you that, if they have attacked us, they might be planning to attack you as well?"

Livingstone snorted his contempt. "I'm not worried about that bunch of pussies," he said defiantly. "I'm just saying it would be bad for everyone's business if they've gone rogue."

The Turk considered this. *"It would, indeed, be bad for business – bad for their business, not mine. Of that, I can assure you, Conrad."*

"I hear you," Livingstone said. "But if things get ugly, I just wanted you to know you can count on my support."

"I am very grateful," Goren said, sounding sincere, *"but a man does not require his friend's support to step on an ant."*

———

Jenny felt numb as she took a cup of mid-morning coffee into her boss's office. Luckily, he was talking to someone on the phone, so she didn't have to worry about making the customary small talk. She carefully placed the saucer on his desk by his elbow, receiving a grateful smile, and left without uttering a word. She liked working for David Forbes. Twenty years her senior, he was a kind thoughtful man and a real gentleman - unlike Edward Maitland.

Jenny had started working for the company five and a half years earlier, having been hired as a PA for Edward. She had immediately found herself bewitched by his alluring manner and magnetic personality. He was everything that her dull policeman husband wasn't - ambitious, ruthless, and well on his way to becoming very wealthy. Edward was not only charming; he was also incredibly handsome.

He had brazenly flirted with her from day one, making it clear that her being married needn't prove an obstacle to their getting to know each other better. She hadn't put up much of a fight against his advances, and within weeks they were sleeping together. To be fair, her marriage was irredeemably broken by that point; at least that was how she justified her actions to herself.

Once she left Jack and moved in with Edward, he decided that it was inappropriate for her to continue as his secretary now that they were officially an item. Accordingly, he arranged for her to move across to one of the other partners, which was how she had ended up with David Forbes.

Over the years, she had come to realise that Edward's charm was purely superficial and that the only person he really cared about was himself. Of course, Jack had spotted that within seconds of meeting the man, and he had warned her that it would end in tears, but she had just thought he was being bitter and petty.

How wrong had she been about that?

When she returned to her desk, her hand reached for the phone, hovered over it for a moment and was then snatched back as though it had just been burnt. *Come on Jen, make the call,* she chided herself. *You're going to have to tell him sooner or later.*

But what was she going to say to him? *Hi. Eddie, remember that night five weeks ago when you forced yourself on me? Well, guess what? I'm pregnant - SURPRISE!*

She buried her head in her hands, thinking, *what a mess.* It was ironic; they had been trying so hard for a baby during the past year, and discovering that she was finally with child should have filled her with joy. Instead, she felt as though someone she loved had died suddenly, and in a particularly gruesome way.

Jenny began to well up as the inner turbulence of her conflicting emotions threatened to overwhelm her. She angrily blinked moisture away from her eyes. *Be strong*, she told herself. *You need to deal with this.*

Perhaps it would be better if she spoke to him in person, she decided, dabbing her eyes with a tissue and hoping her mascara hadn't run.

Taking a deep breath, Jenny stood up, pulled her blouse straight, and checked her appearance in her compact mirror. Thankfully, she looked much better than she felt. She put on some lipstick, wanting to look as strong and confident as possible when she confronted him.

Full of trepidation, she set off along the corridor towards Edward's office on the other side of the building. As a partner, he had a corner office identical to David's. Jenny forced a smile onto her face as she entered the outer office where his frumpy secretary, Shirley, sat. Jenny had insisted that her replacement be middle-aged and unattractive - it wasn't that she didn't trust Eddie, she had told her mother, it was just that she didn't want to tempt fate by putting someone as pretty as her in there for him to oggle.

"Morning Shirley," she said, trying to sound upbeat. "Is his lord-ship free?"

Shirley smiled up at her over her bi-focals. "No, he's having an impromptu meeting with John from advertising. Shall I let him know you called by when they finish?"

Jenny shook her head. "It's not important. I'll catch him later."

She returned to her office, strangely relieved that Eddie had been otherwise engaged. It was only now, as she sat behind her desk, that it occurred to her that she had been so busy worrying what Eddie would say when she told him she was pregnant that she hadn't actually stopped to consider what she wanted to do about the baby. Did she even want it, given the way it had been conceived? If she kept it, would she be reminded of her ordeal every time she looked at the poor child? Would that affect her feelings for it?

Perhaps the most sensible thing would be to say nothing to Eddie and book a discreet termination? Given the circumstances, it really might be for the best.

Suddenly, she felt sick again, and it wasn't just a recurrence of the earlier morning sickness. Covering her mouth, she rushed to the toilet, making it into a vacant cubicle just in time. After she threw up, Jenny leaned over the bowl, wiping her chin and trying to catch her breath. She felt absolutely washed out. That was when the tears came - and once they started, she couldn't stop them.

CHAPTER NINE

PARALYSED BY FEAR

Tyson Meeks' skinny butt was numb with discomfort as he sat on the thin plastic mattress of the wooden cot in his cell. Wallowing in self-pity, he waited for them to come back and get him for the next round of interviews. The Feds were dragging their feet as usual, and he was bored out of his brain. Plus, he was feeling restless and worried, and he needed a joint to sooth his nerves. He had read every bit of graffiti in here, some of it written by people he knew, several times over and he was now seriously considering pressing the buzzer and asking dem Boydem if they had an old newspaper he could borrow - preferably a smutty red-top with lots of topless girl plastered across its pages.

Breakfast had been shite; microwaved sausage and egg - at least that's what he thought it was, but it was hard to be sure. It had looked and tasted like soggy cardboard, and his stomach was still protesting several hours after consuming it. For the sake of his digestive system, he hoped he would be out of here long before they dished up the sloppy gruel that passed for lunch.

Meeks was becoming increasingly angry. His incarceration was a pathetic sham, and it was fooling no one. He was convinced that Goliath knew he was an informer, but no matter how hard he tried to persuade the Feds, they weren't buying into it.

Either that or they just didn't care.

There was nothing to suggest his cover had been blown, the pretty girl cop with the green eyes had patronisingly told him; Goliath couldn't possibly know for sure that he was working for them. Her voice had oozed the same condescending tone that she would have used to reassure a frightened child there were no bogey men or vampires hiding under his bed. Bitch was missing the point; people like Goliath didn't need to know for sure. The slightest suspicion would be enough for them to merk him - that was how life on the road worked.

The custody sergeant had told him that once the interviews were concluded all four males would be bailed pending further enquiries. Off the record, his handler had explained that he would receive a letter in a few days' time, informing him that no further action was to be taken.

Dem Boydem were fooling themselves if they thought Goliath wouldn't come after him once he was released, but Tyson knew better. Now he would have to do a runner as soon as he made bail; if he didn't, he'd end up dead within a week.

As it often did when he was feeling morose, his mind turned to his little brother. They had been so close once, but nowadays Marcel couldn't stand the sight of him; thought he was a failure and a joke. The acrimony between them hurt far more than he would ever dare admit.

The brothers hadn't seen each other in weeks. The last time they had bumped into each other was at a rave near Dalston, and it had rapidly turned into a slanging match, with Marcel going into one because it was coming up to the anniversary of their mother's death. Marcel blamed him for that, and maybe he had a point. When she had sent him out to get some smack from her usual source that fateful night, he had bumped into a new dealer who was trying to whip up some trade. The scumbag offered him a free sample, said it was banging gear of the highest quality. Realising that if he took the free-bie, he could use his mother's cash to buy himself some weed, Tyson had readily accepted. The uncut heroin had been far too pure, and it had killed his mother when she injected it.

Such was the intensity of his brother's hatred for him over his role in their mother's demise that Tyson seriously doubted Marcel would shed a single tear if Goliath wasted him. If anything, he would prob-ably go out and celebrate.

The cell lock turned and the heavy door opened outward, distracting him from his morbid train of thought. When he looked up, Dillon and his pretty friend stood there, staring in at him.

"Morning Tyson. It's time to crack on with your interview," the big man said.

———

It was getting on for lunchtime as Kevin Murray stood on the patch of wasteland staring at the burnt-out wreck of the Mondeo. Even standing upwind, the acrid smell of burning was strong enough to make the back of his throat burn. He could tell at a glance that they would get nothing of forensic value from the car, but he had called out a photographer and the local Scenes of Crime Officer anyway. The charred husk would be lifted onto the back of a low loader and taken away once the initial exam had been carried out, and he would have to wait here with it until it went, which was about as exciting as watching paint dry.

He wondered why Quinlan had allowed Steve Bull to borrow him for this. He appreciated that Tyler's main exhibits officer, Tubby George Copeland, had his hands full but Quinlan's team were on HAT car duties this week and could be called out again at any moment.

Still, on the bright side, it meant he didn't have to worry about bumping into Tony Dillon today. It had come as quite a shock to see the muscle-bound idiot sitting there this morning, and Murray had been absolutely gutted when Tyler announced that he was joining AMIP on a permanent basis. He understood why Dillon disliked him so intently, of course, but the corruption allegation had been fully investigated by Complaints and nothing had been proven against him, so why couldn't the vindictive bastard just accept that and move on?

Murray walked over to the London Fire Brigade crew manager who was standing next to the Mondeo writing his report up on a clipboard. "Where's the lid who called this in?" he demanded sullenly.

The man paused long enough to look down his nose at Murray. "Do you mean the uniform response officer?" he asked curtly.

Murray just about managed to refrain from rolling his eyes; sighed instead. "Yes," he said with forced politeness. "That's who I mean."

The fireman nodded towards the A406 flyover to their left. "He went that way," he said.

"Thanks. Can I grab a copy of your report before you go?" Murray asked.

"Of course," the crew manager replied cordially.

"And just for the record, are you confident that an accelerant was used to start the fire?" Murray asked.

The firefighter became animated for the first time, proving that he did, in fact, have a personality. "Yep, petrol from the looks of it. There's what's left of a jerry can inside the car. I reckon they doused the Mondeo in a couple of litres of unleaded and then tossed in a lit rag to ignite it."

"I don't suppose there were any guns in the car when it was set on fire?" Murray asked hopefully.

The fireman shook his head. "No, nothing like that. Do you think this has been involved in a robbery then?"

"We think it was used in a murder overnight," Murray told him.

The fireman raised an eyebrow, impressed. "Interesting," he said. "I'll get one of my crew to give you everything we've got before we leave."

"Cheers," Murray said and set off to find the first responder.

He found the PC who had attended the scene back out on the road, leaning against his Panda car smoking a cigarette.

"Morning," Murray said, flashing his warrant card. "I'm DC Murray from AMIP."

"Alright mate," the officer responded, moving away from the car. "I'm PC Jones - Trevor."

He was a Welshman from the valleys, Murray realised.

"What's the score with the car then, Taff?" he asked. "Trumpton reckons petrol was the accelerant used to start the fire"

Jones nodded. "Sounds about right, and it's Trevor by the way, not Taff." He stubbed his fag out underfoot and reached for his notebook. "I've got the CAD number and time of the call if you want them," he offered.

Murray shook his head. "Nah, you're alright. I've already got all that information. I don't suppose you've had a chance to canvass the area for witnesses or check out potential CCTV, have you?"

Jones grinned, disarmingly. "No, I haven't, sorry."

Murray grunted. The twat had obviously been too busy smoking his fag to do any police work.

"That said," Jones continued, "I might be able to help you out with a CCTV lead." He pointed to a six-foot high corrugated fence that surrounded an area adjacent to the wasteland, a couple of hundred yards away to their left. From within, Murray could just about make out the roof of a dozen or so caravans. "See that pikey site over there?" Jones asked.

"What about it?" Murray enquired.

"Well, I happen to know for a fact that our crime squad have planted a concealed camera somewhere in this road covering the entrance to the site and this patch of wasteland."

"Have they now?" Murray said. "And why's that?"

"Well, burglaries have gone through the roof since that lot arrived on the ground a few weeks ago and set up site there. Our CID are convinced that stolen gear has been going in there on a daily basis. On top of that, we've had a few stolen cars abandoned or burnt out on this wasteland. Anyway, if my guess is correct, then anything driving onto this patch of wasteland would have had to go right by the covert camera to get here."

"Well done, Taff," Murray said. "I knew you couldn't be as useless as you looked."

———

At three-o'clock that afternoon Jenny Parker went home. Thankfully, she hadn't thrown up again after the first time, but she still felt absolutely awful and she hadn't been able to face eating anything all day.

When David had returned from a late lunch a few minutes earlier, to find his secretary slumped over her desk looking as white as a sheet, he had immediately expressed his concern. Jenny had initially tried to play it down, telling him not to worry; that it was obviously something she'd eaten and that she would be fine. He had fussed around her like a kindly uncle, insisting that she go straight home to bed and telling her not to bother coming in the following day unless she was feeling much better. He was such a nice man, she reflected; Eddie's first thought would have been to worry about who was going to make him his afternoon coffee if she wasn't there. Thanking him for his kindness, she had donned her jacket, gathered up her belongings, and set off for the station.

She still hadn't spoken to Eddie, which she now realised was a blessing in disguise. She needed to give herself some breathing space in order to get her head straight before telling him that she was pregnant; and if she decided that she really didn't want to keep the baby, she would get rid of it without saying a word to him. It wasn't something she that would normally advocate any woman doing but, taking all the circumstances into consideration, she felt that he had lost his right to have any say on whether she had a termination or continued with the pregnancy. Maybe she would feel differently in the morning, but for now that was how she saw things.

Although the train was quite full, it was nowhere near as crowded as it had been during that morning's rush hour. The temperature inside her carriage was stiflingly hot, so Jenny lost no time in removing her jacket, which she then folded and placed on the seat beside her. Opening the window, she sat down and made herself comfortable.

As soon as the train set off, Jenny found herself starting to relax. She was looking forward to a hot bath and an evening chilling in front of the TV. She closed her eyes and leaned back against the headrest. What a dreadful day it had been. Not only had she discovered that the rape – there was no other word for it – had left her pregnant, she had spent the morning being violently sick. What was that old adage of her mother's? *Bad things come in threes.* Yes, that was the one. She hoped that wouldn't be the case today. She doubted she could take anything else going wrong.

———

Marcel Meeks leaned against the wall on the Chingford bound platform at Hackney Downs station. Nine of his friends were sprawled across the benches to his left, joking amongst themselves while they waited for the next train. A few of them were passing a joint around, but Meeks declined the offer, wanting to keep a clear head for what was coming.

The boys were all similarly attired in hooded Echo or McKenzie tops, baggy jeans with low slung crutches, and designer training shoes - Nikes or Adidas mainly. Their baseball caps were pulled down low to shield their eyes. Anyone looking closely would have noticed that they all wore bandannas with homogenous gang colours around their necks. It was the dress code of the streets.

These were Holly Street Boys and they were out grafting. Their leader was a nineteen-year old elder called Ziggy. Tall and muscular, he had a hardness to him that belied his age; it was an unfortunate by-product of his lifestyle and the shocking things he had seen and done.

Like Meeks, most of the others were youngers of fifteen or sixteen, but despite their tender years they had all lost their innocence a long time ago. The youngest of the group, Zane, was only fourteen and this was his first time out running with them, but he was big for his age, and nasty with it, so they were happy to let him tag along.

Zane currently had a can of red spray paint in his hand, and he was busy covering the station's walls with HSB related graffiti.

"Yo!" Ziggy suddenly called out. "Look lively. Train's coming."

Grinning inanely, Zane tossed the almost empty can into a nearby bin and began to get himself ready.

They had started off working the North London Line, hitting trains travelling between Homerton and Stratford, but they had switched lines after a couple of trips, knowing that British Transport Boydem would soon spot a pattern and flood the area with Feds.

As Meeks stepped away from the wall, he instinctively checked the rear of his waistband to make sure the handle of the kitchen knife he'd purloined from the home was easily accessible. The others were off the benches now, looking hyped and ready for action. A few of the less experienced youngers had already started to pull their bandannas up over the lower half of their faces, but Meeks was an old hand at this, and he played it cool. He merely lowered his gaze to stare at the platform floor, knowing this would prevent the passengers getting a good look at his face.

Ziggy had been watching the carriages go by and he had identified the one that was likely to contain the best pickings. Signalling for the others to follow him, he boarded the train and stood there quietly. The others huddled around him, waiting for him to give the word.

As soon as it moved out of the station, he said, "Get ready."

The fastest journey time between Hackney Downs and Clapton was two minutes, although on average it took nearer three. Hoods were pulled up over caps; caps were tugged down to eye level; bandannas were adjusted so that they covered the lower part of their faces. Some of them pulled kitchen knives in readiness, and Switch produced his signature flick knife with its ivory handle and shiny six-inch blade.

On Ziggy's command, they stormed through the carriage, shouting and swearing at the startled and terrified passengers sitting either side of the central aisle to hand over their cash, phones and jewellery. They brutally shoved anyone standing in their way aside, punching anyone who didn't immediately comply. Zane was safely cocooned in the middle of the steamers, and he wore an open satchel over his shoulder into which the rest of the gang were dropping their pilfered goods.

About halfway along the carriage, a slender black man in his twenties stood up and bravely placed himself between his distraught girlfriend and the advancing steamers. Without breaking his stride, Ziggy hit him hard in the face. The man staggered back onto his seat, nose bleeding, eyes full of fear and hate. Switch clambered astride him and held his flick knife against the man's face. "Give me your fucking watch and your money," he yelled, "or I'll stripe you both up."

One of the youngers whooped at this, which seemed to excite Zane. "Shive him," he hollered, eyes glinting with fervour.

The panic-stricken man immediately obeyed, crying with shame for doing so. After relieving him of his possessions, Switch patted his face, said, "Good boy," and moved on. Following on behind, Zane laughed at the pathetic man whose girlfriend was now trying to comfort him.

As the gang worked its way through the carriage, handbags were snatched, phones were torn from the hands that held them, and wallets were demanded at knife point. Watches, rings, and necklaces were effortlessly removed from their wearers. The sheer ferocity of the attack disorientated the majority of the passengers, leaving them over-whelmed and powerless to resist.

Marcel was leading the charge and, as the gang ran amok behind him, his eyes were suddenly drawn to a glint at the neck of a pretty lady who was cowering in her seat a couple of rows ahead. Running up to her, he reached out and ripped a heavy gold chain from it, tossing it back to Zane to add to his growing collection.

Crying out, the expensively dressed woman instinctively raised her hands to try and stop him. As she did, Meeks spotted a diamond bracelet around her right wrist, and what looked like a Rolex on her left. The ring on the third finger of her left hand contained a sparkling diamond the size of a table tennis ball. Grinning beneath his bandanna, he realised he had stumbled across the mother lode. "Gimme your jewellery now," he demanded greedily, signalling with his left hand for her to hand it over.

"Please," Jenny Parker begged him. "The watch was a graduation present from my father. You can have the bracelet but let me keep that."

The only part of Meeks' face that was visible was his eyes, and these stared down at her without an ounce of pity. "Gimme them now or I'll cut your hands off," he threatened, jabbing the point of his knife towards her face.

Jenny recoiled in horror. She started fumbling with the bracelet's clasp, but her hands were shaking so much that she couldn't undo it.

"Hurry!" Meeks shouted, making her flinch again.

When she didn't respond immediately, Meeks angrily backhanded her across the face before grabbing her arm and tearing the bracelet from her wrist.

"The watch," he ordered. "Give me the watch."

Sobbing uncontrollably, Jenny undid the strap as quickly as she could and passed it over with a trembling hand.

"Now, gimme the fucking ring," he demanded menacingly.

Jenny's eyes bored into her assailant's, imploring him to show her some mercy. "Not the ring," she pleaded. She didn't care that it was worth several thousand pounds; to her that was irrelevant. All that mattered was that it was the engagement ring that Eddie had bought her after they'd decided to try for a baby, and it symbolised everything good about their imperfect, sometimes turbulent, relationship. To her astonishment the thought of losing it made her realise that, even after the terrible way he had forced himself upon her that dreadful night, she still harboured deep feelings for him.

Sub-consciously, she curled her fingers into a fist to make it harder for her attacker to remove the engagement ring.

With a snarl, Meeks raised his left hand again, intent on slapping her face a second time. However, before he could deliver the blow, the woman sprang out of her seat and started pushing him away. As he was forced to take a backward step, anger flared inside Meeks and, he lashed out, driving his fist into her midriff. That did the trick. With a startled gasp, the woman immediately stopped struggling.

Switch was by his side in the blink of an eye. It was as though he could smell violence and was drawn to it as a vampire is to blood. Zane was right behind him, cackling excitedly. Even though the woman was clearly incapable of offering further resistance, Switch smashed his right hand into the woman's stomach, hitting her so hard that she doubled over and fell to her knees.

Zane whooped delightedly.

"I got this, bruv," Meeks protested, but Switch ignored him. He grabbed her hair and forced her to look up at him. "Do as my bredrin says and give us the ring or I'll cut your eyes out," he warned, waving a blood smeared knife in front of them.

The ashen faced woman stared up at them in abject terror as Meeks quickly moved forward, grabbed her left hand, and tore the ring from her finger.

The rest of the gang had advanced well beyond them by now, and Meeks and Zane moved quickly to re-join their ranks, the latter sliding on something wet underfoot and nearly falling over.

Switch lingered behind, staring down at the woman who had dared to disobey them with unconcealed loathing. "Do what my bredrin says quicker next time, innit." He drew his foot back, clearly intent on kicking her in the head. An elderly man sitting opposite, who had watched in horror as the two robbers set about the poor defenceless woman, suddenly stood up. He grabbed the back of Switch's hoodie and tugged as hard as he could. "Leave her alone," he screamed, his frail voice quivering in fear. "Can't you see she's badly injured?"

With a ferocious snarl, Switch spun on him and drove the knife he was holding deep into the old man's stomach, just below the sternum.

Eyes bulging, the shocked passenger gasped and staggered backwards, clutching his abdomen. Blood immediately leaked out from between his fingers. As he collapsed onto the floor, landing next to Jenny Parker, Switch gave a grunt of satisfaction and then ran to join the rest of the gang who were now nearing the end of the carriage.

Moments later, the train pulled into Clapton station and glided to a halt. The group of steamers spilled out of the automatic doors the moment they opened. Whooping and cheering, they sprinted along the platform towards the stairs that led up to street level.

As soon as the Holly Street Boys cleared the station, they starburst into smaller groups, removing hats and bandannas and swapping hoodies as they ran. It was a tried and tested tactic to confuse Dem Boydem, who might already have units speeding towards the area to search for them.

Telling Meeks and Zane to follow him, Ziggy crossed the A107 and set off along Ickburgh Road towards Brooke Road. Hackney was their manor and they could find their way around it blindfolded; they would stick to the back alleys and little cut-throughs, avoiding the main drag as much as possible as they circumnavigated their way back to the estate. They would regroup with the others later to go through their spoils and divide the loot between them. The Rolex was safely nestled in Meeks' pocket. It was worth thousands, he knew, and he had decided to keep that for himself, although he knew the penalty would be severe if Ziggy or Switch found out.

————

Although the robbers had now fled, many of their victims still seemed paralysed with fear. Some people in the carriage were standing there crying; others were too stunned to move away from their seats. A quick witted passenger had pulled the emergency cord to prevent the train from moving off. Several others had stumbled out onto the platform, trying to signal for help. A small crowd had formed around the elderly stab victim, and a couple of them were trying to perform first aid on the unconscious man. There was an awful lot of blood on the floor where he and Jenny had fallen.

As Jenny was assisted to her feet, her insides felt as though they had been torn open and filled with burning coals. She suddenly came over faint, and was enormously grateful when the kind man who had helped her up guided her into a vacant seat.

"Call the police," she heard someone shout.

"We need an ambulance too," a woman yelled, her voice riddled with panic.

"Are you okay?" the man who had helped her asked.

Her vision was starting to blur, and she had to blink several times to get him back into focus. "What did you say?" she asked groggily. She was a little breathless, and her skin felt clammy. Was this the onset of another bout of morning sickness, she wondered?

"I asked if you were okay," the man repeated, staring at her intently.

"I don't know," she told him, wondering why her words sounded so slurry.

The man didn't reply. He was too busy staring down at her midriff. "Where is all that blood coming from?" he asked her.

Blood? What blood? It was an effort, but she managed to make her eyes look down to her hands, which were still clutching her midsection. To her surprise, they were covered in blood.

That poor old man must have bled over me, she thought. As she held them up for a closer look, the man in front of her gasped. "Oh my God," he said, staring into Jenny's eyes. "You've been stabbed as well."

CHAPTER TEN

AWKWARD CONVERSATIONS

Paul Evans sat opposite Tulay Yildiz in a dank, windowless interview room located just off the front office at Stoke Newington police station. In common with virtually every other Met interview room he'd ever been in, it was a dirty, unwelcoming environment, populated by an ancient wooden desk and sticky plastic seats that he suspected were deliberately designed to be uncomfortable.

It was a little after three in the afternoon, and they had been sitting there for just over an hour, going through her statement in more detail. Evans had listened to the audio from her key witness interview before meeting up with her, and it had struck him how afraid she sounded on tape. It was clear that the thugs who ran the protection racket her father was paying money to were powerful and far reaching, and she didn't want anything she said to the police to come back and bite her family.

She had given an impressively accurate physical description of the three Turkish men who came into the café, but had been unbelievably vague about what they had been doing there. She had described the sequence of events, as the shooters closed in on her customers and ruthlessly gunned them down, in meticulous detail; she had been less specific about their descriptions. It was obvious to him that she knew more than she was saying, but what? He couldn't put his finger on it, but experience told him she was holding something crucial back.

"Tulay, how long has that café been in your family?" he asked, deciding to try a less direct approach.

She shrugged. "I don't remember it ever not being run by my family."

"And how long have you worked there?" Evans enquired, smiling to put her at ease.

"Since I left school," she informed him.

Tulay was in her early twenties, he knew. "So, a good few years then?"

She nodded.

He leaned forward conspiratorially. "So, in your professional opinion as a barista of some experience, what do you think of the coffee from our canteen?" he asked, jutting his chin towards the polystyrene cup by her hand, which contained the dregs of the cappuccino he had fetched from the canteen a few minutes ago.

Tulay grimaced apologetically. "It's not very nice," she said.

"It's blooming horrible," Evans told her. The face he pulled as he said this earned him a smile. "We could pop out to one of the local cafés for a decent brew if you would prefer. It would be my treat."

Tulay shook her head. "That's very kind of you, but I'd rather stay here."

Evans understood at once. The station was surrounded by some lovely little cafés and bistros, but they were predominantly Turkish. Under the circumstances, she didn't want to be seen with him in one of those, even if it meant putting up with rubbish coffee.

"So, does your family do okay from running the café?" he asked. "Financially speaking, I mean."

"We do okay, but there are lots of overheads: electricity, rates, bills…"

"Protection money?"

"I–"

"Look, Tulay, I understand your reluctance to speak to me, but we both know what goes on out there, so it's silly to pretend otherwise. If it helps, this conversation is just between you and me. It's not being recorded. I'm not writing anything down. I just need to know what you know, even if it means you telling me off the record."

She frowned at that. "My father said nothing is ever off the record with the police."

Evans couldn't help but smile. "That's what my boss always says about the press," he told her.

"Is it true?" she asked.

"About the press? Dunno. That's above my pay grade."

"I meant about the police."

"Oh, I see," Evans said, and scratched his head in thought. "Well, it stands to reason that some things can never be off the record. I mean if someone confessed to committing a murder, that could never be off the record. If someone witnessed a crime and told me what happened, that could never be off the record. In both scenarios they'd be providing direct evidence that's admissible in court. I couldn't keep that to myself. However, in a situation like this, if you wanted to provide confidential information that might help us find the killers, I would be able to respect that."

Tulay bit her lip and thought hard about this.

"How do I know I can trust you?" she eventually asked.

Paul Evans pointed at his countenance. "Does this look like a face that would lie to you?" he asked with great solemnity, and then broke into a beaming grin.

Tulay couldn't help but respond in kind. When the smile faded, she took a deep breath and her shoulders visibly relaxed. He could tell that she had reached a decision and, like the good interviewer he was, he waited in silence until she was ready to proceed. "My father, like most other businessmen in our community, pays money to people to look after our interests," she eventually said. "They call it insurance, but you would call it protection money. The men who were murdered called at the same time every week to collect this money. This week, as they left the café, three masked men were waiting to gun them down."

Evans noted that she was anxiously wringing her hands together as she recounted the story to him.

"Take your time," he said gently.

"It was the most terrifying thing I have ever seen," she continued. "I could see enough of their skin to say they were definitely white, but I can't tell whether they were English or Albanian because the ski-masks hid their features."

"Did they speak at all?" Evans asked.

Tulay closed her eyes and replayed the scene in her head. "No," she said after a moment. "They didn't say a word."

"Is there anything that you can tell me about them that might help us to identify them?" Evans asked her softly. "Anything at all?"

Tulay's face clouded over and she averted her gaze.

Here we go, Evans told himself. *This is what she's been keeping back.* "Tulay, what is it you're not telling me?"

"My father told me not to say anything," she said, hanging her head low. "He said that we should let these people get on with their blood vendetta against Abdullah Goren. My father thinks that if they weaken the Goren clan it will be better for the rest of the Turkish community. Maybe, we would be able to stop living in fear." A tear ran down her face. "I have betrayed my father's wishes by speaking to you like this."

Evans placed a tentative hand on her shoulder. "I'm sorry to put you through this," he said withdrawing his hand, "but if we don't stop these people, there are likely to be other deaths. What precisely doesn't your father want you to tell us?"

Tulay sighed, wiped her eyes and then blew her nose on the tissue that he had just handed her. "One of the masked men was wearing a scarf around his neck," she said. "For some reason, after he shot Erkan Dengiz, he pulled it off. When he turned around and ran back to the car, I got a good look at a tattoo running down the right side of his neck." She demonstrated the location with her finger. "My father said I should keep this to myself in case it helped you find him."

"Tulay, these people are bad men, not modern-day Robin Hoods. Can you describe this tattoo for me?"

"I can do better than that," she said, smiling weakly. "I can draw it for you."

————

Dritan was bored out of his head. The flea pit in Amhurst Park that they had booked into late last night was even worse than the previous dump they had stayed at. Still, the unshaven fat man behind the desk had asked no questions when the three Eastern European men registered under blatantly false names, so he couldn't complain too much.

Dritan had spent the last five-minutes repeatedly flicking through the limited range of terrestrial channels on the ancient TV, desperately hoping to find something of interest and failing miserably. In the end, he gave up, switched it off and put his feet up on his bed, intending to doze for a while. That didn't work either; he couldn't get comfortable and, if truth be told, after all these hours of being confined to his room, he was starting to feel trapped.

The irrational bouts of intense claustrophobia he sometimes suffered from were a by-product of his former life, as were the terrible nightmares in which the demons of his past revisited him while he slept. Sometimes, the dreams were so vivid that they triggered a series of debilitating panic attacks that lasted for several days afterwards.

He tried pacing the room for a while, focusing on nothing but his breathing, but all that did was to make him feel even more anxious.

Dritan had struggled to acclimatise to civilian life following his army discharge, and before long he had fallen foul of the legal system. Before coming to the UK, he had spent the best part of four years locked in a small cell at Gherla maximum security prison in his homeland of Romania. An outdoors type by nature, the gruelling period of incarceration had almost broken him, and he now hated any form of confinement. Having spent his day trapped in a small room, he badly needed to go out for a walk, to escape the walls that were closing in on him and get some fresh air, but they were under explicit instructions not to leave the hotel until the boss had checked in with them.

Something had obviously happened to delay him, because Dritan had expected a call hours ago. The other two wanted to go out and get drunk, but he had forbidden this. It was now four-thirty. He decided that if he didn't hear anything by six o'clock, he would allow them to venture out for some food. They wouldn't all be able to go at the same time, of course, because neither of their rooms was equipped with a safe to lock the guns away in, and they couldn't leave them unattended; they didn't dare risk taking the weapons out with them either.

For want of something constructive to do, he pulled his holdall out from under the bed, where he had hidden it upon arrival, and field stripped his weapons. That killed some time, and it took his mind off the fact that he had been caged in the tiny room for far too long.

As he was placing the holdall back under the bed, his burner phone rang. As before, it was a withheld number. Placing the mobile to his ear, he pressed the green button and waited for someone to speak.

"*Yo!*" the voice said, and he immediately recognised it as belonging to the man he had liaised with the previous evening. "*I've been told to tell you that you boys can chill out tonight. Things are running a little behind schedule so eat, drink and be merry, my man. That's what I'm gonna do. Expect a call with further instructions tomorrow morning.*"

"Are there any problems?" Dritan asked, not liking the man's flippant tone.

The caller giggled, and Dritan suspected that he was either drunk or high.

"*Everything is bliss,*" the caller said, as though he didn't have a care in the world. The man was stoned, Dritan realised, unimpressed by the lack of professionalism.

Dritan hung up and went to get the others. "Go and eat," he told them. "No alcohol, just food." Valmir didn't look happy about that, he noted, but he knew the surly former soldier wouldn't disobey him. "When you come back, I will go."

"We could bring you something back," Lorik offered.

Dritan shook his head. "No, I need to escape this prison and get some fresh air. Give your holdalls to me when you leave."

He returned to his room and switched the TV back on. Flopping down on his bed he started channel surfing again.

———

Detective Sergeant Susan Sergeant was tall and slim with strawberry blonde hair. It was *not* ginger, as some people had made the mistake of calling it, only to be firmly rebuked. Susie, as she preferred to be called, had joined AMIP at the same time as Steve Bull, having transferred in from Leyton in East London. She had been posted to Andy Quinlan's team, and today she was performing the role of late turn HAT car DS. In that capacity, she had been called out to a double stabbing at Clapton train station.

There were two victims, an elderly male who was not expected to survive, and a thirty year old female who was in a life-threatening condition. HEMS - the Helicopter Emergency Medical Service - had been called to the scene, and they had worked on both casualties for some time before declaring they were stable enough to be transported to hospital. The male patient had been air-lifted to The Royal London in Whitechapel by helicopter, while the female had gone by ambulance.

Kevin Murray, who had just arrived from Tottenham, where he'd spent the last couple of hours assisting Jack Tyler's team, approached her. He was clad in a white Tyvek oversuit and he was looking his usual miserable self.

"Scene's contaminated beyond belief," he complained. "The idiots have traipsed back and forth through the victim's blood, and whoever performed first aid on them inconsiderately left bloody fingerprints everywhere. It's going to be a nightmare differentiating between the dabs left by careless witnesses and the ones left by the suspects."

The look Susie gave him ranged somewhere between disappointment and pity. "Kevin," she said in her soft Irish lilt, "I understand your frustration, but moaning about it won't achieve anything. Let's just focus on getting the scene processed as best we can, and then we can leave the scientists to worry about all the rest."

Murray snorted at that, his expression openly implying that she had no idea what she was talking about if she thought it were that easy.

She chose to ignore the look, knowing that she would probably end up punching him otherwise. "Who's the CSM?"

"Sam Calvin," Murray said. "Good at his job but a bloody boring bloke to be with stuck at a scene with."

And you're not? Susie thought. "I'll leave you to crack on," she said, eager to get away from miserable Murray, a man whose non-stop complaining seemed to suck the fun out of any conversation. "I've got to make some enquiries regarding witnesses and CCTV."

Leaving Murray to wallow under his personalised cloud of doom and despair, Susie quickly sought out the local uniformed supervisors who'd initially requested the attendance of the HAT car. Both wore sergeant's chevrons on their shoulder epaulettes. "So, what have we got?" she asked after introducing herself.

The two men looked at each other, and the taller of the two indicated that his partner should do the talking.

The nominated man stepped forward and offered his hand. "I'm PS Tim Brown, late turn Section Sergeant at Stoke Newington. This is my opposite number form Shoreditch, Kevin Spinner. It looks like this is a steaming gone wrong. From what witnesses are telling us, a gang of about ten or twelve black lads got on the train at Hackney Downs and, as soon as it moved off, they set about robbing the passengers. The female victim–" he checked his notes for her name "-is Jenny Parker, a thirty year old from Chingford. We got this info from her driving licence, which was in her purse. She was on her way home, and it looks like she made the mistake of resisting when they tried to jack her engagement ring. She's been stabbed twice, once just below the ribs on her right side, and a second time in the abdomen. The HEMS doctor describes her injuries as life-threatening. The male victim is a brave old sod called Stanley Cotton. He's in his late sixties. Although he suffers from MS, when the steamers started laying into the Parker woman, he didn't hesitate to try and stop them."

Susie winced. "Poor thing, and so brave too. Is it right that he's not expected to survive?" she asked, making rapid notes in her daybook.

"The HEMS doctor thinks it's unlikely, given his age and the severity of his injuries," Brown said. "He was only stabbed the once, but it looks like the blade nicked his heart."

The shorter man, Spinner, spoke for the first time. "We've got the names and addresses of a dozen people so far. Not all of them saw the attack, but they were all victims of the steaming and they all got a good look at the suspects."

"I'll need the clothing seized of any of the first aiders who got the victim's blood over them," Susie said.

Brown nodded. "I've spoken to DI Bell from the Borough's robbery squad, and he's sending a DS and half-a-dozen DCs down to assist. They'll take the key witnesses back to GN, seize any blood stained-clothing and start interviewing them."

GN was the phonetic code used for Stoke Newington police station.

"That's great," Susie said. "Can you make sure First Description Booklets are completed for each and every suspect the witnesses can describe."

The booklets had been introduced to ensure detailed descriptions were recorded during the reporting stage of the investigation, rather than leaving it until officers got around to taking a statement, which might not happen for several days. If an identity parade was subsequently held, the suspect's first description would have to be served on the defence solicitor in advance, and they had learned the hard way that the sooner it was put onto paper the more credence it was likely to be given.

"It's their bread and butter," Spinner assured her, "but we'll reiterate it just in case."

Susie Sergeant thanked him. "What about a continuity officer?" she asked next. "Has anyone accompanied the victims to hospital?"

"We couldn't send anyone in the helicopter with Mr Cotton," Spinner said, "but a PC called Mary Mitchell went in the ambulance with the Parker woman. She's relatively new, but I've fully briefed her about what she needs to do, and I've instructed her to record any dying declarations either patient makes."

"Good. Can you give me a contact number so I can have a word with her?"

"Of course," Spinner said. "Give me a couple of minutes to dig it out and I'll get back to you."

"Great. Thanks. What about CCTV?" Susie asked. "Was there any inside the train?"

Brown shook his head. "No, but there's good coverage at both stations, and the street outside here is well covered by local authority cameras. Not sure about Hackney Downs."

"We'll need to get hold of all the available footage ASAP," Susie said. "Tell me, do you have anyone on this borough who's really good with faces? Someone who might be able to identify gang members just by looking at the CCTV?"

Susie knew from experience that once the robbers got wind that this was likely to turn into a murder investigation, they would immediately dispose of all the clothing they had been wearing and ditch anything distinctive in the loot they had stolen, which meant that speed was now of the essence, and they needed to start arresting suspects as soon as possible.

Brown nodded. "There's a skipper on the Hackney Safer Neighbourhood Team who's got a photographic memory. It's uncanny, he's only got to see a face once and he remembers it forever. He pretty much knows all the main gang members on the ground. I could check to see if he's on duty if you like?"

"Please do that," Susie said. "In the meantime, I'm going to see if I can fast track getting the CCTV seized. Let's talk again in a few minutes."

Leaving them to collate the information that she'd requested, Susie walked a few feet away and dialled the number for Andy Quinlan's job mobile. "Hello boss," she said when he picked up. "I've got a quick update for you regarding the call-out to Clapton train station." She brought him up to date, and then requested more resources. "The main priority at the moment is getting hold of the CCTV from Hackney Downs. Is there anyone you can spare to get to grips with that?"

"*Couldn't we get the locals to handle that?*" Quinlan asked. "*Most of our team are still helping DCI Tyler. Do you really think it's that urgent?*"

"I do, boss," she said. "I think if we can move quickly there's a good chance that we can identify the robbers from the Hackney Downs station footage and start nicking them later today, before they have a chance to destroy any evidence."

Quinlan sighed down the phone. "*Very well,*" he said. "*I'll speak to the borough DCI and get him to send someone over there to seize it, pronto. Do I also need to tell him to start drafting in officers so that we can get some arrest teams sorted?*"

"I think that might be wise, boss," she said. "The boys responsible for causing this carnage are bound to be from a local gang, which means they'll already be in the system. With any luck, I've identified an officer who'll be able to pick them out as long as the quality of the footage is halfway decent."

"*In that case, I'll make a phone call. Let me know if there are any more developments in the meantime.*"

When she hung up, she found Tim Brown standing behind her, waiting to talk. He was holding his mobile phone in his hand.

"Two things," he said. "Firstly, the skipper I told you about, Gavin Mercer, was due to start work at 6 p.m., but I've spoken to him at home and he's going to come straight in."

"That's brilliant," Susie said. "Thank you."

"More importantly," Brown said, holding up the phone. "I've got Mary Mitchell waiting to speak to you. In light of what she's just told me, I think you need to talk to her urgently."

Oh dear, Susie thought, accepting the phone he handed her, it sounds like one of our victims has died.

"Hello Mary, I'm DS Susie Sergeant from AMIP. Tim tells me we need to speak." She listened for a few seconds, and then her face registered shock. "Sweet Jesus," she said. "Are you sure?"

―――――

Samuel Adebanjo stood before the custody officer's desk waiting for his property to be restored to him. The sergeant on duty was the same man who had booked him in the day before. After reading out the bail conditions, he got Adebanjo to sign the bail form and gave him a copy. "Would you show this man to the door?" he asked Christine Taylor.

"Of course," she replied through gritted teeth. Since meeting him, she had developed quite a dislike for the arrogant giant. Every time that she had spoken to him, Adebanjo had responded by smirking. It was as though he was privy to a secret that she would never know, and she had yearned to slap the silly grin off his ugly face. He hadn't spoken a single word during the two interviews she had conducted with him, not even to confirm his name and date of birth. Now, as she escorted him out of the station, the mocking smile was back, and it was bigger than ever.

"Have a nice evening," he smirked as he exited the station.

"Fuck you, asshole," she muttered under her breath.

After a quick detour to the ladies' room to powder her nose, Taylor returned to the custody suite to arrange Tyson Meeks' release. At least he hadn't given her any attitude, although he had got on her nerves a little with his incessant complaining about the rubbish food he'd been given. What galled her was that the food he was so up in arms about was the same canteen crap that she and her colleagues had to pay good money for. In the end, though, she had taken pity on him and popped out to a nearby Mackey Dee's to get him a Big Mac and fries. Upon her return, he had dared to tell her that she'd brought him the wrong flavour milkshake, at which point she had nearly thrown it at him.

"Miss, I can't just go home," he whined as she escorted him out of the custody office after he'd signed for his bail. "I know you don't believe me, but I'm as good as dead unless I can find somewhere to lay low."

"I do believe you," she said, showing him into an interview room off the front office. "When my boss came over and spoke to you this morning about making a statement, so that we could put you in witness protection, you flatly refused. We made it very clear that you were in danger, and the only way we could protect you was to get the Criminal Justice Protection Unit involved and place you in witness protection, but in order to do that you need to actually put pen to paper and become a witness."

"You don't understand," he bleated. "If I do that, everyone will know I'm an informant."

"Why would you care? You'll be alive, and you will be living a brand-new life, making new friends in a part of the country where nobody knows you anyway."

. . .

Meeks remained silent. How could he possibly expect her to understand that the only thing stopping him from doing what she asked was
his brother? Marcel thought little enough of him as it was; what would
he say if his big brother appeared as a witness for the prosecution? The
shame would kill him. Besides, Livingstone might decide that if he
couldn't get to Tyson, he would take his anger out on Marcel instead.

"It's complicated," he told her.

"Only because you're making it so," Chrissy snapped, tiredness turning
her frustration into anger. She immediately felt bad for reacting like
that. Smiling at Meeks, she said, "Look, I need you to wait here. My
boss is on his way over to speak to you." Dillon was going to give
Meeks an Osman warning. Maybe that would do the trick and make
him see sense. If not, at least the organisation would be covered if he
ended up dead. "After that, I'll give you a lift home if you want."

———

Jack Tyler was sitting at his desk, immersed in paperwork. His office
window was open but, despite the breeze coming in, the room felt as
hot as a greenhouse. He had undone the top button of his shirt, pulled
his tie loose, and rolled his sleeves up over his elbows, but he was still
baking. A fresh cup of coffee sat on the desk in front of him, and he
was halfway through a cheese and tomato sandwich that one of the
civilian indexers had kindly brought him back from Tesco when she'd
popped out earlier.

Andy Quinlan knocked on his office door and came in. He closed
the door behind him quietly, and sat down without waiting for an
invite.

"Jack," he said softly.

"Be with you in a sec, Andy," Tyler said without looking up. He
was updating his latest decision log entry and wanted to get his
thoughts down on paper before he was distracted.

"Jack," Quinlan said again, and this time there was something in his voice that made Tyler look up. He frowned when he saw the worried look on his colleague's face.

"Is everything okay?" Tyler asked, putting both his pen and his sandwich down.

"Jack, it's your ex-wife, Jenny. She's been stabbed."

Tyler felt the colour drain from his face. "What?"

"Her train was steamed by a gang in Hackney earlier this afternoon. She resisted when they tried to take her engagement ring, and the bastards stabbed her twice in the abdomen. She's been taken to the Royal London, but the injuries are serious."

"How serious?" Tyler demanded, feeling his stomach tighten with fear. He became aware that his hands had started to shake, and he slipped them under the desk so that Quinlan wouldn't see.

"Life-threatening."

"Oh my God," Tyler said, closing his eyes to shut out the pain. Although he no longer harboured any romantic feelings for Jenny, he still cared about her as a person and, in spite of the fact that she had left him for another man, he still wished her happiness.

Jack stood up, unable to think straight. "I'd better get over there," he said, looking around for his jacket. "Have her parents been informed?"

Quinlan shook his head. "One of my skippers, Susie Sergeant, just phoned me with the news. She had literally just discovered the connection herself."

"Is Susie at the hospital? I'll need some more details before I speak to Jenny's parents."

"Susie's at the scene. There's a divisional officer at the hospital. She spoke to Jenny before they rushed her into surgery, that's when she said she wanted you informed. I've got the officer's number here if you want to speak to her," he said, handing over a yellow post-it-note. "Her name's Mary Mitchell."

"Thank you," Jack said, taking it from him.

"Jack, I'll keep an eye on things here," Quinlan offered. "Why don't you get over to the hospital?"

"I will," Jack said, trying to get his brain to work.

"And it might be a good idea to get someone to drive you," Quinlan added, recognising that Tyler was in shock.

After Quinlan left, Jack wasted no time in dialling the number he'd been given for PC Mitchell. "Hello, Mary?" he said when she answered. "It's Jack Tyler here. Are you free to speak?"

"*Hello sir,*" she said. "*Yes, fire away.*"

"Is there any update on the seriousness of Jenny's injuries?"

"*Not really,*" Mitchell said. "*She has two wounds. One is in her lower abdomen, which has possibly perforated her bowel, the other is an upward blow that went in under the ribs on the right side of her body. The doctors think it might have punctured her liver. That's the injury that's causing most of the concern. Sorry sir, I did try to get more info from the medical team, but they were all too busy working on her and every time I asked, I was shooed away.*" Tyler got the feeling that Mary Mitchell was quite young and inexperienced from the tone of her voice.

"I understand," Jack said. "Tell me, do you know why she asked for me to be informed and not her current partner?"

"*I don't sir. It was pretty manic there, and she was drifting in and out of consciousness. I asked her if there was anyone that I could contact for her, and she specified you. And she was really adamant that she only wanted you told; no one else.*"

Tyler didn't know how to respond to that. It made no sense whatsoever for Jenny to have insisted that he be informed and not Eddie or her parents. They hadn't spoken properly since the divorce, so why would she suddenly turn to him in such a dire emergency? "Have they said how long she's likely to be in surgery?" Jack asked, trying to get his thoughts in order.

"No sir," Mitchell said.

"Okay, thank you. Is there anything else I should know before I contact her parents?"

The lack of an immediate response told him that there was. "Mary…?"

"*Well,*" she said hesitantly. "*I'm not sure if I should mention this or not sir. No disrespect, but I'm talking to you as a former partner of my victim, not in your capacity as a senior officer.*"

Jack could hear the dilemma in her voice. "Mary, listen, if it's not relevant to the offence, and you don't feel comfortable telling me, that's fine. I understand. However, I assure you my ex-wife and I are on very amicable terms, and when I hang up on you, I'm going to have to tell her parents, one of whom is a senior Old Bailey judge, that their daughter is in a critical condition in hospital. They will ask questions, one of which will be why she wanted me called instead of her partner, Edward Maitland. I want to be as prepared as I possibly can be when I speak to them. Will the information you're obviously withholding help me in that respect?"

"*I don't know sir, but it might be relevant to why she wanted you told and not her partner.*" There was a moment's silence, and then Mary sighed. "*Look, when she arrived, I went through her bag searching for family contact details,*" she told him. "*I found a used pregnancy tester inside, and it was positive.*"

"Jenny's pregnant? Is that what you're saying?"

"*I assume so,*" Mary said. "*I can't think of any reason for her to have someone else's pregnancy test inside her bag. But if she is pregnant, she can only just have found out.*"

Jack thought about this. Jenny had just discovered that she was pregnant, that much seemed obvious. But why didn't she want Eddie informed? Did this mean they were having relationship problems? Could it be that the baby wasn't Eddie's? Was she now cheating on him the way she had on Jack?

He ran a hand through his hair in agitation. *Jesus, what a mess!*

"Okay, thank you for telling me that, Mary. It will help me manage how I break this to her family. If I give you my number, will you contact me as soon as you have an update, please?"

"*Of course I will,*" she promised.

Jack gave her his office and mobile telephone numbers, thanked her again, and hung up.

What was he going to say to her parents?

And what about Eddie - as much as he disliked the man, he had a right to know that his partner was undergoing surgery following a life-threatening assault. He took a deep breath to clear his head and then reached for the phone.

This was not going to be pleasant.

CHAPTER ELEVEN

REVELATIONS

Dillon was just about to address Tyson Meeks on the subject of his making a statement when his phone rang. It was Steve Bull. Excusing himself from the interview room, he stepped outside to answer.

"What is it Steve? I'm about to sit down with a witness."

"*Sorry to bother you, boss,*" Bull said, "*but I thought you'd want to know, the fingerprint results have finally come in for the three unidentified victims.*"

"Okay, that's good news." It was five-hours later than promised, but better late than never. "Anything I need to know about them, or are they just low-level gangland muscle like we expected?"

"*That's about the size of it,*" Bull confirmed. "*All three have connections to the same Turkish-Kurdish crime family that Dengiz worked for, and they all have form for assault and the like.*"

"Anything else?"

"*Juliet Kennedy has arranged for the SPMs to start tomorrow morning. They're being carried out over a two-day period at Queens Road*

*mortuary in Walthamstow. Ben Claxton is the designated forensic patholo-
gist. I don't know if you've ever met Creepy Claxton? He's a dead ringer for
the actor, Peter Cushing."*

"Can't say I've ever had the pleasure," Dillon said.

"Well, that's about to change," Bull informed him. *"Mr Tyler asked
me to say he needs a DI to accompany Juliet Kennedy and George
Copeland, and it looks like you get to do the honours."*

Dillon groaned inwardly. He knew that one of the responsibilities
of a DI on AMIP was attending special post mortems, but he hadn't
expected to be thrown into one - let alone four - quite so quickly.
Death and Dillon didn't mix terribly well. Not that he would have
admitted it, but he tended to get a little queasy whenever he visited a
mortuary. It wasn't so much the sights that affected him as the smells.
Every odour associated with death was deeply unpleasant, and he
hated the fact that he always came away from the mortuary reeking of
it. Sometimes, it took him several showers to rid himself of the cloying
scent of decay mixed with Trigene, and his clothing always required a
trip to the dry cleaners afterwards. "That's fine," he replied, knowing
there was nothing else he could have said. "What time's the first one
kicking off?"

*"Juliet Kennedy said for you and George to meet her there at nine-
thirty tomorrow morning, and she asks that you bring the completed
briefing documents for the pathologist."*

Dillon frowned. "And what exactly are those?" he asked. "Bearing
in mind that I'm new to all this."

"We have to complete a briefing note for the pathologist," Bull
explained, *"outlining the circumstances of the death and anything that
might be relevant to the examination. The forms are on the system. If it
helps, I could get them mostly completed tonight, and e-mail them to you
to fill in the blanks in the morning."*

"That would be a massive help," Dillon admitted. "Just out of
interest, where's Jack? Wouldn't he be best placed to fill out these
forms, bearing in mind that he actually attended the scene with the
CSM and saw the bodies in situ?"

"Haven't you heard?" Bull said, sounding surprised. *"He had to rush
out to the Royal London as his ex-wife's been stabbed."*

"Bloody hell!" Dillon gasped. "When did that happen?"

"*This afternoon. She was on a train that got steamed in Hackney.*"

"Shit! How bad is it? Is she going to be okay?"

"*It doesn't sound too good, to be honest,*" Bull said. "*It's not common knowledge either, so don't say anything to anyone yet.*"

"No, of course not," Dillon promised. "I'll give him a call now," he said, "but if you hear anything more, can you let me know?"

"*Of course I will, boss.*"

As soon as Bull had gone, Dillon tried ringing Tyler's number, but it went straight to answer phone. He sent a text telling his friend to call him when he could, and letting him know that he was there for him.

Dillon returned to the interview room in shock. He had been Jack's Best Man at their wedding. Although he had never hidden the fact that he disliked Jenny Parker intensely, he had always made an effort to be friendly to her for Jack's sake. It hadn't been reciprocated and, as far as he was concerned, Jack was far better off without her.

The strange thing was that Jack seemed to have found it much easier to forgive Jenny for leaving him for another man than Dillon had. In his eyes, she was, and always would be, a selfish, conniving bitch.

Forcing his mind back onto the business at hand, he sat down opposite Tyson Meeks. Christine must have realised something was wrong because she stared at him with concern and he could see questions forming in her eyes.

"Tyson," he began, "DC Taylor has explained your continued reluctance to make a statement to me. I'd hoped that, having had some time to consider what I said to you when we spoke this morning, you would have changed your mind."

Meeks shook his head glumly. "I can't do it," he said.

"You told me that this morning. At least give me a reason why. Surely, I deserve that?"

Meeks sighed heavily. "I just can't."

"Listen, Tyson," Dillon said, trying not to let impatience creep into his voice. "I shouldn't be telling you this, but I've really gone out on a limb for you. My boss thinks you're a liar, and that all you're interested in is fleecing us out of money. I defended you when he said that. I stuck my neck out and insisted you were telling the truth, and that we could rely on you. Now you're turning your back on us when we need you the most. Think how that's going to make me look."

Meeks head dropped, but not before Dillon saw the glimmer of guilt that passed across his troubled features.

"I'm not lying," Meeks eventually said, still staring at the floor. "I do want to help you, but I … I just can't."

Dillon sensed that the snout's resolve was waning. "At least tell me why," he said softly. Meeks didn't respond at first. He was too busy weighing up how much to reveal. In the end, the words just came out. "It's my kid brother, Marcel."

"What about him?" Dillon asked.

"He's a Holly Street younger, innit," Meeks said, as though that explained everything.

Dillon shrugged. "So?"

"You don't understand, bruv," Meeks said miserably. "Conrad Livingstone is the Main Man in our ends. He started off as a younger in the HSB but, since then, he's made it all the way to the top. Marcel looks up to him, thinks he's some sort of celebrity. Meanwhile, I'm still down in the gutter, and when my brother looks at me all he sees is a piece of dog shit." His voice broke, and for a moment Dillon thought he might cry. The informant sucked in a deep breath as he struggled to maintain his composure. When he continued, his voice was trembling. "Where I come from, being a grass makes you the lowest of the low. If I make a statement against Conrad, Marcel will hate me more than he already does."

"And that's why you won't make a statement, because you don't want to embarrass your brother or make him think less of you?"

Meeks was squirming in his seat now. "Partly, I guess. Mainly, I'm just scared that I'd be putting Marcel in danger. Conrad's a ruthless bastard, bruv, and if I cross him, he'll want to make me pay. If he can't get to me, he might decide that the next best thing is to hurt my kid brother, know what I'm saying?"

Tyson's unexpected display of altruism came as quite a shock to Dillon. He hadn't seen Meeks as the type of man who would put the needs of a brother who clearly despised him before his own. In fact, Dillon had always assumed that Meeks' sole motivation for informing on Livingstone had been greed. In light of what he'd just been told, he began to wonder if it had more to do with jealousy. Perhaps damaging Livingstone's criminal activities was the only way he could lash out at a man he resented because Marcel preferred him to his own brother?

"Is there anyone Marcel could go and stay with?" Dillon asked.

Meeks shook his head and, as he spoke, his voice curdled with bitterness. "I'm the only family he has, bruv, but he doesn't want anything to do with me so he's living in a shitty children's home in Queensbridge Road instead."

"I'm sorry things are so bad between you," Dillon said.

It suddenly occurred to him that they might eventually be forced to place Tyson's brother into witness protection if Tyson came on board and made a statement, but he dismissed the idea almost at once. It just wouldn't be viable, not if the boy was as embroiled in gang culture as Tyson had suggested.

They could always get him moved to another care home off the division, of course, but what would be the point? In Dillon's experience, relocating a hardened gang member like Marcel would cause more problems than it solved. His association with the Holly Street gang probably gave him a strong sense of belonging, of camaraderie, of worth, and he would undoubtedly gravitate straight back there if they relocated him against his will.

"I've got a proposition," Dillon said. "I've spoken to the lawyers at the CPS, and they're on board with what I'm about to suggest. Clearly, if you ended up giving evidence at court, we would have to think very carefully about the measures we put in place to protect your brother, but for now let's take things one step at a time. The bottom line is that I need you to provide a written statement today-" he held up his hand to stem the objection that had already started. "Just hear me out before speaking," he said firmly. "Okay?"

Meeks nodded reluctantly. "Okay," he said, "but it won't change my mind."

"Make a statement now," Dillon said, resuming where he had left off. "We won't let anyone know that you've done so, so your brother won't be in any immediate danger, and we won't use it unless we believe that doing so will put Livingstone away for life. In the meantime, you get placed in witness protection and moved out of London, which means that I won't have to worry every time my phone rings in case it's someone calling with news that you've turned up dead."

"Yeah, but bruv, it's not like he wouldn't find out I made a statement until his case went to court," Meeks pointed out. "You're forgetting that I've been nicked a few times, so I know how it works, and I know you've got to tell him what evidence you've got during the interviews."

"We can dilute it in such a way that he won't be able to work out that the evidence we put to him came from you," Dillon said. "We'll just say that we have a statement from a witness who says blah, blah, blah."

Meeks sucked through his teeth. "No way, man. His solicitor will go mad if you try that."

"Trust me, Tyson, in serious cases like this, as long as we make it clear what evidence we have and give him a chance to respond, we can avoid revealing the name of the witness and any details that might identify them."

Meeks seemed confused. "But if it goes to trial, his solicitor will have to be told that I made a statement, and then I'll have to give evidence, won't I?"

"Yes, and yes," Dillon said. "But, by then, you'll have a brand-new life set up well away from Hackney, and Livingstone and anyone else who has helped him will be safely banged up. If you do end up having to give evidence, we can apply for a whole range of special measures to protect you. We might even be able to get away with using a video link, in which case you won't even have to go into the court building. If not, you could give evidence from behind screens so that no one would be able to see you except for the Judge and the barristers. Also, we could use a machine to disguise your voice and make you sound like one of the Daleks from Doctor Who. You wouldn't even have to use the front entrance at court, so no one would be able to see you coming or going."

"No one would be able to see me?"

"That's right, not the defendants, not anyone who might be sitting in the public gallery, not even any police officers, apart from your escorts."

"What if I make a statement and then change my mind, bruv?" Meeks asked. "What if I don't want to give evidence when it goes to court?"

He was obviously considering the offer, Dillon realised. At least that was progress from where they had started off this morning. "No one can force you to give evidence," he said. "And if we don't think we need to rely on your evidence by that point, because we've accrued enough from other sources, we won't use it."

"Is that likely?" Meeks asked.

"I honestly don't know," Dillon admitted, "but if we end up with overwhelming evidence against him, I could make representations that we don't need to rely on you anymore." And I would, Dillon thought. With his background, Meeks would get torn to shreds by a good defence QC. If they didn't still desperately need him by then, it would probably be better not to use him at all.

Meeks sat there in silence, chewing his nails as he thought it all through.

"Do you need anything? To use the loo, or a cup of coffee?" Dillon asked.

"Nah, man, just trying to work out what to do, ya get me."

"I thought I could smell burning," Taylor said, smiling.

To her surprise, Meeks actually laughed at that, but then his face turned serious again. "How do I know I can trust you?" he asked.

Dillon shrugged. "Only you can decide that," he replied. "You're the one who might have to stand in the witness box, not me. But, for what it's worth, if you come on board, I will make sure that you're looked after."

Meeks seemed surprised that Dillon had been so candid. He had obviously expected a bigger sales pitch. "Okay," he said, reluctantly coming to a decision. "I'll do it, but you've gotta promise to take care of my brother if I end up giving evidence."

"We will," Dillon assured him.

"You better not be bullshitting me, bruv."

"I'm not," Dillon said, leaning forward to pat him on the shoulder. "Chrissy, pop upstairs and grab Geoff. All he's doing at the moment is stuffing his face in the canteen. While you're gone, I'll take Tyson back through to custody and get him NFAd." They couldn't take a witness statement from him while he was still on bail. "When you get back, you two can crack on with taking a key witness statement from him on tape while I speak to someone at witness protection to see how they want to play the hand over."

When they were alone, Dillon turned to Meeks. "Tell me honestly, Tyson, why did you decide to become an informant? Was it because your brother looks up to Livingstone rather than to you? Were you motivated by jealousy?"

Meeks jumped to his feet, face dark with anger, hands curled into fists. "I'm not jealous of that motherfucker," he snarled, and the hatred in his voice was unmistakable.

Also standing, Dillon raised his hands to placate him. "I'm sorry if this is painful, but I've got to ask. Your credibility as a witness will be challenged if you ever give evidence, and this is one of the tactics a defence barrister will use to try and rattle your cage with."

"I'm not jealous," Meeks repeated, calmer this time.

"So, what's your beef with him then?"

Meeks sat down again, and Dillon followed suit. "When I was a kid, Conrad's best mate was dating mum," he said. "It was an on-off relationship, mostly off. On the night she died, mum told me that she'd been sleeping with Conrad behind her boyfriend's back, and she was worried he was Marcel's dad. I thought she was just chatting shit at the time, but as the years passed, I started noticing similarities between them, not just looks but traits, ya get me?"

"Does Marcel know?" Dillon asked.

Meeks shook his head. "Nah, bruv, not as far as I know."

"What about Livingstone, is he aware that he's Marcel's father?"

"Conrad's never said anything, and he's never done anything for Marcel or me, so probably not."

"But he employs you, surely that counts as doing something for you?"

A harsh, humourless laugh escaped Tyson's lips. "The motherfucker throws me scraps, treats me like shit, and he never lets me forget that it was my fault my mum died."

This was news to Dillon. "How was it your fault?"

Meeks let out a long, troubled sigh and then dry washed his face with his hands. "That night, she sent me out to get her fix, bruv. It wasn't the first time I'd done it for her, but as I left the block, I was approached by a shotter I hadn't seen before. He told me he'd promised mum a freebie next time he saw her as an incentive to switch dealers. Normally, she got her stuff from one of Conrad's people, but I didn't think she'd care where it came from as long as it was good stuff, so I took it. Turns out the Golden Brown he gave me hadn't been cut properly and was way too pure. When she shot up, the smack killed her. I was there; I watched her die and there was nothing I could do to help her other than call for an ambulance."

Bloody hell! Dillon thought. No wonder the poor sod was so mixed up. "I understand your feelings of guilt," he said, measuring his words carefully, "but you were just a kid at the time, and you had no way of knowing the heroin was bad. It's not your fault, Tyson."

"Yeah, man, it is," he said despondently. "I know it is, and I'll never be able to forgive myself for doing that to her." He angrily wiped away a tear. "I understand why Marcel hates me so much, bruv, because to tell the truth, I hate myself, too." Meeks was crying unashamedly now.

————

The hospital had very kindly provided a small, brightly painted side room for Jack and Jenny's parents to wait in. Edward Maitland was there too, pacing up and down nervously, and polluting the room with the musky scent of his expensive, liberally applied aftershave. Edward seemed unable or unwilling to put aside the resentment he felt at having been the last person to have been notified, and his truculence was making the atmosphere feel tense and combative.

"I need to phone work to check in," Jack said, desperate to find an excuse to escape Maitland, even if only for a short while. "I'm going to grab a coffee while I'm gone. Does anyone want anything?"

Brendan Parker shook his head. "All I want is for my daughter to come out of surgery in one piece," he said.

Brendan was a proud, distinguished looking man in his mid-sixties. Like a true Brit, he was staring ahead stoically, trying his best to keep a stiff upper lip, but Jack knew him well enough to recognise the pain etched into his features and the terrible strain in his voice, all of which told him that beneath the calm exterior, the man was suffering in unspeakable agony.

Jenny's mother, Sylvia, also in her sixties, was normally so gay and vibrant, but the dreadful news seemed to have aged her by a good ten-years, making her seem so very old and frail when Jack had hugged her upon her arrival. Even her hand had felt small and brittle when he took it in his.

A few years back, before their marriage turned sour, Jack had jokingly remarked to Jenny that if she looked half as good as her mum when she reached that age she would be doing well. Laughing, Jenny had readily agreed. Now he realised that they might never find out.

Maitland suddenly stopped pacing. "Jenny's been in surgery for a long time," he announced as if he were the only one being torn apart by the wait. "Shouldn't we have heard something by now? What on earth are they playing at? It's a bloody disgrace." As soon as the rant was over, the agitated pacing resumed.

"No news is good news," Sylvia said, trying to comfort him, and Jack could only hope that she was right.

Brendan reached out, took her delicate hand in his and squeezed gently. "She's strong, my love," he said. "If anyone can come through this, it's our beloved Jenny."

"I hope so," Sylvia said, dabbing red rimmed eyes with a silk hand-kerchief.

"I'll ask the nurse for an update when I go outside," Jack offered, "but I'm sure they'll let us know as soon as there's any news."

As he reached the door an ill-tempered voice called out. "Wait. I could do with some air. I'll come with you." It was Edward Maitland.

———

A half-dozen men were seated around the table when Abdullah Goren arrived with his cortege of bodyguards. As soon as he entered the smoke-filled room, they all stood up respectfully, and took turns kissing his hand. It was a practice he had adopted from Abdullah Baybasin, the Turkish crime lord known as The Emperor. Once the formalities were finished, he gestured for his lieutenants to sit down again and took his place at the head of the table, while his protectors took up station around the room's perimeter.

The mood was tense, the occasion solemn.

"Would you like something to drink, uncle?" the man nearest to him, who also happened to be the owner of the restaurant they used for their meetings, asked nervously.

"Coffee would be good, Ahmet," Goren replied.

"Of course," Ahmet said, slipping away to order refreshments for the table.

Although Goren was eager to hear what they had to tell him, in keeping with their custom, no business was discussed until after the refreshments had been served; no small talk was made either.

"I've called you here this evening to discuss the cowardly attack on my youngest nephew and his three associates last night," Goren began. "We all mourn their loss deeply, but it is not enough merely to grieve. We are men of honour, men of action, and we must avenge this attack by finding the people who are responsible and wiping them from the face of the planet."

Murmurs of approval resonated throughout the room.

"This morning," Goren continued, "you were all told to go out and interrogate your contacts, to leave no stone unturned until you had leaned the identity of those who would wage war against this family. I ask you now, what have you discovered?" He looked around the room as he spoke and was disgusted to see that none of the others could meet his gaze. There could only be one reason for that.

"You have all failed me," he hissed. "A whole day wasted, and I still don't know who killed my nephew? Tell me why that is?" As each man around the table attempted to justify his actions, Goren grew increasingly angry with the pathetic excuses he heard.

"We did our best, uncle…"

"No one knows, uncle…"

"I tried uncle. What more can I do?"

"What more can you do?" Goren seethed at Yusuf Kaya, the morbidly obese man who had just spoken. "It is fortunate for the rest of us that you are not running this family, Yusuf, for you are clearly a useless fool."

Yusuf swallowed hard, stung by the scathing criticism. "I–I'm sorry uncle," he stammered, shrinking back from Goren's withering stare.

With the rest of the group looking at him imploringly, Goren's oldest nephew, Mustafa, felt obliged to take on the role of spokesman. "Uncle," he said timidly, "I swear that we have all done everything possible to bring you the news you crave. Everyone we spoke to assumes it is the Albanians, but no one seems to know for certain…" His voice tailed off when Goren turned to face him.

The gang leader's face was the colour of puce as he banged the table with his fist, making everyone around him flinch. "SORRY?" he yelled. "Sorry isn't good enough! I will not listen to such pathetic excuses. I don't care who you have to pay off or torture to get the truth from, but I want to know who did it, and I want to know by tomorrow evening or I swear you will all wish they had killed you instead of Erkan."

"Yes uncle," the men chorused uneasily.

"Now go," Goren said, "before I decide that an example should be made out of one of you for your collective shortcomings"

The lieutenants stood up immediately, each eager to escape the room as quickly as possible before Goren had a chance to change his mind

"Mustafa, you will wait behind," Goren instructed.

"Yes uncle," Mustafa replied, hesitantly sitting down again and praying that he wasn't about to be punished.

"Tell me nephew," Goren asked once they were alone, "do you truly believe the Albanians are responsible for Erkan's death?"

Mustafa considered the question carefully, trying to second guess a reply that would please Goren the most. "In truth, I can't see who else it could be," he eventually said. "The Albanians were most unhappy with the way the negotiations were going. They even threatened you and Erkan before they left the last meeting. Who else could it be?"

Goren grunted. He had been asking himself the same thing all day. "I received a call from Conrad Livingstone this morning," he said. "He obviously thinks it was the Albanians. He called under the pretence of expressing his condolences but, really, he wanted to know what we were going to do about the attack. I suspect he is worried that the Albanians might also move against him."

"Has the Albanian leader been in contact at all, uncle?" Mustafa asked. "To offer his condolences, and to assure you that he is not responsible."

Goren shook his head. "No, he has not."

Mustafa seized on this. "Then isn't that a clear sign of his guilt?" he asked.

"Possibly," Goren allowed, taking a drag from his cigarette and savouring the strong Turkish tobacco. "But he may just be thinking that an innocent man would not need to protest his innocence, and that by doing so he would actually make himself look guilty."

"It is a complicated business, uncle," Mustafa said. "Perhaps you should phone him?"

"Not yet," Goren said. "I will wait and see what information turns up tomorrow. He can sweat until then."

————

They sat opposite each other across the Formica table in strained silence. Jack had ordered a cappuccino, Eddie a double espresso.

Well this is awkward, Jack thought as he took his first sip, and then winced when he realised how hot it was. When he'd visited the nursing station to enquire about Jenny, there had been nothing new to report, which he'd expected would be the case. After letting Jenny's parents know, he'd come down to the canteen to do some thinking, but Edward Maitland had insisted on accompanying him.

"I don't understand why she wanted you called and not me," Maitland said, staring at him intently.

Jack decided to treat the question as rhetorical.

"Aren't you going to say something?" Eddie asked, clearly miffed that Jack was perfectly content to sit there in silence.

Jack shrugged nonchalantly. "Why would I waste my breath on you when I need it to cool my cappuccino?" He gave it an exaggerated blow just to make a point. It had been petty of him, but it had felt undeniably good.

"Ha-ha, very funny," Maitland responded. He consoled himself by taking a large swig of his own coffee, only to pull a face like he'd just been poisoned. "Arrrgh! This tastes like sewer water," he complained, lowering the cup.

"Mine tastes just fine," Jack retorted, just to wind him up.

The silence returned, but Jack knew it wouldn't last long.

"I still don't understand why she wanted you informed first and not me," Maitland bemoaned a few seconds later. He nudged his Styrofoam cup around the table as he spoke, watching the dark liquid swish around inside.

Jack checked his watch and gave his cappuccino another blow, thinking that Eddie was beginning to sound like a broken record.

"If the situation was reversed," Maitland was now saying, "and it was me who'd been stabbed instead of her, she would have been the first person I'd have asked for. So, why didn't she ask for me?"

"I don't know," Tyler said.

"It's tearing me apart," Maitland confessed, being unusually candid.

Well, don't expect me to feel sorry for you, or to start playing the agony aunt and dishing out relationship advice. "We should probably get back," Tyler said, making to stand up.

"How do you do it?" Maitland asked.

"Do what?" Jack asked, reluctantly lowering himself back into his chair.

Eddie shrugged. "Investigate murders. I don't think I could break the bad news to someone that they've just lost a son, or a brother, or a … or a wife." Maitland's eyes misted over and he almost choked on his last three words. "Sorry," he said, sounding embarrassed. "Bit emotional at the moment."

Jack's face softened. "You wouldn't be human if you weren't," he said.

"Please don't be nice to me," Eddie told him. "I don't think I can take kindness at the moment, especially from a man who's got every right to hate me."

Jack sighed. "I don't hate you," he said.

That seemed to surprise Maitland. "Really?"

"Really. I don't like you, but I certainly don't hate you."

"I never liked you either," Maitland confessed. "Even though she left you for me, I always suspected that a part of her regretted it, and I often wondered if she would have gone back to you if you'd asked."

"I doubt it," Jack said. "You two are like peas in a pod; I reckon you were made for each other."

Maitland smiled. "That's very gracious of you to say … oh, wait. That was an insult, right?"

Jack smiled. "Come on, Eddie, let's get back upstairs. We should be hearing something soon."

They took the lift.

"So, how do you avoid losing your sanity, doing what you do?" Maitland asked as the doors closed.

"Eddie, when you do what I do for a living, you quickly learn how to put up barriers, otherwise you wouldn't be able to function. It's not so much that you become hardened to it, but you do find ways of preventing other people's tragedy from becoming personal to you."

"I don't see how that's possible," Maitland said.

"It's not always easy," Jack admitted. "When the victims and their families are decent people, it's much harder to remain detached, and if you're not careful you find yourself being drawn into their pain. Trust me, that's a recipe for disaster."

As they exited the lift, Maitland placed a hand on Tyler's arm and pulled him to one side. "Do you still love her, Jack?" he asked.

Jack stopped in his tracks. "Why would you even think that?" he asked, confused.

"Do you still love her?" Eddie demanded, squeezing his arm fiercely.

Feeling his heckles go up, Jack pulled free of Eddie's grip. "No,

Eddie," he said, trying really hard to keep his voice even. "I don't love her."

Eddie breathed a sigh of relief. "Good," he said, voice trembling, "because I honestly don't know that, given the way things are, she would actually choose me over you anymore if she was given the choice."

"Don't be silly," Jack said, not that he understood why she had chosen an idiot like Eddie in the first place.

As Maitland shook his head, a tear ran down the side of his face. "You don't understand," he said, brushing it away. "Things haven't been going too well lately."

"In what way?" Jack heard himself say, and immediately regretted it.

"We've been trying for a baby for the best part of a year now," Eddie confided, "but we've not had any luck, and it's started to cause a bit of friction between us. A lot of friction, actually. Jenny wants me to get tested; thinks I'm firing blanks."

I really don't want to hear about this! "Maybe you should talk to someone about it," Jack suggested.

"I'm bloody well talking to you, aren't I?" Maitland snapped. "Sorry, sorry," he said, holding his hands up contritely. "Didn't mean to snap. It's just that it's become a bit of a sensitive issue for me."

Jack wondered if he should say something about the pregnancy test Mary Mitchell had discovered in Jenny's bag, but decided now was not the time. "Let's just focus on getting Jenny through this," he said. "Everything else can be sorted out afterwards."

Maitland nodded. "Yes, you're right," he said, trying to pull himself together. "Here's me, feeling sorry for myself when I should be thinking about Jenny."

As they reached the room where Jenny's parents were waiting, Tyler caught sight of Andy Quinlan talking to a man in surgical greens further along the corridor. If he was reading their body language correctly, it was the sort of conversation that results in a murder enquiry being launched. His stomach went cold. "Eddie, why don't you go back in?" he said. "I just want to have a quick word with my colleague and then I'll join you."

CHAPTER TWELVE

COMPLICATIONS

It was eight o'clock.

Marcel sat at one end of the sofa quietly toking on a joint. Switch was sitting at the other end, looking as sullen as ever, and Ziggy was slouching down between them in the middle, eating a bag of crisps. The rest of the group had turned up in dribs and drabs over the course of the past hour, and they were now all gathered in the small lounge, waiting expectantly for Ziggy to carve up the day's takings.

"Oi, young un," Ziggy called to Zane, who was sitting on the floor, jiggling the controls to a PlayStation up and down in his hand, trying to make a tiny animated dragon fly around on the TV screen. "Go in the spare room and get the bag, innit."

Zane glanced up at him, a plea on his face. "But fam, I'm playing Spyro! Can't someone else go?"

"Don't give me no lip, bruv," Ziggy warned. "Just make yourself useful and get the bag."

Discarding the control, Zane stood up and stormed out of the room, clearly unhappy.

Ziggy laughed. He could have sent any of the others, but it was all about control for him. He liked to occasionally remind his posse that he was the boss, and that when he shouted, no matter what they were doing, they jumped.

When Zane returned, he tossed the bag to Ziggy and returned to his game.

"Bruv," Ziggy said, "turn that shit off. We got business to take care of now. You wanna play games like a little boy, you go to your house, ya get me?"

With the others laughing at his discomfort, Zane switched the TV off and glared at the older boys. "I aint no little boy, bruv," he said defiantly.

"We did good today," Ziggy was saying. "Got us some flash new phones and some serious bling." He looked across at Marcel and winked as he said that, and Marcel felt a warm glow of pride at having been the one to *tief* the highest value item of the day - the woman's engagement ring. The Rolex, which was still inside his pocket, was probably worth even more than the ring, but he planned to keep that for himself, at least until he could find a fence of his own to sell it on for him.

"That stuff we took'll go off to a fence tomorrow," Ziggy told them, "and you'll all get your share of the Ps we make from selling it in a few days' time. Now, though," he said, pulling a large wad of cash from inside the bag and waving it in the air, "you all get some lovely readies to go out and treat yourselves with."

Ziggy made a big thing of handing Zane a crisp fifty-pound note. "There you go, bruv. Your first time running with us and you did proper good, so go out and buy yourself some new trainers or one of them computer games you like."

Zane took the money, stared at it in awe, and then beamed at Ziggy, his earlier sulkiness now forgotten.

Ziggy ruffled his hair, and then moved around the room, sharing the rest of the cash out between the other gang members like a modern-day Fagin. He gave Marcel a little something extra for *tiefing* the engagement ring with the huge diamond, and made sure that the share he and Switch ended up with befitted their senior status within the group.

"There's some ganja on the side and some beer in the fridge," he announced when everyone had been rewarded, "so let's have us a little party."

"We're the Holly Street Boys," Marcel shouted, and everyone cheered.

Laughing, Ziggy ushered them all into the kitchen and told them to help themselves to the puff and the booze.

The celebration was interrupted by a sudden urgent knocking at the door. No one heard it at first, such was the racket they were making, but then, as the initial excitement wore off and they began to quieten down, the incessant rat-tat-tat slowly became audible.

The room fell silent. "You expecting someone?" Switch asked Ziggy.

"Nah, bruv, not tonight."

Feeling trapped, their euphoria quickly turned into panic. The flat was full of stolen property and cannabis, and they were all wearing the same clothing that they had steamed the train in. The street door was their only means of egress, which meant there was no way to avoid whoever was banging on it to get in.

"What if it's the Feds?" Zane asked, sounding more like the frightened boy he was and less like the hard-core gangsta he wanted to be.

They all looked at each other, and then at Ziggy. One of the youngers asked him if they should throw the incriminating evidence over the balcony. "If you do that, bruv, you'll follow it straight down," Ziggy responded angrily. While they were arguing amongst themselves, trying to decide what to do, the letterbox was pushed open and a female voice shouted through it. "Open the door you bunch of wankers! It's me, Leanne."

The relief was palpable. "Stupid bitch," Ziggy cursed as he headed towards the door.

He returned to the kitchen seconds later with a slim, mixed race girl of about eighteen. Dreadlocks surrounded her pretty face. Now that the scare was over, the swagger and bluster had returned, and they were all making jokes and poking fun at each other.

"Have you lot heard about dem people getting shanked at Clapton station this afternoon?" she asked, taking off her black biker's jacket and draping it over the back of a chair.

Ziggy's eyes narrowed. "What you talking about?" he demanded.

"A train got steamed by some gangsta boys, and two of the passengers got shanked, innit," she told him.

Ziggy looked around the room questioningly. "That's news to me," he said, noting that Switch and Marcel both looked jittery, while everyone else seemed genuinely surprised. "How'd you know about this anyway?"

"A boy I work with at the petrol garage was on the train," she said. "He was in the next carriage. He's a St. John Ambulance volunteer and he helped out. Said it was really bad. Reckons they might both die. One of dem got took away in a helicopter, innit."

"Shit," Ziggy said, dragging the word out. This was an unwelcome complication.

"Dem Boydem were still down there when I left work to come here."

"Shit," Ziggy said again. If the Feds were still at the train station this long after the incident, it had to be mega serious.

"Right, listen up you lot," he said. "Everyone, go home now. Take the clothing you wore today off and put 'em in a bin liner. It all gets burnt tonight. And I mean everything. Dem Boydem will have CCTV before long, and they will be looking to nick people on the description of their clothing. Zane, put all the loot back in the bag and hide it at yours. You've not run with us before, so they won't be looking for you."

Zane looked terrified. "But what if my mum finds it and–"

"Just fucking do it." Ziggy ordered. "You wanna run with the HSB, then you man up and stop being a little pussy."

Leanne stood up. "What the fuck's going on, Ziggy?" she demanded. And then the penny dropped. "Jesus," she said, running her hand through her hair. "Don't tell me you were responsible for this?"

"Nah, not me," Ziggy said, shooting Switch a scathing glance. "I aint that stupid. But we did steam that train, and the Feds will come looking for us if someone dies. They'll want to charge us all with murder just for being there, even though most of us bare knew anything about the shit that went down."

"Remember, everyone stays schtum," Switch said as the others began to file out of the kitchen, "or we'll all end up facing an L-plate."

They all moved into the lounge and started gathering up their things and getting ready to leave. "Not you two," Ziggy said, indicating Switch and Marcel. "You stay behind. We got tings to discuss."

———

When everyone else had gone, Ziggy flew into a rage. "You stupid motherfuckers! What the fuck were you playing at?" He pointed an accusing finger at Marcel. "I'd expect this of him," he said, aggressively jutting his chin towards Switch, who stared back defiantly, "but not you, blud."

"Ziggy, I'm sorr-"

"SHUT UP!" Ziggy shouted. He turned to Switch. "I'm guessing you're the one who shived dem mans on the train?" he snarled. "Why the fuck didn't you tell me straight away, blud? If you had, we would have had time to get rid of our clobber and get our stories straight for when the Feds came calling." He sucked through his teeth. "You fucking pussy bumbaclot."

"Chill man, it's all cool," Switch said, standing up to face the elder. The confrontational look on his face told Ziggy that the younger was actually considering going head-to-head with him over this. Did the fool think he was a big enough man to usurp him from his position as leader? Ziggy stepped forward and hit him hard in the face, knocking him down. He followed the punch up with a savage kick to the ribs. Switch cried out in pain, but Ziggy didn't stop. He put the boot in three more times.

He stood over Switch, who was writhing around on the floor in agony. "Don't you ever look at me like that again, bruv," he said breathlessly. "I'm in charge of this group; don't you dare forget it. And if you so much as even think of squaring up to me again, I'll deep six you, bruv, ya get me?

Dragging himself onto his hands and knees, blood dripping from his mouth, Switch could only nod; he was in far too much pain to speak.

Ziggy grabbed hold of his collar and roughly yanked him up to his feet. "Now go home and get rid of your clothes. Make sure you lose that stupid flick knife, too. Dumb motherfucker." As he spoke, he frogmarched Switch to the street door and pushed him out onto the landing. When he came back into the lounge, still panting from his exertions, he stared at Marcel in disappointment. "You obviously knew what he'd done. Why didn't you say something?"

Marcel stared back, uncertain how best to play this. He didn't want to find himself on the end of a beating like the one Ziggy had just dished out to his lieutenant, so he could hardly admit that he was the one who'd stabbed the woman, not Switch. Besides, it had been an accident. He hadn't meant to use the knife on her; he had just been so angry at her for daring to resist that he'd lashed out without thinking.

It suddenly occurred to him that Leanne had claimed two people on the train had been shived. The second stabbing must've been down to Switch because he hadn't denied it. Come to think of it, he hadn't denied shanking the woman either, which was a bit strange. Marcel decided that the best thing he could do was stay silent and let Switch take the blame for both stabbings. "I'm sorry, Ziggy," he said, guiltily. "I didn't think it was my place to grass, not with Switch being above me in the pecking order. Besides, I thought he would have told you himself."

Ziggy seemed to accept that. "You should've said something to me, bruv," he scolded, "but it's good to know you aint no grass."

When Marcel was allowed to leave the flat, he rode the elevator down to the ground floor in a brooding silence. With any luck, even if the woman he'd accidentally shanked had died, no suspicion would fall on him. The rest of the gang, including Ziggy, firmly believed that Switch was responsible and, if push came to shove, he was sure they'd all back him up when he claimed to have had nothing to do with it.

Before returning to the children's home to change his clothing, he made a quick detour to the rubbish bins at the base of the block. He had rinsed the woman's blood off the blade the moment they'd arrived back at Ziggy's flat, earlier. Now, before throwing it into the bin, he wiped it carefully to remove his fingerprints. The bin must have been empty because there was a loud clang as the knife landed in the bottom.

As he jogged through the estate towards Queensbridge Road, Marcel Meeks was confident that, even if the Feds found the knife he'd just thrown away, they would never be able to link it back to him.

────────

Everyone in the room, apart from Sylvia, anxiously jumped to their feet the instant the surgeon entered. He was a slim man of Middle Eastern appearance. Iranian possibly, Jack thought, noting that he had delicate hands with long, slender fingers, and the sharp watchful eyes of a hawk.

Another member of the surgical team, a fair-haired woman in her mid-thirties, followed him in. The brief smile she gave them was that of a seasoned professional, neither happy nor sad, just polite. Without saying a word, she took up station behind him.

The room suddenly seemed very silent as four pairs of eyes stared at the two newcomers in nervous expectation.

"My name is Mr Shirazi," the man said, speaking with an Oxford educated accent. "I'm a consultant surgeon specialising in liver, spleen and pancreatic surgery, and I'm here to give you an update on Ms Parker's condition."

Jack's heartbeat started racing, and he became conscious that his palms had suddenly become wet and clammy. Out of the corner of his eye, he caught Sylvia's hand reaching out for her husband's and wrapping it in a vice-like grip.

Ignoring the two younger men for the time being, Shirazi addressed Brendan and Sylvia directly. "Am I right to assume that you're Jenny's parents?"

They nodded tensely, clinging to each other for support. "That's correct," Brendan said. There was an unmistakable note of anxiety in his voice, and it really shocked Jack to hear him sounding so weak and vulnerable.

"These gentlemen are Jenny's partner, Edward Maitland, and her ex-husband, Jack Tyler," Brendan said, completing the introductions.

Shirazi nodded politely at each man in turn. He raised an eyebrow at Tyler, no doubt wondering what on earth the ex-husband was doing there.

"Do you have an update on our daughter's condition?" Sylvia asked, and it almost broke Jack's heart to see her steeling herself for the worst.

"Well, I don't mind telling you that it was touch and go for a while," Shirazi said with a little too much melodrama for Jack's liking, "but, thankfully, Jenny's a strong young woman and a born fighter, so I'm pleased to be able to report that she came through a difficult surgery and is now in recovery. She will be transferred to the ICU shortly."

There were audible gasps of relief from Brendan and Sylvia. Unable to keep it in any longer, she buried her head in her husband's chest and began to sob. Eddie raised a hand to his mouth and whispered, "Thank God." He looked like he was about to burst into tears as well.

Breaking free of his wife's embrace, Brendan said, "Is Jenny going to be okay?"

Shirazi's face remained inscrutable as he framed his reply. "At the moment, Jenny's in a critical but stable condition," he explained. "As I've said, she'll be moving to the Intensive Care Unit shortly. I promise you that she will receive the very best care that this hospital is able to provide but, in terms of her long-term prognosis, we will have a much clearer idea in as few hours' time."

"Can we see her?" Sylvia asked, dabbing at her eyes with a hand-kerchief.

"She's only just come out of surgery and she's still heavily sedated, so not at the moment, but once she's properly settled into the ICU on the fourth floor, I'm sure we can arrange something. My colleague, Janet, will stay behind and go through some more details with you when I leave, including how to arrange overnight accommodation here at the hospital if you so desire."

"What's the nature of her injuries, doctor?" Jack asked. He couldn't help it; it was the policeman in him.

"Jenny was stabbed twice," the surgeon explained. "One of the blows pierced her liver, the other perforated her bowel. The blow to her liver caused extensive internal haemorrhaging and was certainly life-threatening. However, once the bleeding was stemmed, we were relieved to discover that the damage to the organ itself wasn't as bad as initially feared. That said, we were forced to carry out a small lobectomy."

His audience stared at him blankly.

"In layman's terms, we had to remove a small section of her liver," he explained. "I'm honestly not too concerned about that; the liver has a wonderful capacity for regeneration. Indeed, I've known of cases where it grew back to its full size even after patients had as much as seventy-five-per-cent removed."

Eddie's eyes widened in alarm. "That doesn't sound good to me," he said. "How long will it take to grow back?"

Shirazi pursed his lips. "Actually, the majority of the regeneration occurs within the first few weeks. I should stress that, in Jenny's case, we only had to remove a very small section of her liver."

"So, how long will she have to remain in hospital?" Eddie asked.

It was becoming clear to Jack that Eddie was planning to ask a lot of questions, most of which were probably stupid.

Shirazi flashed a brief smile at Maitland, and Jack could have sworn it was the same neutral expression that his colleague had used earlier. He wondered if they received special coaching on how to do that. He could picture the scene in his mind's eye: a row of aspiring doctors sitting in class at medical school, all wearing white coats and stethoscopes, and all being required to stand up, one after the other, to demonstrate the correct facial expression to their instructor.

"I'm afraid that, due to the seriousness of her injuries, Jenny's going to have to remain in hospital for a while," Shirazi was saying, "but I can't give any indication as to how long that will be at this stage."

"What about the perforated bowel?" Jack asked, getting in before Eddie could come up with another pointless question.

"Ah, yes. Well, it was a clean wound, albeit a deep one," Shirazi said. "We were able to repair the damage without having to remove any sections of her bowel, which is very good news. The greatest danger now is infection, but Jenny will be given a strong course of antibiotics and be monitored closely over the next few days."

"So, she should make a full recovery?" Eddie cut in. He was starting to sound desperate.

Shirazi's eyes were full of sympathy, but his voice was non-commit-tal. "Let's not get ahead of ourselves," he said cautiously. "As I explained before, we'll have a much clearer idea of her prognosis in a few hours' time."

"We understand," Brendan said, "and we all want to thank you and your team for looking after Jenny."

"You're very welcome," Shirazi said, bowing his head in acknowl-edgement. "Now, I'm going to have to get back to my patients, but if there's anything you need to know, Janet here, will be more than happy to help you." With that, Shirazi shook their hands and bid them farewell.

Almost immediately, Eddie started bombarding Janet with ques-tions. Leaving him to it, Jack followed Mr Shirazi out of the room. "Excuse me, doctor, can I have a quick word in private," he said, steering the surgeon into a quiet corner.

Shirazi looked uneasy. He probably thought that Jack was going to do an Eddie on him. "As I said, if you have any further questions–"

Jack produced his warrant card. "Forgive me," he said, cutting the other man off, "but in addition to being Jenny's ex, I'm also a Detec-tive Chief Inspector on the murder squad, and I need to speak to you in my official capacity rather than as a relative of the patient."

"Ah, I see. In that case, how may I help?"

"Do you think the same weapon caused both injuries?" Jack asked.

"I can't really say for certain, but I suspect not. The incised wound to her liver appears to have been made by a blade that was noticeably wider than the one used to inflict the lower abdominal injury. My understanding is that she was attacked by a group. Is that correct?"

Jack nodded. "That's my understanding, too."

"In that case, although I can't say for certain, my instinct is that she was probably stabbed by two different people."

From what he'd heard so far, Jack also suspected that was the most likely scenario. "Tell me, did you work on the elderly man who was stabbed while trying to defend Jenny?" Jack asked.

Shirazi shook his head. "No, I'm afraid not."

"So, you have no idea if the knife that was used on him was also used on Jenny?"

"I'm sorry," Shirazi said with a shrug. "I wish I could be of more assistance."

Tyler thanked him for his time and returned to the others. "Now that Jenny's out of immediate danger," he said to Brendan and Sylvia - Eddie was too preoccupied questioning Janet to even notice his return - "I need to be getting back to work. I didn't mention this before because I didn't want you getting any more upset than you already were, but when Eddie and I popped out earlier I spoke to my colleague, and he informed me that the man who was injured trying to save Jenny didn't make it, so this is now a murder enquiry."

Sylvia was distraught. "Oh, that poor, poor man. Is there anything we can do to help his family?"

Jack was deeply moved by her compassion. "I don't know," he said softly, "but if you can ever get a word in, I'm sure that Janet will be able to answer that. If Jenny comes round, let me know. Otherwise, I'll give you a call a little later when I've got more news."

He hugged each of them in turn and left. Janet, still penned in the corner by Eddie, watched him leave, no doubt wishing she could do likewise.

————

Detective Sergeant Jonny Murphy of Greater Manchester Police Major Investigation Team was sitting at his desk booking in the last of the CCTV he'd seized for his London colleagues during the course of the day. It was almost eight p.m., and he was coming to the end of a punishing twelve-hour shift. He was tired; he was cranky; and he needed a drink.

Originally from the Wirral, Murphy had fallen in love with Manchester during the three years he'd spent studying there. After graduating from university, he had decided to stay on, and shortly afterwards he applied to join the local constabulary. Eighteen-years later, he still loved the city, even though it had changed beyond all recognition.

Obtaining a copy of the CCTV from the hotel where Livingstone had stayed during his visit two-weeks earlier had been incredibly easy; getting the footage from Crosby's Club had proved to be anything but. In fact, as he'd fully expected, it had turned out to be quite problematic. For a starter, no bugger had been there the first two times he'd visited, and there was no reply at either of the numbers the licencing team had on file for the owner and the manager.

The manager, it transpired, was a slimy toad of a man called Cyril Jenkins. When he'd finally arrived at the club and been informed of Murphy's intention to search the building under the power bestowed by Section 18 of PACE, he had done everything he could to deter the officers from entering. It was only when Murphy threatened to arrest him for obstructing an officer in the execution of his duties that he finally moved aside and let the stubborn detective and his two colleagues in. Even then, instead of being helpful and facilitating the search, he had jumped straight on the phone to his solicitor, who had demanded that the officers halt the search proceedings until he could get there to oversee it in about an hour's time. Murphy had responded by telling the odious man to sod off.

Having already failed to endear himself to the detectives, slimy Cyril proceeded to hack them off further by claiming that he didn't know how to run off a copy of the footage they'd requested. He wanted them to come back another day, when someone who knew their way around the equipment would be there to help - like he wouldn't immediately get rid of everything the second they left.

"Not a problem, chum," Murphy had assured him in his strong Liverpudlian accent. "I'll call down my tech guys and we'll just take the hard drive away with us."

Unsurprisingly, at that point, the manager suddenly remembered how to do it. Murphy had made a point of checking that the recording actually worked before leaving.

"What's the matter?" Jenkins had demanded, belligerently, "don't you trust me?"

"No," Murphy had responded bullishly. "I bloody well don't."

When he'd returned to the office, the first thing he'd done was make a call to a friend at Trading Standards to report that, not only was the manager diluting the various spirits on sale with water, but there were rat droppings on the kitchen work surfaces.

"I didn't see him diluting the drinks when we were there," Katie Richards, one of the officers who had accompanied him, had observed after he'd hung up.

"Neither did I," Murphy admitted, smiling wickedly, "but you can bet your pension that the horrible gobshite is doing it."

"I didn't see any rat droppings in the kitchen, either," she'd added, but by that point Richards was trying her hardest not to smile

"Maybe they were raisins," Murphy had said. "Either way, I've rarely met a fella who deserved an inspection visit from Trading Standards more. You got a problem with that?"

Richards had grinned broadly, and Murphy had instantly clocked the mischievous twinkle in her eye. "Not at all," she'd said. "I reckon that obnoxious git's as crooked as a corkscrew. In fact, I was wondering if you ought to call Trading Standards back and mention all the sewage leaking out of the toilets. Proper health hazard, that."

In between collecting the CCTV that Dillon had requested from the hotel and the nightclub, and grudgingly spending a few hours investigating crimes that had actually been committed within his own jurisdiction, Murphy had somehow also found the time to pay a visit to Manchester Piccadilly to download a copy of the station's CCTV for the previous day.

He would get around to viewing that in the morning. Right now, though, a cold beer at his favourite bar had his name written on it, and he could hear it calling out to him.

———

When Jack got back to the office, he found Dillon waiting for him, looking deeply concerned.

"How is she?" the big man asked.

"She's out of surgery, but still sedated," Jack said, removing his jacket and loosening his tie. "She's gonna be in the ICU for a few days, at least." He flopped down at his desk and wearily motioned for Dillon to pull up a chair opposite.

"You could have stayed, mate," Dillon said. "I've got everything under control here."

Jack shook his head. "Her parents and Eddie are there with her, so I was surplus to requirements. I figured I might be of more use back here."

"Does the quack think she'll make a full recovery?"

Jack shrugged. "You know what they're like. He wouldn't commit; reckons we'll have a clearer picture in a few hours' time. Hopefully, as long as there are no complications from the surgery–" like she's lost the baby she's carrying, he wanted to say but didn't, "-she will."

Steve Bull poked his head around the door carrying two mugs of steaming hot coffee, which he duly handed over. "Thought you might need this," he said. There was an awkward pause, and then he said, "How's your ex-missus doing, boss?"

Tyler gave him the same update he'd just given Dillon.

"I'll be keeping my fingers crossed for her," Steve told him. "Let me know if there's anything I can do to help."

"Thank you, Stevie, that's much appreciated," Tyler said.

Bull turned to leave, but Tyler called him back into the office and invited him to take a seat and join them. "Did you two hear that the old bloke who stepped in to save Jenny died on the operating table?" he asked, taking a sip of his coffee.

Dillon nodded. "It's very sad," he said. "I spoke to Andy Quinlan a little while ago, and he seems pretty confident that we'll be able to identify the steamers. He's already had the CCTV seized from Hackney Downs, which is where they got on, and Clapton, where the bastards got off. Apparently, even as we speak, a local neighbourhood watch skipper is viewing the footage. Andy reckons this bloke's got a photographic memory, and there's a really good chance he'll be able to identify some of the gang members involved just from watching the CCTV."

"I hope so," Tyler said, although he doubted that would be the case. "It would be nice to get hold of them before they have a chance to get rid of their clothing and offload the stolen gear."

"Andy Quinlan's shot off to The Yard for a press conference that's going out on the nine o'clock news, but Susie Sergeant's over at Stoke Newington and she's promised to let us know straight away if this skipper picks anyone out," Dillon said.

"So," Jack said, reaching for his daybook, "where are we with the Turkish job?"

"The other three victims have all been identified," Bull said. "Fatma tried to establish contact with their next of kin, but they blew her out, just like Erkan's family did."

Jack frowned, confused. "Who's Fatma?"

"She's a Turkish PC from Stoke Newington. Mr Q managed to get her seconded to the enquiry for a few days to facilitate communication with the victim's families."

"Ah, I see," Jack said. "What's she like? Did you ever come across her when you worked at Stoke Newington?"

Bull shook his head. "I saw her around, but never had occasion to work with her. I got the impression that she knew her stuff, though."

"Is she still here?" Jack asked. "I'd like to have a quick chat with her if she is."

"Sorry, I sent her home just before you returned. The poor cow's been on duty for sixteen-hours straight, and she could hardly see straight."

Dillon grinned. "Is that what it was? I just thought she was cross-eyed."

"So not funny," Steve said, shaking his head.

"It was a little bit funny," Dillon insisted.

Bull ignored him. "The SPMs start in the morning at Queens Road mortuary in Walthamstow. I really don't know why the bodies went there instead of somewhere closer, and we drew Creepy Claxton as our pathologist."

"Are you going to be okay to cover them, Dill?" Jack asked.

Dillon shrugged unhappily. "I guess I'll have to be, won't I?"

"Might as well get used to it," Jack said. "It goes with the territory."

"Speaking of territories," Bull said, "Dean's prepared a detailed briefing note outlining the main points we need to know about the three gangs involved in this turf war. He's e-mailed it to everyone on the enquiry."

"Well, that'll make for some interesting bed-time reading," Jack said, dryly. "Anything new come out of processing the scene?"

Bull shook his head. "All the shells are going up to the lab as urgent submissions in the morning. With any luck, we might get some prints or DNA off them."

"I doubt it," Dillon said. "These shooters strike me as being far too professional."

"There is one significant development," Steve said. "Paul Evans spoke to Tulay Yildiz. When pressed, she told him that one of the shooters – the one who gunned Erkan down as it happens – had a distinctive tattoo of a serpent curled around a knife on his neck. She's pretty good at drawing, so Paul Evans got her to produce a detailed sketch. The original's been exhibited and locked away, but Julia has run off some copies for distribution at tomorrow morning's meeting." Julia was one of the civilian support staff who worked in the Major Incident Room as an indexer.

"Would you be kind enough to go and fetch me one now, please, Steve?" Jack asked wearily.

"Of course," Bull said, standing up. "Be back in a second."

"How are your lot getting on with the tasks we set them?" Jack asked Dillon when they were alone.

Dillon leaned back in his chair and took a sip of the coffee Bull had made him. "Adebanjo and the Kalu brothers have been inter-viewed. The smug bastards all went no comment. They've been bailed for three weeks. Tyson Meeks is providing a witness statement as we speak, and I've spoken to the Criminal Justice Protection Unit about getting him into witness protection. As soon as the statement's finished, two of my DCs are going to drive Meeks to a service station just outside London and hand him over to them. They'll put him up in a hotel for a few days, and then relocate him to somewhere remote once they can sort out a suitable placement."

"Any idea where he'll end up?" Jack asked, rolling his neck to ease the pain that had formed at the base of his skull.

Dillon shook his head. "The bloke I spoke to suggested Manchester. Needless to say, I explained why that wouldn't be a good idea!"

"Anything else?"

"We've obtained the CCTV from Euston. DC Perry will start viewing that first thing tomorrow. Oh, the bank played ball about the credit card that was used to pay for Adebanjo's hotel stay. Although they'll still need a court order to hand over the paperwork, the woman my officer spoke to said the application was submitted on Monday the tenth of May. In other words, nine days after Livingstone met up with Adebanjo in Manchester. The funny thing is, the contact number she has on record for Meeks ends in 217, which isn't his number. Reg submitted subscriber and call data requests for me, so we'll see what comes back. Personally, my money's on it being a pre-paid unregistered phone that was purchased on the day of the application."

Steve Bull returned and handed each of them an A4 sheet of paper. "Look at that," he said. "There can't be too many people floating around with one of these beauties on their neck."

"Wow," Jack said, studying the sketch closely. "She's recalled an incredible amount of detail."

The drawing featured a serpent curled twice around a dagger, once around the hilt and a second time around the blade. The snake's head was protruding just beyond the hilt, at the top of the drawing; its tail dangled just below the blade's point at the bottom. The hilt was braided, and the guard that protruded out from either side, where the blade joined the handle, was tapered to a fine point that faced towards the snake's head, making it resemble a bull's horns. The most distinctive feature, however, was a sinister looking skull - minus the lower mandible - shaped pommel at the base of the hilt.

"Steve," Jack said excitedly. "Can you get either Dean or Wendy to run this through the marks and scars index on the PNC. Also, I'd like one of them to do some research and tell me if it's related to any particular gang."

"I'll get them onto it right away," Steve said, standing up.

As soon as he left the room, the telephone rang.

Jack snatched it up, annoyed that his chain of thought had been interrupted just when it felt like they were starting to get somewhere. "DCI Tyler speaking," he snapped. After listening in silence for a few moments, he thanked the caller and hung up. "That was Susie Sergeant," he said, standing up. "Apparently, the Safer Neighbourhood Team skipper from GN has come good for us. He's viewed the CCTV from Hackney Downs station, and he's identified three of the suspects. They're trying to scramble the TSG to carry out rapid entries on their addresses this evening, and we've been invited to join the party."

The Territorial Support Group – or TSG – were the Met's highly trained rapid response and public order unit.

"Fuck me," Dillon said, "that was quick."

Jack grinned. "I heard that's what all your girlfriends say."

Dillon responded by giving him the finger.

Bull reappeared. "Going home already?" he asked.

"Grab your coat and a Log-Book and car keys, Stevie," Dillon said, slipping his suit jacket back on. "There's been a development and we're going over to Stoke Newington."

CHAPTER THIRTEEN

THIS IS A NICE WAY TO SPEND AN EVENING

They met at a little Jamaican restaurant in Kingsland High Street, not far from where Livingstone resided. He was a silent partner in the business, having put up the initial stake to get it going. There weren't many other diners, so they could talk freely, without fear of being overheard.

The bald giant from Manchester sat opposite Livingstone, surveying the menu. His face was calm and serene, as though he didn't have a care in the world. "What would you recommend, fam?" he asked, peering at Livingstone over the top of the menu.

Livingstone shrugged. "Everything here's top notch, bruv," he said. "I recommend it all."

The Kalu twins had been seated at table towards the rear of the restaurant, along with Gunz and Jerome Norris. Livingstone could see the four men were doing their best to make small talk, but intermingling didn't come naturally, and there were long periods of awkward silence as they tried to think of something to say.

Reggae music was playing in the background, and Bob Marley was about halfway through *Buffalo Soldier*.

Goliath raised an amused eyebrow. "Well, in that case, fam, why don't you do the honours and order for both of us."

Livingstone smirked. "Yeah, why not."

The owner, a tall, pencil-thin Rasta in his early fifties, with long dreads protruding beneath the red, yellow, and green crocheted tam he wore on his head, was standing over at the bar, singing along to the Marley tune as he wiped wine glasses with a dishcloth.

Livingstone snapped his fingers several times to get the man's attention. "Yo! Marvin, come over here." His tone was peremptory, as if he were calling a dog.

Marvin ambled over like he had all the time in the world, still singing along to Bob. "Yeah man," he pronounced it 'mon', "what can I get you?" He had an infectious smile that was so bright it could have been used to advertise toothpaste.

"One second, bruv," Livingstone told him, ostensibly double checking something in the menu but, in reality, just making Marvin wait because he could.

"Sure man," Marvin said, unperturbed "Take all the time you need." He stood behind Livingston and resumed his singing.

"Not easy to concentrate with you making that noise in my ear, bruv," Livingstone muttered under his breath.

If he heard the comment, Marvin chose to ignore it.

As soon as Marley finished, Jimmy Cliff started belting out *Many Rivers to Cross* from his 1972 album, *The Harder They Come*. "Oh man, this song is pure bliss," Marvin cooed, and immediately joined in.

"I'm ready to order now, bruv," Livingstone snapped, staring daggers at Marvin until he took the hint and shut up.

Goliath watched on in amusement.

"I think we'll start with the mutton soup," Livingstone announced.

Marvin nodded approvingly. "An excellent choice."

"And… let me see… the curried goat looks good, bruv, but I've decided to go with your famous jerk chicken."

Marvin let out a delighted chuckle, exposing his pearly white teeth again. "It's true my bredrin" he boasted to Goliath, who he seemed to have taken a shine to, "people flock here from all over London just to sample our authentic jerk chicken."

"I'm sure they do, fam," the giant said, high-fiving Marvin.

"I'm telling you, man, it's aromatic, smokey and spicy hot." Marvin was almost drooling as he described the restaurant's signature dish. "The chicken is marinated in our special concoction of spices, including ginger, garlic, cloves, hot peppers, cinnamon and pimento. Then it's slow cooked on an open grill until it tastes like heaven on earth."

"Sound's amazing," Goliath said, smiling indulgently.

Livingstone was eager to get rid of Marvin so that they could talk business. "We'll have rice and beans with it, bruv, and a couple of side dishes. You can choose those."

Marvin rubbed his bony hands together in culinary joy. "How about I fix you some callaloo and bammy, and serve them with saltfish?"

"Sounds perfect," Livingstone said with a curt smile.

Scooping up the menus, Marvin did a little pirouette and danced off towards the kitchen to put their order in.

"He's quite a character, fam," Goliath said as Marvin disappeared out back, now singing along to *Last Chance* by Mykal Roze.

"He's stoned out of his head on ganja," Livingstone said, shaking his head at the owner's flamboyant behaviour. "But I'll let him off as they do make some of the best authentic jerk chicken outside of Jamaica here."

"The next time you come to Manchester, I will take you to a little place I know that specialises in African cuisine. They do a traditional Nigerian dish called Moin-Moin. It's a steamed bean pudding made from a mixture of washed and peeled black-eyed peas, onions and fresh ground peppers. You would enjoy it very much."

"I'll look forward to that," Livingstone said, thinking that it sounded absolutely revolting. He looked around again, just to make sure that they couldn't be overheard, and then leaned in to address the giant. "Let's get down to business. First, here's another burner." He slid a sleek black phone across the table as he spoke.

Goliath picked it up, weighed it in his hand and then turned it over. "Is this a new phone?" he asked warily.

Livingstone shrugged. It was the 217 handset, and he had used it twice. "Newish. I've only made two calls from it. The first was when I phoned Weasel's bank to request a credit card in his name, and the second was to reserve your hotel in Beckton, which was paid for with Meeks credit card."

Goliath considered this. "Maybe I should just get a virgin phone from a shop in the morning."

"Why waste a perfectly good phone?"

Goliath's eyes narrowed accusingly. "You want to risk us getting caught for the sake of a few quid, fam?"

"I don't care about the money," Livingstone said dismissively. "But it's been used for two calls, both attributable to Weasel Meeks, and it can't be traced back to any of us."

Goliath considered this. "And Meeks was given bail like the rest of us," he said with a sly grin, "so if the police did look at the number, and any calls subsequently made from it, they would associate them with him, not me."

"Exactly."

Goliath considered this, then nodded his massive head. "Very well, fam, I will keep the phone, for now."

"Good, bruv. Now that's settled, why don't you tell me how you're gonna fuck up the Turks and the Albanians for me."

Goliath's eyes lit up. "Ah yes, let me tell you about my clever battle plan. Before coming down to London, I carefully studied all the information you provided me with about the Turks and the way their operation is set up. Taking everything into consideration, I have decided that tomorrow night the Albanians–" he used his fingers to add air quotes to the word "–should strike at the family restaurant where Goren and his closest lieutenants usually hold their meetings. That will send a very clear message to them, one that they cannot ignore."

Livingstone wasn't sure he liked the sound of that. Yes, he wanted the Turks and Albanians to go to war, and sooner rather than later, but what Goliath was proposing was fraught with risk. It was one thing to wipe out a lowly group of debt collectors out on their rounds, but quite another to strike at the heart of Goren's empire.

"I don't know about that," he said cautiously. "I mean, if something goes wrong, Goren could end up getting hurt, and that would ruin everything." Despite his ruthlessness, Goren was a savvy businessman, not a mindless thug, unlike those who were likely to take over his operation if anything happened to him.

Goliath's smile was that of a predator. "Do not worry, fam," he said soothingly. "I know exactly what I'm doing. No harm will come to Goren."

"Maybe not, but–"

"Listen, fam," Goliath cut him off, and there was an underlying note of warning in his voice. "You hired me to do a job. Let me get on with it without interruption."

The atmosphere between them suddenly become strained, and for a few moments neither man spoke. "Very well," Livingstone eventually said, staring into his guest's unblinking eyes and trying to fathom what made him tick. "I'll do that, but if anything goes wrong, you need to make sure that nothing can ever be traced back to me."

"Of course," Goliath said, smiling placatingly now that he had got his own way. "I am a professional. You hired me to look after your interests, fam, and that's exactly what I'm going to do."

Livingstone nodded. "Good. Good. In that case, is there anything you need from my people?"

Goliath considered this for a moment. "The shooters will need another stolen car, and also someone to keep an eye on the address and let them know when Goren arrives. It won't have anywhere near the same impact if he isn't inside when my men open fire."

Livingstone glanced over at Gunz. "I'll have my man take care of it," he said.

"There is one more thing I need you to get for my men," the giant said.

"What's that?"

A smile of pure devilment crept onto Goliath's broad face. "An Albanian flag."

Before Livingstone could ask him what he wanted one of those for,

Marvin appeared, carrying two huge bowls. "Your starters, gentlemen," he said, carefully placing one in front of each man.

"Ahh, it smells delicious," Goliath said, unfolding his napkin. As Marvin departed, he turned to Livingstone and smiled amicably. "Now that business has been satisfactorily taken care of, let us relax and enjoy this fine meal together."

"There is one other matter I need to discuss with you first," Livingstone said.

The spoon paused halfway between the bowl and Goliath's mouth, and he looked up, frowning. "Go on," he said, lowering it back into the bowl.

"Tyson Meeks. He's a loose end that needs to be taken care of as soon as possible."

Goliath tilted his head to one side as he thought about this. "Why are you telling me this, fam? I thought we had agreed that when the time came, you would take care of your own dirty washing."

"And I will," Livingstone said. "I'm just making sure you've got no further use for him before I give the order."

"No, fam," Goliath said, enjoying his first mouthful of Marvin's delicious soup. "I have nothing more planned for your little informant, so feel free to do with him as you will."

————

When they arrived at Stoke Newington police station, the rear yard was crammed full of police vehicles, including four Territorial Support Group personnel carriers that had been thoughtlessly abandoned smack bang in the middle, making it almost impossible for Steve Bull to manoeuvre the Omega past them.

"Not the most considerate parking I've ever seen," he complained as the side of the car came within a hairs width of scraping the paintwork on one of them.

In the back, Dillon chortled. "You've got to remember, we employ them because of their considerable talent for smashing down doors and flattening people, not for their ability to master intricate concepts like consideration."

The briefing room was located in the ground floor of the tower block, opposite the station's main building, but the code Bull typed into the security keypad didn't work, and they ended up having to wait ages until someone, who just happened to be passing by, took pity on them and swiped them in.

"I can't believe you didn't know the code," Tyler moaned as they finally stepped inside the building. "You only left this division six weeks ago. How can you have forgotten it already?"

"It's a sign of old age," Dillon pointed out. "You tend to get forgetful when you're as old as him."

"Ha-bloody-ha," Bull replied, firing a caustic look over his shoulder. And then, but with less belligerence, he said to Tyler, "It's not my fault, boss. They've obviously changed the combination since I left."

"They probably did it to stop you coming back," Dillon suggested unhelpfully.

Bull responded by raising his middle finger.

With ten minutes to spare before the briefing was due to start, they made a quick detour to the canteen. Unfortunately, the crews of all four TSG carriers had obviously had the same idea, and they were raucously queuing in a not so orderly line to grab a quick cuppa before the briefing started.

"Look at them," Dillon muttered under his breath as the boisterous officers laughed and jeered and threw things at each other while they waited to be served. "It's like feeding time at the zoo."

The three detectives joined the end of the line, but with so many people standing in front of them, Tyler began to wonder if it was even worth bothering.

Bull gazed along the length of the line and groaned. "At this rate, we're going to miss the first few minutes of the briefing," he warned.

Just then, the TSG officer immediately in front of him ducked to avoid the sachet of tomato sauce his college had chucked at him, and it hit Steve straight in the face. "Do you mind!" Bull shouted angrily.

"Sorry," the man who had thrown the offending article called from the front of the line, where he was squirming with embarrassment. Having apologised, the burly PC quickly gathered up his order and moved away, keeping his head down.

"It's no wonder that their detractors argue TSG should stand for Thick and Stupid Group,'" Steve muttered under his breath as the offending PC and his mate walked past him, sniggering like a pair of naughty children who had just been told off by their teacher.

Tyler checked his watch. "Right, I'm going to have to go and find Susie. I'll see you in the briefing room in a few minutes." He slipped a fiver into Steve's hand. "It's my round, and I'll have a cappuccino."

People were slowly starting to drift out of the canteen towards the briefing room across the hall, and Tyler followed suit, weaving between them to get ahead.

Pausing at the briefing room door, he spotted Susan Sergeant standing by the lectern. A big TV screen had been set up behind her, and he wondered if they were going to play some of the platform footage. Susie was talking to a suited man of medium height and build, who had short sandy hair and a kind, intelligent face. Jack estimated that he was in his early forties, and the crow's feet around his eyes suggested that he liked to laugh a lot.

When Susie saw him standing there, she waved him over. "Boss, this is DI Bell, the head of the borough robbery squad." She turned to Bell. "Mr Tyler is standing in for DCI Quinlan, who's stuck up at NSY and won't be joining us until later."

Smiling, Bell stepped forward and offered his hand. "Call me Ian," he said. "Pleasure to meet you."

"Likewise," Jack responded, noticing that the robbery squad DI had a firm, confident grip.

The smile vanished from Ian Bell's face and he suddenly became serious. "Susie told me about your wife," he said, lowering his voice. "I hope she's going to be okay."

So do I, Jack thought. "She's my ex-wife, and we'll know more in a few hours," he said, suddenly feeling very awkward. "So, what's the plan tonight?" he asked, keen to change the subject.

"I'm just waiting for my DS and the Safer Neighbourhood skipper to join us. They've popped out to recce the three addresses we're going to raid. Once they get back, we'll get the briefing underway."

Tyler's eyes narrowed. "Are you confident this skipper with the photographic memory has identified the right people?" he asked, trying not to let his scepticism show.

Bell nodded proudly. "If Gavin Mercer says he recognises someone, you can bet your savings that he does."

Just then, two men walked into the briefing room and made their way towards Bell. The first was a slender uniformed sergeant with jet black hair that was swept back into a widow's peak, a high forehead, and skin so pale that it was almost translucent. The second was a shortish, podgy man in scruffy plain clothes, with a ruddy complexion, unkempt brown hair, and at least two days' worth of stubble covering his many undulating chins.

"Ah, Cerebral, you're back!" Bell beamed.

The man in plain clothes – presumably Cerebral – raised a weary hand in greeting. "It's looking promising at the first two addresses, boss," he said, breathing heavily, as though he had just been jogging. "Not sure about the last one though. The lights are on, but there's no sign of any movement inside."

The uniformed sergeant stood motionless behind him, saying nothing.

Bell frowned, clearly disappointed, but he quickly shrugged this off. "Well, I suppose now that we've got everyone assembled and ready to go, we'll just have to take a chance that all three of them are in." He turned to Tyler. "Sir, allow me to introduce you to DS Graham Pausey, otherwise known as Cerebral."

Jack shook a soft, clammy hand. It was a bit like holding a dead fish, and when he released it, he had to resist the urge to wipe his palm against his trouser leg.

"Pleased to meet you," he said.

"And this," Bell continued, "is Gavin Mercer, the super recogniser I told you about."

"Sir." The sergeant nodded respectfully, but he didn't offer his hand, and there was no enthusiasm or friendliness in the voice. No emotion of any kind for that matter.

Tyler's first impression of Mercer was that the man verged on the edge of the autistic spectrum.

The room was starting to fill up, and the ambient background noise increased considerably as a stream of TSG and local officers poured through the open doorway and started scrabbling around for chairs in a disorganised fashion.

Dillon and Bull eventually appeared, the latter holding a white Styrofoam cup. Quickly crossing the room to join Tyler, he handed this over. "It might be a little cold," he warned as they all took the seats that had been reserved for them in the front row.

Tyler took a sip and grimaced. Yep. Stone cold.

When everyone was seated, Ian Bell called the briefing to order. He waited until the room was completely silent before beginning. "I want to thank you all for coming here at such short notice," he said warmly, "especially our esteemed colleagues from the Territorial Support Group and AMIP. Tonight, we're going to raid three addresses that are linked to a prolific local street gang called the Holly Street Boys. The intention is to arrest some of the people who were involved in a train steaming this afternoon at Clapton British Rail station. During this incident two people were stabbed, with one of them regrettably dying, and the other receiving life-threatening injuries."

Tyler's phone, which was on silent, vibrated in his pocket. He pulled it out and saw that he had just received a text message. It read: *Thanks for earlier. Would it be possible to have another chat tomorrow?*

He didn't recognise the number, and he had no idea who it was from.

Bell was steadily working his way through the briefing. "The three suspects, Xander Mason, Devon Brown and Curtis Bright, all live on the Holly Street Estate," he was saying, "and the plan is for TSG rapid entry teams in full public order kit to hit each of their addresses simultaneously…"

Tyler tapped out a message on his phone and pressed send. It read: *Who is this?*

"Once the addresses are secure and, hopefully, all three suspects are in custody, officers from AMIP and GN will carry out a thorough search of each address…"

Jack's phone vibrated again. Another bloody message. It read: *It's Edward Maitland. Can we talk again in the morning?*

Jack groaned inwardly. How the hell had Maitland managed to get hold of his number? And why did he want to talk to Jack? He experienced an irrational spike of anger at the unwelcome intrusion, and he jabbed at the keys, translating his feelings into words: *No. Sod off.* His thumb hovered over the send button for what seemed like an age but, even though he really wanted to, he just couldn't bring himself to press it. Maitland might be a complete tosser, but he was clearly going through a bad time. In the end, Tyler deleted the message and retyped: *Busy trying to catch the people who did this to Jenny.* It seemed a bit more diplomatic, so he sent that instead.

"Right, so now we're going to play you some CCTV footage from Hackney Downs train station, showing a group of approximately ten Holly Street gang members waiting on the platform for the victim's train. As soon as that's finished, DS Sergeant and I will talk you through who's going to be going where and doing what." When he'd finished speaking, Bell nodded to DS Pausey, who pressed the play button on the remote control he was holding in one of his podgy hands. Almost immediately, the screen flickered to life, and the footage began to play.

Jack studied the screen carefully, knowing that at least one of the youths he was now looking at had stabbed his former wife.

Jack's phone vibrated again. For God's sake, he thought. Not another bloody text!

Sure enough, it was Maitland. The latest message read: *I know, and I'm grateful.* That made Jack feel bad. At least until Maitland spoiled the moment by sending another message through straight afterwards. This one read: *I really need to speak to you so is it alright if I call you tomorrow?*

On screen, the Holly Street Boys were making the platform look untidy. Most were lounging around on benches, a couple were just standing there waiting, and one cheeky git was spray painting the station wall with graffiti. There was an unmistakable aura of nastiness about them, and it made Jack's blood boil. As he watched, they all stood up and started preparing themselves to board the train that was pulling into the station. Just before they got on, Jack noticed that the one with the spray can had dumped it in a trash bin.

"Can you pause the tape," he called out, conscious that every eye in the room had suddenly turned on him.

Pausey seemed to think this was a trick question, and he glanced uncertainly at Bell, who nodded for him to do as Tyler had requested.

Jack stood up and quickly crossed to the TV. Turning to face his audience, who were all staring at him expectantly, he tapped the screen. "One of them just dumped a can of spray paint into a bin," he said. "Can I just confirm that we've already seized it for fingerprinting?"

Silence.

Bell looked at Pausey, who looked at Susie Sergeant, who looked blank.

"Susie?" Jack asked.

She glanced sideways at Graham Pausey with an apologetic look on her face. "I'm afraid that Hackney Downs was checked out by divisional robbery squad officers, not by us," she said reluctantly.

Tyler fumed. *Bloody typical.* He pivoted towards Mercer, who stared at him unblinkingly, his pale features devoid of expression. There was something very creepy about his corpse-like face, Jack decided. "Is the boy who did the spraying one of the three people you've identified from viewing the footage, Gavin?"

The neighbourhood skipper shook his head unemotionally. "No, sir."

Tyler fixed Ian Bell with a hard stare. "I'll need you to send someone straight over there to retrieve it." A statement, not a request.

Bell nodded, clearly embarrassed by the oversight. "It'll be done as soon as the briefing's over," he promised.

As he returned to his seat, Jack's phone vibrated yet again. He rolled his eyes. Another message from Maitland.

Please, Jack. I don't have anyone else I can speak to.

Eddie was resorting to emotional blackmail now. Great! Against his better judgement Tyler found himself typing out: *Okay. Call me in the morning.*

Somehow, even before he pressed the send button, he knew he'd end up regretting having acquiesced to Eddie's request.

———

It was coming up to half past nine, and the local news bulletin was just drawing to an end. Apart from Dotty, Marcel, and Leroy Apeloko, the TV room in the children's home was completely deserted. It had been jam-packed a half-hour earlier but, within seconds of Dotty changing the channel to BBC1 so that she could watch the nine o'clock news, everyone else had wandered off to sort out their school stuff for the morning and get themselves ready for bed. It was an old trick and it never failed. Tell them they had to go to bed and there would be universal resistance; put something boring on the box and they couldn't escape to the sanctity of their rooms quickly enough. Marcel and Leroy had wised up to this tactic ages ago, but the youngsters still had a lot to learn.

"It's not like you two to watch the news," Dotty said, viewing the two teenagers with suspicion.

"Trying to broaden our horizons, miss," Leroy told her with a grin.

Marcel said nothing, just sat there with his eyes glued to the screen. The train steaming at Clapton had been featured, and a smartly dressed female presenter had stood outside the station, informing viewers all about the terrible incident that had left an old man dead and a woman hospitalised with life threatening injuries. The names of the two victims hadn't been released yet, but there had been quotes from eye-witnesses who had described the marauding robbers as 'a pack of wild savages', 'running amok like animals', and 'low-life vermin.'

His mind was reeling. The woman he had shanked was still alive; that was good. It meant that he wasn't a murderer – at least not yet. Hopefully, she would pull through and he never would be.

The posh sounding TV presenter had proclaimed that the police were examining CCTV from the station and surrounding area, and they were very hopeful of identifying the culprits from that.

Marcel's mind raced as he considered the worrying implications of her words. He had carefully wiped down the kitchen knife before dumping it in the bin at the bottom of Ziggy's block, so even if the Feds found it, they would never be able to link it to him.

He had removed all the clothing he'd worn at the time of the steaming and wrapped it up in a black bin liner he'd taken from the kitchen cupboard. Leroy had taken it to his girlfriend's house in nearby Middleton Road for him a little earlier. They were going to put it in a metal dustbin and burn it tomorrow, while her parents were out at work.

That only left the Rolex to take care of.

It was currently burning a hole in his pocket, but he couldn't risk stowing it away in his room in case the Feds searched it. He couldn't ask Leroy to look after it for him either. Leroy wasn't as streetwise as Marcel; he was a bookworm who studied really hard at school. He wanted to make something of his life by working for it, not by *tiefing* or selling drugs. He had never run with the gang and, as far as Marcel was aware, had never even been arrested. If the Feds put him under pressure, he would immediately fold.

Marcel was at a loss over what to do with the damned watch. If he couldn't hide it in his room, and he couldn't trust Leroy to look after it for him, what the hell was he going to do? If he stashed it in one of the home's many communal areas, there was a good chance that one of the other residents or – even worse – a member of staff might find it. That would be disastrous. And if the Feds did come looking for him, they would probably search the entire premises anyway. Well, everywhere apart from…

A sly smile crept onto his face. They would never dream of looking *there*. He stood up, made a point of yawning. "Right, miss, I'm off to bed."

Dotty stared at him in shock. "Really? But it's only half past nine. Are you feeling ill or something?"

He forced a carefree smile onto his face. "Nah, miss. I'm fine, but I need my beauty sleep, innit."

He sauntered over to Leroy and extended his arm so that they could bump fists. "Night bro," he said, giving his friend a knowing look. "See you in the morning."

As he left the room, Dotty stood up and followed him.

"Marcel, can I have a quick word?" she asked when they were alone in the hall.

Her voice was taut with worry, and he turned around with a heavy sigh of exasperation, fully expecting her to launch into yet another one of her boring lectures about his having bunked off from school again. "What is it miss?"

Instead of berating him about wasted educational opportunities, Dotty stared up into his face, her hazel eyes burning into his. She placed a hand on his arm and squeezed it gently, and when she spoke, there was no mistaking the fear in her voice. "Marcel, my love, please tell me you didn't have anything to do with that awful incident at the train station."

Marcel laughed dismissively, but he couldn't hold her eye. "Nah, course not. I'm a good boy, miss."

Dotty nodded and tried to smile, but failed miserably. "I know you're a good boy," she told him with a brittle laugh. "But the people you're hanging around with aren't, and I'm really worried that if you carry on mixing with them, you're going to end up turning out just like them."

He opened his mouth to protest, but a raised hand from her silenced him. "I'll be completely honest with you, Marcel. It's got to the point where, every time you leave this building, I'm terrified that the next time I see you, you'll either be lying in a coffin or locked up behind bars."

Tears appeared in her eyes, and she moved forward to give him a big hug, almost crushing him despite only being half his size. "Now go and get yourself ready for bed," she said as she released him, "and don't forget to clean your teeth."

Feeling strangely unsettled by Dotty's ominous words, Marcel went up to the first floor and walked quietly along the corridor to the room at the very end. Looking around to make sure that no one was watching, he tried the door handle. Turning it slowly, so as not to make any noise, he pushed it open and peered into the darkness within.

Closing the door behind him, he stood still for a few moments, letting his eyes acclimatise to the darkness. He didn't dare turn the light on in case it alerted anyone to his unauthorised presence.

Marcel had been inside Dotty's room several times before, but never alone. On previous occasions, he had accompanied her there in order to have an item that had been confiscated from him due to his bad behaviour restored.

Dotty was one of the home's two resident staff members. Unlike her sour-faced colleague, Jane Pringle, who had absolutely no faith in any of the children, Dotty had always insisted on leaving her room unlocked to demonstrate that she trusted her young charges completely. In fact, Marcel had recently overheard her boasting to Jane that, in the five years she had been working here, no one had ever broken into her room to steal anything. He doubted anyone had ever broken into her room to leave anything either, but that was about to change.

Marcel knew exactly where he was going to leave the watch, which was now wrapped in a clear cellophane, self-sealing food bag; another item he had purloined from the kitchen. Tiptoeing over to the huge Yucca plant that stood in the far corner, opposite the room's single bed, he removed the Rolex from his pocket. He bent down and, being as careful as he could not to leave a tell-tail trail of dirt all over the floor, scraped out a deep hole in the soil with his fingers.

Apart from his waste of space brother, Dotty was the closest thing that Marcel had to family, and he really didn't like the idea of involving her in one of his illicit schemes, but what else could he do under the circumstances?

After tucking the watch into the hole, he replaced the earth and levelled it off. When he was finished, he stood up and admired his handiwork. "That should do the job," he muttered to himself as he brushed the last residue of dirt from his hands.

————

Ziggy and Leanne were curled up together on the sofa, watching TV, when the street door exploded inwards with a loud bang, which is the way doors generally react when they've just been struck by a heavy battering ram.

"What the fuck…?" Ziggy exclaimed, almost jumping out of his skin. Leanne reacted by wrapping her arms around him and hanging on like a limpet, screaming so loudly that it made his ears ring.

Almost immediately, yells of "POLICE!" were interspersed with the sound of booted feet pounding along the flat's narrow corridor towards the lounge.

There were more shouts of, "POLICE! POLICE!" as the lounge door crashed inwards, banging into the wall, and half dozen burly policemen, all wearing flame retardant public order overalls, dark blue NATO crash helmets with the visors pulled down, and carrying riot shields, spilled into the room.

The lead officer stopped when he spotted the flat's two occupants clinging to each other on the sofa. "STAY WHERE YOU ARE!" he called out.

At which point, lots of things seemed to happen at once.

"Kitchen clear!" someone called.

"Bedroom clear!" another shouted.

"Bathroom clear!" a third voice decreed.

While all this was going on, Leanne jumped to her feet, her hands instinctively springing to her mouth as she started jumping up and down and screaming hysterically.

Ziggy jumped up too, only he was swearing not screaming. In one fluid move, he reached behind the sofa and grabbed the handle of the baseball bat he kept hidden there in case of emergencies. Snarling at them, he drew it back over his shoulder in readiness to take a swing.

It wasn't a particularly wise move on his part.

The first two policemen were carrying long rectangular shields and, as Ziggy raised the bat, they interlocked these and braced themselves to repel his attack. The three officers immediately behind them were all carrying short, circular shields in their left hands and batons in their right. They instantly took up position behind their colleagues, ready to move forward when the time came. "Well, this is a nice way to spend an evening," one of them said casually as he readied himself for the onslaught.

It was a classic 'Violent Man' scenario, something that all Public Order Trained officers practiced during their regular trips to the POTC – Public Order Training Centre – in Hounslow, West London.

Letting out a frenetic scream, Ziggy ran at them, swinging wildly with the bat, but instead of retreating as he'd expected them to, they moved forward to meet him, absorbing the impact of the heavy base-ball bat strikes on the hard plastic shields. In the tight confines of the flat, every hit that landed sounded like a gunshot.

BAM! BAM! BAM!

Keeping their heads down, the TSG officers advanced slowly and steadily, herding Ziggy into a corner of the room. They were completely unperturbed by the blows that clattered into their shields and, as Ziggy began to tire, they continued to shunt him backwards by thrusting the shields into him, repeating this move over and over again.

"STAND STILL! STOP FIGHTING! STOP RESISTING!"

Ziggy carried on swinging for all he was worth.

As soon as the five-man shield unit moved past the spot where Leanne was standing, two of the officers who had remained in the corridor rushed forward, grabbed her wrists and frogmarched her out of the room.

"Gerroff! I aint done nothing!" she protested as she was placed in handcuffs and escorted from the flat.

Inside the lounge, the two officers with the long shields had managed to pin Ziggy against the far wall. Unable to swing the bat anymore, he dropped it and started banging his fists against the shields, screaming and raging at the officers facing him.

To no one's surprise, the punches proved even less effective than the bat.

"Don't be a twat," one of the officers on the long shields told him. "You're gonna bust up your hands if you carry on like that."

"Give it a rest, mate, you're embarrassing yourself," the other one chipped in. "My nan punches harder than that, and she's eighty-two."

Before long, Ziggy started to run out of steam, at which point the skipper in charge of the shield unit instructed the three supporting officers to move in and secure the suspect. They did this expertly, taking control of Ziggy's arms and head. As soon as the shields moved aside, they dragged him face down onto the floor. Ziggy tried to resist, but he was outnumbered and outclassed, and the arresting officers quickly overwhelmed him, applying handcuffs and ankle restraints to stop him from thrashing about.

But Ziggy wasn't quite finished yet. With no other way of lashing out at his captors, he started spitting at them.

"Stop doing that, you dirty git!" one of the officers growled. Then, calmer, "Xander Mason, I'm arresting you on suspicion of the murder of Stanley Cotton, and the attempted murder of Jenny Parker. These offences were committed during a group steaming at Clapton train station earlier today." He cautioned Ziggy and asked if he understood, to which Ziggy replied, "Fuck you, motherfucker."

The officer raised his visor. "I'll take that as a yes, shall I?" he asked in a highly irreverent tone.

————

Ian Bell finished the call and turned to address Jack Tyler and Andy Quinlan, who were both sitting with him in his office on the first floor of Stoke Newington police station.

"That was Cerebral, calling to let us know that Ziggy's in custody."

"Cerebral?" Quinlan asked, looking confused. Having only just arrived from The Yard, he had missed the earlier introductions.

"Cerebral Pausey," Bell explained. "He's one of my DSs."

Quinlan glanced questioningly at Jack, who just shrugged.

"It's his nickname," Bell explained with a cheeky grin. Almost immediately, he wilted under the disapproving glare he received from Quinlan, who clearly didn't think it was an appropriate sobriquet for someone to have. "Er–right–moving on. Have you heard from either of your officers yet, sir?" he asked Tyler.

With three separate addresses to search, their resources had been pooled in order to cover more ground. Graham Pausey had been sent to Ziggy's address as he'd already had a number of previous dealings with the boy and knew him well. Susie Sergeant had been tasked to oversee the raid on Switch's flat, and Steve Bull had been despatched to the home of, Curtis Bright, the third suspect Gavin Mercer had identified.

"No," Jack said. "I haven't heard from them yet, but as all three addresses were being hit simultaneously, we should be getting an update any minute now."

As if on cue, his mobile started ringing. Caller ID told him it was Steve Bull.

"How did you get on, Steve?" Tyler asked without preamble.

"*Yep. We've got one in custody, boss,*" Bull said.

In the background, it sounded like it was all kicking off.

"*AAARGH! Get off me! This is police brutality – I want my fucking lawyer.*"

"Is everything alright there?" Jack asked, concerned.

"*Fine,*" Bull assured him. "*He's just a bit vocal.*"

More shouting and struggling was heard.

"*You can't treat me like this – I'm a juvenile! I know my rights!*"

"*Yeah, well, you've got the right to shut up, so why don't you exercise it you annoying little toad?*" A voice Tyler didn't recognise, so presumably one of the TSG officers.

"Are you sure everything's under control?" Tyler asked as a woman started screaming in the background.

"*What? I can't hear you! – Will you please be quiet! I'm trying to have a conversation!*"

More shouting and screaming. A surprised yell of, "*Look out!*" Crashing and grunting, and then the sound of glass breaking.

Then everything went quiet.

"Steve! Steve! Are you there, mate?"

"*Sorry about that,*" Bull said a few moments later. "*The little sod managed to wriggle out of his handcuffs and they had to restrain him again.*"

"How the hell did he manage that?" Jack asked.

"*Turns out the horrible little cretin has got double jointed thumbs,*" Bull said, sounding utterly revolted. "*He can dislocate them at will, making his hands as thin as his wrists. Anyway, the place is secure now, and Curtis Bright – he's more like Curtis dim if you ask me – is in custody. Once I calm his poor old mum down, I'll get the search started. Any news on the others?*"

"Ziggy's in custody. We're still waiting to hear how Susie got on at Brown's place. Let me know if you find anything incriminating."

"*Will do, boss,*" Bull promised.

As Tyler was feeding Bull's update into the others, his phone rang again.

It was Susie.

"Here we go," Tyler said. "Hopefully, she's calling to say we've bagged three out of three."

"*Boss, we've lucked out,*" Susie told him, sounding totally gutted. "*We spoke to his long-suffering neighbour, who reckons Brown came home an hour or so earlier, but left again about fifteen minutes later.*"

Tyler looked at the others and shook his head, letting them know it wasn't good news. "Any idea where he might have gone?" he asked hopefully.

"*None,*" she told him, "*but the place is secure, and we're going to start searching it as soon as our exhibits officer arrives.*"

Tyler considered this. Section 17 PACE gave them a power to enter premises without warrant in order to arrest someone who was wanted for an offence. Once that person was in custody, Section 32 PACE kicked in; this gave them authority to search any premises that the detainee was in, either at the time of his arrest or immediately before, without a warrant. However, as Brown hadn't been arrested, they had no power to search, unless they wanted to rely on Common Law, but to invoke that, they would have to declare the flat a crime scene. The problem was, if they went down that route and the lawfulness of the search was successfully challenged at court, any evidence that had been found would be excluded.

Tyler sighed miserably. "Susie, you're not gonna like this, but I want you to hold off on the search until we get a Section 8 PACE warrant."

"*What? But surely we can just do it under Common Law and – *"

"Too risky," Tyler said, cutting her off. "Have one of the locals stand on the door and come back to GN and sort out a warrant."

"*But, sir…!*"

"No."

A sulky harrumph. "*Okay. Fine. I'll be back in fifteen minutes.*" She hung up without saying goodbye.

CHAPTER FOURTEEN

ARGUMENTS

The car pulled into the hotel forecourt and glided to a halt. "Here we are then, mate," the driver said, turning to look over his shoulder at Tyson Meeks. "This'll be your new home for a couple of days, until we can sort out something a bit more permanent for you further afield."

Meeks grunted sullenly. He didn't like the two anonymous looking men from witness protection. "What am I gonna do for food and clothing while I'm here?" he demanded petulantly. They hadn't even allowed him to go home and pack some things – said it was too risky in case Livingstone had someone watching the address, ready to tail him off if he went back there.

"Don't worry about that," the unshaven passenger said. He was the one in charge. "This hotel does great food, and we'll open a tab for you – for food only, not alcohol, so don't take the piss, and we've got all your measurements, so we'll pick you up some new underwear and a couple of T-shirts tomorrow morning. That will have to do you until we can sort you out a new wardrobe."

"This is shit, bruv," Meeks complained. "I thought you were going to look after me, not drop me off at a dingy hotel and leave me on my own without any cash or supplies."

The passenger's eyes hardened. "Listen, Tyson," he said, and there was a trace of annoyance in his voice. "Firstly, this is an expensive four star hotel, and you'll be very comfortable here." More comfortable than he'd be at the dump he currently lived in, that was for sure. "Secondly, as I'm sure you can appreciate, this is all a bit last minute, and it will take us a couple of days to get things properly sorted. In the meantime, you're going to have to be patient and bear with us. Maybe, instead of being so negative, you should remind yourself that the Metropolitan Police Service is about to spend a small fortune on keeping you safe. You know as well as I do that, without our help, you would probably end up dead in a ditch before the week was out."

Meeks opened his mouth to fire off a retort, but then it occurred to him that the man was probably right. "Whatever," he said, crossing his arms sulkily.

The passenger held out his hand.

Meeks stared at it suspiciously. Did the Fed think he was going to shake it?

A sigh of impatience. "Hand it over, Tyson."

Meeks sucked through his teeth. "Hand what over?" He knew full well what the man wanted, but he'd been really hoping the Fed would have forgotten all about it by the time they got here.

"When we collected you from the other officers, I made it clear that you would have to hand over your phone as soon as we reached the hotel." There was something in the Fed's bored tone that suggested he had this same pointless discussion with every witness that they took into protective custody. "So, stop wasting my time and hand it over."

―――――

DC Kevin Murray pulled up at the base of the tower block, parking next to one of the TSG carriers. Some of the local residents had obviously paid the vehicle a visit while it was unattended, because the windows had been well and truly bombarded with eggs.

Seeing the state of the carrier, Murray decided that it might be prudent to reposition his pool car, just in case the yobs returned with more eggs. He reversed a little way back, coming to a stop by the bin room at the side of the building.

"Well, this place is a proper shithole," he observed.

"It's not *that* bad," Copeland said.

They were there to act as exhibits officers for the searches at Mason and Brown's flats.

Murray took a moment to let his eyes wander around the estate. The ugly grey monstrosity resembled a badly put together Meccano set. "It really is," he said. Turning the ignition off, he unclipped his seatbelt and let out a melancholy sigh. "Why don't they just build something aesthetically pleasing for a change, and stop dumping people in these concrete hellholes?"

Copeland shrugged, still not getting it. "Some of these sprawling council estates won design awards when they were first erected."

Murray baulked at that. "Surely not! Those bloody tower blocks look like giant tomb stones"

"It's a well-known fact."

"Well, George, if you want my opinion–"

"Which I don't."

"–I can't imagine anyone giving this dump a design award unless they were getting a massive bung for doing so or playing a cruel joke on someone." Murray shuddered. "Jesus. Imagine growing up here. It's no wonder that half of them turn to crime, and the rest become life-long victims."

They alighted the car, removed their respective exhibit bags from the boot, and walked towards the block's entrance, keeping a watchful eye out in case anything was thrown at them from above. "Knowing my luck, all the wheels will have been nicked and we'll find it propped up on bricks by the time we come back," Murray said, clicking the fob to activate the central locking.

The building's foyer was every bit as bleak as its hideous exterior, and the moment they stepped inside, their nostrils were assailed by the throat burning aroma of urine overlaid with pine scented disinfectant.

Copeland turned his nose up. "Smells lovely in here, doesn't it?"

"Very fragrant," Murray agreed as he jabbed the call button for the lift. "I bet the pong's even worse inside there," he predicted.

"I'll take my chances," Copeland told him. "There's no way I'm lugging this heavy bag all the way up the stairs."

Murray rolled his eyes. "You're such a lazy sod. It's no wonder you're so fat."

"This is just relaxed muscle," Copeland insisted, rubbing his wobbly stomach with his free hand.

Murray chuckled at the sight, but his good humour soon evaporated. "This search is going to be a pain in the arse, and it's going to take forever," he complained.

"With a bit of luck it won't take too long, seeing as we've got photos of what they were all wearing."

A selection of stills had been printed off from the Hackney Downs CCTV, and the images clearly showed the clothing that all ten suspects had worn.

"Don't be daft," Murray snorted as the lift arrived. "You know it'll still take ages because nothing ever goes smoothly for us."

"True," Copeland agreed with a wry smile.

The doors opened and Susan Sergeant strode out. From her fierce demeanour, it was obvious that she had the raging hump. "Which of you two degenerates was supposed to be searching Brown's flat?" she demanded, glowering at each of them in turn.

Copeland and Murray exchanged wary glances, each wondering what had happened to put her in such a foul mood.

She huffed impatiently. "Well?"

"That'll be me," Murray said, wishing it wasn't.

"Well, don't bother going up there yet," she told him crossly. "I've got to get a sodding search warrant first."

Murray turned to Copeland and flashed him a knowing look. "See, I told you that nothing ever goes smoothly."

Picking up his bag, Copeland sidled past them and stepped into the lift. "You were also right about the smell in here being worse than out there," he said, gagging at the stench. As the doors closed, he waved farewell to Murray.

Without another word, Susie spun on her heels and stormed off.

Murray dutifully followed, narrow shoulders sagging despondently. "What do you want me to do instead?" he asked when they reached his car. "I came here with Tubby Copeland, so I can't just bugger off and leave him."

"That's okay," Susie said, and nodded towards the bins at the base of the tower block. "You can crack on with searching those till I get back."

Murray's face dropped. "What? Oh, for goodness sa– "

Susie raised a warning finger so quickly that he flinched. "Don't!" she warned, mouth compressed in anger. "I am *not* in the mood to listen to your whinging tonight."

Murray sucked in air as though he she had just slapped him. "I don't ever whinge!" he said, indignantly.

"Yes, Kevin. You do. In fact, that's *all* you ever bloody do." She held her right hand up with fingers and thumb pinched together and pointing them towards him like a puppet's head. Opening and closing them every time she spoke, she said, "Whinge. Whinge. Whinge!"

Murray dropped his exhibits bag on the floor and fixed her with a contemptuous stare. "How dare you!" he hissed, oozing outrage from every pore.

"Whinge! Whinge! Whinge!" she repeated, her fingers opening and closing in sync.

Murray closed his eyes and took a deep breath, exhaling ultra-slowly like a Zen monk centring himself. Opening his eyes again, his face crystallised into a mask of pure disdain. He stood erect and jutted his chin out haughtily. "Okay. Fine," he said, his voice adopting the aloof tone of someone who knows they have the moral high-ground and have, therefore, already won the argument. "Be like that. I'm not even going to dignify your unfair, and frankly pathetic, accusation with a response."

"That'll make a pleasant change," she told him, smiling cattily.

Murray pulled open his exhibit bag and angrily withdrew a sealed set of barrier clothing, which he proceeded to rip open with vigour. "Have it your way. I'll make a start on searching the horrible smelly bins right now, in the dark, all on my own, not that you'll hear a word of complaint from me."

"Good," Susie said, not an ounce of sympathy in her voice.

Murray thrust a leg into a pair of white overalls, nearly falling over in the process. "But just for the record," he said as she turned to leave, "I do *not* whinge."

"You're whinging now," she called out as she walked away.

"Gah!" he replied, thrusting his other leg into the overalls so viciously that he ripped a hole straight through the material.

————

Devon Brown, better known as Switch to his HSB homies, stood in the shadows at the edge of the estate, watching the entrance to his tower block like a hawk.

He had just returned from his girlfriend's place in Dalston Lane. The visit had been cut short by one of their increasingly frequent arguments. It hadn't helped that, after the beating from Ziggy, he'd been in a foul mood and was just itching for an excuse to take it out on someone else.

As he stood there, his hand wandered to the side of his face and he winced with pain. His lower lip had swollen to twice its normal size, making it difficult to speak normally. He gingerly rolled his tongue around the inside of his mouth, grateful that none of his teeth had been loosened in the attack. His head, and the side of his body, ached like hell from the shoeing Ziggy had given him. His pride hurt even more, and he was furious that Marcel had been there to witness his thrashing.

He had intended to take some paracetamol and then spend a little time chilling out on his PlayStation before going to bed, but his plans had been scuppered the moment he'd spotted the four Fed carriers parked up at the base of his block.

Switch had lived on the Holly Street Estate all his life, and it was a fairly common sight to see dem Boydem rock up in strength to carry out raids or searches. However, given what he had been involved in earlier, the sight of the TSG carriers sitting outside his tower block was deeply troubling, and it had set loud alarm bells ringing inside his head. Just to be safe, he'd decided to hang back for a while and observe what was going on before proceeding any further.

When they dragged Ziggy out a few minutes later, his hands and feet bound like he was some sort of animal, Switch swore under his breath. If dem Boydem had come for Ziggy, the odds were that they would be looking for him as well.

As the carrier drove off, Switch pulled out his mobile and dialled his girlfriend's number.

"Yo! Alicia, it's me."

"*What?*" she said frostily.

Gritting his teeth, he forced a smile into his voice and tried to sound contrite. "Look, I'm sorry for being such a dick earlier, babes. I didn't mean it."

"*You should be sorry, too,*" she replied stiffly.

Switch rolled his eyes. Why did women always end up sulking after an argument with their boyfriends? Why couldn't they just take it on the chin and move on?

"Look, I need a favour. Can I come and stay at yours for the night?"

"*No, you can't!*" Her voice wasn't just indignant, it was ice cold.

"Please, Alicia… I wouldn't ask if it wasn't important." He was glad that none of the boys he ran with could hear him begging her like that. They would have thought him weak, and it would have jeopardized his standing within the group.

"*Why would you even ask me if you could do that? You know my parents would never allow it.*" A pause while she thought this through, followed by an angry sigh as she reached the inevitable conclusion. "*Are you in trouble again, Devon? Because I told you after the last time, I don't wanna be involved with no gangsta boy.*"

He hesitated, wondering how much to tell her. "It's complicated," he said, angry that he should even have to justify himself. "Dem Boyden are raiding my ends, rounding up some of the people I hang with, innit."

"*So?*"

He sucked through his teeth, and immediately grimaced at the pain it caused his battered face. Bitch was giving him proper attitude now, and her lack of respect was making him seriously angry. "You don't wanna be talking to me like that," he warned. Girl or not, he had shanked people for saying less.

"*Don't threaten me, Devon,*" she retaliated feistily. "*I only asked you why you suddenly wanted to stay round here when you never have before.*"

He wanted to shout abuse at her, but he knew she would just hang up on him if he did. "Look, I just need somewhere I can lay low for a couple of days while I figure some shit out, that's all. Ask your parents if I can stay over. I don't mind sleeping on the couch."

There was silence at the other end of the line, and he could picture her standing there, brooding at him for having the gall to ask such a thing. And then he heard her doorbell ring.

"*Hang on a minute,*" she told him. "*There's someone at the door.*"

"Don't answer it," he ordered, but she was no longer listening to him.

"*I'll get it mum,*" he heard her shout.

Switch sucked through his teeth again, ignoring the pain it caused him. "I'll get it mum," he mimicked in a girly squeal.

He heard Alicia's footsteps echoing along the corridor, and then the sound of the latch turning as she opened the door.

Her voice, hostile and worried. "*Can I help you?*"

A gruff sounding male, unmistakeably a Fed. "*We're looking for Devon Brown.*"

Switch felt his stomach constrict into a tight ball. He held his breath as he listened, praying that the dumb bitch wouldn't say anything stupid.

"*He's not here,*" she said, defiantly.

"*When was the last time you saw him?*"

A pause. Then her voice again, hesitant and fearful. "*He came round earlier. Left about half an hour ago, said he was going home. Why? What's he done?*"

"*We have reason to believe he was involved in an incident at Clapton train station earlier today,*" the Fed said, trying to be all cryptic.

"*Clapton train... you mean the murder I saw on the news?*"

It was the Fed's turn to pause now. "*I'm afraid so. If you hear from him, please contact me on this number.*"

Switch heard the door slam, and then she was back on the line, her voice trembling with rage. *"I've just had the police here looking for you,"* she seethed. *"They reckon you were involved in that steaming at Clapton, the one where the old man was shanked to death. That's why you wanted to come here, innit? You're on the run for murder!"*

"Alicia, I–"

"NO! I don't want to hear it! I don't want anything more to do with you or your sick gangsta friends. I told you that if you didn't stop running with them, I'd leave you." Her voice had become increasingly emotional during the rant, and now she was starting to get tearful. *"Well, you've obviously made your fucking choice, so stay away from me from now on."*

"Babes! Please! I–"

She hung up on him.

"Fucking bitch!" he exclaimed, staring at the phone in disbelief.

Pacing up and down, he scrolled through the address book in his phone until he found his cousin's number. He hated doing this, but he was all out of options. "Come on, come on, pick up…"

"Wagwan," followed by a long exhalation.

"Gunz, is that you, man?"

"Who's this?" The voice was slurred. Knowing Gunz, he was stoned out of his head as usual.

"It's Switch, man. Your fucking cousin!"

"Oh yeah, auntie Pauline's son. What you calling my digits for, bruv?"

"Cause I'm in trouble, cuz," Switch blurted out, and then mentally kicked himself for doing so. He couldn't let Gunz think he was weak, not if he wanted the man's respect. Putting a bit of swagger into his voice, he started over again. "Some serious shit went down today, bruv, and now the Feds are after me, so I need somewhere to lay low till it all blows over, ya get me?"

At the other end of the phone, he heard laughter, cruel and mocking. *"Whatcha do, little boy? Get caught shoplifting again?"*

Switch didn't like people making fun of him. "Nah, bruv, I killed someone, innit," he boasted. *Which is more than you've ever fucking done,* he thought.

———

Wearing a stiflingly hot set of Tyvek overalls, Murray felt as though he was slowly melting as he entered the dimly lit bin room.

According to the timetable on the door, the refuse collectors had emptied the block's three large communal bins two days ago. With any luck, that meant there wouldn't be too much new trash for him to wade through. As he expected, the bin sitting directly beneath the rubbish chute was the fullest of the three, so he decided to tackle that one first.

The green sign on the door had stipulated that residents were only allowed to use the chute between 8 a.m. and 8 p.m., so as not to disturb the people living next to it, but Murray doubted many of the people living here gave a toss about disturbing their neighbours.

He slid into the bin, sweat dripping from every pore. "I'll be half a stone lighter by the time I finish here," he grumbled to himself.

Murray was soon up to his knees in rotting food, babies' nappies, dog excrement, and a host of other degradable items that were equally slimy and disgusting. He slowly worked his way through it all, manually examining each and every manky item he came across, keeping one ear cocked for any strange sounds that might indicate a sudden influx of waste was about to drop from the gaping mouth of the rubbish chute above his head. It took him the best part of an hour to search the bin properly, and he spent the majority of the time cursing Susie for making him do it in the dark.

"Well, that was a complete and utter waste of my time," he complained as he clambered out of the sludge infested bin, covered in sweat and breathing heavily from his exertions.

A couple of flies seemed to have taken a shine to him, and they followed him out of the bin room, unperturbed by his constant attempts to swat them away.

Murray pulled off the two pairs of nitrile gloves he wore, only to find that the skin on his hands now resembled dried prunes. Then he unzipped his white overalls and flapped the sides to get some air circulating. His armpits were kicking up pretty badly, and he recoiled at the rank odour that wafted out to assail his nostrils.

Wishing that he'd brought some antiperspirant with him, Murray unlocked his pool car, lowered his Victoria mask, and gratefully took a long swig of fizzy water from the bottle he'd left inside. The mineral water was tepid, but it was wet, and that was all that mattered.

When he'd finished, he looked up at the second bin with apprehension. "Please don't be as smelly as your mate," he implored it.

Pulling his mask back up, he donned new gloves, zipped his overalls up, and then climbed up the side of the metal bin. Perched precariously on the top, with one leg dangling down into the bin, he shone his torch into the opening. To his delight, apart from a couple of bulging black bin liners, it was completely empty. "This is more like it," he muttered as he swung his other leg over the side and carefully lowered himself down.

The first bag he ripped open contained general household rubbish. He quickly discarded this and moved onto the second bag. As he picked it up, something glinted in the darkness beneath it.

"Hello, hello… what have we got here?" he said, placing the bag to one side and shining the beam of his torch on the metallic floor of the bin.

Beneath his mask, a huge grin broke out. "Well, well, well," he purred. "Look what I've found."

In the centre of the yellow beam, its blade gleaming as it reflected the torch light, there lay a medium sized kitchen knife with a polished black handle. There was no obvious sign of blood on it, but that could just mean that it had been wiped clean by whoever had dumped it there. Reaching inside his white coveralls, and braving the pong that immediately escaped from his armpits, Murray extracted his mobile phone and dialled Susie Sergeant's number.

CHAPTER FIFTEEN

Thursday 27th May 1999
MEETINGS

The office meeting for Operation Jacobstow, the computer generated name that had been assigned to the murder of the four Turks, began promptly at 8 a.m.

As he got the ball rolling, Jack Tyler found himself thinking about an almost identical meeting that was being simultaneously conducted a little further along the corridor. That one was being chaired by DCI Quinlan, and the subject under discussion was Operation Jaywick, the investigation into the murder of Stanley Cotton and the attempted murder of Jenny Parker.

Tyler had a vested interest in both enquiries, albeit for very different reasons, and he dearly wished that he could split himself in two so that he could attend both of them at once. However, he couldn't, and as this was the case he had been charged with investigating, it was imperative that he give it his full and undivided attention. Having suitably chastised himself for being distracted, he tried to blot all thoughts of the other investigation out of his mind, at least for the time being.

"Okay, let's crack on," he told the assembled detectives.

In addition to his own team and CSM Kennedy, they had been joined by the four SO7 detectives: Christine Taylor, Coleen Perry, Gurjit Singh, and Geoff Coles.

Also present, and looking uncomfortable in a grey, pinstriped business suit from C&A, was PC Fatma Osman, the Turkish speaking Family Liaison Officer who had been temporarily seconded from Stoke Newington in order to facilitate communication with the families and friends of the four deceased racketeers.

Fatma was a pretty girl; slim, with olive skin and shoulder length hair that was worn in a braided ponytail. She had a pleasant, enquiring face, and intelligent brown eyes. Jack could feel them on him as she sat there, studying him intently.

After getting the newcomers to introduce themselves, and welcoming them all into the fold, he turned to the business at hand.

"We're going to kick off by having a quick run through of where we are," he said, making a conscious effort to sound upbeat. "Let's start with forensics. Juliet, can you confirm that the scene has been closed down?"

As per normal, Kennedy was spruced up like she was about to have tea with the Queen, and not attending a meeting with a load of grumpy detectives. "Yes, the scene's all done and dusted," she informed him cheerfully. "It's been photographed and POLSA searched, and the ballistic expert has done his bit. The road was reopened late yesterday afternoon, and if you walked past it now, you would never know that four men were gunned down there a couple of days ago. The Turk's Mercedes was lifted to Charlton Car Pound, and a colleague examined it for me yesterday afternoon. It's being pulled apart by POLSA this morning, but I don't anticipate them finding anything too exciting."

"What about the car that the shooters burnt out on that wasteland in Tottenham, near the A406?" he asked next.

Juliet patted her hair, making sure that nothing was out of place. "Again, taken to Charlton yesterday. It was examined by the local SOCO, but it was just a burnt out husk, so nothing useful for us from a forensic perspective. We did manage to get the Vehicle Identification Number from the chassis though, so that's something I suppose."

Tyler turned to Dean Fletcher. "What can you tell me about the car, Deano?"

Fletcher donned his reading glasses and studied the PNC printout. "It was a Ford Mondeo, stolen from Highbury on the day of the murders. I've checked the crime report, but it's very sparse. Just says the keeper left it locked and unattended when he came home from work the previous night and, when he went to use it the following morning, it was gone. Nothing in the report to say whether the locals checked for CCTV or not."

Tyler scanned the room until his eyes locked in on Franklin. "Colin, get the details from Dean, and then grab all the CCTV from the surrounding area for the relevant times, please."

Franklin made a hurried note in his daybook. "Will do, boss."

DS Matt Blake, a rugged looking man in his early thirties, was the team's Office Manager. As Franklin finished speaking he waved a hand to get Tyler's attention. "Boss, while we're on the subject of CCTV, there's a message from DC Murray stating that the local borough recently installed covert CCTV in an underpass on the A406. It's there to monitor the comings and goings at a Traveller site adjacent to the wasteland where the Mondeo was burnt out. I spoke to the DS who organised this last night, and she said that if Colin wants to give her a bell after eleven o'clock this morning, she'll arrange for him to have access to it. She's quite happy to provide us with a copy of anything that's relevant to our enquiry."

Franklin made another note. "I'll get the details from you after the meeting," he told Blake, who responded by giving him a thumbs up.

"We'll come back to CCTV later," Tyler told them, "but for now, let's carry on with forensics. I understand that the three men in the car with Erkan Dengiz have now been formally identified?"

Juliet nodded. "That's right, Jack. The fingerprints came in yesterday evening, albeit much later than expected. Their names are…" she checked her notes "… Kerim Bucak, Halil Kocadag, and Kemal Yucel – he was the driver."

"Have you started researching them yet, Deano?" Tyler asked.

"Wendy's doing it," Fletcher responded, indicating his fellow researcher with a jut of his chin.

DC Wendy Blake smiled shyly. It always made her uncomfortable when she was required to contribute during a meeting, and she squirmed in her chair self-consciously. "So far, it looks like they're low-level muscle, with lots of form for the sort of things you would expect. Like Dengiz, they're all affiliated to Abdullah Goren's crime syndicate."

"Thank you Wendy," Tyler said with a grateful smile. "What about the sidearms they were carrying?" This question was addressed to Kennedy. "We're happy that none of them were fired, aren't we?"

"We are," she told him. "They were all still holstered, and dead men don't generally tend to re-holster their weapons at the end of a gunfight, at least not in my experience."

Tyler turned to George Copeland, who was looking a little jaded around the edges after a late night spent searching Xander Mason's address in Hackney. "George, are you making an exhibits run up to the lab today?"

Stifling a yawn, Copeland shook his head. "I'm gonna be tucked up for the next couple of days attending the SPMs with Mr Dillon and Juliet," the rotund Yorkshireman said, "but I've typed out the lab forms, so it's just a case of getting someone to run them up there on my behalf."

Jack grunted. Looking around the room, he wondered who he could lumber with that. "Speaking of the SPMs, what's the score with those?" he asked Juliet.

"As George said, they're being done over the next couple of days. We've got two planned for today, and the others for tomorrow. They're being carried out by Ben Claxton at Walthamstow mortuary."

Copeland groaned loudly. "Oh no!" he whined. "I didn't realise Creepy Claxton was doing them."

Dillon picked up on this, and his brow immediately furrowed with concern. "Is that a problem?" he asked, head volleying between Copeland and Kennedy.

"No," Copeland said, dragging the word out gloomily. "It's just that, well, have you ever watched any of those Hammer House of Horror Frankenstein films with Peter Cushing?"

"Yes," Dillon admitted, spreading his hands questioningly. "And…?"

"Well, that role could have been modelled on Creepy Claxton. He's so intense that it takes all the fun out of it."

Dillon stared at Copeland as though he were certifiable. "*FUN!* Are you having a laugh? There's nothing about attending a post mortem that could possibly be described as *fun!*"

George's expression became sheepish. "Yes, well, perhaps fun wasn't the right word," he admitted.

Dillon glared at him.

"Now, now, boys," Juliet intervened. "I think what George was trying to say was that Ben is very intense when he's working, which means that he gets a bit tetchy if people make any sudden noises or move about too much, so it isn't always as relaxed an environment as it might otherwise be."

George nodded vigorously. "That's exactly what I meant."

Dillon let out a sigh of pure misery. "I'm so not looking forward to this," he said to no one in particular.

Jack felt for his friend. The thought of spending a couple of very long days trapped inside a mortuary with a man who had just been likened to Herr Doctor Frankenstein was enough to unsettle anyone.

"Can I confirm that the DNA and fingerprint examinations of the shells recovered from the scene are being prioritised?" Tyler asked. If they recovered a single fingerprint, it would be enough to kickstart the enquiry.

"Absolutely," Juliet said, nodding emphatically. "I've already spoken to the lab and they're primed to expect them."

"Good. In that case, let's move onto witnesses. Paul did some great work yesterday with one of the two key witnesses from the café. Talk us thorough it, please, Paul."

"Well, boss," Evans said, blushing at the praise, "I met with Tulay Yildiz at Stoke Newington yesterday in order to go through her initial statement with her. She was very hesitant at first, but in the end she admitted that she'd been holding something back. The gunman who shot the front seat passenger, Erkan Dengiz, had a very distinctive tattoo on the right side of his neck, and she got a very good look at it when he ripped off his neck scarf. She's made a further statement to this effect and, perhaps more importantly, drew us a very detailed picture of it. The tattoo she saw is of a snake coiled around a dagger that has a skull shaped pommel on the base of the hilt."

Matt Blake interrupted. "Sorry for cutting in, but we've made a number of photocopies of Tulay's drawing. I want you all to stick one in your daybooks. Under no circumstances is it to be disclosed to anyone outside of this enquiry team without DCI Tyler's express permission." He looked around the room as he spoke, allowing his gaze to linger on each of the newcomers to make sure they had got the message loud and clear.

"Well done, Paul. It's a great bit of work," Tyler said, firing a congratulatory wink in Evans' direction. "Speaking of witnesses, have we managed to trace any of the other people who were inside the café when the shooting occurred?"

Matt Blake gave a sorrowful shake of his head. "It's like they never existed."

Tyler was disappointed by the news, but not in the slightest bit surprised. "What about house to house?" he asked next. "How's that coming along?"

DC Richard Jarvis, the youngest and most junior member of the team, raised a hand. DS Charlie White, a diminutive Scotsman with a badly broken nose that made everything he said sound very nasally, immediately reached out and pushed it back into his lap. "You dinnae need to put your hand up every time you want to speak," he whispered, shaking his head in exasperation.

Jarvis glared at him before turning to address Tyler. "The area is mainly occupied by shops and small businesses, most of which had long since closed for the day by the time the shooting happened," he said in his frightfully posh accent. "There are flats above the shops, but not that many, and the residents have all been spoken to. Even though most of them heard a succession of loud bangs that night, not one of them bothered to look out of their windows to see what was going on."

It was hardly surprising; not in that area. Loud bangs and other commotions were common place.

"Thanks for the update, Dick," Tyler said, making a note in his daybook so that he could update his Decision Log after the meeting. "Let's go through the CCTV next. Colin, what can you tell us?"

"I've collected all the local authority CCTV from Hackney and Haringey boroughs as per your instructions, and I've checked all the shops in the immediate vicinity of the shooting. A few had cameras in. Two turned out to be live-time monitors with no recording capability, one was a fake camera installed just to deter thieves, and the last one was a fully functional system that was recording on the night in question."

"That sounds interesting," Tyler said, leaning forward expectantly. "Have you checked the footage yet?"

Franklin nodded dolefully. "I have," he admitted. "Unfortunately, a great big van was parked directly outside the shop at the time of the murder, so all we get to see is the company logo on its side and the neon sign above the café's entrance."

Tyler's face fell, and he sagged back in his chair. The chorus of groans cascading around the room told him he wasn't the only one disappointed by this news.

"Okay, Reg," Tyler said. "It's your turn to depress me now. Let's talk phones."

Reg Parker blew out his cheeks. "Where to begin?" he pondered, rustling through his copious notes. "Okay, so let's start with the cell dump you requested. As predicted, the TIU kicked off massively, and it was only after I warned them you were threatening to get the Assistant Commissioner involved that they grudgingly agreed to your demand. It'll take some time to organise, mind you, and I've promised that we won't ask for any work to be started on the data unless all other options are exhausted. Needless to say, they've demanded a meeting with you up at The Yard before that happens."

Jack rolled his eyes at that. "Let's hope we can solve this case without ever having to go down that route," he said, knowing that the meeting would be painful.

"I've requested a full month's worth of call and cell site data for mobile phones belonging to the four Turkish victims, Conrad Living-stone, and a bloke called Tyson Meeks."

"What about the three thugs who came down from Manchester, Reg? Did you manage to find any current mobile numbers for them?"

"I didn't," Reg admitted, "but Deano did."

"I can't take the credit," Dean said. "Mr Dillon put me in touch with a bloke called DS Murphy up in Manchester, and he managed to get us the numbers."

"Anyway," Reg continued. "As with the others, I've requested a month's worth of data for Samuel Adebanjo, Isaac Kalu and Andre Kalu."

"Any idea when the results will start coming in?" Tyler asked, as impatient as ever.

"Hopefully, later today."

"You know what I'm going to say, don't you?" Tyler asked with a wry smile.

Reg chortled. "I know. It's urgent and you want it yesterday if not sooner."

"That's right," Tyler said with a smile. He was still grinning as he turned his attention to Fletcher. "Dean, talk me through the intelligence picture."

"Well, guv," Dean began, "we've obtained access to all the intelligence that Stoke Newington and Haringey have on the three gangs. There's stacks of it and, to be perfectly honest, most of it's not worth the paper it's written on. I'm still waiting for all the material I requested from the Regional Crime Squad and the Turkish and Kurdish Crime Task Force at The Yard, but I don't anticipate it'll take us anywhere."

"Give us a brief overview of the gangs involved," Jack said.

"The first gang's run by a former Holly Street Boy called Conrad Livingstone. The second is a Turkish crime syndicate run by Abdullah Goren. His mob has close connections to Abdullah Baybasin who, for those of you who don't know, is a major bad-ass and definitely not a man to be messed with. These two gangs are the most established of the three, and they both have their grubby little fingers in all the usual pies: prostitution, drugs, firearms, etc. The final group is a relatively new mob run by an Albanian called Klodjan Asllani. There's not much in the system about him. From what I can tell, him and his family came to the UK as refugees last year, claiming asylum as a result of the Kosovo war."

"Och, well that's just dandy, isn't it!" Charlie White blurted out. "We let the bastard into our country to keep him and his family safe, and this is how he repays our generosity! Why do we keep doing this?" He demanded, shaking his head in exasperation. "We did exactly the same thing with Abdullah Goren, and with his mate, Baybasin." Charlie threw his hands up in despair. "When are we gonna learn? If you ask me, we should deport the lot of them."

"Calm down, Charlie," Steve Bull soothed, grinning at the irate Scotsman.

Dean cleared his throat before continuing. "There's no concrete evidence to back it up, but intelligence suggests Asllani was running with the Albanian mafia back home, and now he's trying to establish a branch here."

Charlie White opened his mouth to make another scathing comment, but Bull placed a restraining hand on his arm and shook his head.

Folding his arms with an angry 'harrumph', White continued to seethe in silence.

"Anyway," Dean was saying, "the RCS shut down a major criminal network operating in that part of North London at the beginning of the year, and as Livingstone and Goren already controlled the surrounding areas, they naturally decided to move in and fill the void. Then, just to complicate matters, the Albanians tried to stake their claim too."

"There's slightly more to it than that," Dillon told the assembled officers. "Livingstone and Goren wanted to carve up the vacant terri-tory equally between themselves, but the Albanians, who had been given permission to operate in that area by the previous controlling gang, tried to claim squatters' rights. The three gang leaders met to try and resolve the dispute by diplomacy rather than resorting to force, but things hit a bit of an impasse when the Albanians demanded they be given an equal share of the spoils instead of the twenty percent on offer. Then the four Turks were gunned down the other night, and now everything is up in the air."

Dean eyed the big man suspiciously. "All it says on the system is that the three gangs are locked in dispute about who should assume control of the vacant turf," he challenged, "so I'd be very interested to know how you obtained that information, and what its provenance is."

"Let's just say that Mr Dillon has access to information that isn't on the system and leave it at that," Tyler said. He couldn't elaborate further without revealing that Dillon had a source buried within Livingstone's setup.

"But –"

"Take it from me, Deano. You can assume that the info is reliable."

Dean's forehead knitted as he processed this, and Jack could imagine him trying to join the dots in his head.

"What exactly does *that* mean?" Dean asked, staring intently at Tyler.

"It means that you don't ask any more questions, Dean," Jack chided him gently. "Moving on, have you got the ANPR results back on Dengiz' Mercedes yet?"

When Dean didn't answer, Jack realised that the stubborn sod was still running the algorithms through in his head, trying to figure out how Dillon knew what he did.

"Dean…?"

"What…? Oh, right. ANPR results… Haven't received them yet, but I was promised we'd definitely have them by the end of today."

"Let me know as soon as they come in," Tyler said. "Have you had any luck running the tattoo though the marks and scars index yet?"

"The request has gone off," Dean said. "I'm just waiting for them to get back to me."

"Well, don't wait too long," Tyler said. "If you haven't heard anything by lunchtime, put a rocket up their arse." He checked his watch: it was getting on for half past eight. "Right, so in summary, we've got two key witnesses, Bilal Yildiz and his daughter, Tulay. Her evidence is pivotal, given that she spotted the tattoo on one of the gunmen's necks. I'm working on the assumption that we won't identify any of the other people who were in the café at the time of the murder." He paused for a moment and shrugged. "But even if we did, does anyone here really think they're going to tell us anything we don't already know?"

"Unlikely," Steve Bull said, even though the question had been rhetorical.

"We don't have any forensic evidence at the moment," Tyler continued, thinking that this was turning into a pretty bleak summary, "and our best hope of getting any is that the lab will recover DNA or fingerprints from the spent shell casings. All four victims were members of Abdullah Goren's gang, and we know they're involved in a three-way turf war with Livingstone's crew and this Albanian outfit run by Asllani. It's not rocket science to make the leap and say that either Livingstone or Asllani are behind the murders so—"

"Hang on a wee minute, boss," Charlie White said. "The shooters were white, so surely we can rule Livingstone out?" He seemed confused by the suggestion that Livingstone could be behind this and, looking around the room, Tyler realised that a lot of the others were thinking the same thing. Their reaction was understandable, given that none of them were privy to the information that he and Dillon had.

"I'm not ruling anything out just yet," he said, and left it at that.

Looking as miserable as sin, White buried his head in his hands. "Och, this is definitely going to be a sticker," he prophesied.

Tyler's face darkened. "I do *not* want to hear anyone on this team using *that* word about this investigation," he said, surprised at how calm his voice sounded considering how annoyed he was. His eyes slowly traversed the room as he spoke, lingering confrontationally on every single person until they nodded their acquiescence. "Yes, I accept it's going to be a difficult one, but that'll just make it all the more satisfying when we finally solve it. Until we get the ANPR, telephone data, and forensics results back, the emphasis is going to be on getting through the CCTV as fast as we can. I'm absolutely convinced that there will be nuggets of pure gold buried within the footage we've seized, and the majority of you are going to find yourselves tied to your desks viewing it for the next few days. I've drawn up a list of people who will be doing the bulk of the viewing, and Steve will go through that with you in a minute, when he starts handing out the day's taskings. In the meantime, I'd ask you—" his eyes flitted back to Charlie White who promptly looked away "–to try and stay positive and focused, and to remember that the job is only two days old, so it's far too early for defeatist talk about throwing the towel in or it being a sticker." He glowered at them again to make sure they had got the point. "Do I make myself clear?"

"Yes, boss," they chorused, like a group of naughty children who had just been given a dressing down.

———

Dritan had struggled to fall asleep the previous night. When it finally came, his slumber had been fitful, plagued by torturous visions of the terrible atrocities he'd participated in. The images of the screaming, terrified faces standing before the firing squads, and their blood soaked bodies lying in mass burial pits moments later, had been painfully graphic. Instead of feeling refreshed and revitalised, he had awoken feeling physically exhausted and emotionally drained.

The nightmares, when they came, were unbelievably intense, and they were always followed by flashbacks that hit him like a series of aftershocks in the wake of a particularly bad earthquake.

The two major side effects of his nightmares were bouts of intense claustrophobia followed by debilitating panic attacks, and the only way he had found to stop himself from falling apart when this happened was to take himself out into the open, where he could feel the sun on his skin and the fresh air blowing around him.

He accepted that it went against all his training to leave the hotel in the middle of a mission, and he would have forbidden either of the others, had they requested permission to do something similar, but he couldn't help it. He had to get out of the building before he lost control, so he took himself off on a long walk, hoping it would clear his mind of the terrors that prevented him from thinking coherently.

The doctors had told him that he suffered from an acute form of PTSD, and the nightmares and severe panic attacks that always followed them were his mind's way of dealing with the things he had seen and done during his military service. He didn't know or care why it helped, but taking long walks had proven to be the most successful of all the coping mechanisms he'd tried.

Although it went against protocol, he doubted there was any real risk involved in his venturing out for a little walk; it wasn't as if anyone in London knew him, and the police still had absolutely no idea who had killed the Turks on Tuesday evening.

As soon as he set foot outside the hotel, the early morning sun that now bathed him in its warm, nurturing glow started to burn away the inner darkness that weighed him down.

Taking a deep breath, Dritan set off along Amhurst Park, walking at a brisk pace in order to raise his heartrate and get his blood pumping. He continued on a straight path for about ten minutes, until the road veered left and merged into Seven Sisters. Squinting against the harsh light, he found himself wishing that he'd thought to bring his sunglasses along.

Walking with growing purpose, Dritan continued past Woodberry Down Estate, eventually coming to the junction with Green Lanes. He paused at the traffic lights, staring longingly across the road into the entrance of Finsbury Park, his intended destination.

Dritan had a deep love for the great outdoors. Back in his homeland, he had enjoyed numerous camping trips in the country's many remote areas of natural beauty. The North London park hardly compared to the wonders of Cozia forest, but it would enable him to spend a little time on his own while he cleared his mind of the guilt demons that lurked within its darkest recesses.

A few minutes turned into a couple of hours. The time passed peacefully, with him sitting alone on a secluded bench, watching the various birds and squirrels do their thing.

By the time that Dritan felt ready to return to the hotel, his mind was in a much better place, and the panic attack that had threatened to cripple his ability to function for the remainder of the day was now firmly under control.

As Dritan reached the exit, he realised that he was ravenously hungry. On a whim that was both dangerous and foolhardy, he found himself walking along Green Lanes towards the spot where he and his comrades had cold-bloodedly gunned down four men.

He was pleased to see that the little Turkish café was open for business. An elderly man and young girl in her twenties were busy preparing food behind the counter, and he immediately recognised them both as having been there on the night of the hit.

There were only three customers inside, two middle-aged Turkish males with thick moustaches, sitting together and drinking coffee, and a white man in a reflective high-viz jacket, who sat alone at a separate table eating one of the greasy breakfasts that the English so adored.

Before he knew it, Dritan had pushed open the door and walked in. The girl looked up at him and smiled a greeting. The old man, working the grill behind her, glanced over his shoulder and then returned to his food preparation, singing a folksong in Turkish. Dritan took a table by the window so that he could look out into the street.

This was utter madness, he knew, but the temptation to come in here had been irresistible.

"Good morning," the ponytailed girl said, appearing by his side. "What can I get you?" She wore a white apron and carried a little pad to write on. Her fingernails were painted black, he noticed.

As a child, having a proper breakfast had always been something of a luxury for Dritan, mainly because his mother only ever prepared food for the family at the weekend. How he had loved coming downstairs on a Saturday morning to find the table laid with a traditional Romanian breakfast of eggs, cheese, meat and vegetables, all just waiting for him and his two elder brothers to devour it. During the autumn months, there would also be zacusca, a vegetarian spread based on open-fire grilled eggplants – the British called them aubergines – and bell peppers, which they would eat on thick slices of franzela bread.

"I would like some scrambled eggs on toast and a side salad, please," he informed her. "And strong, black coffee."

"Certainly," she said with a polite smile. She studied his face for a moment frowning. "I've not seen you around here before, have I? Are you new to the area?"

He knew she was only making polite conversation, but Dritan didn't like being asked questions like that. "Just passing through," he said, wishing that she would go away and leave him in peace.

She seemed to get the message that he wasn't interested in making small talk. "Do you want any bottled water or orange juice with your breakfast?" she asked.

Before he could reply, the door opened and two uniformed police officers walked in, their radios crackling away. Dritan felt his body tense, and he quickly picked up the menu and buried his head in it to shield his face from view. Had he been looking at his waitress, rather than at the menu, he would have seen the colour drain from her face as she spotted the tattoo on the right side of his neck.

"Morning," the older of the two constables, a man in his mid-forties with thick grey sideburns protruding from beneath his helmet, said cheerfully. "We're just dropping these Crimestoppers leaflets off at all the shops in the parade, appealing for witnesses in relation to the quadruple murder from the other night. Would you be willing to put one up in your window for us, please?"

The old man behind the counter seemed hesitant, as though the request had made him uncomfortable. "Well, I…"

"We'd love to," the girl said, walking over to the policeman and relieving him of the flyer.

As soon as the policemen disappeared out of the door, Dritan stood up. "Don't worry about my order," he said brusquely, aware that she was staring at him strangely. "I've just remembered that I'm running late for an appointment."

"Not a problem," she said, sounding almost relieved. He felt her eyes following him out of the door, no doubt thinking that her customer was an absent minded fool.

———

After the rest of the team had been tasked, Tyler met privately with Dillon and Steve Bull in his office to discuss the more confidential aspects of the investigation over a cup of coffee.

Tyler had decided that the time had come for them to take Steve Bull into their full confidence, and he had just finished appraising him of the situation regarding Meeks, the information he had provided, and the working hypothesis that Livingstone was the mastermind behind the murders. As Case Officer, he would need to know about these things at some point anyway, so it made sense to bring him into the fold now, rather than waiting any longer.

Bull was staring at Dillon. "Let me get this straight," he said, scratching his head in confusion. "According to your snout, Livingstone hired a hitman called Goliath to come down from Manchester and take out the Albanians, but it turns out that was just as smokescreen to keep you distracted while a separate team – also under Goliath's control – murdered the four Turks?"

"That's right," Dillon confirmed.

"And you think Livingstone is secretly trying to provoke an all-out war between the Turks and the Albanians, hoping that they'll wipe each other out, leaving him in a position to step in and mop up afterwards?"

"Something like that."

Tilting his head to one side, Steve shot him a look that suggested he wasn't fully sold on this. "And you say this Goliath character has done something like this before?"

Dillon nodded. "Yep. Two years ago, there was a series of drive-by shootings in Rochdale, Oldham, and Tameside that virtually mirror what's happening here. It left nine people dead. It's all documented in a file that I've obtained from GMP."

"You can read it later, if you want," Jack said, "but under the caveat that it doesn't leave my office and you don't discuss its contents with anyone but us."

Bull stared from one to the other in growing incredulity. "So we actually know a lot more about what's going on than has been disclosed to the rest of the team?"

Tyler nodded guiltily. "We do, but we don't have any evidence yet, and until we do, this has to stay strictly amongst ourselves."

Bull let out a low whistle and leaned back in his chair, shaking his head in bewilderment. "I don't suppose your snout would consider making a statement?" he asked Dillon.

"He's already made one," Dillon said, proudly.

"Well, that's really good news – isn't it?"

Tyler let out a mirthless laugh. "Not really, Steve. At least not as things stand at the moment."

When it became clear that Tyler wasn't going to elaborate, Dillon took up the narrative on his friend's behalf. "As it stands, nothing that my snout predicted has actually come to pass, and without a way of linking Goliath to the Turkish killings, and Livingstone to Goliath, his testimony is utterly worthless."

"It's about as much use as a chocolate teapot, to be precise," Tyler added unhelpfully.

Bull pulled his chin in. "That's a rather depressing thought," he said. "So how are we going to make a case against them without any evidence?"

Tyler leaned back in his chair and interlocked his fingers behind his head. "At the moment, I'm pinning all my hopes on the telephone data providing a connection – even a tenuous one – between Goliath and Livingstone. That would give us a solid foundation to build upon, and it might even add some much needed credence to Meeks' statement. With a bit of luck, we'll also find something we can use buried in the mountain of CCTV we've seized. Apart from all the stuff that Colin grabbed yesterday, and the extra stuff we've asked him to collect today, Mr Dillon's mate has been stockpiling CCTV for us from various locations up in Manchester. Who knows what's in that? Any news on when we might get our hands on it, Dill?"

Dillon checked his watch. "I'll give Jonny a bell shortly," he promised. "See how he's getting on."

Bull seemed at a bit of a loss for words. Eventually, he said, "Well, it sounds like everything is as in hand as it can be, given the circumstances, so what can I do to help?"

Jack sat forward again. "You can start off by getting an urgent tasking sent out to the source units at Hackney, Haringey, and the Turkish and Kurdish Crime Task Force at NSY. Let's see if any of them have anyone on their books who's close to Livingstone, Goren, or Asllani. I also want a separate tasking sent out to every single source unit within the Met to see if anyone knows of a white male, probably Eastern European, who has a tattoo of a snake curled around a dagger on his neck."

Bull was scribbling furiously.

"In fact, now that I think about it, get the tattoo tasking sent to GMP's source unit as well, just in case it rings any bells with anyone in that neck of the woods."

"Anything else?" Bull asked. The look on his face implied that he was hoping there wouldn't be.

"I want you to get a Reverse Osman warning drafted out for each of the three gang leaders. I suspect that, at some point in the near future, we might have to go down that line with them, so we might as well have it sitting on the system, ready to go."

"Do you want me to include anything specific in it, or will the generic wording suffice for now?"

Tyler considered this. "Let's keep it fairly generic. Outline that we have intelligence that the three gangs are involved in a violent dispute, and that we will be holding each of them responsible should there be an outbreak of hostilities."

Tyler paused to take a much needed sip of his coffee. "How are your troops getting on with their enquiries?" he asked Dillon.

"They've seized the CCTV of Adebanjo and the Kalu twins arriving at Euston, and Coleen and Gurjit are going to spend the morning viewing that. They'll also go through the CCTV we got from the hotel they were arrested at in Beckton. I've tasked the other two to go back to the hotel and scope out the surrounding area for local authority CCTV."

"Why?" Bull asked.

"Because Adebanjo popped out to a local shop at one point during Tuesday evening, and we think he dumped his burner while he was gone. I've instructed my people to check out any bins, drains, or areas of wasteland they find along the route from the hotel to the shop."

Bull had been thoughtfully rolling his bottom lip between his thumb and forefinger while he listened. Now he asked, "What makes you think he dumped it while he was out?"

"Because my snout reckons that Adebanjo was in touch with Livingstone throughout the day, but he didn't have a mobile on him when he was arrested, and there was nothing found inside the hotel room. That means he must have dumped it when he went on a walk."

"Okay," Tyler said, conscious that time was ticking on. "Dill, I'd better let you shoot off to the mortuary or you're going to be late."

Dillon shuddered at the reminder.

"Steve, I'd like you to crack on with the source unit taskings and the Reverse Osman letters. I'm going to ring Mr Holland with an update, and then I'm going to pop in and see how Andy's team are getting on. After that, I've got to knuckle down and update my Decision Log. Let's all sit down again together later to see what we've got when the telephone data and ANPR results come in."

As the others stood up to leave, Tyler caught Dillon's eye, signalling for him to wait behind.

"What is it?" Dillon asked when they were alone.

"Your man, Meeks," Tyler said. "Am I right in thinking that, when he was young, he used to run with the Holly Street Boys?"

"That's right," Dillon confirmed guardedly. "Doesn't have anything to do with them these days, though. Works directly for Livingstone. Why do you ask?"

Jack shrugged. "I was just wondering if he might know anyone who could shed some light on who stabbed Jenny, that's all."

Dillon's face softened. "I'm sorry, Jack. He just doesn't move in those circles anymore. His younger brother does, but the two of them aren't on speaking terms and, even if they were, there's no way Tyson would ask him for information like that. The boy already hates his guts, and the main reason Tyson was so reluctant to make a statement about Livingstone was that he didn't want his kid brother finding out he's an informant."

"Surely it can't hurt to ask him?" Jack said, reluctant to drop the matter.

Dillon shook his head. "I'm really sorry, mate. You know I would do it if there was any chance he would play ball, but he wouldn't."

Tyler nodded his understanding. It had been a long shot, after all.

"Sure. No worries," he said glumly.

As Dillon closed the door behind him, Tyler's mobile phone rang. Without checking caller ID, he pressed the accept button. "Hello, DCI Tyler speaking."

"Jack, it's Eddie. What time are you free to meet for that coffee…?"

Tyler's heart sank. He had forgotten all about that.

CHAPTER SIXTEEN

A TERRIBLE CONFESSION

When Jenny woke up, she lay there quietly for a while, trying to match her breathing to the beeping of the machines that surrounded her bed. She could feel her heart beating, so she knew she was still alive, but her arms and legs were numb. Curiosity slowly got the better of her, and she prised her eyes open, wincing at the pain that immediately radiated from the swollen one.

Her mind flashed back to the moment the masked robber slapped her so viciously, and the searing pain that spread through her face as it connected. She gasped at the jarringly vivid image, closing her eyes tight to dispel it.

Trembling with fear, she lay still and forced herself to take deep breaths. She was safe now, she reminded herself. The horrible incident was over and she was in hospital, where the robbers couldn't get at her. When her heart rate finally returned to normal, she opened her eyes again, taking in the magnolia coloured walls of the intensive care unit.

Jenny gradually became aware of the soreness in her body, and set about tentatively exploring her torso with her left hand.

Another flashback, this time to the engagement ring being torn from her finger. As tears prickled her eyes, she felt the space where it had been with her thumb, caressing the base of her fourth finger and thinking how strange it felt not to find the band of gold there.

She dimly recalled the doctors speaking to her after she'd come round in the recovery room, explaining what had happened to her and talking her through the operation she had undergone. It was all very blurry, as was her transfer to ICU and everything that had happened between then and now. All she could recall was that she had been drowsy and confused, constantly drifting in and out of sleep.

Jenny also had a dim recollection of screaming at one of the doctors in the recovery room. Her voice slurred from the drugs, she had demanded to know if she had lost the baby. The doctor's response had been all distorted and echoey as he reassured her that neither of her injuries had compromised her pregnancy, and that there was no reason for her to worry about the baby.

Had that conversation even occurred? Could it just have been a dream, an anaesthesia induced hallucination?

And then, as panic started to mushroom inside her, Jenny remembered asking again, after they had settled her into the ICU. The response had been the same.

The relief that flooded through her was indescribable. If anything positive had come out of this dreadful situation, it was that she now knew beyond any shadow of a doubt that she wanted to keep the baby, and that she would love it with all her heart regardless of the circumstances in which it was conceived.

Her head was beginning to feel much clearer now, and she took a moment to take in her surroundings. There were lines and tubes inserted into her veins so that fluids, nutrition, and medication could be provided intravenously. A drain had been put in to remove any build-up of blood or fluid from her abdomen, and a catheter had been inserted into her bladder to drain her urine. She vaguely recalled the nurse who was looking after her saying something about the machines, explaining that they were there to monitor and measure important bodily functions, such as heart rate, blood pressure and the level of oxygen in her blood, but they were nothing for her to worry about.

Jenny knew that the recovery process was likely to be long and slow, but she would get through it because the love of her family would keep her strong. Jenny firmly believed that she could survive just about anything as long as they were there to support her, even the silent hand grenades that exploded inside her chest every time she thought about Eddie, and how they were going to work things out.

Jenny pulled her covers all the way up to her neck, the way she had as a child when a bad dream had left her feeling vulnerable. The bed's cotton sheets were clean, stiff and functional, but not inviting or comfortable. That was okay; she was there to have her body fixed, not to wallow in luxury.

A nurse appeared beside her as if by magic. She was about Jenny's age, slim, with auburn hair, a warm smile, and laughter lines around her hazel eyes. "Good morning," she said cheerfully. "How are you feeling today?"

Jenny considered this. "Tired, and I've got a slight headache and a sore throat."

The nurse nodded understandingly. "Perfectly normal," she reassured her patient. "Anaesthesia often lingers in the body for a couple of days, so don't be unduly worried if you feel very tired today, or if you still feel a little groggy and confused."

That made sense, and Jenny felt immensely reassured to know this.

"Your partner is waiting outside. Would you like to see him for a few minutes?" the nurse asked.

It was as though the air had suddenly been sucked from her lungs. Eddie was here, and wanted to see her. What should she say to him?

"I – I don't really feel up to it yet," she stammered. "Would you mind asking him to come back later, after I've had some rest."

If the nurse was surprised to hear this, her face didn't reflect it. "Of course," she said with another smile. "I'll let him know."

————

It wasn't until the mid-morning lull arrived that Tulay had any time to herself. After the tattooed man's sudden departure, the flood gates had opened and there had been a non-stop deluge of customers who had literally run her off her feet for the past two hours.

Normally so well organised, Tulay had found herself hardly able to concentrate; she had made an endless series of mistakes, serving the wrong food to customers, recording orders incorrectly, overcharging people or giving them the incorrect amount of change. Towards the end, her father had started to get extremely tetchy with her, and they had ended up bickering, which was unheard of for them.

As she finished wiping the tables down, her father came over and gave her a hug. She hadn't expected that, and the sudden act of tenderness reduced her to tears. "I'm sorry, father," she sobbed. "I know I've been a nightmare to work with all morning, but I promise I'll get a grip of myself and do better from now on."

Her father released her from his loving embrace and held her at arm's length, staring at her with paternal concern. "What's the matter, Tulay? Something must be very wrong for you to get so many orders mixed up. It's not like you at all."

She wiped her eyes and smiled at him. "I'm just tired, papa, that's all."

Bilal arched an eyebrow, clearly not believing a word she had said. "Is your lapse in concentration connected to the terrible events of the other evening, my daughter? Are you suffering from this post dramatic stress I've read about?"

Tulay laughed at the old man's unintended malapropism. "Papa, I think you'll find it's called *post-traumatic* stress."

"That's what I said," he lied, and then grinned at her. "Tell you what, let's finish cleaning the tables and I'll make you some lunch." Kissing her forehead, he turned toward a dirty table just behind him.

"Father, I have a confession to make," she blurted out.

Bilal froze, and she sensed rather than saw the shiver that had just ran through him. "You're not pregnant, are you?" he asked, eyes dropping to her stomach to check for a tell-tale bulge.

"No! Of course I'm not!" she said, indignantly. Then softer, "Look, I know you didn't want me to tell the police about the tattoo on the neck of the man who killed Mr Dengiz, but when I met with DC

Evans yesterday, I realised that it would be wrong of me to withhold this information."

Bilal's leathery face clouded over. "You told the police about the tattoo?"

Tulay wilted under her father's reproachful gaze. Feeling ashamed for having dishonoured his wishes, she stared at the floor, the way she had as a little girl on those rare occasions that he'd scolded her. "Please don't be angry with me, Papa," she pleaded.

"Tulay, I am your father, and I expressly forbade you from doing that. By disobeying me, you've dragged us into something that's none of our business." There was anger in his voice, but there was something else too, and unless she was very much mistaken, it was fear. Shaking his head in dismay, the old man threw his cloth on the table and stormed back to the kitchen, muttering under his breath. The only word she managed to make out was 'stupid.'

Watching him go, Tulay realised that telling her father about the conversation she'd had with DC Evans had been a big mistake. She'd only confessed to ease her guilty conscience, but instead of making herself feel better, all she'd done was make him thoroughly miserable. She decided not to burden him further by revealing that she'd been so all over the place this morning because she'd been spooked by the appearance of the customer with the tattooed neck.

There was no doubt in her mind that it was the exact same tattoo she'd seen two nights earlier. Of course, she hadn't seen the gunman's face or heard him speak back then, and while she couldn't swear that today's visitor was definitely the same person, they were of the same general height and build. On top of that, Tulay seriously doubted there were many people walking around North London with a tattoo like that; she had certainly never seen one before. The question was, if he was one of the shooters, as she suspected, why had he returned to the café today?

Perhaps the tattooed man's appearance had been a subtle warning that the shooters were watching them, and that they wouldn't hesitate to take action if Tulay or her father were foolish enough to give evidence against them?

The thought made her knees go weak. If any harm came to her

family because of her, she would never forgive herself. To her surprise, her fear for her parent's safety only seemed to strengthen her resolve not to give in to these mobsters. Paul Evans' departing words echoed in her head; he had told her that these thugs and gangsters were only powerful because their victims allowed them to be, and that if enough people came forward and gave evidence, the police would be able to put them all away once and for all.

Maybe it was time for someone in the community to make a stand, and maybe that someone was her.

———

Tyler sat down and took an appreciative slurp from the delicious smelling coffee that Andy Quinlan had just made him. It was perco-lated, and had a much richer flavour than the instant rubbish his team used.

After closing the door to his office, Quinlan sat behind his desk and steepled his fingers together. "I take it you've heard the latest update from the hospital, that Jenny's in a stable condition and expected to make a full recovery?"

"Yes, that's very good news," Jack agreed. He had phoned the ICU Sister himself earlier that morning, and he had been enormously relieved to hear that Jenny was doing so well. With luck, he would be able to visit her tomorrow.

"How's the investigation progressing? Did anything significant come out during your morning meeting?" he asked.

As Quinlan considered the question, he removed his Joe 90 glasses and began polishing the lenses on a silk handkerchief that had magi-cally appeared in his hand. Without them, his face seemed strangely bare; less professorial and more mole-like as he squinted at his blurred guest.

"Well, as you already know, Mason and Bright are in custody, and they'll be interviewed this morning." He slipped his glasses back on and wiggled his nose to get them into a comfortable position. "Brown seems to have vanished into thin air. He's been circulated on the PNC as wanted missing, and the locals are out looking for him in force, so hopefully his freedom will soon be curtailed."

They both knew from experience that gang boys tended to be very territorial; they rarely strayed far from their natural environment, even when they were on the run.

"Both Mason and Bright's flats were searched last night but, as you know, nothing was found." Quinlan paused to savour a mouthful of coffee. "It's not surprising though, is it?"

"Not really," Jack agreed, "just disappointing."

"Anyway, we've got forensic teams going over both flats with a fine tooth comb this morning." Another sip; another smile of contentment. "They're going to luminol the baths and sinks, just in case they tried to wash away any of the victim's blood in them."

Jack subconsciously turned his nose up at the news. The expression only lasted a microsecond, but that was long enough for Quinlan to pick up on it.

"I take it you don't agree?" he observed.

Jack shrugged, struggling to think of a polite way of saying that he thought it was overkill. "I can't see that yielding anything if I'm honest, mate," he said in what he hoped was a tactful manner. "I mean, it's not like they stabbed anyone in one of the flats or–" he made a hacking motion with his hand "–chopped up a body in the bath."

Quinlan seemed surprised by his reaction, disappointed even. "I thought you'd be pleased that I'm pulling out all the stops to identify Jenny's attackers."

"I am, Andy," Jack said, smiling sincerely and hoping that he hadn't inadvertently caused offence. "I guess I was just hoping you'd found some physical evidence, like clothing or the knife they used."

A thin, slightly smug smile crept onto Quinlan's face. "Ah! Were you? Well, in that case, I might have some good news for you on that front."

"What do you mean?" Tyler asked, leaning forward in anticipation.

"While he was waiting for Susie to get a warrant to spin Devon Brown's flat last night, Kevin Murray searched the communal bins at the base of the tower block. It wasn't a particularly pleasant experience, by all accounts, but he recovered a four inch kitchen knife, and a bin liner full of clothing. Amongst other things, the bin liner contained a red McKenzie hoodie that matches the one Curtis Bright was seen wearing on the CCTV."

"Wow, that really is a fantastic result," Jack said. "Were there any visible traces of blood on either the knife or the hoodie?"

Quinlan shook his head in disappointment. "Nothing visible, but we'll get them properly tested up at the lab and, if nothing else, I'm confident that we'll get wearer DNA from Bright's top."

"Well done, Andy," Jack said, delighted that at least one of them was making some progress.

"The good news doesn't end there, matey," Quinlan told him.

Tyler raised an encouraging eyebrow. "Go on then, tell me."

"Susie just phoned me from Brown's flat. They found an ivory handled flick knife with a six-inch blade hidden under his mattress. It looks like it's recently been cleaned, but Sam Calvin, my trustee Crime Scene Manager, reckons there's still a good chance that the lab will find microscopic trace evidence if it was used in the stabbings."

"That's very encouraging news," Jack said, and he toasted his friend's success with the remains of his coffee.

"More so than you realise, old son," Quinlan said, breaking into a wide grin as he clinked his cup against Jack's. "You won't be aware of this yet, but in his statement, one of the witnesses from the train very helpfully described the stabber as having an ivory handled knife."

"How reliable is the witness?" Tyler asked. He didn't want to be negative, but this sounded almost too good to be true, and he knew that any defence counsel worth their salt would hotly contest the claim's veracity.

"Very," Quinlan said, unable to keep the satisfaction out of his voice. "The boy in question ended up with one of the robbers sitting astride him, pressing the blade of his knife into the terrified lad's face. I think you'll agree that, when someone's holding a knife against your skin and threatening to slice it open, you do tend to notice little things like the unusual colour of the knife handle, especially if it's only a few inches away from your eyes at the time. The icing on the cake is that we have several other witnesses who are adamant that the robber who did that to the boy is the same one who went on to stab Jenny and the old man."

"Wow," Jack said. The case was really starting to come together for Andy. As he digested the new information, he suddenly recalled his conversation with Jenny's surgeon, Mr Shirazi, the previous evening. "Andy, when I spoke to the chap who operated on Jenny, he was of the opinion that two separate knives might have been used on her, which would suggest she was stabbed by two separate suspects. What are your views on this?"

Quinlan was visibly taken aback by the revelation. "Hmmm, I wasn't aware of that," he admitted unhappily. "And it potentially complicates matters as witnesses say there were three robbers with her when she was stabbed. I'll have to get someone to clarify that with him as a matter of urgency."

"When's the SPM for Mr Cotton being carried out?" Jack asked.

"It's going ahead this morning, over at Poplar. Carol Keating's on her way there now."

DI Carol Keating was an extremely experienced detective who also happened to bear an uncanny resemblance to the Carry On star, Hattie Jacques. Universally respected, her no-nonsense approach and brusque matronly manner had made her very popular with everyone on the command. Jack could always tell when she was around because almost everyone at Arbour Square had taken to greeting her with cries of, 'Ooh, Matron!'

"Well," Jack said, standing up, "I'd better get back to my office and update my Decision Log."

Quinlan grimaced. "That's exactly what I'm about to do. How's your job going, by the way? Are you making any progress?"

Jack paused by the door, a pained expression on his face. "It's very slow going," he admitted grudgingly. "And everyone seems to have written it off as a sticker, even though we're only two days in."

Quinlan afforded him a sympathetic smile. "I had heard rumours to that effect," he confessed. "Still," he offered by way of consolation, "all you can do when a case like that comes along is keep slogging away at it until you get a break." He refrained from pointing out that, sometimes, you never did.

————

They had agreed to meet at a no frills coffee shop near Aldgate East, about a minute's walk away from the tube station. It seemed a good compromise, being halfway between their respective work places. As he walked in, the half-dozen or so customers sitting nearest to the door momentarily glanced up to check out the new arrival. Their interest fleeting, they had already returned to their conversations by the time the door swung closed behind him.

The interior was warm and cheery, with a grey tiled floor, dark wooden panelling, and bright green walls, and the warm, inviting aroma of freshly brewed coffee was certainly preferable to the choking fumes of the heavy traffic lumbering by outside.

Tyler decided that he liked the café's chic appearance and eco-friendly ambience, but he reminded himself that he hadn't come here to experience that, or to indulge himself with a mid-morning treat, even though some of the calorie-laden cakes and pastries on display did look very inviting.

Looking around, Tyler spotted Maitland sitting by a window table at the back, looking tired and dishevelled under the harsh glow of the sunlight that was streaming in from outside. He hadn't shaved, his hair looked messy, and he was wearing the same clothing he'd worn the previous day, which suggested that he'd remained at the hospital overnight to be close to Jenny.

Maybe he did have some redeeming qualities after all, Tyler allowed as he weaved his way through the tables to join him. Although, on reflection, he decided probably not.

As if snapping out of a trance, Edward Maitland suddenly jerked his head up and pivoted in Tyler's direction. His eyes were red rimmed and swollen, as if he'd been crying, and he seemed absurdly pleased to see Tyler, which wasn't disturbing at all.

"Jack, so good of you to come," he said, standing up and offering his hand.

Like I had a choice after your emotional blackmail!

"I take it that Jenny's condition is still stable?" Tyler asked, releasing the hand as quickly as he could and taking a seat.

Maitland seemed startled by the question. "What? Oh, yes, she's doing very well," he said, and then frowned. "Unless the doctors have told you something in your official capacity that they've been withholding from me?"

Tyler smiled disarmingly and shook his head. "No. Not at all."

Maitland impatiently signalled to a server standing by the counter before returning to his seat. It was an arrogant gesture, Tyler thought, made by a man who had lots of money and looked down his nose at anyone who didn't.

"You look a little tired," Tyler observed, which was a massive understatement; the man sitting opposite him looked absolutely exhausted.

Maitland responded with a wan smile. "Didn't get much sleep."

Fair enough.

An overly exuberant server appeared beside them. Clad in the standard apparel of a barista, complete with a brown baseball cap emblazoned with the company logo. "Good morning lovely people!" he greeted them excitedly. "And what can I get for you today?"

"I'll have a cappuccino, please," Tyler told him.

"Double espresso for me," Maitland said.

"Can I tempt you with any of our special meal deals?" the server asked, pen poised over his little notepad in readiness to write down their order. The shiny golden nametag on his left breast read: 'Jerry.' It looked like it had recently been polished.

"We do–"

"Just the coffee, please," Maitland cut him off gruffly.

The smile faded from Jerry's face. "Certainly, sir," he said, dropping the false bonhomie like someone had just flicked off the switch.

"You know, life's a funny thing," Maitland said as their server departed.

Tyler surreptitiously checked his watch, conscious that every pointless minute he was stuck in here with Eddie was one less that he would be alive for, and one that could have been spent so much more productively doing his job.

Maitland was far too wrapped up in himself to notice Jack's restlessness. For a long moment, he stared out of the window, watching the pedestrians who were walking past. When he spoke again, his voice was tinged with sadness. "Isn't it strange how, one minute, life couldn't be more perfect; the next…" the words tapered off and he let out a painful sigh. "Well, it's like God has decided to take a giant shit on you just for the fun of it."

Or perhaps he just wanted to give you a taste of your own medicine because you're an inconsiderate wanker? Keeping the thought to himself, Jack sat back in his chair and folded his arms. "Yeah, well. Life is full of ups and downs, Eddie. You need to man up and be strong for Jenny's sake, not sit here moping because something bad happened." He arched an enquiring eyebrow at Maitland, as if to ask, 'what do you think about that?'

Maitland obviously didn't think much of it at all. He dry washed his face, which was pale and drawn. "Jack, I know we've had our differences, but I really need your help. I told you last night that Jenny and I have been experiencing problems and, well… the thing is…" his voice faltered and his eyes brimmed with tears "… I really don't want to lose her."

Tyler was completely unmoved by the uncharacteristic display of emotion. "Then you need to speak to her about this, not me," he said harshly. The last thing he wanted to do was sit there and listen to the man who had stolen his wife go on about their relationship problems, and it angered him beyond words that Maitland had the audacity to think it was acceptable to expect him to do so.

Maitland looked up at him, face like a wounded puppy, and tears began to roll down his cheeks.

Jack groaned, feeling his earlier resolution starting to wobble. Why couldn't Maitland just be his usual arrogant self, so that Jack could enjoy seeing him get his comeuppance, instead of turning on the waterworks and making him feel guilty?

"I can't talk to her, can I?" Maitland clumsily wiped away the tears with the heel of his hand. "Apart from the fact that she's in an Intensive Care Unit, fighting for her life, she hasn't spoken to me for days."

Jack pinched the bridge of his nose, feeling a headache coming on. "Eddie, you do remember that you're not my favourite person, don't you?"

Maitland seemed to shrink in size on hearing that. "I know, I know, and I'm so sorry," he snivelled, before blowing his nose on his napkin. "Stealing Jenny away from you and breaking up your marriage was a terrible thing to do, and I want you to know that I deeply regret causing you all that hurt."

Tyler didn't quite know how to respond to that. It was a most un-Eddie like thing to say. He took a deep breath, using the time to choose his next words carefully. "Look, Eddie, there's no getting away from it, what you did was completely out of order, and it's going to take more than you just saying 'sorry' to put things right between us." Another deep breath, expelled slowly. "But, the truth is, the marriage was already on its last legs long before you ever came into the picture."

Maitland looked up at him, clearly confused. "You mean I've been blaming myself for nothing for all these years?"

Jack's nostrils flared, and he was sorely tempted to lean across the table and slap Maitland around the head, just to knock some sense into him. "No. I don't mean that." *Idiot!* "I'm just saying that, even without your help, Jenny and I wouldn't have lasted much longer anyway."

"I see. That's very kind of you to say so," Eddie said. "Makes me feel a tiny bit better about myself."

Jack couldn't help but roll his eyes towards the heavens as he realised that his message just wasn't getting through, mainly because Eddie's brain seemed to have a filter installed that allowed him to only ever hear what he wanted to hear.

Before he could respond with a suitably acerbic comment, Jerry returned with their beverages, his faux bonhomie firmly back in place.

"There we go," the server said cheerfully, sliding their drinks onto the table. "Let me know if you need anything else." Smiling sweetly, he turned around and headed back the way he had come.

They sat in uncomfortable silence for a while, with Maitland withdrawing into himself and staring down into the blackness of his coffee to avoid having to look up at Tyler. In the end, Jack couldn't bear it any longer. "Eddie, I don't have a lot of time, so if there's something you want to say, I suggest you get on with it."

Eddie sighed, and slumped even further into his chair.

"Eddie…?"

More silence.

Jack took a sip of his coffee; consoling himself with the thought that, although the company was shit, at least the cappuccino was pleasant.

"I told you last night, Jenny and I have been trying for a baby for the best part of a year," Eddie suddenly blurted out, almost causing Jack to choke on his drink.

Not *this* again? Jack held up a hand to stop him. "Eddie, I'm really *not* the right person to speak to about this. Surely, you can talk to your dad? Or your best friend? You *do* have friends, I take it?"

Maitland shook his head miserably. "You don't understand. This isn't the sort of conversation I could have with anyone I'm close to. It would be too … uncomfortable for me."

A raised eyebrow. *Oh, but you're perfectly fine with it being uncomfortable for me?* That was just so typical of Eddie Maitland, only ever thinking about himself.

Eddie looked up, his eyes imploring. "Jack, you have to promise me that you won't speak a word of this to anyone else, not even Jenny." His lip quivered a little at the mention of her name, but he managed to control it.

This was getting silly. "No offence, Eddie, but I don't feel any loyalty to you, so either tell me or don't, I really don't care either way."

Maitland buried his head in his hands and moaned quietly. "Please, Jack… I don't have anyone else to have this conversation with."

There was so much raw pain in Maitland's voice that Jack felt his anger dissipating. Was he really that bereft of people he could confide in? Eddie was actually crying now, and Jack quickly glanced around the café, hoping that no one had noticed his pathetic behaviour. Thankfully the other customers were all enjoying their morning coffee break, like normal people; having fun and not trying to burden the man whose wife they had stolen five years earlier.

"Okay, Eddie. I'll keep what you say between us," Tyler said, caving in against his better judgement. "But I honestly don't have much time, so get on with it."

"Thank you, Jack," Eddie said as a little bubble of snot appeared beneath his left nostril. Jack slid another napkin across the table and Eddie gratefully blew his nose until the tissue was a soggy heap.

Jack was having a slight crisis of conscience. If Eddie and Jenny's relationship problems were purely down to the stress of trying to conceive, then surely his revealing that Mary Mitchell had found a positive pregnancy test in Jenny's bag would put an immediate end to all that? But Jenny's insistence that Jack should be the only person informed about her injuries still troubled him deeply.

Why hadn't she wanted Eddie informed?

And why hadn't she told him about the pregnancy test?

It just didn't make any sense. Tyler had learned to trust his instincts over the years, and right now, they were telling him to hold that information back.

"Eddie, if you two are having relationship issues, whether it's purely related to the stress of trying to have a baby or anything else, why don't you get some expert advice?"

Eddie shook his head. "It's not that simple, Jack." A mirthless laugh erupted from deep within him, full of bitterness and frustration. "Apparently, according to studies, eighty-seven percent of couples having regular sex will get pregnant within a year," he declared. "Well, guess what?" Anger and resentment had crept into his voice, and his normally handsome features twisted to match it. "Me and Jenny fall into the unlucky thirteen percent who don't." He looked at Jack expectantly, waiting for him to pass comment. When he didn't, Eddie just sighed. "Who knows, perhaps that's where the superstition about thirteen being an unlucky number originated? Anyway, when it hadn't happened for us after a few months, Jenny became totally obsessed. She started researching diet, exercise, the best positions to have sex in if you want to conceive – oh yeah, that's right! Apparently, some positions really are better than others. She learnt everything there was to know about the ovulation cycle."

Jack was inwardly cringing but, somehow, he managed to mask his discomfort. It was a good job he hadn't succumbed to the temptation to order cake with his coffee, because all this gross pregnancy related stuff that Eddie was reeling off had killed his appetite stone dead.

"Every bloody morning she would use a basal thermometer to take her temperature, because on her most fertile days it would be higher." Maitland barked out another harsh laugh. "And get this, she refused to get out of bed for fifteen minutes after having sex, doing her best to remain as motionless as a corpse because she had read that lying still afterwards improved your chances of falling pregnant."

This time, Jack couldn't suppress the involuntary shudder that ran through him. He *really* hadn't wanted to hear about that.

"She was taking all sorts of supplements," Maitland continued, completely oblivious to Jack's growing unease. "She was always hopping on the scales, worried that she might be under or overweight. Apparently, women who are either too fat or too thin have more trouble conceiving. I'm telling you, at one point, she had so many ovulation predictors and fertility monitors floating around the house that we could have opened up our own bloody shop!"

Jack smiled politely, desperately wishing that he could just get up and leave. Why was there never a vitally important call from work when you needed one?

"The whole thing became a bloody nightmare, and she ran her campaign to conceive with the precision of a military operation." Maitland paused to run his fingers through his messy hair. "Honestly, Jack, I've been involved in some pretty hostile takeovers in my time, but even the most brutal of them pales into insignificance compared to what she's been putting me through! I mean, listen to this: she made me go on a Vitamin E supplement because it increases a sperm's mobility and its ability to penetrate the woman's egg. She made us both eat Brazil nuts, tinned tuna and lobster on a regular basis, because they contain selenium. Ever heard of that?"

Jack shook his head, wishing he had never responded to any of Eddie's text messages.

"Lucky you. It's an antioxidant that's–" Maitland's voice parodied that of a cheesy American TV voiceover artist "–'good for men because it increases fertility, and just as good for women as it prevents chromo-some breakage, which can cause miscarriage.'"

"I'm sure she meant well," Tyler said, just to fill the silence that followed.

Maitland grunted, clearly underwhelmed by his response. "And then there were the diaries! She kept one for her menstrual cycle; what day it started, how long it lasted, what day it finished, and anything else that she thought might interest the doctor. There was another diary for sex!"

Jack raised a cautioning finger to his lips to warn Eddie that he was getting a little too animated.

The warning went unheeded.

"Who wants to have sex by appointment?" Maitland was saying, far too loudly for Tyler's liking. A woman, two tables away, looked over her shoulder in their direction and frowned disapprovingly.

Jack smiled an apology at her and she quickly turned away.

"There were days when it was taboo," Maitland continued unabashed, "because she considered it a wasted effort; at other times, she made us go at it like rabbits!"

Jack openly cringed this time, afraid the disturbing, and very graphic, image that had just popped into his head would scar him for life.

Unfortunately, Eddie wasn't finished yet. It was as though a damn had burst inside him and, after having bottled everything up for so long, a floodwater of pent up emotion was now pouring out.

"Did you know that if you have sex six days before ovulation, you stand a really good chance of falling pregnant, but if you leave it until the day before, you might miss your chance of conceiving altogether?"

"You learn something new every day," Tyler said, wishing there were a few things he could *unlearn* today.

For the first time in what seemed like ages, Eddie paused for breath. Thankfully, when he continued, his voice seemed less manic. "A few weeks ago, Jenny read an article that suggested taking regular holidays and romantic weekend breaks while trying to conceive greatly increased your chances of doing so." Maitland waved his hand dismissively, as though he considered this to be pure poppycock. "She said it was all to do with placing yourself in a more relaxed environment where you didn't feel under so much pressure to make it happen. Personally, I thought the article was a scam, written by some opportunistic travel agent who was just trying to flog more holidays.

Anyway, we booked ourselves into a luxury hotel for the following weekend. She spent the whole of Saturday having spa treatments and I played golf." He smiled nostalgically. "We had such a lovely day."

A lovely day apart, you mean, Jack refrained from saying.

"That night, we got ourselves all spruced up and enjoyed a wonderful romantic dinner together." He smiled as he reminisced about the meal. "We were both getting a bit fruity by the end of the night, and I thought to myself, what a pleasant change this makes, thinking about making love to Jenny as an act of pleasure, and not out of desperation to procreate. Everything was going extremely well, at least until we returned to our room and I discovered that she only wanted to have sex with me because–" the bitterness returned to his voice with a vengeance "–surprise, surprise, it was six days before her period started, which made it the optimum time to conceive."

"So you've already told me," Tyler pointed out irritably.

Maitland shrugged. "Have I? Well, anyway, I was rather drunk by then – too much wine with dinner, and too many shorts at the bar afterwards, so I said some hurtful things; told her a few home truths about how the constant pressure she was putting me under to make a baby was affecting me. I mean, you're a man so surely you understand?"

Jack assumed the question was rhetorical, as Maitland carried on without giving him an opportunity to respond.

"Her organising the bloody trip to fit in with her menstrual cycle felt like an act of betrayal. It certainly killed off the amorous mood that had been building. To be completely honest with you, what with the drink, and knowing she wanted me to perform to order yet a-bloody-gain, I struggled to… you know, to get it up."

Jack almost gagged. He was beginning to suspect he would need counselling after this. "You really don't need to be *that* honest with me," he snapped.

Maitland shrugged off the admonishment. "My inability to perform sent her flying into a rage. She accused me of being infertile and firing blanks. Said if I loved her I would be willing to make love to her all night if that was what it took to make a baby…"

"Eddie," Jack cut in, unable to stomach any more of this. "Why the hell are you telling me all this? It's not something I want, or need, to know about."

Eddie hung his head in humiliation. "It is, Jack... because it's relevant to what happened afterwards."

Jack spread his hands in perplexity. "Afterwards? What do you mean...?"

Eddie gulped, forced himself to carry on, although it was clear that he didn't want to. "As I said, I was rather drunk, so I don't really remember much about what happened. But I keep having these really bad dreams... like flashbacks..."

Maitland's breathing had become faster, and Jack could see his hands were suddenly trembling. "Jack, I've got a terrible feeling that, later on, to prove to her – and myself – that I was still a man, I might have forced myself on her, that I might have..." he couldn't bring himself to finish the sentence, to utter that final, terrible word.

The vein in Tyler's temple was pulsating as he leaned forward because, suddenly, he understood exactly why the man sitting opposite him had felt unable to discuss this with his family or friends. "Oh Eddie, please tell me you're not saying what I think you are?"

Tears of shame ran down Maitland's cheeks. "I'm sorry, Jack. I'm saying that I think I might... might have raped her."

CHAPTER SEVENTEEN

FOLLOWING UP LEADS

Standing in the blistering heat of the hotel parking lot, Chrissy Taylor squinted up at the artificial ski slopes of the Beckton Alps, which dominated the skyline behind her. The highest man-made hill in London, the dry slope had been opened in the late 1980s, having been built on a toxic soil heap that had been left over from the long since defunct Beckton Gas Works. She had been there herself, a couple of years previously, when she had undertaken a four session training course for beginners as part of the preparation for a real life skiing holiday with her, then, beau.

Sadly, the view from the Beckton Alps summit hadn't quite matched the natural beauty of its Swiss, Austrian, or French counterparts, with nothing but grey concrete council estates and the pollution filled A13 to gaze down upon from up above.

Slipping on her sunglasses, she wondered how much longer Geoff would be. He had popped into the hotel ages ago, to visit the washroom before they set off on their quest to retrace the steps Samuel

Adebanjo would have taken during his trip to the local grocery shop on the day of his arrest.

Chrissy fidgeted restlessly, wondering if she should avail herself of the facilities herself while they were here, but then decided she couldn't be bothered. "How long does it take to have a wee?" she asked herself, watching a figure clumsily zig-zag its way down the dry slope. Of course, it was always possible he was doing the other thing, having a number-two. She quickly pushed that image from her mind.

Dressed in a short sleeved maroon blouse, dark blue skirt, and black, leatherette flat-heel sandals, she was beginning to think that she should have applied some sun screen before coming out. She tended to burn easily, and she could already feel the midday heat cooking the skin on her arms.

Finally, Geoff emerged, holding a bar of chocolate and a large packet of crisps, and looking rather pleased with himself. "Found a snack dispenser in there," he told her gleefully. "And as I was about to put my money in to get a bar of chocolate, these fell out all on their own!" He waggled the packet of Cheese & Onion in front of her face. "How lucky was that!"

Chrissy shrugged, unimpressed. "Little things please little minds, I suppose." It was the only thing that was little about Geoff, she reflected, thinking that he really ought to go on a diet.

As he started to tuck into the crisps, devouring them as though he were in a race to finish them before someone came along and confiscated them from him, she unfolded the local street map she had printed out. "Right," she announced, after studying it for a few seconds, we want to go... that way." She pointed decisively towards a side road off to their left.

Geoff leaned over her shoulder, munching away like Pac Man. "You're holding the map upside down," he said helpfully.

Chrissy frowned, grunted, and turned it around. "As I said, we want to go that way." This time she pointed to their right.

Geoff smiled, and scrunched the now empty crisps bag up into a tiny ball. "You do know I grew up around here and don't need a map, don't you?" he told her.

Chrissy scowled at him. "Now you tell me?" she said, thinking:

moron! "Tell you what, why don't you lead the way?" She nodded for him to take the lead.

"My pleasure," Geoff said, unwrapping the bar of chocolate eagerly.

————

Detective Superintendent Danny Flynn sat at a table on the fifth floor canteen at New Scotland Yard and studied the food in front of him unenthusiastically. He had opted for the chicken curry, with Bakewell tart and custard for dessert. There was nothing wrong with the food; in fact, it looked rather nice, but nowhere near as nice as the pub lunch he had been hoping for, and his glass of blackcurrant juice was definitely no substitute for the cold pint of Guinness that he had been planning to wash his pub grub down with.

"Sorry I'm late," a distinguished looking man in a grey, pinstripe suit, white shirt, and bright red tie announced, placing his tray on the table opposite Flynn. His Etonian education was evident in his upper class voice, projecting confidence and an air of superiority. Like Flynn, he was in his fifties, with greying, expensively cut hair and the chiselled features of a man who kept himself very fit. His warrant card hung from a lanyard around his neck, proclaiming him to be Assistant Commissioner Timothy Galbraith.

"Only just got here myself, Tim," Flynn said with a smile. The two men had started off as probationers together all those years ago, and had, despite their class differences, become friends.

"Ah, I see you went for the chicken curry, too," Galbraith observed as he sat down.

The conversation, as they ate, was genial; they enquired after each other's families, spoke about how quickly retirement age was creeping up on them and whether they planned to take their pensions and go, or stay on for a little while longer, compared notes on who they were still in contact with from the good old days, and chatted about life in general. It was nice to catch up and indulge in a little nostalgia, Flynn decided, wondering at what point he would be able to steer the conversation onto the one subject that he really wanted to discuss.

In the end, he decided it would be better to wait until they had both finished eating. After all, he didn't want to appear too eager.

"Would you like coffee?" Galbraith asked after dessert.

Flynn nodded. "That would be smashing," he said. "White with two sugars, please."

Left alone with his thoughts while his friend went off to get the drinks in, Flynn cast his beady eyes around the room, studying the canteen's other guests as though they were animals in a zoo. There was roughly a sixty-forty split between uniforms and detectives, with all ranks represented, right up to the Deputy Commissioner himself. No doubt desperate to show that he was still 'one of the lads', the Met's second in command had chosen to eat in here with the masses rather than make use of the more secluded senior officer's mess.

"Bloody idiot," Flynn muttered under his breath.

Flynn spotted a group of six naive looking young PCs, all under the watchful stewardship of a crusty old sergeant. Shoes gleaming and trousers sharply creased, they were all smiling enthusiastically as they took in this strange new environment. This was obviously a group of rookie PCs, fresh out of Hendon Training School, who were being taken on a familiarisation tour of The Yard before joining their new division. Their exuberance made the poor sods stick out like a sore thumb. Well, it wouldn't take long for all that positivity to be knocked out of them, he thought cynically. Give it a couple of years and they would be just as miserable and disillusioned as everyone else.

The old lags like him, officers who were coming up the end of their service and more than ready to go, were just as easy to spot. They sat with their shoulders hunched, a weary expression plastered across their prematurely aged faces, looking like they had had more than enough. And yet, each of them had started off just like the fresh faced recruits who were now standing in an orderly line, waiting to be served. He snorted derisively, thinking how drastically thirty years of policing could change a person's outlook.

When Galbraith returned, Flynn decided it was time to cut to the chase. "Tim, while I've got your attention, I wanted to ask a favour of you."

Galbraith immediately became wary. "How can I help?" he asked in a tone that implied helping Flynn was the last thing he wanted to do.

"It's one of my officers, a chap called Tony Dillon. He's about to be promoted – overpromoted if you want my honest opinion – to the rank of inspector. He's due to transfer to AMIP, but I really don't think he's ready for a job that carries *that* much responsibility yet."

Galbraith's eyes narrowed. "Just to be clear, are you saying he's not ready for the rank, or just not ready to be running murder investigations yet?"

Flynn's moustache twitched as he ran nicotine stained fingers through the unruly strip of hair under his nose. "Both. I don't think he should be promoted at all. I mean, I've done everything I can to groom him for promotion, of course, but the man's a dangerous hothead, and I think if he's allowed to transfer to AMIP, he will inevitably make rash decisions that jeopardise important investigations. That won't reflect too well on the Met, will it? Especially with all this unjustified criticism we've come under over the Stephen Lawrence enquiry."

The results of the Stephen Lawrence enquiry, chaired by Sir William MacPherson of Clunny, had been published in February of that year. It was a damning report that had scrutinised the Met's failings in relation to the investigation into Stephen Lawrence's murder, and it had concluded that the Metropolitan Police Service was institutionally racist. The ramifications were still being felt several months later, and everyone agreed the report's outcome would impact policing for many years to come.

"If he's not up to the job, why was his promotion application supported?" Galbraith demanded, not liking the sound of this at all.

Flynn shrugged. "Unfortunately, his yearly appraisals are exemplary. He has numerous commendations, and he was highly recommended by his first and second line managers, so there was nothing I could do to prevent it." He looked around furtively, making sure that he couldn't be overheard. "Between you and me, Tim, I even spoke to contacts on the promotion board, but they said there was nothing they could do unless I had any actual evidence that he was unfit for promotion. Can you imagine that?"

"Do you have any?" Galbraith asked.

Flynn snorted derisively. "Why does everyone keep asking me that? No. I don't. But I have something more important." He tapped his stomach. "A gut instinct that Dillon doesn't fit the mould. He's not fit to lead, I tell you." His face had gone a dangerously dark shade of red, and Flynn could feel a pulse throbbing in the side of his neck like it was trying to break free.

Calm down. Remember your blood pressure, he told himself. It had been way too high during his last visit to the quack, when he'd had his yearly check-up. The fool had put him on tablets, and told him to stop smoking and cut down on the booze, but what did he know?

He could see that Galbraith was starting to look concerned. That was good, it meant that Flynn was finally getting his point home to someone who could do something about this ridiculous situation. As an AC, Galbraith had the clout to have Dillon reposted to a quiet backwater division, where he couldn't do any harm, with a single phone call. He sat back in his chair, breathing heavily, conscious that his forehead was damp with perspiration.

"This man has really got you worked up, hasn't he, Danny?" Galbraith said gently.

Flynn shook his head, realising that he had to tread carefully. If Galbraith formed the slightest suspicion that he had a personal vendetta against Dillon, he wouldn't get involved. "It's nothing personal, you understand."

"Have you spoken to George Holland about this?" Galbraith asked, and the intensity of his stare was making Flynn feel uncomfortable. "He won't want a man like that on his team."

Flynn grimaced, wishing his friend hadn't asked that particular question. He was tempted to lie, but that was way too risky; if he did, and Tim double checked with Holland, it would come back to bite him with a vengeance. "Actually," he said hesitatingly, "I have spoken to George about this. I told him what I thought, tried to warn him, but he said he had every faith in the man and was very happy to have him aboard."

A pain rippled through Flynn's stomach, like he had just swallowed broken glass. Maybe he should get that checked out, in case he was developing an ulcer. That was all he needed on top of his hypertension. No doubt the killjoy quacks would tell him to cut out greasy food as well as booze and fags. How his wife would love that! She had been nagging him to change his diet for years.

Galbraith sat back in his chair, looking mystified. "Well, to be perfectly honest, Danny, if this Dillon character has such an exemplary record, and George Holland still wants him despite you flagging up your concerns, I don't really know what you expect me to do about it."

"I see," Flynn said, bitterly disappointed. He stood up and offered his hand, keen to get away before he said something that might damage their friendship. "Well, it's been lovely to see you, Tim." A cold smile. "Best wishes to the wife and all that. Now, if you'll excuse me, I've got a meeting this afternoon, and if I don't leave now, I might be late."

"Of course," Galbraith said, shaking his hand. "Take care, and I'm sorry I couldn't be of more help."

Flynn shrugged his shoulders, making light of it. "Like I said, it isn't personal." Only it was, and it was becoming more so with every minute. He waited until he was in the lift, alone, before letting out a scream of rage.

———

Chrissy stared down into the overflowing bin and pulled a face. "Are you seriously telling me you've run out of rubber gloves?" she asked Geoff.

He shrugged lamely. "Sorry, I brought loads of them out with me, but how was I meant to know we would end up having to look through so many bleeding bins on our way here?"

Chrissy shook her head in despair. They had been told to search every bin they came across on the route to the shop Adebanjo had visited – every sodding bin! How had he not brought enough gloves to do the job properly? Maybe he had eaten them; she wouldn't have put it past him. "Well, I'm not putting *my* hand in there," she told him, looking at the overflowing bin outside the shop. "You'll have to do it."

"But it's your turn," he said, looking crestfallen.

Chrissy folded her arms and glared at him frostily over the rim of her sunglasses. "Geoff, you were tasked with bringing gloves. You didn't bring enough. Either get me some gloves to wear or search the blasted bin yourself." She tapped her foot impatiently, waiting for him to do something.

Geoff looked at her, then at the bin, then back at her. "Fine," he said. Cursing under his breath, he set off towards the corner shop.

"Please tell me you're not going in there to buy more food?" she yelled.

Geoff stopped in his tracks, and spun around to face her. "Actually, I was going to see if they sold rubber gloves," he informed her, thrusting his chin into the air haughtily.

"Oh," she said. To be fair, it wasn't a bad idea, not that she was going to tell him that. "Well, don't let me stop you then," she told him.

"Gah!" he said, and disappeared inside.

While he was gone, she tried ringing Dillon to see how he was getting on, but there was no reply. She checked her watch: quarter to one. He was probably still tucked up with the first SPM at the mortuary.

Geoff came out, munching on a Twix.

Oh for heaven's sake! Didn't he ever stop?

He tossed her a sealed blue and yellow plastic bag with white writing on it.

"What's this?" she asked, only just about managing to catch it.

"Marigolds," he said. "I got us a pair each."

It was the first useful thing he had done all day. Tearing open the packaging, Chrissy removed the bright yellow gloves and started sliding her hand into one. "Did they come with a free bar of chocolate then?" she asked, sarcastically.

Geoff shook his head. "Nah, had to pay extra for that."

It had taken them the best part of an hour, but they had walked all the way from the hotel to the corner shop, checking every single bin that they had come across along the way. Taking turns, they had rummaged around inside each receptacle in the hope of recovering the burner phone that the boss was convinced Adebanjo had dumped before returning to the hotel. "You know," she said, ramming her hand inside the bin and recoiling at the stench of rotting food, "I was sure that he would have dumped it nearer the hotel."

"Me too," Geoff agreed, now tucking into a KitKat.

More food? Where did he put it all?

"Here, Chrissy, what's the difference between a KitKat and a porn star?" he suddenly asked her.

Chrissy stopped, mid rummage. "What? I have absolutely no idea." What a strange question, she thought, pushing her arm deeper into the squelchy stuff at the bottom of the bin.

Geoff was belly laughing at his own joke before he'd even delivered the punchline. "You can only get four fingers in a KitKat."

Chrissy threw a decomposing banana skin she'd found in the bin at him, taking great pleasure as it thwacked into the back of his head.

"Oi! What was that for?" he shouted, frantically brushing it out of his hair.

"For being so disgusting. Where did you get that horrible joke from, the sewer?"

"Well, I thought it was funny," he said, flicking the remnants of the banana skin off his shoulder.

Chrissy's hand suddenly brushed against something firm at the bottom of the bin, but then it was gone. Probably nothing, but she fumbled around blindly until she reacquired it. It was rectangular and solid, a reasonable weight, too. Surely, it couldn't be...?

Wrapping her hand around the slimy object, Chrissy carefully pulled it from the bin. "Bingo!" she said, holding her arm aloft like Arthur removing Excalibur from the stone, and breaking into a smile of triumph. Covered in what looked like baked bean juice, the mobile phone in her hand was a cheap Motorola, the sort of no frills model that a criminal would use as a burner.

"Is that what I think it is?" Geoff asked, taking a step closer.

"It certainly is," she announced, and did a happy little jig to celebrate. That was when she caught sight of the small camera above the shop's entrance. The bin was directly in its line of sight. "Oh, we couldn't be that lucky, could we?" she said, walking towards the shop entrance.

"Grab me another KitKat while you're in there, would you?" Geoff shouted after her.

———

Dillon squeezed into the tight gap that George Copeland had left for him at the cramped two-person table and stared dolefully at his chicken burger. The first autopsy had finally finished, and they had taken a much needed break, popping out to a fast food restaurant in nearby Walthamstow Central to grab some grub before commencing the next one, not that he felt remotely hungry, having just watched a man whose torso had been already torn apart by a sustained burst of gunfire be further desecrated by Creepy Claxton.

Having now met the man, he fully understood why everyone at AMIP called him 'Creepy Claxton'. Slim and intense, with a hairstyle that could easily have been modelled on Albert Einstein's, and a face deader than the cadaver he was examining on the stainless steel table, the Home Office Forensic Pathologist had triggered an involuntary shudder every time he'd stared at Dillon with those piercing black eyes, as though measuring him up for the slab.

With his little mortuary assistant shuffling around behind him like his very own version of Igor, and doting on his every move, all that would have been necessary to transform the scene into something straight out of a Frankenstein movie was the thunder and forked light-ning from an overhead electrical storm.

"I'm starving," George announced, happily tucking into his double cheeseburger. A spurt of tomato sauce erupted out of the side of his mouth, instantly reminding Dillon of the shredded body they had just spent the last four and a half hours with.

Grimacing at the sight, he picked up his chicken burger and forced himself to take a bite. There was nothing wrong with it but, somehow, the thought of eating meat after watching a man slice up a human body with the same level of detachment he'd have if he were carving a Sunday roast, had robbed him of the urge to eat.

The thing that had surprised him most this morning was just how much fat had been stored inside the Turkish gangster's body. He had expected there to be a layer of fat beneath the skin, of course, with the muscles and organs located beneath that, but it had been *everywhere,* even in the eye sockets, and fat, he had learned today, had a very distinctive, and most unpleasant smell to it. If Erkan Dengiz had been obese, he would have understood it, but he hadn't been, not at all.

"Did you know," George was telling him, "that feeling hungry after attending a post mortem is a perfectly normal reaction that's triggered by our primal instincts? It stems from the days when our prehistoric ancestors hunted their food and, after killing it, chopped it up and ate it raw."

"What a load of bollocks," Dillon replied, unenthusiastically shoving some French fries into his mouth. He chewed on these joylessly while he watched Copeland trying to work a piece of gristle out from beneath his teeth, where it had become stuck. When he finally succeeded, he looked at it for a moment, shrugged, and then chucked it straight back into his mouth.

"Waste not, want not," Copeland said in response to Dillon's quizzical look.

A small group of teenagers, dressed in the uniform of a local school, invaded the two tables next to them, laughing and joking and throwing fries at each other.

Dillon scowled at them, and they quickly settled down.

"Don't be such a meanie," George teased him. "What's the matter? Don't you like kids?"

"I do," Dillon told him with a faux maniacal smile, "but I don't think I could eat a whole one."

George chuckled and wiggled his eyebrows up and down mischievously. "I think I could probably polish off a couple at the moment. I'm absolutely famished!"

"Good job you purchased enough food to feed a small third world country then, isn't it?" Dillon said as George started on his second burger.

His mobile rang, making him jump. After checking the Caller ID, he pressed the green button and raised the phone to his face with a smile. "Hello, gorgeous! How are you getting on?" he asked DC Christine Taylor.

Only it wasn't Chrissie, it was Geoff, using her phone.

"*I'm doing okay, thank you,*" Geoff replied, and Dillon could hear the mocking grin in his voice. "*Chrissy asked me to give you a quick bell to let you know we found a slime covered mobile phone at the bottom of the bin outside the corner shop Adebanjo went into,*" he said. "*And, as if that wasn't a result in itself, the shop has a little spy camera above the door, and we've managed to get some good quality CCTV of him coming out of the shop and dumping something in the bin.*"

The news perked Dillon up no end. "Well done," he said.

"*Don't you mean, well done gorgeous?*" Geoff taunted.

Dillon laughed at the retort. "Well done, gorgeous," he said obligingly. "So, how come you're calling me and not Chrissy?"

"*She's just speaking to the snapper we called out to get it photographed in situ,*" Geoff explained. "*But she wanted to let you know ASAP in case you were going back in the mortuary any time soon.*"

The reminder that he had another session watching Creepy Claxton cut up dead bodies caused the smile to drop from his face faster than a falling stone. Not to be outdone, his good mood plummeted straight down after it, overtaking it on the way. "Have you informed DCI Tyler yet?" he asked.

"*Er, I haven't but I think Chrissy phoned it in before calling out the photographer. I know she's tried to phone you several times but your phone has always been switched off.*"

"It's not switched off," Dillon corrected him. "It's just that I don't get a signal inside the mortuary."

Geoff said something back to him; it sounded like a not very funny quip about the mortuary being an apt place for his signal to die in, but he be couldn't be sure thanks to George choosing that precise moment to start draining his large strawberry milkshake with extreme vigour, and feeling the need to do so right next to his ear.

As he finished the call, there was a ferocious rattle from the straw, which thankfully signalled there was nothing left. Oblivious to the disparaging looks he was now receiving, George carried on sucking for several seconds anyway, just to make sure, then tossed it onto the table and belched contentedly.

"That's better," he said with a smile.

Dillon chewed his last few mouthfuls of food disconsolately, and then stood up slowly, like a man preparing himself for the long, lonely walk to the gallows. "Come on," he said reluctantly, "the sooner we get this second SPM over with, the sooner we can escape that horribly depressing mortuary."

"Until tomorrow," George reminded him. "Don't forget, we're back tomorrow for the other two." He had the nerve to sound like he was looking forward to it.

Dillon wrinkled his nose in disgust. "Great," he said, morosely. "That's just the news I needed to cheer me up."

———

Colin Franklin rapped on Tyler's door before poking his head in. "Afternoon, guv. Just thought I'd let you know, I've got that covert footage of the waste area where the Mondeo was dumped."

"Have you had a chance to look at it yet?" Tyler asked, putting his pen down. He had literally just finished writing up the last of his Decision Log entries, a never ending process that took up so much of his time as an SIO, and he still needed to review all the main operational strategies to see if any required updating. Because of all the time he had wasted with Eddie Maitland earlier, he had fallen way behind where he wanted to be, and his in tray seemed to have grown another foot or so while he had been out.

Eddie's admission had jarred him so much that he been struggling to concentrate on work since returning to the office and, although he'd tried his hardest not to dwell on the implications of Eddie's terrible confession, the tumultuous thoughts his revelation had conjured up were buzzing around inside Tyler's head like a group of angry wasps.

"I had a brief view while I was with the locals," Franklin said. "You see the car drive by the Traveller's site and then go onto the wasteland, but the location where it was dumped is just off camera."

"Typical," Tyler grunted, shoulders sagging with disappointment.

"It's not all bad news," Franklin told him with an encouraging smile. "A few minutes after it arrives, you see the flickering glow of flames, and these illuminate three bald headed blokes who hotfoot it across the wasteland to the road. The three of them walk straight under the camera, so you get quite a good birds eye view of them for a couple of seconds. It looks to me like they're all wearing baggy track suits and carrying small holdalls, overnight bags or something like that. Oh, and get this, you can definitely make out one of them has a mark on his right neck. I'm hoping the lab can do something to enhance the footage, but even if they can't, odds are that this in the bloke Tulay Yildiz described as the shooter with the tattoo."

"Can you go and set it up for me to view in the CCTV room, please Colin," Jack asked him eagerly, "and give me a call as soon as you're ready."

This was potentially very exciting news; if the faces of the gunmen were clear enough to recognise, the footage would be powerful evidence against them. He reached behind his chair and found the statement ring binder for this job, thumbing through it until he came to Tulay's. He skimmed through it until he reached the suspect's descriptions. Sure enough, she had described all three shooters as wearing grey tracksuit type sweatshirts and bottoms, along with dark balaclavas and gloves.

The phone went; it was Franklin informing him that he was ready to play the CCTV. "That was quick," Tyler said, impressed. "I'll be right there."

On his way through the main office, he spotted Steve Bull sitting at his desk going through statements. "Stevie," he called. "You might want to see this footage that Colin's just brought back from where the Mondeo was burnt out."

The two men walked purposefully along the corridor, heading for the building's CCTV viewing room, a very grand title for a space smaller than most broom closets.

As they strode past Quinlan's office, Jack glanced inside and saw that it was still a hive of activity. He promised himself that he would pop in to get another update as soon as he got a free minute.

When they reached the CCTV broom cupboard, they found Colin sitting in a high backed chair, staring at a TV on the desk in front of him. A picture of a dark road abutting some wasteland was flickering on the screen where it had been paused.

There were two other, smaller, chairs in the room, but there wasn't a lot of space, so the three men sat elbow to elbow, all scrunched up together.

When everyone had got themselves as comfortable as possible under the circumstances, Franklin pressed play. The picture unfroze with a jerk and, after a few seconds, a dark coloured saloon appeared, coming from the left of the screen, in which direction lay the slip road from the A406.

"This is the Mondeo," Franklin said, pausing the shot just before the driver initiated the right turn into the wasteland. Whether by luck or skill, he managed to stop it at the optimum moment, providing them with a very clear look at the front of the vehicle and the men inside it.

Bull whistled slowly. "Will you look at that," he said, leaning in for a closer look. The front passenger was leaning back over his right shoulder to address the rear occupant, so his head was partially obscured, but there was a really good quality shot of the driver's face. Franklin advanced the footage a frame at a time until the index came into focus.

"Stop!" Steve called out excitedly. He hurriedly scribbled down the digits he could make out, which was about half of them. They had already obtained the vehicle's registration number from the VIN check on the chassis, but it was nice to have visual confirmation, even if it was only of a partial index.

Franklin let the CCTV play on and, as he had explained to Tyler earlier, the distinctive flickering glow of a fire lit up the bottom right hand side of the screen a short while later. Before long, three white men emerged into the picture, hurrying from the direction of the flames and glancing back over their shoulders periodically.

As they came straight towards the camera, Franklin slowed the play rate down again, advancing it one frame at a time, until they were standing almost directly opposite the camera. Between the eerie glow coming from the flames behind them and the ambient streetlighting of the road they were entering, their features were very clearly captured.

"How about that," Franklin beamed at them. "I've got to say, the picture looks much clearer on this set up than it did on the little monitor the locals used to show me this footage earlier. I reckon the lab will be able to improve it even more, and we should end up with some very clear facial shots of these three lowlifes."

Tyler tapped his pen against one of the figures on the screen. "The one in the middle has got a scar running down the left side of his face from his nose to his lip," he said. "I thought he was smiling at first but, on closer inspection, I think his mouth is being pulled upwards by the scar."

"You're right, boss. And look at this one," Steve said, pointing to the tallest of the three men, the one on the left. "As he turns his head to speak to the others, you can clearly see he's got some sort of tattoo on the right side of his neck."

"That's what I told the boss," Franklin said.

Tyler leaned forward and squinted, then frowned, and then pulled a moue. "I think you're right," he said guardedly, "but maybe we're all just convincing ourselves of that because we already know one of the shooters has a tattoo there?"

Steve shrugged. "Maybe, but I don't think so."

"Me neither," Franklin said as he continued to advance the footage frame by frame. He paused the footage when the three men finally disappeared from sight.

"That's it," he said. "That's all I've got to show you at the moment."

Tyler stood up and patted him on the back. "It's great work, Colin. Get this up to the video lab at Newlands Park straight away. Let's see if they can improve it at all."

CHAPTER EIGHTEEN

ALWAYS LOOK UNDER THE MATTRESS

Back in his office, Tyler sat at his desk in silence, brooding over the unpleasant dilemma that Eddie's earlier revelation had created for him, and trying to decide what to do for the best.

I'm sorry, Jack. I'm saying that I think I might... might have raped her...

For what seemed like the hundredth time, he replayed the conversation that had followed these words in his mind.

Him, incredulous. "What the hell do you mean, you think you *might* have raped her, Eddie? You either did or you didn't!"

It was a simple yes or no answer as far as Jack was concerned and, if Jenny had said no, but Eddie had forced her to have sex with him anyway, then that was rape, pure and simple. Jack had told him that he couldn't, and wouldn't, look the other way if Jenny made an accusation.

Eddie, all pathetic and cringy, making himself out to be as much a victim as Jenny, maybe even more so. "It's complicated, Jack, and it doesn't help that everything's such a blur in my head."

When pushed, Eddie had admitted that, in addition to all the alcohol he'd consumed that night, he had also snorted a few lines of coke.

"Half of what I'm telling you is vague memory; the rest is me trying to join the dots together to make sense of it all."

"So what can you remember?"

"Well, we had a gargantuan argument. It was bad, even by our standards, but we eventually calmed down and decided that, as it was her optimum time to conceive, we ought to have another go at doing it. Everything was going tickety-boo until I accidentally called her by another woman's name, at which point she went into orbit…" At this point, Eddie had shaken his head disbelievingly, as though Jenny's reaction had been completely irrational. "…Anyway, she shouted and screamed at me, insisting that she didn't want me anywhere near her." With a pathetic little snivel, Eddie had wiped the tears from his eyes. "It was like she was playing mind games with me, deliberately getting me to the point of no return and then telling me to stop. Well, I couldn't stop, and I didn't want to. She'd begged me to make her pregnant, and I decided that was exactly what I was going to do."

Him, exasperation turning to anger, reaching over and grabbing Eddie's arm. "Did you force yourself on her?"

There were equal amounts of outrage and horror in Eddie's voice as he said, "No, Jack! I would never do that." Shaking his head vigorously to reinforce the denial. "She was perfectly happy to let me shag her, until I made the silly mistake of calling out a typist's name instead of hers. Then she went all Arctic freeze on me and tried to make me get off."

"And you didn't?"

Eddie, crying again. "I know that I really should've, but I was so angry, and I was at the point of no return anyway, so I pinned her down until I had… well, you know… finished."

Eddie had been right when he'd said it was complicated. Even though societal attitudes had changed for the better over the years, and the public were now generally more enlightened, there were still a lot of closed minded people who secretly thought it wasn't a bona fide rape if the assailant was a spouse or a loved one. Even amongst those who agreed that it most definitely was, there was a sub-conscious tendency to assume that being assaulted by a husband or lover wasn't quite as bad as being attacked by a stranger. The truth was that rape was rape, and it was wrong to make excuses for the attacker just because they happened to be in a relationship with their victim.

None of the lawyers Jack knew were terribly keen on prosecuting domestic rapes, in which the lines between right and wrong were often perceived as big grey areas of uncertainty by jurors, making such cases notoriously difficult to prove. He had seen it for himself, defence QCs exploiting the fact that 'alleged' victims were still in love with - or at the very least, still harboured feelings for - their 'attackers.' Once that particular can of worms was opened, it inevitably muddied the waters at trial.

Then there was the added complication that they had been engaged in consensual intercourse before Jenny had told him to stop. Unquestionably, Eddie should have done so at once, but Jack knew from experience that no jury would convict him if his barrister could convince them that she had told him to stop at a point in time where it was physically impossible for him to comply because he was about to orgasm. If he was perfectly honest, Jack wasn't sure that he would convict on the strength of that, either.

Of course, he hadn't heard Jenny's side of the story yet, and he needed to if he was to take this any further, which brought him to the crux of the matter; what should he do next? Should he just bite the bullet and ask her directly the next time he saw her? Or was it better to wait and see if she came forward to make an accusation of her own accord?

A loud knock on the door brought Jack's mind whirling back to the present.

"Come in," he shouted, trying to marshal his thoughts as Andy Quinlan waltzed in carrying two mugs of coffee in '*I met the Met*' branded mugs.

"I thought I'd stop by for a quick chat to see how things are progressing," he said, handing one over.

"I would have happily made you coffee," Jack said, gratefully accepting the mug from Andy's outstretched hand.

"I know you would," Quinlan said, with a crooked grin. "And as tempting as a cup of that cheap instant rubbish your team seems to enjoy so much might be for some SIOs, my taste buds are a little more refined, which is why I brought my own." He flopped down into the chair opposite Tyler's desk.

From the smirk on his face, Jack could tell there had been a development that Andy was itching to share with him. "Come on then, spill the beans," he encouraged.

Quinlan grinned like the proverbial Cheshire Cat. "The fingerprint results from that can of spray paint you spotted in the CCTV came back earlier, and they belong to a nasty little street urchin called Zane Dalton. He's one of the Holly Street youngers, and even though he's only fourteen, he's already got form for nicking cars, drugs, assault, and burglary."

"Sounds like an ideal candidate for the church choir," Tyler said with a grin.

"I popped in to tell you earlier," Andy said, "but you were out."

Jack's face clouded over as he recalled his painful rendezvous with Eddie. "Yes, I had a rather unpleasant meeting that I couldn't get out of."

"Well, Susie Sergeant took an arrest team over to his house in Richmond Road, a stone's throw away from the Holly Street estate, about an hour ago. She nicked young Zane and promptly spun his address, and..." he let the sentence die off, taking a sip of his coffee to build the tension. "...guess what they found hidden under his mattress? I'll give you a clue: it wasn't porn magazines!"

"A bundle of cash? Some blood stained clothing? A copy of Choirboys Weekly...?"

Quinlan chuckled delightedly. "They found a bag full of property, all of which we think was stolen during the Clapton train steaming. It included wallets with some of the victim's credit cards and driving licences still in them"

Quinlan's words triggered a fond memory of an 'old-sweat' PC who had taken Jack under his wing during his probationary period.

Every time that they had searched a prisoner's house together, he had whispered in Jack's ear, 'remember lad, always look under the mattress'.

"Is the little shit speaking?" Jack asked, hoping that the boy might have spilled the beans on whoever had stabbed Jenny and poor old Stanley Cotton in the hope of rowing himself out of a murder charge.

"He's too stupid for that," Quinlan said. "Claims he'd never seen it before and that the searching officers planted it there."

Jack tutted. The boy's lack of imagination was disappointing. "Hardly an original line, is it? As if anyone's going to believe *that!*"

"Oh, I don't know. His mother seems to have swallowed it. She's doing the outraged parent bit at the moment, claiming that the big bad police officers are just picking on her poor little diddums because he's a disadvantaged young black lad who lives in an impoverished area and therefore fits our stereotype of a street robber."

"Oh puh-lease!" Jack scoffed. "Honestly, what's wrong with these people?"

"Oh it gets worse," Quinlan announced with a mischievous grin. "The stupid cow tried to give him an alibi, claiming he was at home with her at the time of the murder. Trouble is, her five-year old daughter gave the game away by blurting out that mummy was working at Tesco in Well Street that day, and Susie confirmed this with a quick call to the store manager."

"Oops," Jack said. "Well, I think it's safe to say that she's not a suitable candidate to act as appropriate adult for the interviews then, is she?"

Quinlan shook his head. "Nope. She's lucky they didn't nick her for attempting to pervert the course of justice. If it hadn't been for the fact that there was no one else to look after the little girl, I think they might well have done."

"Have they found the clothing he was wearing at the time of the offence?" Jack asked.

Quinlan's face scrunched up with disappointment. "No, afraid not. Looks like he already got rid of them."

"Pity," Jack said. "How are the interviews with Xander Mason and Curtis Bright coming along?"

Quinlan rolled his eyes. "All we got from those two morons was a string of 'no comment' replies, and they stopped saying that once they were shown the Hackney Downs CCTV footage. They must know they're bang to rights for the steaming, and I suspect they're just hoping that we can't pin the murder on them as well."

Jack noticed that he hadn't said anything about the attempted murder. "I take it you'll be speaking to the CPS about charging everyone who was involved with the steaming with Joint Enterprise murder *and* attempted murder?" Jack said, his tone implying that Andy had better be.

Joint Enterprise is a doctrine of common law dating back several centuries, and it's most commonly invoked to convict people in gang-related cases where the prosecution argues that co-defendants 'should' have foreseen the violent acts subsequently committed by their associates during the commission of a crime.

Quinlan nodded affirmatively. "I've already had a preliminary discussion. The census of opinion at the moment is that we sheet them with the robberies as a holding charge, and then grant them technical bail in relation to the murder and attempted murder. Once all the evidence is assembled, and we know exactly what we've got, we can start looking at specific charges of murder and attempted murder for any identified stabbers, and a Joint Enterprise charge for everyone else who was present."

"Don't let the CPS try to talk you out of it," Tyler warned, staring at his friend intently. "If everyone who participated in the steaming gets charged with Joint Enterprise murder and attempted murder, the trial will become a cutthroat, which will be great for us because the defendants will all turn on each other to save their own rotten skins."

Quinlan nodded reassuringly. "I know, Jack. I know," he said softly. "Don't worry, matey, I won't let the people who did this to Jenny get away with it."

Jack nodded, satisfied that Andy would be true to his word.

The urgent trill of a ringtone interrupted the conversation. Quinlan awkwardly fished his mobile from his jacket pocket, squinted at the caller ID, and then pressed the green button. "Hello," he said as he raised it to his ear. He listened for a few seconds, his face a studious mask of concentration, and then he broke into a wide grin. "That's wonderful news," he said, turning to look at Jack. "I'm with him now, so I'll let him know."

Jack scowled at him, but Quinlan raised a hand for him to be patient while he listened some more. "Okay, Susie. Great work. Thanks for bringing me up to speed."

"What will you let me know?" Jack asked as soon as Quinlan had hung up.

"Kevin Murray has just found a pair of training shoes hidden in the bottom of Zane's wardrobe, and the sole of one foot has a big splodge of dried blood on it."

Jack grinned broadly. "Fantastic news."

"His idiot mother tried to snatch them away from Kevin, claiming they were hers," Quinlan said, shaking his head at the woman's stupidity. "When he refused to hand them over, she lost the plot, jumped on him, and tried to scratch his eyes out. She's just been arrested for attempting to pervert the course of justice and assault."

––––––––

When the call from Gunz came through, Dritan was pacing up and down in his little hotel room. If the faded carpet hadn't already been threadbare, it would have definitely ended up that way by the time he was finished. The uneasiness had returned, and he had been contemplating going for another long walk to prevent it from spiralling into a full blown panic attack.

"Yes?" he said tensely.

"*Yo, man,*" Gunz greeted him like they were old friends. "*Looks like we're on for some more fun and games tonight. I've been told to provide you with another car, and when the time comes, you'll find it parked up across the road from the hotel. I'll ring you with the details later, once I've boosted it.*"

With that, he was gone.

Although Dritan hadn't heard from his employer since he had been arrested on Tuesday night, he wasn't overly concerned. The plan had always called for there to be minimal contact between them, and for all logistical and supply issues to be facilitated by the black man's gang. He already knew the second target address, and what he was expected to do there. Goliath would, no doubt, call him with his final instructions later on, but even if he didn't, Dritan and his team would fulfil the mission objectives they had been set in Manchester.

Now that vital preparation needed to be carried out in advance of tonight's deployment, his mind became totally focused on getting the team ready, and that dispelled his anxiety as effectively as a walk would have done.

He strode along the corridor to the room the others shared, rapping on the door in the agreed manner so that they would know it was him.

Lorik answered, a half smoked cigarette dangling from his mouth. He held the door open for Dritan to enter and then, after taking a quick glance out into the corridor to make sure that no one had seen them, closed it firmly behind him.

The television was playing an episode of *Docklands*, one of the mundane daytime soaps that the people in this country seemed to love so much, and Dritan lost no time in switching it off.

"Hey, I was watching that," Valmir protested from the bed on which he was stretched out with his hands tucked behind his head.

"I've just had a call from one of the black men," Dritan announced, brushing Valmir's legs off the bed and taking a seat. "He said that the job's on for tonight, and that he will be obtaining us a suitable car for transport. He's going to call me back when he has it."

"Have you heard from the boss yet?" Valmir asked, stretching expansively.

Dritan shook his head. "No. I expect he'll call later, before we deploy, but we know exactly where we are going and what's expected of us when we get there, so whether he calls or not, we go ahead as planned."

Valmir considered this, nodded. "Okay," he said. "Have I got time to eat before we start making preparations?"

Dritan stared at him in awe. "Do you ever think about anything other than your stomach?" he asked with a crooked grin.

Valmir grinned. "I sometimes think about women," he admitted, "but mostly food."

The three men laughed.

Dritan checked his wristwatch. "You have an hour," he said. "No more. After that, we get ready and remain on standby until called."

Valmir stood up and reached for his jacket. "I will be back long before then," he promised.

"Wait," Dritan called as his subordinate turned to go. "While you're out, I need you to purchase a broom handle and some heavy duty string."

Valmir spread his arms in puzzlement. "What for?"

"We need to make a flagpole," Dritan said, and left it at that.

———

When Jack returned to his office, having just nipped out to use the loo, he found Reg Parker waiting for him, a pensive expression etched into his normally carefree features.

"I've got some results back from the TIU," Parker said. "Can you spare a few minutes to go through them with me?"

Jack inwardly groaned, and the euphoria that Andy Quinlan's recent news had instilled in him instantly evaporated. He had never hidden the fact that he considered phone data to be incredibly boring. In fact, he had gone as far as saying it would make a perfect cure for insomnia if someone could find a way to bottle it. "Yes, of course," he said, trying not to sound too depressed.

Jack settled himself behind his desk and made himself comfortable, wondering how long it would be before he glazed over. He reached behind and turned down the volume on the little radio that was playing on his window sill, knowing that he couldn't afford the distraction of music.

"Fire away," he told Reg.

"Right, I'll kick us off with the phone data relating to the four Turks," Reggie said, sliding over a sheet of data for each of them.

"All four made and received a number of calls throughout the day of the murder, with Dengiz being by far the most active."

Jack followed this sluggishly on the sheet with Dengiz' name written at the top. "Yeah, well, being the boss, I'd expect him to be on the phone more than his lackies," he said.

Reg nodded. "Me too. Before coming in here, I asked Dean to do some basic research to see if any of the numbers the Turks called are known to us. There was only one hit, and that's a number attributed to Abdullah Goren on a recent intelligence report."

"Can you show me which number that is?" Tyler asked.

Reg leaned over and tapped the third number down on Jack's list. "It's the one that ends in 888."

Jack made another note.

"I'll need you to tell me if you want subscriber checks submitted for any of the numbers the Turk's rang, because I have a feeling that it'll spiral out of control if I bung one in for every number that's on their call data."

Tyler stroked his chin thoughtfully. He had considered this earlier, when he'd been reviewing the telephone strategy document. "I think, at least to start with, run every number on the call data through all the intel databases to see if we can attribute it that way. If the calls are to fellow gang members or family, we don't need a subs check at this stage. We'll carry out a daily review of all the unidentified numbers to see which, if any we think need to be further explored."

Reg nodded, clearly relieved that he wasn't going to end up drowning under a sea of subscriber checks.

"What about their movements on the day of the murder?" Tyler asked. "Were you able to look at their cell site data to see where they'd been?"

"I was," Reggie confirmed. "The cell site data shows us that their phones effectively mirrored each other's movements from about six o'clock that evening, which is when I'm guessing they started out on their debt collection round, right up until the time that they were killed."

He passed Jack a sheet of merged data with four different coloured lines that started in the vicinity of Wood Green, where Erkan Dengiz resided, and then worked their way through North London, via the

A406, until they reached the cell that covered the café Bilal Yildiz owned in Green Lanes.

"The cells that the four phones handshake with en route are shown as little Eiffel Tower like edifices," Reg pointed out helpfully.

Tyler looked at the printout and grunted his appreciation. "Can you give Colin a copy of this document please, Reggie. It might help him to narrow down which CCTV cameras he should be focusing on."

Parker nodded. "Of course." He handed another sheet of paper. "This is the list of incoming and outgoing calls for Livingstone's personal phone. There's hardly any traffic at all. As for cell siting, well his phone never leaves the radius of the cell covering his home address in Dalston."

"How convenient," Jack said. He gave it a token glance and dropped it on his desk with the others.

Reg picked up another sheet and, after a moment's hesitation, handed it to Tyler. However, instead of releasing his grip when Tyler tried to take it from him, he held on tightly, earning himself a raised eyebrow and a questioning look.

"This is Meeks' data, and it's much more interesting," he said as he finally let go. And then he did a very strange thing: he stood up and wandered over to the door, which he closed with great solemnity.

Unusual, Tyler thought as he watched Reg turn around and return to his seat.

"In fact," Reg ventured, his tone becoming sinister, "I would go as far as to describe it as rather worrying."

"Why is it worrying, Reggie?" Tyler asked, leaning forward to rest his elbows on his desk.

Reg took a deep breath. "On the day of the murder, Meeks received several calls from Livingstone, and a couple more from a number that intel shows is registered to a lowlife scumbag called Jerome Norris."

"Okay. What's so worrying about that?"

"Nothing. It's the five calls to *this* mobile number that are giving me cause for concern." Parker leaned over and tapped the relevant section of the page with his pen. "The number wasn't known to any of our databases, but it seemed vaguely familiar to me. There were a few calls between the two numbers the day before as well. I was going to ask you if you wanted me to stick in a subs check on it, but then I realised why the number seemed so familiar. It's because it's the number that I wrote for DI Dillon on the contact board when he joined the team."

In the main office, there was a large whiteboard bolted to one of the walls, and this contained the names of every member of the team, along with their pager and mobile numbers. It was located right next to the portrait of Queen Elizabeth II that some disrespectful sod had drawn a curly moustache and goatee beard on. One of Reggie's jobs was to maintain the board and ensure that it was kept up to date, and he had written DI Tony Dillon's details up there himself that very morning.

Tyler leaned back in his chair and let out a disgruntled sigh. Reg had been a bit too clever for his own good on this occasion. "Who else have you told about this?" he asked.

"Not a soul," Reggie said, watching his boss carefully.

Tyler considered this. "Good. Keep it that way, please."

Parker's face creased into a worried frown. "But boss, why would Mr Dillon be in regular contact with a member of Conrad Livingstone's gang? That's so wrong that it's off the scale, especially as he's been investigating them." He paused, and it was obvious that he was deeply troubled. "Can you imagine what CIB would make of that if they knew?" There was something in Reggie's voice that implied they should be told.

The Complaints Investigation Bureau – they were also known by most rank and file coppers as the rubber heelers because you never heard them coming for you – were the Met's internal affairs department, the ones who policed the police, so to speak.

"They wouldn't say anything," Tyler placated his worried colleague. "Reg, it's a very good spot on your part, and I'm genuinely impressed. However, let me reassure you that I already know all about Mr Dillon being in contact with Meeks, and the reasons for it. There's nothing dodgy going on; quite the opposite in fact."

Reg was understandably confused and, as his mouth spluttered soundlessly, Tyler could imagine the queries that were forming inside his head. "I can't answer any questions Reggie, so don't bother asking them. Just trust me when I say that nothing untoward is going on."

"But–"

Tyler raised a stern hand to silence him. "No ifs; no buts. You've stumbled across something that's running in the background on a purely need to know basis and, to put it bluntly, you *don't* need to know. What you *do* need to do is keep your gob shut and not mention this to anyone else on the team. I'm serious, Reggie. You would be putting Meeks' life in danger." Tyler cringed as the words left his mouth, knowing that he had inadvertently given the game away.

Reggie's eyes bulged with enlightenment as the penny dropped, and a slow smile of relief flittered across his cherubic face. "Oh, so you mean he's a registered inf–"

"Reg!" Tyler warned.

"Sorry," Parker said, raising a hand to his mouth.

Tyler wagged a warning finger at him. "Remember, Reggie, not a bloody word."

Parker nodded obediently, and then mimed zipping his lips up and locking them with an imaginary key, which he theatrically threw over his shoulder.

As Parker was walking towards the door, leaving the room a much happier man than when he had entered, Tyler suddenly remembered the number that had been used to order the credit card and book the Beckton hotel for Adebanjo. "Reg, one last thing I need to ask you before you go."

Parker turned around and mimicked unzipping his lips with a cherubic grin. "Ask away, oh great leader."

"Mr Dillon asked you to put a subs check and call data application in on one other number. Have you had a result back on that yet?"

Reg quickly flicked through his daybook. "Ah, here we are: the mobile ending in 217…" He tutted to himself while he double checked. "No. It's not come back yet," he said. "Do you want me to try chasing it up?"

"Please, Reg. If you would. Oh, and while you're at it, can you also chase up the call data results for Adebanjo and the Kalu twins."

CHAPTER NINETEEN

SOMEONE MUST KNOW

At five o'clock, Dritan received another call from Gunz. "*Yo! It's me again. The car you need is a black Vauxhall Vectra SRI, with blacked out windows. It's parked directly opposite the hotel entrance so you can't miss it. The flag your boss requested is on the back seat. After the job, dispose of it like you did the last one. There's a jerrycan of petrol in the boot.*"

While Gunz was speaking, Dritan wandered over to the window. Pulling back the filthy net curtain, he peered out into Amhurst Park down below. Sure enough, a car matching the description his contact had just given him was parked right across the road, but it was far too conspicuous for Dritan's liking. With its flared wheel arches, alloy wheels, and rear spoiler, it would undoubtably draw attention, which was the last thing he wanted.

"Couldn't you have found us something that wasn't so… flash?" he asked, staring at the car disapprovingly.

Gunz laughed. "*Don't sweat it, blud,*" he said. "*I boosted you a fine set of wheels. It's not even a year old. Besides, lots of dudes around here have rides like that so it'll blend right in."*

"I'll have to take your word for that," Dritan said, unhappily.

Gunz was still laughing, and Dritan decided that he would like to put a bullet through each of his kneecaps, just to see how funny he found that.

"*The man you're interested in normally arrives at the restaurant at about eight-ish,*" Gunz informed him, now serious again, "*and he usually stays there for at least an hour. I'll be keeping watch nearby, and I'll call you as soon as he arrives.*"

"Very well," Dritan replied. "We will be ready to move in when we receive your call." He hung up and took another look at the car. "Fucking amateurs," he said scathingly.

———————

It was almost seven o'clock by the time that Dillon returned to the office. He collapsed into the chair opposite Tyler's desk and closed his eyes.

"Arrrrgh! Why did I ever think it would be fun to join the murder squad?" he demanded, glancing up at the ceiling as though addressing the question to God himself.

Jack looked up from his Decision Log. "A bit stressed, are we?" he asked.

"What gives you that idea?" Dillon growled.

"Oh, I dunno," Jack said with a light hearted shrug. "Just a wild guess."

Dillon harrumphed. "The least you can do is make me a cup of coffee," he complained as he struggled out of his jacket. His nose wrinkled as he caught a whiff of the death and decay that had seeped into it. "And this suit will need to go straight into the cleaners tomorrow morning," he said, turning his nose up.

Jack stood up and stretched. "I'll go and put the kettle on," he said, massaging the small of his back. He was half-tempted to point out that Dillon had another couple of SPMs to get through yet, so he might want to hold off on sending his suit to the cleaners for another day.

Mumbling under his breath about smelling worse than a butcher's shop on a hot day, Dillon followed him over to the urn and watched as he spooned coffee into a couple of chipped mugs. "Any developments worth talking about while I've been out socialising with corpses and Frankenstein lookalikes?" he asked.

"Colin found us some cracking CCTV of the shooters fleeing the stolen Mondeo after torching it," Tyler said. "The stills are on my desk if you want to see them."

Dillon grunted. "Maybe later, after I've had a long, hot shower."

"And you already know that two of your officers, Christine and Geoff, recovered the burner Adebanjo dumped, and some CCTV, from the grocery shop?"

"Yeah, I spoke to Geoff at lunchtime."

"The handset's already gone up to the phone lab, so we should get something back on it tomorrow if we're lucky."

The door to the main office swung open and Steve Bull appeared, closely followed by Fatma Osman. Steve was happily talking away, and she seemed to be hanging onto his every word, clearly impressed by whatever he was telling her.

Bull stopped dead when he spotted Tyler and Dillon, and she walked straight into the back of him.

"Oops," Fatma said, blushing.

Bull's face reddened. "How did it go at the mortuary?" he asked Dillon, who was staring at him with an amused smile.

Dillon shrugged. "As well as can be expected."

"I've never been to a post mortem," Fatma told them with a shy smile. "It sounds very interesting.'

"Trust me," Dillon said with a shudder in his voice, "it's definitely not."

Jack noticed Fatma's nose twitch as the unpleasant aroma from the big man's clothing reached her. With a grin, he nudged Dillon's arm and nodded in her direction.

Dillon glanced down at his suit and let out a little sigh. "Yep. Sadly, that sickly sweet smell of death and disinfectant is emanating from me," he admitted. "Yet another reason to avoid attending SPMs if you possibly can."

"I'm sorry if I reacted rudely," she stammered, cheeks glowing with embarrassment, "I didn't mean to cause offence."

"Fatma's just been helping me write up a Reverse Osman in Turkish," Steve said quickly, mainly to spare her any further blushes. "I thought we'd give Goren two copies, one in English and one in Turkish. That way, he won't be able to say he didn't understand what was in the letter."

"That's a good idea," Tyler said. "Fatma, can you make an appointment with Goren's people to drop that off tonight. Do it under the pretext of paying him a FLO visit, and don't take no for an answer if they try to fob you off."

"Leave it with me, sir," she said. "I'll ring them now." She was about to follow Steve over to his desk, but then she paused and looked straight into Dillon's eyes. "Sir, I know I'm only here to help out with the FLO stuff and translations, but there's not a lot of that to do at the moment, and I was wondering if there was any chance that I could come with you to tomorrow morning's post mortem. I think it would be a very good experience for me, seeing as I want to join the CID and eventually work on a murder squad."

Dillon couldn't understand why anyone would choose to do that. "Well," he said, scratching his head as he considered the request. "If the way I smell hasn't put you off, and if you honestly think you can stomach watching a body being dissected, I'll have a word with Steve Bull and see if he can spare you for the morning."

She beamed at him. "Thank you," she said, demurely.

He watched her walk away, amazed that anyone could seem so outrageously happy at the prospect of attending a special post mortem. "She must have a screw loose," he proclaimed.

"She's just super keen," Tyler said, handing him a mug of steaming liquid. "We were like that once."

Dillon shook his head. "I was *never* like that," he insisted.

"I'm going to get Charlie White and Kelly Flowers to deliver the Reverse Osman to the Albanian," he said as they walked back to his office, "but I thought we could drop Livingstone's one off ourselves. I think it's about time we introduced ourselves to the man we think is behind all of this, don't you?"

Dillon's smile was that of a predator. "I like the sound of that very much," he said softly.

"First, though," Jack said, fanning his nose, "you really do need to have a shower and change out of that suit."

———

Abdullah Goren arrived at his nephew's restaurant at eight o'clock sharp. He was in a foul mood and just itching for an excuse to vent his rage on someone. Unless the incompetent cretins who worked for him had been withholding information in order to surprise him tonight, the fact that he hadn't heard from any of them during the day meant that they were still no nearer to establishing who had killed Erkan than they were twenty four hours ago. If that was the case, and they had failed him, someone was going to suffer his wrath before the night was out.

As if having to listen to his lieutenants making pathetic excuses for failing him wasn't going to be bad enough, the police had insisted on coming over to see him at the restaurant this evening, and no matter what he had said to put them off, the Turkish girl he had spoken to had made it clear that her superiors were not going to take no for an answer. In the end, he had relented, agreeing to spare them fifteen minutes of his valuable time, but not a second longer.

Mustafa was at the door, waiting to greet him. The simpering toady was obviously keen to ingratiate himself into Goren's good books, and he probably harboured aspirations of replacing Erkan as his favourite, and therefore most privileged, nephew.

"Good evening uncle," Mustafa said deferentially as Goren swept past, followed by his four bodyguards.

"Is everyone here?" Goren asked, not even bothering to look at the younger man.

"Y-Yes, they are waiting in the back room."

Mustafa seemed unusually nervous, Goren sensed, which only confirmed his suspicions that they had failed him. As his anger flared, he became aware of the vein in his right temple throbbing, as it was prone to do when he was under stress.

One of the thickset bodyguards had moved ahead to open the door for his employer, and Goren breezed through without breaking stride. As Mustafa tried to follow in his wake, the three rear bodyguards closed ranks, blocking his path and forcing him to trail along behind like a lowly servant rather than a valued family member.

The back room that they used for their meetings was crammed with his underlings, and all conversation stopped dead as he entered. Everyone stood up and greeted him, but there was no warmth in their words, only fear. As he stared at them through the smokey haze that filled the dimly lit room, almost all of them averted their eyes.

Cowards, he thought, glowering at them in contempt.

They formed a line and performed the ritual of kissing his hand, and then the owner, Ahmet, was dispatched to bring them light refreshments. The atmosphere was extremely tense while they waited for the drinks to be served, with no one in the mood to make small talk. Many of the men present were fidgeting restlessly as they waited for Goren to take his seat at the head of the table. They were, he thought, behaving like a row of convicted prisoners who were waiting for the judge to pronounce their death sentences.

"Be seated," he finally announced.

In keeping with custom, they finished their refreshments before discussing business, and he could see that the pressure of not knowing who was going to fall foul of his temper was really starting to get to some of them.

"I am not a happy man," he began, deliberately speaking very slowly. "Last night, I gave a clear instruction that you were to do whatever it took to uncover the identities of Erkan's killers, but I can see from the wretched looks on your cowardly faces that you have collectively failed me."

The fear in the room was tangible, and Goren soaked it up, feeding on it like an energy vampire. "DO YOU NOT REALISE THAT THIS IS A MATTER OF HONOUR?" he suddenly shouted, spraying spittle over those sitting nearest to him.

The men sitting either side of him flinched as his fist hammered down onto the table, causing cups to rattle in their saucers.

"Uncle," Mustafa said, nervously trying to appease him, "we have done everything that you have asked of us, but no one out there knows who—"

Goren halted him with a withering look. "Idiot!" he hissed. And then he was shouting again. "SOMEONE *MUST* KNOW. SOMEONE *ALWAYS* KNOWS." His eyes burned into his nephew's with such malice that the younger man instinctively cowered away from him.

Goren turned his attention to the others, snarling at them like a rabid animal. "All you had to do was ask the right people the right questions, but it seems that none of you were capable of doing that one simple thing."

As he berated them, his eyes traversed the table, glowering at each of them in turn. Not one of his lieutenants dared meet his gaze, for they all knew that such an act would be considered disrespectful and would trigger a tirade of abuse, if not something far worse. Instead, each man quietly stared down at the table and nervously waited for the shouting to stop. Some of the younger members of the group wrung trembling hands together until their knuckles turned white.

Breathing heavily, and still shaking with rage, Goren sank back in his chair and stroked the coarse bristles on his unshaven chin. "Tomorrow morning I will telephone the Albanian," he announced. "I will tell him that the word on the street is that he is responsible, and I will give him one chance to convince me he is not." He turned to a stocky man with a swarthy, pockmarked complexion who was sitting to his immediate right. Unlike the others, he seemed completely relaxed. "Mehmet, you will arrange for two car loads of men, all armed with AK47s, to be ready to move at a moment's notice from midday onwards. Do you understand?"

Mehmet Erdogan was a thirty-five year old enforcer of Kurdish descent who had grown up not far from the Syrian border before fleeing the troubled region with his parents to resettle in the UK. One of Goren's most trusted confidants, Erdogan was a brutal man with no conscience and very few inhibitions, and he was the go-to man when Goren wanted acts of violence carried out against his enemies.

"Perfectly," Erdogan said.

"Good," Goren announced with finality. One way or another, he promised himself, someone's blood would be shed in retaliation for Tuesday's attack on his men. Only then would the stain on his honour be erased.

———

Dritan sat in the front seat of the stolen Vectra, with Lorik behind the wheel and Valmir occupying his usual position in the rear. They were wearing the same grey tracksuits they had worn to execute the four Turks. It was a hot evening, but they were already wearing their gloves, and all three had balaclavas tucked into their pockets.

As before, each of them was armed with a Škorpion machine pistol with two spare magazines. Lorik had tucked his weapon into the footwell beside his left leg, but that was fine as he would be too busy driving to join in when the time came to hose down the front of the restaurant. In addition to their Škorpions, Dritan had the 9mm Baikal IZH-79 pistol tucked into the front of his trousers.

They were parked two streets away from the target address, in a quiet cul de sac just off the main road, waiting for an update from their contact, who had phoned them ten minutes earlier to say that Goren had arrived on schedule, but that they should give him time to get settled in before striking.

Being the consummate professional that he was, Dritan had carried out a full reconnaissance of the area an hour before Goren was due to arrive. On his orders, Lorik had driven past the front of the restaurant twice, so that they could see the layout for themselves and work out which way they were going to come at it when the time came. They had also mapped out their primary and secondary escape routes, and worked out where they were going to dispose of the boy-racer-mobile after the job was done.

"I'm hungry," Valmir complained, and as if to corroborate his claim, his stomach rumbled loudly.

Dritan ignored the comment. "Is the prop ready for when it's needed?" he asked.

Valmir held up the broom handle he had purchased earlier and waggled it around unenthusiastically. It had been fashioned into a homemade flagpole, from which the Albanian flag –the Flamuri i Shqipërise – now hung listlessly.

Dritan smiled at the sight. Displaying that while they carried out the drive by shooting ought to be more than enough motivation to convince the Turks to carry out a reprisal attack against the Albanians.

———

"So how are you enjoying being on AMIP?" Fatma asked Steve Bull as they drove through the late evening traffic towards Goren's nephew's restaurant on the outskirts of Wood Green.

"I'm loving it, so far," he said, casting a sideways glance at her. He had worked in the main CID office at Stoke Newington for several years before transferring to AMIP, dealing with rapes, kidnaps, serious assaults and a plethora of other major crimes. "This murder is the first job I've been made Case Officer for since I arrived," he confided with a grin. "I was expecting to cut my teeth on a simple domestic, but it seems I've been thrown straight in at the deep end."

"Does that bother you?" she asked.

"It's a steep learning curve for me at the moment," he admitted, "but the people on the team are all top notch, and Mr Tyler's a great boss to work for so, no, it doesn't bother me at all."

"I'm guessing, as Case Officer, the DCI takes you into his confidence and tells you stuff that the rest of the team don't get to know about?" she speculated.

Bull shrugged. "It depends. Sometimes, some stuff gets held back for operational security, but mostly, we all get to know everything there is to know about a job."

Fatma studied him intently. "So why isn't Mr Tyler ruling out Livingstone's gang? As far as I know, there are no white people in it."

Bull hesitated. How could he answer that without revealing they had a registered informant inside Livingstone's gang who was providing information? "Let's just say that, until we can eliminate the possibility that Livingstone is involved in this, we have to keep an open mind."

Fatma pursed her lips in thought. "So the boss is hedging his bets in case Livingstone outsourced the murders? Is that what you're saying?"

Bull spotted a gap by the kerb and pulled the Omega into it. "That's handy," he said, happy to be able to change the subject. "What a stroke of luck, us finding a parking space only thirty yards away from our destination."

"Should I bring my PPE?" Fatma asked as he turned the ignition off. As a uniform officer she had been issued with an overtly worn web belt for her baton, Quick-cuffs and CS spray, unlike Steve, who wore a shoulder holster under his suit jacket.

His nose wrinkled at the suggestion. "Nah, I really wouldn't worry. I very much doubt Goren's going to be stupid enough to kick off with us on his own doorstep."

"What about my radio?" she asked, holding it up for him to see.

Bull shook his head dismissively. "Put it in the glove box," he told her. They were only going to be there long enough to deliver the Reverse Osman, and he couldn't imagine them needing to call for back up during that time.

Fatma alighted the car and pulled on her jacket. "How do I look?" she asked, pulling the collar down.

Bull gave her a sympathetic smile. "Like you would rather be back in uniform than prancing around in plain clothes with me."

"Not true," she told him, tugging at the hem of her trousers. "It's just that this suit isn't very comfortable, and I feel a little restricted in it."

The green fronted restaurant looked very inviting. As they peered in through one of the four full length windows that faced out onto the street, their faces were bathed in the warm orange glow coming from within. There were already plenty of customers sitting inside. It looked like they also did a thriving takeaway service, and there was no shortage of people waiting at the counter to be served.

As with virtually every Turkish restaurant Bull had ever been in, the obligatory slabs of lamb and chicken were slowly rotating on their giant skewers, with a hairy armed man clad in chef's whites skilfully slicing chunks off of them to fill the warm pita breads lying on the counter in front of him.

"A popular place, from the look of it," Steve said, impressed.

Fatma nodded. "It has a reputation within the Turkish community for serving good food," she informed him, "and you know it has to be *really* good if Turkish people go there."

A stocky Turkish male in his late thirties, who looked like he had been recruited from the local branch of Thugs Are Us, was standing guard outside the front. Looking uncomfortable in his tightly fitting black suit, he stood with his hands clasped in front of him, vetting potential customers to make sure they were suitable for admission. His mean little eyes were constantly scanning the pavement in both directions, evaluating every passer-by to assess whether or not they posed a threat.

Bull suspected that he was only stationed there because Goren was inside, and that made him curious as to whether the man was carrying an illegal firearm. He couldn't see any tell-tale bulges that might indicate he was and, as the ill-fitting jacket was stretched tightly across the doorman's enormous chest, Bull was fairly confident that he would have noticed the protuberance of a holstered weapon.

"Evening," Bull said, smiling at the man. The doorman gave him a surly nod in acknowledgement, but said nothing.

"What's the matter with him?" Bull whispered as they walked inside.

"He probably thinks you're dating me, and doesn't like the idea of a good Turkish girl mixing with someone from a different culture," Fatma explained with a cheeky grin.

"Oh," Bull said. It hadn't, for an instant, occurred to him that anyone would think they were an item.

On seeing his face, Fatma elbowed him playfully in the ribs. "I'm joking," she said, shaking her head at how gullible he was.

"I knew that," Bull said, feeling his cheeks redden.

Inside, just to the right of the door, an unshaven man in a burgundy shirt and black trousers stood behind a small lectern that had the establishment's name emblazoned on the front. He smiled enquiringly at them. "Table for two?" he asked, reaching for a couple of menus.

Bull produced his warrant card. "Regrettably, no. We're here to see Abdullah Goran. He's expecting us."

The smile faltered for an instant, but then it was back in place. "Ah, yes," he said. "I was told to expect you. Please come this way." Gesturing for them to follow him, the maître d – at least that was what Bull assumed he was – guided them to a secluded seating area towards the rear of the restaurant. "Please wait here and I will let Mr Goren know that you have arrived. Can I get you something to drink while you wait? It's on the house."

Bull shook his head. "That's very kind, but we're fine, thank you."

"Of course," the maître d said. "Let me know if you change your mind." With that, he returned to the front of house, where Bull saw him pick up a telephone. As he spoke into the receiver, he glanced back towards them, but quickly averted his eyes when he realised he was being watched.

"Looks like he's letting the boss know we're here," Bull said.

The restaurant walls had been finished in a mixture of elaborate stonework and wood panelling, all very tastefully blended to create a comfortable, relaxing atmosphere. The seating area was very spacious, and the furniture, brown leather effect chairs and wood grained tables, looked fairly new. The wall lighting was soft and low, and the music playing quietly in the background was equally mellow.

"It's actually a really nice restaurant," Bull said, surprised. He had expected it to be a rough and ready place, full of sullen looking Turks with unshaven faces and intimidating stares.

Before long, Bull heard the sound of approaching footsteps and, on turning around, saw a small entourage of people walking toward them. It was like being in a scene from a Mafia film, he thought, watching Abdullah Goren walk towards him with his three bodyguards in tow. They had obviously been obtained from the same supplier as the hired muscle out front, and were even wearing identical dark suits.

Goren was much larger in real life than he had looked in the intelligence photographs that the Turkish and Kurdish Task Force had sent over that afternoon. It wasn't so much that he was a big man; just that he had a big presence. Even though he looked to be in his early fifties, his thick hair was still jet black, as was the thick moustache that covered his upper lip. Goren's eyes were thin slits that seemed to absorb light without giving anything back. His clothes were casual but expensive, and his fingers were adorned in gold. There was something about him that was, well, scary, Bull admitted to himself.

Both officers stood up as he approached and shook the calloused hand that he offered. Fatma uttered a greeting in Turkish, and Goren smiled gratefully and indicated for them to be seated.

He took a seat at the next table and sat side on, facing them.

"This is Detective Sergeant Bull from the Area Major Investigation Pool," Fatma said, her tone polite and respectful. "He's one of the officers investigating the murder of your nephew and his associates."

Goren ran his eyes over Bull with the cold detachment of an undertaker sizing him up for a coffin. "I am pleased to make your acquaintance," he said, and Bull thought the voice was cold, hard and, above all, cruel. "Have you discovered who did this terrible thing to Erkan yet?"

Before Bull could reply, the world around him exploded into chaos.

———

"So, how did Livingstone respond to your request to meet with him?" Dillon asked. He and Tyler were sitting in the canteen at Stoke Newington, waiting for a call from the front office to say that he had arrived.

Apart from the lady behind the counter, who was having a very loud conversation with someone out of sight about changing the oil in the chip fryer before they went home, they had the canteen all to themselves. It was certainly a contrast to their previous visit, when it had been overrun with TSG officers.

A large flatscreen TV had been affixed to the wall behind Dillon's back. Sound muted, it was tuned into the BBC news channel.

"I don't think he was too enamoured, if I'm honest," Tyler replied with a satisfied grin. "He tried to fob me off, of course, but I told him he could either come into the station to meet with us of his own accord, or we would come and find him."

Dillon checked his watch. "He's already ten minutes late," he said, annoyed. He hated tardiness, even in criminals.

Tyler shrugged, unconcerned. "He was always going to be late, Dill. It's just his way of letting us know that he isn't intimidated by us."

"Do you think he'll bring a brief with him?" Dillon asked.

"Who knows? Who cares?" Tyler responded, only half listening as he skim read the news banner that ran along the bottom of the TV screen, something about the Queen not being amused by a topless sunbathing photo of Prince Edward's fiancée, Sophie Rhys-Jones, that had surfaced in the media.

Behind them, the conversation about the chip oil was getting progressively louder as it rapidly deteriorated into a full blown argument over who should change it.

"Shall we go and wait over in the station office?" Tyler asked, glancing over his shoulder at the escalating commotion.

Dillon stood up quickly. "Yeah, let's get out of here before we become witnesses to an assault."

They were halfway across the rear yard when Tyler's phone rang. It was the station officer, calling to say that a very stroppy black man was at the front counter, demanding to see them.

CHAPTER TWENTY

HAVE SOME BULLETS WITH YOUR KEBAB

They showed Conrad Livingstone into the same windowless interview room that Paul Evans had previously shared with Tulay Yildiz. Such was the man's arrogance that he hadn't bothered to bring a solicitor with him.

Tyler studied their guest intently. Dressed in faded jeans and a Ralph Lauren shirt, Livingstone was doing his best to appear angry, but he was overplaying it a bit, like a not very good actor overly hamming his lines.

"What do you want, bruv?" he demanded petulantly.

"Please, have a seat," Jack said.

After fist brushing it with his hand, Livingstone reluctantly lowered himself onto the hard plastic chair that Tyler had indicated. He sucked through his teeth as he glared across the table at the two detectives. Hostility radiated from him like an expanding toxic cloud, but Jack pointedly ignored this.

"We appreciate you taking time out of your busy schedule to fit us in," Tyler said, smiling gratefully, as though Livingstone had actually had a say in the matter.

Livingstone sniffed, and then shrugged as if to say it was no big deal.

Leaning forward, Jack rested his clasped hands on the table in front of him. The surface felt unpleasantly sticky, and he quickly relocated them to his lap, dreading to think what he'd just put his hands on. "We wanted to speak to you because we've received credible intelligence that you're having some issues with a couple of your *business* associates," he said, loading the word 'business' with irony.

Livingstone tensed, suddenly alert. "Nah, not me, bruv," he said adamantly. "I get on with everyone, know what I mean?"

"Well, Mr Livingstone," Tyler continued, all sweetness and light, "I'm not so sure that Abdullah Goren or Klodjan Asllani would be inclined to agree with you."

Livingstone's eyes narrowed to tiny slits, and his demeanour instantly became defensive. "What are you trying to say, bruv?" he demanded. "I got no beef with either of them dudes."

Jack smiled, but there was no humour in it. "I'm sure you're aware that four Turkish men were gunned down outside a café in Green Lanes on Tuesday night," he said.

Livingstone shrugged. It was a short, belligerent motion. "Yeah. Saw it on the TV. So what?"

"The three gunmen were described as white males," Jack said, watching him carefully for a reaction.

It was almost imperceptible, and had he not been looking for it, he would have missed the satisfied smile that flickered across Livingstone's lips for the briefest of moments. There was also a subtle change in his body language, which became marginally less antagonistic.

"Again, so what?"

Cocky bastard, Jack thought. "Let's cut to the chase, shall we?" he said, dropping the pretence of friendliness. "We know that you and the other two men I mentioned are locked in a three way dispute over what you all arrogantly consider to be a vacant territory."

"Nah, bruv, you must be mistaking me for someone else," Livingstone cut in, emphasising his denial with a vehement shake of the head.

Beneath the outer layer of cool, Tyler could see that he was struggling to contain his growing agitation.

Good.

"We know that the ongoing discussions you've been holding with them have broken down, and it's clear that the four murdered men, who all worked for Abdullah Goren, were killed as a result of tensions between your three gangs spiralling out of control. I'm here today to warn you that the Metropolitan Police Service is watching you, Conrad, and that we will take any and all lawful steps necessary to prevent this situation from getting any worse."

Livingstone snorted at that, as if he knew something that they didn't, and his reaction made Tyler strangely uneasy.

"Furthermore, we will hold you, Goren, and Asllani personally responsible for any deaths that occur."

"Enough of this shit!" Livingstone was up on his feet. "This is slander. I don't have to listen to your empty threats. If you want to speak to me again, do it through my solicitor."

With that, he turned to leave, only to find Dillon blocking his exit. Livingston's nostrils flared angrily as he squared off against the bigger man, seemingly ready to go toe to toe with him. "Get out of my way," he warned, clenching his fists.

Dillon leaned back against the door, looking unbelievably bored. "My colleague isn't finished yet," he said, folding his arms.

"I'm nearly done," Jack told him, "but before you go, I have to serve you with a written letter of warning that reiterates what I've just told you."

He held out the Reverse Osman and, after a second's hesitation, Livingstone snatched it from his hand. As soon as he had taken possession of the envelope, Dillon moved to the side. "Have a nice evening," he said with a contemptuous smile.

For a moment, Livingstone glowered at him, his eyes full of unspoken threat.

Dillon responded by winking at him.

Looking like he was fit to explode, Livingstone yanked open the door and stormed out.

"Make the most of that clean fresh air while you still can," Dillon called over his shoulder.

"Fuck you! You pussy bumbaclot!" Livingstone yelled back.

Dillon closed the door behind him and turned to face Tyler. "I think he likes me," he said with a sardonic smile.

———

"Finally," Valmir said, as Dritan ended the call. He slipped his bala-clava over his head and gave his weapon a final inspection.

In the front of the car, Dritan and Lorik did likewise, and then Lorik started the engine, which growled throatily.

"Remember," Dritan warned them, "no one inside the restaurant is to be injured so be sure to aim high."

"What about anyone outside?" Valmir asked.

Dritan shrugged. "Anyone who comes out after us is fair game," he said.

As Lorik set off, Dritan glanced over his shoulder. "Make sure the Albanian flag is seen," he instructed.

Beneath his mask, Valmir smiled evilly. "Oh, it'll be seen," he promised.

It took them just over a minute to reach the front of the restau-rant. As Lorik brought the car to a halt, eliciting unappreciative honks from the cars stuck behind him, Dritan and Valmir calmly alighted from the nearside and brought their weapons to bear.

Almost immediately, Dritan spotted a powerfully built Turkish male standing in the restaurant's doorway. A soon as the Turk saw them coming towards the premises, his right hand flew to the small of his back, reappearing a split second later holding a pistol.

Hostile at eleven o'clock! Dritan's brain screamed and, without breaking stride, he pivoted to his left and squeezed off a short burst that sent the man flying backwards, his centre mass now riddled with bullet holes.

Dropping the pistol, the fatally injured Turk fell to his knees, mouth wide open in shock. For a moment, his hands clawed at the injuries, trying to stem the blood flow, but then he fell sideways onto the floor. He twitched several times as a spurt of blood gushed from his mouth, and then he stopped moving.

While Dritan was neutralising the armed sentry, Valmir opened fire into the frontage of the restaurant. "Have some bullets with your kebab," he yelled, laughing manically as he emptied his first magazine into the four floor-to-ceiling windows, which all promptly disintegrated into a million pieces. Tiny shards of glass rained down on the screaming customers who were unfortunate enough to be sitting beside them.

Relishing the pandemonium that ensued, as panic stricken diners abandoned their meals and dived beneath the tables in search of refuge, Valmir calmly inserted the second magazine and began firing a little more selectively, taking out lights and mirrors, and even a glitzy lectern with the restaurant's name on it.

Dritan joined in, emptying the remainder of his first magazine into the kitchen area. As his bullets tore into the two rotating kebabs, they sent huge chunks of meat flying across the room, showering the kitchen staff who were cowering on the floor and plastering themselves to nearby walls. He used the second magazine to shoot up the refrigerated display cabinets, which flew apart with deafening noise.

Finally, they were both out of ammunition. Standing in a fog of swirling cordite, their weapons still smoking, and listening in satisfaction to the terrified screams coming from inside the restaurant, Dritan nodded to Valmir, who ran to the back of the car and leaned in. He reappeared a moment later with the home-made flagpole in his hand. As he walked towards the nearest window, intending to toss it inside, Dritan called out to him, and pointed to the body of the guard he had shot.

"Drape it over him," he instructed.

Beneath the mask, Valmir smiled. He jogged over to the unmoving Turk and covered his head with the flag, just as his commander had ordered.

Mission accomplished, the two shooters jumped back in the stolen Vectra, which took off with a loud wheelspin.

———

Inside a red Vauxhall Corsa that was tucked into the mouth of a side street almost directly opposite the restaurant, Switch turned to his cousin, eyes blazing with excitement. "That was something else, cuz," he said admiringly.

As the Vectra containing the gunmen zoomed off, leaving a trail of burning rubber in its wake, he gazed upon Gunz with new found respect.

"For real," Gunz said, passing him a spliff to toke on. "But you can't tell anyone I let you come along, ya get me?"

"I won't say shit to no one," Switch promised, hardly able to believe his luck. Of course, he was fully aware that Gunz had only let him tag along to prove how tough he was. It was his response to Switch boasting that he'd shanked someone to death; a means of showing his little cousin that he was also a bad ass.

Switch leaned back in the car's firm Recaro seat and closed his eyes, enjoying the sensation of the marijuana smoke filling his lungs. Seeing the hit go down had made him re-evaluate what he wanted from life. Before this, his ambitions had stretched no further than forming his own little crew, like Ziggy had done. But now his eyes had been opened; why settle for carrying out the odd steaming, or shotting drugs for the elders, when he could be involved in so much more?

Gunz was into some serious shit!

He was playing with the big boys.

And if he played his cards right, Gunz had promised to introduce him to Livingstone's inner circle and help him to gain access to it.

Gunz jerked his thumb over his shoulder, towards the back seat. "Pass me the phone, innit," he rasped, having just sucked in a lungful of smoke.

When Switch looked, he saw two phones lying side by side. Not knowing which one his cousin wanted, he simply grabbed the nearest.

"Press one on the speed dial, little cuz, and pass it to me when you get a ring tone," Gunz said without opening his eyes.

Switch obliged. Almost immediately, it commenced ringing, but before he could pass it over an angry voice was yelling in his ear. "*Why the fuck are you calling my digits from this phone, you useless motherfucker?"*

Recognising Livingstone's voice, Switch couldn't get rid of the mobile quickly enough.

"Wagwan," Gunz said with a grin, but it disappeared almost instantly as the person on the other end launched into a vicious tirade, and then hung up.

Gunz stared at the handset as though it were about to explode in his hand. "You fucking idiot," he snarled. "You gave me the wrong phone, innit."

To his utter horror, he realised that he'd just dialled Livingstone's personal mobile from his own phone, something that he'd been expressly forbidden to do. All contact between them today was to be made via the burners, so that Livingstone could tell the Feds that he hadn't spoken to any of his crew if subsequently asked.

Grabbing the correct phone, he hurriedly called his employer's burner, a look of abject fear plastered across his face. "I'm sorry, bruv," he mewled the moment it was answered.

Gunz listened in silence as Livingstone berated him for a full thirty seconds, and by the time his employer had finished, all colour had drained from his cheeks. Swallowing hard, Gunz tried to ameliorate the situation. "Don't sweat it bruv, the call only lasted a few seconds. No harm done." He immediately flinched at the abuse his ill-considered comment had just earned him. Head hung low, he nodded guiltily. "Yes, bruv. I understand, bruv. It won't happen again, bruv. I just wanted to let you know it all went like clockwork, bruv."

Lowering the phone, he turned to Switch. "Cuz, you've gotta be more careful," he said reproachfully. "You just called his private digits from my phone. You were meant to use the burner. You wanna survive in this game, you can't be doing shit like that. You get me?"

Switch nodded, feeling like a complete fool. "I'm sorry, cuz," he mumbled, hoping that he hadn't scuppered his chances of breaking into the big time.

The sound of approaching sirens reached their ears, galvanising them into action. Gunz quickly started the engine. "We gotta breeze before the Feds arrive," he said, slipping the gearstick into first.

———

All hell had broken loose inside the restaurant. At the sound of the first gunshots, Goren's bodyguards had reacted swiftly, grabbing hold of him and unceremoniously throwing him down onto the floor. Two of them had dived on top of him, using their own bodies as human shields, while the third had overturned a table and used it as a barricade for them all to shelter behind. It was all very impressive, and almost like watching a secret service detail dragging the President to safety in the face of an assassination attempt. Except that, in Goren's case, it was a just bunch of thugs protecting their mobster boss from another bunch of thugs. Bull had half expected them to pull weapons and start returning fire, and he didn't know whether to be relieved or disappointed when they failed to do so.

Seated at the back of the restaurant, they were far luckier than the customers and staff at the front of the premises, who were directly in the firing line. Bull could clearly hear their terrified screams above the staccato roar of the automatic gunfire. Ignoring Goren and his cronies, he grabbed hold of Fatma, who was standing directly in harm's way, too shocked to move, and bundled her behind one of the concrete support pillars. As he did so, a stray round, ricocheted off one of the light fixtures above them and embedded itself in the wall less than a foot from Bull's head.

"Jesus!" he exclaimed, coughing from the brick dust he'd just inhaled.

He reached into his pocket for his mobile phone, but to his horror, he saw he didn't have a signal. "Why didn't I let you talk me into bringing that bloody radio?" he asked Fatma, who was cowering in his arms, flinching repeatedly at the sound of the machine gun fire.

And then, as suddenly as it had started, it was over.

All that could be heard was the pitiful moaning and crying of the people sprawled on the floor, and the sound of glass crunching underfoot as members of Goren's staff gathered up meat cleavers and carving knives and ran out into the street to chase off the gunmen. And then there was the sound of a wheelspin, followed by the noise of a powerful car accelerating away.

Bull tentatively poked his head out from behind the concrete pillar, taking in the carnage that the shooters had caused. The few remaining lights were flickering, and an exposed electric wire somewhere off to his right was continuously sparking.

"Well," he said under his breath as Goren was helped to his feet. "I hope you have adequate insurance."

The maître d' came running over to report to Goren, speaking animatedly in Turkish and pointing back towards the front of the restaurant. If Goren had been angry before, he went into a thermonuclear meltdown on hearing the news, and he began ranting in an uncontrollable rage.

Fatma was staring at Goren, as if mesmerised by his outburst.

Glancing nervously over their shoulders, and trying their best to placate him, Goren's bodyguards moved quickly, dragging him towards the rear of the building and out of harm's way. One of them, the man who seemed to have taken charge of the situation, shouted something at Fatma in Turkish, and whatever it was, it caused her face to blanch.

As Goren was ushered through a door marked 'Private', Steve Bull realised he hadn't even had time to serve the Reverse Osman letter on him. Well, he could hardly worry about that now, so he put the thought to one side.

"Are you okay?" he asked Fatma, taking her by the shoulders and staring into her eyes.

She nodded, obviously still in shock, and he could feel her body trembling.

"Come on," he said, gently taking Fatma's hand and pulling her towards the front of the building. "We need to see if anyone's injured, and then call for backup."

The majority of customers had fled as soon as they'd realised the gunmen had gone, in some cases leaving all their belongings behind. Those that remained were huddled together in little groups, looking totally shell shocked.

As Bull pulled open the door leading out to the street, he almost tripped over something on the floor. Looking down, he saw a pair of legs protruding from beneath a sprawling red flag with a silhouetted black double-headed eagle in the centre.

Bending down, he gingerly pulled back the flag to reveal a corpse underneath. It was the muscular doorman he'd said hello to on their way into the restaurant. "Oh fuck," he said quietly, counting at least four holes in the man's torso.

Thankfully, the doorman appeared to be the only fatality, and there were no signs that anyone else had been seriously injured. That came as a tremendous relief; it would have been a terrible travesty if innocent members of the public had been killed just for being in the wrong place at the wrong time.

Steve slowly stood up. Looking back into the decimated restaurant, he was scarcely able to believe his eyes.

"I doubt they'll be getting any five star reviews on Trip Advisor tonight," he said softly.

"Steve, look at this," Fatma called to him. She was standing a few feet off to his right, looking down at a semi-automatic pistol by her feet.

The doorman had been carrying after all, Bull realised.

"And there's something I need to tell you," she said, her voice quivering. "When Goren's men were trying to get him away from us, and into the back room, they were doing it because he had lost his temper and was screaming that the time for talking was over, and that he wanted someone called Mehmet to organise a retaliation strike on the Albanians. He said he wanted them wiped off the face of the earth for what they had just done."

"Are you sure?" he asked, hoping that she'd misheard, but knowing she hadn't.

Still numb from shock, Fatma nodded slowly, as though she were just emerging from a dream. "The bodyguard who whisked him away warned me to keep what I'd heard to myself, said that I was a Turk long before I became a police officer, and that I would bring shame on my family if I betrayed my own people." The words came out slowly, painfully, as though each one was wrapped in barbed wire.

Bull was incensed. Having worked amongst them, he knew how important the concepts of honour and shame were to the Turkish community. Steve walked over and gave her arm a squeeze. "Come on," he said. "We need to get a grip on the crime scene quickly, before any evidence is contaminated."

Giving her the keys, he sent Fatma back to the car to grab her radio, telling her to call for urgent assistance.

As soon as she had gone, he ran over to the door they had taken Goren through, but it was locked from inside. He wondered if Goren was still in the building, but suspected his lackies would have had spirited him away via a back entrance by now. One thing was crystal clear to him as he walked back to the street: unless they regained control of the situation pretty quickly, the body count was going to go through the roof.

Hands shaking, he pulled out his mobile and called Tyler to let him know what had happened. A gigantic shit storm was heading their way, and they didn't have long to prepare for it.

CHAPTER TWENTY-ONE

Friday 28th May 1999
PREPARING FOR WAR

The daily team meeting didn't start until eight-thirty a.m., having been delayed for half an hour so that Tyler could brief George Holland on the previous night's events.

After receiving the call from Bull, he and Dillon had sped down to the restaurant to take charge. By the time they arrived, the crime scene had been bustling with life, unlike the victim lying on the pavement outside.

Goren had seemingly vanished into thin air, and they had been unable to trace him since, which, given what he had been heard to say by Fatma, had become something of a priority.

The crime scene had been photographed, and the ballistic expert had come along to do his thing. Fiona Grisham, an irascible Scottish lady from the Shetland Isles, had attended in her capacity as the on-call Crime Scene Manager, and she had promptly arranged for a tent to be placed over the body until it could be removed to the mortuary.

As much as Jack would have liked Fiona to attend this morning's meeting, the poor cow was still tucked up down at the scene, and was likely to remain so for the next couple of hours. Juliet was there, though, and she would deal with any forensic issues that arose.

Looking around the room, Tyler was struck by how desperately tired most of his officers were. Most of them had worked well into the early hours, and a few, like him and Dillon, hadn't been home at all.

Still wearing the same clothing they'd turned up for work in the day before, their hollow faces, red rimmed eyes, and listless expressions gave them the appearance of zombies. Tyler could see they were struggling to keep their eyes open but, despite being burnt out, they had refused to go home, knowing that many more lives might be lost if they gave in to sleep.

Holland sat beside Tyler, stiff backed and ready for battle. He had promised to find Tyler another dozen people to help out with, amongst other things, statement taking and CCTV collection. With last night's shooting having occurred in a busy High Street, there was no shortage of it to be seized. Franklin had already contacted the local authority CCTV Control Room to check what coverage they had, and he had been informed that the whole incident had been captured on film, thanks to one of their cameras facing the front of the restaurant. Excited by this news, he had promised that someone would be straight over as soon as the meeting concluded.

"I know you're all exhausted," Tyler began. "And if any of you feel too knackered to carry on, I'll completely understand." He looked around the room to see if anyone wanted to take up his offer. No one did, and he felt proud and humbled by the steely looks of determination on their tired faces. "Okay," he said wearily, "but remember, if you reach a point where you need to go home and rest, especially those of you who have been here since yesterday morning, just let me or one of the other supervisors know."

"Och, I reckon you'll give in long before we do, boss," Charlie White said with a lopsided grin. Charlie was one of the lucky ones; he had finished at 2 a.m., but he still looked as white as a sheet.

"You're probably right," Tyler said with a smile that quickly turned into a face splitting yawn. "See, I'm flagging already."

That drew a few smiles of sympathy.

"Okay, so last night our three shooters struck again, hosing down a restaurant where Abdullah Goren was meeting with family members. One person was killed during the attack. His name is Mesut Anil, and he was a thirty-nine year old Kurdish Turk who was on Goren's payroll. What's he known for, Deano?"

Fletcher picked up a slim docket and flicked through it. "Usual stuff, boss. Assaults mainly, demanding money with menaces, possession of drugs. There are loads of intelligence reports linking him to Goren's crime network, and there are warning markings flagged against him on the PNC for being violent and possessing firearms."

Tyler acknowledged this with a cursory nod. "It appears he was carrying a sidearm at the time of his death. A Browning Hi Power nine millimetre self-loading pistol was found a few feet away from his body, and it looks like he was gunned down while trying to engage the shooters."

Charlie White snorted. "Sounds like just as big a slag as the other four who were killed," he observed. "Were any firearms found inside the restaurant?"

Tyler shook his head. "No, nothing incriminating was found, but Goren and his cronies had all scarpered via a back entrance by the time we went looking for them, so who knows what else was there earlier in the night."

Holland cleared his throat. "Can I clarify whether the Reverse Osman letter was served on Goren before the shooting started?" he asked, looking straight at Steve Bull.

Bull shook his head. "Sadly, no. We'd literally only just met with Goren when the attackers opened fire."

"I see," Holland said thoughtfully. Turning to Tyler, he asked, "But Livingstone and Asllani were given theirs?"

"Yes, that's right," Tyler confirmed.

"Who served the letters, may I ask?"

"Me and Dill gave Livingstone his, and Charlie and Kelly delivered Asllani's."

"What was your impression of Livingstone?"

Tyler didn't hesitate. "Arrogant, cocksure. Not remotely worried about us."

Holland raised an enquiring eyebrow. "Not worried as in he knew he hadn't done anything to be worried about?"

Jack recalled the smile that had flickered across Livingstone's face during last night's meeting. "No. He wasn't worried because he was confident we wouldn't be able to pin anything on him no matter what he'd done."

"And he had a chip on his shoulder the size of a sack of potatoes," Dillon added for good measure.

Holland smiled. "I don't doubt it. And what about the Albanian, Asllani?" he asked, turning to Charlie White.

"To be honest, I was expecting him to behave like a total twat, but the wee scallywag didnae. He was polite and respectful, courteous even," Charlie said. "Mind you, I wouldnae wanna get on the wrong side of him, that's for sure. He's a big lump, almost as big as Mr Dillon, and twice as ugly."

"He gave me the creeps," Kelly Flowers said, barely repressing a shudder. She was a pretty brunette in her late twenties with a heart shaped face. "I got the feeling that, despite his superficial charm, he's not a very nice man."

"Sorry, Kelly," Charlie said with a twinkle in his eye, "are you talking about Asllani or Mr Dillon?"

When the laughter died down, Charlie said, "The thing is, I really didnae get the feeling he was hiding anything. He looked me straight in the eye and said his people had absolutely nothing to do with the attack on Goren's men, and you know what? I think I believed him."

"I hate to admit it," Kelly said, "but I agree. He came across as being completely genuine when he said that."

"But the shooters were all white," Fatma protested, and then blushed as every eye in the room lasered in on her. "Steve and I were there last night, and we saw them for ourselves. Not only that, but they even left an Albanian flag draped over the doorman they shot. Surely there can't be any doubt that Asllani's people are behind the attacks?"

"It's not that simple," Jack said tenderly. He could see the fatigue from having worked so many hours, coupled with the shock of what she'd been through the previous night, was starting to catch up on her.

"I'm sorry for speaking out like this," Fatma said. She paused and looked around the room, clearly conscious that she was the least experienced officer present. "The thing is, I've been working Stoke Newington's ground for five years now, and I know for a fact that everyone in Livingstone's gang is black." Her voice had become slightly strained. "It has to be the Albanians," she insisted. "And we have to do something quickly or Goren will wipe them out."

"We are doing something," Jack placated her. "We've posted ARVs outside the houses of Asllani and his top lieutenants while we track Goren down to warn him off. He might be a ruthless gangster, but he's not silly, Fatma, and he won't sanction a hit if he knows that doing so will put him straight in prison."

It was a short term fix, not a solution to the long term problem, Jack accepted, but they had to do something, and overt armed patrols were the most effective deterrent. Well, that and letting everyone who worked for Goren know they were wise to his plan and would act swiftly if a retaliation hit was carried out.

"That won't stop him," she said defiantly. "He'll just wait until things quieten down and the patrols have stopped."

"Young lady," Holland said, his voice firm. "You need to accept that we're vastly more experienced than you, and that we know what we're doing. Of course this is a stop gap measure, but it will buy us the time we need to gather enough evidence to start making arrests. Now, let's move on."

Fatma drew her chin in and, as the DCS glowered at her, she looked like she wanted the ground to open up and swallow her.

"Things are starting to come together," Jack said. "Colin has produced some stills from the CCTV of the shooters dumping the stolen Mondeo in Tottenham after Tuesday night's shooting. They're up on the wall in the Intel Cell. Please take the time to look at them as they show the suspect's faces very clearly. The priority for us continues to be CCTV viewing, and those of you who were assigned to that yesterday will continue today. This morning, some of the additional officers that Mr Holland has promised us will be tasked with visiting

Goren and Asllani's associates to make sure that they know we're watching them. The rest will be used to take statements and collect CCTV from last night's shooting. We're still awaiting the preliminary results on the ballistics from the lab. Can you chase those up for me, Juliet? And I want to know if the same weapons were used in both shootings."

"I'll put in a call right after the meeting," she promised him. Despite the fact that she was in for another day of Creepy Claxton slicing up cadavers, she was as glammed up as ever.

"I need to have a quick chat with Mr Dillon before he heads off to the mortuary," Jack said.

Sitting beside him, Dillon groaned out loud.

"Steve, you need to be involved in that, too," Tyler added. He turned to Dean Fletcher. "Please tell me you've had the ANPR results back?" His tone implied he would be severely miffed if the answer was no.

"Yep," Dean said in his usual taciturn manner. "Came through just before the meeting started. Give me ten minutes to review the records and I'll come and give you an update."

"Reg," Tyler turned his attention on Parker. "Anything back from the TIU yet?"

"There was a shed load of phone data waiting for me when I logged on this morning," he said. "Let me get it into order while you discuss the ANPR stuff with Deano, and then we can go through it together."

Tyler turned to face Dillon, who was looking thoroughly miserable now that he'd been reminded he had another gruelling day of SPMs to look forward to. "Did you speak to DS Murphy in Manchester about that CCTV he was supposed to be getting for us?"

Dillon slapped his large forehead with the palm of his hand. "Sorry, I forgot to tell you. He's having it sent down to us today. Should be arriving early this afternoon."

Tyler cast his friend a look that said 'it would have been nice to have been told that earlier'.

Dillon gave an apologetic shrug. "Sorry, hanging out with dead bodies all day and then running crime scenes all night makes me forgetful."

Jack chose not to bite. "How did you get on viewing the CCTV from the corner shop where Adebanjo's burner was found?" This was addressed to Christine Taylor.

Taylor, being an SO7 officer, hadn't been dragged down to the Wood Green crime scene with the rest of them, and it showed. She looked fresh faced and perky, dressed in black twill culottes, a red blouse and matching red shoes.

"I viewed it yesterday evening," she informed him. "The footage is absolutely top quality. It shows Goliath arriving empty handed at the shop at 19:15 hours. He's inside for less than five minutes, and when he reappears he's carrying a grocery bag. As he comes out, you can clearly see that he's talking on his mobile. The conversation lasts a couple of minutes and, for most of it, he's facing the camera, looking totally chilled. Then, after glancing all around to make sure that no one's looking, he dumps the phone inside the bin and sets off on a reciprocal route towards the hotel."

"Are we confident it's him?" Jack asked her.

Christine laughed. "Totally. The picture's as clear as a bell, and he's a pretty distinctive looking bloke. It would be very hard to mistake him for anyone else."

Tyler considered what she had just said, stroking his chin thoughtfully. A random idea had just sprung into his head. "Chrissy, you say he was facing the camera while he was chatting on the phone. How clearly could you see his face?"

Taylor seemed bewildered by the question. "Very. Why?"

Jack shrugged. "I'm just wondering if there's any merit in having a lip reader view it," he said. "Perhaps you can show me the tape after the meeting, so I can see for myself."

"Of course, sir."

Tyler turned to Parker. "What about the burner he dumped? Can you tell me anything about that?"

"The lab sent me the SIM details, and from that I was able to obtain the phone's telephone number," Reg told him.

A Subscriber Identity Module – commonly referred to as a SIM card – is a tiny chip that acts as the phone's brain. The telephone number is attributed to this, and not the handset.

"I submitted subs and cell site requests last night, and the results came in this morning. I'll go through the data as soon as we finish the meeting."

"Okay," Tyler said. "Let's all crack on. I'll leave Steve to go through the daily taskings with you. I'm going to view the CCTV of Adebanjo first, then I need to sit down with Mr Dillon and Stevie. Dean, Reg, I'll see each of you in my office as soon as I've finished with them, which means you've got roughly half an hour to prepare. I know we're all fit to drop, but things are finally starting to move, and I'm confident that all your hard work will soon start yielding results–" he allowed himself a wan smile as he stood up "–assuming that we don't all collapse from exhaustion first."

———

Tyson Meeks was bored out of his brain. All he'd done since they'd dumped him off at the hotel was watch TV and sleep. The proposed move to another part of the country had been unavoidably delayed, possibly for as long as another week, they had told him during their visit yesterday evening. He'd thrown a strop, telling them that he was fed up of eating in the hotel. The food was good, but he wanted a McDonalds. After much bleating on his part, the Feds had reluctantly given him an allowance, acting like the money was coming out of their own pockets rather than being funded by the tax payer, so at least he now had some cash.

Most people would jump at the chance of being put up in a four star hotel in a nice area for a week, all expenses paid, they had told him, trying to sweeten the deal. He'd brushed that argument aside, unimpressed. He didn't care what other people would jump at. He felt alienated in Brentwood. They had told him to look on the bright side, recommending that he treat his enforced isolation as a nice little holiday to be enjoyed.

Meeks had spent the rest of the night reflecting on their upbeat comments, trying to buy into the hype they peddled, but the truth was, he was no more convinced by their hollow words now than he had been when they were fresh out of their mouths. The streets of Hackney might not be as pretty as the rural Essex town he now found himself trapped in, but they were his ends, and he was missing them badly.

The worst thing was the lack of human contact. Meeks wasn't exactly blessed with a multitude of friends, but there were plenty of people he could hang out with back in the smoke. True, most of them were low life shotters who worked for Conrad Livingstone, but at least they were someone to talk to or share a spliff with.

Of course, if he were being totally honest with himself, there was one thing that was bothering him even more than the lack of companionship, and that was the fact that he hadn't smoked any weed since he'd been arrested on Tuesday evening. That was three whole days ago! He didn't think he had ever gone that long without a puff before. Well, not since he was a kid, anyway.

The witness protection officers from the Criminal Justice Protection Unit had given him fifty quid, which was more than enough to buy himself some weed. The trouble was, not knowing the area, he had no idea where to go if he wanted to score.

As he sat on the end of his bed, watching breakfast TV, an idea came to him. Why not jump on a train and pop back to his ends to grab some stuff from his flat?

The killjoys from witness protection had warned him against returning to Hackney under any circumstances, but that seemed like stupid advice to him. He could be in and out within a couple of hours, grabbing some clothes and the half dozen family photos that he had of himself and Marcel with their mother before she died. Marcel had been going on at him for years to let him have one of them, but the faded and torn pictures were all he had left of his mum, and he had no intention of sharing them with a brother who wouldn't even give him the time of day.

He also had a secret stash of weed, and a large bundle of cash – nearly a thousand pounds – hidden under a loose floorboard in his bedroom. He hated the idea of leaving it there, and it wasn't as if he could trust anyone to bring it to him. He snorted at the thought;

everyone he knew would just keep it for themselves if he asked them to do that.

He could also get himself a cheap phone while he was there, and then, when he was settled, he could try and re-establish contact with Marcel. Maybe, if they didn't see each other for a while, his younger brother's attitude towards him would mellow a little. What was it they said? Absence makes the heart grow fonder.

His mind made up, Meeks dressed quickly and went through to reception, where he obtained directions to Brentwood train station.

————

Dean was waiting patiently by the door of his office when Jack returned from viewing the CCTV with Christine Taylor. Without breaking stride, he gestured for his lead researcher to go in ahead of him and take a seat.

Following him in, Tyler plonked himself down behind his desk and opened his daybook.

As Christine had said, Adebanjo had indeed been facing the camera for most of the conversation outside the corner shop, and Tyler was cautiously optimistic that a good lip reader would be able to make out at least some of what was being said. Eager to progress this new line of enquiry, he'd instructed Christine to get straight onto the National Police Improvement Agency to obtain a list of approved lip readers. The sooner they drafted someone in, the better.

Buoyed by the prospect of getting something useful out of the footage, Tyler felt like he was starting to get his second wind. It probably wouldn't last long, but he intended to make the most of it while he could. Poor Dean, on the other hand, with his bleary eyes, unshaven face and dishevelled mop of salt and pepper hair, looked like he was in desperate need of his bed.

"So what have you got for me, Deano? Anything I should be excited over?" Tyler made a point of crossing his fingers in front of Dean's face to emphasise his hopefulness.

As always, Dean's face was impossible to read. Without giving anything away, he slipped his reading glasses on, opened the thin blue folder he had brought along with him, and cleared his throat as if he were about to deliver a speech. "These are the ANPR results for Erkan Dengiz' E-Class Mercedes for Tuesday 25th May, the day of the murder," he began ponderously.

Jack had to resist the urge to tell him to speed up, knowing that Dean's anal-retentive personality verged on OCD, and that it would be best to let him get there in his own good time. Hopefully, that would be this morning, and not the middle of next week, which is how long Jack calculated it would take if he didn't start talking faster.

"As requested, I've obtained the registration number of the ten cars following the Mercedes every time it was captured on ANPR." He glanced up to check that Jack was following.

Miraculously, Jack managed to resist the urge to roll his eyes, but he couldn't prevent a tiny sigh of frustration from leaking out.

"I also took the liberty of ordering the registration numbers of the ten cars that preceded the Mercedes, just in case anyone was following him from in front as opposed to behind." It was a technique police surveillance teams used all the time.

Jack nodded, impressed. "Good call," he said. "Did anything show up?"

An irreverent smile crept onto Dean's face as he peered at Tyler over the top of his glasses. "You know, you're very impatient. Did anyone ever tell you that?"

"Just about everyone who's ever known me," Jack admitted.

Dean readjusted his reading glasses. "Okay. So the Merc was caught on ANPR cameras five times after 6 p.m., with the last sighting occurring at a quarter to nine. On the first occasion, a red Vauxhall Corsa was two cars ahead of it. On the four occasions that followed, the same red Corsa was always two or three cars behind it." He passed a still of the Corsa over. The photo had been taken from an overhead gantry camera suspended above the A406. It afforded a front view of the Corsa from above. Unfortunately, the street lighting was reflecting off the windscreen, which meant that most of the driver's face was obscured by the resulting sheen. The only thing he could say for sure was that the driver was a black man, probably in his twenties or thirties. It also looked as though he had longish hair, possibly dreads.

"Are there any clearer pictures of the driver's face?" he asked Dean.

Fletcher shrugged. "Don't know yet. Haven't had time to go through them properly. If I find one, I'll bring it in."

The registration number and keeper details were recorded below the image. "No current keeper, I see?" Tyler said.

"No," Dean confirmed. "But there are several recent intelligence reports that this is a pool car shared by Jerome Norris and Daryl Peters. I haven't had time to go through them yet."

Tyler frowned, deep in thought "Jerome Norris – why does that name seem strangely familiar to me?"

Dean stared at him blankly. "Can't help you there, I'm afraid. Maybe I'll be able to tell you more when I've finished researching them."

Tyler dry washed his face, trying to encourage the weary cogs in his head to turn a little faster. He was convinced the name Norris had previously come up during the enquiry, but he couldn't, for the life of him, remember when or how. "Any chance that the Corsa's presence is a coincidence?" he asked. "Could it be that they were both just travelling in the same direction on the A406 for a while?"

Dean shook his head emphatically. "In my opinion, there's no chance that this is coincidental. Some of the hits are hours apart and in different parts of London. Either they were travelling together in convoy, or the Corsa was following the Merc."

Tyler chewed his bottom lip as he processed this. "Good work, Dean," he eventually said. "Can you let Colin and the other CCTV viewers know to be on the lookout for the Corsa. It'll be interesting to see if it turns up on any of the footage we've seized."

As he showed Dean out, Reggie appeared. "Got some very interesting stuff," he said, waving a thick file of paper at him. "You're gonna wanna see this."

Tyler groaned despondently. It sounded like it was going to be a heavy session. "Give me five minutes to grab a cup of coffee," he pleaded, "and then I'm all yours."

CHAPTER TWENTY-TWO

BREAKFAST AT TONY'S

Marcel Meeks met up with what remained of his crew at their usual meeting place in the estate. He greeted them dourly, and their response was every bit as lacklustre. Without Ziggy or Switch to take charge, there was no cohesion among them and, as they sat there, they all seemed at a bit of a loss as to what to do next.

"Any news on Ziggy and the others?" Marcel asked.

"I heard dem Boydem were still holding them, innit," a slender youth with a large afro said. His name was Carlos Silva and he was a little older than Marcel, but not as tall. "Feds found Curtis' red hoodie and a knife in the bins under their tower block, innit," he said, shaking his head sadly. "Don't look good for 'em, bruv, I'm telling ya."

On hearing about the knife, Marcel's stomach flipped. *Calm down, bruv*, his mind screamed at him. *I wiped the shank, so my prints won't be on it.*

"What about Switch?" Marcel asked. "He still on the run?"

"Dunno, bruv," Carlos said with a shrug. "Aint heard nothing, so I s'pose so."

"Shit!" The word was spat out by a tubby, mixed-race boy called Shaquille Thomas. Glancing around the group uneasily, he pulled the hood of his Mackenzie up despite the heat. "What if dem Boydem come for the rest of us? We get charged with that murder, we're all looking at an L-Plate, bruv."

"Aint no one to blame for shanking dem passengers but Switch," Carlos said bitterly. "Boy never could control that temper of his."

As they spoke, a sleek black BMW coupé pulled into the car park and glided to a stop next to them. With the sun glinting off its shiny paintwork, it provided a stark contrast to the three burnt out wrecks behind it. As they watched, the driver's window came down, allowing the rap music that was playing to escape from within.

The boys stared at the vehicle with undisguised hostility until they recognised the driver, at which point their demeanour instantly became deferential.

"Marcel," Livingstone called out, beckoning him over with an imperious wave of his manicured hand.

"How do *you* know the Main Man?" Carlos asked, unable to prevent a twinge of jealousy from creeping into his voice.

"My brother works for him," Marcel said, pushing himself away from the wall he had been leaning on and strutting over to the car with even more swagger than normal.

"Wagwan," he said, trying to act cool. Inwardly, he was afraid that his useless brother had fucked up again, and that Livingstone was there to punish him for Tyson's shortcomings.

Livingstone smiled disarmingly. "I'm looking for Weasel. Have you seen him recently?"

Marcel shifted uncomfortably, his fears all but confirmed. "Not for a while, bruv. I try to avoid him, innit."

Livingstone nodded understandingly. "You still blame him for what happened to your mother. I get it, blud." He studied the youngster in silence for a while, as though a debate were raging inside his head. Eventually, he seemed to come to a conclusion. "You hungry?" he asked.

Marcel shrugged. He was a growing boy and he was always hungry. "A bit," he admitted.

"Me too," Livingstone said with an infectious grin. "Get in. We'll find somewhere to eat while we talk."

Marcel, glanced uneasily over his shoulder, casting a furtive look at his crew. He was torn. On the one hand, being invited for breakfast with the Main Man would enhance his reputation no end; on the other, he could be walking into a beating, or worse. He could feel the others all watching him with baited breath, wondering why he was hesitating, and wishing that Livingstone had invited them instead.

"You're not scared of me, are you?" Livingstone taunted.

Marcel concealed his nerves behind a quick sneer. It was a defence mechanism he had picked up while running with the gang. "Course not, bruv," he said defiantly.

"Good. Now get in," Livingstone said, and it was clear from his tone that it was less an invite, and more a demand.

Swallowing his anxiety, Marcel walked around to the other side of the car and opened the door. "Catch you later," he said to his homies, hoping that there would be a later. He had heard rumours about people getting into a car with Livingstone and his men for a 'friendly little chat' who had never been seen again.

Tyler handed Reg the mug of coffee he had just made him and settled down behind his desk, pen and paper at the ready. "So, what have you got for me?" he asked.

"I'm going to try and keep this simple," Reg said.

"If only," Tyler said with a wistful smile.

"Let's start with the burner that Christine Taylor recovered from the bin outside the shop in Beckton. I ran a check on the SIM, which revealed the phone is an unregistered pre-pay. The number assigned to it ends in 666."

Tyler smiled inwardly. How appropriate that the mobile in Goliath's possession should end with 666 – the number of the Beast.

"It first became active the day before the murder, so that's Monday

24th May. The 666 phone has only ever been in contact with two other numbers and, as you would expect, both are unregistered pre-pays."

Jack grunted despondently. "No surprise there."

"They end with 109 and 003. The 666 number was in contact with the 109 number several times on the Monday. Cell site indicates that the 666 calls were made from Manchester, and received by the 109 number in London."

"Are you able to tell me the specific areas the phone masts for the making and receiving calls were located in?"

Reg nodded. "Naturellement, monsieur," he said, momentarily slipping into an exaggerated French accent. "The Manchester cell covers the city centre, and the London one covers Dalston."

Jack felt his heart rate accelerate. Dalston! That was where Conrad Livingstone lived. He scribbled a note to find out where in Manchester Adebanjo resided. He had a sneaky suspicion it would be within the radius of the cell that the 666 number had been pinged in.

"Okay, so here's where it starts to get a little bit more complicated," Reggie said apologetically. "At 09:25 hours on Tuesday morning, the 666 number communicated with the 109 number. The 666 number was in Manchester city centre. The 109 number was still in Dalston. Then the 666 number called the 003 number for the first time. That was also in Manchester city centre. In fact, I can narrow that down even further by saying the 666 and 003 numbers were both within the same azimuth of the same cell when the call occurred."

"Remind me what an azimuth is."

"Every telephone mast, or cell, is split into three sectors, with each sector having its own antenna. The antennas are erected at 120-degree intervals to ensure that the cell gets the best all-round coverage. Each 120-degree arc is called an azimuth."

Jack was making frantic notes, unaware that his tongue was protruding from the side of his mouth as he concentrated.

Reg gazed upon him with pity, knowing that Tyler really struggled with processing phone data. "Boss, you don't need to make any notes. I've got printouts for all the telephone numbers I'm going to be talking about. These contain the dates, times and cell locations for all the calls.

I've also got some pretty maps to illustrate the cells they were in when the calls occurred."

"No offence, Reggie," Tyler said, still scribbling away, "but it's easier for me to make a few notes of my own to supplement all the gobbledygook you're going to saddle me with, rather than spend hours going through it, trying to work out what it all means."

Reggie gave him a 'suit yourself' shrug and continued. "About an hour later, 666 was called by 109. It was a brief call, lasting only a couple of minutes. Almost immediately afterwards, 666 rung 003. Here's where it gets even more interesting: 109 was still in Dalston. The 666 and 003 numbers were, yet again, within the same azimuth of the same cell, but they were now a considerable distance way from Manchester, heading south towards London."

"Are you sure?" Jack asked, looking up from his daybook.

Reg raised an eyebrow at that. "Of course I'm sure," he said, tapping the sheet of paper he was reading the figures from. "It's all here in black and white."

Jack pondered this. They already knew that Adebanjo had travelled down to London by train on Tuesday morning. What Reg had just told him suggested that whoever he was speaking to on the 003 number had also been on the train. Could it have been one of the Kalu twins? Surely not.

"Almost as soon as that call ended, 003 dialled a number we haven't spoken about before. It ends in 151. Again, it's a really short call, lasting a minute and a half. The 151 number was in a cell covering Kingsland Road and Holly Street."

Jack paused for a moment. This was getting confusing. "I hate phones," he told Reg, before indicating for him to continue.

"At 12:17 hours, 666 made another call to 003. This one lasted three minutes. Guess what? They were both in London."

"Within the same azimuth of the same cell?" Jack asked.

Reggie nodded, and checked the cell site map. "Somewhere in Central London, so I'm guessing they came down by train because it would take far longer by car."

"They did. If you check, I'm confident that you'll find Euston British Rail train station is in the azimuth they were pinged in."

Reggie scanned the map, his podgy forefinger moving in ever decreasing circles until it finally came to a halt. When it did, he looked up at Tyler with a quizzical expression. "Tell me, did you just happen to know that trains from Manchester arrive at Euston, or is there more to it than that?"

Tyler tapped the side of his nose. "We're back in 'don't ask' territory," he said.

"Fine," Reg huffed, adopting the wounded tone of a man being dealt a blatant injustice. "The 666 number then made another short call to the 109 number. There were a couple more calls between 666 and 109 during the afternoon and evening, the last one being made at 19:15 hours. During both of these calls, 666 was in a cell covering–"

"Beckton," Jack interjected, earning himself a look of incredulity.

"Yes," Reggie spluttered, "but how did you–"

Tyler tapped the side of his nose again, and grinned mischievously. He was actually beginning to enjoy this, which wasn't something he could normally say about one of Reg's tedious sessions on phone data.

"And I'm guessing the 109 phone was still in Dalston?"

Reg sighed miserably. "I don't suppose there's any point in me asking you how you knew that, is there?"

"None at all," Jack said, smiling sweetly. "Carry on."

"The 666 number also made another call to the 003 number, but I suppose you already know which cell it was within the radius of, don't you?"

Jack shook his head. "Haven't got the foggiest," he admitted.

"Seven Sisters and Finsbury Park," Reg said smugly, as though he had just scored a minor but important victory.

Now that's interesting, Tyler thought. The Kalu twins hadn't left their hotel in Beckton all afternoon, and when they did eventually venture out, they were immediately arrested by the SFO team from SO19. So, if the 003 number didn't belong to either of them, who the hell was using it?

Jack thought about this, trying to break the information down methodically. If the cell site data was to be believed, whoever was using the 003 number had left Manchester on the same train as Adebanjo and, by that logic, they must also have arrived at London

Euston at the same time as him. Officers from SO7 had already seized the CCTV of Adebanjo's arrival at Euston, and Coleen Perry had viewed it yesterday, although she had only been looking out for Adebanjo and the Kalu twins, not anyone else. Perhaps, if it was revisited now that they had this new information, the footage would reveal who was using the 003 number. It was a long shot, but worth a try.

"Wait there," he told Reggie. Springing out of his chair, he ran out into the main office shouting Coleen's name.

———

Livingstone took him to a little greasy spoon tucked away in a side street just off Dalston Lane. The faded wavy script on the cracked wooden sign above the door proclaimed the establishment was called 'Tony's'. A bell chimed a quaint ting-a-ling as they entered, and an elderly Maltese man behind the counter smiled at them, revealing a perfect set of gleaming white dentures. "Morning," he said cheerfully.

Livingstone chose a table by the window, keeping as much distance between them and the other customers as possible.

Even this far away from the cooking area, a haze from the café's ancient fryer wafted over, filling the air around them with the smell of burnt chip fat. Lacking adequate ventilation, the windows had become opaque with condensation.

As they sat down, an explosion of laughter came from a table off to their right, which was occupied by half a dozen men in high visibility jackets who were talking animatedly about someone's stag do and what had gone on there.

Marcel looked around, taking in his surroundings without enthusiasm.

Livingstone picked up on this and smiled. "What's-a-matter, bruv? Not what you were expecting?"

Marcel shrugged. He hadn't known what to expect.

"Trust me, bruv, you can't beat breakfast at Tony's."

The man from behind the counter came over, walking with a pronounced limp. "What can I get you?" he asked. He spoke with a faint trace of a Mediterranean accent, one that had been considerably diluted by living in London for so many years.

"Two full English breakfasts," Livingstone said, "and I'll have coffee with mine. Marcel?"

"Orange juice for me," Marcel said.

When they were alone again, Marcel stared at Livingstone earnestly. "Before you ask, I don't know where Tyson is," he said, then added nervously, "is he in trouble?"

Livingstone smiled disarmingly. "Why would you think that?"

Marcel gave a half-hearted shrug. "Because he's an idiot who fucks up just about everything he does," he replied truthfully. He nearly blurted out that the trait didn't run in the family, and that he was nothing like his half-brother, but he managed to quell the urge, knowing it would make him appear weak.

Livingstone laughed at that. "Yes, he does," he agreed, "but I'm not here for him. I thought that, after all these years, it was about time you and I got to know each other a little better."

Marcel frowned at that. *After all these years?* What did that mean? "Why would you want to get to know me at all?" he asked, suddenly wary.

"Tyson's never told you anything about me, has he?" Livingstone asked.

Marcel's brow knitted in consternation. "What do you mean? Told me what?"

Before Livingstone could answer, the limping man returned with their drinks and some cutlery, which he placed on the table for them. "Back in a jiffy with your food," he informed them, his dentures wobbling as he spoke.

Livingstone took an appreciative sip of his coffee and studied his guest over the top of the cup. "What do you know about your father, bruv?"

The question took Marcel totally by surprise; wrongfooting him to the extent that he didn't know how to respond. He was spared having to do so, or at least given a temporary reprieve, by the arrival of their food.

"Eat," Livingstone said. "We'll talk after."

Marcel ate slowly, unsettled by the question, and by Conrad Livingstone's sudden appearance. Livingstone's unexpected question had stirred uncomfortable feelings that were buried deep within him; awakening painful emotions that had lain dormant for many years. The truth was that Marcel knew nothing about his biological father. To the best of his knowledge, he had never even met the man; he certainly had no conscious memories of him. Before his mother had died, the subject had been taboo, to the extent that she flatly refused to even acknowledge the man's existence.

When he had been much younger, Marcel had beleaguered his mother with questions about his unknown father, the two most pressing of which were:

Who was he, and why didn't he want anything to do with Marcel?

Was it his fault that his parents had split up?

Her answers had always been frustratingly evasive, leaving him none the wiser for asking. Later, after her death, he had harboured hopes that social services might help him, but they had been no more forthcoming than his mother. Over the years, the questions had gone round and round inside his head, as if played on a never-ending loop. Not knowing had tortured him until he had finally learned how to block it out.

He had seen a counsellor for a while; a spectacled lady with a nervous twitch, thick tortoiseshell glasses, and grey hair that was always worn in a tight bun that dragged her eyebrows halfway up her wrinkly forehead. She had always reeked of stale cigarette smoke, he recalled. During their twice weekly sessions, she had tried to help him come to terms with the many issues that troubled him. Her name had been Mrs Moody, but she had been anything but, and her saggy face had been set in a perpetual smile.

He remembered her telling him how humans were socially conditioned, and predisposed with a deep need to know both parents; how they had an intrinsic need for family, which explained why people who had been adopted were often compelled to trace their birth parents when they grew up, regardless of how amazing their adopted parents were. It was also the reason that people were driven to visit their ancestral homelands, even though they, themselves, were removed from the place by many generations.

Marcel hadn't cared about any of that. None of what she told him made growing up in a children's home, feeling totally alone and unloved, any easier to stomach. He had resented the fact that most of the other kids at school had at least one parent to go home to, and this had made it harder for him to form meaningful relationships with them. His inability to fit in, and his stubborn refusal to conform to the rules, had led to him getting into fights and falling out with his teachers. He was soon labelled a 'problem child' and sent for counselling, which he knew was just a polite term for correctional therapy.

Many years ago, his well-meaning therapist had asked him to describe his feelings for the man who had abandoned him. Marcel had found it hard to put them into words at first, but over time, with Mrs Moody's help, he had come to understand that what he actually felt for his unknown father was a bitter resentment over his betrayal.

As Marcel shovelled the last mouthful of food into his mouth, he realised that nothing had changed during the intervening years, that his feelings for his unknown father still bordered on hatred. But then, what else was he supposed to feel for the worthless shit who had abandoned him and his mother when they needed him most?

"I don't know nothing about my dad, bruv," he said as he pushed his plate aside.

"But you're curious, right?" Livingstone asked, studying him carefully.

Marcel reacted with a belligerent shrug. "I don't need a father. I've got by so far without one, innit."

"I get it, blud," Livingstone said. "You feel angry, betrayed. And why wouldn't you?"

Marcel stared back sullenly, saying nothing.

"But maybe, if you knew the full story, you would feel differently."

Marcel snorted. "And you know the full story, do you?"

To his surprise, Livingstone nodded. "I do, and I think it's about time you did too."

———

Having hunted Coleen Perry down and instructed her to urgently review the Euston CCTV, Tyler returned to his office, where he found Reg sitting exactly where he had left him, head buried in a small mountain of call data printouts and cell site graphs, muttering away to himself as he worked.

"You alright there, Reg?" he asked from the doorway, wondering if his phones man had finally lost the plot.

"Just tidying up some stuff while I waited for you," Reg told him with a weary smile.

"So where were we?" Tyler asked, settling himself behind his desk and pulling his tie down to half-mast.

"We were discussing the calls between the 666, 003, 109, and 151 phones," Reggie reminded him. "We got as far as the calls that were made from Euston station in the early afternoon, and then you rushed off like a man possessed."

Jack grinned. "Yeah, sorry about that," he said sheepishly.

Reggie stared at Tyler, waiting for him to elaborate. When it became clear he wasn't going to, he grunted in frustration and picked up the next sheet of call data. "At 13:30 hours 003 rang the 666 number, making a call that lasted four minutes. Cell site shows 003 was in the vicinity of Seven Sisters Road, whereas 666 was in Beckton. At 16:00 hours the 109 number called the 666 number. The former was still in Dalston, the latter still in Beckton."

Jack jotted this down in his daybook.

Reg waited for him to finish before continuing. "At 19:15 hours the 666 number rang 109. Their cell locations were the same as in their previous call. Ten minutes later, 666 called 003, which was still within range of a cell covering Seven Sisters Road and Finsbury Park. The last couple of calls—"

Ten minutes later...

"Hang on a minute, mate," Jack said, flicking back through his daybook until he found the notes he'd made about requesting the services of a lip reader. Yep. Sure enough, the time of the call Adebanjo had been having on CCTV was 19:25 hours, which meant that he had been speaking to the 003 number at the time. That was the number of whoever had accompanied him down to London on the Inter-City train earlier in the day. Could this possibly belong to the shooters? It would make sense, his having brought a crew down to London with him? Jack stood up, a frisson of excitement bubbling inside his chest. He needed to let Coleen know that she was looking for three shaven headed men, one with a tattoo on his neck, and one with a scar on his face that made him look like something out of The Phantom of the Opera.

"Reg," he said, striding towards the door, "I'll be back in a minute. Don't go away."

"Really?" Reggie said, scratching his head as Tyler disappeared yet again. "But there's only three more calls to tell you about," he yelled, throwing the call data down on top of Tyler's desk to vent his frustration. To his annoyance, the papers slid right off the end and fluttered down to the floor like a poor man's tickertape parade. Shoulders sagging, Reggie watched them settle by his feet and sighed. "Well, that's just great," he told himself. "Now I've got to pick the bloody things up."

———

Livingstone dropped Marcel back on the estate, but the teenager was no longer in the mood to hang out with his homies, chatting shit and committing minor crimes just to pass the time of day. Instead, he wandered along Queensbridge Road until he came to the entrance that led down onto Regent's Canal. Needing some alone time to think things through, he set off along the canal path, trying to make sense of the bombshell that Livingstone had dropped on him. It was a lot to process, and his mind was reeling.

It couldn't be true, could it?

Surely, there was no way that Conrad Livingstone could possibly be his father?

And yet, the Main Man had seemed quite sincere as he'd told him about his on-off relationship with Marcel's mother, and how she had announced to the world that she was pregnant just weeks after they had split up.

The searing May heat was oppressive, even at this early hour, and

Marcel sat down underneath the shelter of the first bridge he came to. He scooped up a handful of pebbles and threw them onto the canal, one after the other, watching them land with a soft plop and sink without trace.

Following the revelation, Marcel had reacted with vitriol, demanded to know why, if what Livingstone said was true, he had waited until now to reveal the fact, and why he had never so much as sent him a birthday card in the past. "You haven't shown any interest in me for the past fifteen years, bruv," he gushed, his voice thick with fury, "so why the sudden interest now?"

As the workmen filed by on their way out of the café, Livingstone could only offer a lame shrug in response. "Lots of reasons, bruv. Some of them selfish, some not."

Marcel folded his arms across his chest, staring at the older man accusingly. "Like what?" he said, sucking through his teeth in a disrespectful manner. It was dangerous to be discourteous to a man like Livingstone, but the anger raging within made him reckless.

Unperturbed by the insult, Livingstone let out a protracted sigh as he tried to form the right words. "Look, I was a sixteen year old punk and I wasn't ready to be a father. I didn't *want* to be a father. I cared about your mum, but we didn't love each other and… well, our relationship was fiery, blud, ya get me?"

Marcel fixed him with a sneer of contempt. "What, so you just walked away and left her to get on with it, bruv? That what you're saying?"

A flash of anger flickered in Livingstone's eyes, but then it was gone. "What the fuck you expect? I was sixteen, bruv. I could hardly take care of myself, let alone anyone else. When I was a few years older, and a bit more worldly wise, I offered to give her money," he said in a strained voice. "I would have liked to have had a chance to get to know you, but she made it clear she didn't want me in her life and I respected that."

Marcel couldn't imagine Conrad Livingstone respecting anyone else's wishes unless it suited him to do so. He blinked away the moisture that pricked at his eyes, angry at himself for being so pathetic. "And what about after she died, bruv? You weren't a kid any longer, so you can't use that excuse. Why didn't you man up and do the right thing by me then?"

"Because Tyson wouldn't let me," Livingstone said quietly. "He became the man of the house after your mum's death, and he hated me because I was more interested in helping you out than I was him."

Marcel considered this. "But you gave him a job?"

"I've always tried to look after him," Livingstone said. "I'm still trying to look after him, but he's disappeared off the face of the earth and I can't find him."

It was an unwelcome deviation from the conversation they had been having but, to his surprise, Marcel found himself concerned enough to be intrigued. "What's he done now, bruv?"

Livingstone hesitated, as though unsure whether or not to confide in Marcel. "I'm not sure it's a good idea to involve you," he said, waving the question away dismissively.

"Nah, bruv. You don't get to decide that. What's my idiot brother done?"

A pained expression crossed Livingstone's features. "He's dropped some pretty serious players in it with the Feds, blud, and unless I can find him before they do, he's gonna end up very dead."

A look of incredulity appeared on Marcel's face.

"It's true, bruv," Livingstone said. "He's in really deep shit."

Marcel's eyes narrowed suspiciously. "I know he's fucking useless, but not even Tyson would be that stupid. And, if he *has* done what you say, why would you want to help him, bruv? Wouldn't that look bad on you?"

"I don't want to help him," Livingstone said, "but I owe it to you and your mum to try. After all, like him or not, he's the only family you have left."

"Apart from you, you mean?" Marcel said.

Livingstone smiled. "Yeah, apart from me. That's if you're willing to accept me into your life, blud."

Marcel had said nothing. He wasn't at all sure that he wanted to accept Livingstone into his life. Doing so would involve a long painful process of forgiveness, and he didn't know if he wanted to risk reopening emotional scars that had taken so long to heal – or if he was capable of surviving the pain of having his newly rekindled hope extinguished if things didn't work out.

They had agreed that it was a lot for Marcel to take in, and that they would meet in a few days to talk some more, after he'd had a proper chance to digest the news. In the meantime, Marcel had promised him that, if Tyson made contact with him, he would try and arrange a meeting, and then let Livingstone know so that he could come along and attempt to reason with his idiot half-brother.

CHAPTER TWENTY-THREE

THE DAY THAT KEEPS ON GIVING

Inside the cramped CCTV viewing room, Jack leaned over Coleen's shoulder, trying to get a little closer to the TV screen. She had paused the picture as Adebanjo alighted the train at Euston, his right hand glued to his ear.

The camera was looking down along the length of the platform from just above the ticket barrier gantry, and the italic writing in the top right corner of the screen proclaimed the date and time to be: *Tues 24/05/1999 / 12:18hrs.*

"Are you happy that the time shown on the screen is accurate?" he asked her.

"Uh-huh," she answered without averting her eyes from the screen. "I phoned 123 and checked it against TIM when I was at the station. It was only a few seconds out."

The BT Speaking Clock had been a stalwart provider of time checks in the UK since its arrival back in 1936. It was known as 'TIM' because the three letter code was short for 'time', and this correlated to the number that callers dialled on the old-fashioned alphabetic phones that were in use at the time of its invention.

"Do me a favour," Tyler said. "Rewind it to the point where the train pulls in and play it from there. I want you to keep an eye out for three bald headed white men. One will have a tattoo on his neck, and another will have a scar running from his nose to his upper lip, making it curl up like Elvis' does, only without any of the King's charm and sex appeal."

Coleen leaned forward and pressed a button. There was a whirling noise as the tape spun backwards on the spool, and then a loud clunk as she pressed stop. Another button was pressed and the footage resumed playing at the point Tyler had requested.

They watched in silence as the sleek train glided to a halt against platform seven. Almost immediately, doors opened and the first travellers spilled out. About halfway along, Adebanjo's gleaming head appeared as he alighted his carriage, flanked by two massive black men who could only be the Kalu twins. Being as he stood head and shoulder above most of the other passengers, it was relatively easy to see that Adebanjo was definitely holding a mobile against his ear as he walked towards the camera.

They scanned the sea of people surging towards the ticket barrier ahead of him, but none of them remotely matched the description Tyler had given.

As the crowd thinned out, he began to feel a little concerned. Maybe his theory didn't hold water after all?

And then, just when he was about to concede defeat, three white men stepped out of the rear carriage. They lingered at the back of the train until almost everyone else had gone through the ticket barrier before setting off. As they drew nearer to the camera, Tyler saw that they were each carrying a satchel of some sort, and the one in the middle had a hand clamped to his ear. From this distance it was impossible to see if he had a tattoo on his neck, but there was no mistaking the scar on the face of the man who walked a couple of steps behind him.

Jack glanced sideways at Coleen, a smile of triumph plastered across his face. There was no doubt about it, he was looking at the three men who had set fire to the stolen Mondeo in Tottenham.

He barked out a laugh and nudged Coleen's elbow with his. "Maybe this isn't going to be a sticker after all," he told her.

Just then, the door to the CCTV room burst open. Tyler looked up, startled, to find Paul Evans standing there. "Ah, boss, Reggie told me I'd find you in here," he said, closing the door behind him.

Tyler grinned knowingly. "Don't tell me, he sent you to drag me back and finish going through the phones with him?"

"Er, no," Evans said with a quick shake of his head. "I just wanted to let you know that I've had a call from Tulay Yildiz. Apparently, a bloke with an identical tattoo to the one that she drew for us turned up at her café yesterday morning. She thinks it might be the same guy."

Jack's left eyebrow raised itself into an inverted tick. This really was turning into the day that just kept on giving. And then a thought occurred to him. "Why is she only just telling us that now?" he asked.

"Probably because she's conflicted," Evans suggested. "She wants to do the right thing, but she's under pressure from her dad not to get involved."

"Poor cow's involved now whether she wants to be or not," Tyler said with some sympathy, "and we need a further statement and a First Description Booklet from her ASAP."

"I'm on my way over there now to take care of all that," Evans said. "Oh, and she's drawn us a sketch of him, so I'll pick that up while I'm at it."

He turned to go but Tyler called him back. "Paul, have a quick gander at this footage before you go," he said, rewinding the tape a short way. When he pressed play, the three bald men started walking towards the camera. "I want to know straight away if the bloke in her drawing looks anything like one of these ugly buggers."

"Who are they?" Evans asked, studying the clip carefully.

"All will be explained later," Tyler promised. "For now, just get yourself over to the girl and let me know if her drawing matches any of these reprobates."

———

"I'm back," Tyler said.

Reg looked up from his desk in the main office, where he had returned. He didn't seem particularly overjoyed. "So I see, but how long for?"

Sensing that Reggie had the hump with him, Tyler smiled an apology. "I promise I won't run off again," he said, beckoning for his phones expert to join him.

Reg huffed, scooped up his pile of data, and dutifully followed Tyler back to his office. "We only had three more calls to go through," he said, taking the seat he was offered.

Tyler spread his arms effusively. "I'm grateful for your patience, and you now have my undivided attention."

The phone rang.

Tyler grimaced. "Sorry," he said as Reg tutted at the latest intrusion.

The call was from Andy Quinlan. "Andy, I'm just in the middle of a phones meeting. Can I pop in and see you in twenty?" He listened, nodded, and then smiled. "Okay, mate. I'll see you then."

Reg waited until the receiver was back in the cradle, and then picked up a sheet of paper. "Okay," he said. "The last three calls. At 20:46 hours, the 151 number rang 003. It's a two minute call. The 151 number was covered by a cell on the A406. The 003 number was within radius of a cell covering Green Lanes."

Tyler had been jotting all this down, but then he stopped and looked up. "I wonder," he said to himself.

Reggie scowled at him. "Now what?" he asked, and from the accusing tone of his voice it was clear he thought Tyler was about to desert him again.

Ignoring him, Tyler urgently started to rake through the untidy stacks of paper that were scattered across his desk. "Where are you hiding, you little bugger?" he muttered under his breath. Finally, he found what he was looking for. "Ah-ha!" he said, holding the sheet of paper up triumphantly.

Reg stared at him, waiting to be enlightened.

"This is one of the ANPR hits on Erkan Dengiz' Mercedes from Tuesday night," he said, as though that explained everything.

Reg shrugged. "And?"

"Well, it's timed at 20:45 hours."

Reg shrugged again, exaggerating the movement to show his annoyance. "*And?*" A hint of impatience had crept into his voice.

"And a Corsa, which I suspect was being driven by the person following him around that day, was caught by the same ANPR camera. I'm betting that the cell site and ANPR locations will be the same, and that the person using the 151 number was the person in the Corsa. Furthermore, I think whoever had the 003 number in the vicinity of Green Lanes was the shooter."

As he considered this, the expression on Reggie's face transitioned from irritation to enthusiasm. "That would actually make a lot of sense," he admitted, running his finger down the page to check the timings of the next call, "because at 21:10 hours, just a few minutes before the four Turks were murdered, there was another short call from 151 to 003, and this time they were both within the radius of the Green Lanes cell."

"And, as I'm sure you will be able to confirm, so was the café where the murders took place?"

Reggie nodded, getting caught up in the excitement. "Give me ten minutes to compare notes with Dean," he said, standing up. The irony of him abandoning Tyler, instead of the other way around, brought a smile of satisfaction to his face as he rushed over to consult with Dean in the main office.

———

Tyson Meeks cautiously stepped out of the phone shop into Mare Street, his eyes nervously scanning the busy pavement for anyone who might recognise him. He had just used some of the money the Feds had given him to purchase a cheap mobile phone, and with it, he felt reconnected to the world.

Keeping his head down – this was London Fields Boys territory, after all – he walked past the Hackney Empire. The Grade II listed theatre had been built as a music hall in 1901, and he had once seen the comedian, Harry Enfield, perform there. When he reached the Town Hall, he crossed the busy road and came to a halt beside the 55 bus stop. He could catch that all the way to Old Street, from where it was only a five minute walk to his flat.

While he waited, he turned the phone on. After it had powered up, he tapped in Marcel's digits. He listened to the ringtone with baited breath. Quite often, Marcel ignored his calls, but this was a new number, one that Marcel wouldn't recognise, so he hoped his brother would accept the call.

"*Hello?*" His brother's voice, hostile and wary.

"Marcel, it's me. Please don't hang up."

Silence at the other end. And then, "*What do you want, Tyson?*"

Despite the coldness in his brother's voice, Meeks let out a huge sigh of relief. At least Marcel hadn't hung up on him as he'd feared would happen. "Marcel, listen to me," he said, breathing fast. He couldn't believe how nervous speaking to his younger brother was making him. "Bruv, I'm gonna breeze from Hackney for a while, ya get me, and I wanted to speak to you before I went."

Marcel sucked through his teeth "*What trouble you got yourself into this time, Tyson?*" he asked, the words dripping with disdain.

Meeks shook his head. "Nah, bruv, I ain't in no trouble. For once, I'm doing the right ting, innit."

Marcel snorted his derision. "*Bruv, I aint stupid! I know what you've done. You're a grass, innit? You've sold out to the Feds, betrayed your bredrin.*"

"Who told you that, bruv?" Tyson demanded, already knowing the answer. Apart from him, only the Feds and Livingstone knew, and the Feds wouldn't say anything.

"*I spoke to Conrad, innit,*" Marcel said, confirming his suspicion.

Meeks froze. Since when had the boy started calling Livingstone by his first name? Alarm bells rang inside Meeks' head. For as long as he had known him, Livingstone had been using his charm and charisma to draw the gullible urchins who roamed the estate into his orbit, manipulating them until they would do anything to gain his favour. Had his little brother fallen for the spell?

"Marcel, listen to me, bruv," he said, trying desperately hard to keep his voice low and even. "I promise you that you don't know the full story. If you did, you wouldn't be so quick to take his side."

"*So why don't you tell me the full story then, innit?*" Marcel, demanded aggressively.

That caught Meeks off guard. "Okay, bruv," he said. "Let's do that. Let's meet up this afternoon, before I breeze. Just you and me, and I'll tell you everything."

There was a noticeable hesitation at the other end. "*What time you leaving?*"

Meeks wasn't sure. He had already been away from the hotel for too long. If the Feds from witness protection checked in with reception, and he wasn't there, it would cause massive problems. "I aint got long," he said. As he spoke, a big red double decker came trundling towards him and he held out a hand, signalling for it to stop. "Can you meet me now?" he asked, jumping aboard and taking the stairs to the upper deck.

"*Nah, bruv. Not till later,*" Marcel came back at him.

Meeks sighed, unsure what to do for the best. "I need to get back," he finally said. "What about tomorrow? Can we meet tomorrow morning?"

"*Maybe,*" Marcel allowed. "*Call me back this evening to work out a time and place.*"

Before Meeks could say anything in response, his brother hung up on him, leaving him to stare at the phone in frustration.

———

Reg was back in Tyler's office, having dragged Dean along with him for support.

"We've been doing some comparisons between the phone data and the ANPR results," he announced, looking very pleased with himself.

"We've looked at all of Tuesday's phone data for the four Turks and for the 151 number, and we've overlaid the cell siting with the ANPR captures of the Mercedes and the Corsa. There's no doubt that the Corsa is definitely following the Turk's Mercedes. Not only are they both caught on ANPR, but the 151 cell siting mirrors the Corsa's movements."

Tyler nodded. He had already reached this conclusion, but having the physical data to support his theory made it official.

"Also," Dean said, "I've checked those intelligence reports linking Jerome Norris and Daryl Peters to the red Corsa. They're basically just sightings by local officers of them driving along Kingsland Road, but they're fairly recent. I also took a closer look at the rest of the ANPR shots of the Corsa, but none gave a better view of the driver than the one I've already shown you." He handed Tyler two A4 sheets of paper. "These are the most recent custody image photos for Norris and Peters," he said. "As you can see, Norris is a tall, skinny bloke with short hair, but Peters has the right shaped jawline and dreads, so he could be the driver."

Tyler studied the two photographs in silence, paying particular attention to the one of Peters. From beneath thick dreadlocks, a droopy faced stoner stared back at him, rheumy eyed and clueless. Tyler dug out the ANPR shot of the Corsa and compared the images. "Hmmm," he said after several moments of reflection. Dean was certainly right about the jaw being the same shape. While he couldn't actually swear he was looking at two photographs of the same man, his gut told him that was the case.

"And we know the 003 and 666 numbers travelled down from Manchester to London together," Reg continued, "although the 666 number then went off to Beckton and the 003 went to a cell covering Seven Sisters. What's really interesting is the subsequent calls between 151 and 003."

"Okay," Tyler said. "Let me stop you there." He pondered this information in silence for several seconds before coming to a decision. "As you already know, Reg, there are certain matters which haven't been made public knowledge for operational security reasons, but I think it's probably time to divulge more details to the rest of the team. There's no point in us discussing phones or ANPR data any further until everyone's fully up to speed. I'd like you two to spread the word that there's going to be an office meeting at six p.m., and everyone's to attend. With luck, Mr Dillon and George will be back from the mortuary by then."

"I should have the latest batch of call data and cell site for the 109, 003, and 151 numbers from the TIU by then," Reg said. "That'll tell us what, if any, contact there's been between the various numbers since the murder."

Tyler nodded. "Let me know in advance of the meeting if there's anything relevant in it," he instructed, feeling pretty confident that there would be.

After they'd gone, Tyler got straight on the phone to Colin Franklin. He gave his overworked CCTV co-ordinator some very specific instructions regarding a video compilation he wanted prepared in time for the meeting. "And I also need you to fast track viewing the CCTV from the camera overlooking Goren's restaurant in Wood Green for an hour either side of last night's shooting. I'm particularly interested to see if a red Corsa shows up on the plot." He gave Colin the registration number.

As soon as he returned the receiver to the cradle, his phone started ringing, almost making him jump out of his skin. It was a message from downstairs to say that a detective from Manchester had just arrived, and that he was asking to speak to Mr Dillon. "Have him escorted up to my office," Tyler said. It would undoubtably be the messenger delivering the CCTV from up North.

While waiting for the visitor to arrive, Tyler rang George Holland. Things were falling into place at a rapid rate of knots, and maybe it was time to start thinking about making arrests.

————

DS Jonny Murphy looked nothing like the mental picture that Tyler had created in his head. He'd visualised the Manchester based detective

as being short and scruffy, middle-aged and overweight. Personality
wise, he'd envisaged a heavy drinking, chain smoking cynic with a
mean disposition. Instead, the man sitting before him was tall and
slim, in his late twenties or early thirties. Murphy had dirty blonde
hair, mischievous blue eyes, and finely chiselled features. He wore a
crumpled grey suit that looked like he had been sleeping in it, and his
tie was pulled down to half-mast, so at least Tyler had got the scruffy
part right.

The man's Liverpudlian accent threw Tyler at first; he had expected
Murphy to be a native Mancunian, not a Scouser.

"I have to admit," he said, "I wasn't expecting you to come in
person."

Murphy gave him an enigmatic smile. "Ah, well, I had a few days
leave owed to me, so I thought I would bring the CCTV down here
myself, see how you boys were getting on, and then treat myself to a
weekend in London." As he spoke, he reached into his briefcase and
removed three VHS cassettes. "One contains the footage for the hotel
your boy, Livingstone, stayed in. The second contains the footage from
the club, and the last is from Manchester Piccadilly on Tuesday morning, and shows Adebanjo boarding the train."

Jack sat forward on hearing that. "I didn't know we had requested
that," he said.

Murphy winked at him. "You didn't, but grabbing it seemed like a
sensible thing to do, being as Tony Dillon told me you were seizing
the footage from Euston."

Tyler nodded, impressed. Maybe Murphy was more thorough than
he had originally given him credit for, and maybe he really had put as
much effort into catching Adebanjo as Dillon claimed. "Would you
mind if we took a quick look at this now?" he said holding up the tape
marked 'Manchester Piccadilly CCTV'.

Murphy shrugged amiably. "Be my guest," he said, "but I've
already had a peek, and can confirm that Adebanjo and his two thicko
thugs, the Kalu twins, are clearly captured boarding the train."

Tyler stood up and beckoned for Murphy to follow him. "It's not
them I'm interested in," he said.

He set off for the CCTV room, with Murphy in tow. "Dill tells me that you had a similar scenario to our shootings a couple of years ago, up in your neck of the woods," he said, glancing over his shoulder.

"That's right," Murphy confirmed. "Even to the extent that Adebanjo and his two shithead goons were arrested in a raid on the black gang leader's house following an anonymous tip off."

"That's what I was just going to ask you about," Tyler said.

"There are other similarities, too," Murphy continued. "The three shooters were white, and they wore balaclavas and carried out the hits in stolen cars."

Tyler grunted. "And is it right that there was never any evidence recovered?"

"Not exactly," Murphy said. "We recovered a couple of the balaclavas from one of the burnt out cars used in the second shooting. They were in a holdall that must have been blown clear when the petrol tank went up."

Stopping in his tracks, Tyler turned to face the newcomer. "I wasn't aware of that," he said.

Murphy raised one shoulder in a half-hearted shrug. "Why would you be? We got wearer DNA from them, but it didn't come back to anyone in the system. We figured the hitters were probably brought in from abroad and then shipped straight back out of the country after the job was done."

Tyler considered this. "Maybe they've been brought back over to carry out this latest string of attacks. I don't suppose anyone mentioned anything about one of them having a tattoo down the right side of his neck, did they?" Tyler asked hopefully.

"No. Like I said. Our shooters wore balaclavas."

Inside the CCTV viewing room, they found Coleen Perry, staring at the screen with a blank look on her face. Bleary eyed, she looked up at them and forced a smile onto her face. "Guv," she said by way of greeting.

Tyler asked her to stop what she was doing for a moment while they played the footage of Adebanjo boarding the train in Manchester. Stifling a yawn, she swapped the cassette that was already in the machine for the one he offered her, and wound it forward until she located the giant and his two lackies entering the platform. She pressed pause. "That's Adebanjo," she said, pointing to the screen.

Tyler sat down next to her and invited Murphy to do likewise. With Coleen crushed between them, she started to play the tape forward in slow motion.

"Poor you," Murphy said with a flirtatious grin. "A rose stuck between two thorns."

Coleen smiled up at him bashfully, but as she opened her mouth to respond, Tyler pointed at the screen.

"There! Pause the tape!"

Tearing her eyes away from Murphy, Coleen did as she'd been instructed. "What have you seen?" she asked.

Tyler leaned forward and tapped the bottom of the screen with the tip of his Biro. "Look who we've got here," he told her.

"Oh yeah," she said, breaking into a grin. "It's our three baldies again."

Tyler nodded for her to resume the tape. She pressed play, and the three stocky bald men entered the platform and climbed aboard the last carriage of the train. Apart from affording them the slightest glimmer of a side on profile as they boarded, the footage only showed the backs of their heads.

"These three white men boarding the train here," he said for Murphy's benefit, "are picked up leaving the train at the same time as Adebanjo in Euston. And one of them appears to be talking to him on the phone as they alight."

Murphy's eyes narrowed and, from the quizzical expression on his face, Tyler felt sure he knew the question the detective was about to ask him, so he responded without waiting for it to be put to him.

"We have call data and cell site evidence to support my assertion," he said with a reassuring smile. "I'm not just saying it because they are both seen on film with phones held against their heads at the same time."

"I assumed there would be," Murphy said without taking his eyes from the screen. "That's not what I was about to say. I was about to ask if I could see the footage from Euston to see if it gave me a clearer picture of their faces."

"Oh," Tyler said, feeling slightly embarrassed. "Of course. Coleen, would you do the honours?"

Smiling goofily at Murphy, she switched the tapes and forwarded the Euston footage to the point where the two groups of suspects alighted the train.

Murphy watched in silence, staring intently at the screen. He made her play the footage twice more, his brow creasing even more with each repeated viewing.

"You know," he said, and Tyler wasn't sure if he was addressing them or merely thinking out loud. "I've got a nagging feeling that I've seen these three men before. The only question is, where?"

His musings were interrupted by a knock on the door. A moment later, Dean Fletcher poked his head into the room. "Just thought you'd want to know, a burnt out Vauxhall Vectra matching the description of the one used to shoot up Goren's restaurant has been found abandoned in Hackney Marshes," he said.

––––––––––

With Murphy having gone off to grab a late lunch and then sort himself out somewhere to stay, Tyler popped across the hall to Quinlan's team in order to check out the latest developments in Operation Jaywick.

The layout of Quinlan's main office was virtually a mirror image of Jack's own, and just like his, it was heaving with activity. Some officers slouched despondently in chairs, looking fit to drop; others seemed to be buzzing around the room, full of energy. He marvelled at their energy levels, but then realised it was probably just a caffeine rush, and they would crash and burn like everyone else as soon as it wore off.

Most officers he saw were either engrossed in working the phones or writing up reports on computer terminals. One of the girls from Quinlan's Intelligence Cell was busy pinning photographs and CCTV stills of various Holly Street gang members on a whiteboard. Susie Sergeant looked up from the statement she was writing as he entered, pausing long enough to give him a friendly wave, but none of the others seemed to even notice his arrival. Acknowledging her with a smile, he quickly crossed the room, knocked on Andy's door, and walked straight in.

"Thought I'd pop by and see how things were progressing," he said, flopping into the seat opposite Quinlan's desk.

"It's all go at this end," Quinlan said, theatrically mopping his brow to emphasise the point.

"Come on then," Jack said, rubbing his hands together eagerly. "Fill me in on all the grisly details."

Quinlan opened his daybook and ran a finger down a long list of meticulously written notes. "Okay," he said, drawing the word out. "We've finished the interviews with Xander Mason, Curtis Bright and young Zane the pain. All three went no comment. No big deal; we didn't expect any of them to talk. Evidentially, we're in a very good place and I anticipate charging all three before the end of the day."

"That's good," Tyler said. "What evidence have you got so far?"

Quinlan considered this. "Well, for starters, we've got Gavin Mercer's statement identifying all three of them from the Hackney Downs CCTV. On top of that, we've had a preliminary result back on the red hoodie Kevin Murray found in the bin at the bottom of the tower block. We've recovered wearer DNA that matches Bright's, so he's screwed. The preliminary results are also back on the shoe we found in Zane's wardrobe. There's wearer DNA for him inside the shoe, and a match with Jenny's blood on the sole, so he's doubly screwed."

"You've also got all that stolen gear that was found in his bedroom," Tyler pointed out, not that Quinlan was likely to forget.

"Quite right," Quinlan agreed. "Speaking of the loot we recovered, we've had it all forensically examined. The DNA results won't be back for a couple of days yet, but the lab recovered some lovely fingerprints belonging to Mason, Zane, and Devon Brown on various items inside the bag."

"I take it the plan is still to charge the three in custody with multiple robberies and wait until you have all the evidence collated before proceeding with the murder charges?"

Quinlan nodded. "Yes, but we're getting a lot closer to being able to do that." He slapped a hand to his forehead. "Oh, I almost forget to mention, remember the kitchen knife from the bin and the flick knife from under Brown's mattress?"

Jack nodded slowly. "I do."

"Well, they were fast tracked for forensic examination, and the preliminary results came back about fifteen minutes ago. Unfortunately, the lab didn't find any fingerprints."

Jack's mouth turned down in disappointment. "Damn."

"And there was no trace of blood on the blades or handles of either weapon," Quinlan continued.

Tyler felt a wave of disappointment wash over him.

"However," Quinlan said, raising a finger to indicate he wasn't finished yet. "When they unscrewed the handles from the blades, they found microscopic traces of blood in the rivets of both knifes. The subsequent DNA testing of the kitchen knife yielded a partial profile that matches Jenny's DNA. The lab are doing low copy number testing to see if they can improve the quality and raise it to a full profile. The flick knife contained a mixed profile, showing full matches for both Jenny and Stanley Cotton's blood."

"So, the scientific evidence supports the premise that whoever had the kitchen knife only stabbed Jenny, but whoever had the other weapon stabbed both victims, is that correct?"

Quinlan nodded decisively. "That's right. We know that Devon Brown used the flick knife, and I'm confident he'll get nicked sooner rather than later, but we still haven't worked out who was in possession of the kitchen knife that was used on Jenny."

Tyler leaned back in his chair and considered this. "So what now?" he asked, stroking his stubble thoughtfully.

"Well, we know from witnesses that Jenny was surrounded by three robbers when she was stabbed. Between what's shown on CCTV and the information in all the statements, we've managed to compile detailed descriptions of all ten suspects involved in the steaming. We've gone through it all and isolated the three individuals who accosted Jenny. We can conclusively say that two of them are Devon Brown and Zane Dalton, but we still don't know the identity of the third one. I mean, we can single him out on the CCTV, but he keeps his head down at all times, so we haven't got any clear shots of his face."

That was frustrating news. "What about the CCTV at Clapton station, after they decamped from the train, or the footage from the surrounding streets?"

"It's been checked, Jack. The suspect has his head bowed as he runs out of the station, and they all starburst immediately afterwards, taking to side streets that don't have any cameras. To be honest, it looks like a well-practised drill to me, and it's pretty obvious that they've used this dispersal tactic before."

"Bollocks," Jack said, feeling massively disheartened.

"My sentiments exactly," Quinlan concurred.

———

At four o'clock that afternoon, Jack strode through the main entrance of the Royal London Hospital in Whitechapel High Street. He was there to visit Jenny. Earlier in the day, he'd been informed that she was making excellent progress and was likely to be transferred to a normal ward within a day or so, and that she was fit to receive visitors, as long as they didn't stay for too long. He had spoken to Jenny's mother before setting off, to ensure that his arrival at the ICU wouldn't interfere with any visits they had planned. He purposefully hadn't called Eddie, and he was really hoping that he wouldn't find Maitland sitting by her bedside when he arrived.

Although Jack's job had necessitated him spending a fair amount of time in various medical establishments over the years, he really didn't like hospitals. Bleak and impersonal, he found them incredibly depressing places, and they always made him uncomfortable. Apart from anything else, hospitals were too generic for his liking. They all had the same white painted walls, the same squeaky lino flooring, and there was always miles and miles of identical sterile corridors; everything was familiar and yet unfamiliar at the same time.

As soon as he entered the building, he became aware of the charged emotional climate within. Fear, anxiety, anguish, hope, joy, and relief; he saw all of these emotions reflected in the eyes of the people he passed on his way to the lifts.

It was as though, over time, all the trepidation and foreboding that had ever been experienced within its walls had been absorbed into its very fabric.

He wasn't sure what he would say to Jenny when he saw her, and that made him nervous. He thought it best not to mention the conversation that he'd had with Maitland the previous day, but he *was* considering mentioning the positive pregnancy test that PC Mitchell had found in Jenny's bag.

Would that distress her?

Should he wait for her to bring it up?

He would just have to play things by ear, he decided. The most important thing at the moment was for all of Jenny's family and friends to rally round her and help her to get better. Jack had read somewhere that receiving visitors was an important part of the recovery process for most people, and that having them often helped to reduce the stress and anxiety associated with hospital stays. He really hoped the visit would go well but, deep down, he wasn't looking forward to it.

What would he say if she told him that Eddie had raped her?

The more he considered it, the more he suspected that was the reason why she had wanted him informed of her hospitalisation and not Maitland.

Jack ran a hand through his hair and took a deep breath. "God, what a mess," he sighed, wishing that he could just turn around and leave.

When he reached the ICU, he spoke to the sister in charge, explaining his relationship to Jenny. She raised an eyebrow but said nothing.

She probably thinks we're all embroiled in some tacky love triangle, he thought miserably. He decided not to mention that he was also a police officer, in case she thought he was planning to abuse his position as a relative – ex-relative – to question her about the stabbing.

After being made to wash his hands thoroughly, he was shown over to Jenny's bed. A nurse was carrying out routine checks when he arrived, and she smiled at him and told him that she wouldn't be much longer.

He could see that Jenny was surrounded by stacks of monitoring equipment, and that she was hooked up to IV lines and pumps. Oxygen tubes hung from her nose, and she looked very pale and unwell. Her appearance was in stark contrast to that of the vivacious, elegant woman he was used to seeing, and it shocked and saddened him to see her reduced to a shadow of her former self.

The thought of Devon Brown and his scummy little mates surrounding her on the train like a bunch of snarling animals sickened him. That they had been willing to snuff out her life, just so that they could get their grubby little hands on a few thousand pounds worth of jewellery, made his blood boil, and he had to swallow down the anger that rose to the back of his throat like bile.

Susie had played the Hackney Downs CCTV for him before he'd left Arbour Square to come here, and he had looked down upon Devon Brown's feral face with undiluted loathing. He had been shocked by the arrogance in the boy's movements, and the coldness of his stare, recognising the traits of someone who enjoyed violence and didn't need much of an excuse to resort to it. While watching the footage, the only thing that Jack had desired more than being the one to arrest Brown when the time came, was for the worthless scumbag to resist.

As the nurse moved aside, Jack caught his first proper look at Jenny's face. There was a hand shaped welt on one side of it, and her bruised eye was so badly swollen that she could hardly open it. The sight took his breath away. Silently raging, he thought about the damage he would like to inflict on Brown if he ever got the chance, knowing that it went way beyond the definition of 'reasonable force.'

Jack suddenly became aware of a sharp pain in his hands and, when he looked down, he was surprised to see that he was clenching his fists so tightly that his fingernails were cutting into his palms and his knuckles were shining white. With an effort, he forced his fingers to unfurl, flexing them to get the blood flowing again. Perhaps it wouldn't be a terribly good idea for him to be the one to lay hands on Brown after all.

"You can see her now," the nurse said as she slipped away.

"Thank you," Jack said, trying to pull off a smile but failing. He pulled a chair over and sat down beside his ex-wife.

"How are you feeling?" he asked, reaching out to hold her hand.

"Like I was beaten about the head and then stabbed in the stomach a couple of times," she said, managing a weak grin.

He squeezed her hand. "You're going to be fine, Jen," he told her. "We're all rooting for you. Your mum and dad will be up again this evening, and Eddie's been sleeping here at the hospital to be on hand if you need him."

Did something flit across her eyes at the mention of Eddie's name? He couldn't be sure.

"Make sure you get the bastards who did this to me," she implored him. "If anyone can do it, Jack, I know it's you."

He smiled reassuringly and patted her hand. "Don't worry," he said. "We're all over it. We've already caught three of the thugs who attacked you, and it won't be long until we get the rest."

She smiled at him gratefully, but then a frown creased her forehead. She appeared confused, as if struggling to find the words. "What about... what about the old man who tried to help me..? I keep asking, but the nurses won't tell me."

Jack hesitated. He couldn't lie, but if he told her that Stanley Cotton was dead, he knew that she would be devastated. "Jen, let's just focus on getting you well before we start worrying about anyone else. There'll be plenty of time to go into what happened once we get you out of ICU and into a ward."

She nodded wearily, accepting what he had said. "Okay, but promise you'll find out for me before your next visit."

Tyler nodded, relieved that she had assumed he didn't know. "Of course," he said, unable to meet her eye.

"I'm so glad you came to see me," she said, gripping his hand tightly. Even the effort of doing that seemed to tire her out, he noticed.

"Me too," he said.

"Do I look a total mess?" she asked.

Jack couldn't help but smile. It was so typical of Jenny. Despite the fact that she had nearly died, and was now plugged into a variety of machines in an intensive care unit, here she was worrying about her appearance. That had to be a good sign.

"Not at all," he lied. "You look beautiful."

"I'm tired," Jenny said, and closed her eyes.

"Get some rest," he told her. "We can talk more later."

He sat there for a while, holding her hand in silence. Eventually, he realised that she had dozed off. Gently prising his fingers free, he stood up and kissed her on the forehead. "Sleep well," he whispered.

With a farewell glance, Jack was gone.

CHAPTER TWENTY-FOUR

LET'S GET DOWN TO BUSINESS

In the end, the six o'clock briefing didn't take place until seven. Dillon and Copeland had been delayed at the mortuary, and Jack had postponed the meeting in order to give them a chance to get back and get changed.

The delay had proved advantageous in other ways too, as it had given Tyler an opportunity to sit down with Reg Parker and go through all the latest revelations from the TIU, several of which were significant. Colin Franklin had used the extra time to appraise Tyler of an important CCTV development, and incorporate the relevant footage into the compilation he had prepared.

Before the team briefing commenced, Tyler quickly gathered Dillon, Bull, and Murphy into his office for a quick scrum down so that he could share with them his plans for taking the enquiry forward.

"Listen in," he told the assembled detectives when the main meeting started. "I have a significant update to share with you all.

When this job broke, some of you asked me why we hadn't eliminated Conrad Livingstone's gang when the three shooters were white. Well, the truth is, we had classified information to support Livingstone being behind this right from the beginning, but we weren't in a position to share it because doing so might have endangered a source we had within his network. That source has now been removed from danger and placed in witness protection, so I'm finally able to give you the full picture."

Charlie White seemed confused. "So you're saying Livingstone *is* behind the shootings?" he asked.

"There are no flies on you, are there?" Steve Bull teased.

Tyler held a finger to his lips to stop the laugher that had broken out. This was definitely not a time for joviality. "Not only am I saying that Livingstone is behind the two shootings, I'm saying that I think we're finally at a point where we can prove it."

"We are?" White asked, scratching his head. "Och, I must've missed something, cause I cannae see any glaring new evidence."

Jack smiled grimly. "You will do," he promised. "If you stay quiet long enough for me to present it to you."

The rebuke was delivered good naturedly, but White got the message.

"Right, let me start off by introducing DS Jonny Murphy from Greater Manchester Police," Tyler continued.

Murphy half stood from his seat and waved at them.

"He's been investigating Samuel Adebanjo for a number of years. Adebanjo's believed to be responsible for a number of murders up North, but there's never been enough evidence to prove it. Two years ago, there was a turf war in Greater Manchester that's almost a carbon copy of what's been going on here, even to the point where there were three gangs involved. One was black, another Asian, and the third white." Tyler ticked his fingers off as he spoke. "It's believed that Adebanjo brought in three white shooters to carry out a series of attacks against the Asian gangsters, making it look like the white mob was behind it, and this effectively sparked a turf war that left nine people dead and decimated both sides. That left the black gang free to waltz in and take over."

"And that's what we think this Livingstone bloke's trying to do here?" Paul Evans asked.

"That's right," Tyler confirmed.

"Following an anonymous tip off that there were guns at the venue, Adebanjo and the Kalu twins were arrested at the black gang leader's place about an hour before the first drive by shooting occurred in Manchester," Murphy added.

"My former unit had a snout inside Livingstone's set up," Dillon said, taking up where Murphy had left off. "He informed us that Livingstone was bringing Goliath – that's Adebanjo's street name – down to London to take out an Albanian gang leader. We responded by having Adebanjo and the Kalu twins arrested at gunpoint at their Beckton hotel but, as in Manchester, this was a red herring to throw us off the scent, so that the three white shooters could take out the real targets without fear of police interference."

"The real targets being the four Turks?" White asked.

"That's right," Tyler confirmed. "Tensions were already running high between the Turks and Albanians, and Livingstone's plan was to push them over the edge and provoke an all-out war. He started off by having the protection money team hit on Tuesday, and followed that up last night with a drive by on a restaurant where Goren was meeting his family. Just to make sure that Goren was left in no doubt as to who was responsible, the shooters draped an Albanian flag over the body of one of his men."

Kelly let out a low whistle. "It's a very clever plan," she said with grudging admiration.

"It is," Tyler agreed, "and it very nearly worked. If it hadn't been for young Fatma being able to speak Turkish, we would never have known that Goren had ordered a massive retaliatory hit to be carried out today against the Albanians. Thankfully, we've been able to prevent this by flooding the area with Armed Response Units. Goren might've dropped off the grid, but we've pulled in all his top lieutenants and made it crystal clear to them that we know what was being planned, and that we would hold them personally responsible if anything happened."

"With respect, guv," Copeland said, "that might buy us some time, but unless we can identify and arrest the shooters, all we're doing is postponing the inevitable blood bath."

"True," Tyler conceded, "which is exactly what we're going to do."

"Er, boss, we don't know who they are," White pointed out.

Dick Jarvis held up a hand. "Is it possible that the three white shooters who carried out the London hits are the same ones who were used in Manchester?"

"Almost certainly," Tyler said.

"If we arrest them, it'll be easy enough to answer that question," Murphy said. "We managed to recover two balaclavas from the second Manchester based hit. Unfortunately, although the lab retrieved wearer DNA from both of them, there were no matches when we ran the profiles through the DNA database in Birmingham." Murphy allowed himself a grim smile. "I've been busting a blood vessel trying to find these three dirtbags for the best part of two years, so I'd be very grateful if we could catch them this time around."

"We'll do our best for you," Tyler promised. He nodded at Steve Bull, who stood up and started circulating amongst the team, handing out a thick briefing package.

"Let's get down to business," Tyler said. "The document that Steve is distributing to you contains all the information that you need to know. It contains a more detailed version of the synopsis I've just given you. There's also a list of all the phone numbers we've attributed to everyone involved, and a chart showing dates and times of any calls they've made, along with the locations of the phone masts covering them. Please refer to it as I speak and, if you're unsure about anything, check the information in that document before interrupting me." He signalled to Colin Franklin, who promptly inserted a VHS tape into the wall mounted TV / video combo and pressed play. A picture of a train at a platform immediately appeared on screen and he paused it, waiting for further instructions.

"Okay, I'm going to talk you through what we know, and there'll be some CCTV clips to augment the narrative. Before we start playing them, I'd like to direct your attention to page five of your briefing document, where you will see a list of phone numbers."

There was a frantic fluttering of paper as everyone turned to the right page.

"The first, ending 109, is attributed to Livingstone, the second, ending 666, is attributed to Adebanjo. The third, ending in 003, is attributed to the three shooters. There's one other number, which ends in 151. While we can't definitively attribute this burner to anyone yet, we believe it's being used by one of Livingstone's inner circle of thugs, either Jerome Norris or Daryl Peters, aka Gunz. My gut tells me it's Peters, and I'm going to proceed on that basis for reasons that will become clear as we go through the briefing. On Monday just gone, that's the 24th May, there were a few short calls between Livingstone and Adebanjo's burner phones. Cell site shows Livingstone's handset was in Dalston, where he lives, and Adebanjo's was in Manchester, within the radius of the cell covering a nightclub he owns called Crosby's. It seems likely that these calls were made to finalise the following day's arrangements. On Tuesday morning, as you'll see, Adebanjo and the Kalu twins travelled down to London via the train. Play the tape, Colin."

Franklin obliged, making sure he stood well away from the screen so that he didn't impede anyone's view.

"This first clip shows Adebanjo and the Kalu twins boarding the Inter-City train at Manchester Piccadilly on Tuesday morning," he explained, using a long pointer stick to single them out when they appeared on screen. "Now, look at the three stocky white men, all big lumps with shaven heads, who follow them aboard a couple of minutes later." He tapped the screen again to illustrate the targets, not that there was anyone else of remotely similar appearance in their vicinity.

Jack indicated for him to pause play. "A study of the call records and cell site data reveals that Adebanjo's 666 number contacted the shooters' 003 number just before the train departed. There was further contact between them about an hour into the journey, while they were on their way down to London. The train arrived at London Euston at 12:17 hours, and both sets of suspects alighted the train shortly afterwards. When Colin plays the CCTV, you'll notice that Adebanjo and one of the shooters are on their phones. Thanks to the call and cell site data, we can safely say they were speaking to each other."

On Tyler's signal, Colin played the clip, and the team watched on in silence, riveted by the story that was unfolding before their eyes. First, Adebanjo and the twins disembarked from the middle of the train, followed a little later by the three white men, who alighted from the last carriage. As Tyler had told them, both Adebanjo and the lead white thug had phones clasped to their heads.

"Take a good look at the three white males, and remember their faces for later," Tyler instructed them.

"Do you recall the amazing drawing that Tulay Yildiz did of the tattoo?" Dillon asked, looking around the room. He was rewarded by a succession of nods. "It's on page six of the briefing document if you need to remind yourselves. We say the guy on the phone is the one with the tattoo. The ugly bugger with the scar running from his nose to his upper lip is equally distinctive."

Tyler nodded to Reg, who stood up and cleared his throat.

"I'm under strict orders to keep this brief, so I won't go into too much detail, but the bottom line is that there were several calls between Livingstone, Adebanjo, and the shooters throughout Tuesday afternoon and into the evening. After leaving Euston, Adebanjo went off to his hotel in Beckton, and that evening, after speaking to Livingstone and the shooters, he dumped his burner in a bin outside a nearby shop. As luck would have it, he was filmed outside the shop while still on the phone to the shooters."

Franklin played the clip for them to watch.

When Tyler spoke, there was a grim satisfaction in his voice. "Not only do we have call and cell site data linking him to the 666 number, we also have him using the phone on CCTV twice, which provides us with is a lovely bit of corroboration. It's going to be pretty difficult for him to distance himself from that phone now."

Charlie White snorted cynically. "I'm sure some smart arsed, over-priced barrister will have a good go."

"Is he always this optimistic?" Dillon asked.

"Mostly," Tyler admitted.

"Anyway," Reg continued, keen to have the spotlight back on himself, "the shooters' phone went off to a cell covering Seven Sisters Road and Finsbury Park after leaving Euston. What's extremely interesting is that, immediately after Adebanjo rang the shooters during the train journey down to London, the shooters rang the 151 number and spoke to Daryl Peters. Cell site data puts the 151 burner in the radius of the cell covering Peters' last known address, which supports the guv'nor's assertion that he had the phone instead of Norris. It was a short call and, at the conclusion, Peters made two quick calls of his own. The data only came in from the TIU this afternoon, so I haven't had time to submit a subs check on either of the numbers he dialled yet. However, being the brilliant detective that I am, I used my initiative and ran them through Directory Enquiries. Guess what?" He looked around the room expectantly, but got nothing back. "Oh, come on!" he implored. "Play the game."

Bull sighed. "Okay, I'll indulge you: what?"

A big grin broke out on Reggie's face. "The first call was to a grubby little hotel in Seven Sisters Road. I took a chance and rang them, and the woman I spoke to confirmed that three men matching the shooters' descriptions had two rooms reserved for Tuesday night, both paid for in advance by a credit card in the name of Tyson Meeks. They arrived around one o'clock, but checked out in the early evening. There's no CCTV, but the good news is that their rooms haven't been re-let since, and she's promised not to let them again until we've sent a team over to forensicate them."

Now they were looking impressed, and Reggie, who always enjoyed being centre stage, basked in the glory of his triumph. "There's more," he promised. "The second call was to another flea pit of a hotel in nearby Amhurst Park. Guess what?" he asked them again, and this time there were some takers.

"They had a room booked there too?"

"Was it paid for by the same credit card?"

"That's where they went after killing the four Turks?"

Reg lapped the attention up. "Yes, yes, and yes," he beamed at them. "I rang and confirmed that they arrived late on Tuesday night. The rooms were booked for two nights but they checked out on Wednesday evening. As before, the two rooms haven't been re-allocated, and they're not going to rent them until we've forensically examined them."

"It's a really solid bit of police work, Reg," Tyler said. "I've spoken to Mr Holland, and he's organising a CSM and some officers from another team to examine all the rooms for us this evening."

Reg took a graceful bow. And then another. And then several more.

"Okay, that's enough," Tyler said, rolling his eyes. "Carry on and tell them the rest of the stuff that you told me before the meeting."

Reg reluctantly complied, slipping in one last bow before becoming serious again. "Okay. Where was I? Ah, yes! So, at 20:46 hours on Tuesday evening, Peters called the shooters. His phone was cell sited on the A406."

Tyler held up a hand, indicating for Reg to pause his narrative for a moment. "This is relevant because Dean ran ANPR checks on Dengiz' Mercedes and the ten cars that preceded and followed it through the cameras. On five occasions a red Vauxhall Corsa was flagged up. If you turn to page nine of the briefing document, you'll see an ANPR photo of the Corsa. The Corsa is an unregistered pool car used by several people from Holly Street, but there's recent intel showing that Daryl Peters and Jerome Norris are associated with it. The image of the driver isn't terribly clear, but you can definitely make out that he has dreadlocks. If you look at the custody imaging photographs of all our suspects at the back of the briefing document, you will see that Peters has dreadlocks, whereas Norris doesn't."

There was another flurry of page turning.

"The ANPR hit is timed at 20:45 hours," Tyler informed them. "That's literally one minute before Peters rang the shooters. Carry on, Reggie."

"At 20:43 hours, Erkan Dengiz' mobile rang a number we can attribute to Abdullah Goren through intelligence reports. Two minutes later, that's 20:45 hours for those of you who are rubbish at maths, the Merc and the Corsa both passed through an ANPR on the A406. Then, at 20:46 hours, as the boss has already said, Peters rang the shooters. The cell siting places both his and the shooters mobiles within the radius of the mast covering the same section of the A406 that they were travelling along."

"Basically," Tyler explained, "I'm confident that we can prove the Corsa was following Dengiz and his cronies that evening, and that they were communicating with the shooters via unregistered mobile phones during that time."

"Peters' 151 number called the shooters twice more after that," Reggie informed them all. "The first call was at 21:10 hours, at which point the Corsa was cell sited in Holloway Road, so it's about five minutes out from the café where the hit took place. The second was at 23:15 hours, and presumably that was to check in afterwards to make sure that everything went okay."

"Where were the shooters cell sited during these calls from Peters?" Evans asked.

Reggie checked his notes. "For the calls made at 20:46 and 21:10, the shooters were within the radius of a cell covering the café in Green Lanes."

"So they were waiting up at the scene for their targets to arrive?" Copeland asked.

Reg nodded. "Looks that way to me, Georgie boy."

"And for the last call?" Kelly asked.

"The shooters were cell sited in Amhurst Park, which, coincidentally, is where the second hotel was reserved for them."

"There's nothing coincidental about it," Dillon told them.

Tyler nodded his agreement, then took a deep breath before continuing. "As you can see, we can now link all the relevant players together. The call and cell site data shows us the date, time and location of every call they've all made. The Manchester Piccadilly, Euston, and Beckton CCTV conclusively ties the 666 number to Adebanjo, and the 003 number to the shooters. We'll be hearing a lot more about the Corsa and Peters as the briefing goes on but, for now, we have the ANPR photo linking them together."

Charlie White's brow furrowed. "Er, boss, we're going to need more than a grainy ANPR photo to satisfy a court that Peters was driving–"

"Be patient, Charlie." Tyler told him sternly. He turned to face the rest of the team. "Next up, I want you to watch the CCTV footage that conclusively links our three white shooters to the stolen Mondeo they dumped in Tottenham." He nodded to Franklin, who promptly pressed the play button.

The footage of the Mondeo pulling into the wasteland appeared on screen. Franklin dutifully paused it where it afforded them the best view of the index.

"If you turn to page eight in the briefing pack, you'll see a PNC printout relating to the Mondeo. The index and Vehicle Identification Numbers are clearly shown on it, and you will see that the index is the same as the car now turning into the wasteland." He nodded for Franklin to resume playing the tape.

When the three suspects reappeared on screen after torching the car, walking straight towards the camera, Franklin paused it again. "Remember those three ugly white men who got off the train at Euston after Adebanjo? Well, here they are again. You can clearly see the scar on this one's face," he said, tapping the screen with his pointer, "and you can see there is definitely a tattoo on this one's neck," he said, tapping the screen again, "although it isn't clear enough to make out what it is."

"I'd like you all to flip to page seven in the briefing packs," Tyler told them. He waited for them to do so before continuing. "Okay. This is a full face drawing that Tulay Yildiz did for us yesterday evening. The subject's a man who came into her café and ordered breakfast yesterday morning. He got jittery and left when a couple of local plod came in and asked if they could to put up a Crimestoppers leaflet in the window. Young Tulay is a very observant girl, and she noticed that this chap had the exact same tattoo on his neck as the shooter she watched gun down Erkan Dengiz on Tuesday night. I don't know about you unruly lot, but I reckon the drawing is the spitting image of that bloke on screen with the tattoo on his neck."

The eyes of every officer in the room started volleying backwards and forwards between the image in their briefing documents and the one frozen on the TV screen. Eyes squinted, brows creased, and he could almost hear the cogs turning inside their heads as they made the comparison and came to a favourable conclusion. Some actually got up and walked over to the TV to compare the images close up. By the time they returned to their seats, he could tell that no one was in any doubt that the two images were of the same man.

"I would argue," Tyler told them, "that the quality of the CCTV is more than sufficient to invite a jury to compare the two images and conclude it was the same person in exactly the same way that you horrible lot just did."

He allowed them a second or two for the implication of what he had said to sink in. When he was happy that it had, he turned to Colin Franklin. "Play the footage of the second incident."

Franklin obliged, and the team watched on in fascination as the stolen Vauxhall Vectra cruised to a halt outside the busy restaurant. Both nearside doors opened and the two masked gunmen slid out. The picture quality was truly superb. As the gunman to the right began firing into the building, shattering the glass and sending the terrified customers diving for cover, his partner effortlessly neutralised the large Turkish doorman who rushed forward, drawing a concealed pistol from the small of his back.

"So that's where he was hiding it," Bull said to Fatma, who was sitting beside him.

Without breaking stride, the shooter who'd just gunned down the Turk swivelled towards the front of the building and began pouring fire into the kitchen area. Even from a distance, the muzzle flash coming from the two automatic weapons was impressive, and sparks flew as bullets smashed into the kitchen equipment and the two rotating slabs of meat, sending pans and large chunks of chicken and lamb flying everywhere. The glass serving counter seemed to disintegrate, and everything that had rested on top dropped down onto the food sitting in the chiller beneath.

"Look," Dillon said as the lights began to explode one after another, "they're deliberately aiming high, firing into the ceiling mostly, but definitely not at the people lying on the floor."

That was interesting. "Sending a message as opposed to actually trying to kill anyone," Tyler said, staring thoughtfully at the screen. This was the second time that he'd seen the footage, but he was finding it no less shocking to watch.

"Except for the poor wee bugger lying dead on the floor," Charlie pointed out with a cynically raised eyebrow.

"That was different," Bull said, dismissing the observation. "He engaged them, and he was carrying a gun. To them, he was just a threat to nullify."

White wasn't having it. "Aye, well, in a few hours' time it could be one of our SO19 officers facing off against that maniac."

Bull glanced sideways at Charlie White. "Nah, those Muppets are no match for our boys. They'll take care of them, no trouble."

Despite the blasé tone of his voice, Tyler noticed that Bull's slender face was fraught with worry.

"Pay attention to what happens next," he instructed. It was important that they didn't get themselves distracted now.

The shooting was over in seconds. With the restaurant's elegant interior now reduced to rubble. One of the shooters dashed over to the Vectra and removed a flag on a pole, which he draped over the dead Turk. Once that was done, the two shooters calmly returned to the Vectra, which took off with a flamboyant wheelspin the moment the doors closed.

"Bit unnecessary, wasn't it?" Copeland observed.

"Shush!" Tyler growled, and the room fell silent.

Franklin fast forwarded the tape a little way, and the timer in the top corner of the screen showed that three minutes had elapsed. "This is the bit I wanted you all to see," he said as a little red car pulled out of the side turning opposite the restaurant. He paused the tape when it was face on, so that they could clearly read the index and see the two occupants within. They were black males. The driver had shoulder length dreadlocks, and the passenger was a lot younger, with darker skin and short hair. He looked very stocky.

"If you go back to page nine," Tyler instructed, "you'll see that the Corsa on screen is the same as the one captured on ANPR."

"Any idea who the two ball-bags inside the car are?" Paul Evans asked.

"Personally, I think that the driver looks very much like the custody imaging photograph of Daryl Peters," Tyler said with a wry grin. "Before we discuss that any further, I want Reggie to impart some more TIU knowledge upon you."

Reggie had returned to his seat, but now he stood up again. "During the day, there were a couple of brief calls from Peters' 151 number to the shooters 003 number. Peters' was in the Kingsland Road area, the shooters were in Amhurst Park, presumably in the hotel I told you about earlier. At 20:02 hours, and then again at 20:15 hours, Peters called the shooters twice more. Both phones are cell sited close to the restaurant for these calls. My guess, and I know the boss agrees, is that Peters was parked up in the side street where we saw the Corsa pull away from a minute ago, acting as eyeball, and the shooters were parked up a few roads away, waiting to be called forward. He let the shooters know when Goren arrived, which we've confirmed from the staff was at eight o'clock, and then called them in for the strike. The really exciting information is that, in the three minutes that elapsed between the shooters driving off and the Corsa following suit, Peters made two phone calls in quick succession. The first was from his own personal phone, which is registered to him and ends in 141. The call was made to Livingstone's personal number, which ends in 747. This call literally only lasts a few seconds. Immediately afterwards, Peters' 151 burner rings the 109 burner attributed to Livingstone. Cell siting for both of Peters' phones puts him squarely on the plot for the shooting. Both of Livingstone's phones put him within the radius of the cell covering his home in Dalston. Why Peters would have been stupid enough to have rung his boss from his personal phone is beyond me, and all I can assume is that he picked up the wrong handset in the excitement of the moment."

"Regardless of how or why it happened, it did. And it works very much in our favour, because it not only ties Peters to the 151 number, it also links Livingstone to everything that's happened."

"Not wishing to be negative," Charlie White announced reluctantly, "but as compelling as the evidence you've just shown us is, it's still largely circumstantial."

Jack smiled. An eternal pessimist, White was the sort of person who would stare into a cloudless blue sky during the height of a summer heatwave and gloomily predict that it would soon be winter. He reminded Tyler of a younger version of Private Frazer from the BBC TV show, *Dad's Army*. The actor who had played the character had also been Scottish, he recalled.

"Charlie, a few days ago you were the one moaning that this case was going to be a sticker, and yet here we are, not even a week into the investigation, and we're talking about making arrests. Between the witness statements, the call and cell site data, and the ANPR and CCTV evidence, I think we've got enough to ensure that almost everyone involved in the five murders goes down. The only person I can potentially see squirming their way out of this at the moment is Jerome Norris, and that's because all we have against him is that he handed Meeks a duffle bag and the keys to a car. He'll just say he was passing them on for a friend and had no idea that anything sinister was going on."

"Plus," Murphy chipped in excitedly, "if the DNA from your shooters matches the DNA we recovered in Manchester, the MOs and evidence accrued from both investigations can be put before the jury at both trials."

White nodded. "Aye, I suppose you're right," he accepted, although he still looked pretty miserable.

Tyler could only shake his head. What more evidence was Charlie expecting him to produce? A signed confession?

"We've got a uniform skipper called Gavin Mercer coming over from Stoke Newington later," Dillon announced. "He's the bloke with the photographic memory, and he's going to view the footage of the Corsa, to see if he can identify either of the occupants from personal knowledge. That will be far more impactful at court than us saying we think it's the same man from comparing CCTV footage and custody imaging photos. Also, we've got a lip reader coming in on Monday to study the conversation Adebanjo had on his phone outside the Beckton corner shop, so let's see if that turns up anything of interest."

"Okay," Tyler said, still smarting from Charlie's disappointing response, which was the polar opposite to everyone else's. "You now know everything we know. The plan going forwards is this: Reggie, I want you to get straight onto the TIU. We know Adebanjo dumped his 666 phone, but I need all the other phones we've mentioned live monitored from now on. We need to establish where Adebanjo, the Kalu twins, and the shooters are so we can get the bastards nicked."

"What about Livingstone, Peters, and Norris?" Reg asked.

Tyler shook his head. "Don't worry about them for the minute.

My priority has to be taking the shooters out of circulation ASAP, in case they have another hit planned. My guess is that they're going to be shacked up in another flea pit hotel, and probably not a million miles away from the first two. Get their phone cell sited, and narrow the location down to the specific azimuth they're in. Once that's done, let Dean and Wendy know." He turned to address his two researchers. "As soon as Reggie gives you the area they're in, I need you to do some urgent research to work out all the potential hotels they could be using."

Dean pulled a face. "It might not be an exhaustive list," he warned. "We can only go by what we find in the system. There could be loads of little places that are beneath the radar."

"I know," Jack said, looking around the room, "which is why we'll be dividing the outside enquiry team into pairs and sending you all out to conduct a street search to find any other places that have slipped through the net."

"Depending on the radius of the cell, that might be a large area or just a few streets," Reg pointed out. "It might end up taking a fair amount of time if the cell covers a vast area."

Tyler nodded. "Yes, I'm aware of that, which is why, the sooner we get started, the better."

"If it's any consolation," Dillon said, "while you lot are off galli-vanting around London, I'll be stuck here in the office filling in the poxy FA1 forms for the pre-planned firearms operation." He pulled a face like he was chewing a wasp. "I know which job I'd rather be doing."

"And I'll be phoning around, cap in hand, scrabbling together all the resources we're going to need to take these buggers out when we locate them," Tyler added, "so you lot have definitely got the better deal."

There was a lot to do, and time was now of the essence, so he told them all to grab a quick cup of coffee and be back in ten minutes for Steve Bull to allocate the pairings.

Retiring to his office with Dillon, Bull and Murphy, Tyler closed the door and sat down behind his desk.

"The next day or so is going to be crazy," he said, "and bearing in mind that they're already running on empty, I'm concerned that I might be pushing them too far."

"I don't see what choice you've got," Dillon said. "If we send everyone home to get some rest, and the shooters strike again while we're all in the land of nod, the repercussions don't bear thinking about."

"Mr Dillon's right," Steve said. "Better to just press on and hope we can nab the bastards tonight."

Tyler looked at each of them in turn before nodding reluctantly. He really didn't like pushing his team this hard, but the alternative was to risk the killers striking again. "Okay, but let's keep a close eye on them. I don't want anyone making themselves ill."

Murphy coughed to get his attention. "Boss, I know the original plan was for me to just bring the CCTV down and then take a couple of days leave, but I'm fresh and rested, and I'm more than happy to help out in any way that I can. Also, my specialist knowledge of Adebanjo might actually come in useful to you over the next couple of days."

Tyler considered this. "What are your bosses likely to say to that?" he asked.

Murphy grinned devilishly. "I don't know, and I don't really give a toss. I'm perfectly happy to help out on my days off if that'll contribute towards putting Adebanjo behind bars. Besides, after all the effort I've put into nabbing him over the years, I would never forgive myself if I wasn't there at the bitter end."

Tyler smiled at him. He was starting to like Murphy. "That's a very commendable attitude, Jonny, and I'd be very happy to have you with us, but only if your boss sanctions you being here on duty. If you're not with us in an official capacity, and anything happens to you, you won't be covered. Not only that, but any evidence you're involved with finding might be compromised. Tell you what: give me your line manager's number and let me speak to him. It'll look much better if I make a formal request to keep you for a couple of days, on the basis that we need your expertise, rather than you making a personal plea to stay because you want to be in on the kill."

CHAPTER TWENTY-FIVE

WHERE ARE THEY?

Although it was seven o'clock in the evening, the sun still shone brightly in a cloudless azure sky, making the cloying heat outside all but unbearable. It was the fourth day on the trot that the temperatures in London had been well above the seasonal average. The good weather was showing no signs of letting up, and the mini heatwave was now predicted to continue well into the following week.

Livingstone was sitting in his office at the rear of his flat, and even though the large sash windows at the front and back of the property had all been raised as high as they would go, he wasn't getting much of a through draft. The room felt hot and humid, and he had switched on a large electric fan to take the edge off.

The sound of passing traffic filtered up to him from the street below, but he didn't mind. If anything, the continuous noise of vehicles chugging by and people shouting at each other comforted him, reminding him of the hustle and bustle of big city living, and the money that was to be made from it.

"Yo, Gunz," he called from behind his desk, where he was going through a thick red ledger, totting up how much money he had made so far this month. At the moment, it was looking like May's profits were going to exceed April's, even taking into consideration all the extra expenditure involved in hiring Adebanjo and his little team. "I'm starving, bruv, what about you?"

Gunz and Norris were sitting on the leather sofa opposite, immersed in a game of *Grand Theft Auto* on the PlayStation. Thumbs twitching furiously, Gunz manoeuvred the joystick with the skill of an expert. He risked a quick look over his shoulder, beaded dreads swinging wildly. "Definitely. What you fancy eating, bruv?"

Livingstone looked up from his work and rolled his neck to ease out the stiffness. Although he'd left school with no qualifications to his name, he was naturally good with numbers and he found doing the books strangely therapeutic.

"Give Marvin a ring, bruv," he ordered. "Let him know we'll be stopping by in half an hour, and tell him I want curried goat this time."

Norris licked his lips in hungry anticipation. "Cool," he said, and then frowned. "Er, bruv, don't forget we got that hothead younger coming by in fifteen." He was referring to Switch, who Livingstone had asked to meet.

"My cousin's got a name, bruv," Gunz said, clearly irked by the remark.

Livingstone shrugged. "Won't take long to deal with the boy, innit. Who knows, if I like him, I might even let him tag along tonight. Give me a chance to get a feel for him, ya get me."

When Gunz had told him about his young cousin, and his burning desire to work for the Main Man, Livingstone had immediately recognised a way to exploit the boy's eagerness for his own gain. There was a dirty job that needed doing, and with Switch already looking at an L-plate for his role in the recent train steaming, he was the perfect candidate to get it done.

Norris laughed lazily. "Yeah, man. Once you turn on the ol' charm, he'll be putty in your hands."

Gunz paused his gameplay long enough to shoot his partner a

withering glare. "Oi, bruv, what's wrong with you? That's my cousin you're talking about."

"Chill, blud," Norris soothed. "Boy shouldn't be getting no favours just cos he's your cousin. He gotta earn his stripes like everyone else, innit."

"The young un's already shanked one man dead," Gunz said defensively. "That's one more than you, blud. Reckon he's already proved himself."

Norris bristled at the implication that he might be less of a man than the upstart younger. "I aint afraid to shank someone, bruv," he said angrily. "I'll merk any motherfucker who crosses me, ya get me."

Livingstone's mobile started to ring, and he stared at the caller ID suspiciously. He signalled for the two idiots on the couch to stop bickering and raised the handset to his ear. "Wagwan?"

"*Wagwan. It's Marcel.*"

Livingstone allowed himself a little smile of triumph. He hadn't been sure that the boy would call him back. "What can I do for you, Marcel?"

There was a hesitation at the other end of the line, and Livingstone could hear him breathing heavily, battling with himself over what he was going to say next.

"*I've just heard back from Tyson,*" the boy said. "*He wants to meet me tomorrow morning, at the park near his flat.*"

"That's good," Livingstone said, being careful to keep any emotion out of his voice. It was important that he didn't sound eager or excited by the news. "What did you say?"

"*Told him I'd meet him there at ten.*"

"Did you mention anything about me wanting to talk to him?" Livingstone asked. If he had, Weasel would never show up.

"*Course not, bruv.*" There was indignance in the younger's voice. A little belligerence, too. He had spirit, and that made Livingstone smile.

"Do you want me to send someone with you," Livingstone asked, "just to make sure everything goes smoothly."

Marcel became stroppy. "*Nah, bruv. I aint no kid. I don't need a babysitter.*"

"Chill," Livingstone said, eager to pacify him. "It didn't mean it like that. If you don't want no one with you, that's fine by me."

"*I aint no kid,*" Marcel repeated. "*I can take care of myself.*"

"I hear you, bruv. Look, when you meet up with him, you need to persuade Weasel to take you back to his flat. It'll be better if we speak to him there, where he can't make a big scene. You get me?"

There was a lengthy pause. When he spoke, Marcel's voice was full of apprehension. "*You're not planning to hurt him, are you?*"

So much for him not caring about his bumbaclot brother, Livingstone thought, disappointed that the boy's loyalty appeared to be swinging more towards his brother than him.

"Look, younger, if I turn up, Weasel will probably just storm off. Even if he doesn't, he'll go into one, and he won't listen to a word I say. You know what he's like. He'll cause a scene and someone might call the Feds. Get him to take you back to his flat and then call me. He can rant all he wants in there, and when he calms down, we can try and talk some sense into his thick head. That's all I'm saying."

There was another bout of silence while Marcel considered this. "*Yeah, alright,*" he eventually said.

"Good boy," Livingstone said.

The intercom buzzed, long and loud.

"I gotta go, Marcel," Livingstone told the youngster. "Ring me as soon as you get him back to the flat and I'll pop straight over."

He lowered the phone and sat in silence for a moment, pondering how best to play this. Regardless of Marcel's objections, he intended to have someone waiting in the park, ready to intervene if Meeks needed a little gentle persuasion to accompany his brother back to the flat.

Livingstone slid open the top drawer of his desk and fished out a shiny Yale key from inside. It was the spare key to Weasel's flat. The fool didn't have anyone else he could rely on, so he had asked Livingstone to keep it safe for him in case he ever got locked out.

After he'd treated them to a meal at Marvin's restaurant, Livingstone planned to send Gunz and Jerome over to the flat to prepare it for tomorrow. It wouldn't take them too long to cover the small lounge in plastic sheeting, and then it wouldn't matter how messy things got when they killed Meeks.

Norris had trained as a butcher in his younger days, and Livingstone would make sure that he had everything he needed to dismember the body – to chop it up in the bath or whatever - and then remove the various sections in sealed bags. The body parts would go straight into the Limehouse Basin. Weighed down, they would sink to the bottom, never to be seen again.

As far as Marcel was concerned, Livingstone was having second thoughts about his trustworthiness. He was starting to suspect that the boy might not hate his brother quite as much as he professed, and that would make him a liability. Maybe, he ought to tell the boys to take enough stuff to dispose of two bodies, just in case.

It was a pity; he quite liked the boy.

"Bruv, you got a visitor," Norris said, ushering in a stocky teenager with a sullen face and the soulless eyes of a born killer.

"You must be Switch," Livingstone said, indicating for the boy to sit down on the sofa. "Turn that shit off," he said to Norris, indicating the PlayStaion with an aggressive jut of his chin.

Taking his time, he walked around the desk and sat next to the boy, who stared at him with a mixture of awe and fear. "Gunz, where are your manners? A drink for our guest, and maybe a little blow to help him relax."

At the prospect of free drugs being dished out, Gunz broke into a huge grin. He scurried over to a large green safe affixed to the wall behind the desk and withdrew a clear bag of brownish green herbal substance. Placing it on the desk, he started rolling out joints, which he dutifully passed around. Livingstone noticed that he kept the biggest one for himself.

Livingstone studied the nervous younger for a moment as he lit up, flashing a Colgate smile at him as he puffed out a tendril of smoke. "Don't be afraid of me, younger, I aint gonna bite you."

Behind him, leaning against the door frame, Norris' lanky figure shook with laughter. A glare from Livingstone quickly silenced the impertinent sniggering.

"Gunz told me what you did on that train at Clapton, shanking those two fools who disrespected you," he said admiringly. "It's nice to see a younger showing some backbone for a change, and not just taking shit from these mugs, know what I'm saying?"

Switch, who still hadn't spoken since entering the room, shrugged.

"You're a fairly big lump as well," Livingstone observed. "Not the tallest, but pretty hench." He puffed out his chest and flexed his arms like a bodybuilder, smiling at each of the others in turn. As if on cue, Gunz and Norris laughed politely.

"Course," Livingstone said slyly, "it don't matter how big and strong you are unless you got the attitude to back it up." He raised an eyebrow, inviting the boy to respond.

"I got plenty of attitude," Switch said, defensively.

Livingstone chuckled. "That's what I'm talking about, blud!"

"My boy, Switch, wants to join the firm, bruv," Gunz said, blowing out a thick stream of smoke through his nostrils. "Wants to become one of us, don't ya, younger?"

Switch nodded uncertainly. "I want more from life than just steaming trains, bruv," he said, finding his voice. "And I'm willing to graft. I aint frightened to get stuck in, either," he insisted, smashing his right fist into his left palm to emphasise that, by 'getting stuck in', he meant being physical where necessary.

Livingstone nodded appreciatively. "You got a pair on you, younger, I'll give you that. And you're ambitious, too. How old are you? Fifteen? Sixteen?"

Switch's mouth turned down. "I'm seventeen, bruv," he said, unable to conceal his disappointment that the Main Man had thought he was still a kid.

Livingstone's eyes narrowed. "And you think working directly for me would get you respect on the streets? That's what you want, right?"

Switch nodded eagerly. "Yeah, I want respect," he admitted. "But I also want plenty of Ps." As he said this, he repeatedly rubbed his thumb against the tip of his index and middle fingers in the universally recognised gesture for requesting the payment of money. "And I don't care what I have to do to get them."

Ah, and there it was, the opening that Livingstone had been looking for; the clue that showed him which button to press if he wanted to manipulate the boy.

Livingstone leaned back against the soft leather and casually crossed his legs. "Well, younger, if you want to work for me, you'll have to prove yourself first. What would you be willing to do for me, boy? More importantly, how far would you go without questioning my orders?"

Switch thrust his chest out defiantly. "I aint afraid of no one or nothing," he boasted. "If you tell me to do something, I'll do it without question."

"Would you beat someone up if I told you too?" Livingstone asked.

Switch snorted. "Course I would, bruv. I aint got no qualms about knocking people about."

Livingstone nodded thoughtfully as he digested this. He leaned forward until his face was only inches away from Switch's. "And what about if I asked you to snuff someone out?" he asked softly.

For several moments, Switch didn't reply, and during this time Livingstone watched him like a hawk for any signs of weakness or hesitation. The boy surprised him by breaking into a wide grin.

"Fucking right, I would," Switch said excitedly. A disturbing glint had materialised in his eyes, as though he found the idea of being appointed Livingstone's personal executioner irresistibly appealing.

The boy was damaged goods, Livingstone realised. "Then, perhaps I can find a use for you on the firm after all, bruv," he said, patting his knee.

Staring over Switch's shoulder, he caught Norris' eye and nodded towards the safe the marijuana had come from.

Norris lazily pushed himself away from the wall and walked over. He bent down and reached inside. When he stood up, he was holding a black shape in his right hand. He walked over to the sofa and offered it to Switch.

The boy reached up, accepting the handgun nervously. He seemed surprised by its weight.

"Don't worry," Norris told him. "It aint loaded."

Switch stared at the pistol, turning it over in his hands. It was a Baikal IZH-79, identical to the one that had been supplied to Dritan on Tuesday evening.

"What's up? Never seen a gun before, younger?" Norris asked provocatively. A sneer lit up his pockmarked face.

"Stop baiting the boy," Livingstone ordered.

The leering grin dropped from his face, and Norris skulked away to take up his station by the door again.

"See, what I like about you, younger," Livingstone said, now giving the boy his undivided attention, "is that you know exactly what you are, and you aint afraid to embrace it. When I was your age, my teachers, the Feds, even the pussies from social services; they all used to go on at me about changing my ways before it was too late. They spouted all this meaningless bullshit about me being at a crossroads in my life where I had to make a choice. I could either start towing the line and working hard, pass my exams and get a job, or I could carry on as I was and throw my life away." He paused long enough to let out a contemptuous snort of derision. "Like I ever had a fucking choice!"

Mesmerised by his every word, Switch nodded along; his rapturous gaze making it clear that he related to everything Livingstone was saying.

"People like us don't get to make a choice, blud," Livingstone continued passionately. "If we want anything from this fucking world, we have to tief it, or kill for it, cos no one's gonna give us the time of day otherwise. Lots of youngers want the same things as you, bruv, but they don't dare to dream big; they think all they gotta do to build a rep is roam the streets with their homies, mugging old grannies and shotting drugs. Twenty years down the road, most of them roadmen are still doing the same shit. I'm telling you now, bruv, you want people to take you seriously, you gotta make them fear you. I can help you with that. You start working for me, your pathetic little friends are soon gonna sit up and start taking notice of you. Do you like the sound of that?"

Switch nodded enthusiastically, hardly able to contain the smile that had broken out on his face.

Livingstone held up a cautionary finger, wagging it at Switch. "Now we mustn't forget that the Feds are looking for you, and if they pin those train stabbings on you, you're looking at an L-plate."

The smile dropped from Switch's face, to be replaced by a worried scowl.

"Don't worry, young un," Livingstone said, reaching out to grasp his arm reassuringly. "They gotta find you first, and we won't make that easy for them. Besides, if you work for me, you'll have the best barristers that money can buy. Even if you get convicted, you won't do too much time because of your age, and then, when you came out," smiling, he spread his hands expansively, "you'd have the world at your feet. All I ask in return for my protection is that you take care of a little bit of business that I'm about to put your way. Are you up for that?"

The inane grin was back on Switch's face; all thoughts of prison banished by the hollow promises of his host.

"Fucking A!" he beamed.

Livingstone grinned back, privately thinking that the malleable boy smiling at him was about as bright as an eclipse.

———

"Where are they?" Tyler asked, making no attempt to conceal his frustration. "They can't have just disappeared off the face of the planet." But that was exactly what the three shooters seemed to have done.

He gestured impatiently for Reg to step into his office and pull up a seat next to where Tony Dillon and Steve Bull were already sitting. Flopping down in the chair behind his desk, Tyler glowered at his phones man. "I've just spent the best part of twenty minutes on the phone trying to persuade George Holland to sanction my plan, and now that he's finally approved it, you're telling me that the footprint from their phone has mysteriously vanished?"

"I'm sorry, boss," Reg said, his shoulders slumping miserably. "The last activity we had on the 003 number had it cell sited within the Beckton area. There was a three minute call with a number ending 217 at lunchtime, but since then both numbers have gone completely dead."

Tyler frowned. "Hold on a minute. The 217 number? Isn't that the phone that was used to order Meeks' credit card, and then to book rooms for Adebanjo and the Kalu twins in Beckton on Tuesday?"

"It is," Reg confirmed. "It's an unregistered pay-as-you-go, and apart from the two calls you've just mentioned, it's been completely dormant until lunchtime today."

Tyler had to swallow down his anger. "And you didn't think to mention the fact that it had suddenly become active again to me until now?" he snapped.

Reg shrunk under the intensity of his gaze. "I'm sorry boss. I literally only received this information a few minutes ago and I haven't had time to analyse it properly yet."

Tyler could feel his temper simmering, but he knew it would be unfair to vent it on poor Reggie. "What about the other burners? Are the 109 and 151 numbers still active?"

Reg shook his head. "Not at the moment," he said, hurriedly scanning the records to double check. "Although it looks like the 109 number was in contact with the 217 number about ten minutes before it made the lunchtime call to the shooters' 003 burner."

Tyler considered this for a few moments. "Do you think there's any possibility that Adebanjo could now be using the 217 number?" he eventually asked.

"It's possible," Reg conceded, "but without more data there's no way of knowing for sure."

"I don't suppose you know where the 217 number was cell sited when it made these calls?" Dillon chipped in.

Parker quickly checked his notes. "Actually, it was also in the Beckton area. In fact, the 217 and 003 numbers were within the radius of the same cell."

Tyler looked at each of them in turn. "I think Adebanjo's started using the 217 number, and I also think the reason it was cell sited so close to the shooters phone is because they bedded down in close proximity to each other last night, just not at the same hotel."

Reg shrugged his shoulders. "Possibly, but why would they stay at different hotels?"

"Because, that way, Adebanjo would've been near enough to control the shooters, but far enough away to distance himself from them if he had to," Dillon said, catching on to what Tyler was driving at.

Reg glanced from Tyler to Dillon. "I accept that what you're both saying makes total sense, but without more call and cell site data, I'm not sure how knowing this helps us."

Leaning back in his chair, Tyler steepled his fingers over his chest. He took a deep breath, closed his eyes, and forced himself to think things through logically. "We have to be alive to the possibility that they've finished the job they were brought down to do," he told the others. "If that's the case, everyone involved in the conspiracy will have dumped their burners, which would explain why there hasn't been any further activity."

"In that case we need to be ready to move quickly," Bull said.

Still sitting there with his eyes closed, Tyler nodded but said nothing. If the suspects dispersed, he was reasonably confident that Adebanjo and the Kalu twins would head straight back to Manchester, in which case they would still get them; it would just take a little longer. Tracking the three Eastern Europeans down, on the other hand, was likely to be far more problematic, especially if they managed to get out of the UK. If that happened, there was a strong likelihood that they would never be found.

Dillon was obviously thinking along the same lines. "Do you want me to get the three shooters' descriptions circulated to Heathrow, Gatwick and the Channel Tunnel?" he asked. "Just in case they try and skip the country."

Feeling increasingly pensive, Jack finally opened his eyes. "I think we should contact the Old Bill at Manchester airport as well, seeing as they got the train down to London from that part of the world."

"Fair enough. I'll add them to the list," Dillon said.

"Where's your mate, Jonny?" Tyler asked. "Maybe he knows someone stationed at the airport who can disseminate the information directly, and save us all the hassle of making a Force-to-Force request."

"I don't know where he got to," Dillon admitted. "He was in the office one minute, talking to Coleen, and then when I looked around, they'd both disappeared."

Jack remembered that Murphy had been flirting with Coleen Perry in the CCTV room earlier. She had seemed very smitten by him. Surely they hadn't sodded off somewhere to get all gooey with each other? *Sodding coppers!* The randy little gits were all alike. "What about the personal phones we've attributed to Livingstone and Peters?" he asked Reg grumpily.

Reg nervously checked his daybook. "Er, Livingstone's personal number ends in 747, and that's still active. So is Peters', which ends in 141. Both have recently been cell sited in Dalston, which makes me wonder if they're together. Who knows, maybe Peters has popped around to Livingstone's place? Oh, by the way, Livingstone received a call from an unknown number at 19:05 hours tonight. It ends in 086, I was in the process of knocking out a subscriber check for it when you dragged me in here for an update. Let me see what else I've got for you," Reg said, running his finger down his notes. "Ah-ha! Here we go. Peters called a local landline at around the same time. I checked with directory enquiries, and it comes back to a Jamaican Restaurant in Kingsland High Street."

"He's probably booking a table," Dillon suggested.

"Or ordering a takeaway," Bull added, not to be outdone.

"Do you want me to try ringing it, see if that number's known to the staff there?" Reg asked.

Tyler shook his head. "No. Too risky. Bearing in mind how close it is to where Livingstone lives, we ought to assume that he knows the management, and the last thing I want now is for someone to tip him off that we're breathing down his neck. Stevie, can you grab a couple of people and have them hotfoot it over there and scope the place out. Who knows, they might find Peters and Livingstone seated at a table."

Bull stood up. "If they're there, do you want them nicked?"

"For the moment, I just want to know where they are." Tyler responded. Even though they had enough evidence to arrest Living-stone, he didn't want him brought in until the shooters had been detained.

As Bull set off in search of a couple of volunteers for the Stoke Newington assignment, the main office door flew open and Franklin barged through, making a beeline straight towards Tyler's office.

"Boss," he said, excitedly. "You and Mr Dillon might want to come and see what we've just found on the CCTV."

CHAPTER TWENTY-SIX

I'M SURE YOU'VE GOT ROOM FOR A LITTLE ONE

Jonny Murphy and Coleen Perry were already in the CCTV room so, by the time Franklin, Tyler, Dillon, and Bull squeezed in with them, there was literally no space left for anyone else.

"I think we're going to have to take it in turns to breathe," Bull grunted as Dillon's great bulk crushed him against the far wall.

Franklin indicated for Tyler to take the last available seat, and the others all bunched around them, leaning over their shoulders to stare at the screen on the rickety wooden desk. With no air conditioning or windows in the room, it was already stifling hot, and getting worse by the second.

Dillon wiggled his eyebrows up and down in true Groucho Marx fashion. "Let's just hope that no one passes wind while we're all trapped in here together," he said.

Murphy was the only one who found that remotely funny.

"Okay, what have we got?" Tyler asked, keen to get the viewing done quickly so that he could escape the broom cupboard furnace. As he sat there, squashed between Murphy and Coleen's chairs, he felt a rivulet of sweat run down the centre of his back and soak into his boxers.

Murphy said, "I don't know if you remember, but when the lovely Coleen played us the clips of the shooters boarding the train at Manchester Piccadilly and then getting off at Euston a little earlier, I told you that I thought they looked familiar, although I couldn't say why?"

Tyler nodded, becoming increasingly conscious of the body heat from the people leaning over him.

"Well," Murphy was saying, "I had that exact same feeling when we saw the CCTV compilation during this evening's briefing. Anyway, cut a long story short, it finally dawned on me where I'd originally seen the buggers before." He leaned forward and pressed play. "Have a look and see for yourself."

The screen flickered into life, and there, as plain as day, were the three bald headed males Tyler had previously seen in the train station clips and the footage of the Mondeo being torched. All three men were standing outside what appeared to be a nightclub entrance, dressed in ill-fitting penguin suits and vetting customers as they queued up to be admitted. It was probably the clearest footage that he had seen of them yet; even the shape of the tattoo on their leader's neck was clearly discernible.

"That's them," Tyler said, excitedly. "That's our shooters."

Murphy nudged his elbow. "See, I'm already proving my worth. Make sure you let my boss know that when you give him a call."

"When and where was this footage taken?" Tyler asked, unable to drag his eyes away from the screen.

A grin spread across Murphy's face, almost splitting it in two. "This is footage from Adebanjo's nightclub, and it was recorded on Saturday 1st May, the very same night that Livingstone went up to Manchester to meet him."

For a moment, Tyler forgot all about the room's oppressive heat. "Get some stills of their faces printed," he said as he stood up. "I need to start preparing the briefings for the arrest teams."

"Wait! There's more," Franklin said as Tyler tried to manoeuvre his way through the congested room towards the door.

"More?" Tyler said, sounding surprised. Then, eyebrow raised, "Don't tell me you've found something that tops this?"

"Well, I don't know about topping it," Franklin said with a modest smile, "but I reckon it's more or less on a par."

Tyler awkwardly reversed, and sat back down in the cramped space he'd just vacated.

"Sorry," Franklin said, placing a hand on Murphy's shoulder. "We need to swap places."

Murphy stood. Chest to chest, they pigeon stepped their way around each other, stepping on each other's toes like bad ballroom dancers.

"Ouch! That's my foot!" Dillon complained as one of them stomped on him.

Murphy's guilty giggle put him squarely in the frame for that.

When Franklin was finally ensconced in his chair, he quickly switched the tapes and played the clip for them.

By now, Tyler's shirt was clinging to his back, and he found himself hoping that the clip Franklin wanted him to see wouldn't take too long to watch.

The footage was of an urban street at night, and it had been filmed from a lamppost mounted camera that was looking down onto the road. Cars were parked all along it, and there was a junction about half way along, on the left. The date and time stamp in the top right corner showed the clip they were viewing was recorded at 02:00 hours on Tuesday 24th May 1999.

"Okay, this is footage of a residential street in Highbury, just around the corner from the nick. The road on the left of the screen is where the Mondeo was stolen from." As he spoke, a small red car drove into view from the bottom of the screen. It indicated to turn left into the side road. Franklin paused play before it made the turn. "Anyone recognise this car?" he asked.

"It's the Corsa that followed the Mercedes to the café where the first four victims were killed," Tyler said, leaning forward to study the screen intensely. "Pity we only get to see the rear of the car," he said quietly.

"Don't fret," Franklin told him. "You'll get a much better view when it leaves." He pressed the play button and they watched the car disappear into the side road. Franklin then fast forwarded the footage five minutes in time. "Any second now, you'll see the Mondeo pull out and turn right, towards the camera. As it passes under the first street-light, you get a really clear look at the driver's face."

Everyone in the room leaned forward expectantly, and Dillon rested his massive hands on Tyler's shoulders. The heat coming off of them made it feel like he was being branded.

There was a sudden knock on the door, and it opened, crashing into Murphy, who was standing with his back to it.

"Oops, sorry," Paul Evans said, peering in.

Tyler felt a draft of cooler air flood in. It was absolutely blissful.

Franklin quickly pressed the pause button. "It's a bit crowded in here at the moment, Paul," he said. "Can you come back in ten minutes?"

"I'm not staying," Evans said, ushering the slender uniformed figure of Gavin Mercer forward.

In the daylight, Mercer's pale skin looked even more translucent than Tyler remembered. Mercer stared at them, clearly reluctant to enter, and Tyler got the distinct impression that he felt uncomfortable being in such close proximity to other people. It seemed that he wasn't destined to have any say in the matter, as Evans placed a hand in the small of his back and unceremoniously shoved him forward. "I'm sure you've got room for a little one," he declared jauntily.

Mercer looked horrified as he suddenly found himself standing chest to chest with Jonny Murphy, who raised an amused eyebrow and said, "I hope that's just your truncheon pressing into me."

Behind him, Dillon sniggered.

"I'm here to view some CCTV for you," Mercer said, standing rigid and looking down at Tyler with pleading eyes.

"Okay," Tyler announced. "Let's have a rethink. Coleen, can you let Gavin have your seat. In fact, as you've already seen all this footage, why don't you go and wait outside to create a little more space for us."

"Thank you," Mercer said, sounding greatly relieved.

Coleen reluctantly stood up. With much huffing and groaning, they all jiggled around to rearrange themselves into new positions. Finally, when everyone was sorted, Franklin resumed play.

"We're just about to see the stolen Mondeo come out of that turning," Tyler explained to Mercer, leaning forward to tap the screen with his pen. "It would be wonderful if you recognised the driver for us."

"I'll try," Mercer said, voice as expressionless as a machine.

The Mondeo appeared at the junction, indicator blinking brightly. Franklin let it complete the turn and then waited until it was directly underneath the streetlamp before pausing play. The stolen car was being driven by a black man with dreadlocks, who was wearing gloves despite the hot weather, which was hardly surprising, considering he was driving a stolen car.

Mercer's face remained deadpan as he viewed the freeze frame shot. He sat there, silent and unblinking, as if in a trance, for what seemed an age before finally turning to face Tyler. "That's Gunz," he announced dispassionately; there was no excitement, no enthusiasm, just a statement of fact.

"Are you sure?" Tyler asked, studying the man's face intently.

Mercer nodded. Slowly. Just the once. "Positive. That's Gunz, aka Daryl Peters. Lives in Fermain Court on the De Beauvoir Estate. He's Conrad Livingstone's right hand man."

Tyler let out a low whistle. Footage of Gunz stealing the Mondeo used in the murder tied Conrad Livingstone to the crime as effectively as if he had been driving the stolen car himself.

"That's a fantastic spot, Gavin," Tyler said, indicating for Franklin to resume play. "Let's see if you can recognise who's in the Corsa."

Franklin waited until the Corsa had reached the same spot, directly underneath the amber glow of the streetlight, before pressing the pause button. Again, they were afforded a clear view of the driver, who was a slender black man. He appeared scrunched up, as if he were too tall for the little car. All eyes turned on Mercer as they awaited his verdict.

"Jerome Norris," the super recogniser said a moment later. "Another of Livingstone's most trusted thugs."

Tyler glanced over his shoulder at Dillon, and grinned triumphantly.

The big man responded by squeezing his shoulders. "We're gonna put these bastards behind bars for the rest of their lives," he predicted.

At Tyler's request, Franklin swapped tapes, and played Mercer the footage of the Corsa driving away from Goren's restaurant the previous evening.

"Gavin, can you make it three out of three, and recognise who's inside the Corsa in this clip?" Tyler asked with a smile of anticipation.

"I'll try."

Franklin played the footage through once, and asked if Mercer would like to see it again. "I can pause it for you next time, if you like," he offered.

Mercer gave an economic shake of his head. "That won't be necessary," he said. "The driver was Gunz. The front passenger was a Holly Street younger called Devon Brown, aka Switch. He's currently wanted in connection with a murder that happened on Tuesday evening at Clapton British Rail station."

Hearing the name of Jenny's attacker, Tyler sat bolt upright. "Are you sure?" he demanded fiercely. "Are you absolutely sure the passenger is Devon Brown?"

Mercer raised a single eyebrow and pulled his chin in, as though the question had surprised him. "Positive," he replied, staring unblinkingly at Tyler.

––––––––––

Edward Maitland stood outside the entrance to the ICU, taking a few moments to compose himself before going it to see Jenny. He had returned home earlier in the day for the first time since she'd been hospitalised. Showered, shaved, doused in his favourite cologne, and wearing fresh clothing, he was feeling much more like his normal self.

Before coming back to the hospital this evening, he'd popped around to see their elderly neighbours, who had so kindly offered to look after Fritz, Jenny's beloved Dachshund, during her enforced absence. The sausage dog could be a demanding little so-and-so at times, but thankfully, Maureen and Josh had reassured him, Jenny's pampered pooch had been on his best behaviour for them.

Normally, Fritz was such a snooty git, and he invariably looked down his very long nose at any attempts Maitland made to be friendly. Tonight, though, he had been so pleased to see Eddie that he'd exploded with ear shattering howls of happiness.

After washing his hands, Eddie pushed open the door and walked into the sanitized environment of the ICU, nodding a polite greeting to the sister in charge.

Jenny's refusal to see him during the first couple of days following her admission had hurt far more than words could say. Her parents had been mystified by this, and had showered him with sympathy, which at least meant that she hadn't told them why she didn't want to see him.

She had finally permitted him to visit her for the first time that morning, and the sight of her battered and bruised face had shocked him to his core. The spectacle of her debilitated, heavily bandaged body, with all the tubes running from it, had driven home just how close he'd come to losing her.

Jenny's face had tensed up the moment he'd reached out to take her petite hand in his, but at least she hadn't snatched it away, which had afforded him the tiniest glimmer of hope.

They hadn't said much to each other during this morning's visit and, after everything that she'd been through, he had been quite content just to sit there with her. Tonight, though, he planned to broach the thorny subject of their future, assuming that they still had one.

He simply didn't know what he would do with himself if she told him they were over. The mere thought was enough to make his stomach start doing crazy summersaults.

Jenny was sitting up in bed when he arrived, propped up by a stack of pillows. She seemed small and frail, as though the ordeal had diminished her. Her face seemed a little less gaunt this evening, which was reassuring, and it warmed his heart to see a smile pull at her cheeks as she looked up and spotted him.

She raised a hand and waved at him. It was just a simple gesture of greeting, but it melted him, and a lump rose in his throat as he fluttered his fingers at her in return.

"You're looking so much better," he said as he lowered himself into the armchair beside her bed. Without thinking, he leaned over and took her hand in his. This time she didn't resist, and even allowed him to interlock his fingers with hers.

"I'm actually feeling much better," she told him.

She suddenly squeezed his hand, and the unexpected show of affection brought tears to his eyes. He blinked them away, trying not to let his emotions get the better of him. As Jack had told him a few days ago, he needed to man up for once, and be strong for her sake.

"I really thought I'd lost you," he confessed, nearly choking on the words. So much for being strong, he thought as he scrunched his eyes shut to ward off the tears and pulled her hand to his face, kissing it tenderly.

Jenny seemed startled by this sudden outpouring of emotion. "I wasn't sure that you cared one way or another," she admitted, saying the words so softly that he almost didn't hear them.

"Of course I care!" he stammered, horrified that she might think otherwise. Not wanting to release her hand, he clumsily wiped his eyes on his sleeve. "Jenny, I know I've been a complete arsehole, and I know I've really hurt you, but..." his voice gave out on him and he found he just couldn't speak; it was as though he couldn't breathe either.

"I'm sorry..." he gasped. "I'm so, so sorry." He swapped his chair for the edge of the bed, knowing that the nurses would tell him off for sitting there, but not caring if it gave him a few moments of being close to her.

As he leaned over her, tears were streaming down the side of his face. "Please forgive me," he implored her. "I know I don't deserve another chance, but I'm begging you."

She was crying too, he saw, but she was also smiling, and then she surprised him by wrapping her arms around his neck and pulling him down to her.

They stayed that way for what felt like ages, although in reality, it was probably only a matter of seconds. But they were wonderful seconds, during which he was afraid to move or even speak in case it broke the spell.

"Uh-hmmm!"

Maitland glanced over his shoulder to find a stern-faced nurse standing there with her arms folded. "This is an intensive care unit, not a hotel room," she chastised him. "No sitting on the bed with the patients."

He stood up quickly. "Yes, of course," he said. "Sorry."

The nurse lingered a moment longer, giving him the eye. When she was gone, he returned to the not so comfy chair.

"Why didn't you stop when I asked you to?" Jenny asked, taking him by surprise. "Why did you... why did you *rape* me?"

Eddie let out a little groan of anguish. "Please, don't use *that* word."

"What word would you use?" she demanded, and he recoiled at the anger that had suddenly appeared in her eyes.

Maitland shrugged, feeling woefully inadequate. "I don't know, but not *that* one. Look, Jenny, I was drunk. I'd been snorting cocaine, and you'd been putting me under so much pressure–"

"Oh, so it was all my fault was it?" she snapped, her lips compressing into an angry thin line.

Maitland groaned. "No, of course not," he told her, wishing he could make her see things from his perspective for once. "I didn't mean that at all. I was trying to explain that..." his words tapered into silence.

She was staring at him so intently, waiting for him to finish. It was almost as if she were willing him to say the right thing and give her a reason to forgive him.

Staring at the floor, Maitland let out a long sigh of misery. "You're right, Jen. I'm trying to make excuses for something that's inexcusable. When you said 'stop', I should have stopped at once, not carried on." He looked up, tapping the side of his skull. "But my head was messed up, I know that now. The booze and the drugs didn't help, but I was already in a bad place. I'd started resenting you because I thought all you saw when you looked at me was a sperm donor." He squirmed uncomfortably, and then nodded down at his nether region. "I was literally on the point of shooting my bolt when you told me to stop, and I remember thinking, 'you wanted this, you're gonna get it'. It was totally wrong of me, and I'm disgusted with myself so how can I possibly expect you to forgive me?" As he spoke, he reached out a tentative hand for hers, but she withdrew it. Maitland didn't know what else to say or do. He was overwhelmed with emotion, barely able to speak. "Please, Jen. I'll do whatever it takes to put things right between us. I'll even go to counselling if you think it would help. I promise, if you'll just give me another chance, I'll never do anything like that ever again."

————

It was getting on for half eight and the day's oppressive heat was finally easing off.

Kelly Flowers and Paul Evans sat in a battered pool car, which was parked opposite the Jamaican restaurant in Kingsland High Street. Unfortunately, the lower half of the floor to ceiling windows that faced out into the street were heavily tinted, so it was impossible to tell how many people were still inside, or where they were sitting.

"How much bloody longer do we give this?" Kelly asked, checking her watch for the umpteenth time.

Evans shrugged. "Dunno. I suppose we wait here till everyone leaves and see if Livingstone's amongst them."

Kelly thumped the steering wheel. "Boring, boring, boring." She fanned her face with her clipboard to get some air circulating inside the car.

Evans took a much more pragmatic approach to the stakeout. He tuned the car radio to TalkSport and then reclined his seat to get comfortable. "Shouldn't be too much longer," he said, smothering a yawn.

Kelly stared at the crackling radio in disbelief as a discussion about which Premier League players were likely to be bought and sold during the summer transfer window came on. "You're not seriously going to make me listen to this rubbish are you?"

"It's not rubbish," Evans protested with the passion of a sports fanatic. "It's football! What could be more exciting than that?"

Kelly shrugged. "Oh, I don't know?" she said sarcastically,

"watching paint dry, spending the night in a mortuary, maybe even slitting your wrists."

Evans rolled his eyes theatrically. "Don't be like that," he chided her. "Who do you support? You must have a favourite team, surely?"

Before she could answer, a bendy-bus trundled past, and Kelly started coughing uncontrollably as she choked on the diesel fumes it had pumped into the car through its open windows.

"Gah, this is torture," she said, quickly winding her window up. "It's bad enough having to listen to that drivel about football, without being poisoned by bus fumes as well."

Evans grinned. "Could be worse," he said, although he didn't elaborate on how.

The door to the restaurant opened, and four black men filed out. Kelly opened her clipboard and flicked through the stills contained within. "Here we go," she said, sitting up straight.

Beside her, Evans wound his seat back up and killed the radio. He dialled Tyler's number. "Boss, we've got Livingstone and three others leaving the restaurant."

"*Are you sure it's him?*"

"Yep, definitely him. They're standing outside, talking at the moment."

"*Describe the others for me,*" Tyler instructed.

"Er, they're all black. One has dreads, the second is tall and lanky, and the third one looks much younger, and he's quite stocky. Wait, they're splitting up now... Livingstone and the lanky one are crossing the road... Looks like they're heading back to his flat." He craned his neck to get a better view. "The others have gone into a side road and we've lost sight of them. Who do you want us to stay with?"

At the other end of the line, Evans heard muffled voices, and it took him a second to work out that Tyler had placed his hand over the receiver while he spoke to someone in the room with him.

When he came back on the line, Tyler's voice was unusually tense. "*Paul, listen carefully, I'm happy that Livingstone is heading home. Try and house the other two if you can. Whatever you do, don't show out. I think the stocky one is Devon Brown, who's wanted by Mr Quinlan's team for the Clapton train murder.*"

"Do you want us to try and nick him?" Evans asked, urgently signalling for Kelly to start the engine. As he spoke, a little red Corsa appeared at the mouth of the junction and signalled right. "We've reacquired the two who walked off," Evans said. "They're in a red Vauxhall Corsa, turning right into Kingsland High Street towards Dalston Junction." He gave Tyler the car's index. "It's the same car you told us about in the briefing, boss," he said excitedly.

———

Tyson Meeks was laying on the double bed in his hotel room, hands tucked behind his head, wearing nothing but his boxers and socks. He was watching a typical Friday night drama on ITV, but his mind was elsewhere. They had put him in a no-smoking room, but that hadn't deterred him from lighting up a big fat spliff, which currently dangled from the corner of his mouth.

When the adverts came on, he nipped into the bathroom for a quick piss.

The show he was watching was okay, but all he could think about was what he was going to say to Marcel when they met up the following morning. He was acutely aware that he might not get another chance to see his little brother for a long while after that, and he wanted to ensure that they parted on good terms or, at the very least, on better terms than they currently enjoyed.

Flopping back down on the bed, he glanced at the little burner on his bedside table, wondering if he ought to call the younger, just to make sure that he hadn't changed his mind about meeting up. At the best of times, Marcel was a fickle fucker, and Tyson was worried that something more interesting would come up and that his little brother would blow him out in favour of that. In the end, he decided not to. If Marcel didn't show up, there was nothing he could do about it, but at least his conscience would be clear because he had tried. If mum was up there, looking down on him, she would be glad that he had always tried to do his best by the boy, even though his best didn't amount to much.

Those two wankers from witness protection had stopped by to see him again this evening. Thankfully, Tyson had been back from Hackney for over three hours by the time they arrived, so they had no reason to think he was flouting any of their stupid rules.

They were going to pick him up early on Sunday morning, they had told him, and they would be whisking him off to another part of the country so that he could begin a brand new life. The tossers had refused to say where they were taking him, but they had hinted that it was going to be a very long drive, so he should be sure to get a good sleep the night before.

Tyson hated the idea of moving away from his ends, and he had every intention of going back at the earliest opportunity. If the Feds kept their word, and managed to put Livingstone away on an L-plate, there would be nothing to prevent him from returning to London and picking his life back up at the point where he had left it. Could they do it, though? Could Dillon and his pretty assistant outsmart the Main Man and the psycho killer from Manchester? That remained to be seen. If they couldn't, Tyson was unlikely to see his beloved Hackney again for a very long time.

———

Kelly Flowers' glanced at her colleague for the briefest of moments, and then her eyes were back on the road in front. "Please tell me you brought a radio with you," she asked through gritted teeth.

The Corsa was two cars in front of them, and Peters was driving it like none of the usual rules of the road applied to him.

Evans was mortified by the question. "I thought you were getting a radio when you grabbed a Log-Book and keys," he responded, placing his hands against the dash to brace himself as Kelly was forced to brake hard.

They had just cleared Dalston junction, where Kingsland High Street became Kingsland Road, and they were now heading South, towards Shoreditch and the city.

"I told *you* to grab a radio, you doughnut!"

"Oh yeah, I remember now," Evans said, sheepishly.

"I won't be able to stay with him without showing out if he

continues to drive like this," Kelly warned, gripping the steering wheel hard as she swerved towards the nearside to avoid the clapped out old heap that had just pulled out of a side road on her right, cutting in front of her and forcing her to slam on the brakes to avoid rear ending it.

"What's the matter with people around here?" she growled, somehow resisting the urge to hammer her fist down on the horn. "Haven't they heard of the Highway-sodding-Code?"

They were now three cars behind the Corsa.

"You'd better ring the boss back," she told Evans. "Let him know that we're struggling. He might decide he wants us to try and get uniform to stop it."

Evans was clearly reluctant to do that. "But he said that he just wants us to house them," he pointed out.

Kelly felt like pulling her hair out, and she might have tried had it not been for the fact that she needed to keep both hands firmly on the wheel. "Yes, but at this rate, we're going to lose them, and then we won't be housing anyone."

Evans reluctantly fished his mobile out of his pocket. "I suppose you're right," he conceded.

"I'm a woman. I'm always right."

They were passing through a section of Kingsland Road colloquially known as 'the Waste.' In its heyday, it had been home to a thriving Saturday market selling everything from fruit and veg to tools and household cleaning products; from cheap clothes and shoes to knock off DVDs. The market had been the go-to place in the 1950s and 1960s, but it had been in a steady state of decline for the past few years, and now it attracted only a fraction of the traders that had flocked there during its glory days.

At Richmond Road, the car immediately behind Peters' Corsa turned left, and they were back to being two cars behind it. Peters seemed to be driving a little more sensibly now, which was making it easier for Kelly to stay with him.

"He seems to have calmed down a bit, so I think I'm going to hold off on ringing the boss," Paul said.

"Whatever you think best," Kelly said, hoping they wouldn't end up regretting that decision.

On the approach to the Middleton Road intersection, the traffic lights began to change, going from green to amber. Instead of slowing down, Peters slammed his foot to the floor and the little car surged forward.

"Shit!" Kelly said, dropping a gear in anticipation of it jumping the lights. Sure enough, a second after the lights had turned to red, the Corsa shot straight through them.

The car following immediately behind did likewise. Luckily, nothing was crossing its path or there would have been carnage.

Given the way that the old heap had cut her up when it had pulled out in front of her, Kelly was confident that the driver would have no qualms about going through a red light, especially as there was no traffic coming the other way. Anyway, she reasoned, if it was going to stop, she would have seen brake lights by now.

Even as the thought passed through her head, she realised that she was gaining on it way too fast, and that if she didn't lose speed, she would ram it from behind.

Kelly stamped on the brake, sending the pool car into a slide. "Fuck!" she screamed as the wheels locked.

Letting out a yell of panic, Evans stiffened and braced for impact.

The heap in front had now come to a complete stop. The bastard's brake lights weren't working, she realised far too late.

Kelly's mind flashed back to the skid training she had done during her driving course at Hendon Police College. *Brake hard for as long as you can*, her instructor had told her. *Then, if the car starts to slide, or you can see you don't have the room to stop, come off the brake and steer around the hazard.* So she did. Releasing the brake pedal, Kelly steered the car around the outside of the stationary vehicle, and then reapplied the brake. She skidded through the stop line, but came to a halt before she emerged into the junction.

Evans let out a strangled whimper and sagged back in his seat. "I think I've just crapped myself," he said as the smell of burning brake pads reached them.

CHAPTER TWENTY-SEVEN

Saturday 29th May 1999
GOING BACK TO MY ENDS

The office meeting kicked off at eight a.m.

The detectives were all looking slightly more human today, having benefited from a good night's sleep. Even so, the accumulative effect of having worked such incredibly long hours every day since the job had broken on Tuesday were all too evident, and everyone in the room looked utterly knackered.

As the inspector ranks were salaried, the only renumeration Tyler and Dillon were receiving for working over the weekend was a day off in lieu, but everyone else in the room was being compensated very nicely by the payment of double time.

Charlie White seemed full of the joys of spring. "Och, just so you know, I'm very happy for you to keep me here as long as you need me today, boss," he told Dillon.

"I bet you are," Dillon said acerbically.

"Now, now," White teased. "You shouldnae be jealous that us

humble worker bees are getting paid double time. After all, it was your choice to take promotion."

Dillon scowled at him. "You know Whitey, I think I preferred you when you were being a miserable git."

"Right," Tyler said, kicking proceedings off. "Everything we do today is going to be centred around finding Adebanjo and the three shooters and arresting them. I'll bring you up to speed on a couple of developments you might not be aware of, but I don't intend this to be a long, drawn out affair as there's just so much to do." He paused to clear his throat. "Yesterday evening, DS Murphy found CCTV footage of our three gunmen working the door at Adebanjo's club in Manchester city centre on the night that Livingstone visited him, so it looks like the shooters weren't flown in from abroad as we initially thought might be the case. Fingers crossed, if we don't nick them in London, we *might* get a second chance at nabbing them in Manchester. That's assuming that they don't realise we're on to them beforehand. If that happens-" he made a gesture of an aeroplane taking off with his hand "-they'll disappear quicker than Charlie's smile once the double time finishes."

Polite as ever, Jarvis put his hand up and waited for Tyler to acknowledge him before speaking. "Sir, if we know they're going to go back to Manchester, wouldn't it just be easier to plot up on the club and wait for them to arrive?"

Tyler smiled at the boy's naivety. "We only think they'll go back to the club, Dick. We've got no way of knowing for sure. If I gamble on them doing that, and they don't, The Yard will have my guts for garters. Besides, for all we know, their job here isn't finished yet. What if they're planning to carry out more hits in the coming days?"

Jarvis blushed. "Oh, I see what you mean," he said demurely.

"And don't forget," Dillon added, "ideally, we want to catch them with the firearms still in their possession, and get them taken out of circulation"

"Okay," Tyler said, holding his hand up for silence. "That was development number one. The second thing you need to be aware of, is that Livingstone was spotted having dinner with Daryl Peters, Jerome Norris, and Devon Brown at a restaurant near his flat last night. As you know, Brown's implicated as being one of the stabbers in the job Mr Quinlan's team took on Wednesday. I keep asking myself, what's a street gang younger doing meeting with a big hitter like Livingstone?" He looked around the room, inviting suggestions, but none were forthcoming. "Afterwards, Peters and Brown drove off in the red Corsa. Kelly and Paul tried to follow it off, with a view to housing Brown, but they lost it in Kingsland Road." He nodded towards Evans to take up the narrative.

"Basically, Peters was driving like a total twat," Evans said. "He jumped a red light, and it was far too dangerous for us to follow. Peters is believed to live in Fermain Court on the De Beauvoir Estate, so we did a lengthy drive around, but there was no trace of the car."

"Where did that info come from?" George Copeland asked.

"It was Gavin Mercer, the skipper from Hackney, who told us that," Dean said. "When I actually researched this, it turned out that the information was historic rather than current. Peters moved there with his parents when he was twelve years old, but moved out a few years ago. There are several people on the estate that he regularly visits, and of course he still gives his mum's address for bail purposes whenever he's nicked, although he hasn't actually lived there for some time."

Tyler checked his watch, conscious that time was pressing on. "Dill, can you give an update regarding the firearms deployment?"

"Mr Holland has signed off the paperwork, and I've spoken to SO19. They've put a couple of Level One SFO teams on standby for us at Lippits Hill. I've already sent them over a briefing. As soon as we've housed the suspects, they'll deploy."

"I suppose they're all earning double bubble as well?" Tyler asked.

Dillon grinned ruefully. "They are," he confirmed.

Tyler grunted. It seemed that everyone was making a profit out of working the weekend except for him and Dillon.

"Steve, what's the score with hotels and B&Bs that need to be visited today?"

Bull grimaced. "Even after Reg narrowed the search area down to one azimuth for us, there are about thirty potential places that the suspects could be staying in. Dean identified a dozen reputable hotels for us, and the street search churned up loads of smaller establishments. They're all going to need visiting this morning."

"Er, boss, are we expected to go knocking on doors trying to find the shooters without armed back up?" White asked, suddenly not looking so cheerful.

"Don't worry," Dillon told him. "SO19 are sending two ARVs to patrol the area. They can't accompany you as we don't have any authority for that, but they'll only be a couple of streets away if you need them."

White, it seemed, had regressed to his normal negative default setting. "Aye, that's as may be, but they won't reach us before a speeding bullet does, will they?"

Tyler bristled at that. "Listen Charlie, I'm not asking you or anyone else to do anything I wouldn't do myself. All you've got to do is visit the hotels and B&Bs that Steve assigns you and have a quiet word with the reception staff. Show them stills of Adebanjo and the three shooters, and ask if anyone matching their description is currently staying there."

"Aye, I get that, but what if the place is dodgy and we think the staff might tip off yon suspects?"

Tyler sighed, wondering whether Charlie had forgotten to pack his common sense when he'd left for work that morning. "Look, it's a judgement call on your part," he said tersely. "If you think the person you're speaking to is okay, then ask the question. If you pick up vibes that they're in any way dodgy, just walk away. It's that simple. And, remember-" he paused and looked around the room to impress upon them the seriousness of what he was saying "-if you spot any of the suspects on your travels, you are not to engage them under any circumstances. Just act naturally, avoid drawing attention to yourselves, and get the fuck out of there. Then call it in, and we'll deploy the gun nuts to do the necessary for us."

———

It was another fine morning, and Tyson Meeks had just enjoyed a massive breakfast. His dining experiences had been greatly enhanced by the fact that it had been paid for by the taxpayer, and not him. Stomach bulging, he ambled through to reception and waited for the pretty lady behind the desk to finish the call she was currently fielding.

Meeks had been awake since half past seven, which for him was virtually the middle of the night. Like most of the crowd he mixed with, he rarely surfaced from his pit before eleven. Today was different; he was finally meeting his brother for a long overdue talk to clear the air between them. From the moment his eyes had flickered open, he had been full of nervous excitement. Instead of drifting back to sleep as he would have done on any normal day, he'd lain in his comfy double bed, smoking a king sized spliff to calm his burgeoning nerves. The ingestion of marijuana had promptly given him a bad case of the munchies, so he had hurriedly dressed and then scurried along to the restaurant, where he had consumed a large and very satisfying breakfast.

While he waited for the receptionist to finish the call, his thoughts anxiously turned to Marcel. What would he say to him when they met?

Would Marcel even give him a chance to speak? Worry lines creased his forehead as he contemplated this. Tyson knew that the first few seconds of the interaction would be crucial. He needed to choose his opening words carefully because what he said would set the tone for whether things went well or deteriorated into yet another slanging match. Marcel was bound to be stroppy, because he always was, but Tyson had mentally prepared himself for that, and he was determined not to respond in kind.

"Good morning, sir. How can I help you?" the woman behind the counter asked, smiling politely.

"Er, I need you to call me a taxi to take me to the train station," Meeks said, temporarily putting aside his concerns about the forthcoming meeting.

"Of course, sir," she replied, reaching for the phone. "Are you going anywhere nice?"

"Going back to my ends to meet my brother, innit," he said.

A frown appeared on her face. "Your ends?"

He nodded. "Where I live, in Hackney."

———

Dritan hadn't slept particularly well. He had been up since the crack of dawn, pacing his room like the captive he was. The damned dreams had returned with a vengeance, and he knew if he didn't escape his self-enforced prison and get some fresh air soon, he would start to become uncontrollably anxious; he could already feel the dampness in his palms and the restlessness in his blood. Dritan decided that when this job was finally over, he was going to take himself off camping in the Lake District for a few days to try and get his head in a better place.

Goliath had ordered them to join him at his hotel last night, and it was nice to be staying somewhere reasonable for a change, and not in another dive like the previous establishments. That said, although the rooms were undeniably far more comfortable, and they benefited from the additional luxury of having air conditioning fitted, they weren't significantly bigger, and space was all he cared about at the moment.

Goliath's original plan had called for them to return to Manchester later today, but from what he'd said to Dritan, their departure was looking increasingly unlikely. The problem, as Dritan understood it, was that the Turks hadn't responded as they were meant to. Draping the Albanian flag over the body of one of Goren's men should have triggered a swift and deadly response, which would have sparked the all-out war the black man so desperately craved. Yet here they were, on Saturday morning, and not a single drop of Albanian blood had been spilled in retaliation.

Something was obviously wrong - but what?

He knew that Goliath was due to receive an important update from Livingstone this morning. If it was good news, they would be able to go home as planned. If not, Dritan and his two associates would have to remain in London for a little while longer, in order to carry out at least one more attack.

Goliath had promised to inform him of his decision at ten o'clock, which meant that Dritan still had a little over an hour to wait, and he decided that he would go stir crazy if he spent that time cooped up in his room.

Decision made, Dritan opened his wardrobe and removed the bag sitting on the bottom shelf. Both of his weapons – the Škorpion and the Baikal – had been cleaned and oiled, and were ready for immediate use, should they be needed. Taking the bag with him, he went next door, knocking quietly. A few seconds later, the door was opened by Lorik, who still looked half asleep. "What is it? You woke me up," he said, rubbing his bleary eyes.

Dritan eyed him enviously, wishing that he was still capable of sleeping until someone woke him. "Here, take this," he said gruffly, and thrust the bag into his compatriot's arms.

Lorik, seemed confused, but he relieved his leader of the bag. "Why? Where are you going?"

"I need some fresh air," Dritan told him. "I won't be long."

Lorik's eyes widened. "What do I say if Goliath comes looking for you?" he asked nervously. Their orders were to stay in their rooms until he called for them.

Goliath was staying on a different floor, so that seemed unlikely to Dritan. "Say I have gone for some exercise, and that I will be back before ten."

"But-" Lorik protested.

"I've given you an order," Dritan snapped. "Get on with it." With that, he stormed off towards the lobby.

––––––––––––––––

DS Peter Pringle of the Criminal Justice and Protection Unit, which pretty much everyone else in the Met incorrectly referred to as 'Witness Protection', entered the hotel with a spring in his step. He was carrying a duffle bag full of clothing and toiletries for Tyson 'Weasel' Meeks, so that he would have some new stuff to see him through the first few days of his new life when they relocated him tomorrow morning.

Pringle removed his shades as he entered the air conditioned hotel foyer. It was going to be another gloriously hot day, he reflected, feeling glad to be alive.

This should have been his weekend off, but he had agreed to work it in order to service the witness that AMIP had placed with them earlier in the week. All that was actually required of him today was that he drop off some clothing and carry out a quick welfare check on the witness. Tomorrow was going to be a much longer day; he and his partner were driving Meeks to the other end of the country so that he could begin his new life. Still, Pringle didn't mind. He was being well compensated for sacrificing his weekend off with a couple of days at double bubble. It didn't come along very often in his department, so there was no way that he was going to turn it down.

Pringle was hoping today's visit wouldn't take too long. If everything went according to plan, he would be back home in Hertfordshire by lunchtime. His wife, Patricia, would have lunch waiting for him, and then they were going to take the kids over to Paradise Wildlife Park for the afternoon. The kids absolutely loved it there and, as a special treat, Pringle had promised to take them all out for a nice meal at their local Harvester.

"Morning!" he called out to the attractive young brunette manning the reception desk as he breezed through the lobby on his way to Meeks' room.

The room was located on the ground floor, towards the rear of the property. When he arrived, Pringle rapped out a tune on the door and waited for Meeks to open up.

Nothing.

He knocked again, a little harder this time.

Still nothing.

Pringle leaned his head against the door and listened for the sound of the TV playing in the background.

Silence.

He glanced down at his watch and scowled. "Lazy little fucker," he muttered under his breath. Pringle banged the door again, this time using the bottom of his fist instead of his knuckles.

Thump! Thump! Thump!

"Tyson, it's Peter Pringle. Wake up." He was starting to get irritated. After all, he had places to go; people to see.

It was a sad fact of life that many of the 'clients' who came into his care were dysfunctional types like Meeks, bad boys from street gangs who had grown up without any order or structure to their lives. They had never known routine. They got up when they felt like it; they went to bed when they wanted to. It made them unpredictable and unreliable, and it meant that he was forever having to chase them up and cajole them to do the right thing.

It suddenly occurred to him that he might actually be doing Meeks a grave disservice, and that his client could just be having breakfast in the restaurant. With a sigh of frustration, he set off to track him down.

The restaurant was virtually empty and, to Pringle's great annoyance, there was no sign of Meeks in it. Wondering where the missing witness could possibly be, and chastising himself for having been stupid enough to give him the benefit of the doubt, Pringle took himself back to the reception. The obvious answer was that he was still fast asleep in his pit, the lazy so-and-so.

The fair haired woman behind the counter greeted him with a warm smile. "Good morning, sir," she said cheerfully, addressing him in that irritating sing-song voice that hoteliers often use. It was artificially pleasant, intended to convey warmth and eagerness, but all it ever did for Pringle was put him in a bad mood.

"Hi, hope you can help me," he said, leaning on the counter. "I'm trying to get in touch with a mate of mine. His name is Tyson Meeks, and he's staying in room twelve on the ground floor. I think he must still be asleep because he isn't answering when I knock."

"Was he expecting you to call by?" she asked, her 'customer service' smile still plastered to her face.

"Of course," Pringle lied. The hotel had no idea that Meeks was a CJPU witness, or that he was forbidden from leaving the hotel grounds.

"Maybe he's in the restuar-"

"Nope. Tried there already," he said, cutting her off mid-sentence.

The woman, whose name tag identified her as Sandra, seemed unfazed by the interruption. She reached for the house phone. "In that case, I'll try ringing his room for you," she said.

"Thank you. That would be most helpful," Pringle told her.

As Sandra was dialling Meeks' room number, the brunette he had waved at earlier appeared from a small side office. "Excuse me," she said, speaking like a normal person and not a programmed automaton, "but I couldn't help overhearing your conversation. Your friend. Is he, by any chance, a black chap, early twenties, dresses rather scruffily?"

Pringle nodded at her. "Yes. That's the one."

"Ah, well, in that case, he must have forgotten you were coming," she said with regret, "because he took a cab to Brentwood train station about a half hour ago. He said he was going to visit his brother in Hackney."

Pringle reacted as though someone had just thrown a bucket of ice cold water in his face. "I'm sorry?" he spluttered. "Did you say he's gone to Hackney?"

The brunette nodded. "Yes, that's right."

"Are you absolutely sure?" Pringle asked her, feeling the colour drain from his face.

"I certainly am," she told him. "I called the cab for him myself."

———

Livingstone was sitting by the open sash window in his kitchen, eating his breakfast and staring out into Kingsland High Street down below. People watching fascinated him, and he often indulged himself while he ate.

With it being a Saturday, Ridley Road Market was open for business, and the area around it, which included the building containing his flat, was already heavily congested by throngs of sweaty looking shoppers, many of them struggling under the weight of bulging bags and large, unwieldly boxes.

He could hear the gruff, guttural calls of the various street traders. They were screaming at the top of their voices, all trying to outdo each other and tempt passing shoppers to part with their hard earned cash. He caught sight of a small group of hard faced street urchins from Holly Street heading into the market's entrance, wearing hoodies despite the searing heat. They were, no doubt, looking for victims whose pockets they could pick or whose handbags they could snatch. Livingstone smiled nostalgically; he and his mates had done the same thing at their age.

A steady succession of buses, cars, and trucks slowly trundled by beneath his window. If anything, the traffic flow was actually denser now than it had been during the weekday rush hour.

He watched a Traffic Warden engage in a heated argument with a motorist who had dared to park on the double yellow lines beneath his flat. This part of Hackney was a dangerous place to be a Traffic Warden, and they normally patrolled in packs, too afraid to go out alone. To his credit, the scrawny, bespectacled man who wore a uniform that looked two sizes too big for him, wasn't showing any signs of fear as he squared up to the lumbering giant he had just given a ticket to. Nor was he backing down as the aggressive driver towered over him, their faces inches apart.

Livingstone wondered if he was new to the job, and not yet aware of the inherent risks of his chosen profession. Unfortunately, it looked as though he was just about to be educated in that respect, as the increasingly angry driver finally lost his rag and chinned the warden, knocking his glasses from his face. A second punch sent the warden tumbling to the floor. Arms flopping by his sides, the spare tickets he had been holding in one hand blew away in the wind as he lay there, unmoving.

Passing pedestrians were used to seeing such things in Dalston, and they just calmly stepped over or walked around the prone warden, barely even seeming to notice him. Meanwhile, the man who had knocked him out removed the offending ticket from his windscreen and stood over the Traffic Warden as he tore it into shreds, all the time shouting profanities at the man he had just hit. After sprinkling the ticket over the warden's poleaxed form like confetti, he climbed back into his car and drove off with his base box booming.

Up above, Livingstone had watched events unfold with amusement. As he leisurely sipped his coffee, the warden began to stir, clumsily fumbling for his radio to summon help.

Livingstone's burner rang, and he turned away from the window, scooping it up from the table and checking the caller ID.

It was Goliath, checking in at the agreed time.

The Mancunian giant was punctual, he'd give him that.

"Good morning," Livingstone said, moving away from the window so that he could hear better.

"*What's the score, fam?*" Goliath asked, not bothering with small talk. "*Have you spoken to Goren yet?*"

"I have," Livingstone confirmed, smiling he recalled the very satisfying conversation he'd had with Abdullah Goren late the previous night. "Goren's currently keeping a low profile, convinced the Albanians are trying to kill him and take over his business. He aint happy, bruv, you get me? He's ordered a massive retaliation against the Albanians." He could barely contain the excitement in his voice. "I'm telling you, bruv, he wants them wiped off the face of the fucking earth. The only reason it aint happened yet is cause the Feds have been making themselves proper busy, flooding the area with pig patrols and going round warning his men off. Goren's not worried though, innit. He knows the Feds can only keep this up for a short period of time. In a few days, things will revert to normal, and then Goren's men will reduce them motherfuckers to ash."

"*So you are satisfied with the job we have done for you?*" Goliath asked, and it was clear from his voice that the psycho was genuinely concerned about customer satisfaction.

"Very."

"*Good. In that case, I will take my men back to Manchester today as planned. Needless to say, if things do not go as anticipated, you may call me back to finish the job, and there will be no additional expense involved for you.*"

"That's bliss," Livingstone replied, "but having spoken to Goren last night, I'm confident he aint gonna let what happened at the restaurant go unpunished. And, just to add fuel to the fire, I've arranged for word to be leaked to the Albanians. With any luck, that might scare them into hitting out at the Turks first."

"*Yes,*" Goliath agreed, "*that sounds like a very sound tactical decision. Tell me, before I go, what is happening with the leak in your operation? Has it been silenced yet?*"

Livingstone smiled cruelly as he thought about Meeks. "Don't worry about that," he assured the other man. "By this afternoon, it will have been eliminated."

"Good. The sooner that loose end is taken care of, the better. Now, about the hardware you provided for me men to do the job. This will need to be collected from us before we leave."

"What time you going?"

"Around lunchtime."

Livingstone groaned. The timing was awkward, but he would just have to find someone to make the collection. "Very well," he said. "I'll make the arrangements."

"Good. In that case, my friend, I will say goodbye."

Livingstone hung up and returned to the window, drawn by the sound of approaching sirens. As he looked out, he saw a Fed car pull up, blue lights strobing. Two baby faced officers rushed over to help the dazed traffic warden, who was sitting by the kerb, trying to get his broken glasses to stay on his battered face.

Livingstone couldn't help but laugh. As always, the Feds had arrived too late to be of any real help, just as they would be too late to help Tyson Meeks.

———

It was just after ten when Tyson Meeks arrived at Aske Gardens, the little public park in Pitfield Street where they had agreed to meet. Pausing at the entrance, he looked around nervously, hoping to spot Marcel, and praying that he wouldn't bump into anyone he knew. Tyson was banking on the fact that it was still far too early for most people he hung around with to be out of bed.

To his enormous relief, the park was more or less deserted, and he quickly spotted his younger brother sitting on a rickety wooden bench beneath a big oak tree, about halfway along the concrete path that led from the entrance in Chart Street, opposite his flat, to the one in Buttesland Street, on the other side of the park.

As he walked past the empty tennis court, his brother looked up and acknowledged him with a surly nod of his head. There was no warmth in the gesture but, perhaps more importantly, there was no hostility either. That was encouraging.

He sat down next to his brother, being careful to avoid the still wet dollop of pigeon shit in the middle of the seat, which acted as a natural dividing line to ensure they kept their distance from each other.

"Wagwan, bro?" he said, smiling in a way that he hoped wouldn't come across as smarmy, something Marcel had often accused him of being.

"Alright, bruv," Marcel replied with lacklustre.

Tyson risked a sideways glance at his younger brother. This was the first time in almost a year that they had seen each other in daylight, and he was amazed at how much the boy had changed physically. Back then, Marcel had still been a kid, with no facial hair and a squeaky, high pitched voice. Now, he was almost a man. His face had widened, his bones were denser, and there was even some bum fluff on his chin. He was taller too, and broader, with more muscular definition, and his voice was noticeably deeper.

"You're looking good, bruv," Tyson said. "Been working out?"

Marcel shrugged. "A bit. Switch has got some dumbbells in his flat, innit. Let's me use them." He glanced sideways, running his eyes over his brother. "You look like shit, bruv."

Tyson chuckled, but there was no humour in the noise. "Feel like it too, bruv," he confessed, leaning back against the wooden slats of the bench and stretching his arms high in the air.

They sat in awkward silence for a few seconds, Marcel staring at the floor and Tyson restlessly scouring the park's entrances for new arrivals.

"I'm having a bit of a shit time at the moment," Tyson eventually said, removing a small tobacco tin from his back pocket. He prised the lid off to reveal several joints and a disposable lighter. "Fancy a puff?" he asked, lighting up.

"Sure. Why not," Marcel said, holding his hand out. He took a long toke, and then closed his eyes to savour the smoke in his lungs before exhaling slowly. "This is strong shit, bruv," he said, studying the spliff in his hand admiringly.

Tyson relieved him of the joint and took another drag. He swivelled sideways, so that he was facing his brother. "It's really good to see you, little bro," he said softly. "I don't remember the last time we sat down and talked without it ending up in a fight. I wish we did it more often."

Marcel managed a weak approximation of a smile. "Yeah, right."

"No, I'm being serious," Tyson insisted. "I hate not having you in my life, bruv. You're all I've got."

There had been a time when he and Marcel had met up every Saturday morning in this very park, telling each other all about their week and what they had been up to, but that seemed like such a long time ago now.

Marcel's face contorted into a disbelieving scowl. "Yeah, of course you want me in your life, bruv. That's why you're fucking off and leaving me, innit?" He shook his head in disgust. "You're a dreamer, Tyson, and you're just chatting shit like you always do."

———

Charlie White ticked the latest address they had visited off his list and sighed with frustration. "Och, this is like searching for a needle in a bloody haystack," he complained as a trickle of sweat ran from his armpit and travelled all the way down his ribs.

The ancient pool car they were using wasn't equipped with air conditioning, so they had resorted to winding down all the windows to get some air circulating, but it still felt as though they were driving around in a mobile greenhouse.

"How many more places have we got left to visit?" Paul Evans asked from the driver's seat.

"Just a couple," White said, sounding depressed. He ran a finger through his collar, which felt tight against the shaving rash on his neck. "Sod this," he said, undoing the top button and pulling his tie loose.

Evans glanced sideways. "Sore?" he asked.

"Aye. You know when you've had a strong Vindaloo, and the next day it feels like someone's stuck a blow torch up your bum? Well, that's pretty much how my poor wee neck feels right now."

Evans smiled in sympathy. "I wonder how the others are getting on?" he said as he pulled away.

"I'm sure we would have heard by now if anyone else had struck gold," White said, pulling at his shirt to get some air flowing.

Evans nodded his agreement. "I've got a feeling this is going to be a very long day," he said without enthusiasm.

Squinting against the sun, Charlie pulled his visor down to protect his eyes from the painfully bright glare. As he did, he caught a glimpse of his reflection in the vanity mirror on the other side. His face was all pink and shiny, and his neck was redder than a stop sign.

Evans' stomach growled. "Starving, I am," he said by way of explanation.

"Me too," White admitted, scratching his neck and making the rash even angrier. "Tell you what, let's get the last two hotels checked out and then, assuming we haven't struck lucky, we can find a café and have a ten minute pit stop."

Evans grinned. "See, that's why they made you a sergeant, having great ideas like that."

———

"So, come on then, bruv. You said if I met you, you'd tell me what was going on," Marcel said, staring at his brother impatiently. "Or was that just bullshit, too?"

Tyson leaned forward, resting his elbows on his knees. "I'll tell you everything, bruv, but first I need to get something off my chest."

He paused long enough to take a couple of deep breaths, surprised to see that his hands were shaking, despite having just smoked a huge spliff.

Beside him, Marcel shuffled impatiently in his seat, clearly finding the meeting uncomfortable.

"Marcel," he began nervously, "I know you'll always blame me for mum's death and, for what it's worth, I agree with you."

Marcel was taken aback by his brother's candour. His mouth opened, but no words came out.

"My life's a fucking mess," Tyson continued, feeling inexplicably angry with himself for sounding so bitter about it. After all, it was no one's fault but his own. "I'll never be more than a small time shotter, bruv, but you're still young enough to make something of your life."

Marcel glared at him but said nothing.

"On the night mum died," Tyson, said, feeling the stir of powerful emotions, "she sent me out for her smack but, instead of buying from her normal dealer, I accepted a freebie from a new shotter who was hanging around the estate." Meeks buried his head in his hands as he recalled that fateful evening, and when he spoke again, his voice was riddled with more shame and self-loathing than he would ever have imagined possible. "I took it so I could use her money to buy myself some weed," he confessed, "but I swear to you, I didn't know the gear was bad. I would *never* have done anything to hurt mum. I loved that woman, bruv, every bit as much as you."

He was speaking so quietly now that Marcel had to lean forward to follow what he was saying.

"Knowing she might still be alive if I'd gone to her normal dealer, well it fucking tears me apart, bruv, and I'm so sorry for what I did." Tyson bowed his head in penance as he spoke and, when he looked up again, his eyes were red rimmed and moist. "I don't know if you can ever forgive me, bruv. I know I'll never forgive myself, but I keep thinking that, whatever our differences, we should try and get along for mum's sake."

Letting out a tremulous sigh, Tyson reached into his back pocket and gingerly removed a small photograph. He looked at it longingly for a moment before handing it over. It was creased, and a bit dog-eared, and it showed a pretty black woman in her twenties sitting in an armchair, her arms lovingly wrapped around two children. Both were boys. The younger of the two was a carefree toddler, and he was perched on her right knee, staring adoringly into the eyes of an older brother who knelt down beside him, leaning back against their mother's legs. The boys were holding hands and laughing as though they didn't have a care in the world.

"I know you always liked this picture of us with mum," Tyson said, "and I thought it was about time you had it."

A look of shock flitted across Marcel's face as he accepted the small square photograph, and he gently cupped it in his hand as though it was an ancient treasure that might disintegrate if he was too rough with it. As he gazed down upon the image, a sentimental smile slowly pulled at his cheeks. "I don't even remember this being taken, bruv," he confessed, "but I've always loved this picture."

"I remember it," Tyson said, staring at his brother fondly. "We'd all been to church, and there was a birthday party afterwards, with cake and party poppers, and a proper photographer and everything."

Marcel nodded, even though he had no recollection of the event. "We had a happy childhood," he reminisced. "At least, I did."

"Me too," Tyson said softly. "Well, mostly, anyway."

It was a lie; they had been raised by a dysfunctional drug addict who had often neglected them, not that he loved her any less for her failings. And, to be fair, there had been some very happy times, just not that many.

"What went wrong?" Marcel asked, his nostalgic smile inverting into a frown of sadness.

Tyson wished he knew how to answer that question, but all he could offer was a lame shrug. "I dunno, bruv."

Marcel self-consciously dabbed at his eyes with his sleeve, and then used it to wipe his nose. "Who you grassed up, Tyson?" he asked, his voice brittle.

Tyson cringed at the bluntness of the question. "Marcel-"

"Who the fuck you grassed up?" Marcel hissed.

Tyson sighed, not wanting to tell his brother, but knowing he had to. "I gave Conrad up to the Feds," he finally said quietly, seeming to deflate a little more with each word uttered.

Marcel seemed confused by this revelation. "Nah, bruv, that can't be right," he said, shaking his head angrily. "I already spoke to Conrad about this, and he told me you'd grassed up some pretty serious players, and that he was trying to help you."

"He said what?" Tyson stammered.

Marcel became belligerent. "Don't play fucking games with me, bruv. Who did you grass up to the Feds?"

"I told you," Tyson said, confused and exasperated by his brother's refusal to believe him. He could see the boy was growing increasingly angry, but he didn't understand why.

"Stop lying," Marcel shouted, slamming the bottom of his fist down onto the bench. "Why the fuck would Conrad be trying to help you if you'd grassed him up?"

Tyson shook his head. "Conrad's not trying to help me, bruv. He's-"

"Don't nobody move," a cold voice announced from behind.

As Tyson's head spun in the direction of the noise, the lanky figure of Jerome Norris emerged from behind a nearby oak tree and began walking slowly towards them. The pistol in his right hand was unerringly pointed at Tyson's chest and a smug smile was plastered across his lean face. Tyson was furious with himself for becoming so engrossed in the conversation that he'd stopped keeping an eye out for danger.

"Uh-uh," Norris snapped, wagging a warning finger at Tyson, who had instinctively started to rise. "Sit back down, blud, or I'll put a bullet in you. You no good fucking *grass*." The last word was spat out contemptuously.

Reluctantly, Tyson did as he was told. His eyes remained locked on Norris' gun hand as the slender man casually walked around the front of the bench, coming to a halt directly in front of them.

"Well, well, well, bruv. Look what the cat dragged in," he sneered.

"What you doing here, bruv?" Marcel demanded angrily.

Tyson stayed him with a raised hand, wondering why his little brother didn't have the sense to be worried. Everyone knew that Jerome had a screw loose. "It's alright, bruv," he said softly, his eyes never leaving Norris'. "Jerome, you got no beef with my kid brother. Let him go."

Norris found this highly amusing. "Younger aint got nothing to fear from me, bruv," he said, laughing out loud. "He's on the firm now, innit."

"I asked you a question, bruv," Marcel said, standing up confrontationally. "I told Conrad I'd bring Tyson back to the flat on my own. I don't need no babysitter to look after me."

"Don't sweat it, younger," Norris said dismissively. "Conrad thought he might not come without a little gentle persuasion." He wiggled the gun in his hand to indicate how he intended to incentivise Tyson.

Tyson had watched the exchange in total shock but, suddenly, the enormity of what his brother had just said hit him like a punch in the chest. "You sold me out!" he gasped, staring at his brother accusingly. "You betrayed me!"

"No!" Marcel yelled, turning to face his devastated brother. "Can't you see, bruv. I'm doing this to *save* you."

"Enough!" Norris snapped. "Let's take a little walk back to your flat, Weasel. Then we can talk in private, innit." As he spoke, he took a step backwards and indicated for Tyson to stand.

"We can't go back to my flat," Tyson said, too numb to move. "I didn't bring the keys."

Norris laughed. "Let me worry about that." His face suddenly hardened, as though he had ceased to find the situation amusing and just wanted to get on with proceedings. "Up," he said, gesturing impatiently with the gun.

In a daze, Tyson complied without offering any resistance.

As soon as he was on his feet, Norris grabbed hold of his arm and spun him around so that he was standing directly behind him. He leaned forward and thrust the gun into his captive's spine. There was a metallic click as the gun's hammer was cocked back. "I'll be right behind you all the way, motherfucker," Norris whispered. "Put one foot out of line and I'll put a hole in you. You get me?"

There was a cruelness in his voice that suggested Norris was just itching for an excuse to pull the trigger.

"Easy, bruv," Tyson said, wincing as the barrel was jammed into him again. "I aint gonna give you no trouble."

"Good. Now move."

Swallowing hard, Tyson started walking, knowing that he probably only had a couple of minutes left to come up with a way to save his life.

CHAPTER TWENTY-EIGHT

MAKE SURE YOU WASH YOUR HANDS

Tyler put the phone down and slumped back in his chair, feeling a little deflated.

Dick Jarvis had just rung in to say that he'd found the flea pit in Beckton where the Eastern Europeans had stayed on Thursday night after carrying out the restaurant shooting. Worryingly, Gunz hadn't called ahead on the 003 burner to reserve their rooms using the credit card in Meeks' name. Instead, they had just walked in off the street and asked if there were any vacancies. Paying in cash, the shooters had checked out the following day, leaving no forwarding address. It was a major deviation from their previous routine, and the only logical reason for this happening was that the contract had been fulfilled and the shooters were getting ready to leave the capital.

As he pondered this, Reg Parker came rushing into his office, waving a sheet of paper in the air with great urgency. He looked unusually flustered, Tyler noticed, hoping his phones man was going to be the bearer of good news.

"Boss, I've just had the TIU on the phone. There's been some activity on the burner phones."

"What have we got?" Tyler asked, gesturing for him to sit down.

"Firstly, are you still happy that Adebanjo's using the 217 number?" he asked.

Tyler nodded. The more he'd thought about it, the more confident he had become that the giant had replaced the 666 burner with the 217 handset.

"In that case, Adebanjo's 217 burner called Livingstone's 109 number at nine-thirty this morning. They had a four minute conversation. According to the cell site data, 217 was in the Beckton area and 109 was in Dalston, where it always seems to be."

Tyler held up a hand to silence Reggie. "Just to be clear, when you say 217 was in the Beckton area, was it within the radius of the same cell it used to make yesterday's calls from?" Jack asked, studying Reg's face carefully.

Reg shook his head. "Actually, no. This morning's call was made from a cell located about a mile away from the one he used yesterday lunchtime."

Tyler shifted restlessly in his seat. "Dick just rang in to say that he'd found the place where the shooters bunked down on Thursday night. It's right on the edge of the area we've been searching all morning. I'm wondering if, when they checked out yesterday afternoon, they moved to a new hotel within the radius of the cell that the 217 burner used this morning."

"If they have, it would mean we've been searching the wrong area all morning," Reg said, frowning thoughtfully. "You know, now that I think about it, the cell that 217 used this morning does seem vaguely familiar to me. I wonder…" His voice trailed off as he began flicking through his daybook with increasing urgency. "Ah-ha!" he said, smiling triumphantly when he finally found the page he was looking for. "There we go. No wonder that cell seemed familiar. It's the one covering the hotel Adebanjo and the Kalu twins booked into on Tuesday, when they first arrived in London." A trace of excitement crept into his voice. "You don't think they could have gone back there, do you?" he asked hopefully.

A rueful smile appeared on Tyler's face. "Reg, the first thing that Mr Dillon did yesterday, after you told us that Adebanjo was back in Beckton, was phone the hotel Adebanjo stayed in last time. Not only did the manager confirm that they hadn't returned, he made it crystal clear that they would have been turned away if they'd come back."

Reg seemed crestfallen to hear that. "Oh well," he said, "it was just a thought."

Tyler raked his fingers through his hair as he pondered his next move. "Print me out a street map showing the azimuth that the 217 number phoned from earlier. As soon as the troops finish this morning's street search, I'll redeploy them over there. In the meantime, let's get Dean and Wendy to start compiling a list of hotels and B&Bs for them to visit when they get there."

"I'll get straight on it," Reg promised, heading for the door. As he got there, he stopped and turned around. "Oh, I almost forgot to tell you, the 086 number that called Livingstone's 109 burner at 19:05 hours last night, it belongs to someone called Marcel Meeks. You don't think he could be a relative of Mr Dillon's snout, do you?"

————

Valmir had run out of cigarettes, and his craving for one was starting to make him cranky.

"Dritan won't be happy if you disobey him by going out to get cigarettes after he has said no," Lorik warned.

Valmir turned on Lorik, his face flushed with anger. He had covered for Dritan for over an hour during his earlier unauthorised absence, and this was how their leader repaid him, by refusing his request to pop to the shops for ten minutes.

Valmir knew all about his leader's PTSD, and he respected the man's occasional need to take himself off on long walks to settle his nerves. While Valmir didn't suffer from the disorder, he still had needs, and one of these was nicotine.

"I'm going out," he said defiantly, "and if you tell anyone..." he left the sentence unfinished, leaving Lorik to draw his own conclusions.

"I won't say anything," the wheelman said unhappily, "but I'm not comfortable with you disobeying orders."

Valmir, snorted. "The mission is over. Did not Dritan say so himself. We are just killing time now until we leave for the station and catch a train home."

"Yes, but-"

"There's a newsagent's shop two streets from here," Valmir said, cutting him off. "I spotted it when we arrived. I will be ten minutes. No longer. I'm just going to get some smokes. It's no big deal. Do you want anything while I'm gone?"

Lorik shook his head.

Leaving his companion to fret, Valmir stormed out of the room.

––––––––

Dillon had decided to accompany Jonny Murphy and Christine Taylor on their rounds as they visited the venues that Steve Bull had allocated them. They had just left the last one on their list, and were now heading back to Arbour Square.

Murphy was chilling in the backseat. "You know, I really had a feeling that today would be the day we finally arrested Adebanjo," he said, shaking his head in disappointment.

Dillon glanced over his shoulder. "We still might do," he said, trying to sound optimistic.

"Maybe," Murphy allowed, but he didn't sound hopeful.

Christine, who was driving, studied the Liverpudlian in her rear-view mirror. "Bet you're wishing you hadn't offered to work your weekend now, aren't you?" she said with a rueful smile.

Murphy shrugged. "Like the big man says, there's still time."

Dillon's phone rang.

"Dillon speaking," he said, noting that the caller was ringing from a withheld number.

"*Sir, it's Peter Pringle from the CJPU here. I've got some very alarming news for you.*"

Dillon stiffened. Had something happened to Tyson Meeks? He

signalled for Taylor to pull over. "What is it?" he asked, trying to remain calm.

"*It's Meeks. He's vanished, sir,*" Pringle said. *"From what we can gather, the silly git has jumped on a train and gone back to Hackney."*

The muscles bunched in Dillon's jaw. "How the hell did that happen?" he growled. "You're supposed to be looking after him."

"*He's not a prisoner,*" Pringle pointed out defensively. "*We don't have a nurse-maid looking after him around the clock.*"

"Do we at least know when he left the hotel?" Dillon asked, ignoring the questioning looks from the others.

"*Well,*" Pringle began, "*according to the receptionist-*"

A bus rumbled past, drowning out the rest of what he said. Dillon turned away from it and rammed a sausage sized finger in his other ear. "Sorry," he said. "I didn't hear any of that. Can you repeat?"

"*I said the receptionist called a cab for him at about nine o'clock, and he told her he was going back to his ends in Hackney to meet up with his brother.*"

"Have you got anyone checking out his home address to see if he's gone there?" Dillon asked.

"*I'm sorry, boss. We just don't have the resources for that. I went to Brentwood train station and checked the CCTV, and I can confirm he caught a London bound train at nine-seventeen. Apparently, he would have had to change trains, and the journey takes approximately fifty-three minutes, so he could have been there for just after ten o'clock.*"

Dillon checked his watch. It was getting on for ten-thirty. "Do you at least know what he was wearing?" he asked.

"*Yep. He was wearing a black T-shirt, baggy blue jeans and dark trainers.*"

Dillon thanked him and hung up. After venting his displeasure with a string of choice expletives, he filled the others in on what had happened.

Christine frowned, deep in thought. "The other night, when I was taking him to the drop off point to hand him over to the witness protection lads, he was telling me how he and his brother used to meet up in a little park near his flat," she said. "I don't know the exact location, but there can't be too many parks where he lives. We could always have a quick punt over there and see if he shows up. I mean, it's not as if we have anything to lose, is it?"

Dillon considered this. "I'd better check in with Jack first," he said. "In case there have been any developments."

A car drew level with them and honked its horn. It was Gurjit Singh and Geoff Coles.

"What are you lot up to?" Geoff asked, leaning out of the driver's window to talk to Dillon.

"Long story," Dillon said, pulling a sour face. "That twat Meeks has done a bunk from witness protection and gone back to Hackney to meet up with his brother."

That wiped the smile from Geoff's face. "Shit!" he said. "Does Mr Tyler know yet?"

Dillon shook his head. "I was just about to drop that particular bombshell on him when you arrived."

Geoff grimaced. "Rather you than me," he said. With a farewell wave, the Astra pulled off.

————

Dean stuck his head around the corner of Tyler's door. "I've already found a dozen hotels in the new area you asked me to research," he said, placing a list in front of Tyler. "Wendy's also working on it, so we should have some more to add to the list shortly."

"Thanks," Tyler said wearily. "Gurjit and Geoff phoned in a few minutes ago to say they've finished all the addresses on their list, so I'll divert them onto these new venues."

He tried ringing their numbers, but both went straight to answer phone. Either their batteries had chosen to give up at exactly the same time or they were in a dead spot. He decided he would give it a couple of minutes and then try them again. In the meantime, he would call Charlie White. When Whitey had last called in, there had only been one more venue on his list, and that had been nearly twenty minutes ago, so he should be free by now.

"*Hello boss,*" Charlie responded almost immediately. His voice was distorted, like he had his head in a bucket.

"Charlie, where are you? I can hardly hear you."

"*Er, I've just popped into a little café to answer a call of nature. Just using their restroom and then we'll be heading back to base.*"

Tyler raised an eyebrow at the handset and shook his head in disappointment. A quick call of nature! Did Charlie really think he was going to fall for that one? More like they had stopped off for some nosebag. "I've got some more addresses for you to check out, so finish whatever you're doing and then call me back. And Charlie…?"

"*Yes, boss?*"

"Make sure you wash your hands!"

———

Inside the café, Charlie hung up and winked at Evans. "I think he fell for it," he said, feeling very pleased with himself.

Evans grinned, and then took a large bite from his bacon and egg roll. "What did he want?" he asked, spraying food everywhere.

Moving backwards to avoid the spatter, Charlie took a sip of his coffee and shrugged. "Something about having a load more addresses for us to visit in a different area."

Evans groaned. "Really? I was hoping that was it."

"Well it's not," Charlie said, standing up. "I'd better go out to the car and call him back. Be as quick as you can. We dinnae want to anger him today."

He scooped the key off the table and walked back out into the scorching sunshine. Clicking the fob to release the central locking, Charlie sat in the car and wound down his window as quickly as he could. Already starting to perspire, he leaned across and repeated the process with the driver's window. Pen at the ready, he called Tyler back.

"Let me have those new addresses," he said, and proceeded to scribble them down in his daybook.

As he was hanging up, Evans returned, looking grumpy. "You buggered off and left me to pay the bill," he complained.

"Oh yeah, so I did. Must've slipped my mind," White said with an apologetic smile. "Still, you cannae complain too much, laddie. You *are* on double bubble."

Evans grunted. "So are you, you stingy git." He started the engine, which coughed and spluttered as though it was on its last legs. "Come on then, tightwad, where to?"

———————

"DCI Tyler," Jack said, picking up the phone, which hadn't stopped ringing all bloody morning.

It was Dillon, and he sounded stressed. *"Jack, I've just had a call from some DS at the CJPU."*

Jack's first thoughts were that Meeks was having second thoughts about being relocated. "Okay," he said cautiously. "And…?"

"It's Meeks. The idiot has gone back to Hackney to meet up with his kid brother."

Tyler felt his blood run cold. "That boy's not just a fool, Dill, he's a bloody liability. Why would he do something so incredibly stupid?"

"I might be wrong, Jack, but I think he's trying to make peace with his brother before he's relocated. It's all very complicated, but basically it's to do with his brother blaming Tyson for their mother's death a few years ago."

"Well, there's nothing we can do about it," Tyler said. "Either he'll return to the hotel later or he won't, but even if he does, I can't see the CJPU wanting to run with him anymore if he isn't obeying their instructions."

"Jack, I think I know exactly where he's going. He told Christine about a park they always used to meet up in, close to his flat. How about we shoot over there now and-"

"No," Jack said firmly. "Not going to happen. The only reason I agreed to let you go down to Beckton this morning was so that you could take control if and when we housed the shooters. I can't release you from that obligation. If a firearms team's deployed, you'll need to act as Silver. I don't have anyone else who's trained to do that."

"But Jack-" There was desperation in Dillon's voice.

Tyler closed his eyes. He knew how seriously his friend took his responsibility to keep his informant safe but, as far as Tyler was concerned, that obligation didn't extend to circumstances like this, where the snout had deliberately placed himself in danger. If anything happened to Meeks, it was on his own head. "I'm sorry, Dill," he said with a heavy heart. "The answer's still no."

––––––––

Geoff yawned. "I'm feeling a bit peckish," he said.

"Aren't you always," Gurjit responded. The back of the car was littered with the debris from his earlier snacks, which so far had included a drive-through MacDonald's breakfast, two bars of Dairy Milk chocolate, and a packet of crisps.

"Not always," Geoff said with an impish grin. "Sometimes I'm sleeping."

He suddenly indicated left and swerved into a gap outside a small row of run down shops, earning himself a long blast on the horn from the car that had been following behind.

"Won't be a minute," he promised.

Gurjit was appalled. "You've got to be kidding me! Surely you're not buying more food?"

Geoff shrugged. "Just a KitKat. I'll be back in two shakes of a lamb's tail." He had intended to wait until they returned to Arbour Square, but when the boss called and redirected them to the other end of Beckton to start checking out hotels over there, he decided that he ought to top up his supplies. Walking briskly, he passed a Post Office, a charity shop, and a card shop, and then he disappeared into the little supermarket at the end of the parade.

The store was set up in a one way system with five aisles running the length of the shop. The counter with its three tills was set up right next to the exit door, presumably so that staff could intercept anyone who tried to make off without paying, which Geoff imagined happened a lot around here. He entered the first aisle and quickly worked his way down it, passing shelves that were stacked with cakes – tempting – and others with bread and rolls – not remotely tempting. At the end, he came to a large chiller stocked with milk, cheese, yogurts and butter, fruit juice and all that stuff.

Boring.

Geoff tirelessly worked his way up and down the remaining aisles until he reached the one nearest the tills, which was filled with confectionery and crisps. Smiling, he rubbed his hands together. "Come to daddy," he said as he spotted a red packet with white writing on it. Just to be on the safe side, in case he got hungry again later, he grabbed an extra KitKat. On the way to the till, a large bag of crisps also fell into his hands.

There were only two people in front of him – well, three if you counted the screaming brat having a tantrum beside the heavily tattooed woman who was being served. The long haired child was kicking its mother's leg because she had refused to buy him the packet of chewing gum he was demanding. "Scream all you fucking want," she snarled. "You aint getting any, and that's that."

The man standing directly in front of him, a big lump whose scabby bald head resembled a potato, tutted at the outburst, clearly unimpressed by her foul language.

The woman turned on him in an instant, her face contorted with anger. "What you fucking gawping at?" she demanded, spraying spittle everywhere.

The man responded in a foreign language. Although Geoff didn't understand the words, it was clear from the scathing tone that it wasn't complimentary.

The woman unleashed a torrent of abuse at him as she snatched her shopping off the counter and stormed out, dragging the still protesting kid behind her.

"Dute-n pisicii matii!" the bald man shouted after her.

"Next please," the middle aged, overweight man behind the counter called, acting as though nothing had happened.

Stepping forward, the bald man switched to heavily accented English, asking for two packets of Benson & Hedges cigarettes.

After paying, the man scooped up his goods and set off towards the exit, tearing the cellophane wrapping from one of the packs as he walked. He passed beneath a convex mirror that had been set up to allow the cashiers to keep a watchful eye on customers in the aisles, just in case they decided to start stuffing goods under their clothing. As he did, Geoff caught a very brief glimpse of his reflection in it.

The bald man's granite hard face matched his intimidating size, and on it was a nasty scar that ran from the bridge of his nose all the way down the left side of his face to the corner of his upper lip.

"Shit!" Geoff muttered under his breath. The man was the spitting image of one of the three shooters they were searching for. Realising that he needed to get a better look, Geoff immediately set off after him.

"Oi, mate! Oi! You need to pay for that. Oi! STOP!"

Geoff was vaguely aware of angry shouting coming from behind, but he ignored it. It sounded as if someone was trying to do a bit of shoplifting, but he couldn't allow himself to be distracted by that, not now that he had possibly spotted one of the gunmen they were after.

A hand grabbed him by the shoulder and yanked him back, stopping him dead in his tracks.

"What the–"

"I know your game," the man who had rushed out from behind the till said, shaking his head at Geoff in disappointment. "Either pay for that stuff or I'm calling the Old Bill."

Geoff followed the man's eyes down to his hands, which were still holding the chocolate and crisps that he had come in for. In the excitement of seeing the potential suspect, he had forgotten all about them. Without a word, he thrust them into the proprietor's hands and pushed him aside.

Geoff ran out of the shop, ignoring the man's comments about being barred for life. He looked left and right, desperate to spot the man with the scar, but there was no sign of him. He ran back to the car and leaned in through the driver's window.

"Did you see him?" he asked Gurjit, who was sitting in the front passenger seat.

Gurjit was on the phone, presumably to the office, because he was writing more addresses down into his daybook. He cringed at the outburst and made an angry shushing gesture at Geoff.

"Gurjit! Did you see the bald bloke who came out of the shop just before me?" he demanded.

Gurjit sighed his exasperation. "Give me a moment please, Dean," he said into the phone. Then, covering the speaker, he glowered at

Geoff. "What are you bloody well going on about? Can't you see that I'm on the phone to the office?"

"Never mind that," Geoff said, climbing behind the wheel and starting the engine. "I think I just saw one of the shooters."

Gurjit's eyes widened. "You did! Where?"

"He was in the shop, standing right in front of me. I was hoping you might have seen where he went when he came out?"

Gurjit shook his head. "I was on the phone. I'm *still* on the phone," he said holding it up to make his point.

Geoff growled in frustration. If that stupid jobsworth shop assistant hadn't slowed him down, he would have seen where the suspect had gone. Now, all he could do was scour the side streets in the hope of reacquiring him. "Tell the boss," he said, pulling away from the kerb. "See if he can get some more people to the area to help us search. The fucker can't have gone far."

CHAPTER TWENTY-NINE

I'M WORKING FOR MR LIVINGSTONE NOW

Tyson came to a halt, conscious of the gun pressing against his spine.

"Knock on the door," Norris instructed him.

"But there's no one in," Tyson responded, confused by the order.

They were standing on the balcony outside his flat, which was on the first floor of Touchard House. Looking down into Chart Street below, he could see into the public park and tennis courts of Aske Gardens quite clearly.

There was no one else around, but even if there had been, they would have just turned a blind eye to the pistol in Norris' hand and gone about their business. That was the way things worked around here; people didn't stick their noses into other people's business, not unless they had a death wish.

Norris sucked his teeth angrily, and thrust the gun even harder into the small of Tyson's back. "Knock on the fucking door, bruv, innit."

"Okay," Tyson said, flinching. He reached out and worked the door knocker several times, glancing sideways at his brother, who was standing by his shoulder, staring down at the floor. Tyson could see that the boy was unhappy, but he was still going along with this, so he obviously wasn't *that* unhappy.

Within seconds, the door opened inwards and they were greeted by the smiling face of Gunz. He had a spliff protruding from the corner of his mouth, and Tyson caught an envious whiff of it.

"Wagwan, bruv," Gunz said, greeting him like they were still friends.

"Go inside," Norris said, shoving him hard in the back.

Tyson nervously followed Gunz along the narrow corridor towards the lounge at the end. As he entered the familiar room, he spotted the thick plastic sheeting that now covered the walls and the floor. He stopped in his tracks as the cold reality of the situation hit him, taking his breath away.

"What's all the plastic for?" Marcel asked, following his brother in.

Gunz laughed nastily. "We're gonna be doing a bit of decorating, bruv. Thought we might coat the walls in a nice shade of red." He shared an amused glance with Norris, and they both laughed knowingly at the implication of his words.

Marcel's eyes widened with worry. "Conrad told me you weren't going to hurt Tyson."

Gunz grinned slyly, his right index finger flicking between himself and Norris. "Oh, *we're* not going to hurt him," he promised. "*We* won't be laying a finger on him unless he plays up, will we Jerome?"

"Nah, bruv. Not *us*," Jerome said with a cruel grin.

There was hardly any furniture in the room, just an old TV, a cheap fabric sofa, and a scratched coffee table, all of which looked like it was on its last legs.

The curtains had been drawn shut, Tyson noted, wondering how long it had taken them to coat all the walls and the floor with thick plastic sheeting. The unpalatable truth was that, now they had him in here, away from prying eyes, they could take their time, and there was absolutely nothing he could do to prevent the inevitable.

Tyson had considered making a break for it as they'd crossed the road from Aske Gardens, but in the end he hadn't. What would have been the point? There was no way he could outrun a bullet. Instead, he'd walked as slowly as he dared, praying that a police patrol would cruise past. It hadn't, of course; Tyson Meeks wasn't the sort of person who got lucky breaks like that.

As he'd climbed the communal stairs, the barrel of Norris' gun jabbing into him every step of the way, he had slowly resigned himself to his fate. Maybe – just maybe – this was the comeuppance he deserved for having given his poor mother the drugs that killed her all those years ago. Perhaps this was just Karma, and the universe was paying him back for his earlier transgressions.

All he could hope for now, he realised, was that it would be quick and painless, and that Marcel would one day learn to forgive himself for his role in bringing about his brother's demise.

"Oi, bruv," Gunz shouted into the hallway. "Bring in one of dem chairs from the kitchen."

A moment later, a stocky teenager appeared, carrying a hard backed chair. He sullenly placed it in the centre of the room. "Sit down," he said, nodding for Tyson to take a seat.

"Switch!" Marcel exclaimed, surprised to see a fellow Holly Street gang member present. "What you doing here, bruv? I thought you was on the run from dem Boyden."

Switch puffed out his chest proudly. "I aint afraid of them," he boasted. "I'm working for Mr Livingstone now."

Gunz laughed, and wrapped an affectionate arm around the younger's broad shoulders, pulling him in tight. "That's right. My little cuz is in the big league now, aint ya, younger?"

Switch grinned like an idiot. "See, bruv," he said, staring goadingly into Marcel's eyes. "I aint like you. I got family who look out for me. All you got is this piece of shit." He jerked his thumb back over his shoulder at Tyson.

Gunz laughed uproariously and slapped his cousin on the back. "Well said, younger. Now, make yourself useful and get the wire from the kitchen while I dial Conrad's digits."

Switch disappeared into the kitchen, reappearing moments later with a nasty looking roll of barbed wire and a selection of cable ties.

He was carrying the wire gingerly, as though it might attack him at any moment.

Norris pointed the gun at Tyson. "Stand up," he said, smiling ominously.

Tyson timidly complied. "Please," he begged the gunman. "Don't do this."

"Shut up and take off your clothes," Norris ordered.

Tyson hesitated. "My clothes? Why do you want me to take off my clothes?"

"Take off your fucking clothes, Tyson," Norris warned, "or I'll put a bullet in your kneecap right here and now."

Tyson recoiled. "Okay, okay. I'll do it. Please, don't hurt me."

They all stood in silence, watching him undress. Unlike Marcel, who looked like he was going to throw up, the others revelled in Tyson's misery as he tearfully removed his clothes.

As Tyson started to lower his boxer shorts, Norris raised a hand to stay him. "Nah, it's alright, bruv. You can leave your shreddies and socks on."

"Yeah," Gunz added with a chuckle, "we don't want to be looking at your shrivelled pecker, do we."

Norris and Switch both laughed.

Marcel averted his eyes as Norris placed a hand on his brother's shoulder and roughly pushed him back down onto the chair.

"Now cable tie his wrists and ankles to the chair," Norris ordered.

Switch did as he was told, placing a thick, black cable tie around each of Tyson's wrists, and then securing them to the arms that protruded from the chair. Switch pulled them as tight as he could, grinning maliciously as Tyson screamed that his circulation was being cut off.

"Relax, bruv," Switch said with a heartless smirk. "It aint *that* bad."

He repeated the process with Tyson's ankles, fastening them to the legs of the chair.

"Switch, take it easy, bruv," Marcel pleaded. "They don't need to be that tight, know what I'm saying?"

When Switch had finished, Norris inspected his work. Once he was satisfied the ties were secure, he pulled on a thick pair of industrialised padded gloves. Handling it carefully, so as not to injure himself in the process, he then began to wrap the barbed wire around Tyson's body. As it bit deep into his exposed skin, drawing blood and eliciting screams of anguish, Norris laughed heartily.

"Don't be a pussy, bruv," Switch said, stepping forward to slap Tyson around the head.

"Oi, younger," Norris snapped. "No one touches this piece of garbage except for Conrad. You get me?"

"Sure," Switch said, backing off. "That's fine by me."

"You sick fuck!" Marcel screamed, unable to bear his brother's agonised cries any longer. "He's already tied up. There's no need to wrap him in barbed fucking wire as well." He made a grab for Norris, intent on pulling him away.

Switch intervened and pushed him back. As the two boys stood facing off against each other, Switch rolled his thick neck ready to fight. Fists clenched, he strutted forward until their foreheads were touching. "One more word out of you, bruv," he warned, pushing his head into Marcel's.

Marcel was terrified, but he didn't back down.

Gunz quickly pulled them apart. "Easy youngers. Everything's cool," he told them, before shoving Switch out of the room. "Go and wait for me in the kitchen, cuz."

Switch didn't look happy but he complied, lingering only long enough to suck through his teeth at Marcel.

After the younger had left the room, Gunz ambled over to Tyson and ruffled his hair. "I've spoken to Conrad and he's on his way, bruv. All we gotta do now is wait for him to get here, and then the fun can really begin."

———

Charlie White smiled at the attractive receptionist, who reciprocated in kind. "Good morning," he said, showing his warrant card. "My name's DS White, and I'm hoping I could have a discreet word with the duty manager."

"Of course, sir," she said, reaching for the phone. "Would you like to have a seat over there while I give him a call? Won't keep you waiting too long."

White took himself off to one of the many comfy armchairs that littered the lobby and sat down. He studied the hotel foyer with interest, noting that, like all the others he'd visited that morning, it had a pleasant but bland layout. A few prints adorned the walls, and there was a plant pot or two scattered around the perimeter to provide a bit of much needed colour. Music was being piped out of concealed wall speakers to provide some soothing background noise. At that moment, *The Entertainer*, Marvin Hamlisch's catchy tune from the Paul Newman and Robert Redford classic, *The Sting*, was playing.

There was a machine providing complimentary coffee off to his right, and he was tempted to help himself, not because he really wanted one but because it was free. In the end, he decided not to; he'd only just finished a latte at the café, and he would end up pissing all day if he drank too much.

This place was part of a well-known international chain, and Charlie suspected its pedigree would make it a bit too upmarket for the shooters tastes. He envisaged them being more at home in a squalid little dive like the ones they'd used in Seven Sisters and Amhurst Park. Luckily, he and Paul had managed to avoid visiting any dumps like that this morning, so far at least.

The entrance doors were electric sliding jobbies that opened automatically as you approached them, and when he heard them swish, his first thought was that Evans had decided to follow him in. Glancing over his shoulder, Charlie found himself staring at a bald headed brute with mean eyes and an ugly facial scar that ran from the bridge of his nose down to the top of his lip.

Gripping the padded arms of his chair in shock, White felt himself going rigid. "Fuck me!" he muttered under his breath.

Showing no interest in visiting reception, the newcomer made a beeline towards the three lifts that were located at the far end of the lobby, moving with the slow, lumbering stride of a man who lifted too many weights.

As he passed by White's chair, the scar faced man gave the detective a cursory glance. Thankfully, nothing registered in his eyes, and he carried on walking.

A slender, bespectacled white man in his early forties emerged from an office behind reception and ambled over to the girl he'd spoken to upon his arrival. She glanced in Charlie's direction and nodded, and the man's eyes followed.

Accompanied by a soft ping, the doors to the middle lift opened just as the bald man reached it, and he stepped inside without a backward glance. As they began to close, the duty manager smiled at Charlie and opened his mouth to speak.

Please don't call out my name, Charlie screamed inside his head.

If the duty manager referred to him by his rank, the suspect might hear him and be alerted. Thinking fast, Charlie jumped to his feet, raising his left forefinger to his lips and holding his right hand up, palm out towards the manager, who frowned at the strange sight, but said nothing. As the lift doors closed, Charlie let out and enormous sigh of relief and sprinted over to check what floor it was going up to.

The wall mounted dial above the lift indicated that it had stopped on the first floor. Charlie reached inside his jacket for his phone, knowing that he needed to call this in as a matter of urgency.

"Is there a problem?" a voice at his shoulder asked.

Charlie jumped, almost dropping his mobile.

"Jesus!" he exclaimed, spinning around to find the duty manager standing there with his hands on his hips, staring at him accusingly. "Och, behave, man," Charlie complained, clasping his chest. "You could've given me a heart attack, sneaking up on me like that."

The man frowned suspiciously. A gold badge on his jacket proclaimed him to be: 'Albert Peabody. Duty Manager.'

"You *are* the police officer who wanted to speak to me, I take it?" Peabody asked, clearly confused by the odd behaviour he'd just witnessed.

"Aye," Charlie said, "I am." He wrapped an arm around Peabody's shoulders and pulled him in close, lowering his voice to a conspiratorial whisper. "Albert, my old son, I think you and me need to have a quiet wee chat in your office," he said, dragging the reluctant man back towards the reception desk.

"Do we?" Peabody replied unenthusiastically. He shot Charlie a nervous, sideways glance, as though he was unsure that White was even a real police officer.

"The man who just went into that lift," Charlie said, indicating the three lifts with a backwards jerk of his head. "I need to know what room he's in and who's staying here with him."

That earned him a tut of disapproval. "Well I don't know that it would be appropriate for us to divulge such information," Peabody said. "After all, we have a duty to respect our client's confidentiality."

The man had a whinging voice, and Charlie had him pegged as an irritating jobsworth. "Aye, you do," he agreed, smiling sweetly, "unless they're murdering scumbags armed to their teeth with automatic weapons, of course. Then you need to cooperate fully or risk causing a big gunfight inside your posh hotel."

The duty manager stopped dead in his tracks upon hearing that, and Charlie saw the colour drain from his face.

"Oh dear me," Peabody said, suddenly looking terribly worried.

———

Steve Bull pulled the Omega up outside the front of Touchard House, the five storey block of flats that Tyson Meeks lived in. The air condition was blowing full blast, which was a blessed relief because he would have been sweating like a pig without it.

Grumbling to himself, Bull reached behind and grabbed a battered blue clipboard from the back seat. Although he'd been given a verbal briefing by Tyler before being sent here, he wanted to check through his notes before venturing out into the sweltering heat in search of Tyson-bloody-Meeks.

He was seriously unimpressed by the task he'd been given. As Case Officer for five gangland murders, he had far more pressing matters on his mind at the moment, and he could have really done without being sent on a waste of time mercy mission to try and recover Dillon's missing snout. As far as Bull was concerned, if Meeks couldn't even go a few days without succumbing to the urge to return to his old stomping ground, there was no point in witness protection wasting their time trying to relocate him. They might as well cut their losses now and let Meeks get on with it. If his stupidity got him killed, well that was entirely down to him.

When Tyler had called him into his office, and informed him that Meeks had done a bunk to meet his brother in Hackney, Bull had fully expected the boss to write Meeks off as an unreliable witness. Tyler had confided in him that he'd seriously considered doing exactly that, but Dillon had managed to persuade him that someone needed to visit the park where the meeting was believed to be taking place. If that drew a blank, Meeks' flat needed to be checked, just in case he had gone back there. With the rest of the team searching for the shooters in Beckton, Steve had been the only person available to be tasked.

"It'll take you ten minutes to have a stroll through the park and then knock on the door of his flat," Tyler had told him. "Fifteen minutes tops."

Like anything ever went that smoothly!

With a resigned sigh, Bull pulled out the photograph that Dean had printed off for him. It was a custody image from a couple of years back. Steve had never seen Meeks in the flesh, and he hoped that the man's appearance hadn't drastically changed. Folding it up and sticking it in his jacket pocket, Steve Bull killed the engine and reluctantly stepped out into the glaring sun.

———

The phone on his desk rang – again. Tyler had literally been halfway out of the door, on his way to check in with Andy's team, who were also working the weekend, to see what progress they had made.

Growling with irritation, he spun around and stomped back to his desk, wondering why the buggers were all calling him on his landline today, instead of his mobile.

"Tyler," he said brusquely.

"*Boss, it's Charlie. We've found them! We've found Adebanjo and the shooters.*" The Scotsman was speaking quickly, and his voice was brimming with excitement, making it even harder than normal to understand his strong Glaswegian accent.

"Where?" Tyler said, sliding into his chair and scrabbling around for a pen and paper. This was fantastic news, and he felt his palms break out in sweat as the adrenalin kicked in.

"The wee buggers are staying at the fancy hotel you sent us to in Woolwich Manor Way, near City Airport."

"How sure are you of this?" he asked, scribbling away furiously.

White laughed. *"Och, the shooter who looks like The Phantom of the Opera walked right past me while I was sitting in the foyer, waiting to speak to the manager. You couldnae miss that ugly mug, that's for sure."*

His earlier irritation now completely forgotten, Tyler grinned as he considered whether the shooter had thought the same thing about Charlie. After all, the poor sod had a badly disfigured nose that almost sat at a right angle to the rest of his face, protruding ears, and little bowed legs that prevented his knees from touching when he stood with his feet together.

"Has the manager confirmed that he's actually staying there?" Tyler asked, trying to remain calm and not let his excitement get the better of him.

Another chortle from White. *"Aye, yon manager started off by being a right snooty little jobsworth, but he soon changed his tune when I told him what they'd done, and that they were probably carrying enough hardware to start a small war. Adebanjo's booked into one room, under an alias of course. The twins are booked into another room. One of the shooters also merits his own room, and the final two are sharing. Don't know why. Perhaps they're gay."* He proceeded to give Tyler the alias names that were being used: Adebanjo and the twins were listed as Smith, Jones and Jones. The shooters were shown as Brown, Black and Grey. *"I dinnae think they put too much effort into coming up with those,"* he scoffed.

"How long are they scheduled to stay there?" Tyler asked. Hopefully, it would be at least another night, as that would give him time to mobilise the SFO team and work out the best plan of attack.

"Ah, well, according to my new best mate, the manager, they're scheduled to check out at twelve o'clock, but they've paid extra to keep one of the rooms until three p.m."

Tyler glanced at his watch and winced. If they left at twelve, it would be cutting things pretty tight. Two or three would be better, but it still wasn't ideal. "Charlie, I need to go. I've got to let DI Dillon know, so that he can scramble the rest of the team, and then I need to get onto the Tac advisor at Lippitts Hill re deploying the SFOs. Any info you can dig up will be really helpful, especially if you can find out where they're going when they leave the hotel, and how they're planning on getting there."

"*Aye, I'll just go and knock on their door and ask them,*" White replied sarcastically, but it was too late. Tyler had already hung up.

———

Taylor steered the Astra into the car park of the ASDA superstore in Frobisher Road, and drove around until she spotted Geoff Coles and Gurjit Singh. The two detectives were leaning against the bonnet of their car, and Geoff was tucking into a banana.

"That's a bit healthy for you, isn't it?" Dillon said, as he alighted the car.

Geoff shrugged. "My body's a temple," he replied, ramming the rest into his mouth.

"What's the plan for dealing with the suspects now that we've located them?" Singh asked.

Dillon raised a taunting eyebrow. "Now that Charlie's found them, you mean?" he said with a smirk. "If memory serves, you two prats *lost* the one that you found."

Singh cringed at the jibe. "Yeah, well, that's Geoff's fault," he said defensively. "He was so keen to follow the shooter out of the shop that he forgot to pay for the snacks he was holding, and the sales assistant detained him for a bit of shoplifting."

Dillon's eyes narrowed accusingly as he turned to face Coles. "Tell me that's not true?"

Geoff blushed profusely, and then glared at Christine who had doubled over in a fit of uncontrollable laughter. "It's not *that* funny, Chrissy," he snapped.

"It is," she replied, wiping away the tears that were running down her cheeks. "It *so* is!"

Geoff turned to Dillon, squirming under the intensity of the big man's gaze. His face now resembled a beetroot. "Sorry, boss," he said lamely.

"Useless," Dillon said. "Bloody useless." Shaking his head in despair, and hoping that Murphy hadn't formed the impression that all Met coppers were as dim as Geoff, he turned back to Singh. "I've spoken to Charlie. Apparently all six suspects are due to check out at lunchtime, but they've paid extra for a late checkout, which means they might not leave until two or three o'clock. Charlie's going to remain inside the hotel to keep an eye on them until the gun nuts arrive. Speaking of which, we've got a team of SFOs blue lighting it to us from Lippitts Hill. Hopefully, they'll arrive in time to deploy against the suspects when they leave."

Singh checked his watch and grimaced. "It's gonna be tight," he said.

Dillon shrugged. He was very well aware of that, but what could he do?

Two more pool cars pulled into the car park, which had been designated as the RVP. They cruised around lazily until they spotted their colleagues and then drove over to join them.

Dillon's phone rang. There was no caller ID. "DI Dillon speaking," he said.

"*Boss, it's PS Tim Newman from SO19. Just a quick sitrep for you: we're about ten minutes out. Can I confirm the suspects are still inside the hotel?*" The wail of the siren was loud in the background, almost drowning out Newman's words.

There was a sudden explosion of raucous laughter behind him. Glancing over his shoulder, Dillon saw that Geoff was cringing with embarrassment as Christine told the others the story of his having lost the suspect because he'd been detained for shoplifting.

Serves him bloody right, Dillon thought as he walked a few steps away from them so that he could hear better. "Hi, Tim. Yes, they're still inside. We've placed a man in reception, and as far as we know, they're planning to leave between midday and three o'clock this afternoon."

Newman was virtually having to shout to make himself heard

above the sound of the siren. *"I've got someone on their way to recce the venue and the area outside for a suitable intervention point, but we're going to need the road closed off at either end when we put the strike in, so can I confirm you've got local units on standby for that?"*

Dillon groaned inwardly. There had been no time to organise that. "Not yet, Tim, but I'll get straight on it," he promised.

Killing the call, he dialled the number for the Control Room at Newham. The Duty Officer was going to love him, springing an armed operation on the borough with zero advanced warning.

CHAPTER THIRTY

WE MIGHT HAVE A BIT OF A SITUATION HERE

Steve Bull had walked all the way through the park and back again. Wiping his brow, he hit the fob to open the central locking and slid into the car. He started the engine and cranked the air con up to full blast to cool him off. While it worked its magic, he checked the notes in his folder to see what Tyson Meek's address was.

The phone rang. It was Dean, calling him from the office. "What's up, Deano?"

"*It's all go here,*" Dean said. "*Mr Tyler's had the witness protection people on the line, wanting to know if we found Meeks. Apparently, they're talking about kicking him out of the programme if he doesn't turn up soon. Anyway, the boss asked me to give you a quick call and see how you were getting on.*"

"They should kick him out, if you ask me," Steve said grumpily. "Tell the boss the park was a blowout. I'm just about to go and knock on the door of his flat, and then I'll be heading back."

As Bull was reading through his notes, he became aware of a car driving by. He didn't so much see it as feel it, thanks to the ridiculously loud bass from the car's boom box making his chest vibrate. Bull glanced up angrily at the black BMW coupé with its tinted windows. He watched as it pulled into the kerb a little way ahead, disappearing behind a little red Corsa that had seen better days.

Bull frowned. There was something familiar about the Corsa. He grabbed his daybook and began frantically flicking through the pages until he found the registration number of the Corsa that had been following the Turk's Mercedes on Tuesday evening.

Despite the heat, he felt his blood run cold.

It was the same car.

Scooping his mobile off the front passenger seat, where he'd tossed it after terminating Dean's call, he quickly dialled Tyler's number. "Come on, come on," he urged. "Pick up the bloody phone."

And then, things got even more interesting as the BMW's driver door opened and Conrad Livingstone emerged from within.

"Oh shit!" Bull whispered as he caught sight of the gun in Livingstone's gloved hand.

Livingstone worked the breech of the pistol, chambering a round, and then tucked the gun into the small of his back. He reached inside the car, behind the driver's seat, and retrieved a small wooden box, about a foot square and approximately four inches deep. Slamming the door, he set off towards the stairwell for Touchard House, aiming the key fob back over his shoulder to lock the car as he went.

"*DCI Tyler,*" a voice said in his ear.

Bull watched with baited breath until Livingstone appeared on the first floor balcony and walked up to a door about halfway along.

"*Hello…?*"

A moment later, the door opened, just a slit at first, and then wide enough to admit him. After Livingstone had gone in, a black man with dreads poked his head out and quickly looked right and left before withdrawing it and closing the door behind him. Bull only got a fleeting glimpse of the man, but that was enough to identify him as Daryl Peters.

"*Steve, is that you…?*"

What the hell where Daryl Peters and Conrad Livingstone doing at

Tyson Meeks' flat? Were they lying in wait for him, planning to ambush him when he came home?

"*STEVE!*"

Bull jumped, instinctively pulling the handset away from his ear. "Sorry boss," he said, trying to gather his thoughts. "Listen, I hate to be the bearer of bad news, but I think we might have a bit of a situation going on here."

————

Charlie White was standing behind the reception counter, quietly humming along to a piano version of Harold Arlen's 1939 ballad, *Over The Rainbow*, while keeping a watchful eye out for the suspects. Peabody had helpfully provided him with an ill-fitting staff blazer so that he could blend into his surroundings without drawing unwanted attention.

Glancing over in the direction of the lifts, his heart did a little flip as one of the Kalu twins emerged from the nearest one and headed straight towards him, a mean scowl plastered across his chubby face.

Charlie immediately made himself busy. Staring fastidiously at the blank screen in front of him, he started tapping away at the keyboard, pretending to make an entry on the computer. The young lady who was working reception was currently fielding a phone call, so Kalu walked straight up to Charlie. "I need to order two taxis for a twelve thirty pick up," he said gruffly.

"If you'll just wait a wee moment, my colleague will organise that for you," Charlie said without looking up.

Kalu sucked through his teeth to show his displeasure. "Why can't you do it?" he demanded confrontationally. "Is sorting me out a couple of cabs beneath you or something?"

Inwardly cringing, Charlie looked into the man's beady eyes and forced a smile. "Of course not," he said through gritted teeth. "Give me your room number, the details of how many people will be travelling, and where you all want to go, and I'll happily arrange it for you."

Kalu leaned on the counter. "I'm in room 101. Why do you need any other details?" he demanded, glaring at White suspiciously.

Charlie took a deep breath. "Because the cab company will want to know the number of passengers and the destination – they always do," he said patiently.

Kalu's brow furrowed as he processed this, and Charlie had to resist the urge to do a theatrical yawn and look down at his watch to make the point that he didn't have all day.

"Yeah, alright," Kalu begrudgingly said a few moments later. "There's going to be three passengers in each cab, and we're all going to London Euston."

Charlie scribbled this information down on a sheet of headed paper he found on one of the shelves under the counter. "Very well. I'll book them for you now. Do you want a call in your room to confirm the booking?"

The man considered this with irritating slowness. "Yeah, alright," he eventually replied.

"And who should I ask for when I call?" Charlie asked, wondering whether Kalu would be stupid enough to give his real name.

Kalu's nostrils flared in anger. "My name's Mr mind-your-fucking-business," he replied, pushing himself away from the counter.

Charlie blinked in surprise, but recovered quickly. "I see," he replied with a sugar coated smile, "and do you spell that all as one word or is it hyphenated?"

———

A cruel smile of satisfaction crept onto Livingstone's face as he gazed down upon Tyson Meeks, clad in nothing but his boxers and socks, and bound to a chair in the middle of his own lounge. Livingstone noted that the skin of Meeks' arms and torso was criss-crossed with lacerations where the barbed wire had bitten into his flesh, tearing it open a little more every time he moved. Little trickles of blood ran from the worst of the cuts, gradually diluting as they merged with the perspiration that covered his body.

"That's a nice touch," Livingstone remarked. "Whose idea was it to use barbed wire?"

"It was Jerome's idea, bruv," Gunz said. "You know what a sick fuck he is."

Livingstone nodded. He did, indeed. In fact, Jerome was probably the most sadistic person that he had ever met. Not even Goliath could match his ingenuity when it came to dreaming up new ways of inflicting pain on those who displeased him.

"What do you think, Weasel?" he asked conversationally. "Do you think Jerome's a sick fuck?"

Tyson's eyes momentarily blazed with defiance. As he twisted to follow Livingstone's movements, the barb wire cut deeper into his flesh, and his face contorted in a rictus of pain.

"Hurts does it? Having all that wire wrapped around you," Livingstone smirked.

Baring his teeth in anger, Tyson made a feeble effort to spit at him, but the sputum merely dribbled down his chin and landed in his lap.

Although Livingstone laughed at Weasel's feeble display of bravado, Gunz found it less amusing. He stepped forward to slap him hard across the face.

"You need to remember your manners, Tyson, innit," he warned.

As Livingstone slowly circled his captive, he found himself comparing Meeks' predicament to that of Tyrone, the second of the two drug runners Goliath had so casually murdered in front of him during their encounter up in Manchester. Unlike Tyrone, Weasel hadn't soiled himself, although that might well change when Livingstone went to work on him.

"Nice place you got here, Weasel," he said, casting his eye around the room.

Standing behind him, Gunz sniggered.

Marcel, who had been banished to the kitchen while Gunz answered the street door, suddenly came rushing into the room, with Jerome hot on his heels.

"Oi! Come back here, younger," Jerome yelled angrily. When he caught up with the boy, he grabbed Marcel by the scruff of the neck and started dragging him back out of the room.

Livingstone held up a hand to show it was okay, and Jerome reluctantly backed off.

From just inside the doorway, Marcel's eyes darted between Living-stone and his brother. "Conrad, what's going on?" he demanded breathlessly. "You told me you were trying to help Tyson, so why's he trussed up like that?"

Livingstone studied the boy dispassionately. His reaction to the events that were about to unfold would determine whether one or two members of the Meeks family died inside this flat today.

"Marcel, I'm afraid I wasn't completely honest with you," he said, bowing his head apologetically. "Fact is, your brother's a no good grass who betrayed me to the Feds. This worthless pile of shit sold me out to earn himself a few quid from the informer's fund." He glanced contemptuously at Tyson. "Aint that right, bruv?"

Marcel's face registered disgust when the word 'grass' was used. Growing up on the streets, the first thing you learned was that you *never* snitched on anyone, no matter what.

Blinking back hot tears of shame, Tyson seemed to wilt under his brother's reproachful stare. "Marcel, it aint as simple as that. Yes, I *did* give Conrad up to the Feds, but only because he was trying to start a war between the Turks and Albanians. Honestly, bruv, I'm not chatting shit. He was planning to cause a bloodbath just so that he could sell more fucking drugs than them."

Livingstone's voice took on a tone of sympathy. "I know he's your brother, younger, but surely you can see that I can't let Weasel's conduct go unpunished?"

Marcel nodded, timidly. "What are you going to do to him?" he asked.

"I'm going to beat him to within an inch of his life," Livingstone said, studying the boy carefully.

Marcel swallowed hard. "He deserves it, I suppose," he said in a quivering voice.

"He does," Livingstone confirmed. "In fact, he deserves a lot worse than a beating, which is why, when I'm finished, you're going to shoot him dead for me."

Marcel stiffened. "W-what? No way, bruv," he stammered. "I aint doing that." Shaking his head, Marcel took a backward step towards the hallway.

Norris was waiting for him, and he sent Marcel stumbling back into the middle of the room with a firm shove, laughing at the boy's discomfort.

"You have to, younger," Livingstone said with finality. "I need to know that I can trust you, and the only way I can be sure of that is for you to kill him. Otherwise, what's to stop you ratting me out further down the line, just like your brother did?"

Marcel was now shaking his head violently. When he finally found his voice, it was tremulous. "Conrad, I know he's done bad, and I get it that he deserves a beating, but you don't need to kill him, and you can't seriously expect me to shoot my own brother?"

Livingstone smiled indulgently. "Younger, listen to me," he said softly. "Weasel's got to die. That's all there is to it, and you're gonna be the one to pull the trigger." He stepped forward and wrapped a caring arm around the boy's shoulders. Ignoring the boy's attempts to pull free, he hugged Marcel to him. "It has to be that way, so there's no point you fretting over it."

"Nah, bruv. Aint gonna happen," Marcel said, finally managing to shrug him off.

Livingstone held up a finger to shush him.

"I know it won't be easy, but it'll be over in a second, and then, with Weasel out of the way, me and you can finally start getting to know each other a bit better." He stood directly in front of Marcel, placing a firm hand on each shoulder and staring straight into the boy's glistening eyes. "Deep down, you know you'll be better off without that idiot in your life."

Marcel looked away. "I know he's an idiot, but he's still my brother, innit."

"Don't worry," Livingstone reassured him. "You won't be alone. You'll have me by your side." He grinned as he cast Tyson a disparaging glance. "I mean, let's be honest, bruv, who would you rather have looking out for you, me or *that* low-life piece of shit?"

Marcel glanced nervously across at his brother but, as he opened his mouth to speak, Livingstone took a firm hold of his jaw and jerked his head back around to face him.

"I'll tell you what, younger," he said impatiently. "For your sake, I won't give him the beating he so richly deserves. Let's skip past that part of the plan and just put Weasel out of his misery." He nodded at Gunz, to whom he had handed the wooden box he had been carrying upon his arrival.

Holding it out in front of him, so that Marcel could see what he was doing, Gunz undid the two metal clasps that secured it and opened the box. Inside, on a bed of faux velvet, was a gleaming, silver Taurus Model 85 snub-nosed revolver with a chunky black rubber grip and a two inch barrel. He gently removed it and handed it over to his boss.

"You ever fired a gun before, younger?" Livingstone asked, noticing the look of horror that had appeared on the boy's face.

Unable to speak, Marcel shook his head skittishly.

Livingstone levelled the gun at Tyson Meeks, who cowered in the chair, eyes wide with fear.

"Using a gun's no big deal, bruv. All you gotta do is point it at that motherfucker's scrawny chest, cock it like this-" he placed his thumb on the hammer and drew it back with a click, "-and then pull the trigger."

Tyson was frantically shaking his head. "Please, bruv," he begged. "Please don't make my little brother do this."

Livingstone's face contorted with rage. He lowered the hammer and stomped across the room. "You should've thought about how this was going to end before you grassed me to the Feds, bruv," he snarled at Tyson. And then, to ensure that Marcel couldn't hear, he leaned down to whisper in his captive's ear. "I'm gonna make him pull the fucking trigger. And I promise you, bruv, if he doesn't merk you for me, I'm gonna waste him, too."

"You're fucking mad," Tyson snarled, so angry that he hardly even felt his flesh tearing as the barbed wire cut deeper into him.

Livingstone tapped him on the forehead with the barrel of the gun. "Here's the deal, Weasel. Whatever happens, you're dead, but if your brother doesn't pull the trigger when I tell him to, I'll kill him too. And you know what? I'll make you watch him die before I put a bullet in your feeble brain."

Ignoring the agony it caused him, Tyson tried to lunge forward and bite the side of Livingstone's face. "You filthy piece of-"

It was a futile gesture, and Livingstone responded by striking him across the temple with the gun. He immediately followed this up with a backhanded blow across the side of the face. As Tyson's head rocked to the side, blood spilled from a jagged gash that appeared in his right cheek. Succumbing to his rage, Livingstone began repeatedly pistol whipping him about the head and face, only stopping when it was clear that Tyson had passed out.

Breathing heavily, Livingstone stepped back and studied the battered and bloody man in front of him with cold detachment. He felt no remorse; Tyson was a grass and he was getting exactly what he deserved. Behind him, he became aware of Gunz restraining Marcel, who was now sobbing uncontrollably as he desperately tried to reach his unconscious brother.

Wiping his brow with his sleeve, Livingstone walked back over to Marcel, hand extended. "Stop blabbing like a little bitch and take the gun, younger," he ordered. "It's time for you to pick a side."

———

As Gold Commander for the Beckton firearms deployment, Tyler would have preferred to remain in the office where he could coordinate resources and make effective command decisions. However, with Dillon out running the SFO deployment at the hotel, the only person of sufficiently senior rank to oversee the SFO entry in Hackney was him. It was most unsatisfactory, but there was nothing he could do about it. And, as almost everyone from his own team had been sent over to Beckton to help out there, he had been forced to borrow a couple of people from Andy Quinlan's team to assist him with the unfolding situation at Touchard House.

Susie Sergeant had volunteered to drive him there, and they were now making their way down to the scene at warp speed on blues and twos. Kevin Murray had been coerced into joining them, just in case they needed an advanced exhibits officer, and he was currently bouncing about uncomfortably in the back of the unmarked Vectra as it weaved its way through the morning traffic in Hackney Road.

"Bloody hell, Susie," he yelled as she powered the unmarked police car through an extremely tight overtaking manoeuvre. "I'd like to get there in one piece if it's at all possible."

"Stop whinging, you big girl's blouse," she called over her shoulder. "You don't hear Mr Tyler complaining, do you?"

Sitting beside her, Tyler's smile was grim. "I'm too busy praying to speak," he told her.

"Ha-bloody-ha!" she responded, making the car go even faster. "I'm surrounded by wimps, so I am."

Tyler's phone rang. Without taking his eyes from the road, he pulled it from his jacket and answered. "DCI Tyler."

"*Boss, it's Steve. I've got two ARVs on scene with me now. Do you want us to do anything before you get here?*"

Tyler reluctantly released the grab handle above his door and stuck a finger in his ear to block out the noise of the siren. "Steve, I don't want Livingstone looking out of the window and seeing two marked units down in the street below, so get the ARV crews moved, pronto. Tell them to RVP with me at Charles Square, which is just-"

"*I know where it is, boss,*" Bull interrupted. "*I used to work this ground, remember?*"

"So you did. Listen, get them away from the front of the block, sharpish. When you've done that, I've got an urgent tasking for you."

Bull groaned. "*I don't like the sound of that,*" he admitted.

Tyler didn't blame him. "An SFO team's been despatched from Lippitts Hill," he said, trying to make himself heard above the combined din of the two-tones and Murray's whimpering. "It should be arriving at the RVP within the next few minutes. The team leader's asked if there's any way you can do a quick recce for him. He specifically wants to know what Meeks' street door's made of, how many locks are on it, what type they are, and which way it opens. Realistically, the only way you'll get that information is by taking a stroll past the front of the address. As if that's not enough, he also wants you to recce the back of the block to see where it leads."

"*I'll give it a go boss,*" Bull replied, unenthusiastically, "*but I'm wearing a suit so I stick out a bit.*"

"Just do your best," Tyler said. "And listen, only do what you can. I don't want you putting yourself in harm's way."

"*Okay, leave it to me,*" Bull said, glumly.

"One last thing," Tyler added. "Do you have any idea how many people are inside the flat?"

Bull blew out his breath in a long sigh. "*Two for sure, but other than that, who knows?*"

Tyler grunted his thanks and hung up.

Despite Susie's hair raising driving, Tyler retreated into himself for the remainder of the journey.

As he saw it, there were only two possible scenarios. In the first, Livingstone and at least one of his cronies was waiting inside Tyson's flat for him to arrive back home. If that was the case, Tyler would simply put in an armed containment and have SO19 call them out. If they started playing silly buggers and barricaded themselves in for a couple of days before complying, it really wasn't that big a deal. It was the second scenario that was causing him so much angst, because that involved Tyson Meeks already being trapped inside the flat with them. The fact that Livingstone was armed was a clear indication that he intended to kill Tyson Meeks for snitching on him.

If Meeks was in there, Tyler would need to act quickly and decisively, initiating a course of action that could easily endanger both the hostage and the specialist officers he sent in to rescue him.

———

At the RVP in Beckton, Dillon was explaining the situation to PS Newman. The two of them were sitting alone in Dillon's pool car, going through the scenario and discussing options and tactics.

The SFO team had arrived in two dark blue transit vans with blacked out windows ten minutes previously, and the rest of the team where busy checking and double checking their equipment in readiness for the coming deployment.

Newman, clad in his black, fire-retardant Nomex overalls, had been surprised, not to mention a little concerned, to hear that they were about to tackle the same three black men that his team had detained on Tuesday evening.

"Just so I've got this straight in my head, guv," he said, staring at Dillon sceptically. "You're telling me that this Adebanjo bloke and his two associates deliberately set themselves up to be arrested last time, just to create a smokescreen so that the three Eastern Europeans could carry out a hit on the Turks in Green Lanes?"

"That's right," Dillon confirmed, and then he commenced to give Newman an abbreviated version of all the events that had occurred since the SFO's last involvement a few days earlier. "So you see," he concluded, "we think that, as far as they're concerned, the job they came here to do is now complete, and they've regrouped at this hotel in order to travel back to Manchester together."

Newman frowned. "And you think Adebanjo and the Kalu twins will be unarmed?"

Dillon nodded. "We do," he said, but there was a note of caution in his voice. "Of course, we can't guarantee it."

Newman pondered this. "Well, knowing the others have ready access to automatic weapons, we have to proceed on the basis that they're all armed."

"I wholeheartedly agree," Dillon said.

Newman drummed his fingers against his chin. "And you think the three Eastern Europeans will definitely still have their firearms with them?"

Dillon shrugged. "There's no way of telling, Tim," he said with regret. "However, my instinct tells me that they will."

"No offence, but I need hard intel, not instinct," Newman pointed out.

"I know," Dillon conceded. His face became grave. "Listen, Tim, everything I've heard about the shooters makes me think they're former military types, and they acted with such clinical precision during both attacks that I'm genuinely worried they might be prepared for this, and that all hell will break loose when you confront them."

Newman flicked through the photographs that Dillon had handed him, taking a moment to study each face while he composed his thoughts. "You could be right," he finally said. "During my service with the Para's, I came across men like these. Life was cheap to them, even their own."

"We've managed to place a man inside reception," Dillon said. "Through him, we've established that they've ordered two cabs for a twelve-thirty pick up to take them to Euston."

"Okay. That's good. Let's assume that the suspects will all come down to reception a few minutes before their cabs arrive so that they can check out," Newman hypothesised. "Say at twenty past the hour. Will your man be able to give us a live time feed of information as this happens?"

Dillon nodded. "Yes, definitely. He'll be able to watch them from within the duty manager's office and relay their movements to us via the phone."

"That'll be very helpful," Newman told him. "In the meantime, I've sent someone in plain clothes to recce the front of the hotel. When he gets here, we'll work out the battle plan, but my initial thoughts are that the safest place to make the interdiction is directly outside the front of the hotel. As the premises is located within its own grounds, there'll be no passing vehicles or foot traffic for us to worry about. As soon as the suspects leave, your man will have to stop anyone else from leaving the hotel. Can that be arranged?"

"It can," Dillon said, "and I'll discreetly slip another officer into the hotel beforehand to give him a hand."

"What about support from the locals?" Newman asked. "I'll need the road outside closed off in both directions as soon as we move in."

"All taken care of," Dillon said, pointing to the two marked vehicles that were parked a little further along the road. "The Duty Officer wasn't best pleased, but she sent me four officers to assist."

Newman seemed satisfied. "Right, well, in that case I'd better start briefing my troops," he said, grunting at the effort it took to prise open the ancient Astra's creaking passenger door.

———

To the annoyance of Gunz and Norris, who had both been keen to crack on, Livingstone had insisted that they wait until Meeks stirred before allowing the proceedings to continue.

When Tyson's eyes finally flickered, signalling the first signs of returning consciousness, Livingstone walked over and yanked his head up by the hair. "Wakey-wakey, Weasel," he said cheerfully.

"Finally, bruv," Gunz grumbled, making a point of rolling his eyes impatiently.

Marcel recoiled at the sight of his brother's injuries. Tyson's entire face was puffy and smeared with blood, and there were angry purple welts coming up around the jagged cut on his cheek, from which a large flap of skin hung down, exposing the bone beneath. One eye was so badly swollen that he could hardly open it, and his mouth was oozing a steady stream of blood.

"Please…" Tyson moaned, his voice no more than a strained slur.

Releasing Tyson's head to flop back down onto his chest, Livingstone strode over to Marcel's side. Eyes glinting with malice, he held out the hand containing the shiny silver revolver for a second time. "Take it this time, younger," he insisted.

Marcel had flatly refused when it had been offered to him a few minutes earlier, and he had promptly received a black eye for his non-compliance, along with a sinister promise that any subsequent refusals would be dealt with much more harshly.

Marcel reluctantly did as he was told, surprised by the firearm's weight. It felt solid and substantial in his hand. Holding the weapon gingerly, he gazed down at it with trepidation.

"Feels good, don't it, younger?" Livingstone said, smiling at him encouragingly. "Now, be a good boy and point it at Weasel."

The gun wavered unsteadily in Marcel's hand as he began to raise it, but then he faltered and lowered it again, unable to bring it to bear on his incapacitated brother.

Livingstone grabbed his wrist, pulling his arm around until the gun was pointing at Tyson's centre mass. "There you go," he said, as though he had just done the boy a favour. "Now, thumb the hammer back the way I showed you."

"I - I can't," Marcel stammered as tears prickled his eyes.

"Yes you can," Livingstone insisted. Leaning in, he lowered his voice as though addressing a young child with a learning disability, making sure that he pronounced each word slowly and clearly. "Do. It. Now."

Every fibre in Marcel's being called out for him to drop the gun and make a run for it, but he found himself frozen to the spot, as if pinned down by some powerful gravitational force.

Livingstone just stood there in silence, head cocked, listening to Marcel's ragged breathing.

"Please…" Tyson croaked from the chair, his voice frail and brittle. "Let… let the boy go."

Livingstone ignored him. "Cock the gun, bruv," he barked, and there was a dangerous edge to his voice.

Marcel flinched at the harsh command. Hand shaking, he thumbed back the hammer as he'd been told, finding it much harder to do than he'd imagined it would be.

Marcel was painfully aware that Jerome Norris was leaning against the doorframe behind him, watching eagerly. Gunz was standing off to his left and, out of the corner of his eye, Marcel saw him light up another spliff. Dropping the smouldering match onto the plastic sheeting beneath his feet, Gunz puffed out a large plume of smoke.

An insane idea suddenly occurred to Marcel. Maybe, seeing as he was the only one in the room with a gun, he could force the elders to untie his brother and they could make good their escape together.

"Now," Livingstone whispered seductively, "just pull the trigger, bruv. And don't worry about the kick. It aint that bad."

With a huge effort, Tyson dragged his head off his chest and looked up at his brother. Marcel could see that he was badly dazed from the beating he'd received.

"I love you Marcel," Tyson blurted out.

"I love you too," Marcel replied. Like his brother, he was crying unashamedly.

"Very touching," Livingstone said, clapping his hands. "Now. Pull. The. Fucking. Trigger."

"I can't," Marcel sobbed, lowering the gun and wiping at his eyes with his sleeve.

Livingstone put his hands on his hips. "Tyson, remember what I said. You know what'll happen if he doesn't do it."

Tyson swallowed hard. "Marcel, listen to me…" he croaked, chest heaving from the effort of speaking, "I know it's hard, bruv, but I want you to close your eyes… and do as Conrad says."

"No, Tyson. I won't do it," Marcel screamed, horrified that his brother would even suggest something so terrible. It was absurd.

Livingstone stared from one to the other in growing incredulity. Reaching behind his back, he pulled the concealed pistol from his waistband. Crossing to the chair in two quick strides, he jammed the Baikal against the side of Tyson's skull. "Enough is enough, younger," he warned. "I'm telling you, if you don't pull the trigger right now, I swear I will."

At that moment, Marcel finally realised that there was no good way for this to end, and that there was only one thing left for him to do. "Okay, I'll do it," he heard himself shout, hardly recognising the sound of his own voice, so much had the strain he was under changed it. "Move out of the way in case I miss," he said, indicating for Livingstone to step aside with a wave of the gun.

To Marcel's intense relief, Livingstone complied with his request, lowering his gun hand to his side in the process.

"Do it now," the gang leader ordered.

"Okay," Marcel responded with a quivering voice. Licking his lips nervously, the teenager clumsily took aim. "I'm so sorry I behaved like such a dick to you, Tyson," he said, almost choking on his remorse. And then, as his finger tightened on the trigger, he pivoted until the gun was pointing directly at Livingstone's stomach.

The gangster's eyes narrowed. "What the fuck you playing at, younger?"

Gritting his teeth against the expected recoil, Marcel squeezed the trigger hard, easily exerting the six pounds of pressure required to fire the gun.

The explosion that followed was deafeningly loud within the confines of the small room, and it was accompanied by a bright flash that spurted from the end of the gun's muzzle.

Livingstone had been right, he reflected as he squeezed the trigger a second time, the kick really wasn't that bad.

CHAPTER THIRTY-ONE

SHOTS FIRED

The time had almost arrived for them to check out of the hotel, and yet there was still no sign of the man Livingstone was supposed to be sending to retrieve the guns from his men. Adebanjo checked his watch again and then reached for the burner on his bedside table. "It is most unprofessional," he said to himself, tutting disapprovingly.

"Perhaps they've been delayed," Isaac Kalu suggested.

"Yeah, perhaps they've been delayed," his brother, Andre, parroted.

Standing by the door, both men were wearing identical red T-shirts and jeans.

Adebanjo rang Livingstone's number, but there was no answer, which was highly unusual, and he began to wonder if anything had gone wrong.

"Andre," he said, "go and tell Dritan and the others to get ready to leave. Tell them that they may have to take the weapons with them, for us to dispose of later."

The black man nodded respectfully. "Yes, boss," he said, before slipping quietly out of the room.

"Is that wise?" Isaac asked when they were alone.

Adebanjo shrugged. "We may not have a choice. Mr Livingstone is not answering his phone." He lapsed into silence and began pacing the room. "We will just have to take them back to Manchester with us and dispose of them there," he eventually said, sounding less than thrilled by the prospect.

Isaac's brow furrowed. "Won't that be risky, boss? Travelling with the guns, I mean."

Adebanjo's rueful smile exposed his golden canines. "It will be but, unfortunately, it's looking like there's no alternative. Anyway, it's a risk that our Romanian friends will have to take, not us."

"They won't be happy," Isaac pointed out.

Adebanjo shrugged. "They are professionals," he said. "They know the risks. They are being very well compensated for taking them, and if anything goes wrong I will ensure that they get the best lawyers money can buy."

The bedroom door opened, and Andre reappeared. "I've told them," he said sullenly. "Dritan wasn't too keen on the idea of taking the guns with them, but he didn't kick up too much of a stink."

Adebanjo pointed towards the door. "Return to your room and gather your belongings. I will see you down in reception in ten minutes."

He waited until they had gone before trying Livingstone's number again. The response was the same: no answer. He pocketed the phone with a troubled sigh, unable to shake the feeling that something must have gone awry at Livingstone's end.

———

Steve Bull had removed his jacket and tie, pulled his shirt tails out of his trousers, and rolled his sleeves up to make himself look a little less smart. Looking in the Omega's wing mirror, he had repeatedly run his hands through his greying brown hair to make it appear dishevelled.

In search of a prop to help him blend in, he had popped into a local newsagents and purchased a copy of the first newspaper he'd seen. This was now folded under his arm, and he hoped it would make him look more like a local than a visiting policeman.

His recce started with a brisk walk through the back of the estate, taking the concrete path that led from Chart Street through to Charles Square and the base of Vince Court. On his way back, on the pretence of stopping to retie his shoelace, he dallied long enough to check out the rear of Meeks' flat. As Tyler had feared, it would be fairly easy for someone to drop down to the ground floor from inside the flat by climbing out of the windows. The boss would have to place armed officers at the rear of the block to cater for that eventuality.

Hoping that he wasn't taking a monumental risk, and wondering what his wife would say if she knew he was doing this, he reluctantly entered the staircase that Livingstone had taken earlier, jogging up to the first floor landing. Pausing at the start of the balcony, he poked his head around the corner to ensure that none of the residents were out on it. Thankfully, all was clear, but he was acutely aware that could change at any second.

Taking a deep breath to steady his spiralling nerves, Bull stepped out from behind the stairway wall and walked along the landing with feigned purpose. On the approach to Meeks' flat, he slowed down to buy himself the time he needed to evaluate the street door. It was made from solid wood, and fitted with two locks. The first was a Yale, and the second a more substantial Chubb. The door opened inwards, he saw, going from right to left, and he noted that four hinges secured it to the robust looking frame.

Perfect. That was all the information Tyler had requested.

Sweating just as much from his fear of being discovered as from the blistering heat, Bull carried on walking, affording himself a quick glance through the kitchen window as he passed it.

The kitchen was small, cluttered and very untidy. The floral wallpaper had strips missing and was full of air pockets, suggesting damp. A naked bulb dangled from a dust covered wire in the middle of the ceiling. There was a small fridge, an ancient gas cooker that had dried food stains plastered all over the hob, and a washing machine that looked like it needed emptying. The flip top bin by the door was so full that the lid wouldn't close, and it was surrounded by a swarm of buzzing flies. A small sink sat directly beneath the window, and that was stacked full of dirty plates and cutlery. A wooden table rested against the far wall, with two rickety chairs tucked underneath it.

Bull continued walking until he reached the next flat along. He paused by the door for a few moments, as though he were waiting for someone to open it for him, and he then turned around and set off on a reciprocal route along the balcony, stealing another quick glimpse inside Meeks' kitchen as he walked by window.

As he cleared the flat, intent on reaching the staircase as quickly as he could, the unmistakable sound of a gunshot came from within Meeks' flat. Almost immediately, a second one followed.

"Shit!" Bull exclaimed, dropping the newspaper, along with any further attempts to remain low key, and breaking into a run.

———

The SFO team was waiting for Tyler when he and his two colleagues arrived at Charles Square. A blue van with blacked out windows was parked on double yellow lines a little way in from the junction with Pitfield Street, and a dark green VW Jetta containing four tough looking men in dark overalls was directly in front of it.

Susie pulled level with the Jetta and wound down her window. The dark haired, square jawed front passenger in the other car did likewise, fixing her with an ice cold stare.

"Can I help you?" he asked.

"I'm DS Sergeant, and this is DCI Tyler," she said, indicating Jack with a jut of her head.

The man's face immediately relaxed into a smile. "PS Tod Marshall," he said. "I'm the SFO Team Leader."

Tyler leaned across Susie. "Tod, if you follow us down to the park, I'll run you through what we've got," he instructed.

Marshall nodded obligingly. "Lead the way," he said with a gallant wave of his hand.

With the two unmarked SO19 vehicles in tow, Susie drove to the end of the road, stopping beside a walkway beneath the flats that led through to Old Street.

Two marked Armed Response Vehicles, each containing three uniform officers were already there, having been sent to the RVP by Steve Bull a little earlier.

After the introductions were made, Jack indicated for Susie, Tod Marshall, and a uniform skipper from one of the ARVs to follow him.

He led them across the road and stopped by the railings of the small park that occupied the centre of Charles Square. The park's perimeter was surrounded by tall trees, and he picked a nice shaded spot beneath their overhanging branches.

Jack pointed straight through the park to a five storey block of flats on the other side. "That's the back of Touchard House," he said without preamble. "The walkway you can see leads through to Chart Street, and the target address is reached via an entrance on that side of the block."

"It's a first floor flat, is that right?" Marshall asked.

"That's correct," Tyler confirmed. "One of my officers is carrying out a recce for you, and he should be reporting back to me any second now."

"I've already had a look at the front of the premises," Steve Pullman, the ARV skipper, informed Marshall. "I can talk you through it afterward, if you want." He was a solidly built man from the West Country, with a salt and pepper crewcut and wraparound sunglasses, and he had the ramrod straight bearing of an ex-military man.

"Yes, please," Marshall said. "Although I used to work this ground before transferring to SO19, so I'm actually very familiar with the estate."

"That's good to know," Tyler said. "Anyway, to cut a long story short, the occupant of the flat we want you to enter is called Tyson Meeks. This morning, he did a bunk from witness protection in order to meet up with his brother. We think the meet was arranged to take place in a small park directly opposite Meeks' flat-"

"Do you mean Aske Gardens?" Marshall interrupted.

"Yes, I do," Tyler said. "The officer I sent to check the park didn't find any trace of Meeks or his brother, but while he was there Meeks' boss, a nasty piece of work who goes by the name of Conrad Living-stone, arrived and went into the flat. Livingstone's the one that Meeks is giving evidence against, so he has a vested interest in silencing our man, and he was carrying a handgun when he arrived. What's equally worrying is that my man spotted a red Corsa parked outside the flat. It's connected to Livingstone's gang, and was involved in the two Turkish shootings that have been earning your mob so much overtime this week."

Pullman smiled at that. "It's earned me a few quid, that's for sure."

"So you think this chap Meeks is being held inside his flat by Livingstone and some of his gangster friends?" Marshall asked, frowning as he considered the logistics.

"Either that or they're waiting in there for him to arrive," Tyler said grimly.

Marshall considered this. "Do we have any firm intel that your witness is actually inside?" he asked. "If he's not, I'm inclined to move things forward at a slower rate, by which I mean putting in an armed containment and calling the suspects out as opposed to forcing entry, which we'd probably have to do if we thought he was inside and in imminent danger."

A pained expression crossed Tyler's features. "At the moment, I just don't know," he admitted.

"Do you at least know how many people are inside?" Marshall asked.

"Apart from Livingstone, and a thug called Daryl Peters, we have no idea."

The sound of high revving engines made Tyler look up just in time to witness two marked vehicles, an Immediate Response Vehicle and a Leyland DAF Station Van, turn into Charles Square from Pitfield street. In dramatic fashion, they screeched to a halt behind the unmarked SO19 van.

The first person out of the IRV was a slim woman in her mid-thir-ties. She had a pretty, but slightly stern face, and was dressed in the uniform of an inspector. This would be Sue Hillary, the Duty Officer he had been liaising with via the phone. Her driver was a portly male in his mid-forties, with a thick thatch of brown hair and the chevrons of a sergeant displayed on his epaulettes.

Tyler raised a hand in greeting, and indicated for the two local supervisors to join them by the park. However, before he could introduce himself to the newcomers, Jack's mobile went off. Apologising, and asking Susie to bring them up to speed on his behalf, he answered the call. "DCI Tyler speaking."

"*Boss, it's Steve*," Bull said, sounding out of breath and seriously stressed. "*We've got shots fired within the address*," he yelled. "*I repeat, shots have just been fired inside Meeks' flat!*

———

Everything that had happened during the past few seconds seemed to have whizzed by in a blur. Marcel had managed to shoot Livingstone twice before Gunz and Norris had rushed forward to overpower him and wrestle the revolver from his grip. They had reacted faster than him, grabbing hold of his limbs before he could even think about turning the gun on them. It was, he reflected as he stood there, powerless to move, almost as though they had been expecting him to do exactly that.

"Relax younger," Gunz said as Marcel tried in vain to pull free. The spliff he'd lit earlier was dangling precariously from his lip as he grinned at Marcel.

As the thick cloud of cordite in front of his face slowly dissipated, Marcel was able to take stock of his surroundings again. He had fully expected to see Livingstone's bullet ridden corpse lying on the floor in front of him. Instead, the man he had just shot twice was standing there, apparently unharmed, shaking his head in sorrow.

"Marcel, you've let us both down," he said, tucking his pistol into his waistband and moving forward to take the revolver from Gunz' outstretched hand.

Marcel was incredulous. "I don't understand," he panted. "I shot you! Twice!"

Livingstone opened the revolver's cylinder and poured the contents into the palm of his left hand. "Do you think I'm stupid, Bruv?" he demanded, fixing the boy with a contemptuous stare. "Do you honestly think I'm dumb enough to give a punk like you a gun with real bullets in it?" He rattled the five shells in his hand. "These are blanks, bruv. Just blanks."

With a sudden jolt of clarity, Marcel understood that Livingstone had set him up to test his loyalty.

"I told you he wouldn't have the balls to kill his brother," Norris gloated. "Boy's a feeble minded retard, just like Weasel."

"Shut up, Jerome," Livingstone responded, angrily. Then, with a note of resignation, he added, "tie him up."

Switch fetched some cable ties from the kitchen, and bound Marcel's hands tightly behind his back. On Livingstone's instruction, Marcel was dragged over to the couch in the corner and forced to take a seat.

"I'm truly disappointed," Livingstone announced as he looked down into Marcel's terror stricken eyes. "I was really hoping me and you would get to be close, and that you would become my protege. But now…" He let the words taper off, leaving Marcel to ponder his fate.

"Please…" Tyson's plea came out as a scratchy rasp.

Livingstone turned to face him, a look of mild curiosity on his face. "Now what?" he asked impatiently.

"Conrad… he's your son," Tyson wheezed, spraying blood from his shattered mouth. "You can't kill him…" His face was a mask of pain, and he was clearly finding it difficult to speak.

Marcel suspected that one of Livingstone's blows had broken his brother's jaw.

Tyson coughed, and spat out the remnant of a tooth. "I'm begging you bruv," he continued. "If you ever felt anything for our mum, then please spare Marcel's life for her sake."

Livingstone shook his head vehemently. "He's *not* my son, Tyson," he shouted. After pausing for a couple of breaths, he turned to face Marcel and shrugged apologetically. "Sorry, younger. I lied about that, too."

"Yeah, well I'm glad you're not my dad," Marcel responded spitefully.

"But you are his dad," Tyson said with unshakable conviction. "My mum told me you were, and he even looks a bit like you."

"I aint nothing like that piece of shit," Marcel called out, and then flinched when Norris grabbed his hair.

"Show some fucking respect," he bellowed in the boy's ear.

Livingstone waited for order to be restored before continuing. "I don't care what she told you, Tyson. Sure, I shagged your whore of a mother a few times, but that was just in lieu of payment for the smack I gave her. I felt nothing for that bitch. *Nothing.*" A calculating look appeared on his face. "In fact, as neither of you will be leaving this room alive, I think it's about time you both knew the truth about the woman you seem to idolise so much. I reckon you've earned the right to die knowing what a foul creature she really was."

"Don't you dare diss my mum like that, you fucking piece of shit!" Marcel roared, endeavouring to push himself up into a standing position.

Norris casually stepped forward, placed a hand on his chest, and shoved him back down into the chair. "If he moves again," he said to Switch, "feel free to hit him."

A malevolent grin spread across Switch's face. "Be a pleasure, bruv," he purred, taking up station beside Marcel.

Livingstone handed the revolver and shells over to Gunz for safe-keeping. "Your mother," he said, placing a hand on Tyson's shoulder, "was a lot like you, Weasel. She was a grass and a loser, and that's why I killed her."

"That's bullshit!" Tyson screamed. "I was there, bruv. She died of a smack overdose. You didn't kill her."

"I assure you, I did," Livingstone bragged.

Marcel was revolted by the callousness of Livingstone's boast, and it sickened him to think that he had once respected the man so much. "Why you even saying these things?" he cried out. "My mum weren't no grass."

"Ah but she was, younger," Livingstone insisted. "You see, your mum and my best friend, Dwayne Nelson, used to be an item, at least until her drug habit got so out of hand that he dumped her sorry ass." He chuckled to himself, but it was a bitter, unpleasant sound bereft of any humour. "She never forgave him for that, and like the evil scheming bitch she was, she bided her time until she could find a way to pay him back for abandoning the two of you for another woman."

The room had gone strangely silent. Despite their anger and indignation, and the growing desperation of their predicament, both Tyson and Marcel found themselves clinging to his every word.

"Well, she finally got her chance when she found out that Dwayne was going into London Fields Boy's territory to visit his baby mother. Back then, Holly Street and LFB were having a few problems, and we tended to shank each other every opportunity we got, especially if one of us strayed into the other's turf without permission. Anyway, she tipped off the LFB that Dwayne was coming over, and a bunch of them pussies jumped him." He shook his head with great sadness. "He never stood a chance, bruv."

"I don't believe you," Tyson said, defiantly.

Livingstone's face darkened. "Like I give a toss what you believe," he said angrily. "I didn't find out for a long while afterwards, innit, but when I finally did, I took great pleasure in getting rid of your low life snitch of a mother."

"But I bought the smack that killed her," Tyson protested. "There's no way you could've have arranged that!"

Livingstone laughed at the scale of his naivety. "It was ridiculously easy, bruv," he boasted. "She phoned me up to say what time she was gonna send you over to get some gear, so all I had to do was have someone waiting outside the block to intercept you. I knew you'd accept a freebie, and that you'd never realise the shotter was really working for me. It was a piece of piss, bruv," he crowed joyfully. "It was the perfect murder."

"I'm gonna fucking kill you," Tyson sobbed.

"I think you'll find it's the other way round, bruv," Livingstone said with a cruel smirk. He checked his watch and frowned. "Right, now that you both know the truth, it's time for me to take my leave." He removed the Baikal pistol from his waistband and flipped off the safety before handing it to Switch. "Well, younger, it looks like you get to take care of two little problems for me today, instead of one. You okay with that?"

Switch grinned. "No problem, bruv," he said, studying the gun in his hands as though it was a thing of wonder.

Livingstone turned to Norris. "You got everything you need to dispose of the bodies afterwards?" he asked.

Norris nodded. "Don't sweat it. I'll let the younger merk them in here, then we'll carry the bodies into the bathroom one at a time and cut them up. I've coated the floor and walls with plastic sheeting, and I've got a good bone saw and lots of self-seal bags. It shouldn't take too long, two or three hours tops. I'll give you a ring when they've been loaded into the car and we're setting off for the canal."

Livingstone patted him on the shoulder. "When you're finished, make sure the gun is properly wiped down and the car is torched. I don't want the Feds finding any DNA or prints, you get me?"

"Trust me, bruv," Norris promised. "I'll take care of everything, just like I always do."

Marcel's head was reeling as Livingstone and Norris left the room. They were going to shoot them and then chop their bodies up. A wave of nausea came over him as he contemplated this.

He strained at the ties behind his back, but they held firm.

Gunz was leaning against the door frame, puffing on the dregs of his joint. Switch was busy practicing with the pistol, alternating aiming it at him and Tyson like a little child with a new toy.

Marcel cast a nervous glance at Tyson, only to see that his brother had passed out again. Feeling his eyes well with tears, he half hoped that Tyson wouldn't wake up, and that he would be spared any further suffering.

Hearing the street door slam shut, Marcel guessed that it would all be over for him pretty soon and he prayed that, when it came, the end would be quick and painless. He was surprised to realise that, now he had resigned himself to his fate, he felt strangely calm. There would be no escape, and there would be no rescue. This was it for him. All he could do now was try and make it through the next few minutes with his dignity intact.

He suddenly found himself thinking about the woman he had stabbed on the train, and a wave of guilt washed over him. He really hadn't meant to stab her. He had just lashed out in anger, forgetting that the knife was even in his hand. He was sorry for his actions, and he sincerely hoped that she would make a full recovery.

As for him and Tyson, well at least they would die together, their differences finally reconciled and all feelings of animosity as dead and buried as they themselves were about to become. He wished that things could have been different between them. In hindsight, the friction that had driven them apart seemed so unimportant now.

The lounge door opened, and Norris entered. "Are you ready, younger?" he asked Switch.

"Fucking A!"

"Let's do it, then," Norris leered.

With all the enthusiasm of a child rushing to open his Christmas presents, Switch strutted over to Marcel, walking with an exaggerated gangsta boy swagger, laughing all the way. Stopping a few steps short of the sofa, he raised the gun and pointed it straight at his head.

"You've always been a loser, bruv," he mocked, turning his left forefinger and thumb into an L and holding it up against his forehead.

Marcel screwed his eyes shut and began praying, knowing that only a miracle would save them now.

CHAPTER THIRTY-TWO

CHECK OUT

When Adebanjo and the Kalu twins appeared in reception, Charlie White ducked straight into the manager's office. They had shown up slightly earlier than anticipated, and he'd only just finished briefing the woman manning the desk on how to deal with them.

Peering out through one of the plastic slats in the blinds, he watched the three men amble over to reception and complete the checkout process. Adebanjo handled the transaction, while the twins leaned on the counter either side of him, making the place look untidy. There were no additional fees to pay, so the checkout process didn't take very long.

Once they'd finished, they relocated to the little cluster of easy chairs on the opposite side of the lobby to await the arrival of the taxi they had booked. Adebanjo flopped down in the exact same seat that Charlie had occupied earlier in the day. He was way too big for it, Charlie thought, watching the giant squirm uncomfortably.

Charlie immediately called Dillon. "Adebanjo and the twins have just checked out, and they're now sitting in the foyer," he said.

He waited while Dillon passed this information on to the Trojan units.

"*Okay,*" Dillon said a few moments later. "*Everything's in place out here. Let me know as soon as the Eastern Europeans check out. Two Trojan officers are going to be posing as minicab drivers. As soon as you give me the signal, we'll send them in. At the same time, the locals will close the road around the hotel. The plan is to intercept the suspects as they approach the fake minicabs. As we discussed earlier, you'll need to lock the sliding doors as soon as they've left the hotel premises.*"

Albert Peabody had already shown Charlie how to work the electronically operated sliding doors, which could be secured at the flick of a switch. Apart from depriving the suspects of a potential escape route when SO19 moved in, locking the doors would also prevent any guests inside the hotel from inadvertently straying into harm's way. Dillon had sent Christine Taylor into the building to assist Charlie, and she was now sitting at the manager's desk behind him, ready to lock the doors the moment he gave her the signal.

"Don't worry, everything's under control this end," Charlie assured him. "I'll call you back the moment the other three appear."

Terminating the call, he turned to Christine and grimaced. "It sounds a bit tense out there. I think we're better off in here, out of the way."

"I think you're right," she agreed.

Albert Peabody was sitting beside Christine, and his eyes were nervously volleying between the two detectives. "I do hope that this isn't going to turn into *Gunfight At The OK Corral*," he said.

"Och, don't worry your wee noggin, Albert," Charlie said, dismissively. "I'm sure it'll all be over in moments, without a single shot being fired."

Christine raised an eyebrow at that. "Now you've gone and jinxed it," she muttered under her breath.

———

As he descended the stairs to the ground floor, Livingstone pulled out his burner phone and hurriedly dialled Goliath's number. With all the excitement of dealing with Weasel, he had completely forgotten about sending someone to the hotel to retrieve the weapons he'd supplied the giant's men. It was coming up to twelve-thirty, which is when they were due to set off from the hotel, so there was no time for him to make amends for his oversight. All he could do now was send someone to Euston in order to collect the guns before the shooters boarded the train.

The number was dead.

Cursing his oversight, Livingstone jumped into his car and started the engine. Pulling the selector down into drive, he gunned the accelerator and took off like a rocket.

He tried Goliath's number again, and this time there was a ringtone.

"*Where is the man you were supposed to be sending to collect the hardware, fam?*" Adebanjo demanded. He sounded seriously pissed. "*My men are about to leave, and there is no sign of him. That is most unprofessional of you, fam, and I am not happy.*"

"I'm really sorry, bruv," Livingstone said, cringing with embarrassment. "Something cropped up that skewered my plans, but I'll have someone meet you at Euston to relieve you of them. I promise."

There was silence as Goliath considered this. "*Very well,*" he said a moment later. "*But do not let me down again.*" With that, he hung up.

Livingstone bared his teeth in anger. He didn't respond well to people treating him so disrespectfully, although, on this occasion, he grudgingly accepted that it was probably justified. Swallowing his pride, he dialled the number of one of his runners to make the arrangements.

"Yo! Billy. Listen, bruv, I've got an urgent errand for you to run… I don't give a damn what you're doing, you useless bumbaclot. Drop everything, and get your sorry ass over to Euston right now."

———

Steve Bull was feeling somewhat stressed. The moment he'd spotted

Livingstone emerge from the flat, he had tried ringing Jack Tyler, but the line had been engaged.

Now, as he tried a second time, he got the same result.

"You've got to be kidding me," he said, staring at his mobile in agitated disbelief.

The gangster appeared to be in a rush as he jumped in his car. A moment later, the engine roared throatily and the M3 pulled off at speed, leaving Bull in a conundrum over what to do next. Tyler's instructions had been perfectly clear: he was to remain in the car and maintain eyeball on the front of Meeks' flat until the SFOs went in. However, if he did that, the man who had masterminded five gangland murders would get clean away. It was intensely frustrating because he knew that Trojan had their own set of eyes on the front of the building, making his continued presence superfluous to requirements.

Without thinking, he started the Omega. As his hand hovered indecisively over the automatic gear shift, he suddenly spotted the SFOs approaching the stairwell in single file from the rear of the block. Clad all in black, and carrying assault rifles and ballistic shields, they looked more like stealth ninjas than cops.

Reining in his instinct to go after Livingstone, he tried Tyler's number again, and this time he was rewarded with a ring tone. He closed his eyes in relief. "Come on, boss… pick up, pick up, pick up."

Tyler answered on the third ring. "*What is it, Stevie?*" he snapped, as though the call were an unwelcome intrusion, which it probably was, Bull conceded.

"Boss, Livingstone has just jumped in his car and taken off like a bat out of hell," he said, spewing the words out rapidly.

Tyler swore. "*Which way did he go?*" he demanded.

"He's just disappeared around a right hand bend at the end of the road," Bull informed him. "From there, he can only go one of two ways. He'll either take a swift left, which will bring him out into City Road, or he'll go around the block and come back out into Pitfield Street, on the other side of Aske Gardens. My bet is on the latter; that's the quickest way back to Dalston, assuming that's where he's going."

"*Go after him, Stevie,*" Tyler instructed. "*I'll send one of the ARVs from here to support you. If you reacquire his car, get straight on the Main-Set. I don't want it being stopped without armed support."*

Killing the call, Bull tossed his phone into the centre console cup holder and jammed the Omega into reverse. He had to wait for a car that had just pulled into Chart Street to go by him, and then he stamped on the gas pedal, sending the car flying backwards as fast as it would go.

When the speedometer hit thirty, Bull slid his right hand over the top of the steering wheel, bringing it to rest where his left hand would normally be. Then, in one fluid movement, he violently spun the wheel in a clockwise direction, at the same time stamping on the brakes. As the car spun through a 180 degree arc, brakes screeching over the hot tarmac in a manoeuvre commonly referred to as a J-Turn or a 'spin and go', his left hand nudged the selector into neutral. As soon as the Omega was facing the right way, he dropped it down into drive, and transferred his right foot from the brake to the gas pedal, burying it all the way into the floor.

Engine roaring, the Omega skidded sideways into Pitfield Street and quickly picked up speed. Putting the skills he'd learned during his six week Advanced Driving Course at Hendon into practice, he hurtled past a succession of slower cars, ignoring the angry toots he received.

Steve mentally kicked himself for having faffed around waiting for Tyler's permission instead of following his instincts and going straight after Livingstone. He had lost valuable time, and there was no guarantee that he was would be able to make it up.

"Where are you?" he growled, lifting his vision to scan the road ahead. He didn't dare use the covert blues and twos in case he alerted his quarry, and it was proving incredibly difficult to make any real progress without them.

And then, about a hundred yards ahead, he glimpsed the tail end of a black BMW coupé entering the roundabout by St. John's Church. Bull's heart skipped a beat. Could that possibly be Livingstone's car?

From the discomfort of his cramped chair, Adebanjo watched Dritan and his two hulking companions check out. Once that was done, the three Romanians walked over to the exit and huddled together in a little group of their own.

Adebanjo checked his watch and then sighed impatiently. It was almost twelve-thirty, and their taxis should be arriving at any moment. He was keen to get going; the job here was done, and he was looking forward to getting back to Manchester.

He decided to make a quick trip to the restroom before setting off. If nothing else, it would kill a few minutes and restore the circulation to his numb butt cheeks. As he awkwardly levered himself out of the chair, he noticed the door to the manager's office open. A small white male with a badly broken nose crossed to the girl working the counter and bent down to have a word with her. Although he'd pulled the door shut after him, it hadn't closed properly, and through the gap Adebanjo saw two people, a man and a woman, sitting at their desks with their backs to him.

Standing lethargically, he stretched long and slow, like a bear coming out of hibernation. As he lowered his arms, the woman inside the office glanced over her shoulder. Seeing the door was ajar, she quickly stood up and closed it.

Adebanjo remained motionless, staring at the door for several moments after it had closed. The blinds were down, so he could no longer see inside, but he didn't need to. Although he had only seen the woman's pretty face for a couple of seconds, that was more than enough time for him to recognise the female police officer who had dealt with him at Forest Gate police station.

His eyes narrowed to slits.

Her presence here was very bad news.

The only possible explanation for it was that she was spying on him. And if one Fed was on his trail, there would be others. They *never* operated alone.

Adebanjo had no idea how the Feds had tracked him down to the hotel, but if they searched him and found the burner in his pocket, it would be very bad news. His impending trip to the loo suddenly took on far greater importance, as it might be his last opportunity to get rid of the burner before they detained him.

Without a word to the twins, he set off for the men's room, deep in thought. Once inside, he checked to make sure the stalls were all empty and then called Dritan's burner.

"Don't speak," he ordered as soon as the call was answered. "Join me in the men's restroom. Come alone."

While he waited for his subordinate to arrive, Adebanjo removed the phone's chip, dropped it down the toilet and then set about breaking the handset up.

He paused when he heard the door open, but it was only Dritan.

"We have a problem," Adebanjo said. "The female Fed who dealt with me after I was arrested is in the manager's office."

Dritan immediately tensed up. "Are we discovered?" he asked, unshouldering the holdall.

"Not necessarily, fam," Adebanjo said, dropping the last bits of his dismantled phone into the bowl and flushing. "I don't think that they've realised we are together, but we can't take any chances. Firstly, you need to dispose of your burner. The best thing to do is break it up and flush it down the toilet like I did. Make sure you remove the chip first."

Removing the handset from his pocket, Dritan did as instructed, bending it in half and then repeatedly stamping on it with his foot until it snapped.

Adebanjo placed a hand on his shoulder. "If the Feds arrest me and the twins when we leave the hotel, do not try to intercede. Just get in the cab and get away from here as quickly as you can. Someone will meet you at Euston to take the weapons."

Dritan clearly didn't like the sound of that. "I'm not comfortable abandoning you," he said, stern-faced. "In the army, I never left a man behind."

Adebanjo beamed his vampire smile. "I know, fam, but this isn't the army. They've got nothing on me, so even if they do arrest me, I'll be back out in a few hours' time."

Dritan grunted disapprovingly. "Very well, but I don't like it."

"It's too late to cancel the cabs," Adebanjo said thoughtfully, "but if the twins and I leave the hotel from different exits, that should deflect the Feds attention away from you." He considered this for a few moments while Dritan finished breaking up his burner. "Let the others know, and be prepared to move as soon as your cab arrives," Adebanjo instructed. "The twins and I will cause a distraction at that point, so that the Feds will be too busy worrying about us to notice your departure."

"Should we dump the guns now, so that we've got nothing on us if they stop us?" Dritan asked.

Adebanjo frowned. "I have considered this, fam," he admitted. "But if they detain us, I suspect they will search the hotel thoroughly afterwards, as they did last time. If they find the guns, we are all in big trouble, so better to keep them on you."

Dritan's eyes narrowed. "I will obey your orders as always," he promised, "but I will not go quietly if they try to arrest me." As he spoke, he removed the weapons from his bag and began checking them over.

"I understand that, fam," Adebanjo said, placing a massive hand on his shoulder, "but do not engage the Feds if it is at all avoidable."

As soon as Adebanjo left the men's room, he gathered the twins and started issuing orders. A few moments later, he spotted Dritan emerge from the toilet and stride purposefully across the lobby to join his comrades. As Dritan spoke to his team, Livingstone saw their shoulders stiffen, and Valmir glanced nervously towards the reception desk. A few moments later, both Valmir and Lorik set off for the restrooms, moving with grim purpose. Adebanjo guessed that they were going there to ready their weapons in case the police tried to arrest them, just as Dritan had done before them.

———

When he reached the base of the stairwell leading up to Tyson Meek's first floor flat, PS Tod Marshall raised a clenched fist, signalling for the SFOs following in his wake to stop.

Marshall had led a number of armed entry operations like this one and, so far, they had all ended peacefully, without a single shot being fired; he was firmly hoping that today's deployment would turn out to be equally uneventful.

In addition to the standard issue Glock 17 pistols they all carried, most of the team were also armed with Heckler and Koch G36C carbines. They were all dressed in black, fire-retardant Nomex overalls, boots, and gloves, and wore Kevlar MICH (Modular Integrated Communications Helmet) ballistic helmets over their Nomex balaclavas. Their ear defenders were linked to the secure radio system they were using, and the bulging black goggles that gave them such a sinister appearance provided all-important eye protection. To give them the best possible protection against incoming fire – something they all hoped they wouldn't need – they all wore Kevlar body armour.

In addition to a heavy metal battering ram called an 'Enforcer' – often referred to as 'the big red key' – one of Marshall's team was equipped with a Hatton Gun, just in case the Enforcer didn't work and they needed to blow the locks off the door.

Marshall keyed the toggle on his throat mic. "Trojan Bronze to Gold, we're at the stairwell and ready to ascend. Please confirm that the rear of the premises is now secure and that the locals have closed the road, over."

"*Trojan Bronze from Gold, the ARV crew are in place at the rear, and pedestrian and vehicular access to Chart Street has now been halted. You are green to go.*"

"Received. Eyeball from Trojan Bronze, confirm no movement at the front of the premises, over."

"*Trojan Bronze from eyeball, the balcony is clear and there is no sign of movement from within the target address, over,*" the SO19 officer who had been sent to keep observation on the balcony replied.

Marshall cast a critical eye along the row of heavily armed officers hugging the wall behind him. Once he was satisfied that they were all ready, he waved for them to follow him. They ascended the two flights up to the first floor landing quickly. At the top, Marshall paused, raising his clenched fist again to signal another halt. "Trojan Bronze to eyeball. Sit-rep, over."

"*No change. No change. Still all clear.*"

"All received. Moving onto the balcony now."

Moving forward in a crouch, the team stealthily padded along the balcony, their weapons raised to provide cover in case any of the suspects suddenly emerged from Meeks' flat. He halted them just before the street door, indicating for those officers carrying the Enforcer and the heavy ballistic shields to come forward.

"In position. Standby for entry," Marshall whispered into his mic. He held up his right hand and then raised three fingers, one after the other, giving the team a three-second countdown to entry. As soon as he reached three, he pointed at the door, giving the signal for the breach to occur.

As the Enforcer-wielding officer stepped forward, the sound of a gunshot was clearly heard from inside.

"Shit!" Marshall exclaimed, sensing that his cherished 100% record for achieving peaceful resolutions was about to end. He keyed his throat mic. "Shots fired inside the address. Repeat, shots fired within the address. Effecting entry now. Stand by for an update."

He nodded to the officer with the Enforcer, who immediately drove the battering ram into the wooden door with tremendous force. It was a newish door, solid and unyielding, and it took three blows to force it open. As the door finally flew inwards, the officer with the Enforcer stepped aside to make way for the two officers with ballistic shields who raised and interlocked them.

CHAPTER THIRTY-THREE

MAKING ENTRY

"Wait!" Norris called out just as Switch was about to pull the trigger.

"What is it now, bruv?" the youngster yelled in frustration. Nonetheless, he lowered the gun and turned to face the man who had spoken.

A sly grin appeared on the lanky elder's face. "I've decided that we should merk Weasel first."

Switch responded with a petulant shrug. "What difference does it make who dies first?" he demanded. Despite his bravado, he was feeling twitchy and he just wanted to get on with it.

Norris' eyes were angry little slits as he moved forward to assert his authority. "Now that Conrad's gone, I'm in charge, younger, and it's not for you to question what I say. Ya get me?"

Switch was quick to back down. Gunz had warned him that Norris was an unstable psycho, and there was no telling what he would do if provoked. He decided to let him play his little power game and not risk saying anything that might upset him. "Yeah, alright," he conceded, moving away from the couch.

Standing behind Tyson, Norris put his hands on his shoulders and shook him roughly. "Weasel, wake up, you worthless turd."

Tyson, stirred and opened his eyes. "Please…" he begged, dragging his head off his chest and trying to focus his eyes. "Let Marcel go."

Norris laughed raucously, as though Tyson had just told him a particularly funny joke. "Get on with it, younger," he said, making a gun with his fingers and pointing it at Tyson's head.

"Switch, wait," Marcel called from the sofa.

Switch blew out his breath impatiently. "Now what?" he asked in exasperation.

"You can't do this," Marcel implored him. Tears were running down his face, and his voice was trembling with fear. "Me and you are Holly Street Boys, remember? We always got each other's back."

Switch snorted. "Is that right, bruv? Well, if we always got each other's back, why didn't you try and help me when Ziggy was laying into me at his flat? Answer me that."

Marcel opened his mouth, but Switch didn't give him a chance to speak. "Save your breath," he said angrily. "I aint interested in your pathetic excuses."

Norris had watched the childish exchange with growing amusement. "You tell him, younger. You're running with the big boys now."

Gunz lazily pushed himself away from the doorframe. "Look, can we just get this done," he said, sounding bored. "It's gonna take ages to get the bodies chopped up, and I don't wanna be stuck here any longer than necessary."

Norris shrugged. "Of course, bruv. Let's get on with it right now. Younger, do Weasel first."

Conscious that everyone was watching him, Switch took a deep breath and planted his feet shoulder width apart. Holding the gun in both hands, he pointed it at Tyson's chest and began applying pressure to the trigger.

"NO!" Marcel screamed, shuffling forwards so that he was sitting on the edge of the seat.

"Shut up, bruv," Switch hissed, shooting him a sideways glance. Bracing himself for the kick, he gritted his teeth and pulled the trigger.

At the same time, Marcel propelled himself head first from the sofa, throwing himself directly in front of his brother. The bullet hit him in the upper right side of his chest, knocking him backwards into Tyson and sending the chair he was tied to toppling backwards. It landed with a heavy thud, with Marcel sprawled across Tyson's body.

Almost immediately, they both began screaming in agony.

As Switch was about to step forward and finish the job, something heavy crashed into the street door, generating a thunderous boom that resonated throughout the entire flat.

"What the fuck…?" Norris exclaimed as the door was pummelled again.

"It's the Feds," Gunz said, looking around fearfully.

With a snarl, Norris drew his pistol and moved towards the hall door.

"What are you doing?" Gunz asked as he yanked the curtains back and made a grab for the window opener. "We gotta go out the back before they get in."

"I aint running," Norris snapped. "What about you, younger?"

"Switch, we gotta breeze," Gunz said, finally managing to get the window open.

Switch shook his head stubbornly. "I aint running either," he said, defiantly.

Norris smiled at the younger. "Maybe you aint such a pussy after all," he told the boy.

————

The hallway was too narrow for both ballistic shields to enter at once, so PC Danny Spears was nominated to take on the role of point man. As his colleague carrying the second shield stepped aside, Danny positioned his shield at the mouth of the now open doorway. He held there, awaiting further instructions from Marshall.

Marshall had already seen a floorplan of the one bedroom flat, drawn by a local officer who had recently visited a similar address. He knew that the central hallway had five doors in it. The three doors on the left side of the premises led to the bathroom, toilet and bedroom, respectively. The two doors to the right led to the kitchen and lounge. Having looked through the window, they had already confirmed that the kitchen was empty.

"ARMED POLICE. ARMED POLICE. THROW OUT YOUR WEAPONS AND COME FORWARD WITH YOUR HANDS RAISED."

Nothing. No response from inside.

Marshall tapped Spears on the shoulder, and he stepped through the threshold and moved forward, his 11.5 kilo shield held out in front of him. He stopped just shy of the kitchen door. Perched on his shoulder, PC Peter Carmichael aimed his GS36 carbine into the flat.

The silence was eerie.

"I've got a bad feeling about this," Carmichael whispered, his heart pounding.

Marshall was standing directly behind them. "Shhhh," he warned, straining his ears.

There was a creaking noise, like a floorboard moving under foot. Suddenly, from the second door on the right, a tall, black male thrust a skinny arm around the corner and fired off two rapid shots from a handgun, both of which slammed into Spears' ballistic shield with a loud metallic clang.

The shield held firm, which was unsurprising considering it was built to resist the impact of military grade rounds fired from weapons like the M16 and AK47.

"Shots fired at police from inside the address," Marshall transmitted over the encrypted radio channel. Both he and Carmichael had sensibly taken cover behind Spears' shield as soon as the gunman appeared.

Standing up and sighting his carbine on the room that the gunman had disappeared into, Carmichael shouted, ARMED POLICE! THROW OUT YOUR–"

He ducked down again as the gunman broke cover and squeezed off two more rounds.

"Don't think he likes you," Spears said, drily.

As the shooter withdrew back into the lounge, a second black male, much younger but also armed with a pistol, burst out of the room and rushed across the hall into the bedroom opposite, letting off two unsighted shots as he ran. Both bullets smashed into the top of the street door frame, sending wood splinters flying everywhere.

"Is everyone okay?" Marshall asked.

He was immediately rewarded with a thumbs up from Spears and Carmichael, who were still crouching behind the ballistic shield.

"Okay," Marshall said, shaking his head with deep regret. "They've had their chance. If they open fire again, you're free to engage."

Carmichael responded with a grim nod of understanding. He stood up and shouted, "THIS IS YOUR LAST WARNING. THROW OUT YOUR WEAPONS NOW AND COME FORWARD WITH YOUR HANDS RAISED."

The radio squawked in Marshall's ear. "*Trojan Bronze, be advised, we've got an IC3 male with dreadlocks coming out of one of the rear windows,*" one of the ARV officers covering the back transmitted. "*Engaging him now.*"

"Shit" Marshall cursed under his breath. Was this one of the two men who had just opened fire on them, or someone else entirely? "We need to advance," he said, tapping Spears on the shoulder.

Spears and Carmichael shuffled forward, moving beyond the doors that lead into the kitchen and bathroom. Marshall moved with them. The space they had vacated was quickly filled by more carbine toting officers who burst into each of the rooms.

"Kitchen clear!"

"Bathroom clear"

Marshall keyed his throat mic. "Gold from Trojan Bronze. There are at least two gunmen inside the flat. SFOs now advancing along hall. Kitchen and bathroom secured."

The gunman from the lounge opened fire again, this time letting off three rounds in quick succession.

Before the echo from the shots had died out, PC Carmichael sprung up, peered down the ZF 3×4° dual optical sight of his carbine, and calmly discharged two rounds into the shooter's centre mass. The bullets ripped into the startled man's upper body, spinning him around. He staggered sideways before toppling head first into the lounge and disappearing from sight.

"Suspect from the lounge has been hit," Carmichael called out. "Extent of his injuries unknown."

Marshall keyed his mic. "Gold from Bronze Trojan. After second contact, fire returned. One suspect down. Condition unknown."

The hallway was now full of smoke and cordite.

"Help!" someone rasped from within the lounge. The speaker sounded weak and in considerable pain.

"Identify yourself," Marshall shouted.

"My name's… Tyson. Please… we need… we need help in here."

Tyson! That was the name of the witness Marshall's team had been sent in to rescue.

"Tyson, listen to me," Marshall shouted. "I need you to step out of the room with your hands held high,"

"Can't…" Tyson panted. "Can't move…"

"*Bronze Trojan, can you give me an update on the injured suspect yet?*" Tyler's voice in his ear.

"Stand by," Marshall said impatiently.

At that point, the younger male exploded from the bedroom on the left and let off two more rounds.

With his weapon still pointing towards the lounge on the right, Carmichael was unable to return fire. Taking sanctuary behind Spears' ballistic shield, he said to his friend, "The fucker nearly got me, that time."

Indeed, one of the bullets had hit the top of the shield at exactly the point where he had been leaning over it and, had he not moved, it would have struck him in the upper arm or shoulder. The other round had harmlessly embedded itself into the woodwork of the kitchen door frame.

As soon as the shooting ceased, Carmichael jumped back up, shouldering his weapon, but the youngster was too quick for him, and he ducked back behind the wall.

"Shut the fuck up, Tyson, you no good grass," he shouted across the hall.

Marshall signalled for his team to ready themselves for the final

TURF WAR

push. The hostage was clearly incapacitated in the lounge on the right, and there was at least one gunman in there with him. Although said gunman had been shot during the earlier exchange of fire, there was no way of knowing whether he was still capable of harming Meeks.

"Gold from Trojan Bronze, urgent message, over."

Tyler responded immediately, his tone measured. "*Go ahead, over.*"

"We're about to make the final push. Send both ballistic ambulances forward now."

"*All received,*" Tyler said pensively. "*They're being despatched to forward reception point now.*"

It was standard operating procedure to have ballistic injury trained paramedics from the LAS on standby whenever an armed entry was made and, on this occasion, Tyler had requested two ballistic ambulances from the London Ambulance service. These were currently parked at the RVP, but they would now be sent to the forward reception point, which was at the junction of Pitfield Street and Chart Street. That way, when the premises was finally secured, they would be able to provide medical assistance quickly.

Marshall crept back along the hall. He pointed to PC Andrew Simmons, who was holding a second ballistic shield, and then to PC Maggie Cartwright, who was armed with a GS36. "You two, take the bedroom on the left," he whispered. "There's one armed suspect inside."

Both nodded.

He instructed the next two officers in line, PCs Morris and Patel to tuck in behind Spears and Carmichael, and the two after them, PCs Reedy and Niles, to do likewise for Simmons and Cartwright.

"Stand by," he told them quietly. "We go in on three." Raising his right hand, he lifted one finger, then a second, and then a third. "GO!" he said, pushing them forward.

Screaming, "ARMED POLICE! ARMED POLICE! DROP YOUR WEAPONS AND PUT YOUR HANDS IN THE AIR!" at the top of their lugs, the two teams filed along the hallway, their footfall loud and heavy within the confined space.

Branching left and right as they reached the end of the hall, they simultaneously stormed the bedroom and lounge.

At which point, all hell broke loose inside the flat.

————————

Bull was relieved to confirm that it was definitely Livingstone's car up ahead, and now that the gang leader had put some distance between himself and Meeks' flat, he seemed to be driving a little more sedately.

There were two vehicles between them as Bull followed him along Whitmore Road towards the roundabout at the top of Hoxton Market. Keeping his eyes firmly on the road, Bull groped around for the Main-Set's dash mounted mic. Taking a deep breath to compose himself, he thumbed the transmit button and requested urgent armed assistance to stop Livingstone's car.

"*MP from Trojan 501, we're already in Pitfield Street making our way towards Hoxton. ETA less than one minute.*"

The Trojan unit was so close that it could only be the ARV that Tyler had released from the Chart Street deployment to help him.

"*Golf Zero also nearby, MP. Show us assisting.*" An excited female voice squealed over the Main-Set. Golf Zero was the G District dog van, and Bull conceded that having a furry Exocet on hand might prove very useful if Livingstone decided to make a run for it.

But would he?

The gang leader had no idea that they were on to him, so there was a very good chance that he would simply pull over when the Trojan unit tucked in behind him, thinking it was just a routine traffic stop. Still, it was better to be safe than sorry.

When it reached the roundabout, the BMW took the second exit, going straight across into Whitmore Road. One of the cars in front of Bull continued driving around the roundabout, reducing his cover by one.

Bull transmitted an update.

"*Received by Trojan 501. Should be with you shortly,*" came the clipped response.

A few moments later, as they crossed the hump-back bridge spanning Regent's Canal, Bull glanced in his rear-view mirror, hoping to see the cavalry bearing down on him at full pelt. Unfortunately, there was no sign of the ARV. "Now into De Beauvoir Road, towards Downham Road," he said into the mic.

A crackle of static. "*Received by Trojan 501.*"

Bull was fairly confident that Livingstone would turn right when he reached the next junction, which was Downham Road. That would take him down to Kingsland Road, a few hundred yards further along. If he made a left turn there, it was one straight long road all the way back to his flat on the other side of Dalston Junction.

Sure enough, as the BMW slowed to navigate the junction, Livingstone signalled his intention to make a right turn. By contrast, the car between them indicated left, which was inconvenient as it meant that Bull would be losing his remaining cover.

"Suspect now going right into Downham Road," Bull announced as Livingstone made the turn.

He followed suit, hanging back a little so as not to draw attention. "Where the hell's that bloody Trojan unit?" he growled to himself.

Just as he was starting to fret, he spotted the ARV's bonnet protruding from the mouth of a side road up ahead on the right, waiting to pounce like a predatory animal. With a grin, Bull realised that the savvy ARV driver had taken a short cut to get ahead of his quarry.

"Trojan unit, it's the black BMW M3 coupé approaching you now," Bull said, dropping back even further to allow the marked Omega to pull out in front of him once the BMW had driven past it.

"*Received,*" the Omega's operator said as the ARV emerged from the side road and took up station behind its quarry.

Bull glanced down at the dashboard clock. It read: 12:30 hours.

Wasn't that the time that the suspects over in Beckton were supposed to be leaving their hotel?

At that moment the ARV switched its blue lights on.

"Show time," Bull said, feeling the adrenalin kick in.

———

Charlie White wandered over to the three large black men sprawling in the easy chairs opposite the reception desk. Coming to a halt in front of the Kalu twins, he frowned, unable to work out which of the ugly buggers he'd spoken to earlier. In the end, he addressed them both at the same time. "Just to let you gentlemen know, your taxi cabs have arrived and are waiting for you outside."

Glowering up at him menacingly, the twins said nothing.

Awkward.

Charlie coughed. "Right. I'll just let your associates know." As he turned around, he felt the giant's eyes boring into the back of his head, and it was a most unpleasant sensation.

"What makes you think we got any associates with us, fam?" Adebanjo suddenly demanded as Charlie took his first step.

Charlie froze in his tracks, worried that he might have inadvertently said something to give the game away. Swallowing nervously, he ran a finger around his collar, which suddenly felt very tight. Taking a deep breath to calm his nerves, he turned around to face the giant, mustering a saccharine smile

"Well, sir," Charlie said, knowing that it was vital that he didn't come across as being sarcastic. "One of these gentlemen–" he pointed in the general direction of the twins "–asked me to book two cabs, each for three people. As there's three of you and three of them–" Charlie casually nodded towards the Eastern Europeans "–and you all checked out within minutes of each other, I naturally assumed that you're all together. I apologise if my understanding of the situation is wrong."

After a moment's reflection, Adebanjo seemed to lose interest in Charlie, and nodded for him to take his leave.

Offering a farewell smile, Charlie quickly crossed the foyer to the three men standing by the exit.

"Excuse me, pal," he said to Dritan. "The two cabs your buddies ordered have arrived. They're waiting outside for you when you're ready."

Dritan nodded once. "Thank you," he said curtly. Not exactly friendly, but nowhere near as hostile as the three black men had been.

In keeping with his role as a member of the hotel reception team, Charlie tidied up some magazines on a nearby coffee table before returning to reception. Humming merrily to the background music, he disappeared into the manager's office without a backward glance.

"Jesus!" he said, flopping into a vacant chair and pulling his tie loose. "I really thought I'd been rumbled there for a wee minute."

Ignoring him, Christine cautiously peered through the blinds, a phone clasped against her ear. "Tony, all six suspects are gathering their things," she said quietly. "The Eastern Europeans are now walking towards the exit. They should come into Trojan's view in a few seconds. Adebanjo and the others are also heading towards the door. Stand by…"

———

When Dritan emerged from the air conditioned hotel foyer, a wall of energy sapping heat wrapped him in its cloying embrace. The sun was so bright that he screwed his eyes shut to prevent his retinas from being burnt out while he fumbled around for his sunglasses. Slipping them on, he gingerly opened his eyes again, blinking away the sunspots that still lingered.

The Romanian was roasting inside his thick sweatshirt, but it was baggy, and it concealed the gun that was tucked into his waistband, which a T-Shirt wouldn't have done.

"I will be glad to get away from this place," he grumbled to the others as they took shelter under the canopy.

Not many things scared Dritan, but Goliath's revelation that the police were at the hotel had shaken him badly, and the thought of being arrested and thrown in a cell for several days had triggered a wave of anxiety that he was barely managing to control.

Goliath planned to create a distraction to enable Dritan and the others to slip away unnoticed, but the strain of waiting for something to happen was starting to take its toll on the former soldier. He glanced nervously at the two minicabs, which represented his passage to freedom. They were parked tantalisingly close by, with their drivers leaning against them as they chatted to each other. He had been instructed not to approach either of the cabs until the twins distracted the police, but the waiting was killing him.

Finally, Isaac and his dim witted brother emerged from the hotel. They paused by the entrance, no doubt trying to spot the undercover police who were watching them. Then, with a glance in his direction, followed by the subtlest of nods, the twins split up, running in different directions.

As Andre ran past the three Romanians, he was already puffing. He wouldn't get very far, Dritan decided. The man was fatter than an elephant, and there was no way he was going to outrun anyone.

————

Dillon was sitting with Geoff Coles and Jonny Murphy in the control car, which was parked in a remote corner of the local ASDA store. The atmosphere inside the car was incredibly tense, although no one would have guessed that from looking at Geoff, who was happily munching his way through a packet of Chocolate Fingers.

"Doesn't he ever stop eating?" Murphy asked from the back seat. The oppressive heat, and the nonstop sound of Geoff consuming food, was making him irritable.

"Not very often," Dillon said. "I think he's got worms."

"He would have probably eaten them if he had," Murphy responded grumpily.

Geoff just chuckled and stuffed a fist full of fingers into his mouth.

Dillon picked up the encrypted radio that Newman had given him and relayed Christine's message. "Bronze Trojan from Silver. The Tangos are all in the hotel foyer getting ready to leave."

For operational purposes, Adebanjo and the Kalu twins had been designated Tangos one, two, and three, while the Eastern Europeans were Tangos four, five, and six.

"*Received,*" Newman said calmly.

Dillon took a deep breath. "Bronze Trojan from Silver, we are now State Amber. Repeat State Amber. Operational control passes to you, over."

"*State Amber received,*" Newman confirmed. "*I have operational control. B Section, all things being equal, we hit them the moment they approach the cabs, but no one moves without my say so. Please acknowledge."*

"*Acknowledged by B Section*," a female voice replied. The person speaking was PC Louise Richmond, Newman's second in command.

"*Tony, the Eastern Europeans have just walked outside*," Christine said. "*The other three are lingering by the door. God knows what they're doing*."

"Trojan Bronze from Silver. You should have sight of Tangos four, five, and six by now. They've just left the hotel," Dillon relayed the telephone message via the encrypted radio.

"*Affirmative*," Newman replied. "*I have visual control of Tangos four, five and six. All three are standing on the pavement, looking back inside*."

"I wish they'd get a bloody move on," Murphy said from behind. "I've waited sodding years for this moment."

"*Tony, Adebanjo and the twins are at the exit*," Christine's voice whispered in his ear, and he could hear the increased tension in her voice. "*Stand by... The twins are now walking out of the hotel. Adebanjo is held at the door. What the fuck...?*" she suddenly blurted out, her voice raising several octaves in panic. "*Tony, Adebanjo has had it on his toes. He's turned around and is running towards the rear of the hotel... Tony! Did you bloody well hear me...?*"

───────

"We are now state green, repeat state green," PS Newman announced as he watched the Eastern Europeans huddle together just outside the hotel's main entrance.

"*Received by Silver*," Dillon responded over the radio.

All three had their holdalls clasped in their left hands, Newman saw. They were talking quietly amongst themselves, but something about their body language was off. They seemed tense, eyes about, as if waiting for something to happen.

He didn't like it.

Newman had been doing this job long enough to have learned to always listen to his instincts, and right now they were telling him that something was amiss.

"I don't like this at all," he said to the SFOs who were seated in the lead van with him. "Be ultra-vigilant when we move in."

Just then, the Kalu twins walked through the sliding doors into the bright midday sunlight. Newman leaned forward in his seat, frowning. Where was Adebanjo? He keyed his throat mic. "B Section, I now have visual with Tangos two and three. Stand by…"

"*B Section standing by,*" Louise responded.

Andy Marchant and Josh Myles, the two plain clothed officers posing as cab drivers, had just moved away from their vehicles and were now standing together on the pavement by the hotel exit. Newman had instructed them not to wait inside the cars because, if the shit hit the fan, he didn't want any of the suspects being able to jump in and force his officers to drive them away at gunpoint. That would be absolutely calamitous, and it couldn't be allowed to happen under any circumstances.

Marchant was a short, stocky former Marine in his early thirties, with a square jaw, a permeant five o'clock shadow, and a buzz cut.

Myles, tall and slim, with sandy coloured hair and blue eyes, was the team's pretty boy. Unlike Marchant, the twenty eight year old had no previous military experience, but he was tactically astute and had proven himself to be very calm under pressure.

Neither man was married, which was a good thing as far as Newman was concerned, considering the risk they had taken by volunteering for this gig.

If everything went according to plan, as soon as all six Tangos started moving towards the vehicles, Marchant would start patting his head, which was the prearranged signal for the rest of the team to move in. Although he and Myles were carrying concealed Glock 17 pistols, and both wore thin ballistic vests under their sweatshirts, Newman had ordered them to refrain from getting involved if a firefight ensued. Instead, they were to confine their involvement to rounding up any non-combatants who tried to do a runner.

Just as Newman was about to ask Dillon to check in with Christine and confirm Adebanjo's whereabouts, the Kalu twins broke into a run, splitting up and heading in opposite directions. At the same time, the Eastern Europeans marched over to Andy Marchant's cab, shouting at him to get inside and start the engine.

Newman was momentarily caught off guard. "What the fuck...?"

Dillon's voice cut through the silence. "*Trojan Bronze from Silver, urgent message. I think we're rumbled. Adebanjo is doing a runner towards the back of the hotel with two unarmed officers in pursuit.*"

Outside the hotel, Marchant was shaking his head and defiantly waving his arms in the air as the Eastern Europeans shouted for him to get inside the cab. One of them, the one with the tattoo on his neck, suddenly stepped forward and started manhandling him towards the car.

Newman glanced sideways at his driver. "This is all going tits up," he said, reaching for the handset on the dash. It was tuned into a local back to back channel he was using to communicate with the divisional Duty Officer. "Kilo Oscar One from Bronze Trojan, we're about to move in. I need you to lock down the roads, and get the ballistic ambulances up to the forward reception point, ASAP."

A crackle of static, followed by: "*All received. Good luck.*"

Marchant was struggling to pull away from the Eastern European who was now trying to drag him over to his cab. Suddenly, the agitated man pulled a handgun from the waistband of his jogging bottoms and pointed it straight at Marchant's chest.

"Shit!" Newman said, realising that things were spiralling out of control. He keyed his throat mic. "B Section from Bronze Trojan, Tango four has just pulled a handgun on Andy. Move in. ATTACK, ATTACK, ATTACK!"

CHAPTER THIRTY-FOUR

OH GOD, I'M GOING TO DIE

Dillon had strategically positioned the team's four cars, each containing three detectives, around the hotel's outer perimeter. In picking the locations, he'd taken two important factors into consideration. The first had been the ease with which they'd be able to respond when Newman called them forward. The second had been how effectively they'd be able to contain the area if any of the suspects managed to slip past the SFOs. He hadn't actually expected anyone to do a runner, but as it now transpired, three of the buggers had done exactly that.

To his annoyance, Dillon had run out of hands. Holding the phone he was using to communicate with Chrissy in one, and the encrypted SFO radio in the other, he now found that he needed the radio on his lap, which was tuned into the secure murder squad channel.

"Geoff, get us to the back of the hotel now!" he shouted, tossing the SFO's radio over his shoulder to Murphy. Then, as the car screeched across the tarmac towards the exit, he spoke into the murder squad radio. "All Metro units from Dillon, we've got three runners at the hotel. The Kalu twins have gone out the front and Adebanjo's done a bunk via the rear, with Charlie White chasing him. I need you to move in and secure all exits."

As acknowledgements came in, thick and fast, Geoff swerved the Ford Escort out of the ASDA car park and into Alpine Way. Pushing the car through the gears, he accelerated heavily, barely slowing for the left turn into Woolwich Manor Way. Quickly building up speed again, he took a racing line through the roundabout at the junction with Tollgate Road, deliberately inducing a skid and dragging the car around like a seasoned rally driver. He rocketed past one hotel, then a large pub, and then slammed on the brakes as he reached the hotel where the suspects were staying.

Both radios were spewing out urgent chatter, but Dillon largely ignored this, trusting the SFOs and everyone else to do their jobs.

Keeping the phone glued to his ear, he focused on Christine's breathless updates, the latest of which told her that Adebanjo was clear of the hotel and running towards the railway tracks at Beckton station.

"*Newark Knok...*" Christine shouted, so out of breath by now that he could barely understand her anymore. "*He's running into... Newark Knok, with Charlie behind him...*"

"We need to be in Newark Knok, wherever that is," he told Geoff.

Geoff nodded. "I know it," he said, pulling out of the turn he'd been about to make and continuing straight on.

"There have been shots fired," Murphy said from the back, relaying the latest updates from the SFOs.

"Shit!" Dillon said, hanging onto the hand grip above his head as Geoff completed an audacious overtake. "I hope the SFOs are all okay."

———

As PC Spears advanced into the lounge, with Carmichael at his shoulder and two colleagues immediately behind, he saw a fresh trail of blood leading from the doorway over to three black men who were laying in a pile in the centre of the room. The one at the bottom appeared to be tied to a chair, but the others were slumped across the top of him, face down.

None of them were moving.

Spears came to an abrupt halt, with Carmichael directly behind him. The other two cautiously fanned out, weapons raised as they scanned the room for hostiles. There was hardly any furniture in the lounge, and what little there was had been pushed up against the walls. The only possible hiding place was behind the sofa, but the trail of blood led to the middle of the room, not in that direction.

From the safety of his shield, Spears frowned as he tried to work out which of the three men lying in front of him was the shooter. There was no sign of the handgun on the floor, so presumably he still had it with him.

The three black men were all covered in blood, and a dark red puddle was slowly spreading out from beneath them, forming a pool on the thick plastic sheeting.

The two SFOs flanking him slowly advanced towards the pile of bodies, fingers on triggers, ready to react instantly, should anyone move.

A loud battle cry came from the bedroom across the hall, instantly followed by the sound of shooting. At least half a dozen rounds were fired in quick succession, and this ended with the agonised scream of someone being hit. The SFOs were too well trained to be distracted by this, and they kept their eyes fixed on the three men in front of them.

From a tactical point of view, the two advancing officers found themselves faced with a nasty dilemma as it dawned on them that the three men on the floor were so intertwined with each other that they couldn't risk opening fire on any of them for fear of hitting the others. Which is why, for the briefest of moments, they hesitated when the man who was lying on top of the others rolled over and started shooting at them.

———

PC Andrew Simmons entered the bedroom to the left of the hall with his ballistic shield held firmly out in front of him. Maggie Cartwright's carbine felt enormously reassuring as it pressed into the top of his shoulder. He had been expecting to encounter immediate resistance from the hostile, but there was no sign of him.

Stopping just inside the door, Simmons anxiously scanned the room for their target. He took in his surroundings in an instant. It was a standard sized double, square in shape. An unmade bed with a metal frame sat beneath the window in the back wall. A tacky looking bedside table stood beside it. A large, double doored oak wardrobe had been pulled away from the wall nearest the door, and it now stood in the centre of the room, facing towards the SFOs. A million dust motes swirled around the room, sparkling in the sunlight, no doubt disturbed when the heavy furniture was moved.

Blinking away the sweat that was dripping into his eyes, Simmons indicated the wardrobe with a jut of his chin. Although it was possible that the gunman had slid under the bed, Spears' gut was telling him that it was far more likely he was either hiding inside or behind the wardrobe.

Cartwright nodded her agreement.

As Simmons took a second step into the room, a violent scream erupted from the rear of the wardrobe, and it suddenly came toppling down on top of him, having been pushed from behind.

"Watch out," Simmons shouted, but the warning was far too late. With two of their colleagues standing directly behind them, there was no way to reverse, and all he and Cartwright could do was brace themselves for the impact.

Simmons instinctively raised his shield into the path of the falling wardrobe, grunting as it crashed into him. Lowering her carbine, Maggie Cartwright, reached out to take some of the weight off him, leaving both of them vulnerable to counter attack.

Having intercepted the falling wardrobe, they started to push it back up into a standing position, at which point the concealed gunman fired three shots straight through the wood and into them. Purely by luck, the rounds all smashed into Simmons' ballistic shield, doing no real harm.

Screaming with unbridled rage, the gunman then leapt on top of the wardrobe, and the forward momentum he generated sent it crashing down on the two officers for a second time. Clambering over the top of the still falling wardrobe, he pointed his gun straight at Simmons' head.

With the shield now pinned against his chest by the weight of the wardrobe, there was nothing Simmons could do to defend himself. His blood ran cold. Literally. It was as if all the warmth was being sucked out of him by an unseen malignant force.

Oh God, I'm going to die, he thought, lowering his head and praying that the Kevlar helmet would withstand the impact of a bullet being fired at it from such close range.

There were four gunshots in rapid succession, and Simmons body convulsed with every one of them.

As the teenage gunman fell backwards, his torso riddled with bullets, Simmons felt his knees buckle with relief. Moving slowly, as if in a trance, he and Cartwright pushed the wardrobe back into an upright position while their two colleagues rushed around the back to confirm that the gunman had been neutralised.

"Are you alright? "Maggie asked, pulling her helmet and goggles off and staring at her partner intently.

All Simmons could do was nod. He was too numb to speak.

————

In the lounge, the first round that Jerome Norris fired struck PC Patel in the centre of his chest, knocking him backwards. Teeth bared in anger, Norris immediately swivelled to his right and fired two more rounds, this time at PC Morris. They struck him just below his diaphragm and sent him staggering backwards to land on his rump.

From behind the safety of the ballistic shield, Carmichael levelled his weapon at the snarling gunman and took up first pressure on the trigger. However, although he was desperate to take the shot, he found himself unable to return fire for fear of hitting the two men who were buried beneath his target. In the absence of any evidence to the contrary, he had to assume that they were hostages and not hostiles, which is why Patel and Morris hadn't already taken him out.

"Danny, I don't have a clear shot! Move to the right," he yelled at Spears, who immediately shuffled sideways to give his colleague the safe angle he needed to open fire.

The crabbing movement drew the gunman's eye and Norris turned on them in an instant, sitting up and aiming his gun straight at Carmichael. The movement took him clear of the men he had been laying on top of.

As Norris raised his arm, there was a deafening bang, and a bright red hole appeared in his right temple. A millisecond later, the left side of his skull blew outwards with tremendous force as a well-aimed bullet from Patel's carbine went straight through it at high velocity. A cloud of bright red mist filled the air as the gunman sagged to the side, dropping his gun as he fell.

Patel, clearly still winded by the impact from the 9mm slug that had slammed into his Kevlar plated body armour, moved forward, kicking the gun clear.

"You okay?" Carmichael asked him.

Patel nodded. "I'm doing a lot better than him," he hissed through teeth that were gritted in pain.

Morris was up on his knees, clutching his side. "Fuck me, that hurt," he complained, standing up slowly. There were two close cropped impact marks in the centre of his stomach but, like Patel, his body armour had saved him from serious harm.

Between them, Patel and Morris dragged the shooter's dead body clear of the other males.

"Jesus," Carmichael breathed as they gently disentangled Marcel Meeks' from his brother. The barbed wire that bound Tyson had attached itself to the boy's body, cutting deep into his flesh.

While Patel and Morris tended to Marcel, Spears and Carmichael set about freeing Tyson. Both of the males were unconscious, and both were covered in blood, so much so that it was initially impossible to distinguish which one of them had been shot. It was only after the officers cut Marcel's upper clothing away, and carried out a fingertip examination of his torso, that they found the jagged wound in his right shoulder.

"We need the paramedics up here now!" Carmichael called to

Marshall, who had just poked his head into the room, having already checked in with the SFOs in the bedroom.

————

As soon as Dritan pulled the gun on the argumentative cabbie, he realised that he'd made a terrible mistake.

"What the hell are you doing?" Valmir hissed, glowering at him in disbelief.

As a loyal subordinate, Lorik refrained from saying anything, but the look of shock on his face spoke volumes.

"Get in the fucking cab and start the engine," Dritan shouted at the driver, who had backed away, raising his hands.

"Easy mate," the cabbie replied, not sounding anywhere near as worried as he should.

Alerted by the sound of high revving diesel engines, Dritan glanced over his shoulder, still keeping the handgun pointed at the driver. In his agitated state, he made the uncharacteristic mistake of ignoring the second cabbie, who was standing a couple of paces behind his fellow driver, partially shielded from view by the first man's body. Had Dritan been paying closer attention, he would have seen the second driver's right hand start to drift behind his back.

Two dark blue Mercedes Sprinters were now driving in convoy towards the hotel entrance. Dritan squinted his eyes to get a better view of the two men in the front cabin, which wasn't easy with the sun reflecting off the windshield and virtually blinding him. And then he saw that both men wore Kevlar helmets and were clad in dark flame retardant overalls.

A warning claxon sounded in his head.

"Atenție! Polite!" he shouted in Romanian as the first van whizzed by and screeched to a halt just beyond them.

Swerving sideways to provide cover for its occupants, the second van stopped well short of them. Even in his agitated state, the soldier in Dritan recognised that the police had effectively created a pincer movement that would allow them to launch an attack from two flanks.

Simultaneously, the back and side doors of both vehicles sprung open and a horde of heavily armed men in paramilitary attire jumped out.

Valmir reacted in an instant, reaching into the holdall and pulling out the Škorpion machine pistol. The lead van was closest to him, so he moved forward to engage that, seemingly unperturbed by the fact that they were heavily outnumbered.

Lorik was far less enthusiastic as he drew his weapon and started to fire short, controlled bursts at the officers who had alighted from the second van.

Dritan had forgotten about the two cab drivers. Their usefulness to him had ended the moment the two unmarked police vans had swerved in front and behind the minicabs, blocking their exit routes.

As Valmir and Lorik took shelter behind the two mini cabs in order to engage the officers spilling out of the vans, Dritan ran towards the hotel's sliding doors, desperate to find a suitable means of retreat for his comrades.

Just behind him, he heard shouts of, "ARMED POLICE! STOP OR I FIRE!" dropping into a crouch as he spun around, he saw the two cab drivers were now pointing pistols at him.

How could that be?

Squeezing off two shots, Dritan dived to his left, seeking the cover of a thick wooden bench located just outside the hotel entrance. One of the cab drivers – or cops, as he now realised they were – went down, but the other returned fire, and two bullets smashed into the top of the bench's woodwork, sending splinters flying over his head.

Tucking the handgun into his waistband, Dritan dragged the machine pistol from its holdall. He thrust it around the side of the bench and blindly sprayed the area where the policeman had been standing with bullets.

When he poked his head around the edge of the bench a moment later, he saw that the officer he'd fired at was unharmed, and that he was in now the process of dragging his injured colleague around the side of the building and out of the line of fire.

Dritan raised his weapon, intent on taking them both out before they could escape, but before he could take aim, they vanished from view. Cursing, he crawled across the pavement to join Lorik behind the rear cab.

"This is not good," Lorik said immediately. "We are badly outnumbered and have no way of retreating."

Dritan glanced back over his shoulder. "We go back through the hotel lobby," he said breathlessly. "Cover me while I get inside, and then I will do the same for you."

Lorik nodded, and then popped his weapon over the bonnet and fired off a quick burst.

Dritan looked to his left, where Valmir was crouching down behind the other vehicle. As he watched, the former soldier jumped up and sprayed bullets at the advancing officers, yelling maniacally as he fired. Two of the policemen stumbled and fell, but the rest rained fire down on the lone gunman.

Valmir staggered backwards, his chest blossoming in red as several of the rounds found their mark. A gush of blood erupted from Valmir's mouth, and then he dropped to his knees. His head tilted forward, coming to a stop against the side of the car.

It looked as though he were praying.

"Valmir!" Dritan screamed, knowing that there would be no reply, and that his long-time comrade was dead.

Almost as if moving in slow motion, Valmir toppled sideways and collapsed in a lifeless heap on the pavement.

There was no time to mourn. "Cover me," Dritan said, placing a hand on his friend's shoulder. "There is nothing we can do for Valmir, but if we move quickly we can still get ourselves out of this mess."

"Give me a moment," Lorik said, checking his weapon to see how many rounds he had left.

"Are you ready?" Dritan asked.

Lorik nodded. "Go now," he ordered. With that, he rose above the car and emptied the rest of the magazine at the advancing police officers.

———

When Conrad Livingstone glanced in his rear-view mirror and saw the

Omega's bar lights strobing blue behind him, he swore under his breath. This really wasn't a good time to be getting stopped by an anally retentive traffic cop for going a few miles per hour over the speed limit, not with the wooden box lying in plain sight in the front passenger footwell, where he'd tossed it as he'd jumped into the car.

It contained the revolver that he'd told Marcel to shoot his brother with, and although the Taurus had only been loaded with blanks, it was a very real gun, and one that he didn't have a licence for. If the Feds searched his car – as they were bound to – and found that, he would be looking at an automatic five stretch, and he couldn't afford that.

If the gun had been hidden beneath the spare wheel in the trunk, he might well have tried to bluff his way through an encounter with the Feds, but with it sitting in plain sight, there was no way he could risk it.

Licking his lips nervously, Livingstone put the car into sports mode and floored the accelerator, leaving the big saloon to eat his dust trail. The BMW M3 had a straight six cylinder engine that could generate 321bhp, which was effectively half of a McLaren F1 engine. The throttle response was instantaneous, and Livingstone found the deep and throaty exhaust note intoxicating. As it skidded through the junction, turning right into Kingsland Road towards Shoreditch and the City of London, the car gripped the road like glue.

Pressing his right foot into the floor, it went from 0-60 in a mere 5.6 seconds. Unable to contain his exhilaration as he was pushed back into his seat, Livingstone broke into a huge grin and whooped like a cowboy.

––––––––––––

Thankfully, PC Alun Jones, the driver of the Armed Response Vehicle, had been prepared for the possibility that Livingstone would fail to stop, so he wasn't caught off guard. As the BMW pulled away, he calmly put the Omega into sport mode and turned off the traction control. Then he activated the siren and set off in pursuit.

"Here we go," he said with an infectious grin. Being a Pan London resource, ARVs spent a lot of time blatting around the capital at high speed, but chases were few and far between, and Jones intended to make the most of this one.

"MP, MP, Active message from Trojan 501," his operator said into the Main-Set mic. "We've got a vehicle concerned in a shooting in Hackney failing to stop for us. We're in Downham Road, turning right, right, right, into Kingsland Road."

Jones let out a little whistle of appreciation as the BMW accelerated away from them. "It's bloody fast," he said admiringly. The Omega could hardly be described as sluggish. Its V6 engine was capable of going from 0-60 MPH in 7.3 seconds, but even so, it was struggling to stay with the M3 in a straight line.

"Don't you dare bloody lose it," PS Trevor Glynn, a gruff little Cockney, said from the back seat, where he was hanging onto the grip rail for all he was worth.

"Don't worry skip," Jones replied with pride. "His car might be more powerful, but I'm a Hendon trained driver. He don't stand a chance."

The road was relatively clear, and with no traffic to slow them down, the two cars hurtled along at breakneck speed. The speedometer quickly climbed to eighty, then ninety. And then, the bandit car was braking heavily, throwing up a cloud of smoke.

The reason for the sudden loss of speed, Jones saw, was that the traffic lights controlling the four way junction at Whiston Road had just changed to red and several cars were slowing down to stop for it.

Livingstone, it seemed, had no intention of complying with a red traffic signal. With the BMW now only doing thirty, he swerved into the opposite lane, passing the centre island on the wrong side, before taking a sharp left turn into Whiston Road and forcing an oncoming car up onto the pavement in the process.

"MP, MP, Trojan 501, the bandit is wrong side of the road, through red ATS and left, left, left into Whiston Road," the operator, PC Tommy Sands, said into the mic.

"*MP show Golf 1 assisting.*"

"*Golf 2 as well.*"

"*And Golf 3.*"

Sands grinned. "Looks like every pursuit car in Hackney is trying to get in on the act," he said. For every car that had said it was making its way to assist, he knew there would be several others who had started heading towards the chase without transmitting. The bandit car would soon be surrounded.

"The murder squad car's still behind us," Jones told his two colleagues.

"The more the merrier," Glynn said, risking a quick glance over his shoulder to see the green unmarked Omega sitting on their tail, headlights and grill mounted blue lights flashing, siren wailing. "As long as we're the ones who lay hands on the bugger when he finally stops."

CHAPTER THIRTY-FIVE

I'VE WAITED A LONG TIME TO HURT YOU

Head down, Dritan sprinted towards the sliding doors of the hotel. If they could just get inside and take a few hostages, there was still a chance that they could negotiate their way out of their predicament, trading their captives in exchange for freedom.

As he ran towards them, expecting them to swish open and admit him, the hotel doors remained stubbornly closed. "What the…?"

Skidding to a halt, he hammered on the safety glass with his fists, and then forced his fingertips into the gap between the glass and the wall and tried to pull them open, but they didn't budge an inch.

A round fired by one of the policeman smashed into the side of the wall to the left of his head, showering him with brick dust. Dritan instinctively ducked, pirouetted and fired a long burst from his Škorpion.

The police officers were closing in on Lorik, who bravely tried to hold them off. And then, as Dritan watched in horror, a bullet thudded into his friend, knocking him backwards onto the floor. The machine pistol flew from Lorik's hand and clattered across the pavement.

The policemen were on him in a second.

That only left him.

He was outnumbered and outgunned. He knew the sensible thing to do was drop his weapon and raise his hands in surrender, but doing that would lead to his spending the remainder of his life behind bars, trapped in a tiny cell where the nightmares and panic attacks would eventually drive him insane.

Uttering a fierce battle cry, Dritan raised the gun's stock to his shoulder and began walking toward the advancing police officers, firing short controlled bursts, determined to take as many of them with him as he could.

"DROP YOUR WEAPON!"

Dritan ignored the order and continued firing.

Almost instantly, a fusillade of bullets crashed into him, driving him backwards several steps. As he collapsed to the floor, a swarm of black clad figures quickly rushed forward to surround him. Kicking his gun away, they loomed over him, staring down triumphantly.

"Call the paramedics forward," one of them, an authoritative sounding female, called.

Dritan squinted up at the figures gathered around him. They were no more than silhouettes against the glaring backdrop of the afternoon sun. Clad as they were in Kevlar helmets, goggles and balaclavas, it was impossible for him to make out their facial expressions, but he imagined they would all be frowning down at him, confused by his choice to die rather than allow himself to be captured.

As the world around him blurred, and then faded to darkness, Dritan's disorientated mind turned to his two fallen comrades. He hoped that, wherever he was going in the afterlife, they would be there to meet him.

————

"It sounds like utter chaos at the hotel," Murphy shouted from the rear of the pool car. He had the encrypted radio's speaker wedged against his ear as the car careered around a tight corner into Newark Knok, a small road spanning the perimeter of one of the new housing estates that had cropped up in the area in recent years. It ran parallel with Woolwich Manor Way, and they soon found themselves heading back in the direction they had just come from.

Dillon had lost contact with Christine a couple of minutes earlier and, although he had repeatedly tried calling her back, it hadn't been possible to re-establish the connection. It might just be that her battery had died, he conceded, but a more sinister alternative was that Adebanjo had grown tired of running and turned on his pursuers. Christine was feisty enough in a verbal confrontation, but she wouldn't stand a cat in hell's chance against him in a fight and, although Charlie White seemed like a tough little cookie, the diminutive Scotsman was basically a third of the giant's size. Dillon seriously doubted that Charlie would be able to reach Adebanjo's jaw with a punch, even if he were standing on a chair when he threw it.

"All three gunmen are down," Murphy announced tensely, relaying the latest update. "One SFO's injured, but it's not believed to be life threatening."

Dillon was only half listening. "Keep your eyes peeled," he instructed. "They must be around here somewhere."

Geoff slowed the car to little more than a crawl. To their right, the road was populated by an endless succession of houses and low rise blocks, while to their left, there was nothing but a large expanse of grass that was lined at the bottom by thick trees.

About halfway along the road, they came upon a fenced off children's play area. It contained a climbing frame, a slide, and two swings that were hanging from a bright red frame. Two scruffily dressed young girls, neither of whom could have been older than eight or nine, were laughing and squealing as they competed to see who could get their swing to go the highest.

"Pull over so I can talk to these kids," Dillon ordered.

As soon as the car stopped, Dillon jumped out, leaving his door open. "Excuse me, girls," he called, leaning over the park fence and cradling his hands to his mouth. "Can I have a quick word?"

The girl nearest to him, a slim thing with lank brown hair and a dirty, gaunt face, glared at him suspiciously. "My mum said I aint allowed to talk to strangers," she shouted.

"It's okay, I'm a police officer," Dillon said, smiling reassuringly.

The girl furthest away, who was slightly shorter and a bit dumpy, with a short mop of curly red hair and a face full of freckles, scowled at her. "Don't answer him, Janice," she said, fixing Dillon with a mean stare. "Your dad said all policemen are dickheads."

"Charming," Dillon muttered under his breath. "Listen, have either of you seen a big black man with a bald head run this way?" he asked. "There might have been a man and woman chasing him."

"Oh them," Janice said, much to the annoyance of her friend. Using her feet as brakes, she brought her swing to an abrupt stop.

"Janice!" the little redhead scolded, but she too came to a halt.

"Shush, Chelsea," Janice chided her, before pointing to where the road disappeared around to the right about fifty yards further along "They ran that way, mister," she said helpfully.

"I'm gonna tell your dad you spoke to the dickhead," Chelsea snapped, folding her arms huffily.

"Don't you dare grass me up!" Janice admonished, reaching across to shove her friend sideways.

Leaving them to it, Dillon jumped back into the car and signalled for Geoff to follow the road around to the right.

As they drove around the bend, Dillon immediately caught sight of a bent over figure on the corner of the next junction along, about three hundred yards ahead.

"There!" he shouted, nudging Geoff's arm. "I think that's Chrissy."

"I see her," Geoff replied, accelerating the car towards her.

As the pool car closed in on her, Christine Taylor stood up with a groan of exhaustion and raised a hand to flag it down. Her face was bright red and dripping with sweat.

"Where's Charlie?" Dillon demanded, sticking his head out of the window.

Christine pointed into the side road, which was called Downings. About a hundred and fifty yards along, Dillon saw Charlie White standing on the corner of some flats, waving excitedly to get their attention.

Dillon raised a hand to acknowledge him. "You okay?" he asked Christine.

"Knackered," she said, mopping her brow wearily.

"Where was Adebanjo last sighted?"

Cristine jerked her thumb over her shoulder at a three storey block of flats with the big blue security door. "Bastard followed some woman in there," she said. "We were too far behind to stop him, and by the time we got there, the door had already shut. No sod answered when we tried buzzing all the flats, so Charlie's gone around the back of the building to cover the rear exit. I dropped my bloody phone while I was crossing the road and a poxy lorry flattened it, so we haven't been able to call for backup."

Dillon raised an eyebrow. Christine had a habit of dropping her phones. This was the third one that she had broken in as many months. Well, at least that explained why they had lost contact.

"Don't say a bloody word," she warned, catching the look.

Dillon handed her his Job mobile. "Take this in case he comes out of the front," he said, somehow refraining from asking her not to drop it. "I'll radio for backup and we'll do a door to door search as soon as it gets here."

They drove over to where Charlie was standing. He was still wearing the blazer the hotel manager had loaned him, and he looked even hotter than Christine, if that were possible. His hair was plastered to his head, making his ears look even bigger than normal. "Och, you took your bloody time getting here," he complained, striding angrily toward his colleagues as they all jumped out of the pool car. He tore off his jacket and threw it into the car.

"What happened to your bloody phone?" Dillon demanded.

Charlie blushed, going even redder than before. "Aye, well, when Adebanjo did an unexpected runner, I went straight after him. I didnae have time to pop back into the office and collect my phone."

Dillon rolled his eyes. "Are we happy he's still inside?" he asked.

"As happy as we can be," Charlie replied, sulkily. "I cannae figure out why he ran," he added, scratching his head as he spoke.

"Me neither," Dillon admitted. "I mean, there's no way he could possibly know that we've got enough evidence to charge him with all five murders."

"Well, something must have spooked him," Murphy said. "Maybe, when we find him, he'll tell us."

———

Standing in the tastefully decorated kitchen of a ground floor flat at the rear of the block, Samuel Adebanjo listened through an open window to every word that the detectives said.

The Feds were standing less than ten feet away from him, separated by a six foot high wooden fence, and they were making no effort to be keep their voices down.

To his astonishment, one of them had just claimed they had enough evidence to charge him with the murders. The revelation had stunned him, but there was no time to try and work out what had gone wrong. All that mattered now was getting away.

"Do you have a car?" Adebanjo asked Agnes Willoughby, the terrified woman he was holding captive.

When he'd followed her into the block, Adebanjo's intention had simply been to cut through to the back of the flats, but Willoughby had inadvertently gifted him the perfect hiding place when she opened the door to her ground floor flat in front of him. Bundling her inside, Adebanjo had quickly slammed the door shut behind him and, as the terrified woman started to scream, he had grabbed her throat in a vice-like grip, choking off all sound. Pinning her against the wall, he'd demanded to know if anyone else was inside the premises. Willoughby, a slim, well dressed black lady in her late fifties, had almost fainted with fear, and was obviously convinced that the sweating giant looming over her was about to rape or murder her – or maybe both.

Adebanjo had done his best to calm her down, repeatedly telling her that he meant her no harm, and that he would be gone as soon as the coast was clear, but he could tell from the horror in her eyes that she didn't believe him.

He was currently standing directly behind Willoughby, with a massive hand clamped across the lower half of her face to prevent her from screaming. Unable to speak, all she could do was nod in response to his question.

"Good. Where are the keys?"

With a trembling hand, she pointed towards an oak sideboard out in the hall.

Adebanjo dragged her roughly across the room, knocking a chair over in the process. Once in the hall, his eyes scanned the top of the sideboard for a car key, but the surface was so covered in clutter that he couldn't see it.

"Where is it?" he hissed, growing impatient.

Willoughby frantically pushed some bills and a copy of yesterday's newspaper aside and snatched up a bunch of keys that had been buried beneath them. One of them had a Ford emblem on it.

"Good," Adebanjo muttered, extracting the car key from her trembling hand. "Now, tell me, what type of car is it, and where is it parked?" He cautiously relaxed his grip and withdrew his hand a fraction from her mouth. "If you scream, I will snap your neck," he warned her. The words were spoken quietly, in no more than a whisper, but there was no doubting the menace behind them. "Do you understand?"

Willoughby nodded, fearfully. "It's a…" her voice faltered and she started to cry.

Adebanjo growled at her. "I don't have time for your blabbing. Tell me about the car."

Willoughby swallowed hard. "It's a grey Ford Escort, and it's parked out the back," she sobbed.

"Good," he said with a smile, and then punched her hard on the chin, dropping her like a stone. He caught her before she hit the ground, and then carried her limp form into the bedroom, laying her on top of the bed with surprising gentleness. He rolled her into the recovery position so that she wouldn't suffocate, and then rushed back to the kitchen window and listened carefully.

He couldn't hear the Feds talking anymore, so he unlocked the rear door and crept into the small garden. There was a gate in the fence that led out into the car park at the back of the block. Cautiously peering over the top, Adebanjo saw that there were three cars parked against the rear wall, one of which was a newish grey Ford Escort. He pointed the key fob at the car and pressed it. There was a satisfying clunk from the car doors, and the indicators flashed.

Adebanjo gently unlocked the gate and cautiously stuck his head around the corner. The road appeared empty. He slipped out and padded across the hot tarmac to the car. As he was opening the driver's door, he heard hurried footsteps coming from the direction of the road. Looking up, he saw DS Jonny Murphy purposefully striding across the car park towards him, his baton drawn.

For a moment Adebanjo was shocked to see the Greater Manchester Police detective here in London. The man had become the bane of his life, following him around, poking his nose into his affairs, turning a criminal investigation into a personal crusade for justice. Did his presence here mean that the relentless cop had finally discovered some evidence against him? With no time to dwell on such things, Adebanjo rushed around the side of the car to meet his nemesis head on, intending to silence him before he could raise the alarm.

"I've waited a long time to hurt you," he snarled.

————

Livingstone's M3 tore along Whiston Road, with the two police cars in close pursuit. Pedestrians on the pavement turned to stare at the chase, gawping at the three cars as they sped by. Sparks flew from the bottom of the BMW as it hurtled over the intermittent speed humps and landed heavily on the other side. The two Omegas, not having a low slung racing suspension, fared much better over the bumps, and that enabled them to close the gap on their quarry.

This was a busy road, with lots of junctions branching off of it, most of which were obscured by parked cars, making them hard to spot. Undeterred by the prospect of a vehicle blindly pulling out into his path, or a pedestrian running into the road in front of him from between parked cars, Livingstone red-lined the throttle, allowing the M3 to achieve frightening speeds in his determination to escape at any cost.

The lights at the junction of Queensbridge Road were against him on red, but Livingstone bullied his way out, causing traffic crossing his path to slam on the brakes to avoid crashing into him. A car coming from his right screeched to a halt, stopping with inches to spare, but the reactions of the driver in the car immediately behind were nowhere near as good, and it rear ended the first car, shunting it into the middle of the junction, blocking the road and temporarily stopping the pursuing police vehicles from following.

Grinning as he surveyed the carnage he'd caused in his rear-view mirror, Livingstone buried his foot all the way to the floor, enjoying the meaty roar of the engine and the sweet burble of the exhaust as the automatic transmission worked its way through the gears. He drove the length of Whiston Road, watching the speedo climb all the way to a hundred before he reached a point where he had to apply the brakes. At the end of the road, he turned left, skidding into Pritchard's Road. Passing *The Perseverance* Public House on his right, Livingstone took off towards Broadway Market and the Regent's Canal.

He was ecstatic.

He had done it; he had lost the Feds.

Now all he needed to do was chuck the gun in the canal and he would be home and dry. The worst thing they'd be able to do to him was report him for a few traffic offences.

He had almost reached the beginning of Broadway Market when he heard the sirens behind him. Faint at first, they rapidly grew in intensity. Peering in his mirror, he saw the two Omegas turning into Pritchard's Road, about two hundred yards behind him. As his eyes returned to the road ahead, he spotted two more marked patrol cars, Vectras this time. With their headlights flashing alternately and their roof bars strobing, the pursuit cars were hurtling through the market, coming straight towards him.

His earlier jubilation instantly faded. "Shit!" he cursed, stepping on the brakes and causing the BMW to fishtail.

With the cops now in front of him as well as behind, Livingstone's options were severely limited. Glancing left and right, he made a snap decision and turned left into Regent's Row, running parallel with the canal path.

Up ahead in the distance, he spotted a small police van coming towards him.

Behind him, a procession of police vehicles were turning into Regent's Row, and with his path ahead now blocked, there was nowhere for him to go.

"Fuck!" he screamed, bringing the car to an abrupt stop outside Debenham Court. Unfastening his seat belt, he leaned over and retrieved the wooden box from the passenger footwell before jumping from the car.

Emerging from the icy chill of the air conditioned interior into the searing heat of the early afternoon sun, Livingstone felt as though he had just walked into blast furnace.

The most important thing now was to get rid of the gun. With no time for subtlety, he ran to the canal path and lobbed the box into the water but, instead of sinking, it just floated on top of the water.

"Shit!" he exclaimed, staring at in disbelief.

Behind him, police cars were skidding to a halt. Up ahead, the little police van was almost upon him. With a final glance at the box, which was only just starting to go under, he turned and sprinted towards the nearby flats.

From his rear, there were shouts of, "ARMED POLICE!"

From the front, he heard something that scared him even more.

"STAND STILL OR I'LL RELEASE THE DOG!"

Ignoring them all, Livingstone ran onto the footpath at the side of Debenham Court, hoping to lose his pursuers inside the estate.

CHAPTER THIRTY-SIX

STAND STILL

Jonny Murphy had volunteered to remain at the back of the flats and keep an eye open for Adebanjo, in case he tried to slip out the rear before the cavalry arrived. He hadn't actually expected the African to show his face, but now that he had, it was up to him to stop the giant.

His face contorted with anger, Adebanjo lowered his gleaming head and charged forward, arms outstretched to grab the detective.

Murphy instinctively backed away, suddenly feeling very small and frail. The metal baton in his hand seemed woefully inadequate to deal with the human juggernaut bearing down on him at speed.

"GET BACK!" he yelled, raising his baton above his shoulder in readiness to strike. If he'd had the time to think about what he was doing, Murphy might well have done the sensible thing and turned and fled. Instead, he gritted his teeth, stepped to the side, and took a well-aimed swing at the advancing giant's skull, putting everything he had into the blow.

During the twice yearly officer safety classes that every police officer was required to attend, the instructors constantly emphasised the potential dangers involved with delivering a head blow, stressing that these were only justifiable under extreme circumstances and should be avoided if at all possible. That was all very good in theory, but Murphy seriously doubted that anything less than a blow to the bowling ball sized head would have any effect on the enraged giant.

Moving faster than Murphy would have thought possible, Adebanjo intercepted the downward blow, trapping Murphy's wrist in one of his gigantic hands. As he squeezed, Murphy gasped in pain, feeling his fingers go numb. Almost immediately, his hand flew open and the baton fell harmlessly to the floor, clattering across the pavement. Without breaking his stride, Adebanjo grabbed Murphy by the throat and, lifting him clear off the ground with one hand, ran him backwards into a wall.

The air was violently expelled from Murphy's lungs as he slammed into the brickwork. His head whipped back and collided with the wall, causing stars to explode before his eyes. As the tiny glowing orbs faded, the world around him began to swirl and he lurched sideways like a drunk.

"You have messed with me for the last time, fam," Adebanjo promised as he lowered him to the floor. Straddling his unresisting form, Adebanjo wrapped his powerful hands around the semi-conscious detective's neck. With a malevolent smile, he found Murphy's windpipe and began to squeeze.

———

Conrad Livingstone ran along the footpath beside Debenham Court, feet pounding, arms pumping, lungs burning. His face glistened with sweat, and his heart felt as though it might explode at any second.

Risking a quick look over his shoulder, he was astounded to see that the police were still some way behind, and they only seemed to be jogging slowly, not giving it everything they had to close the gap on him. And then, as he heard a low, blood curdling growl coming from his left, he realised why.

Casting a fearful glance sideways, he saw a long haired German

Shepherd tearing across the grass, closing in on him at a forty-five degree angle. The thing was the size of a timber wolf. Teeth bared, eyes blazing with bloodlust, it was gaining on him at an alarming speed.

He had witnessed someone being savaged by a police dog during the Brixton riots in 1995, and it wasn't something he wanted to experience for himself. Redoubling his efforts, Livingstone ran out of the estate, emerging into Pownall Road.

"STAND STILL!" the voice of the dog's handler bellowed at him from a long way behind.

Livingstone ignored the command. He had seen the savage glint in the dog's eyes; it was the look of a vicious predator, and he knew that nothing would stop it from sinking its teeth into him, given half a chance.

He sprinted straight across Pownall Road, heading for the safety of a five foot high wall on the other side. As he ran, he could feel the German Shepherd snapping at his heels.

Livingstone leapt at the wall, grabbing the top with both hands. Pulling himself up, he managed to swing his right leg over, but before he could pull his left leg out of harm's way, the snapping dog launched itself into the air, sinking its teeth deep into his calf. The pain was indescribable, and Livingstone screamed in agony as he felt himself being dragged backwards with incredible force. The sensation of flesh tearing, as he tried to pull his injured leg clear of the animal's jaws, was something he would never forget.

In desperation, he tried to punch the dog's snout, but that just sent it into even more of a frenzy, and it started to shake its large head from side to side, tearing large chunks from his flesh.

Livingstone fell to the ground, landing heavily. Moving in for the kill, the dog released his bloody pulp of a leg, and turned its attention to his arms, which were wrapped around his head.

Livingstone spotted a red telephone box a little way off to his right, and he started dragging himself along the floor towards it. The dog was hanging from his right arm as he tried to stand up, growling furiously. Somehow, Livingstone managed to pry open the creaking door and slip inside the kiosk. Punching and kicking at the snapping jaws, he finally managed to pull his arm loose and drag it inside.

Enraged, and spraying large globules of spit everywhere, the shaggy dog began circling the telephone box, jumping up and barking at the glass in its determination to find a way inside to finish the job. With its foaming mouth and blazing eyes, it looked rabid.

Inside, Livingstone was unable to place any weight on his badly mauled left leg. Holding onto the telephone for support, he looked down at the torn and bloody flesh hanging from his calf.

He was trapped, and he realised that his arrest was now imminent. To add insult to injury, he had to assume that the Feds had seen him throw the wooden box into the canal. If they sent divers in to retrieve the revolver, he would be bang to rights for possessing an unlicensed firearm, which would effectively ruin all his carefully laid plans to increase his power base in North London.

Raising his head to the ceiling, he let out a primal howl of pain and frustration.

A few moments later, half a dozen police officers came running out of the estate. Three of them carried Heckler & Koch 9mm Parabellum machine pistols, which they cradled against their chests. Another had a long lead wrapped around his body. They all stopped running when they caught sight of him, trapped inside the phone box with the police dog glaring in at him hatefully. Laughing amongst themselves, they slowed to a walk and crossed the road.

"Call that fucking dog off," Livingstone cried as it tried to ram its head through a missing glass pane to get inside the kiosk.

"Fluffy, sit," the handler said. The dog complied at once, staring up adoringly at his master, and looking as though butter wouldn't melt in his blood stained mouth.

"Good boy," the handler said, proudly. He leaned down and ruffled the dog's ear affectionately. "You really are daddy's good little boy," he cooed, pulling a ridiculously soppy face and giving the dog a biscuit as a reward.

Fluffy hoovered the treat up and then gave his hand a gentle lick in gratitude.

———

Dillon walked over to join Charlie and Chrissie, who were standing on the corner of Newark Knok and Downings. He had just finished trying the buzzers in the panel by the communal door, emulating Christine's earlier attempt to gain entry to the block. In the end, just like her, he had given up, assuming that the residents were either out at work or stone deaf.

"This is getting ridiculous," Dillon complained, looking down at his watch. Under normal circumstances, the backup he had requested would have arrived by now, but as most of the division's units were still tucked up assisting the SFOs at the nearby hotel shooting, he had been told that he was going to have to wait until they were released.

He reached for his phone, but then remembered he had given it to Chrissie when they arrived.

"Chrissy, love," he said. "Do me a favour. Give British Transport Police at Euston a call, just in case Adebanjo slips through the net here and manages to reach the train station."

With a sigh that said, 'why do I have to be the one to do it?' Christine began dialling.

Wiping his brow, he glanced over at the spot where the Liverpudlian detective was supposed to be keeping watch on the back of the block, but there was no sign of him. "Where's Jonny?" he demanded tetchily,

Charlie shrugged lethargically, too exhausted from all the running he'd done to care. "Maybe he's having a wee look around the car park," he suggested.

"Yeah, he's probably found a nice spot in the shade to stand in," Christine added, shielding her eyes from the sun's glare with her free hand. "I wish I could bloody well do that."

Dillon grunted his disapproval. "I told him to stay where I could see him," he said angrily. With a huff, he set off to find the missing GMP officer.

He strode into the car park a few moments later, fully expecting to find Murphy leaning against a wall, sheltering from the Saharan-like heat and smoking a cigarette. Instead, he saw the detective lying flat on his back by a grey Ford that was parked against the far wall. To his horror, Samuel Adebanjo was sitting astride Murphy, throttling the life out of him.

The reprimand that Dillon had intended to dish out for disobeying his instructions was instantly forgotten. "Oi!" he yelled as he ran towards them, arms outstretched to pull the giant from the defenceless cop.

Adebanjo sprang to his feet with cat like agility, turning to meet him like the dangerous animal he was.

The African's face was strangely calm.

As Dillon skidded to a halt several feet short of Adebanjo, his eyes nervously flickered down to Murphy, and he was immensely relieved to see his chest was still rising and falling regularly.

"It's all over," Dillon said, reaching behind his back for his handcuffs. "Why don't you do yourself a favour and come quietly?"

Adebanjo actually smiled at that. "You are either very brave or very foolish," he said in a matter of fact tone. "I have killed many men, and I do not think that killing you will be too problematic." Rolling his thick neck, he started to walk towards Dillon, the sinister smile on his face spreading to reveal two golden canines.

Dillon scanned the area around them for any possible weapons that the giant could use against him. Satisfied that there were none, he took a half step backwards, inviting Adebanjo to bring the fight to him. The gigantic black man duly obliged, misinterpreting Dillon's retreat as a sign of weakness.

As far as Dillon could see, the only way out of the car park was past him. *Aint gonna happen*, he promised himself.

Unlike Jack Tyler, who hated having to resort to fisticuffs, Dillon was happy to fight anyone, anytime, anywhere. And, if the truth be told, ever since Tuesday night, when he'd compared the size of Adebanjo's biceps to his own back at Forest Gate police station, Dillon had been wondering how he would fare against the giant in a no holds barred fight. Now, it seemed, he was about to find out.

"Samuel Adebanjo, I'm Detective Inspector Dillon from the Area Major Investigation Pool. I'm arresting you for conspiracy to commit multiple murders. You don't have to say anything, but-"

Adebanjo lowered his head and charged, moving with surprising speed for such a big man. He aimed his shoulder at Dillon's chest, clearly intending to drive him backwards and knock him to the ground.

Dillon saw the move coming a mile off. Side stepping, he drove his right elbow into the giant's skull, knocking him sideways. It was like hitting concrete, and Dillon felt a sharp jolt of pain travel all the way up his arm into his shoulder.

Adebanjo had gone down on one knee, but he was up in an instant, seemingly unharmed. Shaking his massive head to clear it, he eyed Dillon with new found respect. "Impressive, fam," he said, rolling his neck again. "Enjoy the moment, because it won't happen again."

Dillon smiled. "As I was saying, you don't have to say anything, but if you don't mention when questioned something which you later rely on in court-"

Adebanjo leapt forward again, but this time, instead of trying to grab hold of Dillon, he drove his right foot forward, aiming for the detective's midsection.

Caught off guard, Dillon instinctively skipped back, trying to block the front kick with a downward swipe of his right arm. He managed to dissipate most of the kick's energy, but Adebanjo's size fifteen foot still connected firmly with his stomach, sending Dillon staggering back several steps.

The giant grinned. "See what I mean?"

Dillon had been winded by the blow, and he doubted he would have been able to continue had he not diffused most of the power by moving back and partially blocking the kick. As Adebanjo walked towards him, Dillon made a point of contemptuously brushing away the dirty footprint the giant had left on his shirt, although in reality he was using the time to get his breath back.

"Let's leave the bragging until we're finished, shall we?" he said, raising his guard.

The two men began circling each other. Adebanjo had a distinct reach advantage, but Dillon wasn't concerned about that. He would do what he was best at, and focus on closing the gap so he could use his grappling skills to his advantage.

He had been caught out by the surprise kick, but now that he knew how lethal Adebanjo's legs were, he would be far more careful. Sure enough, Adebanjo came in with another front kick to the midsection, quickly followed by a roundhouse kick to the side of the head. Dillon sidestepped the first, and raised his arms to absorb the power from the second. It was like being hit by a falling tree trunk, he conceded, knowing that his forearms would be covered in bruises later.

As Adebanjo came in again, this time throwing a haymaker of a right hook, Dillon slipped under it and hit him hard in the stomach, smiling to himself at the surprised 'Oomph!' that came from Adebanjo's lips.

Adebanjo backed off, clutching his stomach. For the first time, he looked a little unsettled.

Dillon could kick too, and he stepped forward and drove the ball of his right foot into the giant's groin. It might not conform to the Marquis of Queensberry rules, but it did the job.

Adebanjo instantly doubled up, but he was far from beaten. Lunging forward with a savage snarl, he wrapped his enormous arms around Dillon, pinning his arms to his body. Before Dillon could react, the giant began squeezing with all his might.

Dillon found himself being lifted clear off the floor as Adebanjo leaned back and put everything he had into crushing Dillon's spine.

With his arms now trapped against his sides, Dillon was powerless to hit out at the man who was trying to snap him in two, and he soon found himself struggling to breathe. As the pressure around his body increased, several vertebrae cracked loudly, and he gasped in pain.

Powerless to use his arms, Dillon tried to drive his knee up into the giant's groin, but they were wedged together so tightly that he couldn't even move it an inch. As his vision began to blur, Dillon drew his head backwards and then rammed it forward again, driving his forehead into the bridge of the African's nose. It felt like he was headbutting a wall, but Adebanjo screamed in agony as the bone shattered with a loud crack and blood streamed from his nostrils.

Dillon repeated the move, and this time Adebanjo's grip wavered, which enabled him to suck in some much needed air. Wriggling like mad, he managed to slide his right hand down towards the giant's groin, and as the hitman started to crush him again, he grabbed hold of his testicles and squeezed with all his might.

Adebanjo held out for several seconds, but eventually, he let out a howl of pain and released Dillon, taking a step backwards and cupping his injured privates.

As the giant stared at him in hatred, Dillon rushed forwards and unleashed an uppercut to his jaw that snapped his head backwards at an alarming speed.

Adebanjo quickly raised his hands to protect himself as Dillon followed this up with a barrage of punches. Most of them were absorbed by Adebanjo's arms, but one of them slipped through his guard and connected with the giant's temple, causing his knees to buckle.

Incredibly, despite being decked for a second time, Adebanjo stood straight up and started trading punches with Dillon. He even landed a few blows of his own as they went toe to toe, slugging it out like a pair of heavyweight boxers.

Eventually, the two men broke apart and began circling each other. Battered and bruised, they were wheezing like old men as they looked for an opening that would tip the balance in their favour.

Dillon's body ached all over, and one of his eyes was starting to close, but Adebanjo looked even worse, and he could tell the giant was waning.

Suddenly, Adebanjo made a desperate lunge for Dillon's throat with his outstretched hands. Dillon ducked underneath and took a wobbly step to the side. As Adebanjo's momentum carried him past, Dillon reached out, wrapping one thick arm around his opponent's head and the other around his neck. Interlocking them, he applied a sleeper hold that worked by applying pressure to Adebanjo's carotid artery, cutting off the blood supply to his brain.

Adebanjo fought back, giving it everything he had, but as he became increasingly starved of oxygen, the intensity of his resistance dwindled. When he finally stopped struggling, the giant's hands, which had been frantically clawing at Dillon's arms, fell to his sides. Adebanjo swayed on the spot for a moment, and then toppled forward onto the floor with Dillon still wrapped tightly around him.

"It's over," Dillon panted, shaking from exhaustion. "You, my old son, are well and truly nicked."

After disentangling himself from the giant's limbs, and making sure that Adebanjo was still breathing, Dillon staggered across the car park to retrieve the handcuffs he'd dropped at the beginning of the fight.

Dropping to his knees, he quickly secured Adebanjo's arms behind his back and then placed him in the recovery position. As soon as that was done, he dragged himself painfully to his feet and, ignoring the protests from his injured body, rushed over to check on Murphy.

CHAPTER THIRTY-SEVEN

LET'S GO AND HAVE A PROPER DEBRIEF IN THE PUB

The station van pulled up next to where Adebanjo was sitting on the kerb with his hands cuffed behind his massive back. Despite being shackled, he still exuded an air of menace, and Dillon cautioned the officers to be on their guard as he was extremely dangerous. Unfazed by the warning, the two burly constables unceremoniously hoisted him to his feet and threw him into the back.

"Where are we taking him, guv?" the uniformed driver asked as he slammed the rear doors shut and wiped his perspiring brow.

"I've reserved cell space for him at Forest Gate," Dillon informed him. "Is it okay if one of my DCs jumps in with you so she can give the facts of the arrest to the custody officer?"

The driver gave him a lazy half shrug. "That's fine by me."

With a weary wave, Christine jumped into the van, sighing with pleasure as the air conditioning wafted over her.

As soon as it had gone, Dillon walked over to the back of an ambulance that was parked behind the flats. In the back, two pretty paramedics were fussing over Jonny Murphy.

"Is he alright?" he asked Charlie White, who was leaning against the back doors, looking bored.

"Aye, he's fine," Charlie said, dismissively. "If you ask me, he's just milking the attention from these wee lasses."

The lead paramedic popped her head out of the ambulance. "I think we'll run him down to A&E just to be on the safe side," she said. She was a petite blonde in her late twenties, with blue eyes and shoulder length hair tied in a ponytail.

"I don't need to go to hospital," Murphy protested from inside. "I've got work to do."

The paramedic looked at Dillon for guidance.

"Take him to hospital," he said flatly.

"But there's nothing wrong with me," Murphy argued.

"Don't worry, laddie. By the time they finish dealing with you in A&E, there will be," Charlie responded, waving as the paramedic closed the back doors on him.

Geoff was waiting for them in the pool car, fretting over the fact that he'd run out of things to eat, and he earned himself a sharp rebuke from Dillon when he asked for permission to make a quick detour to ASDA and stock up on snacks. Sulking over the refusal, Geoff drove them back to the hotel courtyard, which now resembled a war zone, in silence.

Dillon was pleased to see that Newman had everything completely under control. Looking as chilled as ever, despite the searing heat and the recent gun battle, the former Para ambled over to give the detectives an update.

He pointed at Dillon's eye. "Looks like you're going to have a nice little shiner there," he said with a grin.

Dillon smiled back. "You should see the other guy." The smile immediately faded and his voice took on a more serious tone. "What's the damage here?"

"Two of the shooters have been pronounced dead at the scene," Newman informed him, "but the suspect with the tattooed neck is still alive – just."

Dillon grimaced. He'd really been hoping to capture all three without a shot being fired. "Will he survive?" he asked.

Newman's face remained impassive. "Doubt it. The paramedics reckon he's only hanging on by the thinnest of threads."

"What about your troops?" Dillon asked next. "Any casualties there?"

"One of the officers posing as a cabbie was hit in the shoulder," Newman informed him with regret. "Thankfully, it only appears to be a superficial wound, so hopefully he'll make a speedy recovery. A couple of the other lads were hit during the initial assault, but their body armour absorbed the full force of the rounds. Apart from some bruised ribs and a couple of dented prides, they're fine."

"What about the Kalu twins?" Dillon asked, looking around the forecourt. "Where are they?"

"Your people rounded them up after they did a runner," he said. "From what I gather, the fat fuckers didn't get too far before they were detained."

Before long, the duty CSM arrived to take charge of the forensic examination. Her name was Cynthia Alderton, and she was a tall, beanpole of a woman in her early forties. A short brown bob covered an angular face that seemed to be set in a permanent scowl. In spite of her stern appearance, Cynthia turned out to be friendly enough, and he quickly formed the opinion that she was ultra-efficient at her job.

One of the first things that Alderton did was arrange for tents to be erected over the two bodies. Not only was it a disturbing sight for the general public to see, but representatives from the ever increasing media presence were becoming increasingly bold in their attempts to take long range photographs of the dead gunmen.

In dribs and drabs, the scientific support began to arrive. This included several local Scene of Crime Officers, an SO3 photographer, a bushy haired blood pattern analyst, and a studious looking scientist specialising in the recovery of firearms evidence. After a quick, but very detailed briefing, Alderton set them all to work, turning the crime scene into a hive of frenetic activity.

Eventually, the medical team stabilised the critically injured shooter enough to transfer him to the Royal London Hospital, and

Dillon watched the ambulance drive out of the car park on blues and twos.

Unable to raise either Tyler or Bull on the phone, Dillon and the SFO team set off for the Post Incident Procedure, leaving Charlie White in charge.

———

Whenever death or serious injury occurs as a result of police officers discharging firearms, a rigorous Post incident Procedure is carried out. In the Metropolitan Police Service, the designated venue for this is Lemon Street police station in East London.

In addition to the SO19 officers deployed during the shooting, a number of other parties were required to attend. These included the nominated Post Incident Manager – who in this case was a sallow faced inspector from SO19 called Tim Martin – a Police Federation Representative, rubber heelers from the Complaints Investigation Branch, and someone from the Independent Police Complaints Commission.

Tyler and Dillon managed to hold a hurried private conversation before the gruelling process commenced, each running the other through the events at their respective deployments. Both were shocked to hear how badly things had gone at the other location.

Wishing his friend good luck, Tyler walked into the room with some trepidation. He was acutely aware that, in addition to the actions of the SFOs, his and Dillon's decision making processes would also be closely scrutinised. It was an unsettling thought, and even though they had carried out their duties to the best of their ability under the most difficult and challenging of circumstances, he knew the Yard wouldn't hesitate to sacrifice either one or both of them if the findings of the CIB or IPPC enquiries were overly critical.

———

As soon as the lengthy PIP concluded, the two weary looking SFO teams were escorted away to make their provisional notes – full statements wouldn't be taken from them for another forty-eight hours, in accordance with protocol.

Getting out of Lemon Street as quickly as they could, Tyler and Dillon reconvened to a local café in order to compare notes.

The place had a funky décor of orange, lime green, and purple that was so in Tyler's face it was already starting to give him a headache by the time they reached the counter. Glancing around as he waited for the barista to serve them, he wondered if the designer had taken some form of hallucinogenic substance before coming up with the concept. Either that or he had just been colour blind.

At least the garishly decorated café had air conditioning. It was getting on for six-thirty, but the heat outside was still oppressive.

"Bloody hell, Jack. What a day!" Dillon said, resting his elbow on the counter.

"What a week, you mean!" Tyler said with a wry smile.

Dillon leaned in conspiratorially. "You know, I'd much rather be supping a cold beer than a frothy cappuccino. Why don't we go and have a proper debrief in the pub?"

Tyler grinned. That was so typical of Dillon. "I'm afraid we'll have to postpone our trip to the pub until the suspects are all charged."

Dillon's shoulders sagged in disappointment. "Yeah, I know," he conceded, "but it was a nice idea."

"Yes, it was," Tyler said, smiling affectionately.

He became silent as his mind drifted back to the aftermath of the armed entry to Meek's flat in Touchard House. Jerome Norris had been pronounced dead at the scene but, by some miracle, Devon Brown was still alive, albeit in a very bad way. HEMS had been called out, and a section of Pitfield Street had been closed off in order for the helicopter to land safely. Naturally, this had caused chaos with the afternoon traffic flow, but that had been the least of Tyler's problems.

Pamela Bennet, the HEMS trauma doctor in attendance, ably assisted by the ballistic injury paramedics, had worked tirelessly on Brown for some time before declaring that he was stable enough to be air-lifted to the Royal London Hospital in Whitechapel.

Although there was a gaping entry wound in Marcel Meeks' right shoulder, there had been no sign of a corresponding exit wound, and

Bennet had concluded that the slug had become embedded in bone and would need to be surgically removed. Tyler had watched dispassionately as the teenager, dosed to the hilt with a mixture of Morphine and Ketamine, was carefully loaded into the back of an ambulance.

Tyson Meeks had been unconscious when they stretchered him out of the premises. His face had been covered with cuts and contusions, his torso crisscrossed with deep lacerations from the barbed wire that had tethered him to the chair. Although the injuries appeared truly horrific, the paramedic overseeing his departure had seemed quite chilled about them, confidently predicting that her patient would make a full recovery. Her exact words had been, "He might end up looking like one of Frankenstein's monsters, but at least he'll live."

After they'd been served, the detectives carried their drinks over to a quiet table near the back. Tyler sat in an uber stylish chair that was almost as uncomfortable as it was ugly. The designer had definitely been as high as a kite, he decided. There could be no other rational explanation for producing something so grotesque and impractical. He watched in amusement as his friend squeezed his large bulk into the tiny seat opposite.

"I always thought my life on the Organised Crime Group was pretty exciting," Dillon told him, trying to get comfortable, "but you lot have made it seem pretty tame."

Tyler chuckled. "It's not always like this, Dill. I promise."

Dillon studied his knuckles, which were red and bruised, and then flexed his fingers painfully. "Adebanjo's skull must be made of titanium," he complained.

Tyler raised an eyebrow at that. "It can't be thicker than yours, surely?"

Dillon looked up from his hand. "Honestly, Jack. I hit him hard enough to knock out a bloody elephant, but he just kept on coming. In the end, I had to choke him into submission."

Jack shrugged. "So what? You won. That's all that matters."

Dillon grunted. "I suppose you're right," he admitted, looking down at his hand again. The FME had told him that nothing was broken, and that he should just apply ice to ease the swelling. His right eye was also bruised, as was his forehead, and his body felt as though it had been used as a punchbag. "What's the plan now?" he asked, taking a sip of his coffee.

Tyler blew his cheeks out. "Well, we've got three dead suspects, two hospitalised suspects, and three suspects in the bin ready to be interviewed. Once all their addresses are searched, I suppose we crack on with interviewing the first three, and work our way through the others as and when they're fit enough to be released from hospital. Speaking of hospitals, how's Jonny doing?"

Dillon grinned ruefully. "I called him as soon as I got out of the PIP. The hospital's given him a clean bill of health, so he's gone over to join Christine at Forest Gate nick. I told him he should go and get some rest, but he's determined to be involved in Adebanjo's interviews. He said that, after spending so long hunting the bastard down, he wasn't going to let a little headache stop him from being in on the kill."

Tyler couldn't help but grin. "He's a plucky one, I'll give him that."

"He's already arranged for the case file for the unsolved Manchester murders to be sent down. Assuming that the DNA from the shooters matches the unknown profiles found on the two balaclavas he told us about, he intends to deal with Adebanjo for those killings as well while he's in custody.

Tyler ran a hand though his hair as he considered this. He did the maths in his head, not liking the numbers he came up with. "From the sounds of it, you'd better start drafting the application for a warrant of further detention, because there's no way we'll be able to put all that evidence to Adebanjo in thirty-six hours."

Under the Police and Criminal Evidence Act, the police were enti-tled to detain a suspect without charge for up to twenty four hours, which could be extended to thirty-six under certain conditions. However, the fact that Adebanjo had already been arrested for his role in the conspiracy earlier in the week greatly complicated matters, because the time that he'd already spent in custody, some seventeen hours by Tyler's calculation, would count towards the overall period that he could be detained for.

Tyler was confident of getting the twelve hour extension, which could be authorised by a superintendent not directly involved with the case but, if they required additional time to question Adebanjo, which they unquestionably would, an application for a warrant of further detention would have to be made at Magistrates court under S. 44(1) PACE.

Leaving Dillon to his thoughts, Tyler rang Susie Sergeant to obtain an update.

"Hi Susie. What's the latest?"

Her voice, when she replied, was all echoey and distorted. *"Devon Brown's still in surgery,"* she said. *"I've just popped down to the hospital canteen to grab a coffee, but the last update I had was that his condition is critical, and it could go either way."*

Tyler felt conflicted by the news. Devon Brown had stabbed Jenny and murdered poor old Stanley Cotton, and a part of him sincerely hoped the little cretin would die on the table and spare the tax payer the burden of paying for his lengthy incarceration. Another part of him really wanted Brown to recover so that justice could be seen to be done. A trial would give Jenny, and Stanley Cotton's grieving relatives, the satisfaction of being there when he was found guilty of murder and sentenced to spend the rest of his worthless life behind bars.

"What about Marcel Meeks?" he asked next.

"He's out of surgery. The bullet has been successfully removed. His condition is critical but stable and, all things being equal, he should make a full recovery. From a medical perspective, the main concern regarding him seems to be the extent of any nerve damage, and whether he'll ever regain the full use of his arm."

Dillon, who was leaning in close to Tyler's head so that he could hear, chuckled to himself. "He'll just have to learn how to wank with the other hand if that happens," he said, deliberately raising his voice for Susie's benefit.

Tyler nudged him away, and transferred the phone to his other ear. Luckily, there were no other customers around, so at least he was spared the embarrassment of having to apologise for his friend's crude remark.

"What was that?" Susie asked. *"The signal's not very good and I didn't quite hear."*

"Just Mr Dillon making helpful suggestions," Tyler said, glaring at his friend, who was still giggling at the tasteless quip.

"What's the score with Tyson?" Tyler asked, shaking his head in rebuke at Dillon's childishness. "Has the idiot said why he did a bunk from witness protection and went back to Hackney?"

"*We've not been able to speak to him yet, boss,*" she said, stifling a yawn. "*Oh, by the way, I hope you don't mind, but I've taken the liberty of organising armed guards for all three of them. Is that okay?*"

"Of course it's okay," Tyler said. "That was top of my list of things to do once I got back to Arbour Square. You've just saved me a lot of time and effort."

"*My pleasure,*" she said, and he could almost hear the smile in her voice. "*I figured you'd have more than enough on your plate when you finished the PIP. How did it go, by the way?*"

Tyler grimaced. "It was heavy going," he confessed, "but I'm confident both incidents will be declared clean shoots. The general consensus of opinion at the Hackney PIP was that the armed intervention was both necessary and justified, and although it resulted in one gunman being fatally wounded and another seriously injured, the SFO's swift action undoubtably saved the lives of both hostages. I mean, it's hard to argue with the evidence we found. The walls and floor in the lounge and bathroom were covered in thick plastic sheeting, and there were bone saws and a load of heavy duty plastic bags in the bathroom."

"*Gross! Sounds like they were going to shoot them in the lounge and chop up the bodies in the bathroom,*" Susie said, sounding utterly revolted.

"That's how it looks," Tyler confirmed.

She let out her breath in a long sigh. "*Sounds like they had a lucky escape. By the way, I heard a little whisper that a couple of SFOs got shot during the entry. Any truth in that?*"

"Two of them were shot by Jerome Norris as they stormed the lounge, but fortunately their body armour saved them." Both officers had since been examined by the Force Medical Examiner at Lemon Street and given some paracetamol for their bruised ribs, although there had been nothing he could prescribe to ease the pain of their wounded pride. "What's happening with Daryl Peters?"

Peters had been detained by one of the ARV crews as he'd dropped from the lounge window at the rear of the flat. Ironically, considering that his street name was Gunz, Peters had been unarmed.

"*He's been taken into Shoreditch nick and placed incommunicado,*" Susie said.

"Any problems getting that authorised?" Tyler asked. A superintendent's authority was required to hold a detainee incommunicado, and the power could only be invoked if certain conditions were met.

"*None,*" she said proudly. "*I explained that there were other armed suspects not yet arrested, and that we feared they would be alerted if twat features was allowed to have someone informed of his arrest.*"

"Well done," Tyler said. He didn't know Susie terribly well, but what he had seen of her so far had greatly impressed him.

"*Peters' clothing's all been seized, his hands have been swabbed for traces of gunshot residue, and nail cuttings and nail scrapings have been taken,*" Susie said. "*Naturally, he wants a solicitor, but I spoke to the duty brief and told her we're still a little way short of starting the interviews and that I'll call her back when we're ready.*" Unfortunately, keeping a suspect incommunicado didn't stretch to refusing access to legal advice.

"That's great," Tyler said, checking his watch. "Have you spoken to Steve recently, to see what's happening with Livingstone?"

After being savaged by PC Fluffy, Livingstone had been taken to Homerton Hospital to have his wounds attended to. Cell space had been reserved for him at Stoke Newington police station as Tyler didn't want any of the prisoners being housed at the same station, and Peters was already at Shoreditch.

"*Not for a little while,*" she said. "*The last I heard, Livingstone's injuries had been cleaned up and dressed and he was just waiting for a tetanus booster before being discharged.*"

"Okay, That's good to know. Listen, I really need to crack on, so I'm going to say goodbye for now. If there are any developments, please call me at once. And Susie…?"

"*Yes, boss?*"

"Thank you so much for all your hard work today. It's really appreciated."

Hanging up, he turned to Dillon with a lopsided smile, "You might as well dose up on caffeine now, while you've got the chance, because you're probably going to need it to keep you going."

Dillon groaned. "We're not going to get home again tonight, are we?"

"Honestly, Dill. At this rate, I think we'll be lucky if we manage to get home before the middle of next week."

————

After being discharged from hospital that evening, Conrad Livingstone was conveyed straight to Stoke Newington police station. The first thing he did upon arrival, was protest that he was too ill to be interviewed. The custody sergeant rang through to request the attendance of the duty FME, and then carried on booking the prisoner in.

Dr Peter Howell, clad in his motorcycle leathers, and complaining about the heat, arrived a half hour later. Carrying his crash helmet under his arm, he breezed into the custody suite looking like he would rather be somewhere – anywhere – else.

Howell, a slender man in his mid to late forties, had short brown hair and a high forehead, which seemed to be fixed in a permanent frown. He wasn't exactly renowned for his bedside manner and, after conducting a brisk examination, he declared that Livingstone was perfectly fit for detention and interview.

"But look at me, bruv," Livingstone protested as he was escorted back into the main custody area by the gaoler, leaning heavily on the crutch he had been given at hospital and waving his bandaged arm in the air. "I've been savaged," he complained. "I'm in agony."

Howell stared at him without sympathy. "Rubbish," he said, dismissively. "It's just a little dog bite." He turned to Steve Bull and handed over a small wrap of paracetamols. "I've given him a couple of these to take the edge off," Howell informed him. "He can have two more in four hours."

Livingstone glared at him. "How can you have the cheek to call yourself a doctor, bruv?" he demanded indignantly. "Even the Feds have given me more sympathy than you. I'm gonna complain, bruv. You should be struck off."

Howell raised a bored eyebrow. "He's all yours," he told the disinterested custody sergeant.

Livingstone was placed in a cell until his solicitor arrived, and Bull used the time to grab some refreshments from the bakery opposite.

After a very lengthy consultation, Livingstone and his sour faced solicitor were shown into a vacant interview room that was littered with rubbish and smelled like something had recently crawled under the table and died.

The solicitor's name was Audrey Fanshaw. She was an androgynous woman with a short back and sides who was dressed in a man's business suit, complete with shirt and tie. "I want to start off by making it clear both my client and I object to him being interviewed while he's in so much pain," she said in a deep, husky voice.

"Duly noted," Bull said, indicating for them to both take a seat.

While Kelly Flowers removed the plastic covering from the audio tapes and slipped them into the machine, he made sure that there was an 'idiot card' – a laminated sheet of A4 paper containing all the information an officer was required to give a suspect at the beginning of a taped interview – available for him to quote from.

"Everyone ready?" he asked when Kelly gave him the thumbs up.

"Nah, bruv. I aint feeling this," Livingstone complained, nursing his bandaged arm.

Fanshaw placed a restraining hand on his arm, but quickly retracted it when he winced in pain. "We're ready," she said.

Kelly pressed the red 'record' button and there was a long, loud beep that signified the equipment was working correctly.

"Okay, my name is Detective Sergeant Steve Bull, and I'm attached to the Area Major Investigation Pool. The other officer present is…"

"I'm Detective Constable Kelly Flowers, also attached to AMIP."

"The time is 19:30 hours on Saturday 29th May 1999, and we are in interview room number two at Stoke Newington police station. For the benefit of the tape, can I ask you to identify yourself for me, please?"

Livingstone sucked through his teeth. "You know my name, innit."

"For the tape," Bull repeated.

Another suck through the teeth. "Conrad Livingstone."

"Thank you," Bull said curtly. "You have legal representation, Can I ask your solicitor to identify…" he paused, suddenly realising that he wasn't sure whether to refer to Fanshaw as 'him' or 'her' "… themselves."

"I'm Audrey Fanshaw from Cratchit, Lowe and Clarke solicitors. I'm here to protect and advance my client's rights, and to that extent I will intervene if I feel it is necessary because of overbearing conduct or improper lines of questioning."

Bull thanked her, and then, reading from the idiot card, he cautioned Livingstone and explained what would happen to the tapes in the event of him being charged.

"Conrad, you've been arrested for conspiring with Samuel Adebanjo, Isaac and Andre Kalu, Daryl Peters, Jerome Norris, and at least three other men to commit a number of murders. This conspiracy resulted in the death of five men, and the attempted murders of Marcel and Tyson Meeks. Before I ask you specific questions in relation to the allegation against you, I'm going to give you an opportunity to tell me, in your own words, exactly what your role in this conspiracy was. Are you willing to do that?"

"Go fuck yourself," Livingstone snapped.

Bull glanced sideways at Kelly. From her reaction, he could see she shared his opinion that this interview was going to be a very long and very unpleasant experience.

CHAPTER THIRTY-EIGHT

Sunday 30th May 1999
THE WARRANT OF FURTHER DETENTION

As Tyler had predicted the previous day, they found themselves in the unenviable position of having to apply for a warrant of further detention on Sunday morning.

The mechanics of applying for a WOFD were fairly straightforward during the working week, but the process became a complete nightmare once the weekend arrived. This was because, for reasons that Tyler had never fully understood, the British judicial system effectively shut down at five o'clock on a Friday evening, and it didn't resume normal service until nine o'clock the following Monday.

As he'd feared, the only Magistrates Court available to hear the WOFD application on a Sunday morning was the one located at Horseferry Road in Central London. Organising transport and armed escorts for the three high risk prisoners at such short notice turned out to be incredibly problematic, but eventually all the hurdles were cleared and everything was arranged.

Tyler and Dillon drove up to the court together, and upon arrival they were met by Steve Bull, Charlie White and Jonny Murphy, who had each travelled with one of the prisoner convoys.

After their solicitor had been given sufficient time to consult with his clients down in the cells below, the court was called to order, and Adebanjo, Isaac and Andre Kalu were ushered into the glass fronted dock from the cells below. Half a dozen burly guards flanked them, just in case they got any funny ideas.

When the court convened, Tyler carefully studied the three elderly Magistrates who entered from a side door behind the presiding bench, trying to gauge whether they were likely to be pro or anti police. In truth, it was impossible to tell; they all looked as though they had been given a particularly sharp lemon to suck just before coming into the room.

When everyone was seated, the lead Magistrate nodded to the clerk, who looked over to where Tyler and Dillon were sitting and signalled that they were ready for an officer to take the stand.

Tyler stood up, but Dillon placed a hand on his arm. "I'll do it," he said, pushing his friend back down into his seat.

After taking the oath and introducing himself, Dillon took a deep breath and shuffled the papers in his hands nervously. "Your Worships, I come before you today in order to make an application under section 44 PACE for a warrant of further detention to be issued in relation to the three men in the dock, Samuel Adebanjo, Isaac Kalu and Andre Kalu. These men have been arrested for conspiring to commit a series of gang related murders. Some of the killings occurred down here in London, while the rest were committed in Greater Manchester. The London based conspiracy resulted in five Turkish males being ruthlessly gunned down. The Manchester related offences were committed two years ago, and these resulted in nine males from rival gangs being shot dead."

Dillon grew in confidence as he spoke, delivering a powerfully compelling business case for the extension. He then gave the Magistrates a breakdown of how long each man had been in custody, and what had been achieved by the enquiry team during that time.

He talked about the crime scenes that had been processed, the

CCTV that had been retrieved and viewed, the statements that had been taken, and the telephone and banking evidence that had been gathered. He explained that the interviews had begun late the previous evening, but that these had been suspended in order for the suspects to have the sleep period that PACE required. Today, he explained, the interviews would continue, but there was a lot of material to get through. In addition, at least as far as Adebanjo was concerned, a video ID capture would need to be carried out, which would bite into the time left on the custody clock.

When he concluded, the Magistrates asked him a couple of fairly routine questions, and then told Dillon to wait where he was so that defence could cross examine him.

Standing up, Adebanjo's expensively dressed lawyer introduced himself as Bernard Cratchit, a senior partner in the firm of Cratchit, Lowe and Clarke. He was a slender man in his mid-fifties, with an expensively styled haircut and an even more expensively cut suit. Giving off an air of snooty self-importance, Cratchit spoke with a plum in his mouth.

Watching the oration from the side-lines, Tyler found himself wondering if the upper class accent was put on.

With a lavish gesture towards the dock, more becoming of a showman that a solicitor, Cratchit announced that he would be representing the three men in custody, somehow managing to make it sound as though he was doing each of them a very great honour.

Looking around the room with imperious disdain, Cratchit puffed himself up like a peacock on parade. He eventually turned to face Dillon, fixing him with his most intimidating stare.

Dillon made a point of smiling back at him.

"I'm glad the officer thinks this is a laughing matter," Cratchit said, turning to address the bench. "Because, to the three men being deprived of their liberty, it is anything but."

Cratchit then launched into a lengthy diatribe, condemning the police handling of the case and their treatment of his client. He argued that the enquiry team were totally inept, and that it would be unjust to grant them an extension when they hadn't done their job properly in the first place.

Looking on from the side lines, Tyler felt his blood starting to boil.

"If the police had used the time they've already had more effi-ciently, and carried out a more effective investigation in the first place, they would undoubtably have been able to put all the evidence to my clients by now, and we would not now find ourselves in this unsavoury situation. Instead, due to their incompetence, the police have had to come here, cap in hand, to beg for a custody time limit extension." He shook his head as though it was the most terrible atrocity.

Tyler watched the Magistrate's faces as Cratchit spoke, and he got the distinct impression that they didn't approve of him running the police down in this way. With a bit of luck, Cratchit's ranting was doing his clients more harm than good.

Cratchit then accused Dillon of having used excessive force during Adebanjo's arrest. To illustrate his point, the solicitor pointed to the livid bruises that covered the giant's face. "How do you justify the use of such extreme force when all my client wanted to do was cooperate? I think you owe the court an explanation, don't you?"

Tyler rolled his eyes. Cratchit was one of *those* lawyers. His default setting was to accuse an arresting officer of either beating up or fitting up a client. It never worked, and he wondered why some solicitors still persisted in using such a dated tactic to try and unsettle and discredit the officer.

Dillon certainly didn't seem bothered. "Your Worships," he said, smiling at the bench politely. "As you can see for yourselves, Adebanjo is a giant of a man, and he was sitting astride an unconscious colleague strangling him when I arrived on scene. I tried to reason with him, but he attacked me. When he did, I reluctantly used the force that was reasonable and necessary to protect myself and restrain him." He pointed to the beautiful purple shiner on his own face. "As you can see, I didn't exactly come out of the incident unscathed."

By this point, Tyler was confident that the three elderly Magis-trates had grown weary of the solicitor's aggressive outbursts.

"I think we've heard enough Mr Cratchit," the one in the centre drawled. "So, if there are no further questions, we will retire to consider our judgement."

As soon as the three Magistrates had adjourned, Cratchit sat down, looking very pleased with himself.

Tyler grinned inwardly as Dillon returned to his side. "Well done, mate," he whispered. "You did us proud."

Dillon indicated Cratchit with a jut of his chin. "I think that pompous little prick did my job for me," he whispered back.

Tyler didn't want to tempt fate by saying so, but he was quietly confident the bench would award them an extension. The only question in his mind was: how much time would they grant them?

Less than five minutes later, there was a knock on the door, signifying that the bench were about to return.

"All stand," the clerk ordered.

The spokesperson for the bench was a distinguished looking man in his mid-sixties. He had a dashing shock of white hair that kept flopping down in front of his face every time he leaned forward. There was something about the way he kept sweeping it back into place that reminded Tyler of Michael Heseltine. Wearing a dark blue blazer and a regimental tie, he looked very much the retired army officer.

The clerk called the court to order.

"We have listened to the application from Detective Inspector Dillon, and we have carefully considered the representations that were made on behalf of Mr Adebanjo, Mr Kalu and Mr Kalu by their esteemed solicitor, Mr Cratchit. Having given the matter serious consideration, we are satisfied that the police *have* used the time available to them diligently, and that the request for an extension, given the seriousness and complexity of the matters under investigation, is reasonable. We are, therefore, minded to grant a further thirty-six hours of detention in relation to Samuel Adebanjo, Isaac Kalu and Andre Kalu. This case is adjourned."

Tyler winked at Dillon. Both smiled triumphantly at Cratchit.

Huffing and puffing, Cratchit responded by storming out of the court room, complaining that the police had hoodwinked the bench.

After a quick conflab with the three DSs to discuss their battle plan, Tyler and Dillon left the court.

As they returned to the pool car, which had been parked on a single yellow line in a side street near the court building, Tyler saw a parking ticket had been tucked beneath one of the windscreen wipers.

The black MPS Log-Book for the car had been clearly displayed on the dashboard, and there was no way the warden could have missed it. Snatching the ticket up, Tyler swore profusely. Operational police cars were allowed to park on single yellow lines if there were no other suitable places available, as long as they weren't causing an obstruction. Fuming at the pointless inconvenience, Tyler looked around for the warden, intending to give the idiot a stern talking to.

"Don't sweat it," Dillon said, taking the ticket from him. "We'll sort it out later."

As Tyler opened the door, his mobile rang.

"DCI Tyler."

He listened for a short while, saying nothing. "I see," he finally said. Thanking the caller, he hung up and climbed inside.

"Anything interesting?" Dillon asked, slipping behind the wheel.

"That was one of the armed guards at the Royal London Hospital," Tyler said. "The third shooter from the hotel just died."

———

The mobile identification unit that had been sent from Barkingside arrived at Forest Gate at four o'clock that afternoon.

The uniformed inspector and sergeant who were going to perform the ID capture set their equipment up in a room on the first floor. Both were in their late fifties, with grey hair and long sideburns. Both had little beer bellies that had been carefully cultivated over thirty plus years of service, and both were now counting down the days until they retired.

"Right," Inspector Donald Plumb said to Murphy when he was finally satisfied that everything was working properly. "Let's get this show on the road, shall we?"

When Murphy and Taylor got Adebanjo out of his cell and explained what was going to happen next, Adebanjo flatly refused to cooperate. He crossed his massive arms and turned his back on

Murphy like a truculent child. "Take me back to my cell," he told the gaoler.

"That's fine by me," Murphy said, leaning on the custody counter beside him, and smirking up at the giant. "If you don't want to play ball, we'll just use the custody image photograph that was taken when you arrived."

"Is that right, fam?" he asked Cratchit. "Can they do that?"

"I'm afraid they can, Samuel," the solicitor confirmed.

Adebanjo spun around to face Murphy. "I want to speak to my solicitor in private," he said, looking none too pleased.

"Of course," Murphy said with an accommodating smile. "Take your time. Thanks to those nice friendly Magistrates, we've got plenty of it."

Cratchit bristled at the jibe, but said nothing.

After a heated consultation with his solicitor, Adebanjo reluctantly agreed to take part in the ID parade, and several uniformed officers escorted him up to the first floor room where Plumb and his trusty sergeant where patiently waiting for him.

The ID capture involved Adebanjo sitting in a chair and staring straight into the camera. The sergeant doing the filming told him to slowly turn his head all the way to his left, hold it there for a couple of seconds, and then return to face the front. This process was then repeated to his right. Once the front and two side profiles had been filmed, and everyone was happy with the quality of the images, Adebanjo was returned to the custody suite.

Cratchit remained behind while the head and shoulders video clip of Adebanjo was inserted onto a group of eight other clips, all featuring men of similar age and appearance performing the same range of movements that Adebanjo had. When the final edit was complete, Cratchit was asked to approve it, signing off that all the other people in the parade were of sufficient similarity so as not to disadvantage his client when it was shown to Agnes Willoughby later that day.

———

At six o'clock, a very nervous Mrs Willoughby was shown into the room where the ID showing was going to be conducted. After sitting her down and giving her a cup of tea to soothe her nerves, Inspector Plumb explained how it was all going to work. She was going to be shown nine clips of video, each featuring a head and shoulders shot of a bald headed black man looking at the camera. The man would then slowly rotate his head to his left and then to his right, so that she could see both side profiles. Plumb stressed that the man who attacked her the previous day might, or might not, be amongst the people she saw. Plumb was going to show her the footage twice, and after that he would invite her to say whether she could identify anyone on the ID parade.

Cratchit was also there to ensure that the procedure was conducted properly, and that nothing was said or done to steer the witness towards or away from any particular clip. He had asked that Adebanjo be placed at number four in the sequence.

"Are you ready to begin?" Plumb asked Willoughby.

As the video showing commenced, Agnes Willoughby bravely fought back the tears. When clip number four came on, she almost jumped out of her chair, and her hands flew to her mouth. "That's him," she gasped. "That's the beast who attacked me."

"Please, Agnes," Plumb said gently. "Let me play all the clips for you before you pass comment."

Visibly trembling, she sat through the remaining clips in strained silence, shaking her head vigorously as each new person appeared. "It's number four," she said as soon as the film ended.

"I'm sorry. I need to play them all through one more time before I can accept a response from you," Plumb apologised, starting the sequence over again.

———

"So she picked him out then?" Dillon said, when Jonny Murphy phoned in the result.

"*As soon as she saw him,*" Murphy said, sounding jubilant.

"How did Adebanjo take the news?" Dillon asked.

"*Haven't interviewed him about it yet, but his solicitor will have told him by now. They're having another consultation before we get started.*"

"That's a fantastic result," Dillon said. "Looks like we'll be adding charges of kidnap, false imprisonment, and robbery to the list. Well done!"

"*Well done, Agnes, you mean,*" Murphy corrected him. "*She's a brave old biddy, that one.*"

———

Inside the stuffy interview room, Adebanjo sat across the table from Murphy and Taylor, glowering at them hatefully. They were twenty minutes into the first interview and, so far, every question they had put to him had been met with stony silence. He had even refused to confirm his name for the tape.

Cratchit had occasionally tutted, just to remind them that he was there, but with his client exercising his right to remain silent, there really wasn't much for him to do, so he had contented himself to drawing little doodles on his note pad.

After asking Adebanjo to account for his movements between his arrival in London on Tuesday 25th May and his arrest on Saturday 29th May, Murphy asked him about his connection to the Kalu twins, Dritan Bajramovic, Valmir Demaci, and Lorik Kraja. Then he asked how Adebanjo knew Conrad Livingstone, Daryl Peters, and Jerome Norris, and how long they had been in contact with each other.

Adebanjo remained stoic, keeping his emotions to himself.

After a quick toilet break, Christine Taylor started playing the CCTV evidence that Colin Franklin had prepared, beginning with the footage of Adebanjo and Livingstone together at his club in Manchester on the evening of Saturday 1st May.

Annoyingly, Adebanjo refused to look at the screen, choosing to stare at his huge feet instead.

"Too painful to watch, is it?" Murphy asked, hoping to provoke a response. He might as well have addressed the comment to the wall for all the reaction he got.

Taylor played two more clips. The first showed a platform at

Manchester Piccadilly station, and the second featured an almost identical platform at London Euston. The date stamp at the top of the screen showed that both clips had been filmed a few hours apart on Tuesday 25th May. The quality was rather good, and Adebanjo and the Kalu twins could clearly be seen boarding the train moments before the three Eastern Europeans.

Adebanjo seemed unmoved by the footage, but then again he was looking down at the floor and not at the screen.

To establish that Adebanjo already knew Dritan Bajramovic, Valmir Demaci, and Lorik Kraja before boarding the train, the footage of the three Eastern Europeans working the door at his club on the night Livingstone had paid him a visit was shown next.

None of the Romanian shooters had criminal records in the UK, but Murphy had sent DC Katie Richards to the club the previous night, and she had established their names by showing some stills to the staff. Unfortunately, none of them had been willing to put pen to paper and make formal statements to that effect, just in case there were any nasty repercussions later on.

"Who is Dritan Bajramovic?" Murphy asked.

Silence.

"Okay. Who's Valmir Demaci?"

More silence.

"Come on, Samuel. I can see that you want to speak to me. Who's Lorik Kraja?"

Adebanjo opened his mouth and, for a moment, Murphy actually thought he was going to say something, but all he did was yawn

Murphy sighed and ran a hand over his stubbled chin. "Look. We know that these three men have been working for you at your club in Manchester for several years. Isn't that right?"

Adebanjo looked up and smiled. Then he raised the middle finger of his left hand.

"For the benefit of the tape, Mr Adebanjo just gave me a thumbs up sign," Murphy said with a provocative grin. "Are you confirming that they work for you, Samuel?"

Cratchit spluttered and nearly dropped his legal pad. "No, that's not what happened," he hurriedly interjected. "My client clearly raised the middle finger of his left hand, not the thumb."

"Oh! Is that what it was," Murphy said, innocently. "Why don't you clarify that for us, Samuel? Put your solicitor and me out of our misery by confirming which of us was right."

Cratchit had gone the colour of a stop sign. "Are you calling me a liar?" he demanded.

"Let's show our guests the next segment of film," Murphy said, not even bothering to respond to Cratchit's outburst.

Christine pressed the play button, and footage of the three Eastern Europeans disposing of the stolen Mondeo after the Green Lanes shooting appeared on screen.

"Look! It's your three employees again, torching the stolen Mondeo they used to gun down the four Turks in Green Lanes," Murphy said. He was actually starting to enjoy this. "They're very distinctive. All three are big ugly brutes with bald heads and zero personality, a bit like yourself."

Adebanjo's jaw quivered with anger, and the muscles in his shoulders rippled. Murphy could tell that he was just itching to respond.

"Let's see the next part of the compilation, shall we?" Murphy said, leaning back and clasping his hands behind his head.

Christine dutifully played the footage of Adebanjo and the Kalu twins booking into the Beckton hotel the previous evening. "Have a good look at this, Samuel. There's you, Isaac and Andre, all booking into your hotel last night. Tell me, just out of interest, how can you tell the twins apart?"

Adebanjo clenched his fist so tightly that the knuckles cracked.

"This next clip is taken from the same camera, but was filmed thirty minutes after you boys had checked in." On screen, the three Eastern Europeans walked into the hotel foyer and headed over to the counter.

"It doesn't look good, does it?" Murphy said. "All six of you staying at the same hotel together last night."

"I think you'll find that it's your responsibility to prove that there is something sinister about this, and it's not for my client to prove that there isn't," Cratchit said, his voice dripping acid.

Murphy grinned wickedly. "And I gladly accept the challenge," Murphy responded, rubbing his hands together gleefully.

The unbridled enthusiasm with which he said this brought a worried look to Cratchit's arrogant face.

————

It was coming up to ten o'clock when Steve Bull opened the interview room door and gestured for Livingstone and Fanshaw to go ahead of him. "After you," he said, wearily stepping to the side to let them through.

Kelly fell into line beside him as they followed Livingstone's painfully slow progress back to the custody sergeant's desk.

Hop, clunk. Hop, clunk.

"He looks like Long John Silver on that bloody thing," Kelly whispered, nodding at the crutch the gangster was leaning on. "All he needs now is a parrot sitting on his shoulder."

Hop, clunk. Hop, clunk.

Bull laughed quietly. "Oi, Kelly. Why are pirates called pirates?"

Kelly shrugged.

"Because they Arggghhh!" Bull said, slipping into a cringeworthy pirate accent.

It was coming up to change over time, and the custody suite was relatively quiet for once. Behind the desk, a weary looking man was finishing off the paperwork for the prisoners he had processed during the past eight hours. Standing behind him, his night duty replacement was waiting to take over.

"What's happening with your man?" the outgoing skipper asked. From his frosty tone, it was clear that he was hoping that whatever it was, it could wait until he had gone off duty.

"We've finished all the interviews," Bull said. "I believe Mr Livingstone wants a quick consultation with his solicitor, and then he can be returned to his cell while I consult my boss on what we're going to do with him."

"I see," the skipper said. "George, show these two into the consultation room for me, would you?" he called out to his gaoler.

As soon as the door to the consultation room closed behind them, the skipper's face relaxed. "Come on then, Stevie," he said. "What's the plan?"

Bull grinned. "We'll be sheeting him with multiple conspiracy to murder charges," he said, "but I promise I'll wait until night duty come on to formally announce that. That way, you can get off on time and someone else can be lumbered with writing up all the charge sheets."

The outgoing skipper winked at him. "That's music to my old ears," he said with a grin.

"Not so much to mine," the incoming skipper who was standing behind him pointed out.

CHAPTER THIRTY-NINE

Monday 31st May 1999
THAT WENT ALL THE WAY DOWN TO THE WIRE

Adebanjo had been put into a mandatory sleep period at eleven o'clock the previous evening. To ensure there was no time wasting this morning, Murphy had arranged for him to be roused at seven-thirty, given time to shower, and then fed a hearty breakfast at eight.

The plan worked, and the interviews recommenced at nine on the dot.

Murphy took his seat, looking fresh and invigorated. Unlike Adebanjo, who was content to brood in silence, he seemed full of the joys of spring.

"Sleep well, did you?" Murphy enquired with a thin smile, which broadened at the scowl he received in reply.

After going through the introductions and repeating the caution, Murphy explained that the next session was going to focus on the telephone evidence that Reg Parker had compiled.

Murphy knew that it was going to be a long hard slog, but it would deal Adebanjo a heavy body blow, and he was really looking forward to that.

Murphy began the interview by talking about all the various burner phones that had come to light during the course of the investigation. He went into great detail about each one, giving its full number and explaining how each one had been attributed to the various people involved in the conspiracy.

"From this point forward," he said at the end of his summary, "I'll only refer to the last three digits when I speak about a particular phone. So, for instance, your first burner ends in 666, whereas the second burner you used ends in 217. Dritan's phone ends in 003. Livingstone's burner ends in 109. Daryl Peters – you might know him as Gunz – has a burner that ends in 151. With me so far?"

Adebanjo ignored him.

Cratchit had started making notes, and whenever he spotted the lawyer writing, Murphy spoke slowly so that he wouldn't miss anything. It was a courtesy he doubted the other man would have extended him, had their positions been reversed

"As I talk about all the various calls that you lot have made during the past week, I'll provide the call duration and the location of the masts covering both phones. I'll also be showing you some pretty maps as we go along to help you to follow what I say more easily."

Murphy asked Christine Taylor to replay the CCTV footage from Euston, which showed Adebanjo and Dritan talking on their respective phones as they walked along the platform. While the footage played, he recited the call data and cell site information that pertained to the call.

"As you can see," he said when Christine paused play, "the call and cell site data proves that your 666 burner was in contact with Dritan's 003 burner at that time. Thanks to this lovely little clip of CCTV, which you will note is date and time stamped, we can also prove that you and Dritan were the ones making and receiving the call. Anything you want to say about that?"

Adebanjo looked like he wanted to say plenty. He also looked like he wanted to rip Jonny Murphy's head clean off.

Cratchit was now making furious notes, no doubt wondering how even the most experienced barrister was going to be able to refute Murphy's claim.

Having been given the nod by Murphy, Taylor played the next clip, which had been recorded by the camera mounted outside the corner shop near Beckton Alps on Tuesday evening. Not only did it show Adebanjo talking on his burner, but it clearly showed him disposing of the phone afterwards.

"Now why did you dispose of your phone, Samuel? Answer me that." He sat in silence for a few moments, happy to let Adebanjo stew. "I put it to you that you dumped that phone because you knew you were about to be arrested, and you didn't want the police to find anything incriminating on you, especially not a phone that linked you directly to the shooters. Is that right?"

Adebanjo stared down at the floor and sighed heavily, full of restless energy.

Consulting his notes, Murphy read out the times that the call started and ended. Then he showed them a map Parker had produced. "Here's a map of Beckton," he said. "The mast covering the call you made outside the shop is located here." He tapped the paper with his pen. "The big red circle indicates the mast's radius. The yellow dot is the hotel you were staying at, and the red dot is the shop where you were captured on CCTV. Note that the date and times of the call duration match the time stamp on the CCTV. Isn't that interesting? Again, a combination of call data and CCTV conclusively prove that you were using the 666 burner to call Dritan on his 003 burner. Do you want to tell me what you were saying?"

Silence.

"Were you giving Dritan instructions regarding the assassination you had ordered him to carry out at the café in Green Lanes?"

"I object," Cratchit said, angrily. "That's just speculation on your part."

Murphy raised a questioning eyebrow. "Is it?" he asked calmly.

"Of course it is," Cratchit snapped back. "Or are you going to tell me you're a mind reader now as well as a smart arse?"

Murphy laughed at that. "No, I'm not a mind reader," he reassured Cratchit. "I'm not even a lip reader. But a delightful lady called

Professor Eileen Morrison is, and she has very kindly viewed this CCTV clip for us."

Cratchit licked his lips nervously. "This wasn't mentioned in the disclosure you gave me prior to the interview," he said defensively.

"I'm telling you now," Murphy said with an unctuous smile. "I'm now going to paraphrase from her very detailed statement. In it, she states that Samuel Adebanjo said several very relevant things during the call. The first was: 'Get your team ready.' Now, what exactly did you mean by that, Samuel?" he asked, leaning forward on the table and staring intently at the prisoner.

Adebanjo was becoming rattled, and he bared his teeth in anger.

"The professor states that you then came out with this little doozy: 'A dark blue Ford Mondeo with a dented nearside rear wing will be waiting for you in the side street next to the hotel in half an hour's time.'" Murphy let out a low whistle. "I assume that's the stolen Mondeo Dritan's team used during the hit? You know, the blue one with the dent in the nearside rear wing?"

"I should have been told about this in advance," Cratchit spluttered.

"No," Murphy said, bristling at the interruption. "I'm required to give you sufficient information to enable you to properly consult with and advise your client. I'm satisfied that you were given this. There is nothing in the rules that says I have to give you a list of every question that I intend to ask. So, if you don't mind, I'd like to get on with the interview."

Adebanjo had watched the exchange with interest, but still he refrained from speaking.

Murphy took a deep breath. "The last sentence that Professor Morrison picked up on while watching the CCTV is this: 'Your target will be arriving at the location between eight-thirty and nine, tonight.' Isn't that the time that Erkan Dengiz arrived at the café?"

Cratchit placed a hand on Adebanjo's arm. "My advice is for you to exercise your right to silence," he fumed.

"He's doing that already," Christine Taylor pointed out.

"Perhaps it's time for a quick break," Murphy said.

———

Tyler walked into the ward Jenny had been transferred to over the weekend. With everything that was going on, he really shouldn't have come, but he had promised to visit her as soon as she was out of ICU and he didn't want to let her down.

Last night, Livingstone and Peters had both been charged with conspiracy to commit multiple murders. Peters had also been charged with the attempted murders of Tyson and Marcel Meeks. The divers had recovered the Taurus revolver from the bottom of the canal, so Livingstone had been charged with possession of a Section one firearm as well.

Both prisoners had gone to court in custody this morning, and the stern-faced Stipendiary Magistrate sitting at Thames had remanded the pair of them to prison pending trial. Tyler had rushed straight over to the hospital from court, leaving Dillon to go back to the office and mind the fort in his absence.

Tyler enquired at the nursing station, and was shown over to the room that Jenny was sharing with three other women. She was sitting up in bed, watching TV.

When he walked in, her face lit up. "Jack!" she said, extending her hands for him to take.

Tyler leaned in and gave her a peck on the cheek. "You look much better than the last time I saw you," he said with an affectionate smile. The bruising and swelling to her face had gone down considerably since his last visit a few days ago, and she even had some colour back in her cheeks.

Jenny grimaced. "I probably look a total mess, but I'm definitely feeling much better. They're even talking about letting me go home in a couple of days."

"That's marvellous news," he told her, squeezing her hand. When she eventually released it, he pulled a chair over to her bed and sat down beside her.

Jenny studied his face carefully. "You look so tired," she said, sounding concerned.

Jack shrugged. "Work," he said, lamely. "It's been a pretty manic week."

"Have you caught the person who stabbed me yet?" she asked, looking at him expectantly. "You promised me that you would."

Jack nodded. "We caught him on Saturday," he told her. "He was seriously injured in a shootout with armed officers, and he's currently in ICU in an induced coma. His chances of survival are about 50-50 according to the consultant I spoke to earlier."

Jenny's face hardened. "Good. I hope he dies," she said.

Jack was taken aback by her vitriolic comment. "That's not like you," he said softly.

Jenny's mouth compressed into a razor thin line, and her voice became as hard as steel. "Apart from stabbing me, that scumbag killed a defenceless old man who selflessly put himself in harm's way to save me. His daughter came to visit me yesterday, and she was totally devastated, so don't expect me to have any pity for the bastard who killed her dad and ruined her life." An angry tear ran down her face as she spoke.

"Fair enough," Jack said, leaning in and gently wiping it away. He had planned to break the news of Stanley Cotton's death to her during today's visit, having previously withheld the information from her, and a part of him felt relieved that he would no longer have to do that.

Handing her a tissue, Tyler looked around the room to make sure that no one was listening to them. Two of the other women had earphones in, and were engrossed in whatever rubbish was playing on TV. The third, who was in the bed furthest away, was snoring gently.

"Jenny, I wanted to ask you something," he said, broaching the subject carefully.

Her eyes narrowed. "That sounds serious," she said, dropping the tissue into the bin beside her bed.

He took her dainty hand back in his. "Jenny, it's been really bothering me. Why did you ask for me to be called after you were stabbed, and not Eddie?"

Jenny's eyes clouded over. "Jack, I don't think this is the time to talk about that," she said, casting a nervous glance at her roommates.

Jack understood her reluctance to talk about this in front of strangers, but he needed answers. Not only for his own peace of mind but for Eddie. The poor sod was walking around wondering whether or not he was a rapist. One way or another, Jack felt obliged to put him out of his misery.

Jack took a deep breath. "Eddie spoke to me," he said, looking deep into her eyes. "He told me about the problems you two have been having, and about trying for a baby."

The pain that flittered across her face stopped him in his tracks. There was an awkward pause that stretched for a couple of breaths, but then he tried again. "Jen, he told me about the weekend away, and the night he… well, when he didn't stop when you told him to."

Jenny had gone very pale, and he could hear her breath coming in short angry gasps.

"He spoke to you about that?" she sounded shocked, appalled even.

Tyler nodded guiltily. "Look, you know I've never liked Eddie, but I honestly don't think he knows what happened that night. Because of all the booze he'd drunk, and the coke he'd sniffed, he's only got disjointed snippets of memory, and he's terrified that he did something unspeakable. He told me all this, knowing full well that if you made an allegation against him, his confession to me would be admissible. He knows I won't hesitate to arrest him if he's harmed you."

Jenny stared out of the window as she composed her thoughts, and he felt a stab of guilt for pushing her into talking about such an emotive subject when she was clearly reluctant to do so.

While it wasn't his area of expertise, Jack had investigated a few rapes over the years, and he had come to understand that the devastating impact of sexual violence went far beyond the physical side of the attack. The trauma of being raped or sexually assaulted was completely shattering, often leaving the victim feeling scared, ashamed, and utterly alone. Some of the women he'd dealt with had been plagued by nightmares, flashbacks, and other horrific memories for years afterwards. One particular woman had confided in him that the world no longer felt like a safe place to her. She no longer trusted others; she no longer trusted herself. She questioned her judgment, her self-worth and, at times, even her sanity. He had been heartbroken to discover that she blamed herself for what had happened, and that she had come out of the experience believing that she was 'dirty' or 'damaged goods'.

Recovering from a sexual assault took time, and the healing process could be incredibly painful but, with perseverance and support, he knew it was possible for victims to regain their sense of control and rebuild their self-worth, and he would do everything within his power to help Jenny get through her ordeal if it transpired that she had been raped.

"He didn't... he didn't rape me," she finally said, speaking so quietly that he could barely hear her. "Eddie's been to see me, and we've had a long, meaningful talk about what happened. It's true that, at first, I felt violated. Even though he hadn't physically pinned me down and forced himself on me, the fact that he hadn't stopped when I asked him to still amounted to rape in my eyes. Now, I'm not so sure. Anyway, we've had a heart to heart and cleared the air, and we're going to give things another go."

Jack considered this. He didn't want to talk her into or out of making an allegation. "Are you sure?" he asked neutrally.

"Positive," Jenny replied in a tone that brokered no argument.

Jack nodded uncertainly. He believed Eddie when he said that his recall was sketchy at best, and he didn't think Eddie was lying when he said it had been a case of her telling him to stop at a point in proceedings where he was physically unable to. Whether or not that was the truth, he was satisfied that Eddie genuinely believed that's what had happened.

The scenario was a classic grey area, and it would be a nightmare to try and prosecute. That said, if Jenny had been raped, it was his duty to put the matter before a court, regardless of how difficult that might be.

Deep down, he suspected that what Jenny was proposing might be the best outcome for everyone, as long as it was what she genuinely wanted and not something she felt she was being pressured into going along with.

"Jenny, has Eddie put you under any pressure to say that?" he asked as tactfully as he could under the circumstances.

Jenny smiled at him. "Trust a copper to think like that!"

Jack didn't return the smile. "That's not an answer, Jen."

Jenny's face became deadly serious. "No. Eddie didn't ask me to say that. In fact, he told me that, if he had raped me, he should be punished, and he didn't want me to lie just to protect him."

Not for the first time in recent days, Jack found himself being genuinely surprised by Eddie's hidden depth of character.

"Maybe, but just to be on the safe side, I should arrange for you to speak with someone more experienced in these matters than I am? Perhaps, you should talk it all through with a counsellor or something before making a decision."

Jenny shook her head firmly. "No, Jack. It's sweet of you to offer, but Eddie and I are going to make a go of it."

Jack frowned. "Well, if that's what you really want."

"It is."

He wanted to say more, but he decided not to push her. He had done enough of that for one day. Jenny was a strong willed woman. If she had made up her mind, nothing that he or anyone else said would change it.

He checked his watch and pulled a face. "Look, I've got to be getting back to the office. I'll speak to you again soon." He stood up and bent forward to kiss her cheek again.

"I'm having a baby," she blurted out.

Ah, Jack thought, well, that solves the mystery of the pregnancy test in her bag. "That's great," he said, acting surprised. And then a thought struck him. "Does Eddie know yet?"

She shook her head. "I only found out on the day I was attacked," she said with a wan smile. "And I didn't want to tell Eddie until we had sorted things out between us, for obvious reasons."

"I see," he said, and then shook his head. "Actually, I don't. If you've decided to make a go of it, why haven't you told him yet?"

"I'm going to tell him when he visits me tonight," she said, breaking into a wide smile. "I wanted to wait until I was discharged, but I can't keep it to myself any longer." A frown suddenly marred her features. "You won't say anything to anyone, will you? I haven't even told mum and dad yet."

"Don't worry," he reassured her. "Your secret's safe with me."

He walked towards the exit, but then stopped. "Jen, if things really are okay with you guys, why would you wait till you're discharged to tell him something so important?"

She laughed. "You're such a suspicious so-and-so, Jack Tyler. If you must know, the day after we sorted things out, I heard Eddie speaking to my parents. They all thought I was asleep, but I wasn't. Eddie's going to ask me to marry him when I get home. I'm going to say yes, and I thought that would be the perfect time to tell him."

Jack was really confused now. "I thought you two were already engaged," he said, scratching his head.

"We are," she admitted, and then shrugged. "Well, the thing is, Jack, when we got engaged–" she made little bunny ears with her fingers "—it was just for show. We both agreed that there was no need to actually get married, and that we would be content to remain engaged forever. Now, though, Eddie seems desperate to take the plunge, and apparently he wants to set the wedding date as quickly as possible."

Deciding that he would never understand the way Jenny's mind worked, Tyler blew her a kiss. "In that case, I wish the both of you – sorry, the three of you – all the very best."

———

By tea time, Murphy and Taylor had finished putting all the evidence relating to the five London murders to Adebanjo. In addition to the CCTV and telephone evidence that they had covered before lunch, they had now gone through all the relevant witness statements with him. The content of Tyson Meeks' statement had seemed to anger him even more than the account of Professor Morrison, the lip reader.

In his statement, Meeks had described dropping off the car and green holdall to Adebanjo and the Kalu twins in the hotel near Beckton Alps on Tuesday evening. He had then gone into great detail regarding the conversation that he'd had with Adebanjo, who had asked him if the bag contained the guns for the job. Adebanjo had then insisted that Meeks drive him and the twins to the target address.

When Meeks protested, Adebanjo had told him, 'Don't worry, fam. We will let you out of the car before we start shooting.'

Murphy had taken great pleasure in going through the account of Agnes Willoughby. He had described her fear as she was bundled into her flat, her belief that she was going to be raped or murdered. Adebanjo had laughed out loud at that, shaking his bowling ball sized head as if the very idea was too ridiculous to even contemplate.

He hadn't laughed when Murphy described the brutality of the assault he had subjected her to. Reading from the FME's statement, Murphy had listed her injuries in great detail.

Murphy had then produced the Ford key that had been found in Adebanjo's pocket upon his arrest, informing him that this had been checked and it had been confirmed that it was the key to Agnes' grey Ford Escort.

Although Adebanjo's solicitor had already informed him of the outcome, Murphy really enjoyed the defeated expression that crossed Adebanjo's face when he was told that Willoughby had picked him out during the ID parade video she had watched.

———

After a mandatory break for refreshments, Murphy switched his focus to the historic Manchester murders.

In the first interview, all the CCTV relating to the shootings was shown, and Murphy discussed the striking similarities between the MO for the Manchester based killings and their London counterparts, even down to the fact that Adebanjo and the Kalu twins were arrested following a tip off that proved to be incorrect.

Murphy repeatedly bated him for his lack of originality, and for making the arrogant assumption of thinking he could get away with pulling the same stunt twice.

Adebanjo didn't like that, and at one point Murphy began to worry that he might lose his cool and kick off.

Thankfully, he didn't.

At considerable expense, the DNA samples that had been taken from the bodies of Dritan Bajramovic, Lorik Kraja and Valmir Demaci had been fast tracked. The results, which had arrived during the last break, were explosive. The profiles from Valmir and Lorik were perfect matches for the DNA recovered from the two balaclavas used in the second Manchester shooting. This conclusively linked both Romanians to the Manchester murders, and through them, it also put Adebanjo squarely in the frame.

With less than an hour left on the custody clock, Adebanjo was taken before the custody sergeant at Forest Gate and charged with multiple counts of conspiracy to commit murder, both in London and Manchester. He was also charged with the kidnap, false imprisonment and robbery of Agnes Willoughby.

In keeping with the way he had behaved throughout his detention, he remained silent when the custody officer asked if he wanted to say anything in response to the charges.

Incredulously, his solicitor stepped forward and made an impassioned bail application, claiming that his client was a man of good character – which basically meant that no convictions or cautions were recorded against him – and that he didn't represent a flight risk. When the custody sergeant finally stopped laughing, he refused the application point blank.

"Don't worry about him being lonely, Mr Cratchit," Murphy teased. "His mates, Isaac and Andre have also been charged and refused bail. They can all have a big family reunion tomorrow morning at court."

As Adebanjo was escorted back to his cell, Taylor bumped Murphy with her shoulder.

"What?" he asked, staring at her as though he had only just noticed she was there.

"Talk about cutting it close," she said with a weary smile. "That went all the way down to the wire."

CHAPTER FORTY

Tuesday 1st June 1999
MOPPING UP

Sitting at the cluttered desk in his office at Arbour Square, Jack Tyler could hardly believe that it had only been a week since the four Turkish debt collectors had been gunned down outside the little café in Green Lanes. So much had happened during that relatively short space of time that it now seemed like a lifetime ago.

Putting the final touches to his latest Decision Log entry, Tyler lowered his pen and glanced out of the window, taking in the gloomy grey skies overhead. Moving with painful slowness, his joints stiff from having sat at his desk for too long, Tyler stood up and stretched lethargically.

The glorious heat wave that the UK had basked in during the last week or so now seemed like a dim and distant memory. That morning, he'd awoken to discover the perfect blue canopy he had grown so accustomed to being greeted by when he drew the curtains had been replaced by a canvas of mottled grey. It had drizzled for the entire journey into work, and now it was raining properly. The heavy downpour showed no signs of easing off any time soon.

In addition to the rain, the wind had started to pick up, and he could see it bending the trees in the park opposite. It seemed that, after luring them all into believing that they were in for an amazing summer, the fabled British weather had returned to its usual unpredictable self.

Tyler wandered into the main office and stopped by the urn. "Anyone want a brew?" he called out, hoping that no one would.

Six hands went up.

"Bastards," he muttered under his breath.

Across the room, he spotted Steve Bull hunched over his desk, brow knitted in fierce concentration. This was Steve's first time as Case Officer, and the poor sod had been given an incredibly difficult job to cut his teeth on. To his immense credit, Bull had really thrown himself into it, and he had done a cracking job so far.

Tyler grabbed a handful of clean mugs from inside the rusted metal cupboard the urn rested upon. He placed them onto a tray and threw tea bags in. After filling the mugs with water, he added a splash of milk and stirred. Once the tea bags were removed, he distributed the drinks around the office.

Reg Parker seemed disappointed when Tyler handed him his. "What, no biscuits?" he complained."

"Afraid not," Tyler said. "Mr Dillon's mate, Geoff, ate them all."

Tyler finally arrived at Bull's desk. Placing the mug of steaming hot liquid next to a neatly stacked line of box files, he sat on the edge of the desk.

"Thanks boss," Bull said, without looking up.

"It's not sugared," Tyler said.

"That's okay," Bulls replied, taking a big slurp. "I'm sweet enough."

"Is everything under control?" Tyler asked.

Bull looked up. His eyes were red and rheumy from a lack of sleep. Like Tyler, he had been one of the last people to go home the previous night and one of the first to arrive this morning. "It's all coming together nicely," he said. "Although the final report is going to take some time."

Tyler nodded sympathetically. "It's certainly a complicated file to put together," he conceded. "Still, on the bright side, if you can manage a job like this, then everything from here on in will be child's play."

Standing up, he patted Steve on the shoulder and set off back towards his office. "Don't forget we're leaving for court in fifteen minutes time," he shouted over his shoulder.

No sooner had he sat down at his desk than Dillon and Murphy bowled in, laughing and joking like a couple of wayward children.

"Where have you two been hiding for the past half hour?" Tyler asked, eyeing them suspiciously.

They grinned at each other like naughty schoolboys. "We just popped out to a local café to grab some breakfast," Dillon said. "I did invite you along, remember?"

Tyler grunted. "Yes, I do remember, but some of us have work to do."

"What time are we setting off for court?" Dillon asked, sitting down.

Tyler checked his watch.

09:00 hours.

"I've told Steve we're leaving in fifteen minutes," he said, "but there's no need for everyone to go."

"Are you kidding!" Murphy said with a huge grin. "We want to watch Adebanjo's solicitor, Crotchety Cratchit, make a fool of himself by asking the bench to grant his client bail."

Tyler frowned disapprovingly. "So you're only going along for the entertainment value?"

"Of course not," Murphy said with great solemnity. "With all due respect, I've spent the last five years trying to build a case against Adebanjo, and for a long time it felt like I was pissing in the wind. My bosses at GMP told me that it had become an unhealthy obsession, and that I ought to just let it go and move on. Well, I didn't. I persevered, making myself deeply unpopular for doing so. Now, after all this time, he's finally been charged with something that will stick, and there's *no way* on earth that I'm going to miss his first appearance in court."

Tyler thought about this for a moment. "Fair enough," he conceded, knowing he would have felt exactly the same way in Murphy's position.

A devilish smile crept onto Murphy's face. "Although I have to admit, seeing that self-opinionated twerp losing a bail application will give me enormous satisfaction."

Sitting next to him, Dillon guffawed. "I wonder if he'll be any more gracious in defeat this time around than he was after losing the warrant of further detention battle."

"I bloody well hope not," Murphy said with a twinkle in his eye. "Personally, I'm hoping he'll blow a gasket."

———

Tyson Meeks was shown to his brother's bed in the ICU. Laying there, heavily sedated, with his body bandaged and various tubes sticking out of him, Marcel looked incredibly vulnerable. An armed policeman stood by the bed, face impassive, his MP5 cradled ready for use. Two more armed cops were stationed at the ICU entrance.

Tyson sat down gingerly, grimacing as the awkward movement tugged at his many stitches. "Wagwan, little brother," he said, taking hold of Marcel's hand and squeezing it gently.

The policeman did the decent thing and moved away to give them some privacy.

Marcel's eyes flickered and then opened. A faint smile tugged at the corners of his mouth. "Wagwan," he murmured weakly, his voice thin and raspy.

"The doctors said you're doing really well, bruv," Tyson told him.

"I feel like shit," Marcel croaked.

Tyson helped him to take a sip of water. "Well, you're doing much better than that piece of shit over there," he said, nodding to a curtained off bed on the other side of the unit, where the armed officer had relocated to after leaving Marcel's bedside. It contained Devon Brown, who was still in a medically induced coma.

Marcel's face darkened. "I hope he fucking dies, bruv," he said. "I still can't believe he shot me."

"Dem Boydem shot him up pretty good, bruv," Tyson said glee-fully. "The witness protection people looking after me reckon he nearly died."

Marcel sucked through his teeth. "Wish he had, bruv," he said with feeling.

"Yeah, well, they reckon he's out of danger now and gonna pull through," Tyson said, shaking his head as though it were a great shame. "Still, he's looking at an L-plate, bruv. He killed that old man on the train, and he tried to merk me and you, so he's proper fucked, innit."

Marcel managed a feeble laugh. "Yeah, I suppose so."

Tyson became hesitant. "Listen, bruv," he said, "I'm gonna be discharged later today, and the witness protection people are going to send me to another part of the country to live. I was wondering… well, I was wondering how you felt about coming with me?"

Marcel's eyes narrowed and a look of uncertainty appeared in them. "I dunno, bruv. It means leaving my ends, and everyone I know. And what if we end up fighting again?"

Tyson shrugged, and then smiled. "We won't fight, but if we do, I'll let you win."

"Yeah, but we won't know anyone. At least in Holly Street I've got friends, people to hang around with. You get me?"

"What friends?" Tyson snorted. "Friends like Switch?" he nodded towards the bed opposite. "Most of your crew have been lifted for that train steaming, bruv, and from what I hear, you're lucky dem Boydem didn't come looking for you as well."

Marcel's eyes darted to the policeman. "Tyson!" he hissed. "Not in here!"

Tyson chuckled. "Relax, little bro. I aint stupid. No one can hear what I'm saying." He became serious again. "You gotta face the facts, bruv. There's nothing for you here anymore. Come with me. Make a new life for yourself before you end up like Switch or your other HSB homies. Besides, you're at risk in London. What if Conrad has some of his people come looking for you before his trial?"

Marcel became silent, but Tyson could tell he was thinking the offer through. "I've spoken to the officer running my case," Tyson persisted. "He's gonna come see you when you're ready to be discharged. Just promise me you'll listen to what he says, and think it through properly before you make your choice. Will you do that for me?"

Marcel stared at him intently for a while, and then nodded. "Okay. I'll listen, but I aint promising nothing."

A nurse walked over to the bed. "It's time for the doctor to examine your brother, so I'll have to ask you to leave," she said, smiling apologetically.

Tyson stood up. "Okay, miss," he said, turning to go. "I'll come and see you before I go," he promised Marcel.

As Murphy had predicted, Bernard Cratchit became so enraged after his impassioned bail application was refused that he stormed out of court in an undignified rage. It had, Tyler happily conceded, been a rather amusing spectacle to watch.

With Adebanjo and the Kalu twins now safely remanded to prison pending trial, Tyler, Dillon, Murphy, and Bull had returned to the office to find everyone in a party mood.

Every suspect involved in Livingstone and Adebanjo's convoluted murder conspiracy was now either dead or in custody. The only person still to be charged was Devon Brown, and he was under armed guard at the Royal London's ICU. His latest prognosis was more encouraging, and it was starting to look as though he would recover to stand trial with the others after all.

Steve Bull had submitted an initial remand file to the Crown Prosecution Service, and he now had four weeks to get the full file completed and sent to the CPS lawyer assigned to the case at Ludgate House. There was so much work still to be done; so many statements, telephone and financial records to prepare for service, not to mention a humongous pile of CCTV that was yet to be viewed. Meeting the deadline was going to be tight, and it was going to involve a lot of work for the whole team. But that, Tyler decided, was something to worry about tomorrow. Knowing how hard they had all worked, and how shattered everyone was, he told his team to finish off anything important they were doing, and then go home.

Dillon immediately suggested that they should all adjourn to the nearest pub instead, in order to have the proper 'debrief' that he'd been so desperate for after the warrant of further detention application. It proved to be a very popular suggestion and, although Tyler would have been perfectly happy to go home, order a takeaway, and spend a quiet night watching a Bond film, he allowed them to browbeat him into going along.

Murphy, who had been due to return to Manchester that afternoon, managed to persuade his bosses to let him stay another night so that he could celebrate with his London colleagues.

After hanging his jacket up, Tyler wandered along the corridor to Andy Quinlan's office. He wanted to invite Susie Sergeant along to the drink as she had been so helpful during the past couple of days. He was also eager to see how Andy's team were progressing with their investigation.

The room had a more subdued feel to it than the last time Tyler had visited. No one was rushing around like a headless chicken, and looking stressed to the eyeballs; the phones were silent, and the detectives on Quinlan's team seemed pretty chilled as they sat at their respective desks, cracking on with their assigned tasks.

Quinlan was inside his office but, as soon as he spotted Tyler, he came rushing out to greet him, with a huge smile plastered across his face. "I hear congratulations are in order," he said, extending his right hand for Tyler to shake, and patting him on the shoulder with his left.

"Thank you," Tyler said, smiling back. "It all came together rather nicely in the end."

"So I hear," Quinlan said, guiding him back into his office. He closed the door behind them and invited Tyler to take a seat. "I must say, I'm very relieved."

"Me too," Tyler admitted.

Quinlan flopped back down behind his desk. "These gangland murders can easily turn into stickers and, for a while, that's exactly what I thought was going to happen with your one."

Tyler responded with a short, mirthless snort. "I was a little worried myself, truth be told."

"And you also managed to capture our outstanding suspect in the process, I see," Quinlan observed, referring to Devon Brown. He leaned forward, and there was a twinkle in his eye. "I would have preferred that you hadn't shot him up so badly that he's going to be hospitalised for a couple of weeks, of course, but I suppose beggars can't be choosers."

Tyler pulled a sour face, still unsure how he felt about Brown surviving. "Yeah, well, don't forget I want him in connection with my job after you've finished with him," he pointed out.

"Ah, that's right," Quinlan said, raising an eyebrow. "Young Devon has certainly been a very busy boy of late."

"So, how's the enquiry going?" Jack asked, eager to change the subject in case he said something inappropriate about Brown. "Are you any nearer to charging them with murder and attempted murder yet?"

"We are, as a matter of fact," Quinlan responded chirpily. "I had a very productive meeting with our barrister, a charming chap called Jonathan Lacroix, yesterday afternoon. Mr Lacroix is happy that we now have sufficient evidence to charge everyone involved in the steam-ings with the Joint Enterprise murder offences. We've already arranged to produce Xander Mason, Curtis Bright, and Zane Dalton later this week. I can't wait to see their faces when they find out they're being charged with murder and attempted murder. Oh, by the way, we've identified two more gang members involved in the steaming."

Tyler raised an eyebrow. "That's great news. How did you manage that?"

"Their fingerprints came back on the loot that was hidden in Dalton's place. They were arrested this morning. They'll be interviewed over the next couple of days, and then charged with the robberies and the Joint Enterprise murder offences."

"What are these two horrible little oiks called?"

Quinlan glanced down at a note on his desk. "Carlos Silva and Shaquille Thomas."

Tyler shook his head. "Never heard of either of them."

"No, I hadn't either," Quinlan admitted. "Also, we think we've identified all the other members of Mason's little crew."

"Are you going to bring them in?" Tyler asked.

Quinlan shook his head regretfully. "Haven't got any evidence against any of them, I'm afraid," he said, "and I can't exactly arrest them just because they're associates of Mason, can I?"

Tyler remained silent. He would have probably done exactly that if he were running the show, but it seemed Andy favoured a more methodical, and less gung-ho, approach than him.

"We had Gavin Mercer, the Safer Neighbourhood Team skipper with the photographic memory to compare custody image photographs of them to the outstanding suspects on the CCTV, but he drew a big fat blank." Quinlan said, and then frowned thoughtfully. "He's a weird one, by the way. Have you met him yet?"

Tyler couldn't help but smile. "I have," he chuckled. "And you're right, he's definitely a bit odd."

"Anyway, unless Silva or Thomas give up the outstanding suspects in a bid to get a reduced sentence, or more fingerprint hits come back, it's looking unlikely that we'll be able to prosecute any of the others involved."

"Just out of interest, what are the names of the rest of Mason's crew?" Tyler asked.

Quinlan picked up the sheet of paper that he had glanced at earlier and read out a list of names. Most of them meant absolutely nothing to Tyler, but one of them was very familiar.

"Did you say Marcel Meeks?" he asked, sitting forward.

"I did," Quinlan confirmed, staring at him quizzically. "Why? Does that mean anything to you?"

"He's the brother of Tyson Meeks, one of the key witnesses in my job. They were both held at gunpoint over in Hackney the other day, and Marcel was shot trying to save his brother."

Quinlan let out a little whistle. "That's very interesting," he said, stroking his chin thoughtfully. "Tell me, what's he like? Do you think he would talk to us?"

Tyler shook his head. "I have no idea what he's like, but I can't imagine he'd be willing to grass up his mates."

"I just thought that—"

"What? Because his brother's a witness for us, he might be persuaded to go down the same route?" Tyler said, completing the sentence for Quinlan.

"Exactly!"

"You could give it a go when he's released from hospital, I suppose," Tyler said without enthusiasm. "Personally, I think you'd be wasting your time. I mean, if he was there, he's hardly going to implicate himself, is he? And, if he wasn't there, then anything he knows is just hearsay, and would be inadmissible at court."

Quinlan considered his response carefully. "You're right, of course," he allowed. "However, perhaps we should test the waters and ask him the hypothetical question: *If* he was there, and *if* we were able to obtain authority for him to turn Queen's Evidence and testify against all the others in exchange for immunity, would he speak to us?"

Tyler really wasn't sold on that idea. "Andy, if he was involved, he's not going to grass his mates up. It might be different if we had some leverage to use against him, but we don't. And let's face it, if we did have anything against him, we would be charging him, not asking him to turn QE. For me, this is a complete non-starter."

"No. You're probably right," Quinlan conceded grudgingly. "We'll shelve that idea for now."

———

When he got back to his office a few minutes later, Tyler found DCS Holland waiting for him. "Hello, sir," he said, surprised to see his boss. "I didn't realise you were in the building." Although Holland maintained an office there, he was mainly based at New Scotland Yard.

"I've just popped over to congratulate you on a job very well done," Holland said, extending his hand. "Despite the three fatalities, it's a very good result, and it hasn't gone unnoticed at The Yard."

Dillon walked in, carrying three mugs of coffee. "I'm not disturbing anything, am I?" he asked, handing Holland and Tyler a hot drink each.

"No, not at all," Holland said cheerfully. "In fact, I need to speak to you about your position here on the command."

Dillon instantly became wary. "Don't tell me, now that Livingstone, Adebanjo, and all their cronies have been charged, DSU Flynn wants us back at SO7 tomorrow?"

Holland smiled. "He wants his staff back tomorrow, yes."

Dillon's face fell. "Okay," he said with a despondent sigh, "I'll let the others know."

"And by his staff, I mean DCs Taylor, Perry, Coles, and Singh."

Dillon was confused. "What about me? I'm not officially due to join AMIP for a few more weeks."

"Ah, well. There's been a development on that front," Holland said. "It seems that Mr Flynn has been very industriously petitioning some very senior players at NSY to have your posting altered. He feels you would be much better suited to learning your trade as an inspector on one of the quieter outer divisions than here, at AMIP."

Dillon's face darkened and his jaw muscles rippled with barely contained anger. "I see," he said, huffily. "So where am I being sent, if not here?"

Holland permitted himself a little chuckled. "My dear boy, as far as I'm concerned, if Danny Flynn doesn't want you to come here, then here is exactly where you ought to be. I shouldn't say this in front of junior officers, but Danny would have trouble recognising an arsehole if he were staring at one in a mirror. Not only are you still coming to AMIP, but it's been agreed that your move should be brought forward. Allow me to offer my congratulations. As of today you've been formally promoted to the rank of substantive Detective Inspector and posted to this command, and you will henceforth be attached to DCI Tyler's team."

He extended his hand, which Dillon took in a daze.

Then, as it dawned on him what this meant, Dillon's face broke into a broad smile, and he began pumping it vigorously. "Thank you very much, sir," he said.

"You can thank me by not crushing my hand," Holland said, withdrawing it from Dillon's vice-like grip.

"We're planning to adjourn to the local hostelry when we clock off, in order to celebrate solving Operation Jacobstow over a lemonade or two," Tyler informed their boss. "You're very welcome to join us, if you so wish."

"That's very kind of you," Holland said, "but I've got to shoot back to The Yard for a boring afternoon of budget meetings, so I'll have to decline."

After he'd gone, Tyler walked over to his friend and gave him an affectionate punch on the shoulder. "Right then, you big lug," he said with a grin. "We'd better tidy up here and then get the troops over the road to the pub. I believe the first round is on you to celebrate your promotion."

EPILOGUE

It was early August.

Dotty turned on her little bedside table lamp before killing the room's main light. Removing her dressing gown, she sat down on her bed with a heavy sigh. It had been a particularly long and stressful day, and her poor feet ached like hell from all the running around she had done. Kicking off her slippers, she gingerly raised her legs onto the mattress and slid them under the quilt.

Her right knee, the one that always gave her jip, was a little swollen. She was waiting for a referral to see a knee specialist, but the appointment was still two months off. The X-rays indicated that she had damaged her anterior cruciate ligament, one of the four ligaments that connect the shinbone to the thighbone. Her GP had testily pointed out that she needed to lose some weight, and that if she were to shed a couple of stone – stone, mind you, not pounds! – her joints would benefit considerably.

Like that was ever going to happen.

Dotty placed the ice bag she'd brought up with her on the offending knee, gasping at the sudden cold. The bloody thing was getting worse; it had nearly given way on her twice today, and she knew she had been incredibly lucky not to have fallen flat on her face.

After plumping up her pillows, Dotty opened her book and wriggled around until she was comfortable. Hopefully, immersing herself in a chapter or two from *Wuthering Heights* would help her to relax and unwind.

One of the new residents, a spirited ten year old boy called Maurice – he had been nicknamed Little Mo – was having a particularly tough time settling in. He had arrived at the end of the previous week, having been made the subject of an emergency placement order. The poor child's mother had been rushed into hospital suffering from a drug overdose on Thursday afternoon, but she had been pronounced dead upon arrival. Little Mo's waste of space father was doing a ten stretch in prison for armed robbery, and as he had no other relatives, Social Services had been forced to step in and find him safe accommodation until a longer term care plan could be formulated.

Little Mo had been given Marcel's old room, which seemed rather fitting because the boy reminded her of him in many ways. She hadn't seen or heard from Marcel since early June and, as she often did when she got a quiet moment, she found herself wondering how he was getting on. None of the staff at the home had been told much after he had been shot, just that he was being relocated for his own safety until the trial was over.

Although she would never have admitted this to anyone else, Marcel had always been her favourite, and she missed him dearly. Wherever he was, she hoped that he was doing well and staying safe. Her reverie was interrupted by a sudden knock on the door. "Miss," a tearful voice called from out in the hallway. "Can I come in?" It was Little Mo, she realised, and he was crying.

"One moment," she called, placing her book face down on the bed so as not to lose her page. Given that the stiffness of her swollen joint was greatly inhibiting her mobility at the moment, she was unable to respond as quickly as she would have wished. Moving awkwardly, Dotty swung her legs over the side. A stab of pain pierced her right knee as her foot landed on the floor, almost taking her breath away. The damn thing was becoming a liability, she decided, wondering if she should try ringing the hospital in the morning to see if she could get an earlier appointment?

"I'm just coming, Mo," she shouted, clumsily putting her slippers back on and taking an unsteady first step towards the door.

With no warning at all, her right leg buckled under her and she went tumbling forward, crashing into her prized Yucca plant and sending it toppling over with a loud bang.

Despite the searing pain in her knee, Dotty immediately hauled herself to her feet, thinking only of the distressed boy who was weeping outside her door. Brushing dirt from her hands, Dotty limped the rest of the way to the door, ignoring the displaced plant and the pile of dirt now covering the carpet.

As she opened the door, Little Mo collapsed into her arms, sobbing uncontrollably.

"What's the matter, little man?" she asked, gently stroking his head.

"I… I had a… a bad dream, miss," he said between sobs.

Her heart melted.

Dotty gave him a big hug, led him downstairs for a glass of warm milk and a biscuit, and then, when he had calmed down, took him back to bed.

Forty minutes later, she limped back to her room to clear up the mess on the floor.

"Oh dear," she said as she surveyed the damaged stem of her beloved plant. Bending down in a maladroit way, she managed to stand it up, leaning it against the wall for support while she shovelled all the dirt that had spilled out during the fall back into the large pot. As she was bedding the plant back in, she discovered something bulky nuzzled into the roots. Wondering what it was, she scraped away the dirt to find a heavy silver object wrapped in a clear plastic bag.

"What the…?"

Carefully disentangling it, she pulled the bag clear of the plant. It contained a watch, she realised, and an expensive one at that. It was a Rolex if she wasn't mistaken. Turning the bag over in her hand, she noticed an identifying serial number and an inscription engraved on the rear plate. The writing contained the name 'Jenny.'

"How on earth did this get here?" she asked herself, brushing the last of the dirt from the plastic.

Of course, the answer was glaringly obvious: it was a stolen watch that one of the residents had hidden in her room. Her heart sank, because it meant that one of her beloved charges had betrayed her trust, taking advantage of the fact that she never locked her room.

Placing the watch on her bedside table, Dotty climbed back into bed and turned the bedside lamp off. As she lay in the darkness, her mind was too troubled to allow sleep to come. All she could think about was who might be responsible. None of the boys in her care seemed capable of such a terrible thing.

Dotty would have to surrender the Rolex to the police. There was no escaping that. They would probably be able to trace the rightful owner through the serial number and, unless the thief had already wiped it clean, they might even find his fingerprints.

She decided to make an impassioned appeal to the children over breakfast, telling them about the find. It would give the culprit every opportunity to do the right thing and come forward before she went to the police. If no one put their hands up, she would hand it in at the local station. What happened after that was down to fate. Maybe the police would find fingerprints and arrest the culprit, maybe they wouldn't; either way, the rightful owner would get their property back. From the moving inscription, Dotty felt sure that the watch was of great emotional value to Jenny, whoever she was.

FURTHER READING

JACK'S BACK
The first book in the DCI Tyler Thriller series

It's been over a hundred years since Jack the Ripper terrorised the gas lit streets of Victorian London, but when a night watchman discovers the mutilated corpse of a local prostitute at a building site in Whitechapel, it quickly becomes apparent to DCI Jack Tyler that someone has taken up the Ripper's mantle and is emulating the terrible atrocities that gained his namesake such notoriety.

Be afraid.
This is only the start…
Jack's Back.

Written in the victim's own blood, the chilling message catapults Tyler into a frantic race against time. Can he get inside the mind of a monster and find a way to stop him, or will more women end up on a cold mortuary slab?

With the top brass breathing down his neck and hampered by an interfering reporter, Tyler knows that if he doesn't catch the man the media has dubbed 'The New Ripper' soon his career won't be the only thing that's left in tatters.

Perfect for fans of gritty London Noir, Jack's Back will keep you turning pages until the bloody end.

———

THE HUNT FOR CHEN

A DCI Tyler Novella only available from Mark's website:
www.markromain.com

Exhausted from having just dealt with a series of gruesome murders in Whitechapel, DCI Jack Tyler and his team of homicide detectives are hoping for a quiet run in to Christmas.

Things are looking promising until the London Fire Brigade are called down to a house fire in East London and discover a charred body that has been wrapped in a carpet and set alight.

Attending the scene, Tyler and his partner, DI Tony Dillon, immediately realise that they are dealing with a brutal murder.

A witness comes forward who saw the victim locked in a heated argument with an Oriental male just before the fire started, but nothing is known about this mysterious man other than he drives a white van and his name might be Chen.

Armed with this frugal information, Tyler launches a murder investigation, and the hunt to find the unknown killer begins.

———

UNLAWFULLY AT LARGE

The second exciting instalment in the DCI Tyler Thriller series

Claude Winston has been on remand for the past two months awaiting trial for the attempted murder of two police officers. The evidence against him is overwhelming and he knows that he's looking at spending the rest of his life behind bars.

When the unthinkable happens, and an opportunity to escape

arises, Winston seizes it with both hands, leaving an ugly trail of death and destruction in his wake.

DCI Jack Tyler and his partner, DI Tony Dillon, are the murder squad officers who sent Winston to prison, and now that he's unlawfully at large it's up to them to recapture him before he can be smuggled abroad to begin a new life in a country without an extradition treaty.

It soon becomes apparent that this is not going to be easy; faced with a wall of silence on the streets, and having very few leads to follow, Tyler and Dillon find themselves being run into the ground as they battle against the clock to locate Winston before he slips out of their grasp for good.

As the chase goes down to the wire, and things become increasingly frantic, Tyler realises that he is going to have to pull something pretty special out of the bag if he is to prevent Winston from getting away.

GLOSSARY OF TERMS USED IN THE JACK TYLER BOOKS

AC – Assistant Commissioner
ACPO – Association of Chief Police Officers
AFO – Authorised Firearms Officer
AIDS – Acquired Immune Deficiency Syndrome
AMIP – Area Major Investigation Pool (Predecessor to the Homicide Command)
ANPR – Automatic Number Plate Recognition
ARV – Armed Response Vehicle
ASU – Air Support Unit
ATC – Air Traffic Control
ATS – Automatic Traffic Signal
Azimuth – The coverage from each mobile phone telephone mast is split into three 120-degree arcs called azimuths
Bandit – the driver of a stolen car or other vehicle failing to stop for police
BIU – Borough Intelligence Unit
BPA – Blood Pattern Analysis
BTP – British Transport Police
BTNA – Blackwall Tunnel Northern Approach

C11 – Criminal Intelligence / surveillance

CAD – Computer Aided Dispatch

CCTV – Closed Circuit Television

CIB – Complaints Investigation Bureau

CID – Criminal Investigation Department

CIPP – Crime Investigation Priority Project

County Mounties – a phrase used by Met officers to describe police officers from the Constabularies

CRIMINT – Criminal Intelligence

CSM – Crime Scene Manager

(The) Craft – the study of magic

CRIS – Crime Reporting Information System

DNA – Deoxyribonucleic Acid

DC – Detective Constable

DS – Detective Sergeant

DI – Detective Inspector

DCI – Detective Chief Inspector

DSU – Detective Superintendent

DCS – Detective Chief Superintendent

DPG – Diplomatic Protection Group

Enforcer – a heavy metal battering ram used to force open doors

ESDA – Electrostatic Detection Apparatus (sometimes called an EDD or Electrostatic Detection Device)

ETA – Expected Time of Arrival

(The) Factory – Police jargon for their base.

FLO – Family Liaison Officer

FME – Force Medical Examiner

Foxtrot Oscar – Police jargon for 'fuck off'

FSS – Forensic Science Service

GP – General Practitioner

GMC – General Medical Council

GSR – Gun Shot Residue

HA – Arbour Square police station

HAT – Homicide Assessment Team

HEMS – Helicopter Emergency Medical Service

HIV – Human Immunodeficiency Virus

HOLMES – Home Office Large Major Enquiry System
HP – High Priority
HR – Human Resources
HT – Whitechapel borough / Whitechapel police station
ICU – Intensive Care Unit
IFR – Instrument Flight Rules are used by pilots when visibility is not good enough to fly by visual flight rules
IO – Investigating Officer
IPCC – Independent Police Complaints Commission
IR – Information Room
IRV – Immediate Response Vehicle
KF – Forest Gate police station
Kiting checks – trying to purchase goods or obtain cash with stolen / fraudulent checks
LAG – Lay Advisory Group
LAS – London Ambulance Service
LFB – London Fire Brigade
LOS – Lost Or Stolen vehicle
MIR – Major Incident Room
MP – Radio call sign for Information Room at NSY
MPH – Miles Per Hour
MICH/ACH – Modular Integrated Communications Helmet / Advanced Ballistic Combat Helmet
MPS – Metropolitan Police Service
MSS – Message Switching System
NABIS – National Ballistics Intelligence Service
NADAC – National ANPR Data Centre
NHS – National Health Service
Nondy – Nondescript vehicle, typically an observation van
NOTAR – No Tail Rotor system technology
NSY – New Scotland Yard
OH – Occupational Health
OM – Office manager
Old Bill – the police
P9 – MPS Level 1/P9 Surveillance Trained
PACE – Police and Criminal Evidence Act 1984

PC – Police Constable

PCMH – Plea and Case Management Hearing

PIP – Post Incident Procedure

PLO – Press Liaison Officer

PM – Post Mortem

PNC – Police National Computer

POLACC – Police Accident

PR – Personal Radio

PTT – Press to Talk

RCJ – Royal Courts of Justice

RCS – Regional Crime Squad

RLH – Royal London Hospital

Rozzers – the police

RTA – Road traffic Accident

RT car – Radio Telephone car, nowadays known as a Pursuit Vehicle

QC – Queen's Counsel (a very senior barrister)

SCG – Serious Crime Group

Scruffs – Dressing down in casual clothes in order for a detective to blend in with his / her surroundings

SFO – Specialist Firearms Officer

SIO – Senior Investigating Officer

Sheep – followers of Christ; the masses

Skipper – Sergeant

SNT – Safer Neighbourhood Team

SO19 – Met Police Firearms Unit

SOCO – Scene Of Crime Officer

SOIT – Sexual Offences Investigative Technique

SPM – Special Post Mortem

Stinger – a hollow spiked tyre deflation device

TDA – Taking and Driving Away

TDC – Trainee Detective Constable

TIE – Trace, Interview, Eliminate

TIU – Telephone Investigation Unit

TPAC – Tactical Pursuit and containment

TSG – Territorial Support Group

TSU – Technical Support Unit

VODS – Vehicle On-line Descriptive Searching
Walkers – officers on foot patrol
Trumpton – the Fire Brigade
VFR – Visual Flight Rules - Regulations under which a pilot operates
an aircraft in good visual conditions

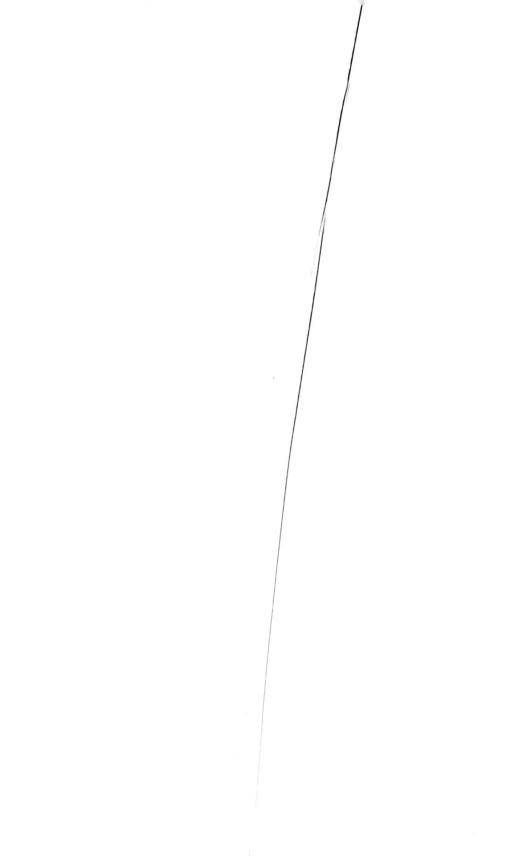

URBAN SLANG / STREET SPEAK

Allow it – stop it
Bare – lots of
Beef – trouble
Blammer – gun
Blower – phone
Blud – mate
Breeze – leave
Burner – cheap disposable phone / pay as you go phone
Dem Boydem – the police
Elder – senior gang member
Ends – home area
Fam – member of the speaker's street family (mainly used to describe associates and friends)
Feds – the police
Golden Brown – heroin
HSB – Holly Street Boys
LFB – London Fields Boys
L-Plate – life sentence
Merk – kill
Ps – paper money

Puff – weed

Pussy bumbaclot – used as an insult, this is a slang term for a soiled tampon

Roadman / Road men – low level street criminals

Shank – stab / a knife

Shive – stab / a knife

Shotter – low level / street level drug dealer

Shotting – selling drugs on the street

Skank – insult for a female

Smack – heroin

Spliff – Marijuana cigarette

Strap – gun

Stripe you up – slash your face open

Tief – steal

Toke – to inhale from a cannabis cigarette

Wagwan – Jamaican patois for 'what's going on'

Younger – junior gang member

AUTHOR'S NOTE

And so we've finally reached the end of the book! I really hope that you've had as much fun reading Turf War as I did in writing it. If you have, can I please ask that you to spare a few moments of your valuable time to leave an honest review on Amazon. It doesn't have to be anything fancy, just a line or two saying whether you enjoyed it and would recommend it to others. I really can't stress how helpful this feedback is for indie authors like me. Apart from influencing a book's visibility, your reviews will help people who haven't read my work yet to decide whether it's right for them.

A lot of readers have told me they like the gritty realism of the DCI Tyler stories, which is good to hear because I try to keep my writing firmly grounded in the real world and ensure that all the police procedural matters are described as accurately as possible. Of course, there are unavoidable times when, to keep the flow of the story going or to maintain the intensity of the drama, I'm forced to apply a little sprinkle of artistic licence, but I endeavour to keep these occasions to the minimum.

Turf War is the fourth DCI Tyler story that I've written. It's safe to say that I've grown rather fond of Tyler, Dillon, and the rest of the team – even Murray – over the years, and I sincerely hope that you'll

grow to feel the same way about them that I do. I'm already fleshing
out the plot for book five, and can't wait to crack on with that!

I'll sign off by saying that if you haven't read them yet, why not
give Jack's Back and Unlawfully At Large a try? And while you're at it,
pop over to my website, www.markromain.com, and grab yourself a
free copy of The Hunt For Chen.

Best wishes,

Mark.

ABOUT THE AUTHOR

Mark Romain is a retired Metropolitan Police officer, having joined the Service in the mid-eighties. His career included two homicide postings, and during that time he was fortunate enough to work on a number of very challenging high-profile cases.

Mark lives in Essex with his wife, Clare. They have two grown-up children and one grandchild. Between them, the family has three English Bull Terriers and a very bossy Dachshund called Weenie!

Mark is a lifelong Arsenal fan and an avid skier. He also enjoys going to the theatre, lifting weights and kick-boxing, a sport he got into during his misbegotten youth!

Mark's debut novel, 'Jack's Back' was published in December 2018. You can find out more about Mark's books or contact him via his website or Facebook page:

www.facebook.com/markromainauthor

www.markromain.com